The Goddess's Choice

The Kronicles of Korthlundia

Book 1

Expanded Edition

By: Jamie Marchant

BEWITCHING FABLES PRESS

The final approval for this literary material is granted by the author.

Expanded Edition

Cover designed by Lou Harper

ISBN: print 978-0-9978624-6-1
ebook 978-0-9978624-7-8
PUBLISHED BY BEWITCHING FABLES PRESS
Printed in the United States of America

To my sister Jalane,

who told me the story of the glass mountain

and my son Jesse,

who brought the mountain to life for me once more

A note on the text: *The Goddess's Choice* was first published in April 2012 by Reliquary Press. When my contract with Reliquary expired in April 2017, I decided that, rather than resigning with my original publisher, I will bring out a new edition of the novel through Bewitching Fables Press, which would give me more control over the content. While the plot remains the same, I have implemented quite a few changes in this edition. To publish with Reliquary Press, I had to cut my original manuscript down by about 100,000 words. Some of those cuts improved the novel, but I also had to delete some scenes that added to the flavor and intensity of the story. This edition restores that material. The editor at Reliquary Press also did a poor job of editing the text, and quite a few errors remained uncorrected. This edition, hopefully, has removed all those mistakes. In addition, I have improved as a writer in the ten years since I first completed the novel, so I have freshened the language, tightened it, and cleaned up some clunky prose.

ACKNOWLEDGEMENTS

The author wishes to express her extreme gratitude to the original members of the Robrek Steele Conspiracy Writers' Group: Peg Daniels, Jim Elston, and Eve Harmon, and to the newest members who helped with this expanded edition: Jack Dickson, Preston Hall, John O'Connor, and Caroline Saxon. (I wrote the names in alphabetical order, so don't go quibbling about order of importance.) Peg and Jim, especially, supported me through every stage of the novel and never let up on me until I got it right. Without them, the novel wouldn't be the book it is today. They said they deserved a full paragraph acknowledgement each (and they're right), but they'll have to settle for sharing the same paragraph and sharing that paragraph with Panera Bread who allows us to occupy a booth every week.

I wish to thank my husband Tim and son Jesse for their love and patience throughout this process and their willingness to listen to parts of the novel read over and over again. I also owe a debt to my oldest sister, Jalane Anderson, who told me the fairy tale upon which this novel is based.

I am grateful to my sensei, Travis Page, who taught me everything I know about fighting and didn't look askance at me when I asked him the best way to kill someone with a staff.

Cheree Castellanos provided excellent editorial assistance, and the cover was designed by Lou Harper.

CONTENTS

MAP OF KORTHLUNDIA

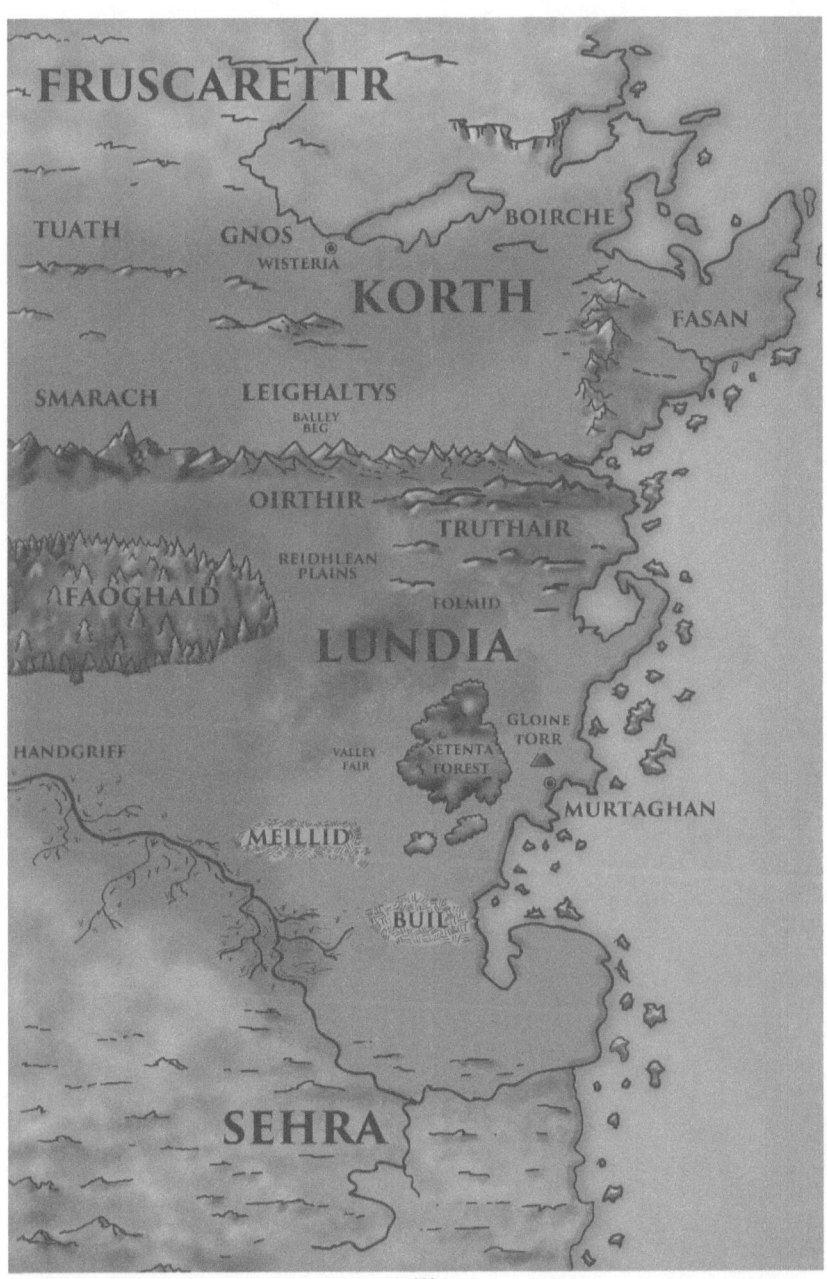

CAST OF CHARACTERS

In Murtaghan

The Royal Family
Britomartus—Solar's second wife (deceased)
Fenella—Solar's third wife; mother of Samantha (deceased)
Kerwin—Solar's brother (deceased)
Lir—Solar's father; former king of Korthlundia (deceased)
Lyonesse—Solar's first wife (deceased)
Maeve—Solar's mother; former queen of Korthlundia (deceased)
Samantha—Crown princess and heir to the throne of Korthlundia
Solar—King of Korthlundia; father of Samantha

The King's Council
Arawn—Baron of Buil; Lundian
Argblutal—Duke of Handgriff; Lundian
Caedmon—Duke of Tuath and Boirche; king's chancellor; Korthian
Kayne—Count of Leighaltys; Korthian
Morgan—Count of Truthair; Lundian
Nola—Count of Meillid; Lundian
Pandaran—Count of Fasan; Korthian
Sheen—Duke of Gnos; Korthian
Teague—Baron of Smarach; Korthian
Torin—Duke of Oirthir; Lundian
Weylin—Count of Faoghaid; Lundian
Ultan—Count of Folmid; Lundian

Samantha's personal guard
Bearach—sergeant

Brice—sergeant
Darhour, aka Ahearn—captain; formerly Master of the Horse
Conroy—sergeant
Kailen—lieutenant
Phelan—sergeant

Other Nobles

Aislinn—Count Morfran's daughter; beloved of Lord Devyn
Briac—Minor Lundian baron
Birkita—Count Nola's wife
Cedric—Duke Sheen's second son
Cyric—Minor Korthian count
Devyn—Duke Sheen's oldest son and heir
Gwawl—Korthian baron
Morfran—Minor Korthian count
Shela—Count Nola's daughter

Palace Servants and Staff

Adalardo—assistant Master of the Horse; later Master of the Horse
Ardra—Samantha's maid
Blaine—Samantha's personal secretary
Calum—royal physician
Cullen—kitchen boy
Druce—chief Librarian
Eilis—palace page
Gilroy—Solar's personal secretary
Gitta—servant in library
Iden—chief palace clerk
Innis Halwnstamm—undersecretary in the palace library
Maggie—chief cook
Malvina—Samantha's maid
Vaughan—stable boy

Royal Guard

Ailbe—member of royal guard
Celyddon—member of royal guard
Errigal—member of royal guard
Faucon—captain of the Royal Guard

Hawk—lieutenant; second in command of the Royal Guard; later captain of the Royal Guard

Liam—member of royal guard

Argblutal's servants and retainers
Clust—Argblutal's retainer
Egan—Argblutal's retainer
Farrell—Argblutal's retainer, sergeant
Herne—Argblutal's assistant and bastard brother
Mahon—Argblutal's servant
Kentigern— head of Argblutal's personal security forces; later captain of the Royal Guard,
Sloane—Argblutal's retainer
Tremayne—Argblutal's retainer; later captain of the Royal Guard

Animals
Muffet—Samantha's horse
Roberta—Samantha's new horse

Foreign nobles and ambassadors
Banki—Massossinan prince
Frare—former king of Saloyna (deceased)
Magnhildr—Massossinan trade negotiator
Phomello--son of Neasarian ambassador
Salome—king of Saloyna

The Priesthood
Anu—Myst's mentor (deceased)
Faolan---assistant to Shylah
Hafghan—chief priest of the Temple of the Mother's Love
Mannix—Leigh's mother's priest
Oriana—Korthian novice
Shylah—High Priest of Korthlundia
Venetia—Oriana's mentor

In the Valley

The Family
Robrek Angusstamm, aka Robbie—an amihealer
Angus Camlinstamm—Robrek's father; richest farmer in the Valley
Boyden Angusstamm—Angus's oldest son
Donella, aka Sphrnztegviza, aka Sphry—Robrek's mother; Angus's wife (deceased)
Robrek of Mahngbhayo —Father of Donella; grandfather of Robrek Angusstamm
Slthethkkne, aka Slathek—Robrek's uncle; Donella's brother

Angus's Servants/Farm hands
Allyn—stable hand
Beacan—Angus's foreman
Cara—kitchen servant
Darien—stable hand
Dillion Briacstamm—Cara's husband; farm hand
Ferchar—farm hand
Trahern—farm hand

Animals
Brazen—mysterious horse
Fancy Man—mysterious horse
Holy Writ—mysterious horse
Ronan—barn cat
Thunder—Angus's favorite mare
Wild Thing—Robrek's horse

The Priesthood
Gildas—chief priest in Valley Fair
Leigh Fergalstamm—novice at the Valley's temple

Other Valley residents
Amergin Kanestamm—Valley framer
Arleen Coalanstamm—Romantic interest of Boyden
Breasal—Valley farmer; Bran's father
Banagher—innkeeper in Valley Fair; father of Davina

Blair Brianstamm—Romantic interest of Boyden
Bran—friend of Boyden
Cullen Bevinstamm—neighboring farmer
Davina—Banagher's daughter
Derry—friend of Boyden
Duffal—maker of pies
Lavena Brianstamm—Blair's sister
Myst—herb witch
Perth Quinstamm—Valley farmer; friend of Angus
Tegan—five-year-old boy
Tully—friend of Boyden
Ula—Valley farm wife

Other Characters

Abenzio—linen merchant
Alair—servant of Baron Briac
Anatloe—Saloynan dealer in the black market
Annkethnnke, aka Annke—captain of Slathek's ship
Aposken—Saloynan assassin
Braeden—Lundian merchant
Bree—servant at the Silk Curtain
Chiamaka—Innkeeper of the Traveler's Haven
Deidre—young girl
Drudwyn—writer of book on magic (deceased)
Dympna—Leigh's mother
Ennis—servant of Leigh's family
Etain—writer of book on magic (deceased)
Fergal Taranstamm—dealer in paipin leaves; Leigh's father
Flynn Idenstamm—king's magistrate
Forsa Duffstamm—writer of book on magic (deceased)
Gitta—servant in the palace library
Irvine Keirstamm—chief magistrate of Murtaghan
Irving—captain; retainer of Lord Devyn
Lorna—servant at the Silk Curtain
Tadc—servant of Count Weylin
Taran—Lundian merchant

PART I

CHAPTER 1

"Please, no!" Robbie Angusstamm screamed as his father's heavy strap came whistling down on his bare back. He tried to yank his hands free, but his brother Boyden held his wrists tightly against the dining room table. *Sulis curse it! Why do I have to be such a worthless weakling?* He promised himself he wouldn't scream again, but he screamed just as loudly the next time the strap hit.

"Sleeping by the river in the middle of the goddess-cursed afternoon! How many times must I beat you before you learn responsibility, boy?" His father brought the strap down even harder.

"I didn't mean to!" But Robbie's explanation turned into screams of pain as the strap landed again and again.

Robbie let out a humiliating whimper when his father finally stepped away and Boyden let go of his wrists. Clutching a chair for support, Robbie struggled to hold back his tears. *By the goddess, don't let them see me cry.*

His father towered over him. "Learned your lesson, boy?" Angus Camlinstamm was the largest man in the Valley, even bigger than the village blacksmith. Although Angus had become a bit round about the middle, he was still strong as a team of plow horses. His blonde hair, flowing past his shoulders, was only just starting to show some gray. His broad face was red, both from anger and exertion. "Well? Have you?" he demanded when Robbie didn't answer at once.

"Yes, sir," Robbie said, ashamed of how pathetic he sounded.

"I'm not going to have to send your brother looking for you again, am I, boy?"

"No, sir."

"All right, then. Stop lazing around like a fool and get your chores done." Angus hung the strap on its peg by the door. "If you finish before dinner's over, I may consider letting you join us."

Like that will ever happen! Robbie clutched at his empty stomach, knowing he'd get nothing to eat before breakfast. Careful of the welts on his back, he pulled on his shirt, which was made from crude homespun. Although Angus could afford better, he didn't believe in wasting coin on workday clothing. His father and brother had better quality clothes for holy days and other special occasions, but Robbie didn't.

As he passed through the kitchen, one of the servants quickly drew the star of Sulis in the air to ward off his evil. He hated it when people did that, but how could he blame them? His reflection in the shiny pots that hung from the kitchen wall showed dark black hair-- the color of night and demons. Green eyes, unlike those of the children of the goddess. Skin, darker than natural. He was also so short his brother called him a worm.

Outside, Robbie drew two large buckets of water from the well. He staggered toward the barn, the weight of the buckets bending him forward and pressing his shirt against his back. Praying none of the servants or farmhands would see him, he set the buckets down and emptied some of the water. His father would beat him again if he knew, and Boyden would laugh at his weakness. Boyden could carry hundred-pound sacks of grain as if they contained feathers. Boyden was everything their father wanted in a son.

Boyden hadn't killed their mother.

When he reached the barn door, he shouted for Allyn or Darien to open it, but no one came. The two farmhands were supposed to help him with the animals, but this wouldn't be the first time they'd used Robbie getting in trouble as an excuse for taking the night off. They knew he wouldn't risk another beating by telling on them.

Robbie sat the buckets down to open the door. The barn was large, with plenty of room for the dozen cows, ten horses, and four mules as well as for the large pig and her half-dozen piglets. When he entered, the cows mooed happily. The horses and mules neighed and stomped their feet in greeting. A bird whose wing he'd mended flew down from the rafters, landed on his shoulder, and nibbled his ear affectionately. The animals' joy seeped into his body like a warm, living current, strengthening him against both exhaustion and pain.

Animals couldn't sense the evilness in his soul. Only here was he loved.

The animals' welcome quickly turned to cries of thirst. Cursing himself for making them wait so long for water, he began filling up the water troughs. He hadn't meant to fall asleep by the river, but he'd been up most of the night helping a neighbor's goat with a difficult birth. "It will be alright. Robbie's here now. Just be patient, and I'll get water for all of you." Knowing they could depend on him, the animals all quieted.

It took several more trips to the well to get enough water, and by the time he'd finished, he saw spots in front of his eyes. But he was far from finished.

When he started the milking, the large, gray-striped barn cat twined around his legs, mewing for attention. "Hello, Ronan. Taking care of the mice and rats for me?"

:*Of course.*: Ronan licked his paws as if getting the last taste of a recent kill. :*Good hunting.*: Robbie didn't exactly hear Ronan's words; it was more that he got an image or feeling from the cat's mind. He didn't know why he could understand animals; he'd always been able to. Perhaps it was another sign of his demon blood.

Robbie placed the milk in the icehouse. He then turned to cleaning the stalls and feeding the animals. When he entered Wild Thing's stall, the mare neighed. :*Wild Thing stomp father bully to mash.*: Robbie hugged his horse around the neck.

With Wild Thing, communication had always been particularly strong, and her mind seemed much more complex than other animals' because Wild Thing wasn't a normal horse. Four years ago he'd found the days-old foal out on the plains, near the body of her dead mother. She'd been half-mad with hunger and fear. Her brilliant coloring, somewhere between chestnut and auburn, and the stars on her chest and forehead made it obvious she was a Horsetad. The herd of wild horses roamed free on the plains of Lundia, and people said they could never be tamed. The origin of the Horsetads was highly debated. Ages ago, some said Sulis herself had ridden her chariot in the land, and her horses had mixed with those of earthly origin. Others said the Horsetads had escaped from the seven hells and their demon masters and were forever unwilling to allow anyone to master them again.

Rubbing his face against her, Robbie choked back a sob. "Wild Thing, girl, why can't I do anything right? Why did I have to be born evil?"

Wild Thing stomped her hoof. :*Not evil. Robbie good.*:

Robbie knew she was wrong, but he didn't argue. Many in the Valley thought Wild Thing was a demon herself.

Very late, he finally stumbled up to bed. Despite his hunger and the pain in his back, he was so tired he fell almost immediately asleep.

* * *

Early in the morning, Robbie stirred. He winced as he sat up. But he knew the pain in his back wouldn't last too long. His demon blood made him heal more quickly than normal people. Struggling to his feet, he carefully got dressed, brushed the tangles from his long, curly hair, and tied it back with a strip of leather. Wondering if he'd ever grow a beard, he felt the smoothness of his face. At sixteen, a lot of boys had at least some hair on their faces. Then again, who ever heard of a demon with a beard?

As he left his room, he was nearly brought to his knees and just avoided crying out. It took him a moment to realize that this time the pain wasn't his own. He blocked it away and hurried outside to find the injured animal. A faint mewing came from the other side of the barn. He followed it and found Ronan covered in blood. Trembling, Robbie knelt beside the cat and stroked his head. *No, not Ronan!* "What happened to you, boy? Don't worry, Robbie's here." Robbie cradled the cat in his arms and carried him inside the barn where he kept his medicines.

As Robbie examined the injury, he sighed in relief. "It's not as bad as I thought, my boy. Some of this blood isn't yours. Got a few licks in yourself, did you?" Ronan mewed feebly, and Robbie saw an image of Ronan fighting several overgrown rats. Robbie cleaned the wound carefully and treated it with one of his salves. Robbie couldn't explain how he knew how to make his remedies. No one had taught him. Certain plants just seemed to make good medicines, and certain medicines felt as if they'd help a particular problem.

As he rubbed in the salve, a trickle of energy moved through his fingers into Ronan. The sensation resembled other men's descriptions of the pleasure to be found with a woman. Ronan's wound began to heal. *Holy Sulis, what is this I do? If being a demon feels this good, maybe I shouldn't mind being one!*

By the time Robbie finished bandaging the wound, Ronan had drifted into a peaceful sleep. He carried the cat to a spot where it could sleep without being disturbed. "You'll be fine, Ronan, my boy. I'm not so sure about me, though." His father wouldn't be happy he'd spent all this time healing a cat, especially after the beating he'd given him yesterday for neglecting his chores. Angus didn't consider cats important animals.

Realizing he'd have to forego breakfast to get the chores done on time, he put his hand over his empty stomach.

* * *

After completing the morning chores, Robbie found his father outside the barn talking to Cullen Bevinstamm, a neighboring farmer. "You think I have no use for the boy myself?"

"Angus, you know I wouldn't ask if I wasn't desperate. This is my only plow horse. If she dies, I won't be able to feed my family."

"Is your horse sick, sir?" Robbie asked.

The farmer glanced nervously at Robbie, and his father snapped, "Stay out of this, boy." Angus turned back toward the farmer. "Just what do I get out of letting him go with you?"

"Angus, you know all my money's gone into seed, but I'll pay you a tetra at harvest."

Angus scowled. "How do you know you'll even have a harvest?"

Robbie clenched his fists. *Why can't he ever think of anything but money? If the horse is sick, I have to help.* "What's wrong with your horse, sir?"

"Boy, I told you to stay out of it!" His father rounded on him. "Do you need another lesson?"

Robbie clenched his fists even tighter, but he didn't dare say anything more.

"Do you have any of your wife's preserves left?" Angus asked the farmer. Cullen's wife was rumored to make the best preserves in the Valley, not that Robbie had ever tasted any.

The man nodded, glancing nervously at Robbie. "Yes, I think there are four or five jars."

"Send all you have back with the boy, and I'll wait for the money." Angus stomped back to the farmhouse without even looking at him.

Cullen licked his lips nervously, and Robbie looked down at his feet. "Your horse?" he asked, still not meeting the man's eyes.

Cullen backed farther away as he explained what was wrong with his plow horse. It sounded like the lung sickness. He fetched his supplies and saddled Wild Thing.

On the ride to his farm, Cullen stayed far away and said nothing. Robbie tried not to mind. Farmers came to him because he was far better at treating animals than anyone else in the Valley, but Robbie knew they wished they had another choice.

When they neared the farm, Cullen rode a little closer. "Just so you know, I've sent my wife and children to her sister's for the day."

Just what do you think I'd do to them? I'd never hurt a woman or a child. I'd never hurt anybody. But even as he thought it, he knew it was a lie. Couldn't his demon blood cause harm even if he didn't mean it to? It had killed his own mother.

They dismounted in front of Cullen's small stable. Cullen had far fewer animals than Angus: a single cow, a few chickens, the sick plow horse, and the old mule he'd ridden to fetch Robbie. The farmer led him inside, still careful to keep his distance. As soon as Robbie entered, his lungs tightened, making it difficult to breathe. A bay gelding coughed and wheezed. Talking in his usual soothing tones, he approached. "Hello, old boy, not feeling so well, are you? It'll be okay.

Robbie touched the horse to be sure of the extent of the illness. "He has the lung sickness, like I thought."

He had the man light a brazier, and he set about brewing a remedy for the horse. "I'll give this to him now, but he'll need the dose repeated three times a day for a week. Come fetch me again if he's not acting better in a day or so." As he put herbs of differing amounts into the mixture, he explained the process to the farmer.

"Sounds a bit complicated," Cullen said. "I'll fetch you some paper and ink, and you can write it down."

"I have better things to do than writing down remedies," Robbie snapped. He wasn't about to admit he was too stupid to either read or write. Father Gildas hadn't allowed him to attend the temple school, claiming the knowledge of the goddess shouldn't be shared with the seed of demons.

* * *

Just after noon, Robbie started back to his father's farm with three jars of strawberry and two jars of peach preserves in his saddlebags. His stomach ached with hunger, and his head swam so badly he feared he might fall off Wild Thing. Cullen hadn't offered him so much as a piece of bread, and healing left him ravenously hungry, especially for sweets. By the time he reached home, the noon meal would be over, and there'd be nothing to eat until supper.

As he took a shortcut through the woods, he got out one of the jars of preserves. "My girl, do you think my father would ever know there were five jars instead of four?"

Wild Thing's ears flicked in answer. :*Robbie hungry. Wild Thing hungry. Nice grass there. Nice jar thing here.*:

Wild Thing was suggesting they stop at the abandoned stable up ahead. He'd found this stable when he was twelve, during one of his wanderings through the woods looking for plants for his remedies. The stable consisted of a small barn with four stalls and a fenced-in paddock with grass for grazing. A small stream ran alongside it, and it had been in surprisingly good condition for an abandoned structure. He'd fixed it up to use as a private retreat. Stopping beside the stream, he opened the jar and reveled in the sticky sweetness of the fruit; it was the best preserves he'd ever tasted. Before heading home, he made sure to wash any sign of the preserves from his hands and face.

* * *

In Robbie's dreams that night, the demon lady came to him. He'd dreamed of her for as long as he could remember. She always dressed in clothing more brightly colored than any he'd ever seen; tonight she wore scarlet, trimmed with bright silver braiding. Like him, the lady had black hair, green eyes, and dark skin. As a child he'd longed for sleep, where he could curl up in her arms and listen to her stories and songs. But as he'd gotten older, the dreams had begun to trouble him. If demons loved him, didn't it mean he was as evil as people said he was?

Tonight she approached through a fog of mist, sunlight forming a halo around her. She hugged him to her chest. "I love you. You won't always be alone."

29

CHAPTER 2

The Princess Samantha sat at her dressing table and glowered at her reflection as her maids dressed her hair. She detested balls and loathed the hundreds of suitors who flocked around her: "I have never seen a lovelier flower, Your Highness!" or "Your eyes rival the brilliance of the stars, Your Highness!" *If I hear that one again, I'll vomit. It wouldn't be quite so bad if even one of them meant it.* Sometimes she wished . . . She pushed the thought away. As the heir to the throne, she couldn't expect romance.

"Let us be painting your face tonight, Your Highness!" Ardra begged. Samantha's maid was as small and slight as the princess herself and had hair so blonde it was almost white. The princess smiled at the quaintness of her speech. Although both Ardra and Malvina had been in Murtaghan for over ten years, they still hadn't lost the peculiarities of their western Lundian accents.

"Yes, Your Highness," Malvina chimed in. "Lady Shela's maids said just yesterday we couldn't possibly be knowing our business 'cause you never be wearing paint." Malvina, more of a typical Korthlundian woman, was tall and broad and not nearly as pretty as Ardra.

"Lady Shela," Samantha snorted in disgust. Shela wore so much paint she resembled some ghastly sea creature. Samantha knew she wasn't pretty, but she was fond of the freckles that speckled her nose and thought the emerald green brilliance of her gown set off her white skin and auburn hair beautifully. Besides being appallingly

30

uncomfortable, paint would absolutely spoil the effect. The princess gestured toward the huge portrait that covered one wall of her bedchamber. "Do you think Danu wore paint?"

Malvina shrugged. "The Princess Danu was said to be a powerful sorceress, Your Highness. She probably didn't need to wear paint to attract men."

Samantha laughed bitterly, as she thought of the army of men waiting below. "I wish not wearing paint was all it took to scare them off. They say Danu never married, and see how happy she is."

Samantha yearned for Danu's freedom. The long-dead princess was laughing as she galloped across the fields with her auburn hair flying out behind her in the wind. The stars on the forehead and chest of her horse shone against its gorgeous coat. Samantha loved this painting, which was just as well because it was bolted to the wall and couldn't be removed without tearing her chambers apart. She'd decorated the rest of her bedroom to match. Tapestries of horses covered the walls. Her dressing table, armoire, and large four-poster bed had horses carved into the woodwork. A quilt, embroidered with horses and stars, was spread over the bed. The mantle over her fireplace sported figurines of horses in gold, silver, jade, crystal, and precious stones. Every new ambassador added to her collection.

"Your Highness, you'll be having to marry one of them eventually," Ardra persisted. "The king won't be letting you hold out forever. You are seventeen, after all. Your mother was only thirteen when she married the king."

"You needn't remind me, Ardra." Samantha picked up her silver-backed brush from the dressing table, a gift from the Neasarian ambassador that was inlaid with an amber Horsetad; diamonds marked the stars at its forehead and chest. She fingered it lovingly. "Do you think it's true Danu rode a Horsetad?"

"So the bards sing of her," Ardra said.

Malvina made an impatient noise in her throat. "And they also be singing she turned suitors into toads with her kiss! You don't really believe such nonsense, do you, Your Highness? Nobody can tame a Horsetad."

"No, I suppose not," the princess sighed wistfully, then smiled at the toads that hopped around the feet of Danu's horse. *How I wish my kiss could do that!*

Finally, her maids were finished weaving the jewels through her hair and had attached the simple gold circlet of the heir. Samantha tried to take a deep breath, but was prevented by the tightness of her corset. "That's it. This is the last time I wear a corset. Have my dresses altered to fit without one. And don't lecture me about fashion. I'd rather be able to breathe."

Before her maids could protest that without a corset she was almost as flat as a boy, she left the room. She passed through her reception room, which was decorated in a similar style to her bedroom and contained more ambassadorial gifts. Pausing in front of her favorite tapestry—a white mare at the edge of the forest, helping her newborn foal stand, she wished she were heading for the stables instead of the ballroom. She forced her face into a court smile and left her chambers.

Her two bodyguards bowed and fell in behind her. The princess couldn't remember a time when she hadn't been followed by two heavily armed men. She'd grown so used to them she often forgot they were there.

* * *

A full crowd tonight, of course. While the possibility of wearing a crown still exists, not even a deadly plague would keep the hordes away.

Behind the dais at the top of the ballroom was the king's standard—a brilliant yellow sun on a field of red. Next to it was a smaller standard in her own colors—the head of a white horse on a field of emerald green. The walls were lined with the standards of all the noble houses of Korthlundia; most sported images of ferocious beasts or weapons of war. *If I'm supposed to be maintaining the peace, why do I have to dance in a room that celebrates war?* Her father claimed they couldn't redecorate the ballroom without the risk of offending one or more of the Korthlundian noble houses. But Samantha doubted she'd like balls any better no matter how the room was decorated.

As she moved through the crowd, the courtiers parted and bowed. All the men attempted to catch her eye, and the smiles of the women failed to mask their jealousy.

As she mounted the dais where her father and members of the royal council awaited, King Solar beamed at her. His long white hair and beard flowed around his head, giving him the appearance of the wise old man from the bards' tales. She bowed to him, and he quickly extended his hand, raised her, and gave her a kiss on the cheek. Despite his insistence that she marry, her father did love her. The princess knew she should consider herself lucky. Most royal children had no choice in a spouse, but her father had left her free to choose among the men of appropriate rank. But as she looked over the sea of hungry male eyes, the thought of marrying any of them nauseated her. *If only marrying them didn't mean I had to bed them.*

Beside the king, Uncle Caedmon smiled at her. Caedmon, Duke of Tuath and Boirche, was her mother's uncle and had been her father's chancellor since she was two years old. He had very bushy eyebrows that gave the impression he was always looking down on people. But he was one of the few members of her father's council she liked, and he was the only one who exhibited no designs on the throne. His only son had married before she was born.

Immediately after the king announced the opening of the ball, Argblutal, the Duke of Handgriff, stepped forward to claim the first dance. No one else ever dared ask her until the duke had had his turn. Like every Korthlundian man, Argblutal was tall, broad-shouldered, and blue-eyed. Many of the girls found him handsome, but she wasn't sure why. He was nearly twice her age. He was dressed in a surcoat of black leather with long black velvet sleeves, trimmed in gold and crimson braiding. He had several thick gold chains around his neck. From the largest of these hung a pendant of a panther, the symbol of his house. In defiance of court fashion, he wore his blond beard and hair cropped short. He and Duke Sheen were her closest living relatives on her father's side, not that they were very close—third cousins or something. Both had thought to inherit the throne until her birth gave Solar a direct heir.

Argblutal bowed. "May I have the first dance, Your Highness?"

"I'd be honored, Your Grace." *Father would throw a fit if I refused.* She smiled her fakest smile and accepted his hand.

As the dance began, the duke bowed low over her hand, sliming it with a kiss. "Your Highness, you are the brightest star in a shining crowd tonight." *It's only the first dance, and I get the star thing already. Is there some book they all read? Fifty-two Compliments for Ladies.* The duke danced stiffly, as if he disapproved of frivolity. "Your dress, it's Saloynan silk, is it not, Your Highness?"

"No, it's Neasarian. I find the weave so much finer. Don't you?" The silk did feel delightful against her skin, but she found talk of fashion and fabric tedious. She'd never understood the other girls' obsession with it, just as she never understood why they giggled so much.

"So I have heard, Your Highness, but it's very difficult to come by. The Neasarians are more interested in trading spices than silk."

This was true, but equally boring, so she smiled and made some inane comment. When the dance finally ended, Argblutal slimed her hand again. "Perhaps we can share another dance before the evening's end, Your Highness." Surreptitiously wiping her hand on her gown, Samantha merely smiled. *Only if all seven of the hells freeze over.*

The next suitor in line was Lord Devyn, Duke Sheen's oldest son. Devyn was only a couple of years older than the princess, but he looked younger. His chin was covered with only the lightest and most delicate of fuzz. The princess thought he'd look better if he shaved. But, of course, he couldn't do that; only the clergy shaved. "May I . . . may I have this dance, Y-y-your Highness?"

As the dance began, Lord Devyn turned a dozen shades of red. "Y-y-your Highness looks just like a-a-a flower tonight." It was obvious he didn't want to dance any more than she did, but Duke Sheen was bent on controlling Korthlundia through his son. She'd heard the duke had threatened Devyn with the lash to force him to court her. Devyn was only comfortable among his paints and canvases. Besides, he was in love with Count Morfran's daughter, Lady Aislinn. She wished just once some man would look at her the way she'd seen Devyn look at Aislinn.

Samantha noticed blue under his fingernails. "And how is your latest creation coming? Working in blues, I see."

Devyn gaped. "I'm doing a seascape, Your Highness, but how could you know?" When she glanced at his fingers, he curled his fingernails into his fists. "Your Highness, how could I have been so neglectful? My father will kill me." Devyn was a nice boy, but she wished his father would leave him to his art and his lover.

After Devyn, the princess worked her way through her father's council—Count Kayne, Duke Torin, Count Weylin, Baron Arawn's son, Baron Teague, and a host of other nobles of varying degrees of importance. Nola, Count of Meillid, looked on wistfully. The count was nearly as round as he was tall, and it was rumored he'd do away with his wife if he thought he stood a chance of capturing the princess's hand. He had a five-year-old son, and Samantha thought it a wonder Nola didn't send the toddler to court her.

After the majority of the king's council had had their turn, ambassadors and foreign envoys began to present themselves. She knew each one was eager to negotiate the most important treaty between their two countries—one that would give them power over the Korthlundian throne. The princess enjoyed the variety of their appearance, but at heart, they seemed little different than the Korthlundian nobles. The vast majority were nearly twice her age, and the talk of stars and flowers sounded little different in a Mintarian accent than in a Korthlundian one. However, the princess smiled when Phomello, the son of the Neasarian ambassador, took her hand. As with all Neasarians, everything from his hair to his skin to his eyes was a deep rich ebony. It was he who'd given her the silver brush and the silk for her gown, and she'd seen him several times in the stables. He seemed to share her love of horses, but the best thing about him was that he could barely speak Korthlundian, so he couldn't bombard her with mindless chatter.

* * *

The king went to bed at midnight, but Samantha was forced to stay and dance with suitor after suitor.

"Might I dance with the stars of heaven tonight?" Count Pandaran, the only member of her father's council with whom she hadn't yet danced, asked. He always danced with her late in the balls; maybe he felt he was saving the best for last. He wore a surcoat of bright turquoise, edged with yards and yards of delicate lace. His hair and beard hung in long, blond ringlets. When the princess took his hand, she cringed at the smoothness of his palms. *The damned fool doesn't even know how to wield a sword.* The hands of most of the men at court were like hers—rough and calloused from weapons training. Knowing she would rule after him, her father had always treated her more like a son than a daughter. Despite what other members of the court might think of it, he had insisted she receive weapons training since she was strong enough to hold a sword.

As they whirled around the ballroom floor, a soft glow of rotten orange erupted around Pandaran. A steaming heat seeped from the orange and poured over her, coating her body with a slime so thick a dozen baths wouldn't cleanse her. The princess nearly cried out in despair. *Not the colors again! I thought I'd gotten rid of them!* It had been several months since she'd spent all night kneeling at the altar in the palace chapel, praying for the goddess's help. She'd felt the goddess's peace and thought the terrifying colors gone forever. But again she'd been wrong. When she'd first seen the colors, she'd gone in disguise to the Temple of the Mother's Love. It was the only time she'd ever given her bodyguards the slip. She'd told a priest about the colors. He'd insisted she was under the influences of the denizens of darkness and that her soul was in great peril and performed an exorcism. It hadn't worked. Nothing had. *Maybe it's not demons; maybe I'm insane.*

The princess was so upset after her dance that she fled the room without giving an explanation. She ignored the questions from her bodyguards and her maids, but she was shaking by the time Ardra and Malvina had finished undressing her and taking down her hair. When she was finally alone, she curled up into a ball on her bed. The colors had to mean something, but after the exorcism had failed, she'd never dared tell anyone else about them. Tonight she again prayed to the goddess for help. At last, she fell into a troubled sleep, her dreams full of people who glowed as brightly as the jeweled horses on her mantelpiece.

CHAPTER 3

On the morning of the Coan Horse Fair, Angus sat at the breakfast table, scowling into his morning bhat. Donella had introduced him to the hot, sweet drink made from roasted bhat beans and sweet cream. With a pang of grief, he remembered the dreamy look of pleasure he'd seen on his wife's face when he'd been able to get her some. The beans had once been difficult to obtain. Now they were common throughout Murtaghan.

He'd loved Donella, but she'd never been at home in his land, and his love had never been enough to make up for the land she'd lost. She'd invaded his dreams last night, angry with him over Robbie again. *Damn her! She never could understand the need for discipline. The boy had no notion of proper behavior.* That damned priest has wanted him killed from the moment he was born. Angus wouldn't be able to protect him forever. She'd never understood things like that.

He took another sip of bhat. *Ah, Donella, my love, why did I ever insist you bear another child?* As he heard Robbie coming down the hallway, he wiped his eyes quickly and left the breakfast table. He didn't want to see those green eyes that were so like Donella's.

* * *

Samantha woke as one of her maids opened the curtains. The sun was just over the horizon, and it seemed just minutes since she'd dropped off. She groaned and pulled the bed coverings over her head.

"I'm sorry, Your Highness," Ardra said. "But you did say you wanted to attend the Coan Horse Fair. You said the Master of the Horse wouldn't wait for you if you were late."

"The horse fair!" Samantha threw off the bed coverings. What did the colors matter? Darhour had told her she'd find some of the finest horseflesh in the joined kingdoms at the Coan Horse Fair. She'd finally be able to replace Muffet with a horse that knew the meaning of the word "gallop." Jumping out of bed, she scrambled into the simple riding outfit her maids had waiting for her.

"What do we say if someone comes looking for you, Your Highness?" Malvina asked.

Samantha frowned. Her father would be furious if he found out where she'd gone. *It would be just like him to send an entire squadron of the Royal Guard to rescue me.* "Tell them I overindulged at the ball, and I'm not feeling well."

"But then wouldn't your guards be waiting outside the door?" Ardra asked.

Samantha drummed her fingers on the dressing table. "We'll just have to hope they don't notice."

Her maids raised their eyebrows, portraying how likely they thought that would be, but Samantha didn't see how it could be helped and just prayed no one too intelligent came looking for her.

After her maids finished braiding her hair, Samantha belted on her sword. It was unlikely anyone would ever get past her guards, but if they did, she was prepared. Samantha took a quick glance at herself in the mirror. She almost looked like a peasant. If she ordered her guards not to wear their surcoats, no one at the fair would ever know she was the crown princess. She threw on a cloak to hide her hair and face.

The Master of the Horse scowled at Samantha. When she arrived, he and his two assistants were mounting up. Most people found Darhour intimidating, if not downright terrifying. The princess thought he liked it that way. *It's not his fault someone carved horizontal lines all over his face, but he doesn't have to wear his hair in those stupid Saloynan braids*. Still, she grinned at him. "You thought you were going to get away without me?"

Darhour scowled deeper, but she saw the smile hidden beneath the scowl. "I'd hoped the late night would cause you to oversleep, Your Highness. You know how His Majesty would feel about this excursion."

She laughed easily, as she always did with Darhour. "I suggest we not tell him. But don't call me 'Your Highness' today. I don't want people to know who I am. A simple 'Milady' will do."

The stable lads brought horses for her and her bodyguards. Vaughan smiled shyly while he held a horse for her to mount. Darhour must have told him not to saddle Muffet because he wouldn't want her recognized either, but the horse was still a tame lady's mare. Since she was going to get the perfect horse today, she decided not to make a fuss. Vaughan was a stringy boy of twelve and gave the impression of having grown too fast. He was nearly as tall as she was, but no bigger around than a fence pole despite the fact that he was constantly eating. As always his hair stood up all over his head and was full of bits of straw.

She pulled up the hood of her cloak. "Let's ride," she said, and took off. Darhour and the other men had no difficulty catching up.

Surrounded by the men, she escaped notice of the guards at the gate who nodded at Darhour. As they left Murtaghan behind, Darhour pulled up beside her. "Did you enjoy the ball, Your Highness? Found that someone special yet?"

The princess shot him a withering glare, and he laughed until she finally joined him. Darhour was the only one who ever teased her, and she usually enjoyed it. But she didn't want to think about the ball, and she certainly didn't want to think about the strange orange glow that had surrounded Count Pandaran. Darhour's presence made it harder for her to push such thoughts away. He was the first person she'd ever seen surrounded by color. She'd been fourteen when she'd gone to the stables, hoping the new Master of the Horse would be more reasonable than the man he was replacing. His back was to her as she entered, and as he turned, he'd suddenly burst into color—the green of a meadow on a spring morning. Part of her had been terrified by the strange colors, but the peace that accompanied the green calmed her fear. She'd known immediately Darhour would become a close friend.

Darhour was happy as he rode beside the princess. He'd had little joy in his life, but every moment he spent in Samantha's presence was a gift from the goddess, both unexpected and undeserved. "I want to thank you, Your Highness, for intervening to save Vaughan's job. His family would have been hard pressed if he'd lost it."

The princess snorted. He'd never thought he'd hear a royal make such an undignified sound, but it only made her more beautiful. "Vaughan's a sweet boy, and it was hardly his fault the older boys gave him so much ale he puked all over Count Pandaran's shoes. I wish I'd been there to see it."

Darhour chuckled. "The count nearly fainted. He wanted Vaughan not only dismissed but flayed. You know how obsessed he is with his appearance. Positively womanish, he is."

Samantha's eyes narrowed. "Why is it that whenever a man is weak, they say he is womanish? Look at these hands." She held up a callused palm. "I can use a sword nearly as well as you. Pandaran is most definitely not womanish! Have you ever seen a woman give birth? Do you think Pandaran could do that?"

While Darhour knew the princess's skills weren't equal to his own, she was far better than Pandaran. "I apologize, Your Highness. How shall I describe the good count?"

The princess wrinkled her nose. "Rabbitish. Smooth, soft, and cowardly. I'd rather sleep with my horse."

"I pray it never comes to that, Your Highness!" Darhour grew hot at the thought of any of those at court touching the princess. In another life he'd have castrated any man that tried. But he'd left that life behind, and intervening in her marriage plans wasn't his place. In fact, he had no right to even take her with him today. If the king found out, it could cost him his job—or worse. But he'd never been able to say no to the princess, just as he hadn't been able to say no to her mother so many long years ago.

"Enough about me, Darhour," Samantha said. "Why have you never married?"

Darhour's eyebrows shot up. "After the Massossinan officer carved up my face, women haven't exactly been eager."

"Surely the right woman would look beyond your scars. Besides, I bet you were quite handsome in your youth."

"Some considered me so, but the life of a soldier isn't one you can ask a woman to share."

"You never did tell me why you ran off and joined the Saloynan army."

"No, Your Highness, I didn't."

The look on his face told her she'd get no farther than usual on that subject. Why would a young man leave Korthlundia and join the army of a king known for his brutality and disregard for the lives of his own soldiers? It seemed a foolish decision, and Darhour was anything but foolish. Despite how much she liked him, he was an enigma to her, and he was the only one around whom she'd seen colors more than once. She mostly saw green, as she had at first, but occasionally there had been hints, shadows almost, of darker colors-- grays and reds that caused a shiver of coldness to come over her. While she was certain that he was her friend, she was equally sure that he'd make a dangerous enemy.

As they left Murtaghan behind, the princess saw Gloine Torr, which rose out of the plains less than a quarter mile north of the road. Unconsciously, she slowed her horse and shuddered at the unnatural blackness of the mountain. It was formed from pure obsidian and rose over five hundred feet from the valley floor. Shaped as an almost perfect pyramid with the top chopped off, its sides were as smooth as glass, which made climbing it impossible except by the staircase carved into one side. Wide ledges circled it at a third and two-thirds its height. It couldn't be a natural phenomenon, but she couldn't imagine how it could have been built either. "Have you ever been to the top?" she asked Darhour.

"No," he answered. "The king still threatening to place you up there?"

Samantha groaned at the long-standing joke. "Regularly. And now I think about it, the old ways of choosing husbands for princesses might not be such a bad idea."

Darhour raised an eyebrow. "You want to stand at the top and see which man can ride his horse up and prove he is the goddess's choice for your husband?"

"Since nobody could do it, wouldn't it prove nobody was the goddess's choice? I wouldn't have to marry at all."

Darhour threw back his head and laughed. Nobody laughed quite like Darhour, which seemed odd considering his appearance. "I guess it would at that, Your Highness. Have you made such a proposal to the king?"

"I'm working on it." Despite her light tone, Samantha had always felt uneasy about Gloine Torr and its legends. Although nobles and commoners alike made pilgrimages to the mountain and climbed its many stairs to visit a shrine to the goddess, the princess had never done so. She made excuses whenever those at court proposed such an outing. Her avoidance of Gloine Torr had even caused whispered doubts about her piety.

* * *

Count Nola shivered as he met Duke Argblutal's cold eyes. He hadn't dared refuse the duke's invitation to breakfast with him. The duke pulled out a knife with a huge ruby in its hilt. Though the only thing he did with it was carve his meat, Nola couldn't help feeling he'd carve Nola's breast just as easily.

"You have a daughter near Her Highness's age," Argblutal said, once the servants had withdrawn.

As Nola took a sip of his *bhat*, his lips tightened. "Shela is just a year older than the princess. They were close as children, but Her Highness grew jealous of Shela's beauty. They haven't had much to do with each other recently."

"Order Shela to renew the friendship."

Nola choked. "Forgive me, Your Grace, but I'm uncertain how my daughter's friendships are any of your business."

"Everything about Her Highness is my business. I will marry her. No chit is going to keep me from the throne that should have been mine by right of blood. I need to know how to attract the princess. If I have a rival, I need to know who." Argblutal carved another piece of meat.

"It's possible Shela might be able to learn such information." Nola shrugged, trying to convey indifference.

Argblutal picked up a piece of meat with the tip of his knife. "Don't think you can toy with me, Nola. You can help me gain the throne and see your estates expanded into the king's lands. Or . . ." Argblutal put the meat in his mouth, and the count lost his appetite.

After Count Nola left, Duke Argblutal summoned Kentigern, the captain of his personal guard. Kentigern had served under his father and was nearly twice the duke's age, but no fat overlay his muscular arms, and there were few younger men he couldn't best with the sword. His eyes were narrowed in a permanent squint, and he was missing his right ear from his days of fighting bandits. Kentigern understood, as Solar did not, that it was the strong who should rule. The captain bowed as he entered. "I want you to return to my estates to recruit and train more men. You must be discreet in this."

"Yes, Your Grace." Kentigern bowed and left, and Argblutal sat staring into his wine goblet. Korthlundia hadn't known war in fifty years. The Royal Guard had grown soft, dealing only with bandits and criminals. If the bitch wouldn't marry him, there were other ways to the throne.

CHAPTER 4

Robbie, Boyden, and Angus rode into the Coan Horse Fair, Robbie winced at the pain in his back. He was healing quickly as he always did, but the hour's ride from the farm hadn't done his back any good. He tethered Wild Thing securely away from the other horses; he didn't want her to wander the fairgrounds looking for him as she had the year before. It made people nervous when she did unusual things.

"Boy!" his father yelled. "Don't stand there dawdling. We have horses to buy."

"Coming, sir," Robbie called. *I wasn't dawdling. Boyden's the one dawdling.* Boyden was ahead with a friend of his, flirting with a group of girls. Robbie averted his eyes. Tonn Tormaidstamm and some of his relatives had beaten Robbie badly a couple of years ago for staring at his daughter too long. He'd had to grovel and swear never to look at a female again before they'd stop. *Why would I want to look at their stupid daughters anyway?*

Shoving aside the unfairness of it, Robbie joined his father. The ring for the horse auction was large and had benches rising in tiers on three sides and the stable filled with the horses on the fourth. As Robbie and Angus took their seats in the middle of the front row, a few people drew the star of Sulis and moved farther away, leaving a bubble of empty space surrounding them. Angus didn't seem to notice, and Robbie pretended not to. He closed his eyes and concentrated on the stable. Even his father's money couldn't get him any closer. Some owners were afraid he'd curse their horses or something. But some of the same men would send for him if any of their animals ever fell ill. *They don't mind using the power of darkness then.*

It doesn't matter. I can tell everything about their horses from here. His father made a noise of disapproval, and Robbie opened his eyes, wondering what he'd done wrong this time and praying Angus wouldn't hit him in front of the crowd. But for once, Angus's disapproval wasn't focused on Robbie. Robbie followed his father's scowl behind them.

Suddenly, he found it difficult to breathe as the most beautiful girl in Sulis's creation took a seat several rows behind them. Her auburn hair sparkled like Wild Thing's coat, and freckles dotted her nose. Her smile glistened in the sunlight, and he felt a tightness in his groin not unlike the pleasant tingling he experienced when healing.

His father elbowed him in the ribs. "What in the seven hells do you think you're doing? You want to dangle from a tree?"

Only then did Robbie notice the five heavily-armed men accompanying the lady; one had a face so badly scarred he looked like something out of a nightmare. Robbie turned quickly away. He'd never survive if that man took offense. *Sulis curse them all! Why is looking so bad?* He shifted uncomfortably in his seat, wondering what it would be like to actually touch a girl.

"Close your mouth, Milady," Darhour hissed. "You're blushing like a silly schoolgirl."

"Just who do you think you're commanding?" Samantha snapped, embarrassed she'd allowed herself to be so undignified over a peasant. But how could she help it? His emerald green eyes had looked at her the same way Devyn looked at Aislinn.

Samantha tore her eyes away from him. As the auction began, she tried to ignore the boy and watch the horses. It almost worked until the air around the boy erupted in color: bronze, silver, and gold blended into an elaborate pattern. *Holy Sulis, what does it mean? Am I truly mad?* She knew she had to be, but her skin prickled with an excitement she'd only dreamed of feeling. She wanted to get closer to him. She glanced around guiltily, but there was no one here who'd take the story back to court. Her bodyguards knew the consequences of gossiping about her, and Darhour was too good a friend to do so.

Before she could change her mind, she climbed over the row of seats in front of her.

"Milady, where are you going?" Darhour objected.

"It's less crowded down there," she whispered, not wanting the boy to hear. Darhour assessed the situation for one of his five hundred and ninety-seven imaginary threats to her safety and then nodded. Followed by her men, she took a seat behind the boy. Fortunately, the peasant was so focused on the horses he didn't notice.

A huge, uncouth farmer sat beside the boy. "Are you going to tell me this one's no better than the last one?" the man sneered. Samantha decided the boy must be the man's servant, but that was no excuse for being so rude. Her father had taught her that treating her inferiors with respect inspired loyalty, something far more valuable than mere obedience.

The boy shook his head and didn't look at his master. "His intestines aren't formed right. His owner's doped him so he acts okay, but the horse is in bad shape, and there's nothing I can do for him."

Samantha could see nothing wrong with the horse, and she considered herself a good judge of horseflesh. The man, however, merely nodded.

A gray stallion was brought out next. "This one?" the man asked in the same sneering tone.

The boy shook his head again. "He's healthy enough. But he wouldn't work well for plowing. Not with his temperament, not even if we geld him."

Again the man accepted the boy's opinion without question. It made no sense. While relying completely on the boy's judgment, the man spoke to him like he was some garbage whose smell he found offensive.

She scooted to the side, so she could see the boy's face better. When the next horse was brought out, the boy briefly closed his eyes. When he opened them, he nodded to his master. "He'd be perfect. Sturdy and healthy. Good temperament." Without asking for more explanation, the man began bidding on the horse.

Just what is he doing? Telling herself she merely wanted to understand how the boy knew so much about horses, Samantha climbed over the final tier of benches and sat near him. "You seem to have an astute understanding of horses," she said.

The boy nearly tumbled over. "Er . . . er . . . Thank . . . thank you . . . Your . . . er . . . M-m-milady."

Holy Sulis! I'm a dead man. Will her men kill me here or ambush me on the way home?

The lady looked between him and her men and rolled her eyes. "Don't worry. My men don't bite." Robbie wasn't at all sure about that, especially the scarred man. But the men said nothing. "Why did you approve this horse and reject the others?" she asked.

As Angus made his final bid on the horse, Robbie wiped his sweaty palms on his trousers. He'd never dared speak to a beautiful girl before. Still, he couldn't just ignore her. "This one is good for plowing, the others weren't."

"But how do you know that?"

Robbie breathed in sharply as his father's hand closed on his thigh in a viselike grip.

"Do you have a problem?" the lady snapped, glaring at Angus.

Holy Sulis, how weak must she think I am to need her to defend me!

Angus abruptly released Robbie's thigh. "No, Milady. I just wanted to remind my son we have horses to buy."

"Your son?" the lady said, as if the idea appalled her. "I fail to see how my speaking to *your son* will prevent you from buying horses." Robbie was shocked; he'd never heard anyone talk down to his father like that. He doubted he'd survive the beating if he tried it himself.

"Forgive me, Milady," Angus said, scooting away and averting his eyes. Robbie could tell his father was seething, but didn't dare say more with Scarface and the rest of the lady's men glaring at him.

The lady nodded and turned back to Robbie. "As I was asking, how can you tell?" Robbie fidgeted and glanced at his father, but the lady leaned toward him and put her hand on his thigh. "Please, I'm only curious, and I promise not to distract you."

Robbie's breath quickened. Nobody ever touched him. Cullen Bevinstamm hadn't even wanted his family near him. His father only touched him to punish him. She looked at him, not as if he were a monster or a demon, but in the same way that girls looked at Boyden. It was almost worth dying for. "I can't explain it. I sort of feel or hear or sense . . . I don't know the word for it, but I can see them from the inside. Know what they're like."

The lady frowned. "Tell me about this one then," the lady said, as the next horse came into the ring.

Closing his eyes briefly, Robbie reached out to the horse. "It's a calm and steady animal. It'd be good with small children. Not too bad for plowing." Robbie blushed as he said that. The lady couldn't possibly be interested in plowing. "But it certainly wouldn't do for riding long distances or racing. You would be hard pressed to get it to go faster than a walk."

The lady nodded. He didn't know what she was thinking, but as each horse was brought into the ring, she asked about it. Her questions showed she knew a lot about horses and liked them just about as much as he did. He felt like crying when his father bought the last horse they'd come for. He wanted to beg to be able to stay with the lady, but his father would never allow it.

"Come along, boy," Angus said, getting to his feet.

Robbie rose slowly, but the lady grabbed his arm. "Don't leave. I'd like to hear your opinion of the horse I mean to buy." She turned to his father. "Surely, you wouldn't mind giving me more of your son's time." She lifted her chin and met his eyes.

Angus glanced at the scarred man, and Robbie couldn't believe his luck when his father walked away without another word.

The lady frowned after Angus. "Not a very pleasant man, is he? I didn't realize he was your father at first. You don't look much like him."

"No, I don't," he answered, biting his lip. "My older brother resembles him more closely."

"That's too bad for him." The lady beamed. "I'm glad I met the more handsome son."

Is she blind? How can she not realize I'm a freak? But if the lady couldn't tell, he wasn't about to argue.

The man with the badly scarred face cleared his throat. "Milady, it's nearly time for the higher quality riding horses."

The lady ignored Scarface. Robbie wondered how she dared do that. But since he'd probably already done enough to either get himself hanged or beaten to death, he decided to savor every moment he could before he had to pay the penalty.

Horses too expensive for his father's farm were led into the ring, and the lady asked his opinion on every one of them. She seemed to drink in his words and repeatedly touched his thigh or his arm when calling his attention to something. He didn't dare touch her back. Remarkably, the scarred man only bid on animals Robbie judged favorably.

"That one's a beauty. Healthy, too," Robbie said, as a fine white mare entered the ring. It was a gorgeous Mintarian with the small head, graceful arched neck, and well defined withers typical of the breed. It moved with a smoothness and ease that seemed almost like dancing. Robbie had seen Mintarians at horse fairs before, but not often.

"This is the horse I recommend, Your . . . Milady," Scarface said. "It is a magnificent animal."

Robbie nodded in agreement. "That she is. A fine mare for a lady. Very gentle. She wouldn't give you a bit of trouble."

The lady turned to the scarred man and narrowed her eyes. "*A fine mare for a lady?*" she repeated, in a tone Robbie didn't understand. The two glared at each other as if having a silent argument.

Scarface snorted, "As you wish, Milady."

Robbie didn't understand what had just happened or why the lady didn't want such a beautiful horse. But she smiled and nodded. Scarface bought several of the horses at prices that would beggar the entire Valley, but the lady tapped her fingers against her thigh. "Why do I have to buy a white one?" she hissed at Scarface.

Before Scarface could answer, another white mare entered the ring. The Korthian Draught reared, pawed the air, and fought to get away from her handler. Robbie whistled in admiration. *What a magnificent animal! She's almost a match for Wild Thing.* The horse had strong, clean-cut shoulders, long, muscular forelegs, and a broad forehead indicating her intelligence. She was sixteen hands high and of a white so pure she sparkled in the sunlight. The lady would look stunning on the horse. It was too bad no lady could ride such a high-strung and spirited beast.

The lady leaned forward and put her hand over her heart. "This isn't a fine mare for a lady, is it?" she breathed.

Robbie shook his head. "No, Milady, she's a glorious animal, but she's very high-spirited. It would take a strong and talented horseman to ride her."

"Or horse*woman*," Milady corrected

Scarface thrust his face between them. "Milady, you cannot . . . "

"You will buy it," she cut Scarface off. Glaring at Robbie as if he intended to disembowel him on the spot, the man bought the horse. Robbie couldn't imagine what it would be like to have a man who looked like that obey him, and he wasn't at all sure buying that horse was a good idea.

The lady stood abruptly. "I'd like to go look at the vendor stalls now." Scarface opened his mouth, but the lady cut him off again. "No need to disturb yourself. I'm sure this boy . . . " She paused and looked meaningfully at Robbie.

"Robbie," he stuttered.

"I'm sure Robbie will accompany me. Won't you?"

He jumped to his feet. He would have walked through fire if she'd asked him to. "Certainly, Milady."

To his intense surprise, the lady took his hand and led him away; two of the armed men trailed behind them. Robbie glanced at them nervously, but the lady paid them no attention.

He noticed with interest that her hand wasn't as soft as he'd expected a lady's hand to be. Testifying that she might know how to use the sword she wore around her waist, her hand was nearly as calloused as his own. Perhaps highborn women were different than he'd imagined.

She drew him toward the vendor stalls, complaining about Scarface. "I can't believe Darhour was trying to get me to buy another lady's mare. But it's just like him."

He has a point. You'll break your neck if you try to ride the one you bought. "That mare will need careful handling."

The lady let go of his hand and put her hands on her hips. "Are you questioning my ability to handle a horse? There isn't a horse in my father's stables I can't handle. Darhour says I'm an expert horsewoman."

"I'm . . . I'm sure you are, Milady," he said, sick at having offended the only person who'd ever wanted him around.

The lady rolled her eyes, and Robbie saw her mouth the word "men." She started walking away. *Why did I have to say something so stupid?* But the lady turned back. "Aren't you coming?" Beaming with relief, he caught up with her. "With the way Darhour was acting I shouldn't blame you. He's just worried about getting in trouble with my father. I blackmailed him into taking me with him today."

"You blackmailed *him*?" Robbie gaped at her.

She laughed, and it was such a beautiful laugh Robbie couldn't help joining her. "He's not as fierce as he looks, and it wasn't blackmail exactly." The lady told him a story of a stable lad vomiting on some count's shoes, and Darhour's request that she save the boy's job.

Robbie couldn't imagine a life that included counts yelling at stable boys. *Her father must be a very important man. Why would she choose to be with me when she could have anyone she wanted?* "Your father will surely have a fine stable with the horses your man bought today."

"Father has a magnificent stable. Fortunately, he doesn't pay too much attention to it. Darhour might be in a lot of trouble if my father found out he lets me ride Horror. Horror requires *a strong and talented horsewoman*, but he nearly flies across the fields. I haven't yet found a fence he couldn't jump. Riding a horse like that makes me feel freer than anything."

Robbie smiled at the image of the lady flying across the field with him and Wild Thing riding beside her. "I know what you mean. My mare's like that."

"She is? Is she here?"

"Yes, she's picketed over that way." He pointed to the far side of the fair grounds.

"Is she a match for my new horse?"

Robbie looked away. "I'm afraid she's more than a match."

The lady laughed again. "You must show me this paragon of horseflesh."

"Certainly, Milady," the peasant boy said. "But we'll have to be careful. She's a bit temperamental."

How sweet! He thinks his peasant horse is an equal to the one I just bought.

The boy's hand was warm in hers as he led her through the fair grounds. It was rough and calloused as a man's hand should be. She paused at a fruit vendor's cart. "Does your mare like apples?"

"Oh, yes, Milady. Wild Thing loves apples."

"Wild Thing?" Samantha paid for the biggest and juiciest looking apple in the pile.

The boy looked away, but with his dark skin, it was hard to tell if he was blushing. "She isn't really tame. She won't let anyone but me ride her."

What more could I ask for—incredibly handsome and an expert with horses? Why aren't any of the men at court like him?

He led her to the edges of the fair grounds. They passed the other picketed horses, and the princess saw one horse off by itself. When they drew closer, she gasped. "That's Wild Thing," the boy said.

She grabbed tightly to the boy's arm. "That's a Horsetad. But . . . but nobody can tame a Horsetad."

The boy shrugged and looked at his feet. "Like I said, Milady, she isn't really tame."

She took a step back. "You're an amihealer, like the Princess Danu!"

The boy's eyes widened. "An ami . . . amihealer? No, I'm not any kind of sorcerer."

"You read horses' minds! You ride a Horsetad! Holy Sulis, Robbie, if you're not a sorcerer, what are you?"

"A demon," the boy blurted. "That's what the people around here all say."

"A demon! That's absurd!"

"Why else . . . " Before he could say any more, the Horsetad neighed and tugged at her picket line. Robbie hurried to the mare's side. She calmed at his touch.

Samantha crept closer. "Is something wrong?"

Robbie scratched the mare's neck. The horse snorted and pawed the ground. "Not really. She just wonders when you're going to stop talking and give her the apple."

Samantha crept closer. "Will she let me feed it to her, or had you better?"

"You can. She says she likes you."

Samantha held her breath as she approached the magnificent animal. A thrill ran through her as Wild Thing ate the apple out of her hand. Trembling, she patted the mare's nose. She couldn't help whispering, "I've always loved the stories about Danu's Horsetad. I never dreamed I'd ever get close enough to actually touch one."

The boy was so close to her their hips touched. "Wild Thing says you can touch her all you want. She'd especially like it if you'd scratch her neck."

Samantha reached up to scratch the mare's neck, but she got the feeling the horse wasn't the only one giving her permission to touch. The expression on the boy's face was hungry. His life must be terribly lonely if people thought he was a demon. His lips were at the same level as her own. It would be so easy to . . . *Holy Sulis, what am I thinking?* She turned away abruptly. She cleared her throat, trying to shake off the urge to take the boy behind the bushes and . . . "How did you get a Horsetad?" she asked.

"I found her when she was just a few hours old. Her mother had been killed by a panther. I brought her home and took care of her. She would have died without me."

"You poor thing." Samantha scratched Wild Thing's neck again. "We're alike, you and I. We both lost our mothers on the day of our birth." The Horsetad neighed and nuzzled against Samantha. "What did she say?"

The boy looked away. "It's kind of embarrassing."

She turned him back to face her. "Please tell me. When am I going to get another chance to talk to a Horsetad?"

Robbie smiled shyly. "She said, if you're lonely without your mother, maybe I could be your friend like I'm Wild Thing's friend."

"That's so sweet." A bubble of warmth formed in the center of her body. "I'd like that. Would you be my friend?"

The boy's face glowed. "Yes, Milady. There's nothing I'd like more."

Samantha's laughter bubbled over. "Come then, my friend, and show me what they sell at a fair." She could barely stop herself from skipping like a small child.

Certain he could only be dreaming, Robbie watched the beautiful lady, who wanted him for a friend, examine the woven baskets. "These are amazing, aren't they, Robbie?" She picked up an ordinary basket and showed it to him. "It looks like they're made by weaving strands of straw together."

The vendor looked nervously from Robbie to the armed men who were still following him and the lady. The man drew Sulis's star to ward against him, but Robbie was too happy to let it bother him, and the lady was so caught up in the baskets she didn't notice. The lady was equally excited about the tin jewelry and the beaded purses. It was odd to see anyone excited by such ordinary things, but the lady's delight was infectious, and Robbie found himself constantly grinning.

"Look at those ribbons," she said, putting down the embroidered shawl she'd been examining and hurrying to the next booth. She picked one up and held it to the side of his head. "It's the same color as your stunningly beautiful eyes. Let me buy it for you. I want to thank you for your help in choosing my horse."

Without giving him time to reply, the lady bought the ribbon and insisted he turn around. An indescribable thrill went through him as the lady's fingers combed through his hair and tied it back with the ribbon. *She likes horses as much as I do. She doesn't think I'm cursed. Why does she have to be a lady?*

As darkness fell, they reached the stalls of the food vendors, and Robbie breathed in the delicious scent of meat pies.

"Are you hungry?" the lady asked.

Robbie didn't meet her eyes; of course, he hadn't a dram. "No, Milady. Not at all. Go ahead if you are, though."

The lady headed for a meat pie vendor. "Four pies, please."

Wishing he could sink into the dirt, Robbie followed her. Boyden would have had money to buy pies for a pretty girl. The lady paid for the pies and offered two to him. "I said I wasn't hungry." He looked away as his stomach announced him to be a liar.

"Of course you are. I've been with you all day, and neither of us has eaten a thing. Take them. What am I going to do with four pies, anyway?"

Robbie hesitated. He'd already accepted the ribbon from her. What would it say about him if he allowed her to buy him pies as well? But he'd never find another person who actually liked him, and he didn't want to offend her. Besides, the scent of the pies was making him aware of how hungry he actually was. "Thank you, Milady. Someday, you must let me repay the favor."

"Count on it." Her eyes sparkled as she bit into the first pie. "These are good."

As they greedily devoured the pies, the band over by the dance floor started playing. "Music?" she asked. "Will there be dancing?"

"Of course, Milady."

"I've never seen peasant dancing before." She grabbed his hand and led the way toward the music.

When they reached the dance floor, the lady beamed at the dancers, a sparkle alight in her eyes. "Dance with me?" she said.

"Milady, I've never really done any danc—"

Milady pulled him onto the floor. "You owe me for the pies, remember?"

* * *

Boyden sat in one of the ale tents with a full mug on the table and Blair Brianstamm on his lap. Blair wasn't as pretty as Arleen, but she had a long neck and large breasts; his hand rested against her plump bottom. He squeezed it, wondering how long it was going to take him to convince her to find some place more private. "So when are you going to marry me, Boyden?" Blair leaned down to drink from his mug and giving him a nice view of her breasts.

He kissed the side of her neck. "My father says after harvest, he'll give me my own lands. Maybe we could think about getting married then?"

"After harvest, is it?" Blair snapped. "Isn't that what you said last year to Arleen?"

"What's Arleen got to do with anything?"

"You don't ever plan on marrying me. You're just saying that so I'll let you have your way with me again."

"No, of course not!" Boyden couldn't imagine why she was in a huff.

"Arleen told me what you said to her, but I thought she was lying because people were calling her a cheap slut." Blair pushed away. "That's probably what they're saying about me now." She ran away.

"Blair!" he called after her. *Damn women! What set that off? Whores are so much easier to deal with.* He picked up his mug and drank deeply.

Carrying mugs of ale, Bran and Derry joined him. Bran had a deck of cards. They were sons of some of the more prosperous farmers in the Valley, so they moved in the same social circles he did, but he wasn't particularly fond of them. Derry was big and stupid; he always had a blank look on his face as if no brain rested inside his overlarge head. Bran was too thin to be a true man, and he had a sly look about him that let you know that he was always plotting something. "How about a game, Boyd?" Bran asked. Boyden clenched his jaw. He hated it when people shortened his name. Bran did it just to annoy him. "We saw Blair running off. Maybe you should try to get yourself a lady instead of a peasant slut."

He picked up his mug. "What in the seven hells are you talking about?"

Derry waved Bran off. "He thinks maybe all the brothers should get ladies."

Boyden stared at him, wondering just how much ale he'd already had.

"You can't tell me you don't know what your brother's doing."

"I have no brother," Boyden growled, wondering what the worm had done to disgrace him now.

Bran laughed. "Well, the highborn lady, who decided to grace us with her presence, can't keep her hands off the runt your father claims as a son. He has her over on the dance floor now."

"You're lying," Boyden said.

"I wish I were. Look, Boyd, we have nothing against you, but your little brother just isn't natural. He decided to go for a lady because he knows if he ever tried his demon tricks with one of our women, we'd string him from a tree."

Boyden drained his ale and slammed the empty mug down on the table. "If you're lying to me, we'll see who swings."

Boyden pushed his way through the crowd. Bran and Derry followed, and they hadn't been lying. The worm was making an absolute ass of himself dancing with a well-dressed lady. A group of girls were laughing and pointing. Others drew Sulis's star. *He should know he isn't welcome among decent people.*

"Moving up in the world? I guess that's why you started thinking you were too good for me."

Boyden turned and saw Arleen. Even in the darkness, he could see how white her skin was. *How dare she throw me over! I might have married her eventually.* Boyden stabbed a finger toward the dance floor. "I had nothing to do with . . . *that.* I'm not like him."

"No, I guess not. Don't have enough of the demon blood to bewitch a lady."

If she hadn't fled laughing into the crowd, Boyden would have punched her. *He's humiliated me for the last time! I'll kill him for this!*

* * *

Since the lady didn't care, Robbie didn't feel the slightest bit embarrassed that he couldn't dance. She whirled away from him, and he swung her into his arms. She laughed, and he wished the night could last forever, but far too soon the lady stumbled and caught hold of his arm. "Should we sit one out, Milady?"

Breathing heavily, the lady nodded. "I guess I'm more tired than I thought."

As Robbie led her back to her retainers, he noticed the grim looks on their faces. The scarred man had joined the two younger ones who'd been following them around. Scarface bowed to the lady. "Milady, we have a long ride back. We truly must leave."

The lady sighed. "I guess you're right." She turned to Robbie. "I had a good time. It was fun."

It was the best day of my life! Please don't leave! Please say you'll come again! "Yes, Milady. It was fun."

"I truly wish I could stay longer, but we do have a long ride, and it isn't fair to keep my men longer," she said. Robbie cursed her men into the seven hells. The lady, however, let go of his hand. She kissed him on the cheek, caressing his face with her soft lips. "Goodbye, Robbie. Remember me," she said, then followed the scarred man off into the darkness.

How could she think he'd ever forget her? Robbie touched his cheek, feeling as if he'd just lost the most precious thing in the world. He hurried away from the dance floor before anyone could see him crying. He wiped his eyes as he threaded his way through the now deserted stalls toward Wild Thing. When he was passing between two stalls, Boyden stepped in front of him. "Getting above yourself, worm?"

Robbie could smell alcohol on his brother's breath. Turning to run, he found Boyden's friends blocking his only escape. Boyden punched him in the gut, doubling him over and driving the air out of his lungs. "Can't have you forgetting that your kind deserves to be wallowing with the pigs, not dancing with a lady." Boyden smashed his fist into Robbie's face, whirling him around. He followed it with a vicious uppercut to the kidney.

Robbie collapsed against the stall quivering with pain and struggling for breath. Boyden tore the green ribbon out of his hair. "Where did you get this?"

"That's mine! Give it to me!"

Boyden held the ribbon out of reach. "And where would *you* get something like this? Did you steal it?"

"'Give it back." He reached desperately for the lady's gift.

Boyden shoved him against the stall wall. "You let that lady buy it for you, didn't you?" Boyden smashed him in the stomach again. Robbie doubled over, gasping for air. Grabbing him by the hair, Boyden yanked him up. He dropped the ribbon at his feet and ground it into the muck. Then he slammed the back of Robbie's head against the wall. "You've become the lady's whore!"

"Don't you dare talk about her like that!" His protest, coming through gasps of pain, sounded feeble even to him. He despised himself for being unable to defend her better.

"You don't think she actually cared about you, do you? Don't you realize you were just her latest toy?" Boyden kneed him hard in the groin, and Robbie keeled over into the mud, exploding with pain and rage. He made a dive for Boyden's feet, but he was too slow. Boyden kicked him hard in the chest.

Robbie tried to fight, but Boyden had always been bigger and stronger. His brother beat him brutally, all the while making obscene comments about the lady. He'd been in pain countless times before, but he'd never hurt this badly. Every time Boyden knocked him into the mud, he prayed he'd simply leave him there, but Boyden dragged him back to his feet again and again. Robbie grew afraid that his brother meant to kill him.

"Please, I didn't . . . " but Boyden refused to let him explain or offer excuses. Robbie turned desperately to Boyden's friends. "Please, help me! Stop him!"

They merely laughed, and Boyden slammed him into the stall wall again. The old wood snapped, sending a jagged chunk into his back. He screamed, fell at his brother's feet, and coughed up blood.

Boyden kicked him again. "Have you learned your lesson, worm?"

"Yes, please . . . yes."

"Prove it. Lick my boots clean."

Struggling not to vomit, Robbie ran his tongue across the filthy boots. Boyden sneered, "There's some more, a little higher up." Robbie strained to reach the spot, and Boyden kicked out, slamming Robbie's head into the stall wall. Darkness overtook him.

* * *

When Robbie awoke, it was still dark, but he could no longer hear the music and dancing. Something licked his face, and he struggled to focus through the small slits in his swollen eyes. Wild Thing was standing over him. He hurt too much to worry about how she'd gotten loose. "Hello, girl," he croaked through swollen lips, almost not recognizing his own voice. When he tried to rise, pain shot through him, causing him to collapse back into the mud, the place he certainly belonged.

"Help me, my girl," he pleaded. Wild Thing tucked her legs under her and sat beside him. As Robbie leaned against the horse's warm side, he saw the green ribbon lying in the mud; he grabbed it. Tucking the lady's present inside his shirt, Robbie boosted himself onto the horse's back.

* * *

Samantha was exhausted when she finally reached her quarters. Malvina and Ardra had a bath waiting. They helped her off with her clothing and into the warm water. They scrubbed the dirt from her body and washed her hair. "Did you have a good time, Your Highness?" Ardra asked.

"I most certainly did." The princess smiled.

"Lady Shela was wanting to speak with you, Your Highness," Malvina said. "We told her you were indisposed, like you said."

Samantha merely grunted. She wanted to think about a handsome peasant boy, not Lady Shela.

After her maids tucked her into bed, Samantha fell into a pleasant sleep. *She laughed with Robbie as they danced the riotous country dance together. As the music slowed, Robbie swept her into his arms to dance the slow and sensuous Saloynan waltz, the one she'd ordered the court orchestra never to play. His body touched every inch of her own. When the dance ended, she took his hand and led him to her rooms. She pulled him down on her bed, and he bent his mouth to hers. Her lips parted, and she teased his tongue with her own. Her breath caught in her throat.*

She awoke dripping with sweat. *Oh, that's why the other girls giggle!*

CHAPTER 5

In the morning, Samantha headed straight for the stables. Darhour was standing at the entrance, blocking her way. Samantha rolled her eyes at him; because of stunts like this, half the men in the palace nearly peed their pants when Darhour looked in their direction. "Your Highness, if anything happens to you because of this horse, I'll personally hunt down your green-eyed friend and disembowel him."

Samantha pushed past him. "Oh, please, Darhour. Enough of the dramatics." Grabbing a couple of apples from the apple barrel, she headed for her new horse. In her stall, the new mare snorted nervously. The princess approached slowly, holding out one of the apples. The mare moved closer, sniffed it, and then ate it from her hand. While the mare sniffed around for more, Samantha stroked the horse's nose. "Good morning. How do you like your new home? Any problems? Complaints?" The horse nickered contentedly. "Well, that's good to hear, sweetheart. Now if you ever do have any problems, you let me know. Samantha wants Roberta to be happy."

Behind her, Darhour snorted, "Roberta?"

"Yes. Roberta. Are you going to disembowel him for the name as well?" Samantha blushed. *I shouldn't let a simple peasant affect me this much. But can anyone who rides a Horsetad be simple? And those colors, what do they mean?* She tried to push the useless thoughts from her mind. However much she enjoyed her time with Robbie, he could be nothing to her. Roberta would have to be the friend she wished for.

She talked softly to and petted the horse for ten minutes. She then presented her with another apple, which the mare ate eagerly. Easing the bridle on, Samantha led the horse out of the stall and continued to talk softly while one of the grooms saddled her. Roberta fidgeted when the man first approached, but settled down as Samantha cooed and stroked her.

When the horse was saddled, Darhour helped her mount. "Let the two of you get used to each other today, Your Highness. There'll be time for a full gallop later."

Rolling her eyes, Samantha saluted in military fashion. "Yes, captain." Fully intending to ignore Darhour, Samantha walked Roberta out of the stables. Followed as always by her bodyguards, she rode to the edge of the king's fields where the open land spread out before her. "Let's go, girl." She gave the mare her head, and Roberta took off at a full gallop, moving so quickly it stole her breath.

Roberta flew across the fields, faster than any horse she'd ever ridden. Imagining Robbie and Wild Thing racing beside her, Samantha laughed as the wind blew through her hair, and Roberta soared over the first fence. She rode far before she realized she'd left her bodyguards behind. *Sulis curse it all! They'll be killing their horses trying to find me!* She didn't want them to get in trouble with her father, so, reluctantly, she turned back.

She reached the stables without seeing her guards. She dismounted and allowed Roberta to drink her fill at the water trough. She brushed back the strands of hair that had come loose from her braid; it would take her maids forever to untangle it. Vaughan came running out. His hair was mussed and full of straw as usual. "Can I get anything for you, Your Highness?"

"Please fetch a brush and a curry comb. Roberta's gotten quite a number of burrs."

"At once, Your Highness." The boy ran to obey. She didn't think she'd ever seen him walk.

While she was waiting, she unsaddled the mare. "It was a nice run we had today, wasn't it, my girl? We make a good pair." Roberta nickered. "Your tail's a mess, but don't worry. I'll fix it for you."

When Vaughan returned with the grooming implements, she asked him to put the saddle away. She rubbed the horse down and began disentangling the burrs. Hearing a horse ride up, she thought one of her bodyguards had finally found her.

"Boy," a voice yelled. "See to my horse at once."

She glanced behind her and saw, instead of her bodyguard, a minor count whose name she couldn't remember. "I wasn't aware His Majesty employed *girls* in his stable. No matter. Don't stand there like a gaping idiot. See to my horse."

Samantha returned to Roberta's tail. "I'm a bit busy at the moment."

"Get over here this instant, or I'll have you flogged."

The princess continued combing Roberta's tail. "I don't think that's likely."

Vaughan came running back out. When he saw the count, he bowed and reached for the horse's bridle. "Can I take your horse, Milord?"

"No, you may not. She will do it." Samantha turned. The count was pointing at her. She leaned back against Roberta's broad flank, keeping her face blank.

"Her?" Vaughan gaped. "But . . . Milord!"

"Yes, her, you idiot boy. She's been most insolent. Fetch the Master of the Horse. I'll have a word with him."

Vaughan just stood there with his mouth hanging open. "Do as he asks, Vaughan," Samantha commanded. Vaughan bowed and ran back inside.

"You could stand to learn a few manners," Samantha said to the count. "It never hurts to treat underlings with respect."

The count turned purple with rage. "One more word from you, wench, and I'll have you on a spit!"

Vaughan came running back out, closely followed by Darhour. Darhour glanced between the count and the princess, and Samantha noticed a spark of amusement in his eyes. "Is there a problem, Milord?"

The count started to speak, but the princess interrupted. "I believe the count wants me flogged for insolence."

"Wants you flogged, Your Highness?" Darhour raised his eyebrows and turned to the count. "You're suggesting I flog the crown princess?"

The count gasped "But she's not . . ." He looked at her face seemingly for the first time. "Holy Sulis, no! I didn't recognize you dressed like that."

At that moment her bodyguards finally found her. The first jumped off his horse before it'd stopped. He put his hand on his sword and stepped between the princess and the count. "Trouble, Your Highness?" Her other bodyguard closed beside the first.

With a look of sheer panic, the count dismounted and bowed low in the dust. "Your Highness, forgive me. I swear I didn't know it was you. I meant no offence."

"You certainly meant to offend someone! Your behavior was reprehensible!"

"Shall we arrest His Lordship, Your Highness?" asked her bodyguard, whose eyes were an icy blue.

Darhour grunted. "I could flog him for you, if you'd like, Your Highness."

The count turned the same shade as the dust beneath his feet. "Forgive me, Your Highness. I apologize most sincerely for my rudeness and submit myself to your mercy. If you grant it, never again will I treat another in the manner I displayed here today."

"Based on your promise, I will grant you mercy, but if I ever hear of you breaking this promise, I'll have the Master of the Horse flog you."

Darhour gave the count his make-men-piss-in-their-pants look, and the count paled further. "I understand, Your Highness."

Samantha dismissed the count, and Darhour chuckled. "You can be wicked, Your Highness."

"Your glare was what nearly made him lose his bowels. Besides, he should have recognized me no matter how I was dressed." She groaned. "I'd best run along. I have to dine with the court."

As she walked toward the palace, the bodyguard who'd offered to arrest the count said, "Your Highness, you must not leave us behind. If Count Tierney had been trouble, we might not have been there in time."

Startled, Samantha looked at the guard. Her bodyguards never reprimanded her; they rarely said anything to her beside greetings. When she met the man's eyes, a chill went up her spine. They were the coldest eyes she'd ever seen. "Next time, Lieutenant Kailen, have Darhour give you Demon." She hoped he'd break his neck when he tried to ride the horse. She wouldn't have stable hands and guards telling her what to do! When she started to turn away, he exploded into colors—pale blue and white. Instantly, she felt warm and protected. But the feeling had to be all wrong. *Holy Sulis, why does this keep happening? I must truly be mad.* But even in her madness, she was certain Kailen was absolutely loyal to her and would gladly die to defend her.

* * *

When she reached her rooms, her maids informed her Lady Shela had called on her. "Again? But she came yesterday!"

"Yes, but she didn't be seeing you yesterday, now did she?" Ardra said. "Your Highness, would it be so bad to have a friend?"

Samantha shrugged as she got into her bath. Meeting Robbie had reminded her how truly lonely she was. Shela had once been her friend, but Samantha no longer trusted her, not since the day she saw her colors. Before she'd realized that all the men at court wanted her only as a means to the throne, she'd been sitting with Shela, talking about them. Samantha would name one, and Shela would give her opinion and giggle. Suddenly, the air around Shela burst into green— not the green of health and life she'd seen on Darhour, but a putrid green. Shela hated Samantha because she was jealous that all the men at court flocked around the princess. Shela only wanted to be her friend because of the prestige and power that came with it. Samantha had cried herself to sleep that night, and never again had she let one of the court ladies close enough to be a friend. *But should I let my madness dictate my friendships? Perhaps I was wrong about Shela.*

While her maids were busy doing the princess's hair, Lady Shela returned. She bowed, and Samantha offered her a seat. Blonde with snow-white skin and blue eyes, Shela was the perfect example of the court lady. Her face was smooth and heavily painted. She was tall with a slender waist and very large breasts, which her low-cut gown displayed irritatingly. She was everything the princess was not.

Shela crossed her feet under the chair in a perfectly ladylike manner. "I hope you're feeling better today, Your Highness."

Samantha forced her face into a court smile. "Much better. I'm afraid I overindulged at the ball and needed to rest. Forgive me if I have my maids work on my hair while we chat. You know how long it can take sometimes."

"Of course, Your Highness. It took my maids ages to get my hair ready for the ball. But didn't you have just a marvelous time? With all those men wanting you, I don't know how you'll ever chose a consort. Duke Argblutal seems completely in love with you."

Samantha rolled her eyes. "Argblutal is only in love with himself and the idea of being king. You're welcome to him or any of the others for that matter." Samantha didn't need the colors to sense Shela's jealousy.

"Your Highness, you can't mean that. Surely there's somebody you favor."

"No, there isn't," the princess answered too forcefully, and to her fury, she found herself blushing.

Shela faked a laugh. "I knew it. Who is he? What does he have that Argblutal doesn't?"

"He respects me. He talks to me like I have a brain." Samantha paused uncertainly. "I mean there isn't anyone, but if there were, that's what he'd be like. Now, if you'll excuse me, I must finish dressing for dinner."

After Shela left, Ardra smiled shyly. "You met someone at the horse fair, didn't you, Your Highness?"

Samantha sighed sadly. "Yes, but he's a peasant. He can't matter to me."

* * *

Count Nola tried to hide his discomfort as Argblutal's servant met him in the entrance hall of the duke's private residence and led him to the duke's office. Nola didn't know why the duke insisted they meet here. Nola felt a lot safer in the palace. As he neared the end of the corridor, he heard a woman crying, followed by a sharp slap. The servant paused outside the door.

"Let me see them," the duke said from within. Nola heard fabric tearing and the woman's quiet sobs. "Yes, she'll do nicely," the duke continued. "Prepare her for me. I won't be long."

The door opened, and Nola was appalled as Herne, the duke's bastard brother, dragged a coarsely dressed woman out of the room. The woman's face was tear-streaked, and her hands tied behind her back. Her dress had been torn open so that her rather large breasts were prominently displayed. Nola couldn't help staring. When the woman whimpered, Herne had the audacity to smirk.

"I'm sorry, Your Lordship, but these aren't for you." Herne grabbed one of the woman's breasts, causing her to cry out. "Although for the right price I could find you some of your own to play with." Laughing, the bastard dragged the woman away.

"His Grace will see you now," the servant announced, as if nothing out of the ordinary had occurred.

Shaken, Nola entered the duke's office. Argblutal was sitting behind his desk, drinking brandy. "Have a seat, Nola," the duke commanded. Nola did so, but couldn't help looking back in the direction of the woman's cries. "Well?" the duke asked, making no acknowledgement of the woman.

Nola cleared his throat. "Yes . . . well . . . It appears the princess does favor someone after all."

"Who?" Argblutal's lips tightened.

"That I don't . . . well, that is to say, Shela couldn't get his name from Her Highness, but apparently he talks to the princess 'like she has a brain.'"

"Which tells me nothing more than he has few brains himself. I need more, Nola." The duke paused. "I'm sure you noticed my evening's entertainment. Did you see the size of her breasts? Your daughter has a rather admirable set herself."

"Just what are you insinuating?" Nola cried.

"You don't want to disappoint me, Nola." The duke stood. "Now, if you'll excuse me, I hate to keep a woman waiting."

* * *

After dining with the court, King Solar returned to his chambers and lit the candles under the painting of Samantha. It was a profile of her, sitting in her window and staring out. Solar knew it was tantamount to idolatry to love Samantha as he deeply as he did, but she'd stolen his heart the moment she'd been placed in his arms. She'd found his finger and fallen asleep sucking on it. No act had ever elicited such tenderness from him; from that moment on, she was *his* child.

No father could ever love a child more than he'd loved Samantha.

Holy Mother, she's so beautiful! Solar could see hints of Samantha's mother in her eyes, mouth, and forehead. Fenella had been a pretty child, but so young he'd never have considered her for a moment if he hadn't been desperate for an heir. The priests had told him a young girl just entering puberty was his only hope, and they had been right in a manner far different than he'd anticipated. Although Solar never knew the name of the man who'd shared young Fenella's bed, he'd always be grateful for the gift the man had given him. It was regrettable he'd had to have his chancellor take care of the unfortunate.

Solar looked at the crossed swords that hung on either side of Samantha's portrait—reminders of the brutal warfare that had secured the peace and stability of his realm. His parents' marriage had finally united the two rival nations of Korth and Lundia, but not all had approved. It had taken fifteen more years to truly meld the two kingdoms. The process had cost him his parents, his younger brother, and all his close relatives. But the peace had now lasted for fifty years. More than anything he wanted peace to outlive him.

CHAPTER 6

Wild Thing licked Robbie's face again. Robbie was very hot, like a fire. *:Wake up, Robbie. Please. Wild Thing scared. Wild Thing need Robbie.:* But the boy just kept sleeping in Wild Thing's stall. The boy hadn't done that before. *Wild Thing no protect. Wild Thing bad. Wild Thing bring Robbie home. But Robbie takes care of hurts. Wild Thing not know how.*

People hurt Robbie; no animal ever would. But Robbie was already hurt so badly he might die if someone didn't help him. *Stupid cat no good.* Wild Thing bared her teeth when the cat drew near the boy, but the cat hissed. Wild Thing thought about stomping the cat, but she couldn't see how that would help Robbie. *:Please, Robbie. Wild Thing not know what to do. Should Wild Thing get people?:*

Robbie didn't answer, and the sun was up. Robbie had been hurt before, but he'd never stayed sleeping after the sun was up. *If people try hurt again, Wild Thing have strong hooves. Protect Robbie.* She rose, reluctantly leaving Robbie in the straw. No one was in the barn, but the door was open. Wild Thing crossed the farmyard to the other barn where Robbie had his stall. She knocked her face against the door and nickered. No one came. She kicked the door and nickered more loudly. One of the female humans opened the door. Wild Thing was glad. Only male humans ever hurt Robbie. The female gasped and looked wild-eyed at Wild Thing.

Wild Thing lowered her head submissively. *:Need help. Robbie hurt. Come please.:* The stupid human looked scared, and Wild Thing was afraid she would run away without helping Robbie. Wild Thing shook her head toward the barn. *:Robbie hurt bad. Come with, please.:* Wild Thing started toward the barn, hoping the human would follow. The human slid out of the house. *Good, not too stupid.*

* * *

Angus sat at the table waiting for his sons to stumble in for breakfast. The strap rested next to his plate. *I know the boy's not too bright. But after what happened with Tormaidstamm, you'd think he'd stay away from women. A lady, for Sulis's sake! If I have to wear my arm out doing it, I'll beat some sense into him this time.* Unexpectedly, Boyden arrived at the breakfast table first. Robbie was usually an early riser.

"G'morning," Boyden mumbled. The stench of ale seeped from his pores. His eyes were bloodshot, and he put his head in his hands as if afraid it'd fall off.

Angus grunted, remembering how many times he'd been in the same condition at Boyden's age. He noticed Boyden's bruised and swollen hands. His oldest son was strong, but sometimes his temper could use a little cooling. "Who was it this time?" he asked. "I take it you came out on top as usual."

"You could put it that way." Boyden picked up the mug of *bhat* the servant placed in front of him, but pushed away the porridge as if its odor were noxious.

Before Angus could get more details, a goddess-awful scream rent the morning air. "Holy Sulis, that sounded like it was coming from the barn." Angus jumped up.

When he ran through the barn door, Robbie's demon-possessed horse reared and neighed wildly, nearly knocking him off his feet. "Robbie, control your damned horse!" Angus shouted. *Why in the seven hells did I ever let him keep the mad beast?*

As usual when there was work to be done, Robbie was nowhere in sight. Allyn and Darien hurried forward and, with extreme difficulty, restrained the animal. "I'm sorry, sir, Robbie isn't going to be able to do much of anything." Allyn nodded toward the open stall. "Someone's hurt him pretty badly."

Afraid the lady's men had gotten to the boy, Angus walked cautiously forward. Cara, one of the kitchen servants, was kneeling on the ground next to something that, beneath all the blood and bruises, looked like his son. "Holy Sulis, is he alive?"

"At first, I didn't think so. But he seems to be breathing," Cara said, her voice shaking.

Angus heard Boyden slogging up behind him and remembered the bruises on his hands. "Tell me you didn't do this!" He pointed at Robbie.

Boyden leaned casually against the stall. "And what if I did? I saw the strap by your plate. Are you angry I got him first? I'll be happy to hold him down if you want to lay a few more on him."

Angus smacked Boyden across the face hard enough to stagger him. "You watch your tone, boy." He stopped as he noticed the servants staring. He turned to Allyn and Darien. "Get the boy inside! Cara, tend to him." As he watched the farmhands carry out his youngest son, the blood against the dark skin reminded Angus of Donella as she lay dead with her newborn in her arms.

When he and Boyden were alone in the barn, he whirled on his oldest son. "You've gone way over the line! You damn near killed the boy! If Robbie needs disciplining, that's for me to do, not you. You'll do his chores on top of your own today and every day until he's fit to do them himself. And you better pray he doesn't die. I'll have no kin murderers on my lands. Do you hear me, boy?"

Boyden glared at him. "Yes, sir, I hear you just fine."

Angus didn't like his tone, but he needed to check on Robbie. No one could replace Robbie's skill with animals.

When Angus entered Robbie's bedroom, the kitchen servant was bending over him. "How is he?" he asked.

"Master Angus, he's not breathing right. I don't know the slightest thing about healing. Maybe . . . maybe you ought to send for someone," Cara said.

Angus scowled. Father Gildas wouldn't touch the boy, and even if he would, Angus wouldn't have trusted him. The damned priest had been trying to find a way to kill Robbie since the day he was born. There was only one other healer in the Valley: the Sulis-cursed, interfering old herb bitch. Sixteen years ago he'd thrown her smelly carcass off his lands and told her to stay the hell away from his family.

While he was trying to come up with another solution, Beacan, his foreman, ran in, looking like he'd seen a ghost. "Sir, the goddess protect us! Demons have descended upon us! A plague of them destroyed all the grain in the East fields!"

"What in the seven hells are you blathering on about? Nothing but fire could destroy that much grain in a single night."

"I swear, sir, it's all gone."

Angus was certain Beacan was overreacting as he always did, but he needed to check on the situation. He looked back at his son, lying without moving on the bed. "Send one of the boys for Myst," he told Cara. *Damn Boyden! I'll make him pay for forcing me to let that bitch back inside my house!*

Angus followed his men. When he reached the East fields, he was certain he wasn't seeing correctly. The day before, the fields had been covered with calf-high grain. Today, nothing was left. Some of the crop appeared to have been devoured, but much of it had merely been torn out by the roots and trampled. *Who or what could have done this? It would take an army of men to destroy this much in a single night.* Angus had the men fan out to look for clues.

"I found something, Master Angus," one of the hands called. But all the fool could show him were a few strands of some kind of very odd hair. It was colored like nothing he'd ever seen—a dull bronze. What it belonged to Angus couldn't begin to guess. The men talked of demons.

"Maybe we should send for the priest," Boyden, who'd joined them during the search, said.

Angus scowled. He hated that fat cow of a priest as much as he hated the herb bitch. But not knowing what else to do, he nodded.

* * *

Please let it stop! Robbie cried. *Let me die! Anything, just let it stop!*

He looked up and saw the demon lady staring down at him. She reached toward him, tears streaming down her face. "Come, my son, come to me. No one will ever hurt you again."

Desperate for relief, he grasped the woman's hand. He felt himself drifting upwards, leaving his pain-filled body behind.

A strange duo of voices stopped the demon lady. "No! His time is not yet!"

"But why must he suffer more?"

"He is still needed there."

"But look what his own brother has done to him! How can I allow this to continue?"

"His brother will answer for what he has done, but it is not this one's time. If you cannot bear to see him hurt, you need not watch."

"No! I am his mother! I won't leave him!"

"Then you must watch him suffer. He must not die."

The demon lady wailed as she released him. Her cries became louder as Robbie writhed with an agony even more intense than before.

* * *

Angus glowered as Father Gildas's carriage stopped at the edge of his fields. A novice jumped from the seat and opened the door. The novice staggered slightly as the priest used him for support stepping down from the carriage. *How in the seven hells could that tub of lard convince the church he was important enough to be assigned three novices?*

The priest smiled the fake pious smile that always made Angus want to kick him in his ample gut, this morning even more than usual. "I see evil has descended on your household, as I have always feared it would," the priest simpered. "I have felt a disturbance emanating from Beyond the Far Mountain for several days now. Clearly, Sulis was trying to warn me of this coming disaster."

"Mightn't it have been more helpful if she'd warned *me* before it had happened?" Angus snapped.

"As blasphemous as ever, I see. It's just such an attitude that got you excommunicated twenty years ago when you brought the demon witch home. The child born of her blood brings this evil upon you now."

Angus laughed bitterly. "I should have known you'd want to blame Robbie. Get off my lands. I don't need any help from a supposedly celibate priest who's fathered half the bastards in the Valley."

"How dare you speak so of Sulis's chosen! Know this, Angus Camlinstamm. Your crops will continue to be destroyed until you rid this Valley of contamination and come to Sulis on bended knee, begging forgiveness." Father Gildas stalked back toward his carriage.

Angus swore under his breath as the carriage creaked away.

"Father, he speaks for Sulis," Boyden said. "Shouldn't we at least consider what he says?"

Angus glared at his son. "That fraud speaks for no one but himself. After what you did to your brother, just how could he have done this? Tonight we'll stand watch, and we'll stop whatever it is."

* * *

Filled with fear and guilt, Myst gathered her things as quickly as she could. The child had said Robbie was near death. It had been sixteen years since she'd failed to save the life of the woman who'd been like a daughter to her. *Donella, I pray I may be more successful today. They say it's the child that is injured now, the sweet babe that killed you.* Myst well remembered when she'd held the tiny infant in her arms seconds after he emerged from his mother's body, little bigger than the palm of her hand; she'd never seen one that small who'd lived.

Donella had smiled at the tiny child with his skin the color of *bhat*. "Promise me," she begged. "Promise me you'll look out for him and Boyden." Myst had tried to insist that Donella would be there to do it herself, but Donella had known what Myst refused to admit. *Oh, Donella, I told Angus another one would kill you, but he refused to listen.*

Later, she'd said this and more to Angus while his wife lay dead in the next room. *I should have held my tongue. He was grieving for you, too, and I poured salt into his wounds.* Angus had thrown her out of the house and warned her never to come near him or his children again.

Having assembled her things, Myst exited her house and practically flew toward Angus's farm. At sixty-five, she felt as fit as she had at twenty-five, and she still had the figure of a young woman. Because she was a healer, the normal aches and pains of one her age didn't trouble her. The only signs of Myst's true age were the grayness of her hair and a few lines around her eyes and mouth.

Her throat tightened as she approached the house and entered Donella's kitchen. When she entered Donella's son's bedroom, she cried out and rushed toward him. "Holy Sulis, Mother of us all! What happened to him?"

Robbie was naked on the bed, and Cara, one of Angus's servants, was cleaning the blood from his body. That he was full grown was shocking enough, but it was his condition that truly appalled her.

"Thank the goddess, you're here," the servant said. "He's not breathing right, and I don't know what to do."

Myst shoved her basket of remedies and herbs at Cara and sat down on the chair the servant had been using. She called on the goddess's power. As she moved her hands over Robbie's body, his life energy flickered. The wound in his back was deep and filled with splinters; several ribs were broken, as was his nose; his entire body was covered in bruises and he raged with fever; his brain had been battered inside his head; but most serious of all, the vessels in his abdomen had ruptured, filling his belly with blood. If they'd waited much longer to send for her, she would have been too late. *Whoever did this to you, child, had better hope I never get my hands on them.*

Myst closed her eyes and entered a healing trance. She gasped as her energy began to vibrate with the boy's. *The boy's an amihealer, like his mother. How dare Angus keep this from me? Who else in the Valley could help him train his gift?* As Myst remembered Donella's last words, shame filled her. Angus had made the promise difficult to keep, but she should have tried harder. *Donella, my daughter, can you ever forgive me for not knowing? Somehow I should have found out.*

With difficulty, Myst shoved her emotions aside so she could fully access her energy and close the vessels leaking out the boy's life. When she emerged from the trance, she was trembling with exhaustion. She told the waiting servant to remove the splinters from the wound on his back and poultice it with an herb mixture she'd brought. She then collapsed on the floor and lost consciousness.

"Holy Sulis, are you well?" Cara cried out and dropped beside the herb witch. She started to shout for help, but remembered that healers were known to collapse after doing their strange work, so Cara tucked a pillow under the old woman's head and covered her with a blanket.

She turned to look at the boy. *He seems to be breathing a bit easier.* She cleaned the wound and poulticed it as the herb witch instructed. She touched his forehead. He was still burning up. Cara thought about what her mother had done for her when she'd had a fever and fetched cold water from the well to bathe his forehead.

She shuddered as she touched his dark skin. He simply wasn't normal. Cara remembered the first time she'd seen him. She'd been in her third year of schooling, waiting eagerly for the first day to begin. Father Gildas had been writing at his desk, and she was talking to her friend Aideen. The room had gone suddenly silent, and Aideen had gasped. Cara had turned toward the door, and Robbie had been standing there beside his older brother. Father Gildas had let out a roar of fury and grabbed the cane he used to punish the children. "How dare you defile the goddess's holy place with your presence? Be gone!" Robbie had turned and run away as fast as the wind. Father Gildas had had the children sprinkle the school with holy water and chant a cleansing ritual before beginning the day's lesson.

And I was afraid to work here, but daddy had needed the money so badly I couldn't turn down the job. Cara had to admit Robbie had never tried anything with her—not that she'd ever let herself be alone with him before today. But now that she thought about it, she'd never heard of him hurting anyone. Some of her fellow servants complained that Master Boyden was too free with his hands, but they didn't say such things about Robbie. Could he truly be evil if he never did harm?

The boy muttered something. Cara wasn't sure if he was saying "Momma" or "Milady." Cara knew he had no mother. With a sudden surge of sadness, Cara wondered if he'd ever had anyone to love him.

But it's not natural for skin to be so dark, and his eyes are enough to steal the soul right out of your body. Can he really feel like others do? Father Gildas says he's demon-cursed. The priests speak for Sulis, don't they? Cara felt painful doubts creeping into her mind. *What demon would allow others to use him so?*

Cara looked down at the floor and saw a filthy green ribbon. Wondering where it had come from, she leaned down and picked it up. There was dried blood on it as well as mud. *Could it be a token from that lady they say he danced with?* Cara couldn't come up with any other explanation for it, so since she didn't know what else she could do for Robbie, she washed it and lay it on the table beside the bed to dry.

* * *

At dusk, all the hands gathered, and Boyden watched Angus arm them with hoes, pitchforks, and scythes. *As if a demon can be fought with farm tools! We are all idiots to listen to him! I should refuse even though the Sulis-damned fool threatened to disinherit me.* Boyden snorted. *Pretending to care about what I did to the worm when I can't even count the times he's beaten the weakling senseless himself!*

Boyden barely listened to his father blathering on about the signal horns and what to do if they saw the beast. He well knew what he'd do, and it wasn't playing some little song for the demon to dance to.

When Boyden learned his father planned for him to stand watch on the far end of the East fields, closest to the woods, he was furious. *Does the old man want me dead or something? Just who does he think the worm's demon will come looking for first?* As he remembered those eerie green eyes looking up at him from the dirt, Boyden shuddered. *A freak like that should never have been allowed to live. How could my father have married a witch?* He looked at his white hand. *At least, Sulis saved me from her demon curse.*

Before it grew dark, Boyden started a fire in order to better see the approaching demon. But outside of its light, Boyden could see nothing but the fires of the other men. Tonight was a full moon, but the clouds blocked all light. As the hours passed with nothing happening, he grew more bored than scared. He sat near his fire and used his knife to whittle a woman out of a branch. He carved her breasts large like Arleen's or Blair's. When he thought of the two women, he threw his carving into the fire with disgust. *Why do women always have to make a simple thing like fucking into a damned marriage proposal?* He struggled against sleep, but the night was quiet, and there was nothing whatsoever to do.

He heard the ground being ripped to shreds, and he wandered out from beneath the trees. A beast of immense size —at least the height of five men— towered above him. Its eyes glowed red. The worm rode on the beast's back, and he too had grown to gigantic size. Robbie's eyes matched the red of the beast's. "You will pay!" he said. "You will all pay!"

"For the strap, old man, you die," Robbie said, and the beast opened its mouth and breathed fire, incinerating Angus. As he laughed over their father's ashes, Robbie turned the beast toward Boyden. Boyden tried to run, but his feet refused to move. The demon drew near, its fangs dripping with emerald green venom. "Hungry, my friend?" the worm asked, and the beast's mouth moved closer.

"Please, Robbie, don't!"

The worm laughed and rubbed his chin. "Prove to me you've learned your lesson. Come and lick my boots clean."

Boyden glanced at the worm's boots; they too were green with venom. "No! Please! Have mercy!"

"What mercy did you show me?" The beast lowered its head. Boyden could feel its hot breath and felt the poison drip against his skin.

Boyden cried out and jerked awake. A light rain was falling. *Infernal dream!* He cursed and tried to shake off the terror of the nightmare.

Almost immediately he realized it wasn't the dream or the rain alone that had disturbed him. He heard a sound like a gigantic jaw ripping plant life from the ground and reducing it to powder. Boyden sprang to his feet and looked frantically across the field. The clouds had parted, and no more than a single acre away in the light of the full moon, Boyden saw the silhouette of an animal of some kind. The beast screamed an unearthly scream and reared toward the sky. The moon illuminated a glittering form on the beast's back. The beast turned toward Boyden, and Boyden ran as if all the hosts of the seven hells were after him.

* * *

As the sun started to rise, Angus watched his hands attempt to sneak back to the positions they'd deserted during the night. He intercepted his foreman and grabbed him by the arm. "Where in the seven hells have you been?"

Beacan wouldn't meet his eyes. "We've been in the bunk house, sir. All of us. We heard what the priest said, and we've agreed we won't risk our souls trying to stop a demon!" Angus wanted to bash the man's head against a rock. "It got the west fields last night. I just came by that way."

"So you all cowered in safety while the demon wreaked havoc? If we don't stop this thing, you fancy starving this winter?"

Beacan raised his eyes to meet Angus's. "More than I fancy trying to stop a demon with a pitchfork. Sir, Master Boyden was in the west fields. Nobody's seen him."

Feeling suddenly weak, Angus grabbed Beacan's shoulder for support. *No, Sulis! Not my eldest!* "Check the house to make sure he's not there. Get everyone to meet me in the west fields."

When Angus reached the fields, a group of his hands stood, staring at the ruined grain. Angus barreled toward them and pointed to the remains of the crop. "This will come out of your wages! And if my son is . . ." Angus couldn't complete the sentence. "Find my son."

The men began the search. After half an hour, they found nothing other than a few metallic bronze hairs. *Please, Sulis, don't let him be dead!*

At last, one of the hands shouted, and Angus hurried toward him. Boyden was lying at the edge of the field. He looked like he'd been dragged through the forest by a runaway horse. His clothes were in tatters; his face and arms were badly scratched, and he had twigs and leaves sticking in his hair. But he was breathing. Angus yelled for water, and someone handed him a canteen. He lifted Boyden's head and tried to force the water past his lips. To Angus's intense relief, Boyden spluttered and opened his eyes.

"I'm sorry, sir," he whispered. "I couldn't stop it."

Angus blinked back tears. "It's alright, son. Just tell me what happened."

Boyden asked for something more powerful than water, and Angus had it brought to him. When Boyden told his story, it was the stuff of nightmares. "I heard this horrible noise. I swear it sounded like demons being tortured. I blew the signal horn, but no one came. At first I could see nothing, but then the clouds parted and the moon shone on it. Holy Sulis, it was the height of five men. Its eyes glowed red, and it breathed fire. It had fangs as long as my finger, and they were dripping with green poison. It spoke to me, if such a horrible noise can be called speaking. It said Robbie had called it up. It said if you don't put Robbie in charge and make him your sole heir, it will destroy everything—the crops, the barn, the livestock, even the house and . . . and all of us. It tore the scythe right out of my hands, and if I hadn't run then, it would have had me. Father, there's nothing we can do against it."

* * *

As Robbie woke, pain shot through him. He kept his eyes closed. He didn't want to wake up, not now, not ever. In his entire life, he'd met one single person who liked him and had only one good day. And for that, he'd been beaten nearly to death. *What's the use of trying anymore? Things will never change.* A spasm of pain passed through him, and he cried out.

A hand grabbed his, and a woman's voice spoke, "Ride out the pain, my son. It will be better soon." He felt a warm tingle, similar to what he felt when treating sick animals, and the pain dulled. He opened his eyes. An old woman was sitting next to him holding his hand. It was the half-breed witch, Myst, the one his father hated. Cara was standing behind her. The witch smiled, but her eyes seemed to be wet with tears. With her free hand, she smoothed his hair back from his forehead. "It's a good thing you inherited your mother's abilities. If it wasn't for your gift, you wouldn't have survived. Cara said your brother did this to you, is it true?"

Robbie just stared at the witch. Although she seemed to be speaking his language, her words made no sense. The tenderness of her touch made even less. He decided he was still unconscious. *If I'm going to dream of someone, why can't it be Milady?*

He licked his lips. They were dry and cracked. "Are you thirsty?" the old woman asked. He nodded, but still didn't say anything. She let go of his hand and poured a glass of water from a pitcher on the table beside the bed. Next to the pitcher was the green ribbon Milady had given him. It had been cleaned and pressed. He grabbed it.

"I cleaned it up for you," Cara said. "I thought you'd want that. I'm glad . . . I'm glad you're not going to die." *Why would she say that? She's never even wanted to be in the same room with me before.*

Robbie closed his eyes again as the herb witch helped him lift his head to drink. He hoped things would make sense when he opened them again. But when the witch lowered him back onto the pillow, the two women were still looking at him with concern and tenderness.

Of course, it was too good to last. The door burst open, and his father pushed Myst aside, grabbed him by the front of the nightshirt, and yanked him out of the bed. "How dare you do this to me?" His father slapped him hard enough that his head snapped back.

"I haven't done anything!" Robbie cried.

"Liar!" Angus lifted his hand to hit him again, but the herb witch grabbed his arm.

"Angus, what in the seven hells do you think you're doing? Boyden nearly killed him. Are you trying to finish the job?"

Angus dropped Robbie onto the bed and threw off Myst's hand. The herb witch stepped between him and his father, and Angus jabbed a finger into Myst's chest. "You won't use your infernal magic on me. No one, least of all you, has the right to interfere between a man and his son. He's called up demons and destroyed half my crop. He will pay for it. Now, get out of my way."

Robbie cowered as far away from his father as he could get. *Holy Sulis! He's gone mad! He's going to kill me!*

"Have you lost your mind?" Myst echoed Robbie's thoughts. "How can you possibly blame what's happened on Robbie?"

"I don't have to explain myself to you, woman!" Several farmhands came into the room. "Throw her off my lands, boys," Angus ordered.

Before the farmhands could touch Myst, the old woman grasped Angus by the throat. "Stand back," she ordered, and the men stopped. Angus's face went white, and he began to choke. "Angus, he's your son. He's Donella's child. What could possibly make you think he's responsible?"

Angus grabbed the herb witch's wrist, but he seemed incapable of removing her hand. His father, the biggest man in the Valley, was helpless against the old woman. "His demon admitted it," Angus gasped out. "Boyden heard it. Now get your filthy hands off me."

What is he accusing me of? Why does he always believe Boyden and not me? Robbie couldn't count the number of times he'd been beaten for something Boyden had done. It had never mattered when Robbie swore his innocence, and he knew it wouldn't matter this time either. The only thing stopping his father from killing him was an old woman.

The herb witch's eyes narrowed. "Boyden nearly beat his brother to death. Robbie wouldn't be alive now if he hadn't inherited his mother's gift. Did it never occur to you Boyden might be lying?"

"Robbie is my son, not yours. Get out of my way."

"I'm going nowhere until you give me your sacred vow to hurt him no further." The herb witch's voice vibrated with power. The herb witch tightened her hold, and Angus trembled.

Angus shot her a look of pure venom. "Get off my lands. Don't ever try to come back, and I won't touch him."

Her eyes narrowed. "I said, your sacred vow."

Angus hesitated, and the herb witch's hand tightened further. Angus cried out as if he were in pain. "I'll give you my vow, you Sulis-cursed interfering bitch. I promise by the goddess and on my mother's grave that if you get the hell off my lands right now, I won't harm the boy."

The herb witch released her hold, and Angus fell against the wall, gasping. "Don't think you can harm him without me finding out."

"Get off my property!" Angus roared.

The old woman turned to Robbie. "If you need me, please, come to me at any time." She gave Angus one last glare and left.

As his father turned back toward him, Robbie cowered away. *Oh, Sulis, no! Please, no!* "Don't think that damned bitch can protect you. You will go out there, and you will stop this tonight, or you better hope you can run fast enough to outpace a mob." Without waiting for a response, Angus stormed from the room.

Robbie collapsed onto the bed. After several minutes, someone entered. He looked up in terror, expecting his father, but it was the kitchen girl, Cara. "What does he think I've done?" he asked.

Cara told him of the destruction of half of their grain and related Boyden's description of the demon.

Robbie put his head in his hands; one of them was clutching Milady's ribbon. *How can he blame me for this? What does he think I can do about it?* He needed to think, and he needed Wild Thing by his side; she was his only true friend. He told the kitchen girl to leave so he could get dressed.

Cara put her hands on her hips. "You're not well enough to get out of bed."

Robbie glared at her. "Don't you think I know that? Now get the hell out of here!"

"Fine. Go out there and get yourself killed. See if I care." Cara stormed out of the room, slamming the door behind her.

When has she ever cared?

Gritting his teeth against the pain, Robbie managed to get himself dressed, carefully placing Milady's ribbon in the pocket of his shirt. He grabbed the table by the bed and forced himself to his feet. Since he didn't immediately fall, he decided he could walk. He opened the door and cautiously looked out into the deserted hallway. Using the wall to steady himself, he walked to the kitchen.

He paused at the door; the barn had never seemed so far. He took a step and nearly stumbled, but caught himself on a large, warm body. "Wild Thing, girl! I've got problems. Can you help me get somewhere private and help me figure out what to do?"

Wild Thing nodded her head in an unusually submissive manner. *:Wild Thing help.:*

Robbie clung to the mare, and the two of them slowly made their way across the farmyard and into Wild Thing's stall. There, Robbie collapsed, and Wild Thing lowered herself beside him. When Robbie buried his face in her warmth, a wild mixture of anger and guilt came from her. "You're not blaming yourself for what Boyden did to me, are you?"

:Wild Thing not stop brother. Wild Thing has strong hooves and strong teeth. Robbie never tie Wild Thing again. Wild Thing never let anyone hurt Robbie. Wild Thing stomp into mash if try to hurt Robbie. Robbie good. Robbie make things feel better, even stupid cats. Brother bad. Lady good, too. Lady give Wild Thing apple. Wild Thing like apples.:

Robbie threw his arms around her neck. "What would I do without you?"

:Robbie never be without Wild Thing.:

"I hope you're right, girl." Comforted by her fierce protectiveness, Robbie rested against her side. He told her about how the crops were being destroyed and how his father was blaming him.

:Be all right. Beasts like Robbie.:

Robbie almost laughed. "Not beasts like that. Boyden said it is the height of five men."

:Who care how big? What beast not like Robbie?:

Not knowing how to make Wild Thing understand, Robbie shook his head. Seeking out the monster seemed insane, but what choice did he have? He curled up next to the horse and fell asleep.

As he slept, he danced with the beautiful lady who found his green eyes stunning. She kissed him and promised to be his and his alone. As he dreamed, he felt the weight of the ribbon in his pocket.

* * *

A bucketful of cold water woke Robbie. He sprang into a sitting position, crying out in pain. His father stood over him. "So this is where you've been hiding," Angus said. "Now get out there and banish that demon back to wherever you called it from or don't you ever let me set eyes on you again." Angus stomped from the barn.

I'll go get myself killed if it will make you happy. Robbie winced as he tried to stand. He was very hungry and thirsty. He doubted his father would let him go into the house and eat before heading for the fields to be torn apart by demons, so Robbie saddled Wild Thing. When he led the mare out of her stall, his brother was lounging against the barn wall. Boyden grinned at him, and he moved closer to Wild Thing.

:Wild Thing protect. Brother not hurt.:

Robbie touched Wild Thing, hating himself for being afraid. He looked past Boyden to see the sun setting. At least his death would prove his innocence. As he walked out of the barn past Boyden, he leaned on Wild Thing.

At the well, Robbie stopped and drew up a bucket of water. He took a long drink, aware that Boyden was watching him. Clenching his teeth against the pain, he swung himself up into the saddle and headed toward the fields.

When he rode out of sight of his brother, he heard someone call his name from the side of the path. "Robbie, wait." He reined Wild Thing in and looked down to see Cara holding a basket. She handed the basket up to him. "I thought you might need this."

Surprised by her thoughtfulness, he took the basket. "Thank you." Before he could say more, Cara faded into the gathering dark.

Robbie rode to the border between the west and the south fields, dismounted, and opened the basket. He found bread, cheese, two apples and a large bottle of *bhat*. The *bhat* was cold, rather than hot like he liked it best, but it was still sweet, rich, and delicious. He devoured the bread and cheese and drank every last drop of the *bhat*. He gave one of the apples to Wild Thing and saved the other for later. He leaned against a tree and allowed Wild Thing to graze nearby, knowing she wouldn't wander far. Staring across the fields, he waited for something to happen. He knew he should stay awake; his very life might depend on it, but no matter how hard he tried to fight it, he felt himself drifting into sleep.

* * *

Cara looked over her shoulder every few seconds as she hurried back to the bunkhouse. While she didn't want the demon to get Robbie, she was even more afraid for herself. As she rounded the bunkhouse, a hand shot out and caught her by the wrist. She squealed.

"Where have you been?" a voice asked out of the darkness.

"Oh, Dillion, you scared me to death. I thought I'd been caught by the demon." She tried to control the beating of her heart as she put her arms around her husband's neck and gave him a kiss. Dillion wasn't exactly handsome, but Cara had always been drawn to the way the sunlight caught the highlights of gold in his hair and the twinkle that was usually in his eyes.

Dillion broke off the kiss. "I said, where have you been?"

Cara removed her arms from his neck. "I brought a basket of food to Robbie. They were going to send him out to face a demon without even the decency of a meal."

Dillion folded his arms across his chest. "Robbie again, is it? You've been spending a lot of time with him lately."

Cara put her hands on her hips. "Just what are you suggesting?"

"My bed was empty the last night. Have you found you prefer the demon boy's?"

"How dare you suggest such a thing!" She stepped back from him. "There's only one man I want in my bed."

Dillion's eyes softened, and he reached out an arm to hug her. "I'm sorry, Cara, I didn't mean it."

She shook off his arm. "You'd better not mean it. There hasn't been a man born yet that could take me from you, Dillion Briacstamm."

"You know what they say about the demon boy's mother. How she bewitched Master Angus."

Cara gestured wildly. "Bards' tales, that's all they are."

"I said I'm sorry, Cara." He reached out for her again, and this time she didn't resist being drawn into his arms.

* * *

Angus was far too concerned about the fate of his farm to sleep, so he spent the night pacing the dining room, cursing his son. *Damn him! I've done everything I could for him. Protected him from that accursed priest. Tried to teach him to behave decently. And now he tries to destroy me.* However, after a few hours, his anger began to cool, and as it cooled, doubts began to creep in. He remembered the sight of the boy's battered body lying at the feet of his Horsetad. *Could he have done anything in that condition? He's Donella's son. Donella wasn't a demon.*

Angus walked to the door and opened it, but stopped before walking out into the night. *Who else can it be? Who else has the boy's power?* Angus had watched the power grow within his youngest son. He was more powerful than even his mother had been. There seemed to be no illness or injury he couldn't heal, and the boy had always been able to coax any wild beast into his hands. Angus closed the door and resumed pacing. *Oh, Donella, have I done right?* If Robbie managed to banish the demon, didn't that mean Father Gildas had been right about him all along? And right about Donella? That she was some kind of demon witch that had lured him from the path of the goddess? He remembered how small and vulnerable she had looked in that room near the docks where she'd been put up for sale; he remembered the way her lip had trembled. No demon would be that afraid.

He clenched his fists. *But what other explanation is there?*

* * *

The moon was halfway across the sky when Wild Thing nudged Robbie awake. He heard a noise that wiped all sleep from his eyes: a horrible grinding sound, followed by an unearthly wail. Robbie stumbled to his feet and looked around wildly. Less than a hundred yards away was the silhouette of a horse with a demon knight on its back. The demon saw him, and its horse reared, pawing the night sky. Robbie froze in panic. He wanted to jump on Wild Thing and not stop running until they reached Murtaghan. But even through his fear, he could feel the horse's terrible pain. He couldn't leave an animal who needed him without trying to help.

"Forgive me, Sir Knight," Robbie said. He slowly approached the demon knight, trying to be as deferential as possible. "Your horse is badly hurt."

The demon knight didn't answer. Robbie instinctively reached out with his mind to the injured beast. Feeling as though his skin had been ripped from his body and his mouth torn apart with a knife, he screamed and fell to his knees. *Holy Sulis, it's hurt bad!*

He struggled to his feet. "Please, Sir Knight. Let me help your horse."

The demon knight still made no answer, but the horse reared and wailed. As it did, the knight rocked, and his helm tumbled off and landed with a thud. *Mother of us all, it has no head!* Robbie nearly fled in terror, but the headless knight wobbled on the horse's back, and Robbie realized it was only an empty suit of armor.

Feeling less afraid, Robbie grabbed the apple he'd saved and approached the horse. "It's okay. I know you're hungry. I know you're hurt. I help hurt creatures. Let me help you." The demon horse pawed the ground nervously, but didn't move. Carefully, so he wouldn't be caught in the horse's pain again, Robbie sent feelings of comfort and safety. "It's okay. I won't hurt you."

He held out the apple. The creature tossed its head and pawed the ground. "Come on, you can have it." The beast shook its head, but inched closer. Nothing Boyden said about it was true. The horse was indeed larger than Wild Thing, but it was nowhere near the height of five men. Nineteen hands at the shoulder, it was large for a horse, but not unnaturally so. Robbie could see it didn't have fangs, and it hadn't yet breathed fire. Its eyes also failed to glow red.

When it was close enough, Robbie patted its nose gently with his left hand while he continued to offer the apple with his right. As the horse took the apple, it wailed that unearthly wail again and threw the apple to the side, knocking Robbie to the ground. It reared, and Robbie scrambled out of reach of its hooves. Something was very wrong with the horse's mouth. Trembling with the pain of his own injuries, Robbie got slowly to his feet. "Your mouth hurts, doesn't it? Let me help." He sent the image of a soothing salve he had in the barn. The horse moved toward him, as if begging for relief.

When Robbie was able to get close enough again, he looked for the cause of the horse's discomfort. It was hard to see clearly in the darkness, but he could tell there was some kind of bit in the horse's mouth. As he fumbled, looking for a way to release the bit, he continued to talk. He found the straps fastening it, undid them, and pulled the bit gently from the beast's mouth.

He couldn't take the horse to the barn. If he was found with it, his father would never believe he hadn't summoned the demon to begin with. Angus would kill them both. Robbie thought of the abandoned stable in the woods where he'd eaten the preserves. He could take the horse there. He would have to leave the horses near the barn and sneak in and get the supplies he needed, but he couldn't see another choice. He put his hands on both sides of the horse's nose, stared into its eyes, and explained his plan. Robbie felt the demon horse's trust. He whistled for Wild Thing, who trotted up to his side. He picked up the empty helm, attached it to Wild Thing's saddle, and swung into the saddle. Holding the other animal's reins, he walked the horses back to the edge of the fields and hid them both in a small clump of trees behind the barn. He impressed upon them the need to stay still and silent. Knowing Wild Thing wouldn't fail him, he could only hope demons were as reliable as Horsetads.

Robbie crept silently into the barn. Not daring to light a lantern, he felt around in the darkness. He found a large sack and quickly selected the things needed to care for the demon horse. He also took a bag of oats to make warm mash.

He returned to the horses, loaded the supplies on Wild Thing, and rode in silence to the abandoned stable. Robbie led the horse inside. When he lit the lantern he kept there, he let out a whistle of amazement. The horse was a bronze-colored mare that looked more like it was forged out of metal than living flesh! But the horse's impossible color wasn't the only thing that struck Robbie. Sores spotted the beast's body; puss and blood oozed from under the saddle. The horse's coat was matted with dried blood. Her ribs stood out in stark detail. *How could anyone neglect a horse so badly?* "Where could you have come from, girl?" Robbie could feel a wail building up inside the horse, so he hurried to take the armor and other equipment off her back, unsaddled her, and removed her harness.

Robbie looked the horse in the eyes. "I need to fetch water and warm it so I can make you feel better. Do you understand?" The horse nodded. Robbie lit a fire in a brazier he used to warm the place in the winter and went to fetch water from the stream. He poured it into two different containers. The first he mixed with herbs that would both cleanse the horse's wounds and deaden the pain. In the other, he poured oats to make the mash. When the herbal mixture was ready, he used it and a large jar of his best ointment to treat the horse's injuries, beginning with the mouth, which was cut and raw. No wonder the animal was so thin; eating anything rougher than mash would be excruciating. As always when he touched an animal in need, he felt the gratifying tingle of energy. Sighing with the pleasure of it, he wondered if this was what it'd feel like to be touched by a woman—by Milady.

"I don't think you're a demon. But I don't know what you are. By the look of the armor you must have been some knight's lady. But what happened to him? Sores like these don't form overnight. If he's still alive, he obviously doesn't deserve a lady like you. So how about it? Will you be *my* lady?" He paused at the sound of his own words. *Milady.* "I had a lady once. For one day, that is. My brother didn't approve—I'm sure he wouldn't approve of you, either."

After treating the horse's injuries, he fed her the warm mash. When she'd finished with it, the horse radiated contentment and gratitude. Seeing the first rays of dawn's light on the horizon, Robbie needed to get back to the farm. He promised the bronze horse he'd return as soon as he could.

The sun was coming up as he reached the barn. He was about to unsaddle Wild Thing when his father and Boyden burst in. Robbie moved behind Wild Thing, despising himself as a coward.

"So!" his father said. "You dare defy me and leave our grain to be devoured by demons. I should . . ." He moved threateningly toward Robbie, but Wild Thing bared her teeth.

"I was out there all night. Nothing happened," Robbie protested, trying not to cower.

"Oh, really?" Angus turned to Boyden. "Saddle the horses, son." He wheeled back to Robbie. "You're going with us, boy, and you'd better not be lying."

When Angus saw undamaged grain, his scowl deepened and he clenched the horse's reins more tightly with his hands. Robbie wasn't surprised. Nothing he did ever pleased his father.

Angus jabbed a finger at him. "You'll watch again tonight and the night after and the night after that, until we're sure the demon won't come back. Get back to the farm and get to bed. You're useless in this condition."

When Robbie reached the barn, he was too tired to do anything other than unsaddle the horse and collapse in Wild Thing's stall.

* * *

Robbie awoke near sunset. When he moved, the pain wasn't too bad, but his stomach ached with hunger. Hearing a mewing, he sat up. Ronan drop a large dead rat near his hand. *:For you. Tasty.:*

Robbie suppressed his nausea. *I hope I'm never that desperate.* He petted the cat. "Why, thank you, Ronan, my boy. That's a very fine gift." Pressing his head into Robbie's hand, the cat purred with pleasure.

Someone opened the barn door and came in. Robbie got to his feet, but made sure Wild Thing stood between him and whoever it was.

"Robbie, are you here?" the kitchen girl, Cara, called out. He was still unsure what to think of the girl's odd behavior, but he decided he was in no danger from her.

"Yes, I'm over here." He came out of the stall and was surprised to see her holding a tray of food that looked a lot better tasting than Ronan's gift.

"Here, I figured you'd be hungry." She handed him the tray.

"Ah, thank you, thank you, Miss. That was very kind of you." Twice in two days, she'd fed him, and they were alone in the barn together, something she'd always avoided.

"You're welcome. How are you feeling? You should be sleeping in your bed and not out in the fields all night."

"And what choice in the seven hells do I have?"

Cara stepped back. "I wasn't blaming you. When your horse brought me back to her stall, I thought you were dead. Damn you, Robbie, can't a woman be worried without upsetting every male in the goddess's lands?"

As Cara whirled out of the barn, Robbie stared after her. He shrugged, certain that he'd never understand women. He sat down and ate his food while Ronan mewed around his feet. "Go find your own dinner," he ordered. Flouncing his tail at Robbie, Ronan stalked off.

With the help of Allyn and Darien, Robbie milked the cows, settled the animals in for the night, and gathered the supplies he needed to care for the bronze horse. After he loaded them onto Wild Thing, he tied the green ribbon around a thin strip of leather, which he then tied around his neck and tucked under his shirt. He knew he'd never see her again, but he wanted the reminder that at least one person in the world didn't despise him.

He was about to head to the forest stable when his father arrived. Robbie tensed and moved closer to Wild Thing. "You're going out there again, and you'll stay there until we come and get you at dawn. Do you understand, boy?"

Robbie glared at his father without answering. *I saved his fields, and still he talks to me like this.*

Angus's face turned red. "I said do you understand, boy?"

"Yes, sir." Robbie didn't bother trying to hide his anger. If Wild Thing hadn't been there, his father probably would have slapped him.

"Good. Get out of here." His father left.

Robbie grabbed an extra blanket, walked Wild Thing out of the barn, and swung onto her back.

When he arrived at the stable in the woods, the bronze horse neighed. Robbie could tell she was hungry and the soothing effects of the salve had worn off. He quickly lit the brazier and started cooking oat mash while he tended the horse's injuries. The horse began to relax as the salve brought relief.

When the mash was ready, he fed the mare. She greedily devoured it and fell asleep. He petted the sleeping horse. "What's your name, my girl? Where did you come from? That was pretty brazen of you to destroy my father's crops like that. Maybe that's what I should call you. Lady Brazen." The mare made no response, and Robbie left her to her rest.

The night before, Robbie had been too exhausted to pay much attention to the equipment Brazen had been carrying. He now examined it. Besides the saddle and armor, there was a sword and a pair of saddle bags. Everything was of exquisite workmanship and gleamed brightly in the lantern light. The saddle was made of expensive leather and tooled with bronze inlays in a pattern of crossed swords. It was in perfect condition. The suit of armor was made of bronze and too big for him, but he thought it might fit him when he reached his full height. Since it was too small for any normal Korthlundian man, he wondered who'd worn it. The sword interested him most. It reminded him of the one Milady had worn. Only rarely had he seen a real sword, and he'd never touched one. The scabbard was of the same leather as the saddle and tooled with a matching pattern of bronze inlays. The sword's hilt was made of bronze, and its pommel was tooled with the identical pattern of crossed swords. He pulled the sword from the scabbard, and its steel blade glittered. Although Robbie knew nothing about swords, it felt comfortable in his hands. *With this, I could make sure nobody ever beat me again.*

He let out a disgusted snort. *Except if I dared show it to anyone, I'd be hanged as a thief.* He could imagine the king's officer's reaction when he tried to explain he'd found it. *I wouldn't even believe myself!* He returned the sword to the scabbard and carefully hung it and the armor in the stable. He looked in the saddlebags, which contained a dagger that matched the workmanship of the sword and clothing of fabric so fine Robbie had never touched anything like it. It shimmered and slid through his fingers. *Could it be silk?* The clothing was also dyed bronze and embroidered with bronze thread in the same pattern of crossed swords. *What would Milady think if she could see me in this?*

Robbie looked at the sleeping horse. While he was pretty sure she wasn't from the seven hells, he had no explanation for her or the condition of her gear. Considering how badly off the horse had been, the gear should have shown some signs of age or wear, but all of the bronze sparkled untarnished, and the leather looked brand new. He yawned, too tired to worry about it tonight. He turned to Wild Thing. "Do me a favor, girl. Wake me before dawn." Wild Thing nuzzled him with her nose. Knowing the mare wouldn't fail him, Robbie wrapped himself in the blanket and fell asleep.

That night as he slept the demon lady came to him again. *She smiled at him. "It is well, my son. She will protect you as I cannot."*

Robbie reached out to touch the demon lady, but when he clasped her hand, it was Milady who smiled at him. He drew her into his arms, and they danced until dawn.

* * *

Robbie reached the undamaged fields just before sunrise, and soon his father and Boyden arrived to meet him. Angus merely scowled at the grain, nodded sharply at Robbie, and rode back to the farm house. Boyden smirked at him before following their father. Robbie followed more slowly. When he reached the barn, he stabled and rubbed down Wild Thing. His stomach growled with hunger. At first he automatically headed for the main house, but he saw Boyden's face, commanding him to lick his boots clean. He smelled the odor of food coming from the bunkhouse and headed there instead.

When Robbie entered the bunkhouse, all conversation stopped. The farmhands stared at him with a mixture of shock and suspicion. Some drew stars over their breasts. Robbie tried not to let it bother him.

The bunkhouse was dominated by one large room divided between sleeping and eating areas. The rear portion contained twenty beds, each with two bunks, five of which were presently unused. Behind the bunks were several smaller rooms, portioned off with curtains for married couples; most of the female servants slept on the second floor of the main house. In the front half of the bunkhouse were four long tables, each capable of seating ten people. A fifth table at the front held food from which the farmhands served themselves. Robbie took a bowl, dished up some porridge and bacon and grabbed a hunk of bread. He sat at the end of one of the tables. Everyone who had been sitting at the table moved elsewhere. Across the room, several of the hands whispered.

After a few minutes, Allyn detached himself from the group and sat across from him. Allyn was only a little older than Robbie, and they'd grown up together, caring for the animals. He wasn't exactly a friend, but he never seemed to be afraid of him like so many of the others, perhaps because he had a large purple mark covering his lower right cheek. "So, any special reason for eating with the hands today?" Allyn asked.

"I like the company better."

Allyn raised an eyebrow and looked down the empty table. Then he looked at Robbie's bruised face and nodded. "I see. I guess that makes sense." Allyn walked back to the others.

CHAPTER 7

Samantha awoke with the vague memory of having dreamed of dancing with the peasant. As she dressed, a page arrived with a message that her father would like her to breakfast with him. Samantha frowned, hoping he hadn't found out about the horse fair. She'd hate Darhour or her bodyguards to be punished for it. She finished dressing quickly and hurried to the king's rooms.

As she entered his breakfast room, she assumed the smile that had always got her out of trouble and greeted the king with a kiss on the cheek. "Good morning, Father." The king's expression was grim. *Sulis curse it all! He does know.*

"Good morning, my dear. You've fully recovered from the ball?" The king raised his eyebrow at her, as if he doubted she'd been ill.

She hastily reached for a pastry as an excuse for not meeting his eyes. "Yes, Father. I'm afraid I overindulged, nothing more."

"A ball that would tire you so thoroughly must have produced some depth of thought." He looked at her expectantly. *Not the consort thing again! Why can't any of the men at court be more like Robbie?* "Samantha, you know what your duties are."

The princess gritted her teeth. "Yes, I must maintain the peace. War is bad. People die in war. We shouldn't have war." *But I will not marry one of those fools. Holy Sulis, I'd vomit if I had to let one of them touch me.*

"Samantha, my dear, I have told you I'll allow you to make the choice, but you must decide and soon."

"If the choice is truly mine, I've made it. I choose to marry no one." She jumped to her feet and stomped from the room, ignoring his calls.

* * *

Solar sighed, staring out the window toward the stables. Samantha would appear there shortly. She always went riding when she was angry. *Why is she being so stubborn? Can I even remember what the world looked like at seventeen?* He'd been twenty when his father decided it was time for him to marry, and Solar had rebelled at the thought of marrying "that bitch." His father had never even asked him, merely announced to him the date of his marriage and the name of his bride. *But I'm not demanding she marry anyone in particular. I'm giving her the choice I never had.*

"Your Majesty, we were discussing the coming Massossinan trade delegation," Caedmon said from behind him.

The king started; for a moment he'd forgotten his chancellor was there. *I'm simply too old. How long before my mind deserts me completely?* The king kept looking out the window. "Samantha will be handling that. I'm not wrong in thinking she needs a consort, am I?"

"No, Your Majesty, she's too young, and she's a woman. She will have extreme difficulties if she attempts to rule alone."

Solar hit the window frame with his fist. The blow seemed feeble, as did everything about him these days. "Why can't she see this? If I were my father, I'd force a consort on her."

Solar heard Caedmon shift in his seat behind him. "She'd hate you for it." Caedmon was right, which was why he couldn't do it. Lir would think him weak, and maybe he was. Perhaps his love for her would ruin all he'd built over his long reign.

* * *

After changing for riding, Samantha stomped down to the stables, fuming at her father. *I won't marry any of them. He can't make me.*

When she neared the stables, she heard a commotion coming from the other side—a wild nickering and snorting. She had heard that sound before. As she rounded the corner, she saw Darhour overseeing the breeding of two of the palace horses. As the stallion, with a savage look of pleasure, thrust his way into the mare, she watched with both fascination and horror. The mare's expression was more difficult to read. She looked frightened and helpless, but she also looked as if some intense need were being satisfied. Samantha stopped at the fence beside Darhour, and after a few more thrusts the stallion let out a wild neigh of pleasure. He backed away from the mare looking both satisfied and spent. Grooms jumped into the paddock to care for the two animals.

For the first time, Darhour noticed her. "Your Highness, what would your old governess have said if she knew I'd allowed you to witness such a sight?"

Samantha ignored Darhour's question, as she watched the mare being led away. "Is it like that, Darhour? I mean, when humans mate?"

A blush crept over Darhour's scarred features. "Your Highness, I'm not the one you should ask such questions."

"Who should I ask?"

Darhour turned away. "Normally, a girl's mother would be the one."

Samantha turned the Master of the Horse toward her. "I have no mother, so you tell me, Darhour. Is it like that?"

Darhour seemed to steel himself. "Your Highness, in some ways, it's very much like that. The intensity. The need to join. To become one. But it's also very different, or at least, it should be. For humans, it should be much more than the animalistic impulses you just witnessed. It can and should be the highest expression of love and tenderness between two people. Usually, it's also a good deal gentler."

Samantha hugged herself. It wouldn't be such an expression of tenderness with her. There could be no love for her in marriage. The thought of rutting like an animal to produce an heir nauseated her. She remembered the gentle touch of Robbie's hands on her in her dream. *Things would be different if I could mate with him.*

But that could never be, so Samantha thrust the thought away and entered the stables. As she saddled Roberta, Phomello, the son of the Neasarian ambassador, entered. The blackness of his skin stood out sharply against the brilliant white of his riding outfit. His nose and lips were wide, which Samantha found attractive because it was so different from Korthlundian features. Without noticing her, he walked toward his own horse, which grooms were busy saddling. As he glanced back, he recognized her. "Highness." He bowed and looked over her horse with admiration. Samantha smiled at his attention to her beloved mare. "Ride?" he asked, gesturing between their two horses.

Not being able to think of an excuse to avoid him, she shrugged. "I would be pleased." She swung into the saddle. He mounted and rode alongside her.

"It's lovely weather we've been having," she said, as they rode toward the king's fields with her bodyguards in tow.

"Lovely, Highness." Phomello smiled and nodded. Samantha couldn't tell if he was agreeing with her about the weather or comparing her to it. "Race?" he asked.

The princess grinned. "I'm warning you, Roberta can beat any horse."

Phomello cocked his head as if he didn't understand what she was saying. "Stream?"

"The stream," she agreed. She shouted and touched Roberta with her heels. The mare shot forward.

Samantha laughed as Roberta sped across the fields, at least until Phomello's stallion pulled even and passed her. *Oh, no you don't!* She leaned forward on Roberta and urged her to quicken her pace. The mare seemed to have no more desire to be beaten than the princess did and edged ahead of the Neasarian stallion. For most of the distance to the stream they remained neck and neck. As they were nearing it, Roberta surged into the lead again, and her hooves touched the water a full head in front of the stallion. Samantha reined her in, laughing, as the Neasarian ambassador's son came splashing up beside her.

He too was laughing. "Good horse, Highness." She flushed at the praise to Roberta. "Good rider," he said, and his eyes traveled over her in a way that made the princess think he wasn't talking about her riding skill. He leaned off his horse's back and picked a flower and handed it to her. "Like Highness."

Her stomach sunk within her, but she forced a smile and accepted the flower. *Even with his terrible Korthlundian he still manages to compare me to a flower. If it were nighttime, he'd have pointed to the stars.* While the race had been fun, Phomello was no different from the others.

* * *

Kailen panicked as he watched the princess and the foreigner pull away from him and his fellow guard. He'd had the uneasy feeling of being watched all morning, and he didn't trust the Neasarian. He urged his horse to match the speed of the princess's, but he found himself being left behind. *Sulis curse it! How can I protect her if I can't keep pace with her?*

Kailen came pounding up next to the princess in time to see the Neasarian give the princess a flower. Although the Neasarian hadn't tried anything untoward, Kailen again had a feeling they were being watched. He looked to the left and saw a figure on horseback disappearing into the trees.

Before he could investigate it, the princess and the Neasarian turned their horses to the right, away from the trees. There was no place for anyone to hide in that direction. Now that their race was over, the princess and the Neasarian rode their horses at a far more leisurely pace—one that his own could match.

* * *

Herne bowed as he entered his brother's presence. It was late, but he knew Argblutal would want to hear his report. He'd followed Phomello after he parted company with the princess, and he'd been very amused at where the Neasarian had led him. *What would her Virginal Highness think if she knew who her lover boy spent his nights with?*

"What news?" Duke Argblutal asked.

"The princess has been very cautious in pursuing this affair, but I believe I've found the man. His name is Phomello."

The duke's lip curled with disgust. "Isn't that a Neasarian name?"

"Yes, Your Grace, he's the son of the Neasarian ambassador."

The duke poured himself a goblet of wine and drank it as if trying to remove a foul taste from his mouth. "You're sure?"

"I don't see how it can be any other. He's the only foreigner at court she's been seen with outside of official duties. She danced with him at the ball, and this morning they met in the stables. They rode out together and participated in a horse race that the Neasarian allowed the princess to win. He picked a flower for her."

"What else do you know about this *Neasarian?*" Argblutal sneered the word.

Herne looked toward the wine bottle, and Argblutal nodded. "He has no official duties and seems to live mainly to squander his father's money," he answered, while pouring himself a drink. "He spends a great deal of time at the brothels and gambling houses near the harbor."

"That is a very dangerous part of town, is it not? Full of thieves, pickpockets, and murderers?"

Herne drank his wine and nodded. "It'll be taken care of, Your Grace."

* * *

Solar sat with Caedmon at the breakfast table. Samantha hadn't responded to his request to breakfast with them. *What am I going to do about her?*

There was a knock on the door, and the king's secretary, Gilroy, entered. "Your Majesty, I've just received distressing news. The son of the Neasarian ambassador has been found murdered."

"Inside the palace?" the king asked.

"No, Your Majesty, he was found in an alleyway behind one of the harbor brothels. Your Majesty knows I regularly warn all foreign envoys about that part of town. The murder has the appearance of a simple robbery."

There was something about the way his secretary said "has the appearance" that caught the king's ear. "You have reason to believe it wasn't."

"I don't, Your Majesty, but Captain Faucon is seeking an audience. He has an intense young lieutenant accompanying him."

Solar turned. "Send them in at once, Gilroy."

Gilroy returned a few seconds later, trailed by the captain of the Royal Guard and a young man with the coldest eyes the king had ever seen. Solar felt a chill as the men went down on one knee. Solar had them rise. "What is it?" he asked.

Captain Faucon answered, "Your Majesty, while acting as Her Highness's bodyguard, Lieutenant Kailen has had some concerns about the princess's safety."

Solar gripped the arms of his chair. Samantha had always been his one weakness. He could tolerate anything but losing her. "Speak," he ordered.

"Your Majesty, yesterday, the dead Neasarian met Her Highness in the stables. They went riding together. I'm sure the princess and this Neasarian were being watched. I felt eyes on us since we'd entered the stables, and I'm certain I saw a figure disappearing into the trees after the Neasarian offered the princess a flower. It may mean nothing, but I didn't feel I should keep silent if there's any chance Her Highness's safety is in jeopardy."

The king nodded, pleased with the guard. "And could you identify this figure you saw fleeing?"

"No, Your Majesty. He was too far away and appeared too briefly."

The king nodded. "What is your name?"

The man bowed his head lower. "I am called Lieutenant Kailen, Your Majesty."

Believing good behavior should always be rewarded, the king took a ring from his finger and handed it to the guard. "I thank you, Lieutenant Kailen, for bringing this to my notice. I assure you I'll give it all the attention it deserves."

Some of the coldness left Kailen's eyes, and he clutched the ring in his hand. "Thank you, Your Majesty."

The king dismissed the guards and turned to Caedmon. "You don't think Samantha favored this Neasarian, do you?"

"Absolutely not, Your Majesty. She did joke that since he could barely speak the language, she liked him better than the others. But she held no special fondness for him."

The king sighed heavily. *I'm too old for this.* "Caedmon, do you think there may be some among the princess's suitors who would consider murder to rid them of a rival?"

Caedmon paled, but nodded. "Certainly, Your Majesty, I do see that as a possibility."

"Investigate this death, Caedmon. But be discrete about it. We don't want to cause problems with the Neasarians unnecessarily."

"Of course, Your Majesty, I'll see to it at once."

After his chancellor left, the king called his secretary in. "Gilroy, has Her Highness been informed of the murder? Handling condolences would fall within her duties."

"Yes, Your Majesty, Duke Argblutal was present when I received the message. He asked to relay the information to Her Highness."

The king drew his eyebrow together. *Why would the duke do such a thing? Can I never do enough to protect her?* The king had insisted on a constant bodyguard on the princess since her first day of life, but her guard had always consisted of rotating members of the Royal Guard.

Solar now wondered if the princess would be better served by a select group, separate from the regular guard, who were dedicated to her protection alone, a group whose loyalty to the princess surpassed even their loyalty to the monarch. His choice to lead the group would surprise many, but the king's long peaceful rule had depended upon knowing things most people missed.

* * *

Samantha bristled as, with the help of her maids and her dressmakers, she carefully went over her wardrobe. She had to admit she was a bit nervous about handling the Massossinan trade negotiations. Although she'd participated in trade talks for years, she'd never been the principal negotiator before. If she could secure a favorable treaty, perhaps she could convince her father that she didn't need a consort.

There was a knock on the door, and her maids informed her Duke Argblutal was requesting an audience. "He says he has an urgent message, Your Highness."

Samantha grimaced. Hoping the urgent message didn't involve stars or flowers, she told her maids to let him in.

Argblutal bowed as he entered. "Your Highness, I wanted to offer you my condolences."

"Condolences?" she asked, trying to keep her voice steady and gripping her hand mirror tightly. *Not my father!* "I wasn't aware I needed condolences."

"Haven't you heard, Your Highness?" The duke's voice was soft and tender, something she'd never heard in his voice before. She put her free hand on her abdomen and tried to prevent herself from shaking. "I'm sorry to be the one to tell you this, but Phomello was found murdered near the docks."

Samantha released her grip on the mirror and nearly laughed with relief, but she resumed an appropriately grave expression. "I hadn't heard. Is the Neasarian ambassador blaming Korthlundia for the death?"

"Not that I know of, Your Highness. The murder appears to have been a robbery. Still, I'm sure his father will be devastated by the loss."

It was terrible that that the young man had been murdered, but it came at a very inconvenient time; she had too much to do to get ready for the Massossinan delegation. "It's certainly a tragedy for anyone to die so young, especially so senselessly. I suppose I should offer his father condolences. I wonder what a Neasarian would consider appropriate for the occasion. I don't suppose you know anything about Neasarian burial customs? Surely, Neasar is too far for him to consider taking the body home."

"As it happens, I do. Neasarians preserve the bodies of their dead in a process involving a lot of salt and other preservatives. They feel the need for a great many burial gifts, including food, weapons, and things of beauty."

Samantha tapped her fingers on her dressing table; it seemed like a great deal of unnecessary trouble. Surely Sulis would provide for the souls of the dead once they'd traveled Beyond the Far Mountain. "The crown will certainly have to do its part to show Korthlundia's goodwill," she sighed. It was hard to hide her irritation that this had happened on the eve of the important trade talks.

"The dead do have a way of interfering with the actions of the living."

The duke's words betrayed how completely her face had revealed her thoughts. She hurriedly assumed a more compassionate expression.

"If Your Highness desires it, I could handle the official acknowledgement of Korthlundian sympathy toward the bereaved father . . . unless you believe it's something you should handle personally."

"Oh, would you? That would be most helpful." As she looked at the duke, she started to wonder if she had misjudged him. Even if the conversation had been about death, it was far better than mindless talk of stars and flowers.

* * *

Darhour was going over records of supplies and expenditures in his office when a page arrived informing him he was wanted in the king's chambers immediately. *Sulis curse it, he's found out about the princess's new horse. If I'm out of a job because of this, I'll hunt down that green-eyed boy and teach him about interfering. That is, if the king doesn't toss me in the dungeon.* Darhour spent the entirely too short walk to the king's rooms trying to figure out how to justify his actions and cursing himself for being unable to say no to the princess.

The king's secretary ushered Darhour into the king's private reception room. Darhour went respectfully down on one knee before his sovereign. The secretary shut the door behind him, leaving them alone—a surprising move. Solar almost never saw anyone without his guards present. A dressing down over taking the princess to the horse fair would hardly merit a private audience.

The king didn't leave him kneeling for long, but offered him a seat—a move which further disconcerted Darhour. One of his station wasn't usually permitted to sit in royal presence. In the entire time he served the Saloynan king, Frare had never offered him a seat. Solar sat silently surveying him, and Darhour had difficulty sitting still. Solar had an air of authority that Frare, for all his ruthlessness, had lacked.

At last, the king said, "I know of your services to the former King of Saloyna."

At this completely unexpected opening statement, Darhour's palms began to sweat. *Just how much does he know? What does he want from me?* He responded carefully, "I served in King Salome's stables, as I now do in yours, Your Majesty."

The king raised an eyebrow. "I don't mean King Salome, but his father. The Ghost is legendary. They say he could walk through walls, although you appear pretty solid to me."

Darhour's chest tightened. *How in the seven hells did he find out who I am?* "I no longer care to pursue that line of work."

"Then it's lucky I'm not presently in need of an assassin. I want you to protect a life, not take one. I have watched you with my daughter. I don't know what she has done to win your loyalty, but she has it, heart and soul."

"I would sacrifice all that I have, all that I am, for Her Highness. I'd gladly give my life for hers." Wondering what the king would do if he knew of his true relationship to the princess, Darhour's hands twitched.

"I am asking for nothing less. I am far too old. This makes my daughter more vulnerable than she realizes. I have done my best to prepare her to take the throne young, and she is far wiser than I was at her age. Still, she lacks the reason that can come only with experience. They say there is no assassin trick you do not know. You will use that knowledge to protect your future queen. I am giving you responsibility for her safety. You will swear your allegiance to Her

Highness, the Crown Princess Samantha, and her alone. You will owe me no further allegiance."

"None, Your Majesty?"

"I'm older than anyone has a right to be. I cannot know if age will rob me of the strength of my mind, as it has already taken the strength of my body. If you ever see me acting contrary to my daughter's well-being, you will know this has happened, and you will have no conflict of loyalty. You serve the princess, not the king." The king handed him a scroll. "This documents your change of allegiance and authorizes you to do whatever you deem necessary for Her Highness's protection. Her Highness will be guarded by the Royal Guard no longer, but by her own personal guard. All members of this guard will answer to you. I suggest you consider Lieutenant Kailen for your second-in-command. He has demonstrated fierce loyalty to the princess. But in this, you answer to Her Highness only."

"I am honored by Your Majesty's trust."

"You may have slit your fair share of throats, but your loyalty to Her Highness is unquestionable. You have already shown your willingness to place her before me. Her new horse is testament of that." Darhour's eyes widened, and the king laughed. "Don't tell Her Highness I know. It pleases the young to believe they've put one over on their elders."

Darhour smiled. Although he'd once hated King Solar for ruining his life, he'd always respected him. Now he was starting to like the man as well.

"Take today to settle matters in the stable with your assistant, Adalardo. He will assume the duties of Master of the Horse. You will take up your duties with Her Highness on the morrow."

As soon as the king dismissed him, Darhour returned to his office at the stables and called Adalardo to him. He informed his former assistant of his promotion, then showed Adalardo the record books and discussed the duties of the Master of the Horse. He also showed his former assistant a trap door he'd found in the corner of his office. He opened it to reveal a ladder. "It leads to a small underground room. I have no idea what it was built for, but I understand the palace and the entire grounds are riddled with such secrets. It's useful for storage, if for nothing else."

"Or for certain forms of entertainment." Adalardo winked.

Darhour frowned. "I've always found my bed more useful for entertainment of that sort, but if you prefer the cold and the dark, be my guest."

Adalardo laughed, and Darhour dismissed him. Darhour climbed down the ladder. He didn't bother bringing a light; the darkness was no hindrance to him since King Frare had had his personal sorcerer perform magic on Darhour's eyes. It had been incredibly painful, and Darhour had feared the magician was blinding him. Frare hadn't bothered explaining beforehand. But as soon as his eyes had healed, Darhour discovered he had an acute ability to see in the dark, even the complete darkness of the cave—an asset for an assassin. At the bottom of the ladder, Darhour opened his trunk and looked over his weapons and the new leather armor he'd ordered made for the practice ring. He'd always preferred leather. It didn't protect as well as chain mail or metal plate, but it was far lighter and didn't impair his movement. He got out his sword and his many knives. When he'd served King Frare, he'd worn these hidden all over his body.

Darhour sat in the darkness to clean and sharpen his weapons. The fact he still had them demonstrated the depths of his hypocrisy. Even greater evidence lay in the bag that had been placed under the knives. The bag contained many of the tools of his former trade, including several made by Saloynan sorcerers. Why did he still have these things if he'd been sincere in his vow?

He remembered the scent of wood and incense that filled the small shrine where he'd made his feeble attempt to heal his damaged soul. When he entered the shrine, it had been empty. He'd walked to the front and knelt at Sulis's holy altar. He'd tried to pray, but the words wouldn't come. There could be no forgiveness for one like him. Even entering Sulis's holy place was blasphemy.

He'd been about to leave when he heard a rustle of robes, and an old priestess knelt at his side. "You're troubled, my son."

Darhour's hands trembled, and he couldn't meet the priestess's eyes. "Yes, Mother. I've done horrible things."

"My son, Sulis longs to forgive you and welcome you back into her arms."

Darhour lowered his head on the altar. "I don't deserve forgiveness."

"Is a mother's love ever based on what her children deserve? Does a child need to earn his mother's care? Open your heart and let her inside." The priestess touched him gently on the arm.

Darhour jerked away. "Don't contaminate yourself by touching me." He held up his hands. "These hands have dealt death to more than I can remember. The blood of those I've slain cries up to Sulis for vengeance. I have well earned my place in the seven hells. Nothing else would be just."

Darhour had expected the priestess to recoil from him, but instead her eyes filled with compassion. "My son, taking a life is a grave sin, but the goddess is more merciful than just. If you accept her back into your heart, her love can cleanse even this."

Darhour merely stared at his hands.

"If you truly believe forgiveness is impossible for you, why do you kneel at Sulis's altar?"

Darhour's voice shook. "I want to make a vow."

"A vow can be a two-edged sword. It can destroy as easily as save."

Darhour jerked upright. "I have already destroyed myself."

"Then why take a vow?"

He rested his head back on the altar. "To have peace. I can't live in this torment." Darhour clenched the altar cloth tightly. "I would vow never to take another life."

"No matter the circumstances? You can't know what the future will bring."

Darhour slowly raised his head. "A man such as I has no future and no past. I am Darhour, the exiled one. I'm nothing more than a ghost, a shadow. But this vow I must take. Never will I kill again. I'll allow myself to be murdered in an alleyway first."

The priestess touched his arm gently again. "I see your determination, my son, and I'll help you. But, remember, Sulis doesn't demand this of you."

The priestess had prayed with him, and kneeling at that altar, he'd made the holy vow, and he'd kept it despite the problems it caused him with the Saloynan king.

Darhour paused in sharpening his knives and touched the braids he still wore in the Saloynan fashion, two on either side of his face—a symbol of what he'd been and the vow he'd taken. *Will I need to kill again to keep Samantha safe? Holy Mother, is this what you intend for me? It* didn't matter. For his daughter's sake, he'd take on the goddess herself.

* * *

When Argblutal returned to his rooms, he grabbed Herne by the neck and slammed him against the wall. "Your Grace," Herne protested, as Argblutal drew his knife with the ruby-encrusted hilt and pressed it against the bastard's throat.

"I dislike being made a fool of," Argblutal said.

Herne glanced at the knife, and Argblutal was pleased to see him trembling. "What do you mean, Your Grace?"

"You told me you'd taken care of the one the princess prefers to me."

"I-I assure you I h-have, Your Grace. I killed the Neasarian with my own h-hand."

The duke pressed the knife into Herne's neck until it drew a small trickle of blood. "The princess cares nothing for this Neasarian. She's asked me to arrange proper condolences for his father. Is this the action of a woman grieving for her lover?"

"Then p-perhaps the Lady Shela was mistaken. P-perhaps there's no one the princess prefers. I assure you, Your Grace, the Neasarian was the only foreigner it could have been."

"For your sake, let us hope so." The duke withdrew his knife from Herne's neck and pressed it lightly to his brother's groin. "If I hear of her betrothal to someone else, I'll cut your balls off and feed them to you. Am I understood?"

"P-perfectly, Your Grace."

The duke released Herne, who slid to the floor, clutching the small wound on his neck.

The bastard had his uses, but he was further proof that only those whose blood was unsullied had the strength or intelligence to rule.

CHAPTER 8

Myst called out to Robbie as he rode his horse through the trees. He didn't turn, and she thought it unlikely he'd heard her. Guilt tugged at her as she followed the path his horse had taken, hoping he'd stop soon so she could catch him. She'd been trying to see him every day since Angus had ordered her from his sick bed, but his worthless excuse for a father hadn't allowed it. *Foolish, vain, old woman!* she chided herself. *Do you really think it possible to make up for sixteen years of neglect? I don't deserve Donella's forgiveness. Oh, Holy Mother, I should have tried harder to get past the obstacles Angus put between me and his children. I should have known about Robbie's gift and his difficulties.* She'd heard him referred to as a demon child, but she'd never dreamed his own father believed it.

Ahead she heard the boy talking to someone—or perhaps to himself since there seemed to be no reply—but she wasn't yet close enough to understand his words.

As she emerged from the trees, Myst gasped. Robbie was talking to the most wretched looking horse Myst had ever seen. It was also the most unnatural one. It appeared as if sores of flesh had erupted on a bronze statue.

Robbie whirled. "What—what are you doing here?" His eyes darted around the clearing, as if looking for an escape route or a place to hide.

"The bronze hair they found," she whispered, too awed to speak louder. "This must be . . ."

107

"You can't tell him she's here! She's not a demon, and he'll kill her!"

It broke her heart to think of what she'd allowed him to suffer. She drew the star of Sulis. "I promise on the goddess and my mother's grave I will tell no one what I've seen here today. But where did the beast come from?"

Her vow did little to ease the panic in his eyes. "I don't know. She's hurt, and she needs help."

"That, I can see. What about you? I've been worried about you, and your father has refused to let me near you."

"Why?" he asked, still looking around like a cornered deer.

Myst sighed. "He never liked me, and we had a horrible fight . . ."

"No, I mean, why would you worry about me?"

"My child, how could I not after what that beast of a brother did to you? Holy Sulis, child, if it weren't for your gift, you wouldn't have survived."

"I'm fine now." Robbie grabbed a jar of ointment and seemed to cling to it for safety's sake. "You can leave now."

Myst approached him slowly, wondering how she could convince him to trust her. But as she drew near she sensed something that stopped her dead in her tracks. *Surely not!* She carefully took the ointment from his hands. She shook her head in disbelief. She sensed Adder's Tongue, Comfrey, and Bruisewort in the mix, but that wasn't all. "Where did you get this?"

"I made it," he snapped.

"By the Holy Mother, how? Who taught you?"

"I'm not as stupid as everyone thinks." He glared at her as if she too had questioned his intelligence. "I can tell things about plants. I didn't need anyone to teach me."

Myst gaped at him. "And the magic in them?"

"Are you saying the medicine is cursed by my demon blood?" Robbie's eyes flashed with rage, but underneath the anger, Myst could see his pain and loneliness.

"Cursed? Holy Sulis, no! They contain the goddess's holy magic. Who told you you had demon blood?"

"Are you blind? My skin, my eyes, my hair. What child of the goddess looks like this? I killed my own mother! Isn't that evil enough for you?"

Myst backed away. Unable to bear up under the weight of her shame, she collapsed onto a stump. "My child, I am so sorry I left you alone to believe such lies. It isn't your fault your mother died. If anyone is to blame, it is your father. I told him after Boyden was born that another child could kill her. She just wasn't suited for giving birth. Some women aren't. Your appearance has nothing to do with the seven hells. You look just like your mother, and she was no demon. She was merely from a far distant land whose name I never could pronounce—Manhayo or some such thing. She thought it was the Korthlundians that looked odd. She used to say, 'The gods ran out of paint when they created this land.'" Tears ran down her cheeks as she thought of how Donella would feel if she knew of her son's pain. "She loved you, my child. As she lay dying, her last thoughts were of you. She gave you her beloved father's name—Robrek."

The boy looked away from her, but she could see him trembling. When he spoke, his voice was cold. "I have to go. My father will beat me if I'm not at work by noon." He put away his things, fumbling in his eagerness to get away.

She called after him. "Robbie, when you can get away, please come and see me. You know where my cottage is, don't you?"

"Yes," he said, but he didn't look at her as he rode away.

* * *

That night his father stopped insisting he stand guard, and Robbie curled up in the bunkhouse. *Can it be true that I'm not demon cursed? Am I really not responsible for my mother's death? Did she truly love me and look like me? Is everything I've always believed about myself nothing but a lie? Was Milady right in calling me an amihealer rather than a demon?* He'd heard the songs bards sang about amihealers who calmed the wild beasts with their touch. *Isn't that what I do?* Wild birds regularly landed on his shoulder. A fox had once brought her injured pup to him. They said no one could ride a Horsetad, but he did. Tossing and turning half the night, he was unable to come to any conclusion. When he finally fell into an uneasy sleep, the demon lady came to him again. *"Believe her, my son,"* the woman said to him. *"I love you. I've always loved you."*

* * *

The hands gathered outside the bunkhouse. "Why do you think he's sleeping in there now?" Dillion whispered.

"Must not like your wife's cooking!" Allyn joked. "Or the way she washes the sheets!"

"About the only things he doesn't like about her," Ferchar said.

"What are you suggesting?" Dillion glared at the other man.

Ferchar raised his eyebrows. "You can't tell me you haven't noticed the way he watches her."

Dillion went for the other man, but Allyn and Darien grabbed him and held him back. "Dillion, get a hold of yourself. You could get thrown off the farm. Who cares if he watches her?"

Dillion shrugged off the men holding him. "If he touches her, I'll kill him."

"Calm down," Allyn said. "If Robbie was after your wife, moving in here doesn't make sense. He'd see a lot more of her if he stayed in the main house."

"I don't like it," said Trahern. "How am I supposed to sleep at night with him in there?"

"Just what do you think he'd do?" Allyn asked. "Snore on you?"

"You've heard what the priests say about him." Trahern's voice shook.

Darien sighed and rolled his eyes. "He's not a monster."

"And the crops just destroyed themselves, did they?" Dillion's voice rose.

"I'm not sleeping with a demon," Trahern muttered.

"Fine," Allyn said. "I'm sure Master Angus won't mind you sleeping in the barn."

"Why should I sleep in the barn? He's the one that doesn't belong." Trahern gestured toward the bunkhouse.

"Yes, but in case you haven't noticed, he happens to be the master's son," Darien said. "Are you going to wake up the master's son and tell him he's got to go?"

The men knew he had a point. The last person who'd called Robbie a demon in Angus's presence was given half an hour to pack his bags before Angus booted him off the farm. Most of the hands shrugged and headed back in and took their bunks, but Trahern and a few others grabbed their blankets and headed for the barn.

CHAPTER 9

When Darhour reported to the princess's rooms, he found Lieutenant Kailen waiting. Kailen saluted as was appropriate for Darhour's new rank, but Darhour could tell the younger man wasn't happy about it. Despite the fact they were nearly the same height, Kailen lowered his eyes in such a way as to convey the impression of looking down on him. "The princess is dressing," he said in an icy cold voice. "This door and the windows are the only ways in. The windows are nearly fifty feet off the ground with nothing near that could conceivably be climbed."

"What about the servants' entrance?" Two sets of corridors wound their way through the palace—those used by the nobility and those used by the servants. In his work as an assassin, Darhour had made frequent use of servants' corridors.

"The princess was given these quarters because they are not connected to the servants' corridors. The king wisely believed a single entrance would make the princess easier to defend. The servants' corridors end there." Kailen indicated a door nearly hidden in the wall a few feet away. "The Princess Danu had the servants' entrance permanently walled off three centuries ago. This door and the windows are the only ways in."

Darhour nodded. "You've been thorough."

Kailen didn't respond.

* * *

As her maids carefully braided the last ribbon into her hair, Samantha looked in the mirror. She shot a sour look at Malvina who towered over her. "Do either of you know how tall Massossinans are in general?"

"I've heard they're just a mite bit shorter on average than Korthlundians, Your Highness," Ardra said.

Unless her maid meant something different by "a mite bit" than it normally meant, they weren't short enough. *It's difficult to command respect when I come to their chin.* She shrugged. *What can't be helped can't be helped.* She took one last look at herself and headed for the door.

When she emerged into the corridors, she stopped short. "Darhour, what on earth are you doing here?"

"His Majesty did not tell you he appointed me to be captain of your personal guard?"

She creased her forehead and shook her head. "Last night at dinner he was saying something about a change in my guards, but I was too busy thinking about today's negotiations to pay much attention." *And too afraid that paying attention would lead him to talking about consorts.*

As Darhour explained the king's new idea for her protection, Samantha rolled her eyes. "He sees assassins in every alcove. Still, why would he appoint *you* to head such a guard?" Samantha blurted. "I mean, I can't imagine anyone I'd rather have following me around. I just thought you were happy in the stables." She hoped that sounded more diplomatic.

Darhour smiled. "My career has been a varied one, Your Highness. His Majesty believes I possess certain skills that would be an asset in protecting you."

Like the ability to make a man faint by merely glancing at him. I guess a man wouldn't have developed such a look if he'd spent a lifetime saddling horses. "You have too many secrets, Darhour. Someday I'll pry them all out of you, but for now the trade delegates await." She started down the hall, and the two men fell in on either side behind her.

Darhour tensed as they approached the Massossinan delegation. He touched one of his hidden knives. At the head, a young noble man and a middle-aged woman waited. They were presented as Prince Banki and Ambassador Magnhildr. Magnhildr would undoubtedly be the negotiator. Massossinans thought men were good for brute force, but little else. The prince's role wasn't hard to guess. *Samantha will marry a Massossinan over my dead body.*

The prince inclined his head to the princess. "Your Highness, may I present a small token of our esteem?" The prince's Korthlundian was good, but oozed with a heavy Massossinan accent.

Almost unconsciously, Darhour caressed his sword hilt. It'd been a long time since he'd heard the accent that had filled his nightmares for years.

The prince's servants wheeled in a box big enough to fit a horse. They were accompanied by a detachment of the Royal Guard. Darhour caught the eye of the officer who gave him a small nod, indicating they'd searched the box to make sure it contained no surprises. The prince's servants opened it to reveal a life-sized horse made of smoked crystal. It had a gold mane, tail, and hooves. It wore a gold saddle studded with emeralds. It was exactly the kind of present that would appeal to Samantha. She beamed at it. "It's gorgeous."

Darhour glowered as the prince chuckled. "We were told Your Highness is fond of horses."

Don't think you can buy your way onto the throne. Or charm your way there either. Darhour made a note to discover where the Massossinans would be quartered. Anywhere within the palace should be relatively simple for him to access. He froze, as he realized what he was doing. *He's barely spoken a word, and already I'm plotting his death.* But the most disturbing part was the rush he'd experienced. Since the day he'd been forced into exile, nothing had made him feel more alive than plotting the death of another. *Holy Sulis, I'm a monster. How could I ever think my vow would change that or cleanse me of the blood guilt of so many?* He removed his hand from his sword.

The princess signaled a falconer forward to present the prince with her own gift—a hooded gyrfalcon, a very large and rare bird. "What a magnificent bird! Is it a skilled hunter?" The prince smiled like a predatory hawk who had found an unprotected nest of eagle chicks.

"So I have been told." Samantha signaled again, and the imbecilic Count Weylin stepped beside the princess. She presented him to the prince. "He is an avid hunter himself and has graciously volunteered to introduce Your Highness to our best hunting areas."

"Excellent. I do so love the hunt."

Then you should be a match for Weylin. Darhour despised the count, but since Samantha did as well, he was no threat.

Samantha also presented the prince with a fine hunting bow and a boar spear. After the endless series of formalities, the princess led the Massossinan delegation into the banquet hall for the welcome feast. Of course, the Massossinan prince would be seated next to Samantha. Both he and Kailen took up their positions behind her. He scanned the room for threats and noted with approval that Kailen did likewise.

* * *

Samantha listened to her father welcome the Massossinans. When the king finished, the high priest, Father Shylah, stood. To appease the religious members of the court, Samantha had given him leave to begin the banquet with an invocation of Sulis's blessing. As the high priest cleared his throat, she regretted doing so. Father Shylah was a thin, miserly sort with a habit of rubbing his hands together as if he were counting gold. Given that the clergy had taken vows of poverty, Samantha found this particularly unappealing. His clerical attire also belied his professed poverty. He wore long, flowing robes of rich blue satin, embroidered in gold thread with the stars of Sulis. In the center of each of the five-pointed stars was a diamond or ruby. Having the high, thin, raspy sound of a gelded goat, his voice was even more annoying. "Your Majesty, Your Highnesses"—the priest bowed to the king, the princess, and Prince Banki—"members of the court, and honored guests, at the beginning of these festivities, it is proper to invoke the blessing and support of the goddess of this land, the high and holy Sulis, may her name be praised forever." As the priest went on in agonizing detail about the virtues of Sulis, Samantha noticed Prince Banki shifting uncomfortably in his seat.

When at last the priest finished and resumed his seat, the princess signaled, and the servants immediately came forward with the first course. At least their guests could find nothing to object to in the food. Maggie, the chief cook, had outdone herself. She'd even researched several Massossinan dishes to add to the Korthlundian fare. The princess stared in distaste at one dish on the table. Prince Banki, however, beamed. "Ah, pickled lamb's blood. I'd no idea you were so civilized."

They eat blood? Samantha fought to avoid visibly gagging.

Banki ignored Count Weylin and turned all of his attention on her. She was certain she'd have to endure another round of the usual drivel about stars and flowers. In this, she was wrong. It seemed in Massossina, tales of hunting prowess were the preferred methods for making women swoon in admiration. By the time the third course arrived, she was beginning to wonder if Massossinans ever did anything other than hunt.

"Your Highness, did I tell you about the boar hunt we held just before sailing?" The prince leaned toward her.

"Oh, no, you haven't." She smiled a court smile. "Was it anything like the stag hunt last winter? Or the bear hunt in the spring? Or perhaps it was most like the lion hunt you described in such magnificent detail?"

The prince tensed. "I see I have bored Your Highness."

Samantha groaned inwardly, trying to think of a way to cover her breach of etiquette. "Oh, no, it's not that, Your Highness. It's just that I was hoping to hear more about your homeland."

"Massossina is a place where we have a great appreciation for the challenges of the hunt, as Korthlundia apparently does not," the prince said.

"Really?" the princess asked, trying to project enthusiasm. "Do you have any rituals surrounding the hunt? I've always been fascinated by hunting rituals." *Every bit as much as I'm delighted by eating blood.*

The prince snorted, but he had even more reason than she did for wanting the negotiations to succeed. "Of course we do. Proper ritual is essential to a successful hunt," he said. "We always begin the hunt with an invocation to Skadi, the goddess of the hunt. As I am sure you are aware, we worship a multitude of deities." He said this as though Korthlundia was deficient in its piety by having only one. He described the invocation in excruciating detail. She completely lost her appetite as he told about the proper way to dispose of the dead animal's blood and entrails in a manner pleasing to Skadi. As far as Samantha could tell, Skadi seemed to feast on these entrails when they were burned on an altar properly soaked with the animal's blood. The prince droned on and on about the various sacrifices required for different occasions until Samantha feared she might vomit. Apparently, Massossinan deities had a great need for all sorts of dead animal parts.

* * *

Darhour breathed a sigh of relief when the dinner was over and the Massossinan prince had bidden Samantha good night. He hadn't realized how much tension he'd been holding until his muscles relaxed. *Get a hold of yourself, or you'll never make it through the visit without killing someone.*

When they reached the princess's quarters, Darhour entered first and gave them a thorough inspection. The princess followed him into her bedroom as he was checking the painting of Danu. "Why is this bolted to the wall?" he asked, without turning.

The princess sighed and sank into a chair. "I'm sure it's not because Massossinans have hidden behind it. Banki wants to marry me, not kill me."

Darhour faced the princess, irritated she'd sensed his tension. "I assure you, Your Highness, I will not let personal feelings interfere with my duty."

Samantha rolled her eyes at him, a habit that Darhour found endearing since the princess was the only one in decades who'd dared to treat him so casually. "Don't get formal on me. I get enough of that from everybody else. Since I've had to endure the most boring dinner conversation of my life combined with you breathing down my neck like a mother panther, you owe me at least one of your secrets. Tell me how it happened." She pointed to his scars.

Darhour scratched at the scars on his cheek. "It's a rather grisly story, Your Highness. It happened when I served in the Saloynan army. I'll spare you the details."

Narrowing her eyes, she spoke with the same air of command Solar had. "I don't want to be spared." She gestured to the seat opposite her.

As always, Darhour found himself unable to refuse her. He took the seat and told her the truth, or at least as much of the truth as he could bear her to know. "Your Highness knows Saloyna has had border wars with Massossina for centuries." The princess nodded. "My unit was sent across the border on a . . ."—he paused, searching for a term that would obscure the nature of his mission without being entirely false—"to scout the Massossinan camp. We'd been betrayed. They were expecting us. Only two of us survived the ambush. We were taken to the Massossinan camp. My companion was tied to an altar and had his heart cut out. Freya, their god of war, promises success in battle to those who eat of the hearts of their enemies. I thought I would be next." *I wanted to be next. Sometimes I blamed him more for not killing me than for anything else he did.* "But their officer claimed since I wasn't Saloynan, Freya didn't find me a fitting sacrifice. He had me stripped, beaten, and tied by my wrists to a post in their camp. He smeared honey over my body, which attracted every biting, stinging insect within a hundred miles, or so it seemed. I was left hanging for three days. Every morning and evening, he took his knife, and . . . Well, you see what he did with it. These"— Darhour touched his right cheek—"are only the beginning of the scars he gave me."

The princess put her hand to her mouth, looking as if she might vomit. He wished he'd left out some of the details. "Why?" she asked.

Darhour looked away, unable to bear the pain in her eyes. "I believe he did it for the pleasure of hearing me scream. Massossinans believe mercenaries lack honor."

"That's awful. I'd like to hunt that man down and teach him a few things about honor."

"I'm afraid you're too late, Your Highness. I killed him." *Killed him far more slowly than I'd killed any other man, but still more quickly than he deserved.*

Darhour bade the princess goodnight and turned to see Kailen glaring at him with his icy blue eyes. Darhour was impressed; few dared to look at him that way. *He* will *be a powerful ally in protecting the princess, if I can get him to trust me.*

At the door to the princess's rooms, the two men he'd temporarily chosen to stand night guard—Bearach and Conroy—were waiting. He briefed them and turned to Kailen. "Lieutenant, dine with me." Kailen looked as if he'd refuse, but Darhour snapped, "It's not a request." He motioned the younger man toward his rooms. He'd been given quarters in the same corridor as the princess's, not more than a hundred feet distant.

Darhour took off his glove and rubbed a finger across the door jamb near the lock. He'd coated the spot with a Saloynan potion that would give the wood a greenish tinge if the door was opened without first being touched in this manner. He'd treated the princess's door similarly. He regretted his Saloynan bag hadn't contained a *kleidaria* to place inside the lock of Samantha's door. He'd need to go to the Saloynan sector of the city and see if he could purchase one on the black market. They were both rare and expensive.

Darhour unlocked the door and motioned Kailen inside. He offered Kailen a seat at his table, which contained meals for both of them. Since he was hungry, Darhour began to eat, but Kailen merely stared at him with his arms folded. Darhour met the lieutenant's glare. "Your loyalty to Her Highness is evident, and I know of your skill. I'd like to retain you as one of Her Highness's guards."

Kailen leaned toward him. "You'll remove me from my position over my dead body."

With the speed of long practice, Darhour palmed a knife and threw it. It made a shallow cut along the right side of Kailen's neck and buried itself in the chair behind him. As Kailen's hand went for his sword, Darhour palmed another knife. "If you make killing you necessary, I'm more than capable of obliging you. Now, remove your hand from your sword."

Kailen glared murderously. "What is it you want with me?"

"I want your assistance in protecting the crown princess. But make no mistake. The king has put me in charge. If one of us has to go, it will not be me," Darhour said.

Kailen glanced at Darhour's knife, as if gauging if he could draw his sword in time to counter it.

"Don't waste your life on the vain notion that you could best me in any kind of fight. I've seen you train. You are very good, but you aren't my match. I spent ten years in the Saloynan army, and the only one who could match me was sacrificed on the altar of the Massossinans' barbaric god. And do you know how I killed the man who ate his heart and did this to me?" He scratched at his scars. "I crossed the lines and pursued him deep into Massossina, entered his mansion, and killed him in his own bedroom. If you try to fight me, you will die. Your death will not serve the princess well. Now, remove your hand from your sword."

Kailen grunted, as if to convey disbelief.

Darhour sighed. "It wasn't my service in the army alone that caused His Majesty to choose me, nor was it only on the battlefield that I took men's lives. His Majesty discovered a secret that I thought well hidden. My killing the Massossinan officer who tortured me nearly derailed peace talks and brought me notoriety throughout Saloyna. It particularly impressed the king's chief assassin. He trained me as his replacement and called me the best apprentice he'd ever had. I can't imagine how Solar learned of this. Those who knew the identity of Frare's last assassin can be numbered on one hand. Most spoke of him only by the nickname he'd earned. Although I assure you I'm entirely corporeal, Saloynan myths gave me the ability to walk through walls."

Kailen opened his mouth, and his eyes clouded with fear. "You're The Ghost!" He carefully removed his hand from his sword and set it on the table in plain sight.

Darhour nodded in approval. "Who knows the tricks of an assassin better than one whose infamy has spread the world over? I can say without arrogance I am the best. Being exiled from my homeland left me no reason to live. For fourteen years I did nothing but train and kill. I became a monster all men feared." Darhour paused and met Kailen's eyes. "But I'm a monster completely devoted to Her Highness. And not merely because she is the crown princess and our country's only hope of avoiding the violence I witnessed in Saloyna. From the moment I entered His Majesty's service, she has shown herself worthy of my loyalty. I honor her as my queen." He leaned across the table. "But there's more than that. I love her like the daughter I never had. I would gladly give up my life and my soul for her sake." *If Kailen only knew just how truly she was his daughter.*

Kailen pulled Darhour's knife from the chair and put his hand on the small cut on the side of his neck. He silently stared at the knife for quite some time. Darhour ate, allowing the other man time to think. Finally, Kailen spoke, "His Majesty knows you are The Ghost?" Darhour nodded. "What about Her Highness?"

"No, and I'd prefer it remain that way unless circumstances make it necessary for her to know." *I don't know if I could bear the disgust the knowledge would invoke in her.*

"King Solar is the greatest king in Korthlundian history. Should I question his wisdom?" Kailen didn't seem to expect an answer, and Darhour didn't give one. "Her Highness likes and respects you. Would you be willing to swear a sacred oath that all you have told me is true and that your loyalty to Her Highness is absolute?" Kailen held out Darhour's knife.

Darhour took the knife and rolled up his left sleeve, revealing a forearm covered with thin scars. "I, Darhour, vow to the goddess and on my mother's grave that I have spoken nothing but the truth this night and that my loyalty to Her Highness, the Crown Princess Samantha, is absolute." Darhour made a quick slash across his arm and handed the knife back to Kailen.

Kailen rolled up his sleeve. "And I, Kailen, vow to the goddess and on my mother's grave that my loyalty to Her Highness, the Crown Princess Samantha, is absolute, and that I will submit myself to Captain Darhour's authority." Kailen cut himself in the same manner. Pressing their arms together, the two men mingled their blood.

"With our blood we seal this oath," they said in unison. Darhour felt a quiver of something in the air and believed the goddess herself had witnessed the oath.

Darhour retrieved an old shirt, slashed it with his knife, and gave half to Kailen, wrapping his arm with the other half.

Kailen wrapped his own wound. "Please forgive my disrespect. I am used to being the most skilled fighter in any group of which I'm part. It has made me arrogant. But my arrogance doesn't serve Her Highness well. I see I must learn humility."

* * *

Litha, the summer solstice, marked the final day of the Massossinan delegation's visit. As a traditional part of the celebration, the court gathered to collect wild herbs and flowers. Argblutal observed the princess and her horde of suitors. Shela claimed the princess favored one, but Herne had been unable to determine who. Argblutal suspected his bastard brother's efforts to spy on the princess had wavered since that scarred monstrosity had been made captain of her personal guard. But Argblutal saw no reason to be intimidated by a man who'd done nothing more than been carved like a work of art.

Still, her behavior had in no way revealed her favored suitor. It certainly wasn't the Massossinan prince. Banki was as furious as Magnhildr was pleased. She'd succeeded in obtaining a favorable treaty whereas he'd failed miserably.

The duke watched as the princess and Weylin were gathering flowers nearby. "I want to thank you, Weylin," the princess said, "for the time you've taken to entertain our Massossinan guests."

The air of authority in her voice grated on the duke. His groin tightened as he imagined her naked and tied to his bed. Her breasts were a good deal smaller than he preferred. But as he imagined thrashing them with his cat-o-nine, no breasts had ever excited him more. Dismissing the enticing picture, he joined her and the count.

The princess smiled a court smile at him, and he bowed. "You've done a masterful job with the Massossinans, Your Highness. I was impressed with your ability to win concessions on the price of spices." He commented on several important points of the negotiations, trying to treat her as if she had a brain—something Shela said the princess desired in a man.

"Why, thank you," she said, and her smile became genuine. He'd have Herne get him a small-breasted woman tonight, one with auburn hair.

CHAPTER 10

Slathek had been in the barbaric capital for nearly a month and had disposed of all his cargo; the bhat beans had sold for an incredible profit as they always did. He vaguely wondered what the barbarians had drunk before his father had started bringing the beans that had made him a wealthy man.

Now he merely needed to fill his hold for the return home. Smiling, he sat at a table in the Clothmakers' Guild Hall. Litha was an excellent day for conducting business. Something about the holiday seemed to make the barbarians very amenable to trade in his favor. He'd concluded another successful negotiation that would make this year's trip even more profitable than last year's.

"A pleasure doing business with you," Abenzio said. The merchant dealt in linens, a very profitable item in Mahngbhayo, and Slathek had been trading with him for many years now. "Am I to see the lovely miniature of your sister again?"

Slathek tensed at the request. "You've seen it every year for the last ten. Do you think you'll suddenly remember something you had forgotten?" Still, he pulled his copy of her miniature out from under the tunic. Before allowing it to be passed around, he opened it and stared into the emerald green eyes of the sister he had adored. Her long, curly black hair fell in waves over her shoulders, and her skin was the rich, creamy color of hot *bhat*. Even though she'd disappeared when he was only eight years old, he still missed her every day.

"Such a lovely girl," Abenzio muttered sadly. "Your older sister, wasn't she?"

"Yes," Slathek answered, taking the picture back.

The barbarian shook his head with insincere sadness. Slathek could see the gleam of lust in the man's eyes. "So much evil in the world to corrupt innocence like that."

Slathek's lips tightened. He gathered his papers and held out his hand in the fashion of the barbarians. "I'll expect the merchandise delivered to the docks in the morning."

"Yes, yes, of course." Abenzio shook his hand.

Walking back through the crowded streets of Murtaghan toward The Traveler's Haven, where his father and he always stayed, Slathek felt tears at the corners of his eyes. He didn't like being reminded of the fate of his sister. Although he and his father had traced the men who took her to Murtaghan, they'd never been able to find any sign of her. He hoped she'd died quickly. Because of her, he'd never slept with a whore. Among the numerous stalls lining the street for the holiday, Slathek caught sight of an herb seller. The sight and smell of rosemary and comfrey brought back the time he'd spent in Sphry's stillrooms grinding herbs into powder for her and watching her make her medicines and salves. *By the Mother and the Father, why did the pirates have to take you of all people?*

He walked on until he came to the docks. There, he paused and looked out over the many ships that dotted the harbor. Fifty yards from the shore was a small rock where sea lions were playing. "Sphry," he spoke into the roar of the sea, "did you find any comfort in them, as you did in the dolphins that played in our waters? Did they sing you their songs and tell you their stories?" Slathek's eyes flashed with anger. "No, there could have been no comfort for you in this land of barbarians."

When he returned to the inn, his father was waiting at their usual table. His own locket containing an identical miniature of Sphry lay open on the table before him. He grabbed Slathek's arm as he sat. "Had the merchants any news of her?"

Slathek looked away. By the Father and the Mother he hated these conversations. "Father, I loved her as much as you did. But she's been gone for over twenty years. You can't possibly think she's still alive."

The old man leaned back in his chair. "I know you think me a foolish old man, but a father knows things. As sure as I stand here and breathe, your sister did not die in a brothel. When I'm in this land, I dream of her. I see her happy and surrounded by small children."

"Sphry is dead, Father." Slathek headed for the door. He too dreamed of Sphry in this land. But he wasn't foolish enough to believe in dreams.

As he opened it, he heard the innkeeper address his father. "Master Robrek, will you be desiring anything else?"

* * *

On the morning of Litha, Robbie ate breakfast in very low spirits. Holidays always depressed him because he'd never been allowed to participate in the public celebrations. Soon after he sat down to breakfast in the bunkhouse, Allyn and Darien sat down across from him.

"Oh, boy, you got it bad," Allyn said to him.

"Got what bad?" His eyes darted around the room, but in the holiday excitement, none of the other hands were paying attention to him.

"Milady, oh, Milady, oh, oh, ohhhh." Allyn laughed and thrust his hips suggestively. "A man can't get any sleep with the way you carry on at nights."

Robbie blushed deeply. "I talk in my sleep?"

"Do you ever!" Darien rolled his eyes. "Sure sign you're in need of a real woman, I'd say."

Robbie dropped his spoon into his bowl of porridge. "Where would I get one of those?"

"No need to get so worked up about it. It's Litha. I'm sure we could work something out," Allyn winked.

Dillion appeared at Allyn's shoulder. "Not even the whores will take his kind." Dillion turned and stomped out of the bunkhouse.

Allyn turned to Darien. "Now there's another man who isn't getting enough of what he needs."

"He and Cara still fighting?" Darien asked.

"Off and on," Allyn shrugged. "Those two don't do anything small. When they're off, you can hear them shouting from one end of the Valley to the other."

"And when they're on, you can hear them just as loudly." The two farm hands laughed, and Robbie blushed again. He'd been avoiding Cara, but somehow Dillion still seemed to think he was the cause of the problems he was having with his wife.

Robbie looked across the bunkhouse and saw Cara whispering with some of the other female servants; they were probably planning on hurrying to the village to weave fresh greenery and flowers over the outside of the shrine. Several children danced around the bunkhouse, singing about the fire wheel.

"Chasing the fire wheel is alright for children," Darien told one of them. "But when you're older, Oran my friend, you'll realize the fire wheel is merely an excuse to start the dancing."

The talk of dancing made Robbie think of Milady, the only woman who'd ever danced with him. *Sulis curse them all! If I'm not a demon, shouldn't I be able to go to the celebration with everybody else? It isn't fair.* He'd seen the fire wheel and the dances, but only through the leaves of the tree he'd hidden in; Boyden had always gone out of his way to emphasize how much fun he'd had.

Robbie hurried from the bunkhouse. He went to Wild Thing's stall and wiped his eyes against her side. "We don't need them, do we, my girl? Let them have their stupid celebration. We'll have our own. Just you, me, and Brazen. It will be fun, won't it?" Wild Thing nuzzled him, trying to comfort him.

As he rode toward the stable, he knew he was lying to himself. Brazen was nearly healed now, and he couldn't keep her hidden much longer. Myst had already found her. How long would it be before someone else did? As he came through the trees and saw Brazen shining as if she'd been forged from the purest metal, he thought that losing her might well be the hardest thing that had ever happened to him, but if he tried to keep her, he'd certainly be hanged.

Robbie greeted the horse and started grooming her, wondering how he could make Brazen understand the need to leave.

:*Why grieve what you have not lost?*: Robbie started as he heard the mind voice that wasn't Wild Thing's.

He stared at the bronze mare. Other than basic needs, such as hunger or pain, he'd never gotten anything from the Brazen's thoughts. "Was that you, Lady Brazen?" he asked.

:Why grieve what you have not lost?: the voice said again, and this time he was certain it was Brazen's.

"But I have to lose you soon. Someone other than Myst is bound to find you." Robbie spoke slowly, trying to picture the problem so the horse could understand. He knew it was probably futile; Wild Thing was the only animal he'd ever known with a mind capable of understanding complex thought. But when Brazen opened her mind to him, he realized she'd been hiding her intelligence. His mouth fell open; no animal had ever been able to keep him out, and her mind felt even less like that of a normal horse's than Wild Thing's. "What are you?" he asked.

Brazen ignored his question. *:Why grieve what you have not lost? I am safe here.:*

"No, you aren't. You don't know these people. When they find you, they'll kill us both."

To Robbie's frustration, Brazen repeated herself. *:Why grieve what you have not lost? I am safe here. I cannot be found unless I allow it.:*

"I don't know what you are, but people come through these woods. You will be found."

:I am safe here. I cannot be found unless I allow it.:

"I'm not the most popular person around here. All Father Gildas needs is an excuse to kill me, and most of those in the Valley would eagerly drag me to the gallows. My own brother would probably donate the rope. And you're in as much danger as I am."

:I am safe here. I cannot be found unless I allow it.:

Robbie tried for nearly an hour to get Brazen to understand the problem, but she simply kept repeating the same things over and over again until Robbie thought he'd go mad. Finally, he flung up his hands in defeat. "Fine, then. Get yourself killed, but don't expect me to come here anymore so I can die with you." Robbie swung into Wild Thing's saddle and galloped away.

But after putting some distance between himself and the incomprehensible horse, he reined Wild Thing in. He didn't want to go back to the farm and the festive holiday spirit. He looked at the dark skin on his hands and arms. *Are they right to reject me because I'm cursed? Or was Myst telling the truth about my mother?* He thought about the demon lady from his dreams. She loved him like a mother. She and the animals were the only things that had kept him from completely despising himself.

* * *

Boyden slipped through the back door of the temple to find Father Gildas in his office. "Good morning, Father."

The priest simpered at him, but the arrogant bastard didn't ask him to be seated. "Good morning, my son. You understand the importance of what happens here today?"

"Yes, Father. I won't let him destroy what's mine."

"My son, it's the will of the goddess that should concern us, not our own gain." Father Gildas leaned his vast weight toward the young man. "A ritual of purification can be nothing but a mockery as long as we allow evil to remain in the Valley, as I will tell the people today. You understand what you are to do?"

Boyden fidgeted and didn't meet the priest's eyes. "Yes, Father, but what if my father won't listen?"

"You must make him listen. Or you must act yourself. Angus stands in the condemnation of excommunication. Can I expect better of you?"

Boyden tried to hide his uncertainty. "I'll do what I can, Father."

The priest drew the star of Sulis. "Remember, Sulis will not protect you if you do not act on what you know to be right. Do not disappoint the goddess."

* * *

Cara laughed with the other women as they wove greenery and flowers over the outside of the temple. Young girls played around their feet or tried to help. "Do you think the goddess will bless us today?" she asked one of the other newly married women.

"The way you and Dillion go at it, there's no reason why she shouldn't," the other woman winked. "Now, my Cael's so lazy it would take a miracle to get me with child."

They both laughed. When they were finished, the women stepped back to admire their work as the men and boys approached through the village streets. The men and women lined up on opposite sides of the temple door.

When everything was ready, the doors of the temple swung open, and Father Gildas, flanked by his novices, greeted the crowd. "Welcome, my children, to the temple of Sulis, the Mother and protector of us all. On this, the longest day of the year, let us celebrate her blessings, purify our hearts, and express our faith in the promise of the harvest to come. Come forward, my children, be cleansed with the waters of life and receive the first fruits of her blessing."

One by one the members of the crowd came forward and knelt before the priest. He sprinkled each Valley resident with holy water and pronounced the blessings of purification upon them. Afterwards, each man and woman took a small piece of fruit from the baskets the novices held and filed into the temple. Cara smiled shyly at Dillion as she took a seat directly across the aisle from him.

After all the villagers had received the water of purification and a taste of the goddess's blessing, Father Gildas mounted the pulpit. A large basket of fruit and vegetables covered the altar, which was also decorated with fresh greenery and flowers. The priest spread his arms wide as if to embrace the entire crowd. "My children, the goddess is pleased with all of you who have come here today and purified yourselves in her name. It is the utmost desire of my heart that all in the Valley be as pure and faithful as you are." His arms dropped, and his face fell. "If you look around the temple today, you will see many of your friends and neighbors here, but you will notice others that are missing. Others that lead lives stained with contamination. This very spring one who is absent today suffered the consequences of his refusal to abide by the will of the goddess. The evil that exists on his land caused a horrible curse to smite the fruits of his labor. Despite what Sulis caused him to suffer, he has rejected the goddess's aid and still clings to evil."

Cara found herself shaking. While she took care of Robbie after he was injured, she'd realized that she'd been wrong about him. *A demon would never allow himself to be beaten like that. Boyden would no longer be alive if his brother were a demon.*

"Although the one cursed by demons would not dare approach Sulis's holy shrine, he still moves and breathes in the Valley. The blessings of the goddess cannot rest upon us if we allow this evil to move through our streets, if we invite it into our homes and our barns."

How dare he tell them not to allow Robbie to heal? It's because of him that so few farmers lose their animals to illness or injury. A demon wouldn't help like that. But as Cara looked around the room, she noticed that the crowd, including Dillion, was nodding in agreement.

"My children, Sulis wishes to bless you. Sulis wishes you to grow in wisdom and prosperity, but she is held back by your willingness to ignore the evil among us. Only when we are strong and righteous enough to confront and destroy those who bear the marks of demons on their skin will the blessings of Sulis run free among us once more. Walk with Sulis, my children, and may she lead you in the paths you need to take to cleanse our community and receive of her blessings."

Cara gasped, unable to believe what she heard. *He's trying to get the villagers to kill Robbie or at least drive him from the Valley. This man doesn't speak for Sulis.* Cara ran out of the temple and fled in the direction of the woods with tears streaming down her cheeks. Behind her, she heard Dillion call her name, but she didn't stop until she reached the shelter of the trees. There, she threw herself on the ground and cried in the dirt.

Dillion dropped down beside her. "What's wrong, Cara?"

"Did you not hear the priest's lies?"

Dillion took a step back and gaped at her. "Careful, Cara, you know as well as I do the priests speak for the goddess."

"I know no such thing." She gestured wildly in the direction of the shrine. "Dillion, he's wrong about Robbie. There's no harm in him."

"Cara, how can you defend him?" Dillion asked icily. "Just look at him. He's not natural. For Sulis's sake, he rides a Horsetad. I don't want to hear you speak his name again. You're my wife, and you will obey me."

Cara glared at her husband. "You're wrong, Dillion, and so is Father Gildas."

"Damn it, woman! Keep your voice down. Do you want the entire Valley to hear your blasphemy?"

"I don't care who hears it. I won't sit in that temple and listen to priests who tell lies ever again."

"You will do what I tell you to do." He raised his hand and slapped her across the face.

Cara reeled under the blow and turned and stared at her husband in shock. "Do that again, and you'll find out just how cold your bed can get." She turned and stalked away.

* * *

Sitting in the shadow of a small wood, Myst's cottage was a small one-room structure beside the road between Valley Fair and Murtaghan. On two sides of the cottage, the herb witch had gardens, bursting with vegetables and herbs. Combined, the gardens were easily four times the size of the cottage itself. They were surrounded by rock walls to keep out rabbits and other animals. The cottage backed onto the woods. Near the large window, Myst had painted a pair of crossed hands—the sign of a healer.

Today neither the mushrooms of the woods nor her gardens interested her. She sat in a chair, staring out the front window. The glass in her windows made the cottage a bright and cheery place and was the one luxury she had indulged in, as most peasants covered their windows in simple oilcloth. But today the sunlight streaming through did nothing to lighten her mood. She'd dreamed of Donella last night. Her dead friend had assured her Robbie would come today. She glanced at the table behind her, on which she had laid out the cakes she'd spent all morning baking. A kettle for tea was warming over the fire, but the road leading to her cabin was empty. She must have merely dreamed what she wished would be true.

She had tried to purify herself that morning, but the goddess didn't hear her pleas. The goddess had deserted her for her failure to keep her vow. She had tried again to visit Robbie at the forest stable, but she hadn't even been able to find the stable, let alone the boy. *Oh, holy Sulis, I know I've done wrong. Please, give me a chance to make it right.*

As she stared down the road, she saw a horse approaching. Even at this distance, the Horsetad was unmistakable. *Oh, thank you, Holy Mother! You are truly merciful!*

She hurried to fetch the teakettle from the fire. A knock came at her door. She bustled about and opened it. She smiled as she saw Donella's green eyes shining from her son's face. "Come in," she laughed. "Come in."

Robbie was distressed at the sight of the table set with tea. *I should have known she wouldn't want to see me today. Surely, she has better things to do with her holiday.* "You're expecting someone. I'm sorry. I'll go."

"Oh, no, my child. I was expecting you. Please, sit."

Robbie raised an eyebrow. *What would have made her think I'd come today? I didn't know I was coming myself until a few minutes ago.* Still, he eyed the cakes hungrily. He was usually sent from the table before dessert was served. The herb witch offered him a seat. He perched on the edge of the chair. He had no idea what to say and couldn't figure out what to do with his hands.

The herb witch placed a cup of tea and a hunk of the cake in front of him and sat down herself. He reached for the cake, but froze when Myst asked, "And how is that great horse?"

He picked up the cake and took a bite in order to delay answering. It was delicious. Obviously, she hadn't told anyone about Brazen, and the beast was so Sulis-cursed frustrating he needed to tell someone about her or he'd burst. "She's determined to get us both killed. She says she is safe at that stable and that nobody can find her. Now does that make any sense?"

Myst's eyes widened. "The horse talks to you? Holy Sulis, your gift is strong."

"What gift?"

The herb witch laughed. "My dear child, you communicate with animals. You ride a Horsetad. You can tell a plant's properties merely from sight and smell. You make medicines imbued with magic despite the fact you've never had a teacher. Not to mention that a magical horse has come seeking you. How can you not know you're an amihealer? In fact, you're the strongest amihealer I've ever heard of outside of legends and bards' tales."

Robbie almost choked on his tea. He snorted and looked away. *I'm not a little boy who believes in bards' tales.* He took another sip of the tea in order to have something to do, but the stuff tasted like boiled weeds. He could barely gag it down.

The herb witch reached across the table and touched his arm. "My child, I have neglected you for so long that I don't deserve the privilege, and you have grown stronger than most purely by acting on instinct. But with a teacher, you could become stronger still."

Robbie looked at Myst, and her eyes held something close to desperation. He didn't trust her, but she was offering him what he'd wanted since he was five years old. He hated being ignorant. "You don't want to be my teacher. I'm not very smart."

"I doubt that very much. How about we give it a try?"

Robbie shrugged. *Why is she being so weird?*

"I'd first like to see how much you already know. Let's start with your knowledge of healing herbs. Go over to my bookshelf"—she indicated the one in the corner—"and fetch my herbal. It's the one that says *Herbal Healing in the Joined Kingdoms.*"

Robbie's stomach plummeted. *Now, she'll find out how stupid I am and want no more to do with me.* Praying that somehow he'd be able to guess the right volume, he went to the shelf she indicated. He stared at the books covering the shelves, the symbols on their coverings meaning as little to him as they ever had. *Some legend!*

"What's wrong, child? It's the one near the middle that says *Herbal Healing in the Joined Kingdoms.*"

Robbie put his hand randomly on a volume. "No, my child, not that one. What's the problem? Can't you read?" Myst laughed as if it were a joke, laughed as Boyden had always laughed at his ignorance.

He rounded on the old woman. "No, I can't! Do you find that funny?"

Myst abruptly stopped laughing. "Every child in Korthlundia is taught to read."

Robbie clenched his fists, his whole body shaking. He longed both to strangle the old woman and to disappear into the boards that made up the herb witch's floor. "Every child but the one that defiles the goddess's holy places with his presence! I won't waste any more of your time." He stomped toward the door.

Moving quicker than Robbie imagined her capable of, Myst interposed herself between him and the door. "Did Father Gildas's say that to you? That ignorant fool! A priest of the goddess of healing, he calls himself! What blasphemy! One jar of your ointment contains more of Sulis's holiness than his entire shrine. If you walk out this door, do so because you have judged me unworthy to be your teacher, not because an arrogant fraud has convinced you you're unworthy to be taught." The herb witch stepped aside.

Robbie tensed, unsure of what to do. He'd craved the ability to read since he'd first seen his brother doing it, but the passion of the herb witch frightened him. "But what if I can't do it? What if I'm too stupid?"

"That would be the biggest surprise you've presented me with yet." He didn't resist as she led him back to the table. He sat, and she fetched a book from the bookshelf. Myst sat beside him again and began to teach him sounds and letters out of what appeared to be a simple storybook. Despite his misgivings, he found himself relaxing in the old woman's presence.

Two hours later, he was already stumbling through the first few pages. He was amazed there wasn't some greater mystery to it. The herb witch patted his arm. "My child, never call yourself stupid again."

When he left, she lent him the book, asking him to study what he'd learned that day. "Come back as soon as you can."

"I will, Mistress, I promise." *If I'm not stupid, maybe I'm not evil either.*

* * *

As Robbie neared the farm in the late afternoon, Allyn and Darien stepped out into the road. "I wouldn't go home right now if I were you," Allyn said. "It might not be safe."

"Why not?"

Allyn shrugged. "Just might not be."

Looking askance at Allyn, Robbie slid off Wild Thing, left the road, and crept up to the farmyard from behind the barn. Most of the farmhands, servants, and his brother Boyden stood in front of the main house.

His father emerged. "You have something you want to discuss with me?"

"Yes, Father," Boyden said. "This morning we all purified ourselves at Sulis's holy shrine in celebration of Litha. Now we ask you to allow us to purify the farm."

"It's your holiday. You can sprinkle holy water or waste it any way you want!" Angus turned to go back inside, but stopped at Boyden's voice.

"Holy water can't purify if the contamination isn't first removed. Father Gildas warned we wouldn't be under the protection of the goddess as long as you insist on keeping the seed of evil on our lands."

Angus whirled to face Boyden. "I won't have you repeat that lying fraud's words. You will respect your mother." Angus turned to the crowd. "These are my lands and anyone who has a problem with the way I run things is free to leave. But I will not hear anything against my wife or my son. Nor will I tolerate him being harmed." If things hadn't been so tense, Robbie would have laughed at the irony. His father had harmed him far more often than anyone else. "If you don't have anything better to do than stir up trouble, maybe you should all get back to work. So which will it be? Are you going into the village for the feast, the fire wheel, and the dancing? Or do I have you head out to the West fields and repair the fence that needs attention?"

The farmhands hesitated, but soon started to drift away. Angus treated his hands better than any other farmer in the Valley, better than he treated Robbie. Boyden didn't move, but stood arguing with their father, although too quietly for Robbie to hear. To Robbie's shock, Angus slapped Boyden. He'd never seen his father hit Boyden.

"You'll regret this!" His brother stomped away.

Robbie turned to Allyn and Darien, who'd crept up behind him. "What's going on?" He forced the words through clenched teeth, his hands forming fists.

Allyn scratched his head. "Father Gildas pretty much said until you were gone, we're all cursed."

"What have I ever done to anyone?" He fled toward Wild Thing. As he leaned against her, he tried to decide what to do. He didn't dare sleep in the bunkhouse, and he wasn't about to move back into the main house. But he was too angry and frightened to plan further than that. For the first time in his life, he didn't want to leave the farm. He didn't want to leave the herb witch who'd promised to be his teacher, but he didn't want to die, either. So he headed toward the one place he could feel safe.

* * *

When he reached the forest stable, Brazen was waiting by the paddock fence as if she expected him.

Still irritated with the horse, Robbie didn't say anything as he unsaddled and started rubbing down Wild Thing.

:Fetch the sword,: Brazen commanded. :You will learn to fight with the sword.:

Robbie stopped in mid-stroke. "Are you mad? In case you haven't noticed, I'm a peasant. I can't carry a sword, especially one like that. I'd be arrested and hanged as a thief."

:Fetch the sword. You will learn to fight with the sword.:

"If no one can find us unless *you* allow it, why would I need the Sulis-damned sword?"

Brazen didn't even seem to notice his mocking tone. :Fetch the sword. You will learn to fight with the sword. It is your destiny.:

Robbie put his hands on his hips. "What destiny would that be? Getting my throat cut in my sleep?"

Robbie turned away from her and tried to ignore her, but all the while he groomed Wild Thing, Brazen kept repeating herself. He went inside the stable, wrapped himself in a blanket, and put another one over his head to block out the horse's absurd demands. But since the voice was inside his head, the blanket didn't help. Brazen followed him inside, stood next to him, and kept repeating herself until Robbie couldn't stand it anymore. "Fine." He jumped to his feet. "I'll get the Sulis-cursed sword if it will shut you up."

He grabbed the sword and went out into the paddock. Brazen followed him and corrected the manner in which he was holding the sword. Images of sword thrusts and parries came to him from Brazen's mind, and he tried to follow her instructions. Despite his irritation, it wasn't long before he started enjoying himself. The blade flashing in the light of the setting sun exhilarated him.

After some time, he dropped on the ground, panting. He was used to hard physical labor, but the muscles used in swordplay were different from those required by farm labor.

:*A good beginning.*:

Robbie merely rolled his eyes, put the sword away, and fell into an exhausted sleep. In his dreams, he met Milady. With shining swords in both of their hands, they fought off their enemies and then made love under the stars.

CHAPTER 11

Returning to his rooms after trying to get an audience with the king, the High Priest Shylah slammed his hand down on his altar. The king had to be made to recognize the essential connection between divine and earthly authority, but this evening the king had even refused to see him. Shylah fingered the fine silk cloth that covered his altar. It was embroidered with a gold star, which was surrounded with baskets of fruit and roses of the deepest scarlet. Finding a red that bright and true had been difficult and costly, but the effect was worth it. He knelt on a plush crimson and gold rug before the altar and lit the candles on either side of the statue of Sulis. The candlesticks were of gold, inlaid with silver roses and rubies. The statue itself was three feet tall and made of pure white alabaster. It depicted Sulis dressed in the long, flowing robes similar to the one Shylah was wearing. In contrast to most depictions of the Holy Mother, it lacked the curves that differentiated a woman's body from a man's. The goddess's hair, traditionally depicted in long braids interwoven with flowers, was here hidden under a priest's cowl. The statue's face had a strong chin, a pointed nose, and a stern expression. Indeed, it looked far more masculine than feminine. Its sculptor had seemed to understand the truth about Sulis as very few did.

The priest bowed his head. "Sulis, why have you allowed the king to live so long? He has never shown the slightest interest in you or your ways. The church courts need the power to enforce sound doctrinal practices. If only we knew who the future king would be!" He touched the statue. "How you must rage at Korthian heresy. How dare women claim to speak in your name!" The northern priestesses corrupted the people's understanding of the place of women. They needed to go, and once they were gone, Shylah could begin to attack the far more dangerous and deeply-rooted heresy—the idea that Sulis was female. Shylah was certain the true power of the divine could not inhabit a weak female form.

Bringing the truth about Sulis back to the joined kingdoms had been Shylah's mission since he'd been a novice studying in the libraries of the monasteries of Wisteria. He had always wondered, if the goddess was a woman, why women themselves were so weak and unintelligent. Among the books, he'd found his answer. He'd come across a very old copy of Writ that used both the male and the female pronouns to refer to deity. Shylah felt as if the heavens themselves had opened that day. He'd discovered the answer to all doctrinal inconsistencies and a key to the disappearance of magic from the joined kingdoms. Of course Sulis would withdraw *his* powers if the people had drifted from *his* paths!

Elated in his discovery and intent on sharing the good news, he'd taken the manuscript to his master. The priest had immediately burned the offending volume and cautioned Shylah about even entertaining such heretical notions. But Shylah was certain what he'd found was not heresy, but a forgotten truth. Shylah had devoted the next few years to searching every ancient library for more old copies of Writ. He'd yet to find any old enough to use exclusively male references to deity, but he'd found several manuscripts—all very old and nearly crumbling in his hands—that referred to Sulis as the Mother *and* the Father, which, of course, was nothing less than the beginning of the heresy that turned Sulis from male to female.

"Ah, my god, it's time the princess marries. The people need to know who will lead them when Solar finally travels Beyond the Far Mountain. He gives far too much heed to a mere girl's desires."

Shylah paused. He chided himself for not taking advantage of this obvious fact. As a female, the princess should really have no more importance than a vessel for the peaceful transfer of power between the king and his son-in-law. However, the king had given his daughter complete charge of the important trade negotiations, demonstrating how far the king was from seeing this truth. "Yes, it's heresy, but can we not use this heresy to advantage?"

He called in Father Faolan, his most trusted assistant. "Go to the princess and summon her to meet with me at half past seven."

* * *

Samantha scowled at her reflection as her maids dressed her for a private dinner with her father and Uncle Caedmon. Things had been tense with her father since she refused to name a consort, and her success with the Massossinans hadn't changed that. Knowing her father and the duke were going to gang up on her, she dreaded the dinner.

She heard a knock on her outer door and prayed it'd be someone giving her an excuse to avoid the dinner. Ardra answered the knock and informed her Father Faolan, the high priest's assistant, was asking to see her. When the priest entered accompanied by her bodyguards, he bowed, but only very slightly.

"Your Highness, His Excellency, the High Priest Shylah, bids you wait upon him in his chambers this evening at half after the hour of seven."

Yes! I can go there instead of dinner! She'd opened her mouth to agree when it hit her just how grossly she was being insulted. Only someone above her in status could summon her. *That Sulis cursed bastard! Just who in the seven hells does he think he is?* "I'm sure you misspoke. You meant to say His Excellency requests an audience with me. You may tell him he may have one at ten tomorrow morning."

Father Faolan took a step backwards. "But, Your Highness, His Excellency wishes to speak to you this evening."

The princess kept her voice steady and cold. "We all wish a great number of things we cannot have." She turned from the priest. He started to argue, but a glare from Kailen's icy blue eyes chased him from the room.

"Can you believe the audacity of the man?" Without giving her maids a chance to finish with her hair, Samantha hurried to her father's chambers.

She burst into the king's private dining room. "Do you know who just summoned me? Some bastard of a priest sent by His Excellency himself."

The king's eyes narrowed, one of the few signs of anger her father ever showed. "I hope you had sense enough to refuse."

"Of course." She folded her arms.

Caedmon shook his head. "Shylah is hungry for power. Truly, it doesn't surprise me he sees himself above the crown princess. Female inferiority is his most cherished and oft-preached doctrine. He is rabid in his denouncement of the Korthian priestesses."

Samantha snorted. "As if a female goddess would create women to be inferior! The entire idea is absurd."

"So my mother believed, as does most of Korth, but I've heard he believes Sulis is male. He has been constantly badgering me to give the church courts power beyond that of excommunication. I've gotten so tired of the old bag I told Gilroy I wasn't available to him anymore."

Samantha snorted again. "So he decides to command me? I'd like to strangle the presumptuous imbecile."

Caedmon laughed, but the king drew his eyebrows closer together. "Using such words to refer to the high priest is politically dangerous. However, he does need to be put in his place. You will do so tomorrow. Now, sit down, and we'll discuss the matter of your consort."

Haven't I been upset enough for one evening? "What is there to discuss? I've told you my choice." She stomped from the room before either of the men could stop her.

* * *

For her meeting with the high priest, Samantha chose a regal, midnight blue dress embroidered in gold. She put a large chain of gold around her neck and had her maids dress her hair in a way that emphasized the heir's gold circlet.

Ten o'clock arrived, but the high priest did not. *Does he think I have nothing to do all day but wait for his pleasure?* Samantha was due at town hall at eleven to hear petitions from the commoners—a duty she performed weekly. She turned to her maids. "When His Excellency arrives, inform him one does not keep the heir to the throne waiting. If he has something he wishes to discuss with me, he can come to city hall and place his name on the list with the others. With any luck, his turn will come up some time next week or the week after that."

Ardra giggled. "With pleasure, Your Highness. But perhaps you should have a clean-up crew on hand. He'll be so angry he'll probably explode, and I don't want to clean blood and brains out of the carpet."

* * *

Samantha returned to the palace in the late afternoon. Unsurprisingly, Shylah hadn't joined the line of petitioners at city hall. She was glad because she'd barely held it together when one of the petitioners had erupted in a sickly purple. Evidence and testimonies from witnesses contradicted each other widely, but the putrid nature of the purple told her immediately who was lying. *But how could I have known that? Holy Sulis, what does it mean? Does madness reveal truth? But if I'm not mad, why do I see these things?*

She'd barely had a chance to change before Darhour reminded her about the bout he'd arranged for potential members of her personal guard. Like the mother hen that he was, Darhour was anxious to have her guard filled with men he could trust. When they entered the practice arena, the twelve men assembled all bowed deeply to her. "I have judged each of these men suitable for your personal guard," Darhour said, "and all have expressed an eagerness to serve in this capacity. I believe four should be chosen for now. We can add others later, if we deem it necessary."

Samantha nodded, knowing she was in no condition to make a judgment and wishing she'd just told Darhour to do the choosing. Darhour had the men pair off against each other. She and Darhour stood to the side, and Darhour commented on the abilities of the different men. He pointed to the first couple. "I wouldn't judge Bearach simply by his sword work. He is good with a sword, but more importantly, he's the best archer in the guard." Samantha had always liked Bearach. He blurted out whatever he thought while most of the guard hardly dared say a word in her presence. "Phelan is a mute, but he'd take on an entire army to protect you." Phelan had always reminded her of a big dog. He was unusually tall, and his odd yellow eyes promised complete devotion whenever he looked at her. Bearach noticed her watching and winked conspiratorially. Phelan took advantage of the moment's inattention to land a blow to his rib cage. Bearach swore loudly and then blushed as he realized she'd heard him. He didn't bother to apologize, though, but focused his attention on beating Phelan back.

"Ailbe is better than Conroy." Darhour pointed to the next pair. "But Conroy is better than most, and he's rock solid steady. He'll keep his head in a crisis." She nodded and glanced at the next pair. "Brice is fast," Darhour said. Indeed, his sword was nothing more than a blur. "And Celyddon . . ."

Samantha didn't hear what else Darhour said because at that moment four of the guards burst into color, glowing with the same light blue and white she'd earlier seen on Kailen. "No!" she screamed. She'd never seen more than one person glowing before. She must have truly lost her mind this time. The entire room went still. Darhour and Kailen drew their swords and tensed for battle, but her madness wasn't something they could protect her from. She ran from the arena with Darhour and Kailen in pursuit.

The princess fled to her rooms without answering her guards' questions. Slamming the doors, she yelled at them to leave her alone. *I'm mad! Four at once! It's getting worse! What am I going to do?*

Samantha collapsed next to her bed and wrapped her arms around herself to stop shaking.

After a while she looked up at the Princess Danu. "How can I be mad? My father needs an heir."

Danu's expression seemed to mock her, and she knew she could hide from the problem no longer. She had to figure out what was causing the colors, but since she didn't dare ask anyone, she'd have to do the research herself.

She dried her eyes, washed her face, and stuffed all her turmoil behind a court mask. When she opened the door to her quarters, Darhour touched her on the arm. "Your Highness--" he started to say, but she cut him off with a look. Too distressed to do anything more about his breach of protocol, she headed to the library without a word.

* * *

Blaine, the most junior of all the junior undersecretaries in the library, was busy with another tedious task Druce, the chief librarian, seemed determined to reserve just for him. He heard the doors of the library open and heard his master's overly cheerful voice. "Oh, Your Highness, so nice of you to drop by. Whatever can we do for you today?"

He jumped to his feet at the words, knocking over an ink bottle in the process. He ignored the mess and bowed with the rest of the library staff. The princess was somewhat disheveled, but Blaine thought she looked more beautiful than ever. He prayed she wouldn't look in his direction. *Her eyes hold the fire of heaven, so to speak.*

The palace library was huge. The walls were lined with bookcases that reached from the floor to at least ten feet above her head. More bookcases nearly as tall stood row upon row in the center of the room. A staircase led up to a second floor which was also lined with books. As Samantha entered, the library staff bowed to her. She felt as if every one of them was seeing her madness. One of them knocked over an ink bottle in his haste to rise, and when she looked at him, he turned a brilliant crimson. She tried to keep her voice casual when she addressed the chief librarian. "I have heard some rumors about my family's history I'd like to verify. It would be better done in private."

"Of course, Your Highness." Druce gestured to the rest of the library staff. "You heard Her Highness. Everybody out." The library staff disappeared.

She turned to her bodyguards. "Now back up, the two of you," she said.

Darhour crossed his arms. "Your Highness, we cannot leave you alone."

She jabbed a finger at him. "You both can and will."

Darhour glared at Druce, sizing the man up. To her intense irritation, Kailen looked to Darhour, and only when Darhour nodded did he move away. She kept waving them farther back until they were out of earshot. She gestured Druce into a seat at a nearby table and sat near him.

Samantha kept her voice low. "I've heard rumors the princess Danu might have been insane."

Druce chuckled and spoke loudly enough she was sure her guards would be able to hear. "You can rest assured the rumor is false, Your Highness. The historical record gives no evidence of insanity."

She whispered through clenched teeth. "The rumor stated Danu would see colors explode in the air around people."

The librarian briefly wrinkled his brow, but seemed to get the hint. When he responded, it was in a much quieter voice. "Colors, Your Highness?" After he paused for a brief moment, his eyes lit up. "You mean auras, I believe, Your Highness. The projection of a person's essence into the air surrounding them, which manifests itself as a pattern of colors and reveals a person's true character."

"Yes, that's it." Samantha wanted to laugh out loud. There was a name for what she saw!

Druce chuckled again. "I assure Your Highness, Danu was no aurora—that's the name we use for a woman who sees auras. Whoever spread this rumor had no respect for the princess. It's tantamount to calling her a bastard."

Samantha's relief withered. "Whatever do you mean?"

Druce chuckled yet again, and Samantha swore she'd ram her fist through his mouth and out the back of his head if he did it one more time. "Your Highness, auroras only arise from the mixture of common and noble blood. Since the nobility of Danu's mother is not in doubt, Danu could only be an aurora if her mother had been welcoming someone other than her husband into her bed."

The room spun, and Samantha feared she would faint. *No, that can't be true!*

"Are you alright, Your Highness? You've gone white."

"I'm fine." Samantha tried to smile and hoped it didn't look as false as it felt. She breathed deeply and reminded herself who she was talking to. Her tutor had called Druce a "muddle-headed imbecile."

"I'd like to read more about Danu. I'm sure she must appear in some of these books." She gestured toward the nearest set of shelves.

"Danu has always held great fascination for the historian. She's said to be a powerful sorceress, although I'm sure the frog story is apocryphal. To my knowledge, no one has written a book exclusively about Danu, but many histories devote entire chapters to her. A rare thing for someone who wasn't a reigning monarch. Shall I assemble our holdings on Princess Danu?"

Samantha nodded. "Please do. And while you're at it, I'd like to see whatever you have about auroras. I've never heard of one before."

"I'm not surprised, Your Highness. It is an extremely rare ability. There hasn't been an aurora in Korthlundia in at least a century." Druce bowed and left to fetch the books.

Druce brought her books with references to Danu first. To make her interest in Danu seem legitimate, she opened a book on the history of Lundian royalty and moved her eyes over the page, but she didn't have the slightest idea what it said or even if the portion of the book she opened to had anything to do with Danu. *If he's right . . . ? If I'm a bastard . . . ? No, it's not possible! Druce is never right. He catalogues books beginning with the nationality of the author.*

When Druce delivered the first book on magic, Samantha had to breathe slowly to stop herself from pouncing on it. She kept her eyes on the history book and continued to turn pages at regular intervals until Druce placed the last book on the table in front of her. "There you are, Your Highness. Ten books for Danu and ten for magic. Is there any other assistance I can provide? If you'd tell me the exact information you're looking for, I'd be more than happy to do the research for you."

I want to know if these colors mean I'm a bastard. Should I have you research that? "No, I'll do it myself." Her voice came out far colder than she'd intended, but right now anger was her only defense against falling apart.

"Well, I guess I'll leave you to it, Your Highness. I'll be in my office if you require further assistance." Druce spoke politely, but Samantha could tell he was offended.

When the door closed behind Druce, Samantha slammed the book on Danu shut and reached for the first volume on magic, *Magical Abilities and Their Origins* by Father Drudwyn. To her intense frustration, Father Drudwyn hadn't provided an index for his immense work. After searching for what felt like hours for the section on auroras, she decided her first order of business as monarch would be to hang writers who didn't index their books.

Finally, she found the pages she sought and read silently:

The aurora is a person of the female sex gifted by our high and holy goddess Sulis, may her name be praised forever, with the capacity to see the very currents of the air that vibrate from our corporeal being as we reposition ourselves through the space of this world and as we inhale and exhale the substance of life. Our high and holy goddess Sulis, may her name be praised forever, has seen fit in her infinite wisdom and continuous care of us, her children, who despite our defects and blemishes which make us forever unworthy of her attention . . . .

Get to the point, you daft old man! If you aren't already dead, I'll see you hanged for such abominable prose!

She struggled through Father Drudwyn's nearly incomprehensible explanation of an aurora's powers. He claimed the onset of an aurora's power came when a girl began to bleed in the way of a woman. Samantha paused. She hadn't made the connection before, but she had just begun to bleed the day before she first saw Darhour's aura. The book further claimed a mature aurora could call forth a person's aura at will; this maturity came when the aurora bore a child. Before an aurora's maturity, auras would simply appear at seemingly random intervals. Two things made the appearance of an aura more likely: blood ties and necessity. It was almost always the auras of family members an aurora saw first, and the more an aurora needed to know a person's character the more likely an aura would be visible.

Finally, toward the end of the section, the princess found the passage she was looking for:

As with all gifts of a magical nature, our high and holy goddess Sulis, may her name be praised forever, has seen fit in her infinite wisdom to bestow this gift only upon those whose life fluid has been adulterated. When the blood of one from the far and frozen northlands intermingles itself with the blood of one from our fair southern climes and when in the additional part if one or the other of the adulterating pair possesses the blood of a most lofty and exalted nature, which debases itself by mingling with blood of the lowest and most ignoble variety, our high and holy goddess Sulis, may her name be praised forever, will, as it pleases her in her infinite mercy, bless the offspring of the debased union, if the results are a child of the female gender, with the gift of the perception of auras.

Samantha slammed the book shut. *Lies! It isn't true! How can I trust someone who writes such nonsense as "if one or the other of the adulterating pair"? Besides, Old Father Drudwyn, may he rot in the seven hells, was a priest! Priests can't be trusted on anything about magic, since they're mostly responsible for its disappearance because of their "purity of blood" nonsense!*

Samantha shoved Drudwyn's book aside and picked up the next volume, which was clearly newer and wasn't written by a priest, but by a man named Forsa Duffstamm. She could tell at once that Forsa knew more than old Father Drudwyn. Forsa had provided an index, and it took her only a few moments to find the right pages. The first words on the page further convinced her of Forsa's greater intelligence; they were written in clear, simple Korthlundian. Samantha skimmed the page to the section that described the origins of an aurora's power.

> While certain aspects of the mixture necessary to produce an aurora have long been the subject of debate among scholars, the one universally agreed upon fact is that it must come from the mixture of noble and common blood.

Idiot! The princess slammed the volume down. Who cared if Forsa could write an index? He obviously knew nothing more than Father Drudwyn. *"Universally agreed upon?" Scholars can't universally agree that the sun will come up in the east tomorrow!*

It hit her. *They are both men! If all auroras are female, what can men know about them?* Samantha searched the volumes for one written by a woman. She found two. The first was written by a "Mother Etain, a priestess and an aurora in the service of Sulis, who is also the illegitimate child of Winfred, the count of Boirche, and his chamber servant." That description made the princess nervous. Mother Etain was a bastard. Of course, she'd say that being a bastard was necessary for one to be an aurora. Not surprisingly, Mother Etain made the same foolish claims as the two men. The second volume was by the Countess of Faichlundia, but she was no better.

Samantha was desperate. Four out of the ten volumes had now said the same thing. She sank her head in her hands. Another idea dawned on her. Maybe she wasn't really an aurora after all. Maybe the colors she saw were a completely different kind of colors. She ignored the fact that Father Drudwyn's description of an aurora fit her so well. She hadn't really read the description of the aurora's talent in the other books. Eager to prove herself not an aurora, she went back to Forsa Duffstamm's *Magics of the Joined Kingdoms*. But it was of no use. Forsa described what she experienced all too well, as did Mother Etain and the Countess of Faichlundia. *This is impossible. The king is my father. He loves me.*

* * *

Hours later, Samantha put down the last volume. She had no doubts. Although the books disagreed on some minor aspects of an aurora's power, it was "universally agreed upon" that she was a bastard. This was much, much worse than being mad. Her mother was little better than a whore, and she wasn't the heir. She was a fraud, an imposter, some foundling foisted on the king without his knowledge. She wanted to scream, tear the books to pieces, and dissolve into a flood of tears, but she was too devastated to move.

My poor father! This will kill him! She didn't know how many times Solar had told her of his long wait for an heir. He'd insisted if he had died without one, competing claimants would tear Korthlundia apart. *My father worked his entire life to prevent this, and I have failed him. Who knows how many thousands will die because of me?*

As she lifted her head and looked out into the blackness of the night, a new thought occurred to her. *Is it possible he already knows? Would he have taken another man's child as his own if that was the price of preserving the peace?* Samantha knew he wouldn't have hesitated. The joined kingdoms were far too important to him. *Could a fifteen-year-old girl truly have carried on an affair without his knowledge?*

Samantha put her head back in her hands. She didn't know what to do. If her father did know, he'd be angry she'd found out. If he didn't know, what would it do to him? He was nearly ninety. There was no chance of him having another heir. She needed advice, but could think of no one she dared turn to. *Is it okay to be a fraud if it is the only way to avoid war? Does the good of the people demand I continue to live a lie? Holy Mother, what do you want me to do? I'm not certain I can live with either choice.*

The stillness of the night brought no answer, but the consequences were too great for her to make the decision rashly. The books were right about one thing. Earlier today, her need had made her ability operate. She needed men loyal to her. She picked up a quill and dipped it in ink. On a sheet of paper, she wrote the names of the four men whose auras she'd seen—Phelan, Brice, Bearach, and Conroy. She called Darhour and handed him the paper. "Add these to my guard."

These men, like Kailen and Darhour, would loyally serve a bastard; she wished she knew if she were damning herself by allowing them to do so.

CHAPTER 12

"I thought you were going to take care of this problem for us," Father Gildas said, as he sat at the desk in his office. Boyden stood on the other side of the desk. Again, the damned priest wouldn't offer him a chair.

"I told you, my father won't listen. He threatened to disinherit me."

"So you decided that your earthly welfare is more important than your soul? We often need to sacrifice to do Sulis's bidding."

"But how? The land isn't mine. I can't make the worm leave."

"You can think of no other way of ridding this Valley of its contamination?" the priest asked.

Boyden felt a chill at the priest's expression. "Do you mean kill him? Doesn't Sulis condemn most severely those that murder their blood?"

The priest nodded. "That is generally the case, but here there are other factors. First, we must consider whether a blood tie actually exists. I look at you, and I see a child of the goddess. Do I see a child of the goddess when I look at him?" The priest shook his head. "Do you think the Holy Mother would condemn one who acts to purify her people and protect them from harm?"

"Are you saying the goddess will approve if I kill him?"

"You must let Sulis guide you, but the goddess will not hold you blameless if you have the power to rid her people of contamination and do not act." The priest paused. "Think about your duty to the goddess and to her people. That is all that I ask."

* * *

With the rest of the hands, Robbie helped to load the harvest into the wagons. When the task was nearly finished, his father called. Robbie dragged his feet as he went to him. He'd barely spoken to his father since the attacks on the crops had ceased in the spring.

"I've heard that you've been spending time with the herb witch."

"Have any of my chores been neglected?" Robbie asked, cursing himself for not being more careful.

"I won't have that bitch interfering with my family. Keep away from her. Do you understand me, boy?"

Robbie looked down at his feet and didn't answer. He couldn't give up what Myst was teaching him no matter what his father said. Angus grabbed him by the shoulder and shook him. "I said, do you understand me, boy? Or do I have to drag you back in the house and teach you another lesson in respect?"

"I understand, sir," he answered. But the herb witch was the only one who cared about him.

"Your brother and I are going to Murtaghan in the morning to sell the harvest. If I hear that you've been anywhere near that witch, I'll rip you apart."

Robbie looked away and didn't answer.

* * *

Angus ignored the boy's scowl, but he wouldn't have that bitch turning his own son against him, as she'd once tried to turn his wife. He watched as the hands loaded up the last of the harvest. He didn't have the yield he'd hoped for in the spring, but there would be enough to pay the hands, and no one would go hungry this winter.

When night fell, Angus took the best of the grain and his finest apples and went to pay his respects to the woman he still loved. As always, he went alone. As he trimmed the grass around her headstone carefully and laid out his offerings, he felt the pain of her loss tearing at his heart. Although, it'd been over sixteen years, he still missed her as much as he had on the day she died.

He'd fallen in love with Donella's combination of strength and vulnerability that day at the auction. Her eyes had held a spark of defiance, but her lower lip had quivered with fear. He hadn't gone there intending to buy, but simply to see the newest whores brought from abroad. But the trembling of her lip had appealed to the protector in him, and he couldn't allow her to be ruined by hundreds of other men. He'd searched the city for a priest willing to marry them and located a drunk who would have done anything for the right price. Even though it was a man's right and duty to chastise his family, he'd never hit her. He'd loved her, and because of Robbie, he'd lost her. He felt a coldness in the night air that caused him to shiver. Donella was angry with him again, angry that he'd forbidden Robbie to visit the herb witch. *Damn that bitch! She had better leave me and mine alone.* He stalked from his wife's grave without the feeling of comfort and peace he craved.

* * *

Slathek watched from the deck of his ship as they followed the Korthlundian pilot boat out of the treacherous harbor. He sighed as the shore of the land of barbarians flew behind him. He was weary of the lies that filled his dreams at night. He was afraid that, like his father, he couldn't accept Sphry's fate. He looked over at his father, who'd sat on a bench and was staring at the departing coast.

"I'm afraid this may be my last trip, my son." Robrek had tears in his eyes. "I'm growing too old to make such long voyages. It will be up to you to find her."

Slathek looked away and didn't answer. *Why can't he allow Sphry to rest in peace?* He stared back toward the shore. *Why can't I?*

* * *

"Why are you teaching me this?" Robbie asked for the dozenth time, panting against the stable wall and holding the bronze sword.

Brazen answered as she always did. :*It is your destiny.*:

Robbie rolled his eyes and returned the sword to its scabbard. "What destiny requires the son of a peasant farmer to know how to use a sword?" The horse didn't answer, as Robbie knew she wouldn't. Since Litha, Robbie had slept at the forest stable, but the bronze mare was driving him mad by endlessly repeating the same nonsense.

As he walked down to the stream to bathe, he shivered. The nights were getting steadily colder. When his father returned from Murtaghan, he would pay off the hands, and those hired only for the growing season would disappear for the winter. The long-time hands were less wary of him than those that had only served the family for a season or two. Surely, it would be safe for him to return to sleeping in the bunkhouse. Still, did any place exist where every eye wouldn't turn when he passed? If he went to Murtaghan like he'd once thought to do, would he fit in any better? There was only one person in his life with whom he had felt normal. He stared up at the stars and thought about Milady. *Does she even remember me?* He shook his head, knowing the answer. *Why would she?* Still, he fell asleep with the memory of her kiss on his cheek.

The next morning he returned to the farm to help care for the stock. He spent a long time with Thunder. The mare was pregnant again. She'd nearly lost her last foal, and she wasn't having an easier time with this one. She shouldn't have been bred so soon. He'd tried to tell his father this, but Angus wouldn't listen.

When Robbie had her settled as comfortably as he could, he realized that, with the harvest over, there was no other task required of him on the farm until evening chores. He saddled Wild Thing and headed for the herb witch's cottage. He didn't care what his father said: he would go see the herb witch if he wanted to. He would just have to be more careful about it.

He'd grown over the summer, and now that he wasn't so harried, he noticed that his clothing no longer fit. There were inches between the end of his trousers and his feet, the sleeves of his shirt were much too short, and his shirt wouldn't stay tucked in. His coat, which he'd put on to meet the chill of the fall morning, was similarly small and threadbare.

The wind had picked up, and he was thoroughly chilled when he arrived. Myst fussed over him, gave him the seat closest to the fire, and warmed him with tea and cakes. He wished there was some *bhat*, but the herb witch probably couldn't afford the beans. Her cake was delicious, though.

"Oh dear, my child, you've grown. You must have new clothes."

"I know, but I can't bring myself to get down on my hands and knees and beg my father for them."

"My dear child, why should you beg for what you have clearly earned? Does anyone else work on the farm for nothing more than food and a place to sleep?"

Robbie opened his mouth to argue, but could think of nothing to say. Why *did* he continue to work for his father if he wasn't paid? His father obviously had no appreciation for what he did. "He'd never pay me, and if I went in and tried to demand it, he'd beat me raw. He probably will anyway. He told me I'm not allowed to come here anymore."

The herb witch pursed her lips. "Damn the man and his arrogance!" Robbie's eyes widened. He had never heard her swear. "Robbie, you have a gift. You must learn how to use it." She paused. "Robbie, if he won't pay you and he treats you so horribly, why stay?"

Robbie stared at her and stated the obvious. "Because I have nowhere else to go."

"Of course you have. Most apprentices live with their masters. I'd be delighted to have you."

Robbie looked around the small cottage. "I couldn't do that, mistress. You can hardly afford to feed and clothe yourself. I won't be a burden to you."

The old woman laughed. "You'd never be a burden, and I doubt I'd need to either feed or clothe you. How much was your father paid for the foal you helped deliver just last week?"

"Half a tetra and a barrel of apples," Robbie answered.

"You could buy a new shirt or two for that, and I do love a good apple."

Robbie just stared at her. Although he often resented his father taking everything he was paid for healing, it hadn't occurred to him that farmers would pay him directly. Still, he shook his head. "Two of my father's mares are in foal. One of them has had a difficult time in the past. If I'm not there, she could die."

Myst smiled. "You have the marks of a true healer, but do you think your father will risk the lives of his valuable animals by refusing to pay what he must know in his heart you are worth?"

Robbie looked away from her. *He'll have me on the ground begging to be allowed to live before he's through with me.* He pushed away the herb witch's cakes.

"Your mother would never stand for you being neglected like this."

"Maybe. But my mother's dead. If she hadn't wanted me to have a brute as a father, she shouldn't have married one." `

153

"Don't you dare judge your mother! You have no idea what she went through."

"No, I don't. No one will talk about her. Not even you."

Myst's mouth opened to protest, but she realized she did change the subject whenever Robbie brought up Donella. "Your mother's story isn't a pretty one."

Robbie met her eyes. "Neither is mine."

Myst turned away, not able to face the young man who looked at her through Donella's eyes.

"Why would she have a name like Donella if she came from far away? It's a Korthlundian name."

"Donella wasn't her given name. It was something very long with very few vowels in it. Spregrita or some such thing. I never could pronounce it. Neither could Angus. He's the one who started calling her Donella. She thought it was sweet when she found out what it meant—elfin girl."

Robbie snorted in disbelief. "Sweet" wasn't a term she'd ever use for Angus, either, but Donella often had. He might have been a different man, if she'd lived.

"But how did she meet my father?" Robbie asked. "There certainly isn't anyone around here who looks like me, and my father only goes to Murtaghan once per year to sell the harvest." Robbie looked her straight in the eyes. "Mistress, she's my mother. I deserve to know."

Myst sighed and sat down. "I guess you do. Your mother was younger than you when she was kidnapped from her native land and brought to Murtaghan with a lot of other young girls to be sold to the brothels. Even though slavery has long been illegal, King Solar has never been able to completely stamp it out. Your father saw her at the auction and bought her. She was always grateful to Angus for saving her from the brothels."

She looked away, not able to meet the shock and anger in Robbie's eyes. "My father purchased my mother like a cow! How dare he pretend to have loved her!"

"We had our fair share of arguments on that subject. I told her she didn't have to stay with Angus. He didn't legally own her. But your mother would never hear anything against him. She claimed his love for her was real. In your father's defense, he did marry her before he touched her. She was completely alone and vulnerable. He had no need to make her his legal wife."

Robbie's hands formed fists. "I'll kill him."

The depth of his rage almost frightened her. "Your mother never felt a desire for revenge against your father, and even I think killing him is taking things a little too far. But you shouldn't allow him to treat you the way he does. My child, you're a strong and talented amihealer. You can easily support yourself without your father's money. He needs you far more than you need him."

* * *

Robbie watched from the bunkhouse window as his father and brother drove in from Murtaghan. He watched the hands take care of the wagon and horses and his father and brother head for the house and the noon meal. *I won't be treated like dirt by the man who thinks a wife can be bought like an animal!* He hurried toward the house before he could change his mind.

For the first time since he'd moved his meager possessions out, Robbie opened the front door and went in. His father and Boyden were talking at the dining room table. Conversation stopped abruptly. "To what do we owe the pleasure of this visit?" his father demanded.

Robbie took a deep breath. "I have come to inform you I expect to be paid with the rest of the hands in the morning."

His father leaned back and folded his arms. "Have you?"

Robbie looked at his father's hands, the ones that had so often hit him, and thought of them touching his mother. He allowed the rage to mount within him to combat the fear. "You reduced me to the status of a farmhand long ago. Now you will pay me, or I'll do what any farmhand would do in my position."

His father laughed. "Just who do you think will hire you, boy? Most around here think you're a demon. Now, get out of here before I give you the beating you so richly deserve."

Robbie clenched his fists and fought to keep his voice from trembling. "They may think me a demon, but even now, they pay for my services. I can live well enough without you. You will pay me, or you will find someone else to care for your animals."

Angus jumped to his feet and slapped Robbie across the face, knocking him to the ground. "Damn you, boy! I wouldn't take this from Boyden, and by the seven hells, I won't take it from you!"

Robbie tasted blood in his mouth as he slowly got to his feet. He looked his father in the eyes, allowing his hatred of the old man to fill them. "Tomorrow morning I'll line up with the rest of the hands to receive my wages. You can pay me the twenty tetra due experienced hands, or you can watch me ride away. If you ever hit me again, I will leave." Robbie turned his back on his father.

"I won't be dictated to! Come back here, damn you!" his father yelled after him.

Robbie ignored the shouts and headed for the bunkhouse. He half expected Boyden to intercept him and drag him back for the worst beating he'd ever received from his father. But he reached the bunkhouse unscathed and collapsed on his bunk, shaking with the aftereffects of fear and rage.

* * *

Next morning, Robbie awoke sick to his stomach. Since his father would view his actions as treason, he couldn't imagine Angus letting him get away with it. His back ached with remembered pain, and his mouth grew dry as he imagined Boyden holding him to the dining room table. *Will I even be able to walk when he's through with me?*

But even as he imagined the beating, he knew he wouldn't take back what he'd done yesterday. He would be treated as a human being. If his father did beat him today, it would be for the very last time.

When his father came out of the house carrying the sack of coin, Robbie lined up with the others. His father didn't look at him, as one by one the men stepped up and received their pay. When Robbie reached the front of the line, his father counted out twenty tetra, but didn't push them to Robbie's side of the table. "If you choose to be no more than a hired hand, reach across and take your money," Angus said. "But if you do so, you'll be my son no longer."

"When have you ever treated me like a son?" He swept the coins into his hand and returned to the bunkhouse.

But as Robbie sat on his bunk looking at the coins, he didn't feel the triumph he'd expected. A part of him had always believed that someday his father would change, that one day he'd look into his father's eyes and see them shining with love and pride. As Robbie looked at the coins, he realized that day would never come. He blinked quickly to rid his eyes of tears. He wasn't going to cry like a baby over a stupid fantasy.

He took an old pair of trousers, cut a large piece of cloth from them, and put the coins inside. He gathered it up into a makeshift purse and tied the top closed with a strip of leather. Putting the coins in his pocket, he headed to the barn to saddle Wild Thing.

The small village of Valley Fair was only a few miles away, and Robbie reached it before midmorning. He'd rarely been there and never alone. He ignored those who stared at him or drew the star of Sulis as he went by and bought the things he needed. When Robbie rode out of town, his grumbling stomach reminded him he'd had nothing to eat that day; he hoped he'd arrive at Myst's cottage in time for lunch.

* * *

Before Myst would feed him, she made him tell her what happened with his father and bring in his purchases and show them to her. She fussed over him and had him change into a set of his new clothing. Although Robbie was uncomfortable with all the fuss, a part of him was pleased by it. He'd never had anyone who cared enough about him to fuss over him before. When he was properly dressed, he looked at his reflection in the shining pot over the fireplace. For the first time, he didn't see a demon-cursed runt; instead, he saw something of the young man Milady had wanted to spend time with. Through the fabric of his new shirt, he fingered the ribbon that hung around his neck.

Myst came up behind him and put a hand on his shoulder. "You look quite grown-up. You have your mother's eyes. I always found their color stunning."

"That's what Milady said."

The herb witch's face darkened. "Robbie, do you realize . . . ?"

"Realize what?" He whirled away from her. "That she's out of my class? That I'll never see her again? What kind of fool do you think I am?"

Myst shook her head. "My child, I just don't want to see you hurt."

"Boyden is the one that hurt me that day. Not Milady."

CHAPTER 13

Count Weylin sat across the table from Duke Argblutal. He tried to maintain a court mask, but he could feel sweat beading on his forehead. He knew the duke hadn't requested "the privilege of dining" with him for the pleasure of his conversation. The duke's servants laid the table and withdrew. They always had a hint of fear in their eyes that Weylin often wished he could produce in those who waited upon him.

"You've spent a great deal of time hunting lately," the duke said as soon as they were alone.

Weylin nodded. "I've always enjoyed a good hunt. Prince Banki and I did manage an impressive take."

"The princess seemed grateful to you for keeping the Massossinan bore off her hands." Using a particularly large knife with a ruby-encrusted hilt, the duke cut his meat. Rumors that couldn't possibly be true claimed he did unspeakable things with that knife.

"I wish only to serve The Crown," the count replied, struggling and failing to keep his eyes off the knife.

The duke laughed in a way that completely destroyed what little appetite Weylin had. "You wish only to *wear* the crown, but you never will. I will rule Korthlundia, as is my right by blood."

"Perhaps that would have been true if the crown princess had never been born. Now whoever weds Her Highness will rule." The count tried to take a causal sip from his wine goblet, but the trembling of his hand ruined the effect.

"I believe you've a mistress living on your estates with several little bastards running around."

"So what if I do? You want me to believe you have lived the life of a priest?"

"As far as I know, I have no bastards," the duke said, and Weylin thought it was probably true. Rumor also had it that Argblutal's women didn't live long enough to beget children. "I've heard you are rather fond of yours, though, even so much as to pay for their education. I would hate for anything to happen to them."

Weylin straightened in his chair "Are you threatening me?"

"Not at all." The duke's smile reminded Weylin of the panther pendant around Argblutal's neck. "Didn't your grandfather have a long dispute over lands with Count Tierney's family?"

What is he trying to trap me into? "And if he did?"

"The dispute was settled in favor of Count Tierney, and your house lost some of its best grazing land."

"My family received a seat on the council in exchange."

"A most unjust exchange when a man could have both the position and the lands." The duke paused and took a sip of his wine. "I will be king. If you support me, I will restore what Solar took away. And since your lands are so near mine, I can help to ensure the safety of all your little bastards."

Weylin picked up his wine glass and gulped down all that remained. "I can think of no one I would rather have on the throne."

* * *

Samantha sat in the clerks' office, staring at, but not really seeing, the papers on the desk in front of her. The king's ninetieth birthday coincided with the traditional harvest festival of Mabon. *He deserves the greatest celebration in the history of the joined kingdoms! But how can a bastard give him that? I can't even concentrate on a single subject for more than a minute any more. Oh, Holy Sulis, what would you have me do?* She'd been at the point of going to the king dozens of times, but she hadn't been able to bear the thought of breaking his heart.

A young man entered the clerks' office, blushed deeply when he saw her, and bowed far lower than strictly necessary. He had light brown hair, hardly any beard, and severe acne. He dressed in shabby scholar's robes. He looked vaguely familiar, but the princess couldn't place him. He delivered a message to one of the clerks. As he walked out, he burst into colors—light blue and white with a hint of yellow.

She felt the same warmth she'd experienced with the members of her guard, but there was an additional feeling of order and precision about the colors. His aura proclaimed not only would he be loyal to her, but he also had a tremendous gift for details and organization. *He has what I no longer do. Holy Mother, is he an answer?*

"Who was that young man?" she asked Iden, the chief clerk. She learned his name was Blaine, and he was an undersecretary to the chief librarian. Samantha now remembered him as the one who had knocked over the ink bottle when she'd visited the library. "And how do you find his work?" she asked.

"Your Highness, I don't know much about him. Perhaps you should ask Druce. I believe Druce has had some difficulties with him."

Druce's difficulties were recommendation enough. She gathered her things and sent a page to summon Blaine to her quarters.

* * *

Blaine busied himself carefully copying Master Druce's lists. It was a futile task: nobody would be able to make any sense of them. They offended Blaine's sense of order so profoundly he couldn't suppress a groan.

"What's wrong?" Innis, his fellow junior undersecretary, asked.

"It's these lists," Blaine whispered. "With the slightest bit of rearranging, they would be so much clearer."

"You aren't going to say anything, are you?" Innis whispered back.

"Of course not! What kind of a fool do you take me for?"

Innis didn't answer, but Blaine knew Innis thought he was a fairly big one. Innis had warned him not to go to Druce the last time, but he hadn't listened. The section of the library catalogue he'd been given to copy that time was horrendous, involving maps and architectural diagrams of the palace and other important buildings throughout the joined kingdoms. The palace itself was a nightmare to anyone interested in order. It had been built and expanded over five centuries. New walls had been put up and old ones torn down in a seemingly haphazard manner. There were so many secret corridors, hidden rooms, and forgotten stairwells that no one truly knew half of the palace's secrets. *And they aren't going to learn them fighting their way through the jumbled mess in this library.* Blaine had gone two full weeks, sleeping only a couple of hours a night, and had come up with what he still considered a brilliant plan for making these materials orderly and accessible to anyone.

When Blaine had brought the plan to him, Druce had shouted at Blaine for close to an hour. "The king most certainly did not put me in charge of the library to be questioned by a mere boy just out of temple school. If it weren't for my friendship with your father, you'd be thrown out the palace gates right here and now." Blaine had been forced to apologize repeatedly and utter the near blasphemous claim that Druce's ordering of the library was far superior to anything he could think of. Blaine needed the job. He'd been alone in the world since he was fourteen and had been hungry every day for nearly four years. He'd keep his mouth closed over far worse disorder if it meant going to bed with a full belly every night.

The door of the library opened, and Blaine glanced up to see one of the palace pages enter. The page spoke to Druce, who looked surprised but pointed in Blaine's direction. Blaine froze as the page crossed the library toward him, followed by Druce.

"You're the undersecretary Blaine?" the page asked. When Blaine nodded, the young page puffed up his chest. "Her Highness, the Princess Samantha, requests you attend her in her quarters at once."

"Her . . . Her Highness? The . . . the p-princess wants m-me?" Blaine stammered, knocking over his ink bottle. He tried to clean up the mess he'd made, but in his nervousness, he made things worse. "But why?"

"Do you think the princess confides in me?" the young boy snapped and left.

Druce regarded him narrowly. "How have you offended the princess?"

"I-I don't know. I-I had no intention of doing so. I-I did see Her Highness in the clerks' office earlier, but I did bow, and I'm sure I did it appropriately. At least, I-I think I did. I did it exactly as you said I should if I ever passed her in the halls. At least, I think I-I did," he stammered, still trying and failing to clean up his mess.

"Stop that immediately!" Druce ordered. "You don't keep the heir to the throne waiting because of spilled ink. Change into clean robes and wash up, and be quick about it! You'll report to me immediately after she's through with you. That is, if she hasn't had you thrown out of the palace or into the dungeon."

Blaine shuddered. "Yes, of course, Master Druce."

As Blaine sprinted to the cramped room at the back of the library he shared with the rest of the undersecretaries, Innis gave him a look of sympathy. He changed as quickly as he could into his best robes, which weren't very nice, and despaired at his inability to scrub the ink stains from his fingers.

* * *

The young undersecretary trembled and bowed repeatedly as he was ushered into Samantha's rooms. When the princess offered him a chair, he sat on the very edge.

"I'm happy you arrived so quickly." She smiled, attempting to alleviate some of his nervousness.

"I-I-I . . . Your H-highness . . . I-I-I . . ." he stammered, seeming to search around desperately for an appropriate response.

"How do you enjoy your work in the library?" she asked, suspecting the disorder drove him mad.

Something close to terror flashed into his eyes. "I-I-I am happy to serve in any c-capacity."

Samantha smiled at the neutral comment. "Good, because I'm appointing you to a new one. The king's ninetieth birthday celebration will take place at Mabon," she told him. "It's very important to me that it be spectacular. However, I'm having difficulties handling all the small details of organization and planning. I need someone to organize this mess." She indicated the scattered piles of paper that littered the table between them. "As my personal secretary, this will be your first duty."

"P-personal s-secretary?" The young man nearly fell off his seat. "Y-your Highness, surely you have made a mistake. I'm only a junior undersecretary in the library!"

"I know what you are, and you are the one I want. I've arranged an office for you just around the corner with sleeping quarters behind. I'll have a page help you fetch your things and move them into your new quarters. I want you at work on this by this afternoon." She again indicated the papers.

"But Y-y-your H-h-highness? I-I'm not . . ."

Samantha cut him off. "Be quick. There's much work to be done." Samantha dismissed him before he could make any further protest.

After the young man left, Darhour turned to her. "Your Highness, I repeat my objections. You know nothing of this boy."

"Boy?" Samantha raised her eyebrow at the chief of her guard. "Darhour, he's older than I am."

"But he's still a boy. Didn't you see how nervous he was?"

"It would have helped if you hadn't looked ready to slit his throat," she snapped. "Darhour, the choice is mine. I won't discuss it."

Darhour glared at her. "At the very least, give me leave to investigate the boy."

Samantha rolled her eyes. "If it'll make you feel better, investigate him to your heart's content."

* * *

Fearing he'd vomit, Blaine hurried back to the library. *The princess's personal secretary? Please, Sulis, don't let it be true. I'll make a disastrous mess!*

As he hustled through the library to his quarters, Druce intercepted him. "Well, do I need to look for a new junior undersecretary?"

Blaine nodded, unable to speak.

"I always knew you'd amount to nothing," Druce sneered. "I would have dismissed you myself if it hadn't been for your father."

"Her Highness didn't dismiss me," Blaine croaked. "She's made me her personal secretary. Now if you will excuse me, I can't delay."

Sputtering, Druce followed. "But this isn't possible! You aren't qualified!"

Blaine faced the chief librarian. "I tried to tell her that, but she wouldn't listen. Now, if you please, she wants me at work as soon as possible." Blaine hurried toward his cramped quarters, feeling the chief librarian's eyes boring into his back.

While he was packing, Innis slipped into the room. "Did I hear right? Her Highness's personal secretary?"

Blaine nodded.

"But that's unbelievable! The only higher position is secretary to the king himself. That's wonderful!"

"It most certainly is not!" Blaine didn't understand how any friend of his could see the beginning of his complete and utter ruin as a good thing. He began shoving his robes into a sack.

"Why are you bothering to pack those?" Innis asked. "Surely, you'll need better if you're the princess's secretary."

"I may need better," Blaine snapped, "but I haven't exactly got the coin to buy any. You know how little we're paid."

Innis laughed again. "As Her Highness's personal secretary, don't you think you'll be paid a good deal more?"

Although the princess hadn't mentioned his wages, Innis was probably right, and his old robes were certainly not fit to be worn in her presence. He threw the sack of robes at Innis. "You keep these, then. Wear them, sell them, cut them down into rags, do whatever you like." He looked around for anything worth packing. He opened his single drawer and found a couple of books, his comb, a brooch that had belonged to his mother that he meant to give to his wife someday, and the papers that represented his two weeks of work reorganizing the architectural holdings of the library. He handed the papers to Innis. "And take these, too. If Master Druce ever dies, perhaps the library catalogue can be rewritten so it's actually useful."

"Blaine." Innis's face was suddenly serious. "You'll be fine. You have a gift for this kind of thing. Master Druce may have been too blind to see it, but obviously Her Highness has clearer vision."

Blaine sat next to him. "But Innis, how could Her Highness know anything about me? Until she summoned me, I'd never even spoken a word to her, and you know Master Druce didn't recommend me. He'd rather be boiled in oil, so to speak."

"She's the crown princess." Innis shrugged, as if that explained everything. "Blaine, for whatever reason, she made a good choice. Just do what you do best." Innis lifted the papers that represented Blaine's work.

Somehow Innis's words made him feel less like he was teetering on the edge of a cliff. He pulled Innis into a quick embrace, grabbed the small sack that contained everything he owned, and followed the page that would take him to his new quarters.

* * *

Argblutal listened to High Priest Shylah complaining about the princess's blatant disrespect of him personally and the priesthood in general. The duke hid a smile; he found the little chit's antics amusing. "I know, beyond belief," Shylah said, obviously misinterpreting Argblutal's expression. "She's a mere girl and doesn't understand the place Sulis has reserved for women. I actually believe she thinks to rule herself rather than properly submitting her authority to a consort. If she continues to act like this, who knows the damage she can cause? We can't have that heresy taught by the Korthian priestesses filtering into Lundia. Women aren't meant to be man's equals."

Argblutal froze with his wine goblet at his lips. While he planned to thoroughly enjoy putting the little bitch in her place, the high priest was coming awfully close to treason. Argblutal quickly adjusted his court mask and sipped his wine.

Shylah continued, "What the princess needs is a strong man to teach her the appropriate duties of a woman. Once she's carrying an heir, nature alone will tell her to submit to a man such as Your Grace, one with the strength of vision needed to guide this people toward the truth."

The duke carefully set down his goblet. "I have made no secret of my ambitions."

"Yes, but you lack the means to achieve them. The princess is indifferent toward you," Shylah said.

Argblutal clenched his fists. He didn't appreciate being reminded of how little the bitch regarded him.

"It is purest blasphemy that the king is letting her chose her own consort. However, with my magic, I could see to it that His Majesty learns the folly of such a course. I have preserved in the libraries on my estates the secrets of powerful ancient magics that can bend the mind of another to the will of the sorcerer. The king, taking proper control of his daughter, will send a strong message to those who question the place of women."

Argblutal swirled the blood-red wine around in his goblet. "I will be blunt. It is well known your magic is weak to non-existent."

Shylah pressed his lips into a fine line. "Strong magic is not needed. Merely time. I could make the potion at my estate while the court is in Wisteria for the winter. In the spring, it will be ready. If you agree to support religious orthodoxy, I can hand you the throne."

The duke paused before answering. By spring, he'd certainly know if he could win the princess without such aid. "Sulis should have the full support of the crown."

* * *

When Samantha returned from court, she found Blaine poring over the piles of papers she'd shown him earlier. He jumped to his feet and bowed repeatedly, glancing nervously at the papers he'd been working on. She couldn't help noticing the shabbiness of his robes. "Y-y-your Highness, I hope I haven't been too forward. Y-y-you asked me to be quick. Y-y-you said these needed organizing."

"Yes, that's definitely what they need. What do you think so far?"

"I'm sure Your Highness knows what she's doing, and if you like things this way, I'm sure it's a perfectly fine way to have them. I know I have very little experience, and Your Highness must have a very good reason for having—"

"Blaine," the princess interrupted. "If you have a suggestion, by all means make it."

Blaine hesitated for a few seconds, then picked up a stack of papers, and brought them to her. "These lists, Your Highness, 'From the Potter's Guild,' 'From the Butcher's Guild,' 'From Duke Torin.'" He laid the lists on the table in front of her. "They're like pieces of a puzzle, so to speak. It's difficult to see how things stand when they're scattered about like this. If I were to organize them in this manner . . ." He laid several new sheets of paper down headed by words such as "Meats," "Wine," and "Entertainment." On each list, he'd begun to categorize the offerings from the different Guilds, Merchants, and Nobles. Samantha was impressed by the simplicity of it. Blaine blushed, mistaking the look on her face. "I-I'm sorry, Y-your Highness, I shouldn't have presumed. It was wrong of me to think so, but it just seemed to me that, organized like this, it'd be easier to see the big picture, so to speak. I'll destroy them at once." He reached for the lists.

Samantha put out a hand to stop him. "Blaine, this is wonderful."

Blaine froze. "You think so, Your Highness? I would never presume to question Your Highness's judgment."

"Blaine, only a fool thinks she's always right. If you see a better way to do things, it is your duty to propose it. Take these papers to your office and continue what you've started."

"With pleasure, Your Highness." Blaine turned a deeper red as he began gathering up all the papers. "I'm so glad you liked my idea. It did seem to make things ever so much clearer."

"I'll have Gilroy send a page with your first month's wages. You may have some expenses in settling into your new position."

Blaine looked at his robes. "I have need of little, Your Highness, but I did think some new robes might be in order." He turned to leave, but stopped at the door and bowed deeply. "Your Highness, I'll try to be worthy of your trust."

* * *

It was nearing midnight as Blaine finished organizing the princess's vast papers into a few simple lists. The meal he'd hardly touched sat beside him on the desk, as did a bag of coins with the wages the princess had promised him. He hadn't opened it, but he didn't need to to know it was far more than a junior undersecretary to the librarian was paid in a year. He'd use some of it to buy suitable robes so his shabbiness wouldn't disgrace the princess. He'd keep the rest just in case the princess demanded he return it when she dismissed him.

As he looked at the lists he'd created, he was quite pleased with the results. They were clear and organized, as all things should be. *Will the princess recognize the beauty of such simplicity, as Master Druce never did?* His stomach let out a rumble, reminding him he had yet to finish his meal, but before he could turn to it, the door of his office opened to reveal four heavily armed men. Two he recognized as the guards that had been with the princess earlier; the other two he'd never seen before. They were scowling and had their hands on their sword hilts. Blaine jumped to his feet, knocking his tray of food to the floor. The men fanned out in front of him. "C-c-can I help you?" he asked.

"Do you know who we are?" the one with the heavily scarred face asked.

"Well, I-I-I can't say I so much as know your name, but I saw you with Her Highness earlier."

"I am Captain Darhour, the captain of the princess's personal guard," the scarred man said. "Her safety is my responsibility."

"I am Lieutenant Kailen, second in command of the princess's personal guard," a man with cold blue eyes said. "I value Her Highness's safety above my life."

The third man casually drew a knife and began paring his nails with it. "I am Bearach, member of the princess's personal guard."

Blaine's eyes flitted to the fourth man. "And I'm Conroy. There is nothing I wouldn't do for Her Highness."

Am I about to die?

Captain Darhour leaned across the desk. "Guarding the princess is both our duty and our pleasure. I have no idea why Her Highness chose you, and I can't override her decision, but know this, junior undersecretary from the library: if you ever lift your hand against her, tell a single one of her secrets to her enemies, pass on so much as a bit of idle gossip about her, I will personally rend you limb from limb."

"And I'll butcher the remains," the man with the icy blue eyes said, and the other two nodded in agreement.

"How dare you!" Blaine thrust out his chest. "I may not be able to rend a man limb from limb. The only thing I may be good at is organizing lists." He indicated the results of his meticulous labor. "But I assure you I'm no less loyal to the princess than any one of you. I'd give my life before I betrayed so much as the color of Her Highness's bed coverings. All the forces of the seven hells couldn't torture the information out of me."

Blaine paled as Darhour, too, took out a knife. "Would you be willing to take an oath on that?" He cut himself across the forearm and handed the knife hilt-first to Blaine.

"Most certainly." Blaine grabbed the knife and rolled up his sleeve. He cut himself and felt a little faint at the sight of his blood. Still, his voice was steady as he spoke. "I vow my loyalty to Her Highness, the Princess Samantha. On the goddess and my mother's grave, I vow that I will never harm her or betray her in any fashion whatsoever." He grabbed Darhour's arm and mingled their blood. The tension in the room eased.

"We welcome you," Darhour said. "But break that vow, and you'll learn in detail how I got these scars." He reclaimed his knife and bowed slightly. He and the others left.

Blaine fell trembling into his chair. *How dare they think I'd betray the princess! I'd cut off my right arm first!* The princess had been his idol since he'd first caught sight of her as a small child. He'd been five at the time, the princess three. His father had taken him to watch the royal procession on its trip to the northern palace. Sitting on his father's shoulders, he'd been stunned by the little girl riding with the king. She'd smiled at him, and Blaine had fallen immediately in love. He'd remained so to this day. Of course, he was unworthy even to be her secretary. *Surely, I'll fail her. But betray her? Never.*

* * *

After receiving the secretary's vow, Darhour returned to his rooms, where he was expecting two visitors—members of his rapidly growing network of informants. He heard a knock before he'd even had the chance to unbuckle his sword belt. He opened the door to the servants' corridors to find Gitta, an old woman whose principle responsibility for nearly forty years had been to keep the library free from dust. Darhour invited her in and offered her a chair. "Can I offer you anything?" he asked. Darhour had long ago learned that having his informants' favorite drinks available helped to loosen their tongues.

"I wouldn't say no to some wine or a spot of brandy, if you have it," Gitta said.

Darhour opened a bottle and poured her a glass. "What can you tell me about this Blaine?"

"I can tell you the library is in a right buzz about him, I can." Gitta laughed. "He being made personal secretary to Her Highness! The lad's nineteen, and he's only worked in the palace since Ostara. Master Druce is none too fond of the lad. Nearly had an apoplexy, he did."

Darhour tensed. "What does Master Druce have against him?"

"Master Druce is one that likes things done his way. Blaine had some ideas for improving the library, he did, and the lad wasn't bright enough to keep them to himself. Master Druce hasn't forgiven him for saying that the library wasn't orderly."

Darhour waved the objection aside; the library was a disordered jumble. "And what do *you* think of the lad?"

"He's always seemed a nice enough sort to me. He's a bit on the clumsy side, has quite a number of accidents, but he's always good about cleaning up his own mess, he is. I've always felt a bit sorry for the poor lad actually, if you want the truth. He was left all on his own in the world at fourteen, you see. He worked himself ragged trying to keep himself fed and still complete his education, he did. Before he showed up in the library at Ostara, I doubt the lad had had a square meal in five years."

Darhour questioned her further, but found out nothing else of interest. Still, the princess's choice grated on him. She'd seemed to decide on this unknown boy after a mere glance at him in the clerks' office—a demonstration of dangerous flightiness that seemed unlike the princess, just as her attraction to the peasant amihealer at the horse fair had been. Tomorrow, Darhour would look into the place where the boy had supposedly worked himself ragged.

After Gitta left, he didn't have long to wait for Tadc's arrival. Count Weylin's servant had been particularly eager to spy on his master, whom he blamed for debauching his sister. She was some kind of servant on Weylin's estates and, apparently, his mistress.

"What do you have for me?" Darhour asked after offering the man a seat and providing him with his favorite variety of ale.

"The count's given up the princess. He's opened discussions with Count Nola over his daughter, Lady Shela—round, pleasing breasts and a hefty enough dowry, I suspect."

Darhour drew back. "Not that I believe Weylin ever had a chance with the princess, but why has he abandoned the pursuit?" There'd been a dearth of weddings among the highest class of Korthlundian society for the past several years, as every eligible man weighed his chances to capture the ultimate marriage prize.

"I think Duke Argblutal convinced him on that. When His Lordship came back from dining with the duke, I could tell he was shaken, though he tried to hide it."

"Interesting." This was hardly the first time Darhour had heard something troubling in relation to Argblutal. "And what do you know of this duke?"

Tadc shuddered. "If you want to discuss that one, you'd best go elsewhere. I'll not say a word against him."

Darhour noted the fear in the man's eyes, and no matter how he questioned him, he got no additional information about Argblutal. His other sources had been just as tight-lipped. That in itself spoke of something very rotten.

* * *

"You have to stop him," Lady Shela whined.

"And why would I interfere with your father's right to dispose of you in whatever manner pleases him?" Duke Argblutal narrowed his eyes at her, although he couldn't help noticing the bitch was displaying her breasts most becomingly.

"I could make it worth your while." Shela leaned forward, revealing even more of her admirable cleavage. "I've learned the ways of pleasuring men."

"Such a little slut you are," Argblutal sneered. "Quite the bitch in heat." He rarely enjoyed a willing woman. But this one needed a lesson.

He drew the lady toward him, ran his hand up her side, and across her breasts. He slipped his hand under her bodice, grasping the fullness of her bare breast. The slut gave a small sigh of pleasure. He put his other hand around her back and pulled her into him while taking her nipple between his fingers and pinching.

"You're hurting me!" She tried to pull away.

"Not nearly as much as I intend to."

Shela screamed as he dragged her toward his bed.

* * *

When the duke had finished taking his pleasure with her, Shela curled herself into a ball. Argblutal wasn't the first man she'd welcomed into her bed, but never had it been like this. Her breasts ached, and she felt sharp pains inside of her where the duke had pounded her. She hurt almost everywhere else, too. He grabbed her by the hair and pulled her face back toward him. *No, not again! Please not again!* she pleaded silently. He'd hit her when she'd begged earlier. He pulled her bruised mouth against his and forced her mouth open with his tongue. She didn't dare resist.

He broke off the kiss, but he held her face close to his. "You acted like a common whore, so I treated you as such. You understand, do you not?"

Shela closed her eyes and said nothing. *How could I ever have thought he'd help me? How could I ever have wanted to lie with him?*

The duke slapped her. "I asked a question, slut! Do you understand you only got what you deserved?"

"Yes," she cried out. "I deserved it! Please don't hurt me anymore."

"I will do with you as I please." The duke grabbed one of her aching breasts and twisted cruelly. "Now and at any time in the future."

Shela heard him reaching for something on his bedside cabinet and opened her eyes to see him holding a knife with a huge ruby in its hilt. He ran the flat of the blade over her nipple. "Do we understand each other?" he asked.

Shela whimpered.

The duke moved the cold blade over each breast as he spoke. "That Count Weylin is trying to marry you speaks well of him. He understands the throne will be mine. But I have given you an assignment you haven't yet fulfilled. I need the name of the man you claimed the princess favors and anything that will help win her. If you don't get it for me soon, I'll have to find more ways to motivate you." He leaned over her and bit deeply into her breast, drawing blood. Shela cried out and closed her eyes so she wouldn't have to watch what he did to her. "And should you breathe a word of this to anyone"—he lowered his knife down between her legs—"I'll slit you open."

* * *

As she walked through the palace corridors followed by her guards, Samantha pulled her robe more tightly around herself. As was common these days, she hadn't been able to sleep. A desire to view her mother's portrait seized her. She paused just outside the Royal Gallery to examine a painting of Gloine Torr. In the painting, an unnamed princess tossed one of the gold Apples of Airh toward a knight toiling up the steep side of the mountain. Beneath the painting was a glass case holding the Apples of Airh themselves. Except for being made of gold, they looked quite ordinary. She shook her head and continued into the gallery itself.

"Light all the torches," she instructed Phelan. As he did so, she heard the jangling of arms, and Darhour joined them. She rolled her eyes. Brice must have sent a message to him. "You needn't have come. I'm sure Phelan and Brice will be adequate protection from any bogeymen lurking among the portraits."

"One can't be too careful, Your Highness."

If he wanted to drag himself out of a warm bed, it was his business. She walked slowly down the line of paintings of the members of the Royal House. She passed the wedding painting of Lir and Maeve, her grandparents. Lir looked every bit as stern as her father had described him. Maeve looked defiantly back at the painter. Solar claimed his mother soon lost this defiance and was completely cowed by her domineering husband. Next hung a painting of Solar and his younger brother Kerwin as children. Solar stood protectively behind Kerwin, his hand resting lightly on his shoulder. They were ten and five in the picture. Kerwin had only been eighteen when he'd thrown himself in front of Solar, taking the arrow meant for his older brother.

Next hung the wedding painting of Solar and his first queen, Lyonesse. She looked as proud and haughty as the king had often described her, and the king looked so young, his blonde hair pulled back in a long braid. He and his bride were not touching, and neither looked happy. The next painting was markedly different. It was of Solar and his second queen, Britomartus. Solar was about twenty years older. His hair had started to gray, but that wasn't what was so different about it. Solar and Britomartus stood with clasped hands, staring into each other's eyes.

Finally, Samantha came to the first of the two paintings she'd come to see. It was the wedding portrait of King Solar and her mother. Solar was seated on the throne, his long white hair and beard flowing around his head. Next to the throne stood the child queen Fenella. Although Samantha had seen this painting countless times, it had never before struck her how very young her mother had been. She looked far more like the king's granddaughter or even great-granddaughter than his wife. Her mother's eyes were haunted by a profound sadness mixed with anger. The king had never told her how her mother felt about marrying him. In the romanticism of childhood, she'd always assumed her parents' marriage was one of the great love stories, but the expression in her mother's eyes gave lie to that thought, as did her later infidelity.

Samantha drifted to the next painting. The sign under it read "The Mother of the Heir," and the painting was of Fenella, vastly pregnant. Her mother looked at her with blue eyes that were shaped exactly like Samantha's own. She had the same mouth and forehead. But her chin was different, as was the shape of her face. Her mother also didn't have her freckles and auburn hair. These traits must have come from her father. Her mother had been only fifteen in this painting, and she'd died only a month or two later. Samantha's eyes clouded with tears. *She was far too young.* Samantha forgave her mother for betraying the king. She considered Argblutal far too old, and he was decades younger than the king had been. As Samantha examined the swelling under her mother's dress, she thought about the man who had put it there. *Mother, what was my father like? Why did you choose him?*

In her mother's face, Samantha tried to find some clue to her father's identity. There seemed to be a sly pleasure in her eyes as the young queen's hand rested on her swollen belly. *Was she thinking about her lover when she stood for her portrait? Did she love him? And my father? Did he love the sad, young queen?* When she tried to imagine her father, she pictured a handsome young man with auburn hair and freckles, perhaps an artist or a poet. It was always so in the bards' tales. *Surely, he must have made the queen laugh and removed that sadness from her eyes. Were you found together, mother? Did you see your lover killed? Or is it possible my father could still be in the palace today? No, he's dead. Surely if my father were near me, I'd know it.*

Darhour watched his daughter stare at the portrait of the young girl who'd once been his lover. He'd been foolish, as only the young can be, to think no one would discover the affair. At the time, Darhour had believed he was in love with her. He'd longed to make up for all that was missing in her lonely life. He'd been foolish enough to believe she loved him, too. He hadn't realized she was merely using him to get her revenge on her father and the king. She'd ruined his life, but as he stared at the swelling that had become Samantha, he found he had no anger left against Fenella. Samantha was worth all he'd suffered in Saloyna. He would suffer it again and far worse to keep her safe.

"I never knew her," the princess said; her voice was choked with the effort of holding back tears. "No one ever speaks of her."

"She would have been proud of you, Your Highness. I'm sure of that," Darhour said. Fenella would have supported her daughter's refusal to marry. Her daughter being the sole monarch of the joined kingdoms would have pleased her.

"How can you know that? Did you know my mother, Darhour?"

Samantha stared at the strangled look that distorted Darhour's features. "I witnessed her betrothal procession, Your Highness, but I hardly think that qualifies as knowing."

Samantha walked slightly farther to the painting of herself as an infant in the cradle. "What about me, Darhour? Did you witness the celebration of my birth?"

Darhour had an odd sadness in his eyes. "No, Your Highness, I heard of the birth of the Korthlundian heir on the battlefields of Saloyna."

Samantha continued down the line of portraits of herself. For the first time, it struck her just how many there were. While her father had only a single portrait of himself in his childhood, he'd had portrait after portrait painted of her over the years. The portrait of her in the cradle. One of her at two years old on the lap of the king. Another at four astride a horse. At six sitting in the throne of the heir. At eight in the palace gardens, picking flowers. At ten dancing with an imaginary partner. At twelve looking into the mirror as her maids dressed her for her first Royal Ball. At fourteen in her armor reviewing the members of the Royal Guard.

There was another one of her at sixteen wearing the simple gold circlet of the heir and sitting on the window seat in her rooms, but it wasn't here in the Royal Gallery. It hung in the king's chambers, as all of these paintings once had before they were replaced by more recent ones. *He must love me! Why, oh Holy Mother, could he not be my true father? Is it a sin that I continue holding onto the crown?*

The night held no answer. She wandered back to the portrait of her pregnant mother and realized something else for the first time. The young queen's name wasn't mentioned on the plaque beneath it. She was no longer Fenella. She was the "Mother of the Heir." Somehow that struck the princess as terribly sad, especially since the queen never got the chance to truly be a mother. "She died because of me, Darhour."

"Your Highness, any parent would consider their life well worth yours." Darhour's voice was curiously intense.

As she looked at her mother's hand resting on her belly, she wondered if her mother had thought that death at fifteen was "worth" it. She'd always felt a small emptiness in her life she thought her mother would have filled, but tonight that emptiness felt like a vast chasm. The king wasn't her father. She was an orphan who had never known either of her parents.

* * *

The king breakfasted alone with his chancellor. "She'll barely talk to me these days, and when she does, she's always formal. She actually called me 'Your Majesty' the other day. Things have never been that way between us."

"Have you talked to her about it?" Caedmon asked.

Solar sighed. "I've tried, and she either insists nothing is wrong or gives some flimsy excuse. I've lost track of how many slight headaches she's had this summer. Also, she's been making some rather odd decisions, making some junior librarian her personal secretary."

"Your Majesty, the princess is at the age when children feel the need to prove they're no longer children. I remember some of the things my own did at her age. Absolute menaces, they can be. If making an odd choice of a secretary and being a little more distant is all the trouble she causes, you have much to be grateful for."

The king nodded thoughtfully. He'd hated his own father when he was seventeen. Of course, he never remembered a time when he hadn't hated his father. He shuddered as he realized his father had been half his present age when he'd died. It was truly absurd to live as long as he had. If only Samantha were older, he'd have been perfectly content to journey Beyond the Far Mountain. Much more content than he was at the thought of journeying to the cursed Winter Palace. "Perhaps, Caedmon, we won't go to Wisteria this year."

"But Your Majesty, won't having your birthday celebration here in Lundia and then keeping the court south for the winter cause hard feelings in Korth?"

"You misunderstand. The court will travel north as always, but perhaps you and I will not. This winter would be a good time to begin the transition from the rule of Solar II to Samantha I."

* * *

Grasping her dress in her clammy hands, Lady Shela made her way toward the banquet hall where the princess was rumored to be overseeing the decorating for tomorrow's celebration. Shela wore a dress with a collar so high it nearly choked her. Her father thought she'd finally developed a proper sense of modesty. She couldn't let him know what had happened. If her father didn't kill her for it, the duke certainly would. And it was all her fault.

The princess had been too busy to see her over the last several days, or at least that's what her secretary had said. She put her hand over her breast where the duke had bitten it. *Please, Sulis, let her see me tonight.*

Samantha frowned as she surveyed the hangings on the wall behind the high table. It was late, and she was tired. She'd had someone else see to the rest of the decorations, but the idea for the wall hangings had been her own. "What do you think?" she asked her secretary, who no longer stuttered *every* single time he spoke.

Blaine blushed. "Well, Your Highness, it looks . . . it looks . . . I'm sure that it seems . . . It's certainly quite . . . "

"Ordinary," she finished.

"Yes, I'm afraid so, Your Highness. It's as ordinary as a rainy day in the spring, so to speak."

"Damn it to the seven hells, Blaine," she swore, and Blaine's eyes widened. "Why does it look so ordinary? The colors are brilliant enough." And they were. The king's gold sun on its red background. The golds, browns, and oranges of Mabon.

"Your Highness." Samantha swore again as she recognized Lady Shela's voice. *Can't she understand some of us have more important duties than sitting around and giggling all day?* Blaine faded into the background as the lady approached, but her guards drew closer, as if they expected Shela to be overcome with an insane rage and leap at her.

Shela bowed and glanced up at the wall hangings. "Your Highness, they look positively lovely."

"No, they don't," Samantha groaned in frustration. "They look positively ordinary."

"Now that you mention it, the colors are brilliant, but the hangings are all the same length, all the same width. With a little variety, the effect could be stunning."

She's right. That's the problem. "Do you think it can be fixed?"

"It wouldn't take much, Your Highness. Just shorten a few here and there. Fold others in half." Shela's eyes darted between the hangings, the princess, and the floor. *What is wrong with her?* "If you'd like, I could do it for you."

"Please." Samantha gestured toward the hangings. She was too busy to worry about Shela's trivial problems. The count's daughter hurried forward and began directing the servants. Samantha fell into a chair and watched.

Blaine stood beside her. "The lady has the fashion sense of a peacock, so to speak."

"Yes, she does, and I have the sense of a boar." To her annoyance, Blaine didn't disagree.

In far less time than Samantha imagined possible, Shela had rearranged the wall hangings, and the effect was dazzling. She joined Shela as the lady directed the finishing touches. "That's far from ordinary. I can't thank you enough."

"It was no trouble, Your Highness. I'm glad to be of help." Shela smiled, but the smile didn't reach her eyes. Samantha also noticed that, for the first time since they were twelve years old, Shela wore a dress that didn't reveal at least half her breasts. It was also wrinkled as if she'd been clasping it, something that was very unlike Shela.

Samantha turned to Blaine. "Is there anything else?"

"I don't think so, Your Highness," Blaine said, as he looked through the lists that he always carried. "This was the last detail that needed seeing to."

"Go off to bed." She nodded her dismissal. She wished she could get rid of Shela as easily, but Shela looked like she would burst into tears at any moment. "Would you care to join me for a cup of tea or a glass of wine?" she offered.

"That would be lovely, Your Highness," Shela said, with far too much enthusiasm.

The princess sent a page to order a pot of herbal tea, wine, and cakes sent to her quarters.

Soon after they reached the princess's rooms, servants arrived with the refreshments. The princess poured herself a large mug of the steaming chamomile tea, and the lady chose a goblet of wine.

"Will your man be riding in the procession tomorrow?" Shela glanced shyly over her wine goblet.

"My man?" The princess raised her eyebrows.

"Yes, Your Highness, the one you spoke of."

Samantha fought a wave of longing. Surely, she'd never again be as happy as she'd been on that night when she danced with the peasant. "I have no such man. I never truly did." But thinking about Robbie made the princess long to speak of him. "Can you keep a secret?"

There was such sadness in the princess's voice Shela felt guilty about worming her way into her confidence. "Of course, Your Highness."

"You've seen my mare, haven't you? I got her at a horse fair in the Valley."

"His Majesty let you go to a common horse fair?" Shela couldn't imagine her own father's reaction to such an outing.

The princess laughed, but her laughter rang hollow. "He had no idea I was going. I dressed very plainly so no one knew who I was. I met a handsome peasant there who knew a great deal about horses. He helped me choose Roberta. I danced with him."

"You danced with a peasant?" Shela tried to keep her face expressionless, but the thought of the heir to the throne dancing with common trash was appalling.

The princess looked away. "He was the one I had in mind the last time we talked, but as you can see, he can mean nothing to me."

"Oh, Your Highness, that's so sad," Shela said, repressing her revulsion.

"I'll have to marry some man at court, but it's so hard to know which one."

"And what would you like in a man, Your Highness?" Shela asked.

"My first concern has to be for the people. I need a consort who sees the people as his highest responsibility and will rule beside me in justice and peace. He should be generous and kind. He should respect me both for myself and as the monarch. But there's no man like that at court."

"Your Highness, surely you'll find someone." Shela fought twinges of guilt. The princess was a nice person, but Shela refused to be used like a whore again.

* * *

It was a bright, sunny day and very warm for the time of year. The weather suited Argblutal's mood perfectly as he rode behind the princess and the king in the royal procession that marked the beginning of the celebration of Mabon. Gutter scum thronged the street, throwing straw and grain in front of them, as was traditional for the celebration of harvest. They chanted, "Long live King Solar! Long live Princess Samantha!" *Soon it will be my name on everyone's lips.*

180

After the procession, the court gathered in the town square, where the guilds had set up tables for breakfast and entertainment. Argblutal ate while watching an insufferable play by the Butcher's Guild. As a member of the king's council, he was seated near the princess. He leaned over and whispered to her. "You've done very well, Your Highness. Planning a celebration of this magnitude is no easy feat."

"Thank you," the princess said.

"The people love your father. He's always been a just and good king, ruling with the best interests of the people at heart. All monarchs should, but too few actually do."

"So I've always thought." The princess smiled a seemingly genuine smile. A surge of blood rushed to his loins as he imagined taking her in the manner he had Lady Shela.

* * *

The celebration was every bit as magnificent as Samantha had hoped. Music and dancing filled the streets. An abundance of food and drink was available. The only stain to her happiness came during their traditional visit to the Royal Graveyard. As she placed the apples and grain on her mother's tomb, she again experienced the sadness she'd felt while gazing at her mother's portrait in the Royal Gallery. *Oh, mother, can you help me now? Am I doing the right thing?* Suddenly, an unexpected wave of peace came over her. The bards did say that the veil between this world and the next was thinnest at Mabon. The king put his arm around her shoulders. "She would have been proud of you, my dear," he said, echoing Darhour's words from the Royal Gallery.

* * *

"No, I won't go without you," Samantha protested the morning after Mabon. "If you aren't well enough to travel, the court will stay south this winter. My place is by your side." *At least, it used to be, when I thought I was your daughter.*

The king smiled at her. "Samantha, you know I've never wanted you absent from me for a day of your life, but your place is where I say your place is, and this winter that place is in Korth, not in Lundia with an old man."

"But father, what if . . . ?"

"'What if' nothing. I'll be here in the spring to make the announcement of your betrothal. I know you've been avoiding me."

Samantha couldn't meet the king's eyes. She was again on the verge of telling him everything, but the king didn't give her the chance.

"Samantha, I love you. I've loved you from the very first moment I laid eyes on you. You've been the greatest joy of my life."

Samantha burst into tears; she would have promised him anything at that moment. "Father, I love you, too." She hugged him and felt the comfort of his arms around her. "And I promise, at the Ostaran ball, you may announce my betrothal. When I return in the spring, I will have chosen your future son-in-law."

The king held her tightly. "My daughter, you've never been a disappointment to me, and who knows, I might yet live long enough to have your heir suck on my finger."

* * *

"Report," Duke Argblutal ordered Captain Kentigern, who'd come to Murtaghan with news from the duke's estates.

"Recruitment is proving more difficult than we'd hoped, Your Grace. I presently have two hundred men, but many of them are very raw and will need a great deal of training. The most talented young men usually try for a position with the Royal Guard."

"Two hundred is insufficient."

"I assure you I've given it my utmost effort. The princess and the king are popular with the people. It's no easy task to find soldiers discontented with how things are run. There are only so many that will respond to threats, and your treasury will only support a certain level of bribery. An army of even this size is expensive to maintain."

Argblutal's eyes bore into Kentigern's. The man was good at following orders, but he had no ability to think for himself. "Once I'm king, I'll have the royal treasury at my disposal."

"Of course, Your Grace. Many will fight for a delayed reward. I'm sure that by spring I'll have better news for you."

Since Argblutal didn't share Kentigern's certainty, military action seemed a risky course.

CHAPTER 14

"Bless you, child," Myst exclaimed as Robbie entered her cottage. "With such a storm, I didn't expect you today. Get out of those wet clothes at once and sit by the fire, or you'll catch your death of cold." She handed him a warm blanket and turned her back.

"No, I won't. I never get sick," he said, taking off his wet things anyway and wrapping himself in the blanket.

"No, I don't suppose you do. A healer as strong as you wouldn't." The herb witch hung his wet clothes over the fire to dry.

"What's being a healer got to do with it?"

Myst set out tea and cakes. "Everything, child. Healers are immune to almost all illnesses. We also heal from our injuries much more quickly than others. Still, being warm never hurt anyone. Drink up." Myst pointed to his tea. "Drink it straight. No honey or cream today."

Robbie drank it with a grimace. This cup of tea was probably the worst he'd ever tasted. "If you're worried about me warming up, maybe you should add a splash of brandy," he said, hoping it'd make the tea taste better.

"Holy Sulis, no, child! Healers can't tolerate alcohol. As powerful as you are, a splash of brandy would probably lay you out for a week. Your father's never given you alcohol, has he?"

"No, I thought it was because he didn't like me well enough to waste it on me."

"No, he simply showed good judgment for once in his life." Myst paused and closed her eyes. "I'm sorry, my child, I shouldn't criticize your father. It isn't my place."

Robbie shrugged. He didn't care who criticized his father. Angus seemed to have forgotten that Robbie existed; he hadn't spoken a single word to him since the day he'd handed him his wages.

Myst settled herself into her chair and picked up her own cup of tea. She seemed to savor the aroma. "Finish your tea, and we'll continue your lesson on seeing your energy. I've put some chamomile and lavender in it. I'm hoping the herbs will help you relax further today, so drink it all."

If it tastes this bad, it better do something. Myst had started teaching him the relaxation rituals over a week ago, and he hadn't yet been able to "see" anything.

"I'm sorry, my child. Maybe a healer can't teach an amihealer. The healing of people and of animals seems so similar, I never dreamed we'd encounter difficulties."

"It doesn't make any sense a person can't heal both. Why would there be any difference?" he asked, choking down the horrible tea.

Myst shook her head. "That's one of Sulis's many mysteries. Only in legends have I heard of anyone whose power is strong enough to heal both." She got the look on her face he didn't like—the one that said he might someday be the hero of such a legend.

When he finished the last of the awful tea, Myst directed him to close his eyes. He felt very relaxed, almost sleepy.

"Look inward," Myst said. "Relax, and look to the very heart of your being."

Robbie drifted inward. While he barely moved a muscle, his sessions with Myst always left him more exhausted than the sword practice with Brazen. To his frustration, he saw nothing yet again. But the tea was helping him relax and drift deeper inward. He gasped as he "saw" something.

"What is it, child?" Myst asked. He heard her as if he were at the bottom of a deep well. He was too far away to answer.

The thing he saw wasn't like the pure light Myst had described. Instead, it was like a huge dam stopping the energy's flow as if his magic was a river of power. He could see the edges of his energy building up behind the dam, straining to break free. He reached for it, as Myst said he should, but he felt as if he were beating his head against the dam. Myst had warned him against trying to force the process, but he was tired of sitting there day after day accomplishing nothing. He slammed his mind against the dam.

He screamed and fell writhing on the ground, as his whole body exploded with pain. He hurled himself away from the agony and forced his way back to the surface of consciousness. The pain stopped as suddenly as it'd begun. He opened his eyes and found himself naked and panting on the floor of the herb witch's cottage.

The herb witch was kneeling at his side. "My child, are you alright?"

Reaching for the blanket to cover himself, Robbie sobbed, "What happened?"

Myst resumed her seat and took such a long while to answer Robbie grew afraid. Perhaps it meant he was a demon after all. "That, my child, was your power. As I told you, it can't be forced." The herb witch fell silent and refused to meet his gaze.

"What aren't you telling me?"

"I have always thought of myself as a powerful healer. But, my child, what I just saw in you makes my energy look like a small stream next to the great ocean. I would never have imagined a human frame could contain that much. When you are able to access it, I have no doubt that some day the bards will sing of you." She paused again, and she looked at him, almost worshipfully. "My only question is, what they will sing? I know you've been treated appallingly, but power like yours can't afford the luxury of hatred. Remember the power to heal is also the power to harm." Myst took hold of his hand. "The touch of this hand can bring health or illness, life or death. But if the gift of the goddess is used for evil, it will twist and mangle your soul until nothing of your true self remains. Once I almost destroyed myself this way. Be smarter than I was. Don't allow your father's brutality to warp the goodness of your heart. My child, when the bards sing of you, be the hero of their tales, not the villain."

Robbie pulled his hand free, reached for his clothes, and dressed quickly. "You expect too much of me." He fled the cottage.

As he drew closer to the farm, the muscles in his abdomen clenched painfully. Thunder had gone into labor, and she was in trouble. He galloped into the farmyard and vaulted from Wild Thing's back. When he ran into the barn, he found his father, Allyn, and Darien crowded around the pregnant mare.

"Where have you been, boy?" Angus bellowed. "If she dies, I'll have your hide for it."

Robbie clenched his fists. "And who was it that insisted on breeding her so soon? Have you learned nothing about when females are fit to give birth?" Angus lifted his hand to strike Robbie, but Robbie jumped back. "Don't think you can bully me, old man." Robbie folded his arms and glared at his father, but Thunder's cry caused him to relent. *:Save my baby.:*

Robbie dropped beside the mare and touched her. The afterbirth had torn away from the wall of the womb, causing Thunder to bleed profusely; the foal was suffocating in its mother's blood. *Holy Sulis, what can I do? They'll both die.* If he was going to have a chance of saving them, he needed the energy he'd "seen" on the other side of the dam.

He closed his eyes and breathed deeply. The mare's pain pulled against something deep inside of him, and he felt a trickle of his energy. It wasn't enough. *Thunder, help me! Show me where it is.* Robbie followed the path of the mare's pain deeper into the heart of his being, searching until he found the dam. *It's no use.* But joined to Thunder's need, he saw something he hadn't at Myst's cottage. The dam didn't block all of his energy; a small stream flowed from behind it as if a sluice gate had been opened in the dam.

He grasped it and began sending it into Thunder. His body flooded with joy, and Thunder's life signs became stronger. He found and closed the vessels that were leaking the horse's life and strengthened the muscles needed to expel the foal.

His father leaned down and patted the mare. "It'll be okay, Thunder. It'll be okay, my girl." *He threatens to beat me while he talks like that to his horse! How dare Myst tell me I'm not allowed to hate!* He heard Thunder gasp. Without realizing what he was doing, he'd wrapped his energy around her heart and was crushing it. *Holy Sulis, no!* Panicking, he gathered up his anger and shifted it aside, and the energy flowed back into its previous pattern. The foal slipped from its mother's body.

Abruptly, Robbie collapsed into the straw, shaking with fear. *I guess we know how the bards will sing of me.* The world went dark.

Angus looked down at the exhausted form of his youngest son. He tried to be furious that the boy had blamed him for Thunder's difficulties, but guilt pressed against him. *Is it my fault Donella died? Or is it his?*

Angus had felt the energy at work as Robbie helped Thunder deliver her foal. Donella had had energy, but what he'd felt from his son wasn't anything like his wife's. It had been both more powerful and darker. For a moment Angus had the impression Robbie was on the verge of killing the horse. *Are they right about him being the spawn of demons after all? That damned witch! What is she teaching him?*

* * *

When Robbie regained consciousness, a blanket had been thrown over him, but he was still lying on the floor of the barn. As he sat up, he heard the soft noises a mare makes to her baby. He wanted to be happy he'd made it possible, but it scared him how close he'd come to killing the horse instead. *Just what have I become?* He didn't have an answer, but he knew precisely when the changes began. Brazen would never say where she'd come from, but he was starting to think it was the deepest level of the seven hells.

He got shakily to his feet, saddled Wild Thing, and headed for the forest stable. It was freezing cold, but the moon reflecting off the snow provided plenty of light. When he reached the stable, Brazen was waiting by the paddock fence. He didn't greet her, but went straight inside the stable, pulled the bronze sword from its scabbard, and went back out into the night. "Brazen, I've had it. You will tell me what you're doing here, or . . ."

:You are ready.: Brazen interrupted.

Robbie heard a noise behind him. He whirled to find a knight less than six feet away, holding a bronze-hilted sword and wearing bronze armor. The visor of his helm was closed, so Robbie couldn't see his face. There was no other explanation. Brazen's owner had finally tracked her down. "Milord," Robbie stammered and bowed. "I found your horse."

Without saying a word, the knight lunged. Robbie barely got his own blade up in time to parry. "Milord, I didn't know who she belonged to. I've been taking care of her!" The knight's only response was a sword thrust toward his heart, which Robbie avoided by a quick move back and to the side. "Please, Milord, let me explain."

The knight swung a brutal blow toward his head. Robbie ducked and fought for distance. It was immediately clear both that the knight was better than he was and that the knight's goal was to kill him. Robbie called to Wild Thing for help, but the mare seemed completely unconcerned. Even more maddening, he could feel Brazen in his mind, directing him toward the next movement. "Damn you both! Help me!" But both simply stood there, watching as if his death were a mildly entertaining show.

Robbie saw the killing blow as if it were in slow motion. He'd parried far too widely, throwing himself off balance and leaving his entire left side unprotected. The knight swung his sword, and Robbie screamed as it cut through his side and into his heart. When the knight pulled his sword free, it was red with Robbie's blood. But Robbie didn't collapse as the dead should, and when he looked down, there was no wound. His coat hadn't even been torn. He looked in disbelief at the knight, who saluted him with his bloody sword and then disappeared.

"What . . . ?" he gasped.

:A good beginning. You have done well. Tomorrow, I will teach you more.:

"What . . . what happened?"

:You were ready. To improve your skills you now need an opponent.:

Robbie pointed his sword at Brazen's throat. His whole body was shaking. "So that was just an illusion! You could have warned me. I thought your owner had come to claim you over my dead body."

:You were ready.:

Robbie stomped back inside the stable and slammed the sword back into its scabbard. *Damn her to the seven hells! I'll never come here again.* But he knew he was lying.

He felt Brazen in his mind, replaying the battle. The horse showed him what he'd done well and where he'd made the mistake that would have cost him his life. As he watched, he couldn't help feeling a growing sense of pride. While he'd lost the fight, he'd learned much.

* * *

"Are you with me in this or not?" Boyden asked Dillion, as they met in the shadows behind the bunkhouse. "Or are you going to wait until he's actually doing your wife?"

Dillion glared angrily. "Father Gildas said murdering the demon boy isn't a sin?"

Boyden's nostrils flared. "You heard his sermon at Litha yourself. You can't tell me you don't think you have a right to protect your wife." He thought he could probably take Robbie on his own, but he'd grown nervous since the demon within him seemed to be growing stronger. "Do you want to help me now or wait until after he's already implanted his demon seed in her womb?"

"Damn him!" Dillion turned away. "We can't do it anywhere near the farm. If Cara finds out, she'll leave me."

Boyden nodded. "Agreed. My father's threatened to disinherit me if I touch him. Robbie goes into the woods often enough. He'll just disappear, and no one will know what became of him."

CHAPTER 15

The court settled in at the Winter Palace, and the first afternoon at court Samantha felt as if she were on display, the word "bastard" tattooed on her forehead. The first matter before the court involved a dispute over cattle between two minor Korthian counts—Morfran and Cyric. These two men possessed neighboring estates near Wisteria. They had wanted royal permission to kill each other since before Samantha had been born. Dueling was banned in the joined kingdoms, except by royal sanction. Her father said it set a bad precedent to claim justice could be won by force of arms and had always resolved the arguments between the two counts without violence.

"Your Highness." Morfran bowed before her. "I demand justice. I have been robbed."

"Your Highness." Cyric bowed as well. "He has besmirched my honor, and I demand redress."

The princess turned to Morfran. "What is it you allege?"

"He has stolen one hundred head of my cattle. They are—"

"You lying bastard," Cyric interrupted. "Your Highness, there is no—"

"Count Cyric, you'll have your turn to be heard," the princess said, using the tone of command her father had taught her. She just wished she didn't feel so much like a fraud.

"Forgive me, Your Highness." Cyric glowered at his rival.

Samantha turned to Morfran. "Proceed."

190

"As I was saying, Your Highness, one hundred head of my cattle now graze in his pastures. I sent my servants to reclaim them, but his servants put up a fight. One of my servants now lies dead. Count Cyric is a thief and a murderer, and I demand justice, Your Highness."

Samantha turned to Cyric, who was turning red with rage. "Your Highness, he is a liar. The cattle in question are mine and have always been mine. His servants carelessly allowed his cattle to stray into a bog where they became mired and froze, so they came to steal mine. He has besmirched my honor. I demand satisfaction."

How can I know which one is telling the truth? Neither one of them knows the meaning of the word. She could feel Duke Sheen below her, waiting for her to issue an inane ruling. Of the council, he was the most vigorous opponent to a woman on the throne, which was strange since he was from Korth, which generally viewed women more favorably. To buy herself time, she turned to Count Morfran. "Describe the cattle you claim as stolen."

"Your Highness, they are . . . cattle." Suddenly, Morfran glowed a sickly purple, and bile rose in her throat. She nearly laughed in relief. He was lying. Again, need had brought forth her gift.

Knowing he was lying, she knew what line of questioning to pursue. "So you have said, Morfran, but what type of cattle?"

"Well . . . Your Highness. They are . . . they are . . ." the count stuttered. "They are Korthian mountain cattle, of course, Your Highness. Why would I have any other variety?"

"They are not, Your Highness," Cyric protested. "The cattle his servants tried to steal are a special breed I have been developing from Mintarian black bulls and Neasarian mountain cattle. They give more meat than the traditional Korthian mountain cattle, but are as well adapted to our cold winters."

Samantha let her gaze bore into Morfran in the manner her father—no, the king she'd once thought was her father—had taught her. "Do you wish to retract your claim? Or do I send someone to examine the cattle?" With her eyes, she let him know how poorly it would go for him if she proved him in a lie.

Morfran managed to look shocked, apologetic, and angry at the same time. "It is quite possible I'm mistaken. My men may have been negligent, as the count suggests. I will chide them for it."

"And after you have chided them, you will compensate Count Cyric for his losses. I'm certain you are eager to demonstrate your sincere regret for the error of your men."

Morfran looked as if he'd prefer to be boiled in oil, but he bowed. "Of course, Your Highness."

Samantha turned to Cyric. "I'm certain you understand how such errors can be made and will happily accept just compensation."

Looking murderously at his rival, Cyric bowed his head and attempted a smile. "We are all prone to error, Your Highness."

After determining the amount of compensation, the princess dismissed the two counts. Duke Argblutal leaned in and whispered. "Expertly done, Your Highness. I doubt His Majesty could have handled it better."

Why can't I just accept being the heir? Holy Sulis, let me know what I should do! But the only answer she heard was Darhour reminding her it was time for weapons practice. Ever since being given charge of her personal guard, Darhour had insisted she keep her own fighting skills as finely honed as possible. She followed Darhour to the practice arena where he paired her with Brice. Brice, assigned guard duty during the midnight hours, was usually sleeping when the princess trained, so she hadn't trained against him before. He was the smallest member of her guard, but also the fastest.

"Shall we dance, Your Highness?" Brice put his sword at the ready position.

Samantha didn't answer, but tried to take him off guard with a sudden attack. To her complete surprise, she got through his guard, taking him in the side. "Well done, Your Highness."

She felt rather pleased with herself, but the feeling faded as she managed to score on him a second time. When she touched him a third time, she lowered her wooden sword. "What is the meaning of this?" she demanded.

Darhour strode over from where he'd been training against the ever silent Phelan. "Is there a problem, Your Highness?"

"Yes, there's a problem. Brice is playing with me. I've scored on him three times already." She glared at Brice.

"Is this true?" Darhour, too, glared, and Brice paled under their joint scrutiny.

"But Captain, she's . . . she's the princess. Why does she need to train? We will die to a man before we let anyone in reach of her sword."

Darhour gave Brice the look that had caused many men to think dark thoughts of their impending death. "What happens after we're dead and nothing stands between Her Highness and her enemy except her own sword?"

Brice first looked offended, then thoughtful. "I suppose the enemy could attack with several times our number." He turned and bowed to the princess. "Forgive me, Your Highness. I'll play with you no longer." He raised his sword. Samantha nodded and raised her own.

She decided to attempt a quick lunge again. This time she didn't come close to touching him. His blade moved with such speed she didn't even see it. Her own blade went flying out of her hand, and before she realized what was happening, she was lying flat on her back with his sword at her throat. *Damn, he's fast!*

Phelan fetched her sword while Brice helped her to her feet. Phelan handed back her sword with a silent bow. "Your Highness," Brice nodded. "If I may say so, you're holding your sword too loosely. I shouldn't have been able to disarm you so easily. If you'd hold it like this"—he placed her hands in a slightly different position—"your grip will be more secure."

Later in their bout, Samantha again found herself flat on her back with Brice's sword against her throat. This time, however, the tip of her own sword was at Brice's breast. "Your Highness, that was much better. You may have gone down, but you'd have taken me with you." Brice surveyed her sword position with approval. "You aren't all that bad with a blade, Your Highness. You could take at least half the Royal Guard."

Darhour had approached and helped her to her feet. "That you could, and Your Highness, you'll have one additional advantage if anyone ever does manage to get past us."

"And what is that?" she asked.

"You're a woman. Your opponent is bound to underestimate you."

* * *

On Solstice morning, Samantha led the court through the streets of Wisteria. Children lined the streets jumping and shouting with joy. From a sack beside her she handed out small toys, sweetmeats, and coins. The other members of the court did likewise. It was a tradition she looked forward to all year.

"Your Highness, did you notice these boats I had made especially for the occasion?" Count Pandaran asked, as he handed one to a child with an elaborate bow.

She should have been happy that morning, but Samantha felt as if a vast weight was pulling her under the surface of a surging river. Pandaran hadn't been the first to point out to her how generous he was being. *How can I marry any of them? Why did I promise my father I would?*

As the children jostled for a position to receive their gifts, the princess noticed a small girl being pushed aside. The girl fell down on the ice and began to cry. Before Samantha could say anything, Argblutal dismounted and went to the crying child. He set her on her feet, took out his silk handkerchief, and wiped the blood from the child's knee. The child's tears turned to smiles of delight, as the duke gave her a doll and placed a coin in her hand. Samantha noticed that it wasn't a dram, but a full drachma. The duke patted the child's head and remounted.

The princess fell back to ride beside him. "That was extremely kind." With a small sense of shame, the princess noticed the sack containing Argblutal's offerings was larger and filled with finer things than her own. Unlike so many of the others, he hadn't pointed it out to her.

The duke turned away as if embarrassed she'd noticed. "Your Highness, I must admit I've always had a weakness for children. They're Korthlundia's future, and I can't bear the thought of a single child being left without a gift."

* * *

That night at her dressing table, the princess struggled not to cry. That morning had convinced her who her consort should be. None of her other suitors had even noticed the child being pushed aside. After the last few months she'd become convinced that Argblutal respected her and that he understood what it meant to rule. Also, he would very likely have taken the throne if she'd never been born. If she married him, maybe it wouldn't matter so much that she was a bastard. But despite being kind and respectful, the duke was old, formal, and no fun; she couldn't imagine lying with him as she did with Robbie in her dreams. But she couldn't have Robbie, and unless she announced her bastardry to the world, she had to marry someone.

Her maids dressed her hair with fine white lace studded with diamonds. "Ardra, send a page to Argblutal, asking him to lead the men in the Solstice dance."

Ardra giggled as she took the message to a page. The request was a clear sign of her favor. The court would take it as the closest thing to a betrothal announcement. It was the right decision. She only wished she could be happier about it.

* * *

In the palace courtyard, Samantha stood quietly with a torch in her hand while the priestess spoke the words of the Solstice ritual. She'd purposely chosen a priestess to lead the ritual this year to show High Priest Shylah where her loyalties lay. The priestess brought the ceremony to a close, "Oh mighty Sulis, we dedicate this night and this dance to you. Let our fires and our energy feed the sun and bring it back with the strength of summer."

Samantha touched her torch to the waiting wood and watched the flames begin to lick the sky. She gave the torch to an attendant and, as was customary, began the Solstice dance alone. She danced around the fire, giving her energy to the ritual. When she'd completed three full circles of the fire. Argblutal joined her. The duke smiled as he began to move with the music. In time, the rest of the court followed. Samantha danced wildly with the abandonment allowed by the holiday; she strove to forget, if only for a moment, that she was the crown princess. But the looks on the faces of the men as she passed breathlessly from suitor to suitor couldn't help but remind her.

Argblutal seemed stiff and formal, almost as if he disapproved of her lack of restraint—a marked contrast to the one she'd rather be with. She wondered jealously how many girls Robbie would be dancing with that night and what he'd do after the dancing. Would he participate in the other ritual? The mingling of a man and a woman on Solstice night was said to be pleasing to Sulis: the energy produced by the mating encouraged the sun's return. Would Robbie be with another in the way he was so often with her in her dreams?

She prayed he would be happy. She doubted she'd ever be.

* * *

Robbie set fire to the wood he'd gathered at the forest stable. He'd never been allowed to participate in the ritual bonfire and dancing. In previous years, he'd watched from afar, but now he was too old to watch from shadows and envy those who hated him.

He watched until the flames seemed to reach the sky, then began to dance around them in the manner he'd seen others do so many times. He wondered who Milady would lie with tonight or if that part of the ritual was even practiced among the highborn. Robbie was sure she'd forgotten him months ago. He'd never see her again, and he was destined to always be alone.

* * *

The next morning, Robbie tried to shake off his depression by searching for a particular fungus that grew only in the winter. Because of the thickness of the trees, he'd left Wild Thing back at the farm. He was just moving into a small clearing when Boyden emerged from the trees in front of him. "Worm, you thought you got away with summoning the demon, didn't you? You may have fooled the old man, but you haven't fooled me."

Robbie turned and thought about running, but Dillion was cutting off his escape. "Father Gildas says it's time to rid the Valley of your kind. Did you really think I'd stand by and allow you to bewitch my wife?"

Robbie could tell from the looks on their faces that he was in serious trouble. *Damn Brazen! Why didn't she teach me to fight with something I could actually carry?*

He looked down in the snow and saw a strong, thick branch. He grabbed it as Boyden closed in. "I'm going to break every bone in your worthless body and leave your remains to be devoured by wolves." Boyden swung, and Robbie stepped to the side and brought his branch up, blocking the blow. He swung the branch around into Boyden's thigh, stepped behind him, and knocked his leg out from under him. Boyden landed face first in the snow.

As Boyden fell, Dillion moved in, aiming a blow at his face. Robbie again sidestepped and blocked the punch with his branch. He whirled and bashed it into Dillion's unprotected side. Dillion cried out, but Boyden launched off the ground. Robbie jumped out of the way and smashed the branch down on the back of Boyden's shoulders, knocking him to the ground again.

As Robbie fought off the attack, he realized with surprise that neither man had any true skill at fighting. Sidestepping, blocking, jumping, and rolling, Robbie was able to avoid most of their blows. Those that did strike him hardly hurt, at least not in comparison to the blows given him by Brazen's illusions. His own strikes almost always hit their target, and it wasn't long before both men were on the ground at his feet.

"What are you?" Boyden croaked.

"The one who has your life in his hands." They were now at his mercy, as he'd been at Boyden's mercy last spring. *He certainly didn't show me any. Why should I?* He raised the branch to crush Boyden's skull. But a wave of nausea swept over him, the strength of his rage reminding him of how close he'd come to killing Thunder. *But this is different. He deserves it.* Boyden had made him crawl through the mud. Boyden had made him lick his boots. Boyden had nearly killed him. Still, he lowered the branch and stepped back. He was a healer, not a murderer. "I have no desire to harm either of you, but you will both leave me alone. Boyden, I had nothing to do with what happened in the spring. Our mother wasn't a demon, and neither am I." Robbie turned to the fallen farmhand. "Dillion, I have no designs on your wife. It's you Cara loves, not me." He turned and stalked away, still carrying the branch.

The branch didn't feel quite the same as a sword, but it'd be a weapon he could carry with him at all times. At the forest stable, he carved a staff out of the branch. He was no longer Robbie, the demon child. He would use the name his mother had given him.

He was Robrek, the healer. Robrek, the warrior. Robrek, the bronze knight.

PART II

CHAPTER 16

:A good beginning.: Brazen said as Robrek felt the wrenching pain of a sword through his heart. He'd been fighting with his staff this morning. Since Boyden and Dillion had attacked him, he'd insisted Brazen alternate between teaching him the sword and the staff. Surprisingly, Brazen hadn't objected.

"Does it have to hurt so much?" He bent over, covering his heart with his hand.

:If it didn't hurt, you would not take care to avoid the blows.:

Robrek had to admit this made sense, but he didn't like it. Still, he was in a good mood this morning. The first hints of spring were in the air. The snow was starting to melt, flowers were peeking through, and he heard the sounds of birds returning from the south. Nature was coming to life around him, and Robrek had decided it was time for him to come to life as well.

He sat on a stump. "Lady Brazen, things around here have calmed down a bit, but it won't take much to set them off again. Boyden wants me dead, and so does the priest. I've been thinking it might be a good idea if we moved on. You know, went to Murtaghan."

:The time to leave is not now. You must stay.:

"Now, hear me out. I've got some money saved up, and I'm sure I could find work in the capital. I won't leave you behind if you want to come."

:The time to leave is not now. You must stay.:

"There's no 'must' about it. I'm not a little boy, so . . ." His argument was cut short by a scream of pain that brought him to his knees. It took him a few seconds to realize the scream wasn't an audible one. A horse had been badly injured nearby. Robrek jumped onto Wild Thing's back and rode hard in the direction of the scream.

* * *

Darhour heard the snap of a bone breaking and watched helplessly as Samantha flew off her horse into the muddy roadway. "Your Highness!" he cried, bringing his mount to an abrupt halt and vaulting from the saddle. He knelt beside her. The princess stirred and groaned without opening her eyes. "Thank the goddess, she's alive." He turned to one of the others. "Conroy, we passed a cottage with a healer's sign some ways back. Go fetch him."

Off to the side of the road was a large rock with an overhang. This could hide them from anyone approaching from the direction of Murtaghan and keep the princess out of the cold wind. Silently cursing Samantha for her insistence on traveling in these conditions, he carried her there and had the rest of the men fan out to form a perimeter. Three weeks ago, a message had arrived at the Winter Palace informing Her Highness the king was dying. Samantha had demanded to leave immediately without giving him time to assemble a proper escort. It was sheer idiocy for her to travel all this distance with only her personal guard and her secretary, but if he hadn't agreed, she'd threatened to go alone. In addition to an inadequate number of men, it was far too early in the season to travel between the joined kingdoms. They'd had to go far out of their way to find a pass free from snow. It was sheer luck they hadn't run into bandits. Ironically, it was now, when he thought they were safe, that the princess was injured.

Darhour brushed the princess's hair back from her face and covered her with his cloak. He wasn't sure how he felt about Solar dying. Samantha was too young for the full pressure of the monarchy, but part of him relished the idea of being her only father.

Lieutenant Kailen stationed himself near the roadway. Bearach, Brice, and Phelan fanned out to encircle the rock under which the princess sheltered. Their position seemed reasonably good.

When he was sure the perimeter was safe, he turned his attention to the injured animal. The mare writhed in pain, its leg bent at an odd angle. Kailen hesitated, knowing of Her Highness's love for the horse, but his hesitation was cruel. Drawing his sword, he approached the great beast to end her suffering.

As he raised his sword, he heard a horse approaching rapidly across the meadow from the shadow of a small woods. A single rider rode into sight, and Bearach, the best archer among them, nocked an arrow and awaited Kailen's command. When the rider came within arrow range, Kailen called out in a loud voice, "Halt! Identify yourself!"

The rider ignored the warning and continued to approach at a full gallop. Kailen nodded, and Bearach loosed the arrow.

Robrek, his mind near bursting with the horse's pain, saw the horse writhing in the mud. Suddenly, Wild Thing wheeled beneath him. The sting of an arrow grazing his shoulder brought him back to full awareness of his surroundings. For the first time, he noticed the armed men and an archer nocking another arrow. He dropped from the horse's back and lay flat in the snow. "I'm unarmed!" he shouted. "I mean no harm!"

Robrek remained on the ground with his hands in plain sight as two men approached. The men grabbed him and tied his hands behind his back. They half-dragged, half-carried him to the muddy roadway and forced him to his knees.

A man only a little older than himself with cold blue eyes put his sword inches from Robrek's throat. "Why did you not halt as commanded?"

Robrek could scarcely understand the man's words over the screams of the injured animal inside his head.

"The horse. It's hurt. Let me help it."

"The only thing that can be done for it is to put it out of its misery."

"No!" Robrek cried. "I'm an amihealer! I can heal her!"

The cold-eyed man laughed. "Charlatan. Her leg's broken. No herbs and chanting are going to help."

"Please!" he begged. "What harm could I possibly do to a horse you mean to kill?"

To Robrek's relief, after a brief hesitation Cold Eyes nodded, and one of the others cut the cords that bound his hands. "If he makes one suspicious move, kill him," Cold Eyes ordered.

Robrek stumbled over to the injured horse, which continued to writhe hideously. "It's okay, girl. Robrek's here now." At his touch, the horse relaxed. Above the break, he constructed a block that would stop the pain. But the leg was broken in several places. He'd never healed anything this serious.

Robrek reached with his mind into the horse's body and soon lost awareness of everything outside of himself and the horse. As he studied the injury, he saw the edges of his energy well up inside him, as he had every time since he'd healed Thunder. As he became one with the injured animal, he saw the bone as if it were a moving current. He could make the bone fluid and reweave the damaged tissue. Carefully, he straightened the bones into their proper alignment. Feeling the rush of pleasure that always accompanied healing, he wove the bone back together. At last, the leg was straight and whole. Releasing it, he dropped out of the trance.

The sun had advanced some hours in the sky, and only two of the armed men remained. He staggered away from the horse and dropped onto a relatively dry patch of ground. "The mare will be alright. She should be allowed to rest until morning, and she shouldn't be ridden for a week." He collapsed and allowed darkness to overtake him.

* * *

Samantha dozed in an uncomfortable bed. The mattress felt stuffed with straw instead of feathers, and the blankets were rough and harsh. A similarly rough garment covered her body, and her head was pounding. *Where am I?* She opened her eyes. Darhour and an old peasant woman hovered over her.

"There you are, my child," the woman said. "Just a bump on the head. My name is Myst, and I'm an herb witch. Drink a little of this." The old woman helped her lift her head to a mug of steaming tea.

As she sipped, Samantha remembered the sound she'd heard as she vaulted off Roberta's back. *How could I have been so careless?* Fighting back the tears, she turned to Darhour. "Did Roberta suffer much?"

"We met an amihealer, Milady. He claimed he might be able to save her. He's with her now."

"An amihealer?" She grasped Darhour's arm. "Is it . . . ?" She didn't finish the question; he would have told her if it was Robbie.

"The herb witch says you need to rest until tomorrow morning at the earliest. I've sent Blaine ahead. He should return before nightfall with news of your father."

Her head hurt so badly she didn't argue, but she clutched her heart as she thought of the news Blaine would bring. Three weeks ago her father had been dying. What were the chances he was still alive?

The herb witch placed the cup back to her lips. "Here, Milady. Drink the rest. It'll help the pain and allow you to rest."

She swallowed obediently. Soon the pain lessened, and she drifted into sleep.

* * *

At the sound of the door opening and the heavy tread of one of her guards, Samantha jerked into wakefulness. When she opened her eyes, Bearach was facing away from her, holding someone in his arms. Long curly dark hair trailed over Bearach's arm. "Robbie!" she yelled, struggling to sit up. The sudden movement renewed the pounding in her head. Bearach turned slightly, and she saw the creamy darkness of the peasant's skin. "Robbie, how can it be you?"

Robbie's eyes were closed, and as Bearach laid him in front of the fire, she noticed his right shoulder glistening with blood. "What have you done to him?"

She tried to get out of bed, but Darhour restrained her. "It's a minor wound, Milady. Let the herb witch tend to him."

Feeling faint, Samantha gave up her attempts to rise. "But why is he bleeding?"

The old woman removed Robbie's mud-covered shirt and examined the wound. "Because your men shot him," Myst said, sounding far less friendly than she had earlier.

Samantha glared at Darhour. "Why in the seven hells would you shoot him?"

"Milady, you were unconscious and vulnerable," Darhour said. "He ignored commands to halt. We did what we thought necessary for your protection. It's only a light scratch."

"Are you saying you ordered the peasant be 'lightly scratched'? You can't just kill people! Who fired the shot?"

"Milady, your safety can't be compromised. The peasant's life is nothing compared to yours." Darhour glared at her in the way that caused men to lose control of their bladders but had no effect on her.

Looking uncomfortable, Bearach cleared his throat. "The peasant amihealer healed your horse, Your H— Milady. He says she needs to rest for several hours and shouldn't be ridden for a week. I've left Brice with her."

The spark of joy that rose in her as she learned Roberta was going to be alright didn't distract her from Robbie's injury. She glared at Bearach. "Did you fire the shot?"

Bearach looked to Darhour. The captain of her guard's lips narrowed. "Milady, no one knew who the peasant was when the order was given. I will not let you blame Bearach."

Samantha hardly heard him, for she caught sight of the ribbon she'd given Robbie around his neck. *He hasn't forgotten me!* Even covered in mud, he was so staggeringly handsome it hurt to look at him. Although he still had no beard, he'd grown since last spring. He was taller and broader across the shoulders. His dark curly hair, loosed from the thong, fell gracefully over the hearthrug; she remembered how smooth it had felt as she'd tied the green ribbon around it last spring. She ached to touch him again.

The herb witch cleared her throat. "I'll need to remove the rest of his clothing and bathe him. I'm sure he'd prefer a lady like yourself not watch." Although the woman smiled, a hint of hostility flashed from her eyes.

Samantha nodded and closed her eyes. She heard the splash of water and smelled the soothing aroma of soap. She couldn't help imagining the old woman's hands moving over his body and wished they could be hers. She felt the smoothness of his chest, the curve of his buttocks, and the firmness of his thighs. *What will one glance hurt?* She opened her eyes; the peasant was lying naked on the rug, looking every bit as gorgeous as he did in her dreams. Darhour glowered at her. She went red and closed her eyes again.

She didn't open them again until the old woman touched her on the shoulder. "I see you've met my child before. You must be his 'Milady,' the one he danced with at the horse fair last spring."

"He speaks of me?"

Myst snorted. "Sometimes he speaks of nothing else. The boy has known little kindness in his life." The herb witch paused, and the hostility in her eyes was now unmistakable. "You are a lady, important enough to travel with a bodyguard of six armed men who'd kill without hesitation to protect you. For all of his talent, Robrek is a peasant. Did you consider how a peasant boy dancing with a lady might be viewed by his own?"

"I didn't think it would matter."

"That's right. You didn't *think*. It mattered quite a bit to his older brother. A large brute. Nearly twice his size. His brother beat him so viciously he wouldn't have survived if he weren't a talented healer. And he's only alive today because your man missed."

"I would have had him, but the horse veered at the last second," Bearach said, and Samantha glared at him. Bearach blushed furiously. "Which is a very good thing, is it not? I'd better check the perimeter."

Samantha had a hard time meeting the anger in the old woman's eyes. "I'm sorry, Mistress. Robbie's the last person I want to see hurt."

"Then leave the boy alone. He needs no more pain." The old woman got up abruptly, as if trying to prevent herself from saying something harsher. She took both Samantha's dress and the boy's muddy garments outside to wash.

Darhour grunted from beside the princess. "If you truly care for him, you'll listen to the herb witch."

Samantha remembered Robbie's loneliness, his pain growing up among people who thought he was a demon. It hurt to think she'd added to his problems. Watching him sleeping by the fire, she couldn't help thinking of his nakedness underneath the blanket the herb witch had thrown over him. She didn't want to cause him more pain, but she craved his touch one more time before she'd have to let him go forever.

Darhour watched the boy sleeping beside the fire. *Can he be trusted?* The guards had insisted he'd done nothing suspicious at the horse fair, and Bearach assured him he'd done nothing other than heal the princess's horse. They all claimed he'd acted like a simple peasant, but Darhour's instincts told him there was nothing "simple" about this one. Healing Roberta's leg proved how powerful he was. With his skills, the boy could have a position of prestige with any lord in the land. When he was Master of the King's Horse, he would have welcomed a lad like him into the king's employ. But despite his powers, this strange boy hid among the peasants and just *happened* to run into the princess at the horse fair and again today? It couldn't be merely a coincidence.

The princess's feelings for the boy complicated the situation. Darhour couldn't count on her to keep her head. She barely knew him and, like most adolescents, had mistaken infatuation for love. If the boy's intentions weren't honorable, he'd find the princess an easy mark.

A portion of Darhour devoutly wished Bearach hadn't missed.

The herb witch returned to the cottage. "Robrek has exhausted himself. He likely won't wake for some time. He'll be missed. I'd take the message myself, but I have two patients on my hands, and the boy's father has made it quite clear I'm not welcome on his land."

Sending one man would still leave five, and five could defend this small cottage as well as six. "I'll send a man with word." Darhour went to the door and called Bearach in.

The old woman gave Bearach directions to the boy's farm. "It'd be better for him if the injured horse belonged to a lord rather than a lady," she added.

Bearach looked at Darhour, who nodded.

"As you wish, Mistress."

* * *

Angus was in the barn, looking over the seed and plows for the planting that would begin in a couple weeks' time. He wanted to talk with Robbie about the animals that would be needed for plowing, but the boy was nowhere to be found. "Where is he?" Angus demanded of Darien and Allyn. "Is he with that damned witch again?"

"He didn't say where he was going, sir, but he spends a great deal of time there. He says she's teaching him."

Angus glared at his underlings. "I'm aware of that." *The gall of the boy, pretending to be a hand rather than a son of the family. How dare he take wages as if he were nothing more than a servant! And if he's nothing more than a servant, how dare he think he can call his time his own!* He heard a horse galloping into the farmyard; hoping it was Robbie, he went out to tear the boy apart.

Instead of his youngest son, a heavily armed stranger addressed him, "Are you the father of Robrek, the amihealer?"

Robrek? Amihealer? What nonsense has the boy got in his head now? "My son Robbie has a little skill with animals. But he isn't here now."

"I've brought word of him. My lord's horse fell and broke its leg some miles up the road. Robrek was close at hand and healed it. The amihealer collapsed with exhaustion afterwards, and we've taken him to the cottage of the herb witch, who says he will likely not wake for some time."

Another noble. The boy had a habit of attracting useless parasites—the lady at the horse fair last spring and now some lord from the seven hells. "He won't, eh? And who does *your lord* think is going to do the chores around here? He uses my son up and thinks I've no use for him?"

The man reddened. "My lord would be happy to pay for his services. He saved the life of a valuable animal."

"That would be most proper." Angus waited.

"I don't have my lord's purse. I'm sure my lord will reimburse you properly for the loss of his services." He spun the horse around and galloped away.

Only after the man left did the full impact of his words sink in. *Healed a broken leg? Has the boy gotten that powerful? Donella couldn't have done such a thing.*

* * *

Warm and comfortable, Robrek didn't want to wake. Around him, he heard a mutter of several male voices and two women. The first was Myst. The familiar scent of drying herbs confirmed he was in her cottage. He knew who the second woman sounded like, but it meant he had to be dreaming. He shut his eyes tighter to hold onto her voice, but then she laughed, and Robrek knew it was no dream.

He opened his eyes. She sat at the table. "Milady!" he cried, sitting up. The blanket dropped from his shoulders, and Robrek realized he was naked. He hurriedly covered himself.

"Robbie!" Her eyes sparkled. "I was hoping you'd wake soon. You must be terribly hungry." She picked up a bowl of soup and a hunk of bread and brought them to him.

Her hands touched his as she handed him the food. They were as warm and calloused as he remembered. "How is it you're here, Milady?"

"You saved my mare's life." She smiled, and Robrek's entire body started to glow.

He grinned shyly. "I thought she seemed familiar. Are you okay, Milady? You must have taken quite a fall."

"Just a slight bump on the head." She pulled back her hair to reveal a red lump.

"Oh, Milady." He reached up, but drew back as he realized the impropriety of touching her, especially when he was naked.

The lady let her hair fall back over the lump. "I had quite a headache, but mistress's tea worked wonders."

"Mistress Myst is a rare healer."

"And a very good cook, too. Eat up before it gets cold." The lady fetched her own food and joined him on the hearthrug, sitting so close he could touch her hair if he dared. *Holy Sulis, she's beautiful!*

He heard a grunt and looked up to see the other inhabitants of the cottage. There was the herb witch and two armed men--the archer who'd shot him and the scarred-face man from the horse fair. Just as at the horse fair, Scarface was glowering at him. Robrek pulled the blanket more closely around himself and couldn't help wishing for his staff. He looked out the window to avoid the man's gaze and noticed the gathering darkness. He swore softly. Remembering whose presence he was in, he stammered, "Forgive me, Milady." He tried to get to his feet without exposing himself. "My father will be angry. I must go."

"Your father's been taken care of," Milady said, and put out her hand to prevent him from rising. He settled back down. Her touch on his arm sent heat through his body and made him very aware of his own nakedness.

The second man at the table grunted; he was at least fifteen years younger than the scarred man, but he seemed nearly as dangerous. "I brought him word. A right unpleasant fellow, your father. Downright rude, in fact."

"Bearach!" the scarred man snapped. "You forget yourself!"

"It's okay, Milord," Robrek assured him. "My father is rude."

"It's not 'okay' to insult someone's kin in front of them, and I'm no one's lord."

Robrek paled under the hostility in the man's eyes.

"Look, Captain, I'm just saying I don't know why he'd put up with him. My own father was only about half that bad, and I took off when I was fourteen, and I'm no damned amihealer. What he did with Milady's horse was the most amazing thing I've ever seen. There's not a lord in the land that wouldn't take him. I'm sure he'd even be welcomed at the king's stables, and to stay . . ."

"Enough!" the scarred man shouted, seeming far angrier than the occasion warranted.

Robrek stared at the archer who called him an amihealer. It shocked him to realize the man respected him, but what he said about the king's stables had to be fantasy. Looking away from the men, he leaned back against the hearth to eat his soup and bread. His hand shook slightly, and he spilled a little soup on the blanket. The lady sat her own food down. "Myst told me how much energy healing takes. Let me help you." She reached for his bowl. Her smile made his body respond in ways he feared would get him killed. He was glad the blanket completely hid his reaction.

She scooted closer until her thigh touched his. Only her dress and the blanket separated them. She held out a spoonful of soup, and they both laughed when she spilled far more of it on the blanket than he had. When she brought up a second spoonful, she was shaking so hard with suppressed laughter she spilled it all on him.

Feigning outrage, he reached for the bowl. "Let me take that. I'll starve to death with you feeding me."

"We can't have that, or who would help with my horse problems?" She relinquished the bowl, but she kept her thigh pressed against his.

Even without seeing her for a year, Robrek felt as comfortable with her as he had when they'd danced together. "I guess I'll have to hope you have a lot of horse problems," he said, taking a spoonful and smiling when he didn't spill a drop.

"Is your Horsetad here?" she asked.

Robrek felt for Wild Thing's presence. "Yes, Wild Thing's outside, not too far away. She wants to know if Apple Lady has any more apples."

"Apple Lady? I wish I did. She is magnificent," the lady sighed. "It's too bad Roberta broke her leg."

Robrek froze with the spoon halfway to his mouth. *Roberta? Could Milady have named her horse after me?*

Noticing his reaction, the lady blushed. "If you hadn't been there, Darhour would have stuck me with another lady's mare. I'm still amazed at how perfectly you understood her. Roberta flies across the fields. No horse in my father's stable is her match. I would have loved to see how she could hold up in a race against a Horsetad."

"I'm afraid Wild Thing would leave her in the dust."

The lady hit him lightly on the shoulder and rolled her eyes. "Men. I wish I could make you either prove or eat those words."

"I'd be happy to prove them any time you like. Give Roberta two or three weeks to make sure her leg's strong enough, and you know where to find me." Robrek was shocked at his own daring.

The lady laughed and then sighed sadly. "You don't know how I wish I could. I've never had more fun than I did with you at the horse fair." The lady reached over and pulled the ribbon she'd given him out from under the blanket. "I see you haven't forgotten it either."

He leaned closer, wanting to wrap his arms around her and touch her as he had when they'd danced together. "It was the best day of my life."

A knock on the door interrupted the moment. Robrek jerked away from the lady, as the archer, with his hand on his sword, rose to answer it. Scarface was glaring at Robrek murderously. Robrek couldn't believe that for a moment he'd forgotten the two men were there. When the door opened, another of Milady's guards entered. This man was slightly smaller than the others, but he moved with the quick grace Robrek associated with Brazen's illusions. Robrek glanced at the man's sword, wondering how good he was with it.

"Your . . ." the man began, but stopped abruptly. "Milady, your horse is outside. She awoke, so I walked her down. She seems tired, but steady."

The lady jumped to her feet. "Come with me, Robbie. I want to see her." She reached out to help him to his feet.

Robrek blushed. "Perhaps I should get . . ." He looked up at his clothes.

"Oh." Blushing, the lady put her hand over her mouth. "I guess that would be best. Hurry up, though." She left the cottage, followed by her men.

Robrek got up, trying to keep the blanket around him. As he reached for his clothes, Myst frowned at him. "I should check on the horse, Mistress," he said.

"Is it the horse or the lady you're checking on?"

Robrek didn't answer as he put his trousers on and reached for his shirt, which was ripped where the arrow had grazed him. Only Wild Thing's sudden movement had kept that arrow from hitting his heart.

"My child, I'm worried . . ."

"I'm not your child, and I can take care of myself." He pulled the shirt over his head, pulled on his boots, and went outside into the early spring night. The white mare was near the garden wall to the right of Myst's cabin. Milady was petting the horse's nose and talking softly to her. Cold Eyes was standing between him and Milady as if daring him to approach. Milady turned and reached for him. Forcing Cold Eyes to move aside, she drew Robrek toward the horse.

"I can't thank you enough for saving her. She means the world to me," Milady said, seemingly oblivious to her men's hostility. "I'm so sorry Bearach shot you," she said, looking at his shoulder.

"It's little more than a scratch, Milady." *Holy Sulis, I love you. Why do you have to be a lady?* Bearach, Cold Eyes, and Scarface had surrounded them, wearing decidedly unfriendly expressions. He was relatively certain if he did what he wanted to, these men would see it as suspicious enough to merit a death sentence. He backed away and sat on the garden wall some distance from her, trying to control the beating of his heart and the part of his body that threatened to reveal his interest all too clearly now that he had no blanket to hide it.

The lady joined him on the wall, sitting entirely too close for his comfort. The men followed her, their hands resting on their sword hilts. Still, she seemed unaware of them. To break the tension, he asked her what she was doing in the Valley.

"I'm hurrying back to my father. I've had word he may be dying. I don't know what I'll do without him." The lady's eyes filled with tears.

"Milady, I'm sorry." He couldn't resist the urge to touch her arm. "You must love him dearly to risk travel at this time of year."

She nodded, taking his hand and intertwining her fingers with his; heat passed through her fingers and traveled up his arm. "The herb witch seems to be an amazing woman," Milady said, evidently not wanting to talk about her dying father. "Has she been your friend long?"

"She was a friend of my mother's, but I didn't know her until she healed me last spring." He paused. "You see, I had . . . an accident . . ."

Milady put her other hand on his thigh. "I'm so sorry. I never imagined someone would object to my dancing with you."

Robrek tensed. "She told you?" He hadn't wanted the lady to know how his brother had humiliated him. He glanced at her bodyguards. *How can she want anything to do with me when men like these surround her?*

The lady took his hand in both of hers. "I don't want to be responsible for anything else happening to you. Myst warned me to leave you alone, and I'm sure I should."

He grasped her hand tightly. "I wouldn't want that, Milady."

"I wouldn't want it, either." The lady smiled and looked away. She noticed for the first time how close her guards were. "I'm in no danger," she told them. "Back away."

"Milady," Scarface said. "We know little of this boy, except that he's powerful enough to be a threat even without a weapon."

"You can't think I'd harm her!" Robrek protested.

Milady silenced him with a touch. "I'm perfectly safe. You will back off and watch for real threats."

The man didn't look happy, but he nodded to the other two, and they moved a short distance away, although they were still watching him rather closely.

The lady turned back to him. "It's amazing you could heal Roberta's leg. When I met you last spring, I didn't realize you were that powerful."

"I wasn't." He wasn't accustomed to admiration from anyone, but from Milady, the woman he loved, it was enough to send his soul flying high into the star-filled sky. "Myst only recently took me as her apprentice. She's taught me how to see my energy, so I can use it more effectively. I can't see it all yet. Just the barest edges of it. Myst says something's blocking me, but she doesn't know what. Our gifts aren't the same. Maybe I need another amihealer to teach me."

The lady shook her head. "I'm not certain where you'd find one. I've never known of anyone who can heal as you do, even in Murtaghan."

Her lips were turned toward him, and he wondered if kissing her would cost him his life. He decided a kiss from her might be worth dying for.

Samantha felt the heat of the boy's leg next to her own. Staring into his eyes, she saw the sadness of his life reflected in their emerald-green depths. *What can it hurt? None of his people are nearby.* She leaned toward him and pressed her lips into his. He responded greedily, hungrily. "Ah, Robbie," she breathed as she ran her lips along his cheek. She nibbled on his ear, and he buried his mouth in her neck. *Who will it hurt to take him now? Do I have to save my maidenhead for a man I don't love?* She allowed her hands to roam freely.

Robbie kissed his way down her neck, and her body throbbed against his. His hand moved up her side and brushed her breast. "Yes, Robbie," she whispered.

But he broke away abruptly and jumped off the wall. "I'm sorry, Milady. I don't know what came over me."

Jumping down, she followed him. "It's okay. I want you, Robbie." She touched his face gently and leaned toward his lips. But he glanced at her men.

"Milady, I can't." He whirled away and ran into the darkness.

"Robbie, no, don't go!" Samantha shouted. She heard a whistle, and then a horse galloping away. *Please, don't go! I need you!* Darhour put his hand on her shoulder. "Darhour, no! Why did he go?"

"He understands his place."

She shrugged off Darhour's hand. "What? You don't think he's good enough for me?" She fled back into the cottage and flopped down at the table. Darhour and Kailen followed her inside. Myst offered her another cup of tea, which she ignored. As she stared out the window into the blackness of the night, she heard horses approaching. Darhour and Kailen went to the windows. Soon, she heard three owl hoots. Both Darhour and Kailen relaxed. It was Brice, letting them know all was okay. About twenty riders, wearing the gold sun of the king, came to a halt in front of Myst's cottage.

There was a knock on the door, and Blaine and a man she recognized as Lieutenant Hawk entered. They both bowed. "Your Highness," Blaine said. "His Majesty is ill, but is in no immediate danger of traveling Beyond the Far Mountain, so to speak."

As relief washed over her, Samantha heard a plate breaking. She turned to see Myst staring at her wide eyed, the dish shattered at her feet. "I'm sorry, Mistress, I should have told you. Still, I'd appreciate it if you not tell Robbie."

The old woman bowed deeply. "I won't, Your Highness. The boy has enough problems without knowing he's fallen for the crown princess."

Samantha turned back to her men. "Go on, Blaine."

Blaine shifted uncomfortably. "His Majesty didn't seem pleased you were returning so early and accompanied by only your personal guard. He sent Lieutenant Hawk and a squadron of the Royal Guard back with me."

Lieutenant Hawk was young for his position as second-in-command of the Royal Guard, thirty at most. Her father had to be very worried to have sent him. The young lieutenant bowed to her and saluted Darhour. "Your Highness, Captain, my men and I are at your service."

"Very good, Lieutenant." Darhour turned to her. "If you'll excuse us, Your Highness, I'll see to setting the watch." He left the cottage with the rest of the men.

"You should rest, Your Highness," Myst told her. "You may take my bed for the night. My cottage is small, but your men may make use of whatever space is available."

"Thank you for your kindness, Mistress." When she slid under the covers, Samantha wrapped her arms around herself, wishing it could be Robbie holding her. She wept silently at what could never be until she fell asleep.

CHAPTER 17

When Samantha entered the king's bedchamber, he was lying in his bed with his eyes closed. She crept quietly across the room and sat beside him.

He opened his eyes and smiled at her. "Samantha, my dear."

"Father, how are you?" *He looks so old! Please, my goddess, don't let him die! Not yet!*

"My dear, I'm fine." His voice was barely a whisper, and Samantha had to lean forward to hear him. "Why have you come so early? You should be in Wisteria for another month."

"Uncle Caedmon said you were dying." She touched his hand.

Annoyance passed briefly over the king's face, to be replaced by the utmost weariness. "I should have him flayed. And the captain of your guard as well for allowing you to travel without a proper escort."

"Don't blame Darhour, father. He argued most strenuously against it. Besides, nothing happened."

The old king examined her as if searching for an injury. "But I heard you were hurt."

"Just a bump on the head. A larger escort wouldn't have protected me from my own clumsiness."

The king sighed. "If something had happened to you, I couldn't have borne it. But I can't say I'm sorry you're here. The palace is a bleak place without you."

Tears welled up in Samantha's eyes. *He loves me. Can he know I'm not his true daughter?*

"Samantha, the promise you gave me in the fall has become increasingly urgent. You must have a consort."

From the sight of him, she really couldn't doubt he had little time left. Still, she wasn't willing to accept his death. "Father, I met someone when Roberta broke her leg—a real healer, Father. She's an herb witch, and she has healing magic, true magic. Let me send . . ."

The king shook his head. "Samantha, my dear, Calum has been my physician for thirty years." Samantha tried to interrupt, but the king silenced her with a hand. "Besides, you're changing the subject. We were talking about your consort. Who will it be?"

She crossed her arms. "Don't be so Sulis-cursed stubborn. You let me send for the herb witch, and I'll tell you the name of my consort."

The king chuckled weakly. "Taught you well, haven't I? All right, my dear, if it would make you feel better, send for this herb witch. Now, who do you have in mind?"

"Duke Argblutal," she said, but she couldn't meet the king's eyes.

"You don't seem happy, my dear. Is there one you would rather marry?"

Samantha laughed bitterly, got up, and crossed to the window, thinking of Robbie's kiss and the silky smoothness of his hair. "Yes, but I can't marry him, so it doesn't matter."

"And why not?"

Samantha stood with her back to the king and didn't answer.

"I see. He's outside of our class."

When she didn't turn, he called to her. She turned and met his eyes.

"You know I love you, and I wouldn't ask you to do this if it weren't necessary." His sadness told her he understood what marrying the duke was costing her.

Samantha crossed back to his bed and sat. "I know, Father, and I'll do my duty."

"Does the duke know about his coming good fortune?"

She shook her head. "I wanted to talk to you first, but I did choose him to lead the men in the Solstice dance."

"Then he knows, as does all of the court. The question is how to handle the formal announcement." The king smiled. "What better time than Ostara to announce a marriage that will renew the joined kingdoms?"

"How will we break the news to Argblutal?"

The king chuckled. "The same way we'll break it to everybody else. You will be the regent, my dear. He is merely your consort. By making the announcement public, he will understand this." The king patted her arm. "A monarch's marriage is the business of all the people." The king paused. "But who she chooses to share her bed is nobody's business but her own."

"Father!" the princess gasped. "Do you think Argblutal would accept a rival in the marriage bed?"

"Do not forget who reigns, my dear. Don't let him forget it, either."

* * *

Captain Tremayne sat in Duke Argblutal's office with his feet on the duke's desk and a glass of the duke's best brandy in his hand. He spilled the brandy all over himself when Sergeant Farrell gave him the news. "What do you mean he's back? He isn't due for a month!" Tremayne jumped to his feet. He'd nearly been dismissed last year for getting drunk. He'd promised the duke never to touch another drop. And he'd kept that promise, at least when the duke was in town.

"That may be," Sergeant Farrell said. "But he entered the stable yard not two minutes ago."

Captain Tremayne quickly shoved his brandy glass out of sight as the duke swept into the room. "You've made yourself at home," Argblutal observed. Tremayne tried to hide his shaking hands as the duke walked to the brandy decanter and poured himself a glass.

"Your Grace, we weren't expecting you."

The duke sipped the brandy slowly. "It is exquisite quality, is it not?"

Tremayne licked his lips nervously. "Your Grace would have nothing less than the finest."

"You'd do well to remember how I dispose of anything that doesn't serve me well." Argblutal took another sip of the brandy. "The king? Does he live?"

"Yes, Your Grace, but he's been ill all winter."

"Sulis curse him! If I'm going to inconvenience myself by traveling this time of year, he should at least have the decency to die. The princess has arrived?"

"Yes, Your Grace, she arrived about noontime today."

"Excellent. Have my servants prepare a bath. In the morning, you'll accompany me as I pay my respects to the princess and assure her of my utmost concern for her father's health."

* * *

"Robbie, wake up!" Allyn shook him by the shoulder. "Your father isn't going to be happy if you aren't at work again today."

Robrek came awake reluctantly. He'd been dreaming of Milady. *What a fool I was to run last night. Nobody will ever want to touch me like that again.* He got up, dressed, and followed Allyn and Darien toward the barn. Before he was halfway across the farmyard, one of the hands from the neighboring farm rode in. "Master Robbie, my master's mare is having difficulty dropping her foal. Can you come at once?"

"Your father won't like it," Darien told him. "He was quite put out that you were gone all day yesterday."

"Please," the hand begged. "The mare's in a great deal of pain, and Master Kanestamm's worried we'll lose them both."

"I'll come at once." Robrek headed to the barn to saddle Wild Thing.

* * *

Myst heard the horses approaching in the late afternoon and went to her front window. She was surprised to see a man wearing the golden sun of the king and leading an extra horse. She opened the door.

"Are you Mistress Myst, the healer?" the man asked.

"I am." The herb witch wondered if the princess had managed to fall off another horse.

"Her Highness, the Princess Samantha, summons you to the palace in Murtaghan. The king is ill, and she wishes you to attend him. We're to leave at once. We can make it at least as far as the traveler's inn before nightfall. Gather your things."

Myst didn't know whether to be pleased or annoyed. That the princess wanted her to care for the king bespoke great respect. Still, she'd have rather have been asked than commanded. Did the princess even consider what Myst's absence would do to the people of the Valley? Or to Robrek?

Nevertheless, in all her sixty-five years, she'd never been inside a palace. She'd answer the princess's summons if only for the adventure of it. She promised herself she wouldn't be gone long. How much trouble could Robrek get into in a few days?

She gathered the items she'd need and gave them to the man to pack onto the waiting horses; as he did so, she got out a piece of paper, ink, and a quill. What to tell Robrek? She decided being vague was best.

My dear Robrek,

I've been called away. I shouldn't be gone long. Feel free to make use of my cottage and books in the meantime.

With love,

Myst

* * *

Robrek returned to the farm after sunset. It had been a difficult birth, and it had taken him some time to stabilize both the mare and the foal. Despite his exhaustion, his body vibrated with the intense pleasure that came with healing, and his pocket jingled with the coin the farmer had given him. He hoped Allyn and Darien had already cared for the animals because he wanted to do nothing other than eat and fall into his bunk. He hoped to dream of Milady again.

His father emerged from the main house.

"Where have you been, boy?" Angus demanded.

Robrek bristled as he dismounted. "I have a name, you know."

"You what?" Angus spluttered.

"I have a name. Would it really hurt you to call me Robrek or even Robbie, instead of 'boy'? I'm not a boy anymore."

Angus laughed. "A man doesn't run off on his duties."

"I haven't. I'm a healer. My duty is to heal."

"Your duty is what I say it is. Hand over what you got in payment from Kanestamm, and from now on, you go nowhere without my permission." Angus held out his hand.

Robrek grabbed his staff. "No."

"I'll have no more of your insolence!" Angus swung, but Robrek blocked the blow easily. Angus looked at his hand in shock.

"You won't hit me," Robrek said. "I'll keep the money I get from healing, and I'll heal whenever someone comes for me."

"You'll treat me with respect, or you'll get off my lands."

"Fine!" Robrek whirled in the direction of the bunkhouse.

"Where in the seven hells do you think you're going?" Angus thundered after him.

"I'm going to get my things and get off your land." Robrek went into the bunkhouse. Packing his small bundle took only a couple of minutes. The hands stared at him, but nobody said anything. When he went back out, his father was waiting for him.

"You won't last a week on your own. If you ride out tonight, don't think I'll let you come crawling back."

Robrek swung up into Wild Thing's saddle. "I'll bear that in mind." He rode away without another word. He knew Brazen would be angry, so he headed to the one person who could help him decide what he should do now.

Robrek felt a pang of loss as he approached the place where the beautiful lady had kissed him. His groin ached with the remembrance of her touch, and he cursed himself again. *Surely, there's no bigger idiot in the entire joined kingdoms.*

Myst's cottage was dark, and no smoke came from the chimney. He dismounted and knocked. No one answered. She wouldn't care if he waited for her, so he made Wild Thing comfortable and went inside.

He shivered as he lit the lamp on the table. He saw a note and read it. *Called away? Who would call her away?* The note said she wouldn't be gone long, and since it specifically said he could make use of her cottage in the meantime, he decided to settle in and wait for her. He fetched some wood, lit a fire in the fireplace, and grabbed some bread and cheese from her pantry. Feeling truly exhausted, he rolled up in blankets in front of the fire..

* * *

Samantha undid her own hair that night while thinking about Robbie. Ardra and Malvina were still in Wisteria. She'd sent for Myst and hoped the herb witch would arrive early the next day. After undressing herself, she collapsed onto her bed and stared at the painting of the Princess Danu on her Horsetad. "Could I really have him for a lover?" she asked the long-dead princess. She knew her father hadn't been faithful to any of his wives, not even to Britomartus whom he claimed to have loved. With the memory of Robbie's kiss on her lips, she fell asleep.

Robbie took her in his arms and kissed her gently. He undid her dress, and it fell to her waist, leaving her breasts bare to the touch of his hands and his lips. "Oh, Robbie!" she cried. "I will marry the duke, but you are my only love." She wanted to feel his maleness inside her. As she moved her hands to remove his trousers, her father burst into the room, followed by her personal guard.

"Whore!" he shouted. "Just like your mother! Neither of you could keep your hands off common trash!" He turned to her guard. "Take him away and hang him as I hanged her father!"

"No!" Samantha screamed. "Father, you can't! You said it was okay!" Her father merely glared at her, as Darhour and Kailen grabbed Robbie. "Darhour, Kailen, I forbid this! Let him go!"

Darhour spat at her. "To think I pledged my loyalty to a whore."

"I told you you could never be mine!" Robbie cried. As Darhour and Kailen dragged him from the room, she could hear Robbie cursing her name.

Duke Argblutal appeared behind her father. "If you're determined to whore yourself," the king said, "so be it. But you shall at least be a noble's whore, not a peasant's slut." He turned to the duke. "Finish what the peasant scum started."

"With pleasure, Your Majesty." The duke leapt upon the bed and wrestled her down.

The princess screamed and pleaded as the duke's rough hands mauled her. He ripped off what clothing remained and forced her legs apart. She struggled to push him away.

She awoke and sat up quickly in bed. She was drenched with sweat, and her heart was pounding. She quickly assured herself her nightdress remained firmly around her and lay back. "It was only a dream," she said to herself. Still, she shuddered at the look in Argblutal's eyes and the touch of his hands. *The duke is nothing like that. Dreams mean nothing.* She repeated the words over and over again. It was quite some time before she could get back to sleep again.

* * *

Samantha awoke very early. Foolish as she knew it to be, she was still shaken by her dream and felt too restless to sleep anymore. She dressed herself in her riding clothes. When she emerged from her rooms, Phelan and Brice were still on duty.

They followed her down to the stables; it was so early that few of the stable boys and grooms were up. She picked up an apple and went straight to Roberta's stall. The mare nickered happily. She stroked Roberta's pure white coat. She wanted to go riding, but Robbie'd said Roberta shouldn't be ridden for a week, so she grabbed a shovel and began mucking out the stall. The distraction of physical labor helped her think. *It was only a stupid dream.*

She heard a stir behind her and turned to find Vaughan gaping at her. "Your Highness, there's no need for you to do that. I'll get to it at once."

"It's okay, Vaughan. I like doing it."

"You like shoveling horse shit?" His jaw dropped, and he glanced up and down the long line of stalls.

She laughed. "I suppose if I had to muck them all out, it'd lose its appeal."

The boy raised both eyebrows. "I guess one isn't bad. But you needn't do it, Your Highness. I'd be honored to shovel your horse's shit."

"Thank you, but I couldn't sleep."

"Is something wrong, Your Highness?"

Samantha started to say, "No," but the innocent friendliness of the boy's question made her want to confide in him. "I'm so worried about my father, and his illness means I need to get married right away. My betrothal will be announced at the Ostaran ball. I know it's my duty, but I don't want to do it."

The young boy frowned. "If you think shoveling horse shit is better than getting married, why get married, Your Highness? You're the crown princess. You can do whatever you want."

"I wish I could. Sometimes I think I'm the least free person in the joined kingdoms."

Before Vaughan could ask her to explain, Roberta let out a neigh. Samantha handed her shovel to Vaughan. "What is it, Roberta?" Roberta nuzzled her, and she could tell the mare wanted to be groomed. She had Vaughan fetch her a brush. "Oh, Roberta, what would I have done if he hadn't been there to save you?"

"There have been the most unbelievable rumors going around the stables," Vaughan said. "Her leg wasn't really broke, was it?"

"Yes, it was. An amihealer healed it." Samantha was still amazed Robbie was powerful enough to have done so.

"Like the bards sing of?" Vaughan asked, his eyes wide.

"Yes, just like the bards sing of. Robbie's so powerful and exotic that the bards would probably love to write songs about him. He doesn't look at all like a Korthlundian. He has brilliant emerald green eyes, curly black hair, and creamy dark skin." She sighed as she remembered the peasant boy's beauty in the moonlight.

"Would you rather marry him, Your Highness?" Vaughan asked.

Samantha blinked back tears. "If I were truly free, he is the one I would marry. I love him."

* * *

Samantha spent the rest of the morning helping Vaughan and the other stable hands with their chores. Since the rest of the court was still in Wisteria, she didn't have any official duties, and she wanted to be on hand when the herb witch arrived. When the sun was fully up, Darhour and Kailen relieved Brice and Phelan. She sent a page to see how her father was doing. The page informed her the king was still sleeping.

Finally, she heard horses approaching. *Thank you, Sulis.* But when Samantha emerged from the stable, it wasn't Myst. "Argblutal, what are you doing here?"

The duke dismounted. "Your Highness, when I heard the king was ill and you had gone to his bedside, do you really think I could have stayed in Wisteria? Have you arrived in time?"

Can it be true he actually cares about me? "Yes, my father still lives."

"Thank the goddess," Argblutal said, drawing the star over his breast. "It's hard for me to imagine Korthlundia without King Solar on the throne. Even my father knew no other monarch. Is there any hope for recovery?"

Samantha blinked back tears. "I don't know. I've summoned an herb witch with true healing magic. I pray to the goddess she can do more than Calum. I can't lose him. How can I ever hope to rule half as well?"

The duke patted her on the shoulder. "That, Your Highness, is the least of Korthlundia's worries. You, as his heir, are the finest parting gift a great king could leave to his people."

To think I let a silly dream affect me so. He isn't at all like my nightmares. She was on the verge of telling him about the betrothal plans when Myst arrived. "Mistress, I can't thank you enough for coming."

"It's my pleasure, Your Highness." The herb witch bowed as she dismounted, looking very tired and worn.

Samantha chided herself for not sending a carriage for the old woman. "I'd like you to see my father as soon as possible, but I've arranged rooms where you can first refresh yourself and eat." She turned to the duke. "Your Grace, I thank you for your concern, but I must attend to my father. Would you dine with me this evening?"

The duke bowed. "With pleasure, Your Highness, but if the king has need of you, don't spare a thought for me."

* * *

In the darkness of the night, Darhour observed Argblutal's residence from the roof of the neighboring house, grateful to the Saloynan magic that allowed him to see in the dark. On the ground below, a couple of guards were on duty, but there was an attic window that would allow him easy access. He still knew far too little about the man his daughter intended to marry, but his instincts shouted the man was evil. As an assassin he'd learned to trust his instincts. Despite a thorough search of the duke's quarters at the palaces both in Murtaghan and Wisteria, he'd been unable to obtain evidence to substantiate his suspicions. *Whatever secrets he's hiding, this must be where he keeps them.*

Darhour leaped lightly across the space separating the roof he was on from Argblutal's and crept to the attic window. Hiding in the shadows, he carefully oiled the hinges so they wouldn't squeak. He slipped one of his wires in through the gap and lifted the latch. Two maidservants were sleeping in the attic room. He entered quickly and shut the window before the cold night air could disturb them. Without a sound, he crossed to the door, where he again oiled the hinges. He opened the door and stepped out into the corridor.

As Darhour searched the house, he felt the familiar excitement of the chase, the rush of stalking his prey, and the anticipation of the kill. He'd almost forgotten the simple joy of the artist doing a job to perfection. *This is wrong! I am no longer The Ghost! I have made my vow!* He found the duke's office and searched methodically, being careful to leave no sign of disturbance. He found several hidden panels in the duke's desk and the walls of the room, but disappointingly these were either empty or filled with jewels or other valuables. There wasn't a single scrap of paper, not even the typical reports from the duke's estates. The lack of paper screamed that the duke was hiding something, but Darhour wasn't sure he could get Samantha to see it that way.

Finished with his search, he left the duke's office. In a room ahead, he heard a game of cards in progress. Automatically, he found himself planning the best way to kill those men. They weren't expecting anyone. It wouldn't be hard. He froze with a knife in his hand. He didn't remember drawing it. *Holy Sulis, no!* He replaced the knife and slipped silently past the room.

Darhour came up empty-handed again when he searched the duke's bedroom. He went methodically over the rest of the house. In a storage area, he found several sets of the duke's livery. He purloined one; it might come in handy. He found nothing else of interest until he ventured into the cellar. At first, Darhour thought it was nothing more than an ordinary wine cellar, but he found a door at the back that opened into a torture chamber. There was a rack against one wall, a cat-o-nine whip on a hook next to a wall with hanging manacles, and various other instruments of pain. At the back of the chamber was an empty cell. A thin layer of dust covered everything, and some of the devices showed signs of rust. But of course, the duke had been in Wisteria for months. Somehow, he doubted this alone would be enough to convince the princess she was making a mistake. Having torture devices in a cellar would be unremarkable in any of the old houses. They harkened back to a time when the nobility had fewer restrictions.

Darhour hit the wall. He needed more.

CHAPTER 18

"That's enough, Darhour!" the princess snapped, as she brushed Roberta's gleaming white coat. "You've told me a hundred times none of them are worthy of me. I have to marry someone."

"It doesn't have to be Argblutal, Your Highness. I told you what I found in the basement of his private residence." Despite all of his efforts, Darhour had no more damning evidence than the unused torture equipment.

"And what were you doing crawling around in the duke's house anyway? How would I have explained the captain of my guard doing something like that?"

"I wasn't caught, Your Highness."

The princess put her hands on her hips. "That isn't the point. You've overstepped your authority. You know as well as I do that a lot of old houses have that kind of thing lying around. You said yourself it was covered in dust."

"The duke has been in Wisteria all winter, Your Highness."

"And now that he's back, you think he has started rounding up people, torturing them, and locking them up?" Samantha didn't bother hiding her sarcasm. "Argblutal may not be the most exciting man in the world, but he's not like *that*. I'm not the idiot you seem to think I am."

Darhour bowed his head in defeat. "Your Highness, I would never question your intelligence."

"You've done little else since you were made the captain of my guard. Remember when you thought I was a fool to choose Blaine? You nearly scared the poor boy to death, and for what?"

"Your Highness, this is different." Even to himself, his objection sounded lame.

"How?"

Darhour leaned against the support column. Tonight was his last chance; tomorrow at the Ostaran ball, his daughter's betrothal would be announced. "I beg you, Your Highness. Pick any one of the others. I could keep you safe from them."

"You've got to be kidding. Darhour, you have been more than my guard; you have been my good friend, but this is getting ridiculous."

"Your Highness, please . . . ."

"Darhour, I will hear no more."

* * *

Ostara dawned bright and warm. Myst found King Solar on the palace balcony. He wouldn't be joining the procession to the city square, but he was well enough to preside over the ball and announce his daughter's betrothal that night.

"Your Majesty," Myst said, bowing. "You're well this morning?"

"I haven't felt this good in years," the king said.

The two of them, with the king's attendants, watched the procession move out of the palace grounds. Samantha riding her white mare in the lead, her bodyguards surrounding her. "She's a daughter worthy of a king," Myst said.

The king beamed down at his daughter. "Yes, she'll make an excellent queen."

"Your Majesty, your health is stable, and I've made enough of my potions to last for some time. It's time I went home. There's a young man there, just a year younger than your daughter. Your Majesty knows how young men are at that age—thoughtless, reckless. He has no one else to provide him guidance."

The king nodded. "Send for the young man. Certainly, we can find some position at the palace for him."

"Your Majesty, I thank you for your offer, but I don't think that would be wise."

"Why not?" The king stared at her with his piercing eyes that missed little. He nodded. "Ah, he's the one, isn't he?"

"I'm sorry, Your Majesty?"

"The peasant amihealer my daughter has fallen in love with. The one she met at the horse fair last spring." King Solar laughed at the surprise on the herb witch's face. "Samantha doesn't think I know about the horse fair, either. You may leave in the morning, but you will return at a moment's notice if I summon you."

* * *

Argblutal's face twisted with fury, but Herne told himself at least his brother wasn't angry with him.

"The bitch's father will announce it before the entire court tonight, as if I were some underling." As his manservant dressed him for the ball, the duke glared at his reflection. "When I have her under me, she'll learn the price of insulting me. I'm not a dog to obey her call."

No, you're a panther, as is the symbol of our house. Herne seethed that even though he too was a son of the house, he didn't have his brother's freedom and power.

"Is Lady Shela prepared to do her part?" the duke asked.

"Yes, Your Grace, she assured me she'll talk to the princess before the ball. She'll let you know if anything is amiss." Next time, Herne hoped his brother would give him a turn with the wench. He'd like to get his hands on those breasts.

* * *

As her maids wove fresh flowers through Samantha's hair, Malvina shook her head. "You don't look like a girl should on the night of her betrothal, Your Highness. I know it don't be my place, but why be you doing this?"

"You're right. It isn't your place." Samantha stared sadly at her reflection.

Her maid blushed. "Duke Argblutal isn't unattractive, Your Highness."

"No, he isn't."

There was a knock on her outer door, and Blaine announced Lady Shela. The count's daughter had been looking paler and more fragile all winter. She looked deathly white tonight, and again she was wearing a dress with an unfashionably high neckline.

"Your Highness." Shela bowed with a false brightness to her eyes. "You look as lovely as any girl should on a day such as this."

"Whatever do you mean?" Samantha asked.

"Your Highness, you don't think it's any secret you're to be betrothed tonight?" The forced smile on the lady's face was painful to behold.

"I'm sorry my marriage will throw yours to Count Weylin into the shadows."

"Your Highness, I wouldn't want all that attention anyway," Shela said, which further worried Samantha. Since they were children, Shela had done her best to attract as much attention as possible.

The princess touched the lady's arm. "If your father is forcing you into this marriage, I can put a stop to it."

Shela jumped away. "Oh, no, Your Highness! Please, don't think of doing any such thing. My lord count has promised I can retire to his estates after we're married. I love the flowers and the quiet. I can't wait to play the shepherdess and walk among the lambs."

Samantha wasn't sure Shela would even recognize a lamb unless it was cooked in brandy with mint sauce. Shela didn't feel safe at court any longer. Who couldn't Count Nola protect his daughter from? The possibilities were few and disturbing. Whether the lady liked it or not, the princess would have to find out. But she didn't have time to press the matter tonight.

* * *

With nearly all her suitors looking like they'd gone into mourning, the Ostaran ball proved to be the most intolerable of all the balls Samantha had suffered through. The only one who didn't seem affected was Lord Devyn, who was happier and more at ease with her. He didn't stutter once during their dance. But he barely looked at her. When she followed his gaze, she saw his eyes resting on Lady Aislinn, Count Morfran's daughter. Duke Argblutal would never look at her like Devyn looked at Aislinn. Only Robbie ever had.

Samantha was relieved when Argblutal finally came forward to take his dance.

"You'll forgive my saying so, Your Highness, but you do look exceptionally lovely," the duke said as he drew her onto the dance floor. *Malvina is right. He may be old, but he isn't unattractive.*

Although the duke danced with perfect correctness, his stiffness indicated he didn't enjoy dancing. Then again, neither did she—at least not the formal dances of the court. The wild country dances were another matter. *Stop thinking of him! You're about to be betrothed.*

Halfway through the dance, her head exploded with pain. She stumbled, and the air around the duke blazed with color—rotten orange and blood red. Steaming heat coated her body. She felt as if she'd been raped and then carved up with the ruby encrusted knife that even now he wore at his belt. *Holy Sulis, Mother of us all! He's worse than even Darhour painted him!* Samantha fought against retching. Her court mask slipped, and she stared at the duke with utter revulsion.

"Your Highness." The duke's voice barely pierced her horror. "Are you all right?"

"No, I don't feel at all well. I'm . . ." *How does one speak to a monster?*

Darhour and Kailen appeared at her side. "Are you all right, Your Highness?" Darhour asked.

She grabbed his arm, fearing she would faint. "Get me out of here, Darhour!" she cried.

Darhour nodded, and the rest of her bodyguards materialized out of the crowd and surrounded her.

"Samantha!" the king called from the dais as they led her out of the room.

"Conroy, tell him I'm sick. Tell him I have to lay down."

After a nod from Darhour, Conroy detached himself from the group. The ballroom had gone silent, and every courtier was staring at her. But she couldn't worry about what they were thinking. *Holy Sulis, I am* the fool Darhour thinks me!

Kailen and Darhour followed her into her rooms, checking for intruders as they always did. She collapsed on the sofa, trembling. Soon Darhour was kneeling at her feet. "Your Highness, what happened? Did he do something to you?"

Samantha was certain if she said, "yes," Argblutal would die before morning. She shook her head. "No, I just felt ill suddenly."

She was certain Darhour didn't believe her, but he didn't press. "I'll summon your maids to get you to bed. We'll make sure no one disturbs you tonight."

She nodded, feeling too numb to make further response. After her maids undressed her, she crept under her blankets and shivered uncontrollably until sleep finally took her.

* * *

Shela had just returned to her parents' quarters when Duke Argblutal burst through the door. Screaming, she pushed her father between herself and the duke.

"What is going on here?" her father demanded, but he didn't put up a fight when Argblutal pushed him aside.

The duke grabbed the front of her dress with those awful hands and slapped her. "What did you tell her?"

"Now see here . . ." her father started to protest, but a mere glance from Argblutal shut him up.

"Please, I didn't tell her anything!" She hated how pathetic she sounded, but she couldn't bear him being so close to her again.

"Perhaps you have another explanation for what just happened?"

"I don't know," Shela cried, tears streaming down her cheeks. "When I talked to her before the ball, she was planning on becoming betrothed tonight. She apologized that her wedding would overshadow mine."

Argblutal slapped her again, and still, her father did nothing. "You will go to her in the morning and discover the cause of this. You will mend this error."

After the duke left, Count Nola sent his daughter to bed. When he turned to his wife, tears were forming at the corner of her eyes. "Is doubling the size of your estates really worth sacrificing your daughter?" she asked.

"Whatever are you nattering about, woman?"

Countess Birkita clasped her hands together. "Haven't you seen the change in her? The way she dresses now? Her eagerness to marry the man she once despised? Her terror in the duke's presence?"

"Are you suggesting Argblutal had his way with her? You think he has so little respect for me that he would use my daughter?"

"Argblutal respects no man but himself."

"He wouldn't dare!" Nola paced and muttered in outrage for several minutes. He stopped abruptly. "I'm sure you're mistaken. But even if it's true, do you realize what gaining the king's lands will do for our son? Surely, with an estate that vast, the king will bestow the title of duke on him. He'll be one of the most powerful men in the joined kingdoms."

"So you're willing to sacrifice Shela for your son's and your own ambitions?"

"I've made my decision, woman, and you won't question it."

* * *

The High Priest Shylah smiled when his servant reported Duke Argblutal was in his reception room demanding to see him. "He has learned he needs us, has he? Tell him I'll be there momentarily."

When he emerged into his reception room, Argblutal was pacing like a caged panther. "You have the potion you spoke of?"

"Of course." Shylah picked up the large flask of purple liquid from his altar.

"How long does it take to work?"

"It starts working immediately, but when it reaches full control varies based on the individual's strength of mind. A couple of weeks, a month at most. That is, if the subject isn't tampered with. The herb witch who has been treating the king has the smallest touch of magic. There is a remote possibility that she could counter its effects."

"I'll take care of the herb witch. You take care of the king."

After the duke swept out, Shylah summoned his most discreet servant and handed him the flask. "Take this, as we discussed, and exchange it with the potion the herb witch made for the king."

"Yes, Your Eminence." The servant bowed his way out.

Shylah touched the statue of Sulis on his altar. "Soon, my god, both priestesses and herb witches will be things of the past, and you will be free to show your true power through your priesthood. Then we will stop the blasphemy that deems you female."

* * *

Ardra woke Samantha early. "I'm sorry, Your Highness, but His Majesty wants to see you at once." The princess groaned, her head pounding abominably.

As they helped her dress, her maids offered compassionate glances. When they'd finished, she was reluctant to leave the safety of her rooms. She turned to the painting of the Princess Danu. "Wish me luck." Danu's eyes seemed to sparkle with approval.

When she emerged into the hallway, her entire guard was waiting for her. "We're with you, Your Highness," Darhour said, and she knew he didn't just mean physically. Still, she felt like a prisoner being escorted to her execution.

They reached the king's quarters far too quickly. Frowning with disapproval, Gilroy let her know the king was expecting her in his reception room.

Her bodyguards forced to wait at the door, Samantha entered alone to find her father glaring at her. She bowed formally and didn't think it prudent to approach with the usual kiss on the cheek. "Good morning, Father."

"Explain yourself! And don't tell me you took ill suddenly!"

Samantha looked at her feet. "I can't marry him."

"And why not? Did dancing with him remind you of your peasant lover?"

Samantha's mouth fell open. "This has nothing to do with Robbie."

"Did you perhaps have some other reason for causing a scene?" The king's voice was icy. He'd never talked to her like that before.

She tried to meet his eyes, but found she couldn't. "I'm sorry. I can't marry him. He's evil."

"Samantha, this melodrama is inexcusable. You have five minutes to convince me you had a good reason for your actions last night, or I'll go to court today and announce your betrothal."

Samantha finally managed to meet his eyes, and he wasn't bluffing. "I don't know how to say this. Maybe I should have come to you when I first realized it, but I didn't know if that would be the right thing. Father, I'm an aurora. I saw the duke's aura last night when I danced with him. It was the foulest I've ever seen."

The king's face, red when she'd entered, went white. "Where in the seven hells did you dig up this nonsense? I forbid you to ever speak of it again." His eyes bored into her. "You are my daughter, and it is treason for you or anyone else to claim otherwise."

"Father—"

"You have three days to name a consort, or I will chose one for you, as my father chose for me." He called in her guards without giving her a chance to say anything more. "You will escort Her Highness to her rooms. She is to remain there until I say otherwise." The king nodded his dismissal.

* * *

Samantha sat in her window seat staring out at the castle grounds. *I shouldn't have told him. I should have found some other way to make him understand.* But a part of her was glad the secret was no longer between them. His accusations of treason told her he'd known all along about her mother's affair. *Holy Mother, why did you make me an aurora? If you hadn't, I would never have known he wasn't my father.* But the thought of how close she'd come to handing both herself and the joined kingdoms over to a monster made her so sick she doubled up in pain. *Maybe I should let my father choose. What kind of queen would be so blind?*

Samantha straightened as she heard a knock. "Unless it's a message from my father, I'm indisposed," Samantha called to her secretary.

A few moments later, Blaine appeared in her doorway. "Your Highness, it's Lady Shela. When I tried to send her away, she looked as if the world was coming to an end, so to speak."

Of course. Her sudden friendliness and high necklines. Argblutal displaying all the qualities I told her I wanted. "Show her into my reception room, Blaine."

As she entered, Shela bowed. "Your Highness, you gave me quite the surprise last night. I thought your betrothal was to be announced," she said with false enthusiasm.

The princess had the lady sit close to her. "Shela, I need you to tell me the truth. Duke Argblutal . . . hurt you, didn't he?"

Shela drew away, trembling visibly.

"Don't be afraid. Just tell me what happened. We can go to my father, and he can protect you."

"I haven't the slightest idea what you're talking about." The lady refused to meet her eyes and began twisting her dress between her fingers.

"Shela, I know *someone* hurt you. I didn't know who until last night, but I've discovered what the duke is like. Please, if you'll tell me the truth, I can help you."

"Are you some kind of witch?" The lady fled.

* * *

"Which one of them would you recommend, Caedmon?" The king sank wearily into a chair, cursing Sulis for allowing this to happen. All his hopes for the last eighteen years had rested on

Samantha, the daughter he loved. He would allow nothing to threaten her now, not even Samantha herself. She had to get married as soon as possible, giving a strong man a vested interest in keeping her on the throne.

The chancellor shook his head. "I must admit I'm puzzled. Has she given any reason for her sudden change of heart regarding Duke Argblutal?"

The king shook his head. This wasn't a secret he could trust even Caedmon with.

Caedmon licked his lips. "Your Majesty, I was watching the princess's face when she danced with Argblutal. One minute she seemed entirely calm, the next she was staring at Argblutal as if he'd suddenly morphed into a hideous creature." Caedmon paused and hesitated before going on. "I had a great-aunt who never married, never had any children, but every now and then she'd get flashes, sudden insights into a person's character."

Solar gripped the arms of his chair. "What are you suggesting?" He hoped he didn't have to have his long-time friend executed.

"Your Majesty, I love Her Highness like a daughter, and my loyalty to her is unwavering. I've kept the secret of her birth for nearly nineteen years, and I have no intention of revealing it now. But I was with my father the day he found the stable groom with Fenella."

The king closed his eyes. "A stable groom, was it? I never asked."

"This does change things. Her Highness needs to be counseled on exercising more caution in regards to her ability, and she needs to marry as soon as possible, but, given the circumstances, too strong a man could reduce her to a consort. I would recommend you consider Lord Devyn. Devyn cares far more about art than politics. But such is not true of his father. Sheen would do anything to see his line established on the throne. Once Her Highness's reign is secure, well . . . he's old enough to die from any number of things."

Solar shook his head tiredly. "And I thought I was ruthless. I will give Samantha the day to consider the matter and discuss Devyn with her tomorrow." Devyn might be a perfect fit for her in other ways as well. He was in love with Lady Aislinn. Theirs could be a marriage in which they were both free to pursue a relationship with the one for whom they really cared.

After Caedmon left, Solar sank back into his chair. Things weren't as desperate as they'd first appeared. He could surely manipulate the situation to Samantha's advantage. If only he weren't so tired. He needed rest, a long sleep from which he'd never wake. But he couldn't go quite yet. The king rang for a servant. "Fetch the strengthening potion the herb witch left for me."

* * *

Shela paced her room frantically. *She knows. And if the princess won't marry him, he'll think it's my fault. She says she can protect me, but nothing can stop him. Not the princess. Not the king. Nobody. Certainly not Father. He cares more about the lands the duke promised him than he has ever cared about me.* Shela fell to her knees beside her bed; she retched as she remembered the duke inside her, using her like a common whore. Nothing would stop him from using her again. *Unless . . .*

She tore the sheet off of her bed and began twisting it into a rope.

* * *

Lord Devyn watched the beautiful curves of Lady Aislinn's backside, as she bent to examine the painting he'd completed the day before. It was of a ship sailing out of the Murtaghan harbor headed for some far distant land—a land without fathers and kings. The smell of paint was strong in the air, and his paints, brushes, and canvases littered the room.

Aislinn stood with her chin in her hand. "It's probably your best piece yet."

"I was inspired by the princess's coming betrothal, which would free me to sail away from this Sulis-cursed place." Putting his arms around her waist, Devyn kissed the side of her neck. "Damn it, Aislinn! Why did she change her mind?"

"You can't tell me you want that great horned toad as king."

Devyn pulled away. "Better him than me."

"You'd willingly bow the knee to that gutter slime, that swamp-goop-encrusted pile of toad shit? I told you what he did to Lady Shela." Aislinn's eyes flashed. When she got angry like this, it always set his groin on fire. She had the passion and the strength he knew he lacked.

"You also told me Lady Shela denied it. Surely, Argblutal wouldn't rape another council member's daughter."

"You think everyone's as pure as you are, my sweet boy." Aislinn touched him gently.

Devyn laughed bitterly. "I know better than that. But damn it, Aislinn, don't you see? I thought once the princess's betrothal is announced, I might be able to open negotiations with Count Morfran for the hand of his amazingly beautiful, warm, and inviting daughter." He put his arms around her as he said this and kissed his way up her neck to nibble her ear.

"Devyn, my boy," Aislinn sighed with pleasure. "It's a nice fantasy, and though Count Morfran would jump at a marriage of such advantage, my dowry is nowhere near large enough for the oldest son of his great pompous dukeship."

"Aislinn, what do I care about the size of your dowry?" Devyn pulled away. "I will marry you, Aislinn. We'll run away if we have to."

Aislinn ran her fingers through his hair. "It's sweet of you, but your father will cut you off without a dram if you marry without his permission."

"We can live without his money."

"You know nothing of poverty. You'd despise me within a year. I love you too much to allow you to destroy yourself. You'll marry who your father commands, and the best I can hope for is to be your mistress." Aislinn put her arms around him, but he held himself stiff. She stroked his cheek, and he bent toward her mouth, but as he tasted the sweetness of her lips, he heard footsteps pounding in the corridor.

He swore quietly. "It's my father. Quickly." He grabbed her and shoved her into the closet. He just managed to get the door closed when Duke Sheen burst into the room without even the courtesy of a knock.

"The goddess lives and guides us after all." Duke Sheen was nearly jumping up and down in excitement. "Argblutal is furious, but the opportunity is ripe for you."

Devyn looked away. "Father, I've told you I don't want to be king."

"What you want doesn't matter. You'll waste yourself on this nonsense"—he waved his hand at the paints and canvas—"and that slut no longer."

"I won't hear you speak of Lady Aislinn like that."

Sheen raised an eyebrow. "Are you trying to convince me she hasn't warmed your bed and that of half the court as well?"

Devyn clenched his fists tightly; Aislinn was his and his alone. "You will not defame her like this! I won't stand for it!"

"You'll stand for whatever I say you'll stand for. Your mother was a fool to ever allow you to waste your time on paints and a worse fool for her kindness to Count Morfran's poor talented daughter. I should have thrown the slut out of the house before she crossed the threshold—her and your art master both. They've made you soft in the head. You have the chance to be king!"

Devyn struggled to stop himself from trembling. "Despite what you might wish, the princess isn't foolish enough to marry me."

"She's a woman, for Sulis's sake, and can be led even into marrying an incompetent imbecile if you put forth the smallest amount of effort. The day the princess's betrothal to someone else is announced, I'll consign the entire lot to the fire." He gestured toward Devyn's paintings.

"You wouldn't!" Devyn protested, knowing full well his father would. Devyn had seen some of his best work go up in flames or cut to pieces by his father's sword.

"And if I catch you with that slut again, I'll have you both stripped and beaten raw." The duke swept out of the room.

Devyn collapsed into a chair as Aislinn emerged from the closet. "Aislinn, what am I to do?"

She put her hands on his shoulders. "You'll do as your father commands."

"You would see me in another woman's bed?"

"Before I'd see you destroyed, yes. The princess wouldn't be a bad choice for my sweet boy. She's a strong woman with a kind heart. She could protect you from your father. I won't see your back in that condition again."

There were tears in Aislinn's eyes, and Devyn winced at the memory of what had happened when he'd refused to attend a royal ball nearly a year ago. He still bore the scars. He couldn't allow his father to do that to Aislinn.

* * *

"Is the herb witch confined as I ordered?" Argblutal asked him as Herne returned to his brother's rooms in the palace.

"Yes, Your Grace, things have gone more smoothly than I anticipated. The herb witch had the king's leave to depart this morning. She won't be missed."

"Good." Argblutal smiled in the way he always did when someone was about to die. "If you wanted to kill the princess, how would you do it?"

Herne's right hand twitched against his leg; he needed some paipan leaves, but he'd been too busy with the herb witch to visit his supplier. "It'd be most difficult, Your Grace. She's always accompanied by her guards. Assuming our assault team is small enough to make it through the palace without arousing suspicion, her guards are more than sufficient to defeat them."

"I wasn't suggesting killing the princess in the palace corridors. You're convinced that while every other room in the entire palace has at least two entrances, Her Highness's only has the one?"

"So they say, Your Grace."

"This palace contains a labyrinth of passageways. If there's another way in, you'll find it."

How am I supposed to do that? But since his brother didn't allow excuses, Herne merely bowed his head.

* * *

The king drank deeply of his strengthening potion as his servants prepared him for bed. He looked at his reflection in the mirror and was again surprised at just how old he'd become. But that wasn't what upset him—physically, he felt better than he had in years. But as he looked at his reflection, he noticed that there was something wrong with his eyes. He knew there was something he'd meant to do about his daughter, but he couldn't remember what. *I'm losing my mind. No, that must not happen. Samantha still needs me.*

CHAPTER 19

A few days after Robrek moved into the herb witch's cottage, he heard a mewing at the front door. He opened it to find Ronan carrying a dead mouse. The cat dropped the mouse at his feet. Robrek bent and petted the big gray cat. "Ronan, my boy, brought me a present, I see."

:Found. Good.: Ronan rubbed against his leg and began purring. The cat let Robrek pet him for a few minutes, then flounced off, plopped down on the rug in front of the fire, and began licking himself.

Robrek laughed. "Of course you may stay. I saw a mouse in the pantry earlier. See that you check on it for me." Ronan merely purred and continued licking himself.

Robrek picked up the dead mouse by the tail. Before he could determine what to do with it, he heard a small scream from the doorway. He looked up to see a woman. "It's just a dead mouse." He put the mouse behind his back.

"Is Mistress Myst at home? I have a rash that needs tending." The woman's voice quavered. Her hands and arms were bright red and covered in bumps.

"No, she's been called away. I'm her apprentice. I could look at it."

"Sulis protect me, no!" The woman drew the star of Sulis and fled as if the hosts of the seven hells were after her.

Robrek threw the mouse out the front door and slammed it. He collapsed on the rug next to Ronan. "You've come all this way to find me, but people flee in terror at the sight of me. Why, Ronan?" Ronan just purred and continued cleaning himself. Evidently, the actions of humans were unimportant.

* * *

Leigh Fergalstamm answered the knock on the temple infirmary to find a woman whose arms were covered in a horrible rash. It looked like the type of rash caused by Nimh weeds. Although he'd studied herbals enough to know the proper salve to use for it, Father Gildas had explicitly forbidden him to treat even minor injuries.

He'd been assigned to this temple against Father Gildas's will. When Leigh had told his father he wanted to be a priest, his father had laughed at him, pulled strings in the capital, and got him appointed a novice in the most backward corner of the joined kingdoms. His father thought that after a month Leigh would come running home to Murtaghan and become a dutiful son like his older brothers. Leigh vowed he'd never do that. His father dealt in paipan leaves—a scourge on the children of the goddess.

He wouldn't have minded being in such a nowhere place, except the priest didn't seem to like half-breeds and wouldn't allow him to do anything except the most menial of tasks. Leigh cursed his narrow, pointed nose that announced to the entire world his mother was Saloynan.

The suffering woman shouldn't be made to wait until the priest finished with morning devotionals, but if he ever wanted Father Gildas to begin training him, he had to obey orders.

While she waited for the priest, Ula thought she would go mad from itching. She prayed, knowing Father Gildas would need the goddess's aid if he were going to get things right.

Finally, the novice with the strange, pointy nose led her into Father Gildas's consulting chamber. She curtsied to the priest, who sat while leaving her standing.

"How can I help you, my child?" Father Gildas asked.

Ula held out her arms. "I have this rash, Father. It's about to drive me mad with the itching."

The priest barely glanced at the rash. "I see, and have you been arguing with your husband lately? You know, my child, it's Sulis's will that a woman submit herself to her husband, and you've repeatedly tried to usurp your husband's place. This rash is Sulis's way to teach proper subservience." The lectures were another reason Ula always avoided the priest. Ula was sure the rash had nothing to do with Sulis. She'd been pulling some weeds at the edge of her garden the day before, and she thought there might've been some of that poison plant Mistress Myst had warned her about. To hurry him up, Ula placed the expected donation on the priest's desk; it was all the ready coin she had.

Father Gildas smiled. "I see you're starting to develop the proper attitude." He took down a small jar from the shelf behind him. "The only thing that will truly solve your difficulty is to make your heart right with Sulis and with your husband, but this should help in the meantime."

Ula took the jar eagerly. "Is this like the ointment Mistress Myst gave me last time?"

The priest's eyes flashed. "Do not mention that heretic in Sulis's holy house! Her witchery may give temporary relief, but at the danger of your immortal soul. You did right to come to me for this problem."

"She wasn't there. Her apprentice said he didn't know when she would be back." Ula clapped a hand over her mouth. She shouldn't have admitted seeking the herb witch's help first.

"What apprentice?"

"She's taken on the demon child."

The priest suddenly looked like a demon himself. "Does he dare lay his unholy hands on the children of the goddess?"

Ula shrugged. "He offered to treat my rash."

"Sacrilege!"

* * *

Robrek dozed in bed the next morning with the comforting presence of Ronan at his feet. While he was deciding whether to get up, he heard a knock on the door. He quickly pulled on some trousers and answered it. It was the same woman who'd come the previous morning.

"Has Mistress Myst returned?" she asked, nearly weeping from pain. Her hands and arms were redder than the previous day, and they were running with fluid.

"No, she hasn't. I can help if you'll let me."

The woman hesitated.

"Look, I know what people say about me, but I'm no demon. I heal using the same methods Mistress Myst does."

"Can you truly help? I'm likely to go mad." The woman still kept looking behind her as if contemplating fleeing.

Robrek invited her inside. She came slowly, her eyes darting around the cottage. He had her sit at Myst's table and examined the rash. "You got into Nimh weeds, didn't you? Why on earth would you use nettle juice salve on it?"

"Father Gildas gave it to me."

"And he calls me a demon?" He handed the woman a bar of soap. "You'll need to wash yourself thoroughly to get the salve off. While you're doing that, I'll make you a proper treatment for the rash. My name is Robrek."

"They call me, Ula." While she went outside to wash, Robrek put some sunflower oil in the kettle over the fire. He added Burdock root, red clover, and heartsease. Then he closed his eyes and added the ingredient that would make the mixture into a truly powerful medicine: his magic. By the time it was ready, the woman had come in from washing. He poured the ointment into a jar and brought it to the woman. Her hands and arms already looked somewhat better; the soap he'd given her also contained healing herbs and a great deal of magic. Once the ointment had had time to cool, he rubbed it into her rash. As he did so, the fear left her eyes and she sighed with pleasure.

When he was finished, she smiled broadly, displaying several missing teeth. "It doesn't itch anymore. How did you do that?"

"Unlike Father Gildas, I'm a true healer."

Ula looked away. "I gave the last of my coin to the priest. Mistress Myst always let me pay her with fresh-made bread and honey from my bees. Will you do the same?"

"I'd be happy for both."

"My eldest was getting the bread ready to bake when I left. As soon as it's ready, I'll have my boy bring you over a couple of hot loaves and a nice jar of honey." Ula smiled at him. "No matter what the priest says, you really aren't a bad sort."

* * *

Flynn Idenstamm, the king's magistrate, rode into Valley Fair on the day of the annual horse fair. He'd serviced this backwater region for six months, marking his time until a posting in a more visible and civilized region of the joined kingdoms came available. He'd have to check in with the mayor first, who conveniently also happened to be the innkeeper. The mayor would have a record of all cases that awaited his judgment, usually such things as one person complaining that his neighbor's dog ate his chicken. He sighed as he passed the village shrine on his way to stable his horse at the local inn. Unfortunately, he'd also have to pay a courtesy visit to the village's priest. His superior insisted that even though the priests had no legal authority, they had to be treated with due respect since they often wielded a lot of influence. On his two previous trips, Father Gildas had wanted him to prosecute someone the priest hadn't found sufficiently pious.

* * *

Father Gildas pursed his lips as the king's magistrate entered his office. He had hoped that, since the demon child was no longer under Angus's protection, he could use the civil authorities against him. To accomplish this, he'd also been hoping for a new magistrate. This one was far too young and uncouth to trust with such an important task, and he'd demonstrated his lack of piety in the past. It was blasphemy that this backwards land gave the clergy no choice but to trust in those that didn't owe their first allegiance to the goddess.

"Is there anything I should be aware of?" the man asked, sitting without waiting to be offered a seat.

"Yes, I'm afraid we have quite a suspicious set of circumstances. Our local herb witch has gone missing."

"The mayor mentioned that, but he didn't have any details." The magistrate flipped through his book. "The herb witch would be a woman by the name of Myst, the woman you've accused of 'selling adulterated medicines and defrauding the unenlightened'?"

Father Gildas tapped his fingers against the desk. "The woman is a heretic, but that doesn't mean her disappearance shouldn't concern us. She hasn't been seen in several weeks, and her apprentice has taken up residence in her cottage. This apprentice is a dangerous young man, and it's my fear he's done her violence in order to take her property."

"And what does the apprentice say happened to her?" the magistrate asked as he wrote in his little book.

"As far as I know, he hasn't explained himself."

The magistrate nodded noncommittally. "Who is this apprentice?"

"His name is Robbie Angusstamm." Father Gildas spat out the name.

"Robbie Angusstamm?" The priest didn't like the hint of amusement on the magistrate's face, as he flipped back through his book. "You've lodged a string of complaints against him for years. And back here, it says his father complained you wanted the boy exposed at birth."

"And so he should have been!" Father Gildas leaned toward the magistrate. "He's the child of an unholy union! His appearance clearly shows the taint of his demonic blood, and now he seeks to usurp the right of Sulis's own by using his unnatural powers to heal!" Father Gildas instantly regretted his hasty speech. Less fervently, he continued, "But it isn't for his unsanctioned healing I seek the aid of the king's officers. I fear the herb witch no longer lives."

The magistrate nodded again. "I'll admit that does sound a bit suspicious. The mayor has a list of cases that I need to hear this afternoon. I'll start my investigation this evening."

* * *

The morning of the annual Coan Horse Fair dawned bright and clear. Instead of looking forward to it as he had in the past, Robrek found himself dreading returning to the place where he'd met Milady. But if he was going to support himself, the community needed to know where they could find him.

When he reached the fairgrounds, he left Wild Thing untethered upon her promise not to bother any of the horses or humans. Carrying his staff and a bag of herbs and medicines he'd prepared, he entered the fairgrounds. A farmer immediately approached him. "Ah, demon boy. I hoped I'd find you here."

Robrek bristled under the greeting and the smell of alcohol on the man's breath. "My name is Robrek."

The man shrugged off the information. "My horse has a slight indisposition of the foot. Would you mind taking a look at it?" He gestured toward the far side of the fair grounds. Robrek went with him. They passed the stall of an herb seller who seemed to stock anything he hadn't brought with him.

Robrek swore when he saw the man's horse and staggered slightly before he could block out its pain. The horse was underweight, and its sides showed evidence of frequent whipping. But neither of these were the animal's major problem. The horse had lost a shoe and had been ridden in that condition over rough roads. The hoof was split, cracked, and bleeding. "What in the seven hells did you think you were doing riding on a hoof like that?" Robrek demanded.

"Had to get here somehow. Too far to walk, isn't it? She made a right fuss, too."

"Any horse in this condition would make a fuss," Robrek snapped. The horse bared its teeth as he approached. Robrek reached out with his mind and calmed the horse. He touched the animal's leg and blocked its pain. Robrek knew he could use his gift to heal all of the damage, as he'd healed Roberta's leg, but he noticed other farmers gathering around and hoped some of them might have animals in need of attention. He also didn't want to exhaust himself in a place where he might need to defend himself. So he sent the farmer for hot water, clean rags, and some herbs. When the farmer returned, Robrek mixed calendula and comfrey in the warm water, adding his magic to increase its potency. He divided the remaining magically enhanced herbs into three different pouches. He told the man he needed to get fresh hot water every hour for three hours, mix it with the herbs in one of the pouches, and keep the horse's hoof soaking in the mixture. "After the herbs have a chance to do their job, I'll come back to complete the treatment."

"Why, thank you, demon boy." As Robrek turned from the drunken farmer, another man nervously approached.

* * *

After treating about a dozen animals with varying illnesses, Robrek returned to the horse with the cracked hoof. Most of the ailing animals had been treatable with herbs, so he'd expended only a small amount of his healing energy. This was fortunate because the farmer hadn't followed his instructions. Nor was he around. A small boy, probably no more than five, was in charge of the horse. The horse's hoof was still soaking in the original herb mixture, which was now filthy. The pouches of herbs he'd prepared were gone. Not surprisingly, the hoof looked worse. "What happened to the other herbs?"

The boy cringed and began to sob. "My pa said he was thirsty. He'll beat me if the hoof isn't better when he gets back."

Robrek remembered himself at that age, being forced to remove his shirt and climb on the dining room table. His legs hadn't reached the ground. Boyden had held his wrists tightly against the table, as his father beat him nearly senseless, all because he'd thrown rotten fruit at the priest who'd driven him from the school. He'd hardly been able to move for two days.

Robrek ruffled the child's hair and assured him he could help. Robrek was hungry, and the boy looked awfully thin, so he sent the boy with a coin for six of Mistress Duffal's meat pies. When the boy left, Robrek entered a healing trance. Everything disappeared around him, and he became one with the injury. He killed the infection, eliminated the swelling, and melded the tissues of the hoof back together. A rush of pleasure filled his body. *How could I ever have believed that something that feels this good was evil?*

When he emerged from his trance, he was tired, but not to the point of collapse. The boy was staring at him with wide, wondering eyes, all six pies untouched before him. "How did you do that, mister?"

Robrek basked in the child's admiration. "I'm an amihealer. It's a gift from the goddess."

The boy nodded, as if this made perfect sense. "My pa said you was a demon, but my ma says my pa lies a lot." The boy handed him all the pies. Cursing himself for assuming the boy would know half were meant for him, Robrek quickly returned three of the pies and bid the boy eat. The boy bit into one hungrily.

"I'm Robrek. What's your name?"

"Tegan." The boy looked at his feet and barely whispered. When the pies were gone, he noticed the boy's lip start to quiver.

"What's wrong? If you're still hungry, we can get more."

The boy began to sob. "I'm a lousy, good-for-nothing, low-down thief." He reached into his pocket and pulled out two drams—the change from the pies. The boy gave them to him and began to sob harder. Through his sobs, the boy told Robrek how his mother had been sick all winter, and he and his father had come to the fair to sell one of their goats to get medicine for her, but the boy's father had gotten too thirsty and had drunk away all the money they'd gotten for the goat. "I don't want to be a thief, Master Robrek, but my ma's going to die, and nobody will love me."

Like no one ever loved me. Robrek put his arm around the boy. "If there's anything I can do about it, your ma's not going to die. Tell me what's wrong with her."

Hiccupping with diminishing tears, Tegan described the illness. By the time he was done, Robrek was pretty sure he knew what was wrong and which treatment would help. He went to the herb seller's booth to purchase the supplies he needed. As he approached, he saw the herb seller holding the pouches he'd made for the horse's foot and talking to a male customer. "No, I can't accept less than five tetras for them. The demon boy himself imbued them with the powers of the infernal realm." Both the herb seller and her customer caught sight of him. They froze, and their eyes darted around as if looking for an escape.

"My magic comes from the goddess, not the seven hells!"

"From the goddess?" The man looked very doubtful, but he handed five tetras to the herb seller and disappeared as soon as possible.

The herb seller bit her lip and took a step backwards. Ignoring her, he selected the items he needed. The herb seller calmed when he made no move to blast her into dust. "I'll give you those free of charge if you'll make up some more pouches for me," she said.

"You expect me to help you make money while you tell lies about me?" Robrek gave her a coin and walked away.

He was fuming as he returned to Tegan. He combined the herbs into different pouches, but found himself blocked as he tried to add healing magic. Tegan beamed at him. "These will make my ma well, right, Master Robrek?"

Tegan's trust salved his anger. No other child should suffer as he had. He closed his eyes and shifted his anger aside. It wasn't easy, but he was able to add his magic to the herbs. "I can't promise, but I hope they will."

"Thank you, Master Robrek." Tegan threw his small arms round Robrek's neck. "But what if my pa gets thirsty again?"

He hugged the boy back. "I'll make sure he doesn't."

He released the boy, picked up his staff, and headed for the stalls that sold alcohol. On the way, he bought a small dagger. Through the crowd, he caught sight of the drunken farmer. Robrek walked up to him, grabbed him by the back of the shirt, and hauled him into the alleyway between two of the stalls. He slammed the bigger man against the side of one.

The drunken man laughed. "I'm sorry, demon boy. You won't get a dram off me. I've already drunk everything I had."

"I haven't come for payment, old man. I've come to ensure the medicines I have provided for your wife will get to her." He drew out his new dagger.

The farmer paled. "Now, look here. Those cursed with demon blood can't just go about threatening children of the goddess."

"Cursed with demon blood? Or possessing demon blood with the power to curse?" Robrek pulled up his own sleeve and cut his forearm.

"No!" the man screamed and tried to wriggle free, but Robrek held him firm.

Robrek allowed the blood to fall on the man's groin. "If the medicines I've given your son do not reach your wife and stay in her hands, I curse you by this blood that your testicles will shrivel up and fall off."

"No! Please, get it off me!"

Robrek bled on each of the man's hands. "By this blood, I curse you that if you ever raise your hand in violence to either your wife or your son, the hand that strikes them will rot. I seal this curse with my blood." He wiped his bleeding arm along the man's forehead and let the man go. The man fled unsteadily in the direction of the stream.

Only after the man disappeared did Robrek notice a crowd had gathered. Fear covered all their faces, and many drew the star of Sulis over their breasts. Robrek wondered if he'd just done something extremely foolish.

He made his way quickly toward Wild Thing. The mare looked with concern at his bleeding arm. "It's okay," he assured her. "I did it to myself."

:*Why cut self?*:

"Because I was trying to help a boy and because I'm an idiot," he said as he swung into the saddle. As he rode off into the dark, he heard music start up. He ached with loneliness for the one woman who didn't think he was a demon.

Milady, where are you tonight?

* * *

Flynn Idenstamm rode out of Valley Fair in the direction of the herb witch's cottage early the next morning. He'd paid the place an initial visit the day before, but the apprentice hadn't been at home when he'd come calling. He'd later found out that the young man had been at the horse fair creating quite a scene. At first Flynn hadn't believed the story, but it got repeated by an increasing number of people who claimed to have seen the apprentice cut his arm and curse a man with his blood.

Bleeding on a man didn't seem to violate any of the king's laws, but it did add to the already suspicious circumstances concerning the disappearance of the herb witch. The magistrate hoped he wouldn't be forced to order another hanging.

* * *

Robrek was awakened early by loud knocking. "Demon child! We know you're in there! Open up!" Ronan jumped off the bed and scurried underneath it. Recognizing Dillion's voice, Robrek tensed, and from the sounds of things, he wasn't alone. *Why in the seven hells did I do something so stupid?* He grabbed his staff and wondered if he should jump through one of the back windows and run for it. Before he could make a decision, someone kicked the door open, and Dillion and a dozen other men spilled into the herb witch's cottage. Robbie backed against the wall, knowing he could never fight them all.

Dillion looked at the other men. "He won't escape what's coming to him this time, boys."

"Halt in the king's name!" An unfamiliar man, wearing the red and gold uniform of the king's magistrates, shoved his way to the front of the crowd. "I'm Flynn Idenstamm, the king's magistrate. If the apprentice is guilty, he'll answer for it. But his fate will not to be decided by a mob."

The men in the cottage muttered angrily. "He's a demon!" Dillion insisted.

The magistrate held up a hand to placate him. "I'll handle it." Robrek wasn't sure if he was any better off in the magistrate's hands. Had what he had done at the horse fair been illegal?

The magistrate faced him. "Now, son, I've heard several suspicious reports concerning you." Robrek was slightly irritated at the man calling him "son"; the magistrate wasn't more than ten years older. Robrek offered the magistrate a chair, but remained standing himself. They wouldn't take him without a fight.

"The first thing we need to discuss is the events at the horse fair last night."

"I hurt no one," Robrek said.

Dillion grabbed the back of the magistrate's chair. "He called down a demonic curse on a poor innocent farmer!"

The magistrate glared at Dillion. "I'll handle the questioning." The magistrate turned back to Robrek. "I've heard dozens of reports of the incident, and now I want to hear one from you. Did you curse a man with your blood?"

Robrek shifted his weight and looked at his feet. "It's not as simple as that."

"Have him roll up his sleeve, and see the evidence for yourself!" Dillion yelled. "I saw him do it with my own eyes!"

The magistrate rounded on Dillion. "I've warned you. You'll remain silent or be thrown out." Despite his relative youth, Flynn Idenstamm had a sense of authority that commanded respect, and Dillion backed off, although he did continue to mutter. The magistrate turned back to Robrek. "Did you or did you not curse the man?"

Robrek pounded his staff into the floor and gritted his teeth. "Yes, I cut myself and bled on the drunken brute, but I didn't hurt him. I can't put curses on people, but I had to do something to protect the boy and his mother."

While the crowd muttered angrily, the magistrate got out a quill and ink, and made some notations in his book. "Just how does bleeding on someone protect anyone?"

"He abused his horse, his son, and his wife. I wanted to stop him, and I thought that if he was afraid of me, he might. It was the only thing I could think of." Not expecting the magistrate to believe him, Robrek glanced at the back window planning how he could escape through it.

"Go on, son. I'm listening." Flynn paused with his quill poised above his book.

Robrek started at the beginning and told all about the horse with the cracked hoof.

Flynn Idenstamm's face darkened and his eyebrow drew together as Robrek finished.

"I didn't want this child to lose the one good thing in his life. What in the seven hells is so wrong with that?"

The magistrate nodded, his face softening. "While it certainly wasn't wise, I don't see that you've violated any law. It was yourself you cut and not the other man. I believe that clears up my *first* concern."

"Like hell it does!" Dillion raised his fist into the air. "We'll allow his kind among us no longer!"

The magistrate got slowly to his feet and drew his sword. He pointed it at Dillion. "You've interrupted this interrogation for the last time. You'll leave now, or be arrested not only for obstructing the king's justice, but also for inciting a riot and trespassing."

Robrek tightened his hold on his staff, but one of the men near Dillion touched him on the arm and whispered, "Dill, we'll see justice done."

After Dillion left, Flynn addressed the mob. "Anyone else that can't hold their tongue is free to leave as well." The crowd stared back at him in stony silence. "Good," he said. He sheaved his sword and sat down again. "As I was saying, that resolves my *first* concern. There's still the whereabouts of your mistress we need to discuss."

"I don't know where Mistress Myst is. She left with nothing more than a note nearly a month ago, and I haven't heard from her since."

"Might you still have this note?" The magistrate again lifted an eyebrow.

Glad he'd kept it, Robrek crossed to the bookshelf and fished out the note. He handed it to the magistrate.

Flynn Idenstamm read over the vague note. "Do you have any idea who might have called her?"

"No, I'm worried about her."

The apprentice did look genuinely concerned. Besides, Flynn had started to warm to him. What he'd done at the horse fair might have been stupid, but it showed compassion, to say nothing of courage. "Do you have anything written by the herb witch to compare the handwriting to?"

"Yes," Robrek said. He crossed to the shelves and pulled out a couple of volumes and slammed them down on the table in front of him. "Mistress Myst keeps notes on all her treatments. She has journals going back for nearly fifty years."

Flynn carefully compared the note to the volumes. The same person had certainly written them, and he doubted the apprentice would have gone to such effort to forge all of them. "And you swear you had nothing to do with her disappearance? Father Gildas has made accusations against you."

"Father Gildas!" The young man laughed without humor. "He's been trying to get me killed since the day I was born. He didn't like my father marrying a foreigner. Now he doesn't like the fact I'm a better healer than he is." The apprentice looked away. "Mistress Myst is my friend and my teacher. She's the closest thing I've ever had to a mother. I'd never do anything to harm her."

Flynn noticed the apprentice struggling not to cry. *No one is that good an actor.* "I'll tell the priest I see no evidence of guilt, and I'll see if I can find anything out about Mistress Myst on my circuit."

He got up and turned to face the mob. "It's the judgment of the king's magistrate that the herb witch's apprentice, Robrek Angusstamm, has violated no law. Any action taken against this innocent man would be answerable to the king. I advise you all to return to your houses or be arrested for trespassing." There was some muttering, but the men started drifting away. Eventually, all the men left, and he was alone with the herb witch's apprentice.

The young man sighed and sat down for the first time. He seemed to collapse from within. "I was afraid they were going to kill me."

"If I hadn't been here, I think they would have. Listen to me, son. Though you've violated no law and the herb witch's note gives you every right to stay in her cottage, I'm not sure that's best for you. If the people choose to take the law into their own hands, I'll do my best to see that justice is served. But justice won't bring you back to life if they hang you from a tree. Take my advice, and get out of here while you still can."

As soon as the magistrate left, Robrek put his head in his hands. Ronan climbed out from under the bed and hopped up on the table next to him. The cat butted his head against Robrek's hand, but Robrek ignored it. He sat there without moving for several minutes. Then he jumped abruptly to his feet and went to saddle Wild Thing. He had to make the bronze horse see reason.

When he reached the stable, he jumped off of Wild Thing's back and faced Brazen. "I know you wanted me to stay, but I can't. This destiny of mine you're so fond of won't do me much good if I'm dead."

The force of the thoughts coming from the horse nearly brought him to his knees. *:You must stay.:*

"There's no 'must' about it. Damn it, Brazen. I'm not a child any more, and what you're asking me doesn't make sense. I'm not staying."

:You must stay. Soon you will know why.:

Robrek turned away and mounted Wild Thing. "If I die because of this, I'll haunt you until the end of time."

CHAPTER 20

Awakening with the sun shining on her face, Samantha was certain her father had had time to calm down now and would be able to see reason. She got dressed, but before she could send a page requesting an audience, Blaine entered, followed by Darhour. "Your Highness, there's a novice asking to see you," Blaine said. "She won't state her name or her business, but insists it's important."

"She?" Samantha asked, knowing all Lundian clergy were male.

"Yes, Your Highness, a young girl. At least, her body is young. Her eyes are as old as the Setanta Forest, so to speak."

When the novice entered, Kailen trailed behind her with his hand on his sword. The novice looked quite young--about fifteen, the age Samantha's mother had died. Although she couldn't say quite what, something about the young novice reminded her of the portrait of her mother in the Royal Gallery. The novice wore long, flowing white robes, and her hair was confined in hundreds of small braids, as was the fashion among the Korthian clergy. But hers were the eyes of a very old and very wise woman, which gave Samantha the bizarre impression that her other, youthful features were merely an illusion. The girl bowed. "Your Highness, my mistress sends her greetings." Samantha asked her to be seated and offered refreshments. "No, thank you, Your Highness. My mistress bids you to accompany me to her temple so she may provide you the Holy Mother's guidance."

"Your Highness, a mere priestess does not summon the crown princess." Darhour's growled. "If she has something to say to you, she should request an audience with you here at the palace."

"My mistress has her reasons. She said if you had any doubts, I was to touch you." As the novice reached toward Samantha, Darhour leaped forward and caught the novice's wrist. Kailen drew his sword and pointed it at her breast.

Samantha jumped back in alarm. "What in the seven hells are you two doing?"

"You can't allow her to touch you!" Darhour protested. "She may have a poisoned needle."

The novice looked at Darhour with her wise, old eyes, far too calm for a girl with a sword at her heart. "You're free to search me. The princess must be protected at all costs. She is the only hope for our people."

Darhour's scowl deepened. "Your Highness, do not allow her to touch you."

Darhour did have a point, and he'd been right about Argblutal. Still, Samantha felt as if the Holy Mother herself were looking through the novice's eyes. "You may check her however you feel necessary, but I will touch her."

Darhour's nostrils flared, but he didn't argue. Instead, he felt carefully over every inch of the novice's hand. Finding nothing, he turned to Kailen. "If she so much as twitches, run her through."

Darhour extended the novice's hand toward her. When Samantha touched it, the novice's aura exploded around her—a brilliant white. Peace and light flowed from the novice. "We'll accompany her at once," she panted. "Release her."

Darhour flung the novice's hand away. "Your Highness, this is madness! I won't allow you to be led into a trap!"

Samantha stood and looked Darhour in the eyes. "Darhour, do you owe me your allegiance or not?"

Darhour loomed over her, his scars standing out sharply in the light of the room. "My allegiance demands I protect you from all dangers. I will not allow this!"

Samantha stepped around Darhour and pushed Kailen's sword aside. "I will accompany her," she said coldly. "I'll allow you to come, if you desire, but you won't stop me."

Darhour clenched his fists as if he were thinking of strangling her. "I beg you, Your Highness. Don't do this." Samantha merely took the novice's hand and held it in her own. He sighed. "You must go in disguise. Borrow one of your maid's dresses, and we'll arrange for inconspicuous horses."

"Ardra," Samantha called to her maid. "Fetch me your plainest dress, if you don't mind." She turned back to Darhour. "We'll go as soon as I've changed."

* * *

When Samantha emerged from her bedchamber, she was dressed in Ardra's dress with a peasant scarf over her hair. Kailen was guarding the novice. He had removed his surcoat with her colors on it. "Where's Darhour?" she asked.

"The captain's making arrangements, Your Highness." He glared at the novice, making it clear he, too, thought she was making a mistake.

A short time later, Darhour returned, having also removed her colors. "All is in readiness, Your Highness." When the novice rose, Darhour grabbed her arm. "If any harm befalls Her Highness, I will personally rend you limb from limb."

The novice met his eyes with complete serenity. "As I've told you, the princess is the only hope for our people."

At the door of her rooms, Brice and Phelan, also stripped of her colors, awaited them. Darhour led the way into the servants' corridors so they could sneak out of the palace. They exited through a little used servants' entrance and left the grounds through the small garden gate where Bearach and Conroy awaited with the horses. Bearach had his bow out and an arrow nocked.

Darhour placed the novice on the saddle in front of Kailen. Samantha saw him whisper to Kailen. Samantha was certain that if anything happened, the novice would die instantly. She was even more sure that nothing would. Kailen, with the novice, and Bearach took the lead. Darhour let them get several yards ahead before he allowed her to proceed, flanked by himself and Conroy. Phelan and Brice fell in some paces behind. They rode in silence through the city streets and down to the docks. When the novice directed them to a small fishing boat, Darhour again objected. "Your Highness, you can't know where she's taking us."

Ignoring him, Samantha stepped in. Her guard had no choice but to follow. They sailed far out into the harbor, and the novice directed the craft expertly through the dangerous reefs. After they left the harbor, the novice sailed the craft up the coast. When Samantha caught sight of a small wooded island, she gaped in surprise. She'd sailed up and down the coast many times and never noticed this island. She looked at her men and noticed Conroy's mouth was hanging open. He drew the star of Sulis over his breast. The novice steered to a simple dock and jumped out to tie up the boat.

Four of her guards disembarked and fanned out to check the area. Only when they were sure it was safe did Darhour allow Samantha to disembark. The novice pointed to a path that Samantha would have sworn hadn't been there when they'd landed. From the expression on Darhour's face, he hadn't seen it either. "The shrine is in that direction. Simply stay on the path. I'll remain with the boat."

Darhour whispered in the princess's ear. "I don't like it, Your Highness."

Samantha ignored him again and forged up the path. Her guards surrounded her. After only a few minutes, they reached a small shrine. A priestess emerged. Like the young novice, the priestess wore long, flowing robes of sparkling white. Her blonde hair was streaked with gray and braided into hundreds of small braids. Her face was smooth and unwrinkled, but it seemed as if all the ages of the earth looked through her eyes. "She who seeks the goddess's aid, come now," the priestess said in a calm, clear voice. "Your men may accompany you. The goddess would have no secrets between you and them. This is a holy place, however, and their weapons must remain outside."

Darhour started to protest, but when the priestess looked at him, he felt a jolt of raw power, as if his insides were being scoured with light. He knew this priestess spoke for the goddess. He nodded to his men and began to remove his own weapons. The priestess smiled. "All of your weapons." Somehow, Darhour wasn't surprised she knew he'd planned on keeping his hidden knives.

Soon there was a pile of weapons outside the door. After looking each man in the eyes, the priestess nodded and disappeared inside.

The building was furnished with wooden benches and a small wooden altar, lacking all the pomp and grandeur that typified the temples in the capital. Yet the small building was imbued with a spirit that was loving, comforting, and awe-inspiring. Samantha gave in to a compulsion to remove her shoes. Barefoot, she stepped forward. Except for the priestess, who knelt near the altar, the shrine was empty.

Samantha walked forward and knelt at the priestess's side. Her men knelt behind her. The princess closed her eyes, feeling welcomed and loved. She could have knelt forever in that peace.

Some time later the priestess addressed her. "Samantha, my child, you are deeply troubled. The weight of the future of this land rests on shoulders too young to bear such a burden. The goddess will not leave you to carry the weight alone."

Samantha's hands shook as she laid them on the altar. "But should I . . .? Is it right for me . . .?"

The priestess touched her arm gently. "You have been plagued with doubts since you discovered the king isn't your true father. The goddess judges not by the blood that runs through one's veins, but by the heart which strives to serve her. It is her will that you should reign."

Samantha burst into tears of relief, all misgivings dissipating in an instant. As she cried, Samantha felt arms of love wrap themselves around her, but they weren't the physical arms of the priestess—Samantha knew the Holy Mother herself was present.

Before addressing her again, the priestess allowed her to cry herself out. "You have also been troubled by the choice of one to reign beside you. None of those who flock to you are pleasing to Sulis. In time, the goddess's choice will appear before you, and when he kneels at your feet, you will know. Until that time, you must wait and believe in the goddess's promises."

"But my father?"

"The king has ruled this people well. But evil men work upon his heart and mind. He will oppose you, but you must stand strong." The priestess brushed Samantha's hair back from her face. "My child, dark times are ahead for you. You must guard against hatred and the desire for revenge. Does not the Writ say, 'Avenge not yourselves, but leave it to the wrath of the goddess. Vengeance is mine'? My child, do you know why Sulis reserves vengeance unto herself?"

Samantha shook her head.

"Because the one dedicated to vengeance twists and mangles her own soul, and the Holy Mother will not see her children destroy themselves. Sulis seeks a better life for you. The goddess will walk the path beside you, and your friends will stay true to you when many turn against you. Sulis has provided you the six who accompany you here. At the palace are three more who have dedicated themselves to your service."

Samantha knew she meant Blaine and her maids.

"You will need their aid, so you must trust them. Take comfort in the goddess, my child."

The priestess touched the princess, causing light, peace, and love to flow into her until Samantha was certain her body would burst into flames, and her soul fly free Beyond the Far Mountain. She felt no fear of death. Reunion with the goddess would bring the purest joy. Her frame shook until she was no longer able to bear such close contact with the divine, and she sank into unconsciousness.

As Darhour watched his daughter and the priestess, he felt as if he'd been doused in an acid bath that had burned away his impurities, but also had stripped him of his strength. He gazed in awe at Samantha. How had she known the novice would lead them into the goddess's presence? Was his daughter one of what the Saloynans called "the god-touched"? He briefly panicked as the priestess revealed the king wasn't Samantha's true father, but the spirit in the shrine calmed him. When the princess sunk to the ground, he wanted to rush to her assistance, but the goddess's presence kept him firmly on his knees.

The priestess got up and turned to face the princess's guards. She looked each man in the eye, and Darhour shook even more violently. "As you have all heard, the king's blood does not run in her veins. However, the Princess Samantha is the goddess's choice to rule when the present king passes Beyond the Far Mountain. You have all sworn an oath to the princess. This, the Holy Mother asks you to renew here today, as you kneel at her sacred altar, and you will uphold it with no thought to your lives. Some of you will travel

Beyond the Far Mountain before the princess takes the throne, but if you keep your oath, you will be welcomed into the Mother's loving arms."

The priestess touched Darhour's face. At her touch, his trembling immediately stopped, and he felt satiated with love and light. "Do you, Darhour, swear your loyalty to the goddess and the princess? And will you sacrifice your life and honor in the eyes of the world to her protection?"

A shiver went through Darhour's frame. *How does she know my name?* Despite his shock, his voice was firm and steady as he replied, "By the goddess and on my mother's grave, I so swear."

The priestess smiled and moved to the next guard. She touched his face. "Do you, Kailen, swear your loyalty to the goddess and the princess? And will you sacrifice your life and honor in the eyes of the world to her protection?" Tears were streaming down Kailen's face as he swore.

The priestess moved down the line of guards, touching each one, calling him by name, and asking for his oath. By the time she'd accepted Phelan's mute oath, all of their faces were stained with tears.

The priestess smiled. "The goddess is pleased with you. Remember, her arm carries the strength of nations and never falters. Go forth with her blessing."

The men arose, wiping their eyes. Darhour gathered the princess in his arms. The priestess touched his arm and whispered so only he could hear. "She will have a special need for her father."

Darhour nodded. "I'm sure the king—"

"I wasn't referring to the king."

* * *

Count Nola walked through the corridors of the duke's private residence to answer the duke's summons for his daughter. Somehow, he'd make the duke answer for what had happened.

When he was ushered into the duke's office, Nola found him behind his desk reading a letter. The duke turned the letter over before facing him. "I asked for Lady Shela."

"My daughter hanged herself last night." Nola stared into the cold eyes of the duke. "My countess wants me to call you out over it."

The duke laughed. "She wants to be a widow? Why would the good Countess Birkita lay this at *my* feet?"

"Shela hasn't been the same since Mabon. Birkita insists you forced yourself on her."

The duke stroked the pendant at his neck. "I assure you I had no need to use force. She was distressed because she didn't want to marry Weylin. She stuck her ample breasts in my face and promised to make it worth my while if I helped change your mind. I took what was offered, although I made sure she came to regret it. But if you want to call me out over a slut, feel free."

The duke might be lying, but Nola had seen how Shela threw her breasts into men's faces. *Damn you, Shela!* "Well, then . . ." Nola trailed off, unsure of how to extricate himself from the situation.

The duke smiled icily. "Your daughter has cost me the easiest means of claiming the throne. Since she is dead, who should pay for this? If someone else takes the throne, my vengeance won't be sated until your entire house has traveled on to meet your daughter."

Nola trembled. "Your Grace, I've always been loyal to your cause. What would you have me do?"

* * *

King Solar looked from the High Priest Shylah to Duke Argblutal. *What are these men doing in my rooms?*

"Drink up, Your Majesty." The high priest put a goblet of some purple liquid into his hand.

No, I'm not drinking anything you give me. Despite his internal protest, the king watched himself raise the goblet and drink. It had a sickly sweet flavor, and after he'd finished it, he felt a strange, pleasant floating feeling. *There's no reason to be concerned. Everything is well,* a small voice inside his head seemed to say.

The duke was speaking. "Did Her Highness tell you why she changed her mind?"

Solar looked at the duke. *Why would he ask me such a question? Why would I answer?* The king found his mouth opening. "She said you were a monster."

The duke leaned over his chair in a manner that violated the respect of his person, but Solar found himself unable to object. "She lies. She needs to be taught responsibility. You won't allow her to participate in any gathering of importance until she repents of her foolishness and retracts her lies."

The king frowned. This didn't seem right. "But Caedmon thinks I should marry her to Lord Devyn."

"Caedmon doesn't know his place. For the good of the joined kingdoms, he must return to his own estates. You need a chancellor such as I, one aware of the loyalty he owes his monarch."

The king nodded, wondering why it'd taken so long to notice. *I should let her choose, as I've always promised I would.*

When Argblutal and Shylah left, the king stared at his tapestry on the wall. Britomartus, his second wife, had woven it, and it had always been his favorite. It depicted a heron drinking from a fountain, surrounded by blue, red, and yellow flowers.

* * *

Samantha awoke warm and comfortable in her bed with no memory of the trip home. The peace and love she'd felt in the temple lingered. She smiled as she looked out the windows at the palace grounds. *I don't have to marry any of the fools at court! It's the will of the goddess!* Still, the priestess had announced her illegitimacy in front of her guard. How had they taken it? As her maids dressed her, she asked them to summon her entire guard. "And Blaine as well," she decided. The priestess had told her that she must trust her people.

Within a few moments, they were all assembled. Brice and Phelan were fighting yawns. Her maids moved to retire, but she signaled for them to remain. "Your Highness," Darhour said. "I have grave news."

"It will wait." She faced all of those assembled. "As most of you learned yesterday at the shrine, I am not the king's true daughter. My mother had an affair, and the king chose to ignore it and accept me as his own." Blaine and her maids looked shocked, and Darhour opened his mouth, but Samantha silenced him with a look. "I discovered this last summer when I learned that the colorful glows I see are called auras and that an aurora has to be of mixed blood. I need to know if my bastardry makes a difference to you."

Darhour's eyes shined as he looked at her. "I can speak for your guard. Last night, each one of us renewed our sacred vow to you before Sulis's holy altar. You are our queen." The rest of her guard looked at her as if she were the goddess herself.

She turned to Ardra and Malvina. "Your Highness don't be thinking this could make any difference to us, do you?" Ardra said.

Malvina nodded fervently. "We've served the princess, and we'll be serving the queen."

When she turned to Blaine, he pulled up the sleeve of his scholar's robes to reveal a scar across his forearm. "When the captain doubted my loyalty, I vowed by the goddess and on my mother's grave. I sanctified that vow by an exchange of blood. I'll do so again today if anyone still doubts me." He glanced at Darhour.

The princess felt as if the weight holding her down had been released. Surely, with her people behind her, she needn't fear. "Darhour, you mentioned news?"

Darhour nodded grimly. "Your Highness, Lady Shela hanged herself the night before last. Her maids found her body yesterday morning."

Samantha gasped. "Holy Sulis, this is my fault! I should have made her tell me what happened and protected her."

"Go to the king, inform him," Darhour said. "He will see to it Argblutal is dealt with."

Samantha turned to Blaine. "Blaine, request an audience with my father. Tell him it's urgent."

* * *

Duke Caedmon sat with the king in his private quarters. He was trying to discuss Lord Devyn, but the king kept staring at his tapestry. Gilroy entered and announced the princess's secretary was requesting an audience. "This may be an ideal opportunity to mention Lord Devyn to Her Highness, Your Majesty."

Solar nodded to Gilroy. "Send him in."

The princess's secretary scurried into the room and went down on one knee. The boy looked ridiculously young, and he was sweating profusely. "Your Majesty, Her Highness, the Princess Samantha, requests an audience with you at your earliest convenience. She said to tell you it's urgent."

"Has she chosen her consort?" Solar asked.

Caedmon looked askance at the king. *Why would he ask such a question?*

Blaine blanched. "I'm sorry, Your Majesty. She confided no such thing to me. She merely asked me to request an audience."

The next thing that came out of Solar's mouth made Caedmon wonder if Solar was drunk, a state he'd never witnessed in the great king. "You may tell Her Highness she should use the freedom from attending council meetings and court today to consider her most important duty. Tell her I expect her to bring me the name this evening." He nodded a dismissal. When Blaine hesitated, the king nodded to his guards. "Get rid of him."

The boy's eyes widened, and he rapidly fled the room.

Caedmon cleared his throat. "Your Majesty, I must admit I'm confused. You've never refused Her Highness an audience, and I thought we agreed to promote Devyn as her consort."

The king's eyes narrowed. "Did we ask for your opinion?"

"Your Majesty, have I offended you?"

"We have been too permissive, and those under us have begun to think they have the right to question our decisions. That ends today. You will remove yourself to your estates immediately."

Caedmon gaped at the king. "Surely you aren't banishing me from court, Your Majesty?"

"We are."

"Your Majesty, what have I done to warrant—"

"We said you will leave immediately. Guards!" the king bellowed, and his guards snapped to attention. "Escort Duke Caedmon to his quarters so he may begin packing."

"But, Your Majesty, certainly—"

The king ignored him. "See he has left the palace before nightfall." The king nodded to the guards, and Caedmon had no choice but to accompany them.

* * *

When Blaine returned, he was trembling and wouldn't meet her gaze. "When will my father see me?" she asked.

"Y-y-your Highness, he refused to see you until, until . . ."

"Until when?"

"Until this evening. He said you should use your freedom from attending council and court today to think about your consort. He wants you to bring him the name this evening."

"What in the seven hells did he mean by my 'freedom from council and court'?"

"I believe he meant you shouldn't attend. Sh-should I go back and ask him?" Blaine looked like he devoutly wished she would say no.

She growled in frustration. "I'll just wait; by this evening, he should have calmed down. Attend council and court in my place. Bring me word of anything of note."

Blaine paled. "Of course, Your Highness."

After Blaine left, the princess started pacing. *What in the seven hells is my father up to? This isn't like him.* Samantha took a book off her shelf and tried to read, but found herself reading the same sentence three times without having the slightest idea what it said. She slammed the book closed and returned to pacing.

After Samantha paced for what felt like an eternity, Blaine returned, accompanied by Darhour. Darhour looked ready to slit someone's throat, and Blaine looked even worse than he had earlier.

"What's happened?" she asked.

Blaine drew the goddess's star across his breast. "Holy Sulis protect us all! When it rains, it pours, so to speak. First, the king has banished Duke Caedmon to his estates."

"That's absurd!" Samantha snapped. "Have you been chewing paipan leaves?"

Blaine put his hand over his heart as if she'd stabbed him.

"I'm afraid it's true, Your Highness," Darhour said.

She stared from Darhour to Blaine, hoping one of them would explain why they were lying to her. When neither did, she pointed accusingly at Darhour. "Caedmon has served as my father's chancellor for nearly twenty years, and his father was chancellor before him. Caedmon is my father's closest friend. Tell me what reason he could possibly have to banish Caedmon."

"I believe it would be better if Blaine were to finish his report first."

Blaine gulped. "Count Ultan has been appointed to the empty seat on the council."

"But he's a Lundian!"

Blaine nodded vigorously. "I know, but he was sitting right there in the council meeting, as plain as day, so to speak."

Samantha massaged her temples. "That would disrupt the balance between Korthians and Lundians on the council for the first time in my father's sixty-five year rule. My father wouldn't do that. He has lectured me countless times on the dangers of showing favoritism."

"And . . . er . . ." Blaine seemed to be having trouble with his tongue.

"There can't possibly be more."

Blaine nodded. "H-he appointed Argblutal chancellor."

"Have you gone stark raving mad?"

"The news is indeed disturbing," Darhour said. "But I'm afraid it is true."

Samantha felt dizzy and collapsed into a chair. "But I told him Argblutal was a monster." She looked from one of her men to the other; they were so different they couldn't possibly be suffering from the same delusion. "Darhour, you said you knew why my father banished Caedmon."

Darhour glared at Blaine, who took the hint. "I-I have things to do elsewhere, don't I?" Blaine stammered and left.

Darhour sat across from her. He didn't seem at all the fierce warrior who'd sent Blaine running, but the compassionate man no one else saw in him. "Caedmon objected to the king's refusal to see you this morning."

"And . . .?"

Darhour sighed. "His Majesty banished the duke."

"My father wouldn't banish him for that."

"All my sources attest to it."

"What sources?" Samantha asked, feeling as though she'd woken up in a different reality.

"Your Highness, under King Frare I developed certain skills that were useful in gathering information." Darhour hesitated. "I've been acting on your behalf, but without your knowledge or permission."

"You were a spy?" Samantha shook her head, begging Darhour to begin talking sense.

"In a manner of speaking, yes, and I have established a network of informants to update me on anything that might affect Your Highness's safety. I should have asked your permission. I'm afraid I'd grown used to seeing you as a child. I assure you it won't happen again."

"How good are you at spying?" Samantha asked.

"In all honesty, Your Highness, I'm very good."

"Find out what's going on. Help me make sense of this." A cold chill seized her heart. "What if he tries to force me to marry Argblutal?"

"I will never permit that, Your Highness."

"And how could you stop it?"

"I was also Frare's assassin."

Now Samantha was certain the world had gone mad. Darhour—her friend—offering to commit murder on her behalf? But looking into his eyes, she could doubt neither his willingness nor his ability.

* * *

As evening fell, Samantha and her guards made their way to the king's rooms. When she arrived, Gilroy bowed. "Your Highness, His Majesty has instructed me to ask for the name your consort."

"I'll discuss the matter with the king."

Gilroy placed his hands together. "With all due respect, Your Highness, His Majesty instructed me that before allowing you to enter, you must present me with the name of your consort."

"We'll see about that!" She made for the doors into the king's inner chambers. The king's guards blocked her. "Get out of my way!" she ordered. "I will speak to my father."

"We're sorry, Your Highness," one of the guards answered. "But we have been instructed not to allow you to enter unless you have complied with the orders he gave Master Gilroy."

She rounded on Gilroy. "Tell the king I have a matter of great importance to discuss with him."

Gilroy shook his head. "I've been instructed to convey no message but the name of your consort."

Samantha gaped at Gilroy. Her father wouldn't act like this, but she could see no way of getting past them, except to have her guards fight her way in. While she was relatively certain they'd succeed, someone would probably get killed. She glared at Gilroy. "Tell my father I must speak with him in the morning. Tell him there are matters that can't wait." With all the dignity she could muster, she swept out.

Darhour and Kailen followed her back inside her rooms. Samantha collapsed onto a sofa and stared at her bodyguards. "What's going on?"

"Your Highness, I will find out," Darhour said.

When they left, she sat staring at nothing. *Surely, he'll talk to me in the morning.*

* * *

Herne chewed a paipin leaf as he sneaked into the library in the dead of night. His brother hated him using the stuff. *Damn him! If he didn't make impossible demands, I wouldn't need it. If the entire court claims there's only one way into the princess's rooms, why in the seven hells does he think there might be another one?* He shuddered as he thought of his brother's ruby encrusted knife. Herne had seen too often what became of those who failed the duke. He touched himself to make sure he was still intact.

He lit a lamp and made his way to the large catalog on a stand in the center of the great library. If any of the old architectural plans revealed another entrance to the princess's rooms, he'd surely find them here.

Three hours later Herne was tempted to burn the entire library to the ground. He'd never encountered such a disorganized mess in his life.

"Can I help you?" A voice caused Herne to jump.

He jammed the book he'd been looking at back onto the shelf and rounded on a young man, a mere boy. "What are you doing here at this time of night?"

"I'm a junior undersecretary in the library. I saw the light and wondered if I might be of assistance. If you tell me what you're looking for, I'm sure I could locate it for you."

"What I am looking for is no business of yours."

The junior undersecretary tugged at his ear. "Perhaps not, but I also know how disorganized the library is. I've made careful notes of everything the library contains on architecture, and I'm sure that with my help it'd be far easier to locate what you need."

"I have need of nothing. I merely couldn't sleep and thought I'd browse the library." Herne picked up his lamp and headed for the door before the nosy boor could get suspicious.

The imbecile didn't take the hint, but hurried after him. "I'd love to be of service to the duke. I can be most discreet."

"If the duke ever has need of your services, I'll bear that in mind."

* * *

Myst stared into the darkness. She'd lost all sense of time in this place where no sunlight reached. The cell reeked of human waste. There was only a small hole to relieve herself in, and in the pitch blackness, she couldn't always locate it. She was afraid she'd been left to die. She saw no one, except for an occasional glimpse of a hand when her food was shoved in or her tray taken away. She'd tried to talk to the guard, to get him to explain why she was being held or to beg him to take a message to the princess, but he never responded.

With the continued absence of light, Myst found herself dwelling on her worst memories: Donella's life bleeding into her hands, her laugh going silent, never to be heard again.

Worse were the memories of her own poor, mad mother.

Her mother had been a young girl of fourteen when she went out to gather firewood in the forest and came across a band of mercenaries fighting the king's wars. At least a dozen of them had taken their turn with her. Myst's grandfather had found her the next morning, barely alive and covered in blood and the fluid of manhood. He'd taken her to the priestess for healing, but would never speak to her again. In his eyes, she'd been "ruined." Under Mother Anu's care, she'd eventually healed physically, but her mind never recovered. Myst remembered her mother as a frightened, incomprehensible being. At times, she would hold Myst tightly and cry. She'd tell her young daughter she was the most precious thing in the world. At other times, she'd fling Myst from her and revile her, tell her in detail what those men had done to her. "Your fathers were raping, rutting bastards! You half-breed daughter of infidels!"

Mother Anu had been a second mother as well as a teacher. She sheltered Myst as best she could from her poor mother's mad ravings and assured the young child none of it was her fault. So, despite her mother's madness and her grandfather's callousness, her childhood had been a fairly happy one. Mother Anu had given her the unconditional love all children need, and she'd taught Myst of her wonderful gift. Only later did she understand that her mother's sanity had been the price of that gift. Whenever she healed, a part of her still imagined the brutalized body of her child mother.

Myst felt tears on her cheek. She hadn't been able to have Mother Anu or her mad mother long enough. That horrible day had taken them both and everyone else she'd known as a child. She vigorously pushed that memory out of her mind. *I won't think of that. Not now. Not ever.*

CHAPTER 21

Robrek spent the day after the king's magistrate's visit wandering through the woods, thinking about his dreams and about Milady. With Myst gone, he ached from loneliness. He was avoiding the bronze horse, who insisted he stay among people who wanted him dead. Even the magistrate thought it was a bad idea for him to remain in the Valley. Surely, in Murtaghan life could be different for him.

He didn't return to the herb witch's cottage until the sun was beginning to sink beneath the horizon. When he arrived, he found Dillion pacing before it. Robrek grabbed his staff and prepared to fight or run. No matter what that damned horse said, he wasn't about to stand around and let them kill him. But when Dillion saw Robrek, relief spread over his face. "Thank the goddess, you're here. It's Cara."

"What's wrong with Cara?" Robrek glanced around, but he saw no sign of an ambush.

"The baby's too early. She's bleeding badly. You have to help her."

"You think I'm going to let you lead me into a trap?"

"No! I swear, by the goddess, this isn't a trick. I don't deserve anything from you, but damn it, Robbie, she does. She's going to die if you don't come." Robrek still hesitated. "By the goddess and on my mother's grave, I swear I'm telling you the truth."

Dillion's vow and the desperation on his face convinced Robrek that Cara really was in danger. "Dillion, I've never treated a woman, just animals."

"I know that!" Dillion snapped. "But there isn't anyone else. Myst is off goddess knows where, and the priests won't touch women in Cara's condition. Robbie, you're the only one. Please, you have to help her."

Robrek got his things.

When they arrived at his father's farm, Angus was in the farmyard. "So you found you can't survive on your own, have you? Come to beg me to let you come back?"

"No," Robrek said as he dismounted. "I happen to be doing quite well without you."

"Then to what do we owe the pleasure of this visit?" Angus sneered.

"It's Cara, sir," Dillion interrupted. "She's dying. Robbie's got to save her. Please, sir, she's bleeding something awful."

He was surely mistaken, but Robrek thought he saw tears in Angus's eyes as he stepped aside.

"Thank you, sir." Dillion grabbed Robrek by the arm and practically carried him through the kitchen door.

Dillion led Robrek to the room where Cara lay, doubled over. Another female servant was sponging her forehead. "Cara, I've brought Robbie. Everything will be okay," Dillion said.

When the other servant saw Robrek, she gasped, drew the star of Sulis, and fled. *Sulis curse them! Why do they have to do that?*

Robrek knelt beside Cara. The bed was covered in blood. The baby was surely already lost, and if the bleeding didn't stop, Cara, too, would die. He shook his head, not sure where to begin. "I'll have to examine her." He blushed.

"Do it, then!" Dillion shouted.

"Cara?" he asked for her permission.

Her face was pinched by pain. "Please, Robbie, anything."

She's female. A mare is female. There can't be that much difference. Robrek pulled down the covers and pulled up Cara's nightdress. He was shocked at the amount of blood still pouring forth. Healing energy was the only thing that could stop that much bleeding. Cara moaned, and Dillion shouted, "Please, don't let her die, Robbie!"

"I'll try." He put his hands on her womb and slipped into a healing trance. He practiced Myst's exercises and tried to become one with Cara's body, as he could so easily with the body of a mare. But he had difficulty concentrating. *Why'd that damned servant have to look at me like I'm a monster? Just what does she think she needed to draw that star to protect her from?* He tried to shove the other woman out of his mind and focus on Cara, but he felt as if he were floundering in quicksand. The situation was hopeless. Cara was going to die.

No, I refuse to make her pay for what others have done to me. He tried to shove his anger aside as he had when he'd healed Thunder. If Cara had been a mare, it might have been enough. But Cara was human, and he still sensed nothing. He tried harder to push the anger away, but it wasn't working. Since he couldn't push it away, he tried imagining a room in his heart and shoved his anger inside, but the room wasn't big enough. *I'm not getting rid of it. I'll let it out later.* As he thought that, he was able to enlarge the room so it held all of his anger. He closed the door. He felt like a part of himself had been amputated, but at the same time freer than he'd ever been. More importantly, he saw his energy burning more brightly. He seized his power, and with a rush of intense pleasure, he merged with the woman's body. It wasn't so different from a mare's after all. He knew instantly what was causing the bleeding and poured all his energy into sealing the vessels. Cara relaxed under his hands.

* * *

Robrek heard a confused shout of voice and opened his eyes. Dillion was standing between him and his father, Boyden, and several of the other hands. He could see more spilling into the hallway. As he struggled into a sitting position, nothing made sense. He heard the words "demon" and "Cara" being thrown about. When he moved, his father pushed Dillion out of the way and advanced on him. "What have you done?"

"Done?" Robrek said, shaking his head.

Dillion pushed between Robrek and his father. "He saved my wife's life. He couldn't have had anything to do with the crops."

As Robrek sank into unconsciousness again, he was jerked to his feet. His father was screaming about demons, curses, and how he should have exposed him as a child. "I've got to rest," Robrek mumbled.

His father let go of him, and he dropped to the floor.

* * *

When Robrek next awoke, the room was quiet. Certain he'd dreamed the earlier chaos, he struggled to his knees to examine Cara. She was sleeping peacefully. He sighed and sank onto the floor. He couldn't remember ever being so tired. He put his head in his hands and began working out the herbs Cara would need. He was in the middle of a mental list when Dillion burst into the room.

"I've got your horse ready. If it happens again tonight, I'm not sure anything will be able to stop them."

"If what happens?" Robrek asked.

"The fields have been attacked again," Dillion said. "Some of the hands wanted to hang you for it."

What in the seven hells does Brazen think she's doing? He gave Dillion instructions for caring for Cara, and Dillion helped him to his feet. Angus burst into the room. Dillion stepped between him and his father. Without Dillion's support, Robrek fell to the floor. "Until you take care of this mess, you're going nowhere," Angus yelled. "I don't know if you summoned the demon or not, boy, but you can and will stop it."

Robrek glared at his father. "What's it to me if your grain is destroyed?"

"If you won't do it for common decency, boy, how much will it cost me to buy your oh-so-special powers, Master Amihealer?" Angus sneered.

"I wouldn't take a dram from you."

"If it happens again tonight, do you really think you'll be safe anywhere in the Valley?"

"And just how many tears will you shed over my grave?"

Angus gaped at him, clenching and unclenching his fists. "I can't afford the same losses I suffered last year. I know you hate me, but do you really want to see everyone who depends on me starve? I'm asking you, will you send the beast back to wherever it came from?"

"When you need me this badly can't you even say 'please'?"

Angus's face turned red, and he headed for the door. He stopped in the doorway with his back to Robrek. Robrek could see the tension in his shoulders. "Please, Robrek, will you stop this thing?"

Angus hissed through clenched teeth. Without even turning to look at him, Angus left.

Robrek looked up at Dillion. "Help me to Wild Thing. What fields were attacked?"

"The East fields."

Robrek swore. *The fields closest to the forest stable. I'll kill her for this!* Dillion picked him up like a child and carried him out of the house. Robrek was too tired to protest. He also had to accept Dillon's help to mount Wild Thing.

He nearly fell off the horse as he rode through the ruined fields, but his anger at the bronze horse kept him going. He reached the forest stable and found her waiting as calmly as ever. He didn't dismount, uncertain he'd be able to get back up without help. "You reckless cull! You nearly got me killed! Go back to the seven hells! I don't want anything more to do with you!" He turned to ride away.

:Another comes: Brazen's voice bored through his skull.

Robrek turned Wild Thing around. "Another what?"

Brazen merely repeated herself like she always did. *:Another comes.:*

Robrek's vision began to swirl as he realized what she meant. "You're not serious? I don't even want one of you."

:Another comes. It needs you. Come here and touch me: Brazen commanded.

Robrek wanted to curl up and sleep for a week, letting both the humans and the horses fend for themselves. None of them deserved his aid, but he couldn't leave an animal in the condition Brazen had been in the previous spring. Though he had no idea why Brazen wanted him to touch her, he was too tired to deal with her endless repetition, so he rode closer to the fence and put his hand on her shoulder. His weariness flowed out, and energy flowed in. Within a few moments, he felt restored, but Brazen looked like she was about to collapse. *:I cannot do that often. But tonight your need is great.:*

"I'll go and fetch your partner."

Brazen snorted, and Robrek got the feeling she didn't entirely approve of this "other" that was coming.

The sun was starting to set as Robrek rode back to his father's land. Brazen hadn't begun her attacks until the middle of the night, so he thought he probably had some time to wait. He set Wild Thing to walking along the edges of the fields. Soon the monotony of finding nothing set his mind to wandering. He thought about Dillion and Cara and grew unreasonably jealous. It wasn't that he wanted Cara. It was the love between them Robrek envied. He touched Milady's ribbon under his shirt. *Holy Sulis, why does she have to be a lady?*

* * *

After several hours, his musings were interrupted by a sound so loud it shook the night air—the sound of plants being ripped from the earth and ground into powder, followed by an unearthly scream. Robrek's eyes darted around, and he saw it, not more than a hundred yards away. The horse had what appeared to be a knight mounted on his back, but Robrek was certain it was another empty suit of armor. Surprisingly, this horse appeared to be an ordinary gray, and it was slightly smaller than Brazen. He dropped from Wild Thing's back and reached out carefully with his mind so as not to get overwhelmed by the horse's pain. "It's okay, my friend. Robrek's here. Let me close, so I can help."

He sensed the bit tearing apart the horse's mouth and sent images of him removing the source of the animal's pain. It moved toward him, whinnying sadly. He stroked the horse, and it looked into his eyes, pleading for the promised relief. Because this horse's gear appeared to be identical to Brazen's, he had an easier time releasing the bit. When he'd loosed it, he mounted Wild Thing and led the other horse to the forest stable.

When he arrived, Brazen was fast asleep. Robrek lit a lantern and brought the injured horse inside. He let out a low whistle. The horse was no ordinary gray, but a dull silver—a silver that would probably gleam as brightly as Brazen's bronze once the horse was healthy. He also noticed a troubling fact. The horse was a full stallion. Housing a stallion and a mare so closely together was bound to cause problems, but he had no choice. Besides, the silver horse was in too bad a shape to do much at the moment. He took its gear off—it was identical to the gear Brazen had been carrying, except it was silver and bore a design of leaves and vines instead of crossed swords—and unsaddled it. Everything from its emaciation to its damaged mouth mirrored Brazen's injuries.

"Where did you come from? Is there some kind of demon knight that abuses and abandons magical horses? Because one mysterious, magical horse is one more than a person should meet in a lifetime, and you're my second." The horse let out a small squeal of pain.

"Don't worry. I'll take good care of you. I suppose it's too much to hope you'll explain yourself any more than Brazen does." He thought he sensed a soft, pain-filled chuckle, but decided he must be mistaken: Brazen didn't have anything approaching a sense of humor. After he finished with the horse, Robrek curled up in the straw and fell asleep.

* * *

The next morning after caring for the silver horse, Robrek rode to the herb witch's cottage to fix his own breakfast. He was in the middle of eating when he heard a knock. He answered it to find his father. He stood aside and allowed Angus to enter.

"Well?" Angus said. "Did you banish the demon?"

"There was no demon, but your fields are safe." Robrek sat and resumed eating.

"Safe, are they?" Angus looked like he didn't know what to do with his hands, and Robrek had never seen his father so unsure of himself. "The hands wanted to kill you."

"So I understood. Did you want to join them?"

"Just what are you?"

"I'm an amihealer, as was my mother before me."

"Your mother had some skill with animals, but you're something different, something more."

"I really have a great deal to do today. If there is nothing else . . ." Robrek gestured toward the door.

Angus gaped at him, then left without another word.

* * *

Because of Robrek's growing skill, the new horse healed much faster than Brazen. Two days after he'd found it, it nickered in greeting when he arrived at the stable. Brazen snorted; she still wasn't happy about the new arrival. Robrek wasn't sure why.

"Greetings, Lady Brazen and Lord Silver. I'm glad to see you're feeling somewhat better, Milord."

Robrek prepared the oat mash and herbal wash. As he cared for the horse, unexpected emotions came from the stallion. Before, all he'd sensed was pain, hunger, and gratitude. Today the horse seemed mournful. "What's wrong, Milord? Your sores can't pain you as much as they did."

The silver horse hadn't said a word to him yet, so Robrek didn't expect a response, much less the one he received. *:I look positively dreadful. Hair rubbed off. Ribs sticking out. No shine to my coat.:*

The sentiment was so unlike Brazen Robrek almost laughed. In fact, Brazen snorted with disgust. "Milord, don't worry. I'll have you back to your old self in no time. Brazen looked as bad as you do when I first found her and look at her now. You'll be as shiny as she is soon."

:Don't compare me to that nag. If you'd seen me at my best, you'd know how much more attractive I am. I shine and sparkle in the sun. All the mares swoon when they behold my magnificence.:

Brazen snorted even more loudly and turned her back on the stallion.

:All mares except her, that is.:

This time Robrek did laugh. He didn't know why he'd expected the new horse to have a personality identical to Brazen's. "Oh, do they, fancy man? Maybe that's what I should call you—Lord Fancy Man."

:Yes, I like that. I'll be Lord Fancy Man.:

"As you wish, Milord." The stallion's mention of the swooning mares brought up Robrek's initial concern. "Milord, Milady, is this joint stabling going to work out?"

They both snorted. Robrek sensed Brazen's disgust, and Fancy Man's fuller commentary. *:With that hag? Not if she were the last mare on earth. I'd mount you first.:*

His crudeness startled Robrek into laughing again. "I'd appreciate it if you didn't, Milord."

Robrek swore the horse winked. *:Don't worry. Not when there's a pretty thing like her around.:* Robrek gaped as Wild Thing raised her tail flirtatiously at the stallion.

"I'm not sure that's such a good idea."

:Don't worry, human child. I'd be gentle with her, and I never take what isn't freely given.:

:Very handsome.: Wild Thing seemed to have no problem with the idea.

Robrek reddened. He was destined to live his life alone, while even his horse could find companionship.

After he was done caring for Fancy Man, he went to fetch the new silver sword. The sword was lighter and easier to handle than the bronze one, but it did less damage when it hit. He supposed there were different names for different types of swords, but he didn't know them. The techniques were similar enough that Robrek had only small problems adapting. Brazen paired him with two fierce opponents. As always when he fought, Robrek's mind became completely focused. For some time now, he'd ceased to think of his weapon at all. It became merely an extension of his body as he entered a state that was in some ways similar to a healing trance. As mere illusions, his opponents were tireless, and Robrek fought until he was ready to drop. To cool himself, he stripped and went to bathe in the stream. The exercise had helped somewhat, but he still ached with loneliness.

* * *

Leigh jumped as Father Gildas slammed his hand down on his desk. "How could a magistrate be so incompetent? You can't tell me the demon child's innocent of the herb witch's blood. He calls the inhabitants of the seven hells to attack his own father's grain, and now he has corrupted the purity of a married woman."

Leigh continued dusting the shelves and didn't say anything. He wasn't at all sure how to feel about the stories he'd heard. What they claimed this peasant had done in order to heal the woman was beyond scandalous, but when did demons start helping people?

"This has to be stopped," the priest continued. "Before she fell under the influence of the demon boy, Cara had always been a faithful follower of the goddess. Now, she's rejected the judgment of the goddess upon her and accepted the aid of demons. The demon boy defiled her and laid his unholy hands where no man's hands but a husband's should ever go. The woman still lives, but I fear her soul has been forever lost."

Certainly, that was the answer. A demon would help in order to steal a soul. "What are you going to do?" he asked.

"She will be excommunicated, of course. As will her husband for allowing it."

CHAPTER 22

"You can't tell me you don't see it?" Count Kayne gestured wildly as he sat facing the Korthian duke. "The king's ninety years old. Is it any wonder his mind isn't what it once was? It's time to crown the princess as regent."

Sheen snorted. "She's a child, not fit to reign on her own."

"Far more fit than the king at the moment," Kayne insisted. "He's allowing Argblutal to take over. The princess has been completely marginalized, and we Korthians are being squeezed out."

Sheen's lips narrowed. "I can't say I'm happy with the imbalance on the council, but the princess only has her own stubbornness to blame for her exclusion. If she'd merely agree to marry as she ought, she'd have no further difficulties."

"Your Grace, I know you want her to marry your son. I once had ambitions myself, but there are far more important issues at stake. I need your support to put a motion before the council to have the king declared incompetent."

"Kayne, what you need is to control your hysteria. Some could see it as treasonous."

"Treasonous?" The count jumped to his feet. "I won't sit back and allow Argblutal's power to increase unchallenged. Korth will become a subject state to Lundia over my dead body."

* * *

Duke Argblutal watched as the High Priest Shylah gave the king another dose of the purple potion. The king drank it obediently as he always did, and the familiar look of glassy unconcern washed over his face.

"The deadline you gave the princess for choosing her consort has passed, Your Majesty," Argblutal said. "It's time you gave the order for her to marry me at Litha."

"But the princess said she didn't want to marry you," the king said, his face reflecting idiotic confusion.

The duke leaned over the king. "What the princess wants doesn't matter. The good of the joined kingdoms is at stake."

"Yes, the princess must marry." The king nodded. "I've told her that. She must make her choice."

"No!" Argblutal brought his fist down on the arm of the king's chair, causing the king to jump. "She must not be allowed a choice! Only I am fit for the throne!"

The king seemed to retreat farther inside himself and began muttering nonsense, as he always did when Argblutal pressed him on the subject of the princess's marriage.

The duke straightened and turned on the high priest. "Why is he muttering like this?"

"You must exercise patience, Your Grace."

"I have little left for your nonsense," the duke sneered. "At this very moment, Count Kayne is spreading rumors the king is no longer sane. He's working to have the princess crowned as regent. I'll silence Count Kayne before others begin to think as he does. But your potion had better work soon, or I'll resort to other measures."

The king fought against the pleasant floating feeling that was fogging his brain. He knew something was wrong, or perhaps he merely dreamed it was. Yes, that was it. They were merely dreams, but such horrible ones. He dreamed he'd banned his daughter from court and council meetings. The worst nightmares were those in which he refused to speak with her at all. But if they were merely dreams, why hadn't he seen her lately?

He heard voices in his rooms and turned toward them. Duke Argblutal and the High Priest Shylah were standing there. *What are they doing in my rooms?* With a jolt of shock, he realized that his nightmares hadn't been dreams after all.

Oh, Samantha, my dearest, how will you ever forgive me? I'll make things right for you.

Be careful of making promises you can't keep, Solar.

This is a promise I will keep if I have to run the lying bastard through with my own sword.

Killing him is the only thing that will stop him, so if you're going to do it, now would be as good a time as any.

The king moved to place his hand on his sword, but a fly buzzing across the room caught his eye. He watched it move in and out from behind his favorite tapestry, the one depicting a large white heron drinking from a fountain. He marveled at the beautiful blue, yellow, and red flowers that surrounded the heron. His hand dropped back on the edge of his chair.

* * *

Shylah lay the signed documents on his altar and knelt down to praise his god. "Sulis, this is the first step. Soon we will have all we've ever dreamed of." Argblutal knew nothing of the documents the high priest had gotten the king to sign and certify with the royal seal. Neither did the king, for that matter. Solar had been staring at his tapestry and had simply signed the two documents without reading them. One granted Shylah's messenger an escort by the Royal Guard, and the second rid the priesthood of those who had no right to it.

Father Faolan entered and knelt beside him. "He signed as you hoped?" the younger priest asked.

Shylah nodded. "Praise be to Sulis!" He handed the two documents to Father Faolan. "Speak nothing of the purpose of your mission until you reach Korth. Then show the documents to the officer in charge of the Royal Guard who will accompany you."

* * *

Conroy grabbed Samantha from behind. She ducked, aimed a kick at his kneecap, and threw him over her shoulder, drawing her practice sword and aiming for his heart. Conroy rolled out of the way and came up in a crouch, drawing his sword as he did so. He came at her fast. She knocked his sword away and scored a hit on his upper arm. She parried Conroy's next blow, looking for the slightest opening.

Conroy was the least skilled member of her guard, and she wanted to beat him badly.

She feinted for his head and then came in low, but she didn't fool him. He not only parried, but also followed with a thrust of his own. She was only just able to block it. She circled the room, judging distance as both her childhood weapons master and Darhour had taught her. Conroy came at her, and she sidestepped the attack. Using a new move Darhour had taught her, she tripped Conroy with her foot as he passed. He fell to the ground, but before she could take advantage, he'd rolled to his feet again. But he dropped his sword too low, leaving his left side vulnerable. Samantha went in for the kill. Too late, she recognized the trick for what it was. Conroy knocked her sword aside and followed his parry by striking her a bit too hard in the stomach.

"Oomph," the princess groaned, collapsing against the wall of the practice arena. "Sulis curse it! Damn you all to the seven hells!"

"Your Highness!" Conroy ran to her side. "Have I hurt you?"

"I'll live." She waved Conroy off, slamming her practice sword back into its place on the wall and sliding down the wall to sit panting on the ground. Her stomach did hurt, but that wasn't truly what was wrong. "What are all of you staring at me for?" she snapped. "Do you enjoy seeing your princess murdered again?"

"Your Highness," Conroy apologized. "I'm sorry. I should have pulled the blow more effectively. I'm afraid I'm not as good at that as some of the others."

Samantha laughed bitterly. "I can't believe after all this training, I still can't beat even you." Since the king had relieved her of official duties, she'd done little other than train.

Conroy looked stricken, hanging up his own practice sword. "You're improving, Your Highness. As am I."

"Go and clean up," Darhour ordered, and Conroy bowed out of the room. Darhour turned to her. "Your Highness, Conroy feels his inadequacy enough without having you throw it in his face. He has a steadiness that will allow him to keep his head in a crisis, and only when you compare him to the rest of your guard does he lack skill. We're on your side. We don't deserve to have you take your dissatisfaction out on us."

"I'm not doing that," she snapped, and looked to Kailen and Blaine for support. They became interested in their feet. She sighed. "I guess I have. I just wish I could best one of you!"

"You best me every time, Your Highness," Blaine offered.

"There is that," Samantha muttered. Darhour had begun to train both Blaine and her maids in self-defense. Ardra and Malvina had made some progress, especially with knives, but Darhour had almost given Blaine up as hopeless—he still closed his eyes whenever he saw a blow coming.

Samantha leaned against the wall, struggling against tears. "Do you think it's true, Darhour? Has my father lost his mind?"

Darhour sighed and sat next to her. "The signs all point to it, Your Highness. You will remember it was this fear that caused His Majesty to insist your personal guard owe their allegiance to no one but you."

"In the spring I feared he was dying, but this is worse. He refuses to see me, and Argblutal is using him. Do you think I should push to become regent?"

Before Darhour could answer, a member of the Royal Guard entered and bowed. "Your Highness, Count Kayne sent me to inform you that he's been arrested for treason."

"What?" Samantha jumped to her feet. "Of what is he accused?"

"He has expressed the opinion that the king is no longer sane. He was making noise about naming you as regent. He is being tried before the king's council within the hour."

"No he won't! I won't allow it!" Followed by Darhour, Kailen, and Blaine, Samantha sped to the king's rooms. She burst through the doors of the king's outer room. Gilroy was at his desk. "Where's my father?" she demanded.

"His Majesty is in his rooms. If you'll give me the name of your consort, I'll be happy to bring it to him."

"Gilroy, this is no childish game! Kayne has just been arrested for treason! I'll see my father!" Samantha approached the door to the king's inner chambers. The king's guards blocked her way. "Stand aside," she ordered with the full force of royal command her father had taught her.

"I'm sorry, Your Highness, we have our orders."

"And I'm giving you new ones. You will stand aside, or you will be removed." Darhour's and Kailen's hands rested on their sword hilts. The king's guards paled. Everyone in the room knew who would win if it came to a fight. "You know I'd do my father no harm. I don't want anyone to get hurt, but I will speak to my father."

The two guards glanced at each other, then nodded. "If your guards will remain out here and you'll surrender your sword, we won't stand in your way."

"Fine!" She unbuckled her sword belt and handed it to Darhour. When she entered the room, she saw the king sitting in a chair, staring at the heron tapestry that had always been his favorite.

"Father," she strode across the room toward him. "What is going on?"

The king smiled. "Samantha, my dear, you're just the one to help me. Do you think the blue flowers in this tapestry are the most beautiful? Or the red ones?"

Samantha moved between him and the tapestry. "Father, Kayne has been arrested for treason. You know as well as I do he is no traitor."

"Kayne?" The king's eyes glazed over for a moment; then he nodded. "You're blocking my view, but perhaps you are right, maybe it's the yellow flowers that are the most beautiful. Or perhaps it's the combination of all the colors together that makes this tapestry so brilliant."

Samantha felt as if a knife were ripping through her guts. Even with the rumors, she hadn't dreamed he'd be this far gone. "Father, look at me!" she demanded. "Argblutal is using you! He is working against me, and I need your help in stopping him."

The king looked at her with confusion. "No, it's this tapestry; it presents an unsolvable puzzle."

Before she could say anything else, Argblutal swept into the room surrounded by a dozen guards she didn't recognize. Darhour and Kailen entered ahead of them and placed themselves between her and the duke. Argblutal bowed. "Your Highness, how nice to see you!" He turned to the king. "Your Majesty, the council is assembled and awaits you. Come with me now."

The king's eyes suddenly came into clear focus. "But of course," he said. "We won't be betrayed."

Samantha started at the king's use of the royal "we," a pompous affectation he never used. "Father, no." She grabbed the king by the shoulder. "Can't you see what's happening?"

"Send the princess to her rooms," Argblutal commanded. "She seeks to interfere with the justice of the council."

Samantha tried to force the king to meet her eyes. "Father, you are king! A mere duke doesn't command you!"

The king ignored her and addressed the guards with Argblutal. "Six of you escort Her Highness back to her own quarters and see she stays there until these proceedings are over."

"Father!" she cried, but the king swept out of the room without another glance at her, leaving six guards behind. Darhour's and Kailen's hands were on their sword hilts, ready to draw at her command. She shook her head. They were now outnumbered three to one, and even if they did manage to fight their way past these six, how many more stood between them and the council chamber? "No, we'll go to my rooms." Blaine watched nervously from the doorway. "Blaine, get to the council at once, and let me know what's going on."

"Of course, Your Highness." Blaine bowed and hurried after the king.

As soon as she entered her rooms, Samantha sank into a chair and put her head in her hands. "I thought I knew all the members of the Royal Guard," she told Darhour. "Did you recognize those who escorted me here?"

"The king has increased the size of the Royal Guard over the last few days by about two dozen men, Your Highness. Most of the new men were once Argblutal's retainers."

"Damn him! I won't allow him to take over! Assemble my guard!"

Darhour bowed and carried out her orders.

Soon all six members of her personal guard arrived, and she had them be seated. She took a deep breath. "I didn't want to believe my father could be mad, but after seeing him today, I have no doubt. Argblutal is using him. Any suggestions would be most welcome."

The room fell silent for a few moments. Phelan twitched uncomfortably. "M-m-m-m . . . M-m-m-m . . . M-m-m-m . . ." He struggled to speak as all eyes turned to him. "M-m-m-myst-t-t-t." He looked humiliated, and Samantha realized for the first time why he never spoke.

"Myst?" she asked, and Phelan nodded gratefully. "Of course! She might be able to cure his madness. I'll have a messenger sent to her."

Darhour shifted his feet. "I wouldn't trust the mission with anyone but one of us."

She nodded. "Bearach, go at once, but don't wear my colors. Stand out as little as possible."

After Bearach left, Samantha turned to Darhour. "What about Captain Faucon? He's a Korthian, and his family has always been close to Kayne's."

Darhour nodded. "I believe Captain Faucon would at least listen, but he'll certainly be in attendance at Kayne's trial."

"They can't execute Kayne immediately, can they?"

"Argblutal is capable of doing most anything."

"Do you have any other suggestions?" she snapped.

He didn't, so she sent Conroy with a message for Captain Faucon, dismissed the rest of her men, and let out a prayer to Sulis. As she prayed, a loving presence surrounded her, but the words that came with it were far from comforting. "*Oh, my child, it pains me, but dark times are ahead for you. The path ahead of you will not be easy, but it is a path only you can tread.*" "Easy or not," she whispered fiercely, "I won't allow Argblutal to execute Kayne."

* * *

Devyn lay on his bed, his hand tracing the smooth lines of Aislinn's naked hip. Her body was a work of art he despaired of copying, although he'd made numerous attempts. He snuggled close to her and cupped one of her breasts.

"What are you going to do about your father?" she asked.

"I told you there's nothing to worry about." He nibbled the side of her neck. "He's been called to an emergency council session that should last for hours." They'd had to be careful since Ostara, and he'd been feeling her absence acutely.

"That isn't what I meant. You know Kayne's right. The princess should be crowned as regent."

Devyn suppressed a groan. "And what do you expect me to do about it?" He tried to distract her by kissing the spot on the back of her neck that always drove her wild.

She pulled away and turned to face him. "Devyn, I'm serious. You have to get your father to support Kayne."

Devyn fell back against the bed. "Aislinn, you know he never listens to me."

"He would if you were the princess's betrothed."

Devyn jumped off the bed. "Damn it, Aislinn, you're the only woman I want in my bed. Besides, only you and my father think Her Highness is foolish enough to take me."

Aislinn sat up, her naked body tormenting him. "You could try. It's a very good match. The princess might see that."

Devyn grabbed his trousers and started putting them on. "If you're tired of me, there are easier ways to tell me." He grabbed a shirt and stalked out of the room, ignoring her calls. He'd take a swim in the river. He only hoped it was cold enough.

* * *

Waiting for Blaine to return from Kayne's trial, Samantha sat in her window seat. Conroy had informed her there was no possibility of getting a message to Captain Faucon until after it was over.

Finally, Blaine, Darhour, and Kailen entered her room. Blaine was pale as snow and trembling from head to foot. "Blaine, what is it?" she asked, getting to her feet.

"Your Highness, I . . ." Blaine broke off abruptly and rushed toward the basin on her side table. He retched noisily into it for several moments. He straightened, wiping his mouth. "Please, forgive me, Your Highness. I've never seen a man die before. I mean I saw my father's body, of course, but he was sick, and then one morning when I went to check on him, he was just lying there dead. There wasn't any of the blood or the screams or the . . ." Blaine broke off and began retching into the basin again. When there didn't seem to be anything left in his stomach, he straightened. He swayed, and Darhour caught him by the arm.

"Sit down, son," Darhour said with unusual gentleness.

"Get him a glass of wine," Samantha ordered Kailen.

Darhour had Blaine sit with his head between his legs for a few moments, and then Kailen put the wine into his hand. Blaine started to gulp it down, but Darhour restrained him. "Slowly, son. Too fast, and it'll do you more harm than good." Blaine nodded and took a small sip of the wine.

Samantha sat across from him. "What happened?" she asked. She felt sick herself, and the odor of Blaine's vomit didn't help.

"I'm sorry, Your Highness. I'm not used to this kind of thing. I organize lists and make nice orderly plans. I don't rend men limb from limb, or watch other men do so." Blaine stopped abruptly. "I'm sorry, Your Highness. I don't presume to criticize. I'll serve you in whatever capacity you require. I—"

"Just tell me what happened," Samantha urged.

Blaine nodded. "Kayne was found guilty, Your Highness. They chopped his head off. Do you know how much blood spurts out when they do that? And his head. It just kind of rolled into a basket and stared at me." Blaine got up and rushed back to the basin. When he'd finished vomiting, he turned to her. "I'm sorry, Your Highness. It's just . . . I'm not . . ."

But Samantha had stopped listening to him. *How could Argblutal have managed this?*

There was a knock on her door, and Kailen answered it. He returned, trailed by Captain Faucon, whose jaw was clenched so tightly it looked painful. "Your Highness." He bowed, and the princess offered him a seat.

"Blaine, get rid of that." She gestured to the vomit-filled basin and turned back to Faucon. "My secretary informs me Count Kayne has been executed."

" I thank you for your efforts on his behalf, as I'm sure his family would. But they'll be struggling for survival shortly, since Kayne's estates have been confiscated and given to Count Morgan."

"A Lundian count has been given an estate in Korth?"

"Yes, Your Highness, and he'll take Kayne's place on the council." Faucon froze. "I'm sure His Majesty has only the best interests of the joined kingdoms at heart."

"My father always did, but my father isn't in control anymore."

Captain Faucon drew himself up in his chair. "What are you suggesting, Your Highness?"

"Captain, you know I've been kept away from my father," Samantha said, and Faucon nodded. "I forced my way in to see him today and tried to discuss Kayne's arrest, but he was only interested in which flowers in his tapestry were the most beautiful. I'm afraid . . . I fear he's gone . . ." She couldn't complete the sentence.

Faucon's face relaxed. "Thank Sulis, the king hasn't turned on us. The Royal Guard serves Solar *and* his heir. How may we be of assistance?"

"I've sent one of my men for the herb witch who treated the king before Ostara. It's my hope she can restore the king's mind. But I may need your help in getting her near the king."

Faucon bowed. "That should be a simple matter."

* * *

Robrek saw Ronan look up from where he was sunning himself on the herb witch's garden wall. Knowing the cat had keener hearing, he straightened from tending the plants and followed the direction of the cat's gaze. Soon he, too, heard the sound of an approaching horse. Robrek brushed the dirt from his hands. His mouth opened in surprise as the rider got close enough to recognize. It was one of Milady's men, the archer who had shot him. He grasped his staff, which was never far from him.

The archer caught sight of him and dismounted. "Ah, Master Robrek, what a pleasant surprise!"

"What can I do for you?"

The man smiled in a friendly manner. "It's actually Mistress Myst I seek. Is she at home?"

"Is Milady ill?"

The archer looked at him blankly, then shook his head. "No, no, Milady is well enough. Is the herb witch around? I'm in a bit of a hurry."

"I'm sorry, Milord, sir . . ." Robrek faltered, unsure how to address the man.

"Bearach will do."

"I'm sorry, Bearach. Myst left the day after I healed Milady's horse. I haven't seen her since."

"She never came . . ." He stopped in mid-sentence. "I mean, you haven't seen her all spring?"

"No, do you know where she went?"

"No, no idea," he answered too quickly. He looked uncertain for a moment. "I guess I'd best get back."

"Are you in need of a healer? My skill with humans isn't what Mistress Myst's is, but I am her apprentice." Robrek's heart beat faster at the thought of seeing Milady again.

Bearach hesitated, then shook his head. "I was asked to fetch Mistress Myst, no other." Of course, Milady's men wouldn't want him anywhere near her. Bearach turned to leave, but looked back.

"By the way, I don't think I ever apologized for shooting you. That would have been a tragic waste. Healing Her . . . I mean, Milady's horse was the most amazing thing I've ever seen."

Robrek shrugged. "There isn't even a scar."

"Well, good." Bearach nodded. "I really must be returning to the pal . . . to Milady."

"Tell her . . ." *Tell her what? I can't tell this man I love her.* "Tell her I'll never forget her."

Bearach nodded, but Robrek thought it unlikely Milady would get any message. Looking embarrassed, Bearach mounted his horse. "You take care of yourself, Robrek. You deserve better than a place than this."

* * *

It had been so long since she'd seen any light, Myst wondered if she'd forgotten how to see. She was starting to hear voices at times—Mother Anu's, her poor mad mother's, Robrek's. "Robrek," she whispered into the darkness, thinking she saw him. "Are you okay, my child?" *No, he isn't here. I need to get back to him. Power like his needs to be guided by love, not hate.*

She heard the jangle of keys in the lock. "Mother Anu," she called out. *No, the priestess is long dead.* The door opened, and a light blinded her. She shielded her eyes from it.

A cold voice spoke from behind the glare. "How do your accommodations suit you?" Myst couldn't tell if the voice was real this time, so she didn't answer.

A second man spoke. "Clean this woman up, and bring her to my office. Don't allow her to touch you." He walked away.

"Certainly, Your Grace," the cold voice answered.

Myst's eyes were slowly becoming accustomed to the light. She saw her prison door surrounded by armed guards with drawn swords. One of them ordered her out of the cell. Myst decided this was real, but she began to wish it was another hallucination when she emerged into a small chamber that seemed to vibrate with pain. On one side was a rack. A head vise and thumbscrews lay on a table nearby. A Judas cradle stood in the corner. Myst turned her head away, not wanting to see any more.

Surrounded by guards, she walked into a large wine cellar, up a staircase, and into the corridor of what appeared to be a well-appointed mansion. Thick carpeting covered the floor and rich tapestry lined the walls. The colors in the tapestries were so rich and vibrant Myst felt drawn to them, until she looked at one closely enough to see the depiction of a naked woman being savaged by dogs. Myst tried not to look at the others. Just down the hall from the staircase, the guards led her into a very small room with nothing more than a small cot and a table containing a basin of water and a bar of soap. A clean dress lay on the cot. There were no windows and only the single door. "Clean and dress yourself," one of them commanded. "You have five minutes; after that I open the door, and we all watch. Not that a one of us wants to see your wrinkled old body." He turned up his lip and shut the door.

Myst struggled to clear her mind. She hurriedly took off her filthy clothing and trembled as she washed herself. She hadn't realized how weak she'd become. The water was icy cold, but it was good to be clean. She'd just had time to pull the dress over her head when the door opened. The man gestured her out of the room with his sword. The guards took her to the end of the corridor, and one of them knocked on a large door. He opened it at an order from within and gestured her inside. She entered and the man who had been talking to the princess when she'd first arrived at the palace sat behind the desk. She thought he was a duke, but she didn't know his name.

The duke gestured at her to be seated. Three of the guards entered and stood behind her. The duke narrowed his eyes. "I know of the power of you healers. If you try to rise from that chair, my men will disembowel you."

"What do you want from me?"

The duke pushed a thin book across the desk toward her. "I want you to read this and tell me what this potion will do. You have until morning to present me with a full analysis. Do not disappoint me." The man's eyes were so cold no further threat was needed. The duke rose quickly and addressed his underlings. "I have to return to the palace. Watch her closely. Kill her if she tries anything. Take her back to the room down the hall when she's finished."

* * *

A knock on the door to the servants' corridors woke Darhour. He got to his feet, drawing his sword. Before he reached the door, the knock came again. "Captain, it's me." Recognizing Bearach's voice, Darhour lowered his sword and opened the door.

"Have you brought Myst?" he asked, as he invited Bearach inside.

"She wasn't there, Captain," Bearach said. "I found the amihealer at her cottage, and he hasn't seen the herb witch since before Ostara."

"Argblutal," Darhour said automatically.

Bearach wrinkled his forehead. "Why would the duke have her? How could he have known His Majesty would lose his mind?"

"I don't know." Darhour began pacing the room. "She's in Argblutal's cellar. She has to be. If I'm not back by first light, let the princess know where I've gone."

* * *

Darhour crept through the streets of the capital. Under his cloak he wore the duke's livery he'd purloined on his last visit. The scars on his face were covered with wax and makeup. He also carried a bottle of a special wine of his own making, as well as his sword and all of his knives. Still, he prayed to the goddess he wouldn't have to kill anyone.

He turned into the alleyway that ran behind the duke's residence. From a few blocks away, he could see the guards stationed at the duke's back door. There were two of them, just as there had been last time. He imitated a drunken stagger and began singing loudly a bawdy song about a girl named Deidre, the heat of whose love could turn a Korthian winter into spring.

When he neared the duke's mansion, the guards stepped out. "Quiet down, you sot. You've no right to disturb decent people."

Darhour giggled and put his finger to his lips. "No, no, wouldn't want to disturb decent people. It's only the indecent I have any interest in." He winked and pretended to drink from his bottle. "Care for a nip to take the chill off the night air?" Darhour wafted the bottle in front of their faces. It was one of the finest of Korthlundian vintages. "I stole it from my lord's cellar. Damned good stuff." The guards glanced at each other. "Go on," he urged. "A swallow or two won't hurt."

With no more urging, the first guard grabbed the bottle and took a long pull. "Damn good," he agreed and passed it to his fellow. The second one drank as well. Darhour took the bottle back and began spouting drunken nonsense while he waited the few seconds it would take for the wine to have its effect. Soon both men were lying at his feet. The drug would only give him about an hour, but the guards would awake without realizing they'd been drugged. He slipped the keys from one man's belt, took off his cloak so the duke's livery was clearly visible, and slipped inside the back door.

The house was nearly silent. He walked confidently through the corridors toward the staircase that led to the duke's cellar. He'd long ago learned that one of the best ways to be unnoticed was to dress like a servant and act like he belonged.

As he neared the staircase, he saw two guards in front of a door at the end of the corridor. He staggered toward them. "Out drinking a bit late, aren't you?" one of them asked.

"What's it to you if I have been?" Darhour slurred, drawing himself up indignantly. "Not going to tell his dukeship on me, are you?"

"For a nip of whatever you've got there, we might be convinced to let it pass."

Darhour smiled as he handed over the bottle. Soon they, too, lay at his feet. Whatever they'd been guarding deserved a look before he proceeded to the cellar.

When he opened the door, he stopped short. The herb witch knelt beside a cot. "Mistress," he whispered. "I've come to get you out."

Her eyes widened. "Who are you?"

Not having time for explanations, he grabbed her by the hand and pulled her to her feet. "I've come from the princess. Quickly."

* * *

At dawn, Herne went to the kitchen to retrieve the witch's breakfast. He'd arranged Faucon's accident the night before and then arrived to take charge of his brother's prisoner. He'd found everything quiet, and nothing disturbed his sleep during the night. Carrying the tray and backed by a handful of guards, he nodded in greeting to the two guarding the duke's precious asset. "Any problems?"

"None, sir. It was a quiet night," one of them said. Herne had the men draw their swords and unlock the door. As the door swung open, he dropped the tray. The small room was completely empty. "Where is she?" he shouted.

The two guards looked into the empty room. "She must be here somewhere," one said, though the room held no possible hiding place. Still, the guards began searching as if she'd somehow shrunk to a size sufficient to hide under the mattress.

"Find her now!"

The guards scrambled out of the room, but before they could move farther, the front door slammed open, and a dozen footsteps approached. Herne froze as his brother turned the corner, flanked by his usual contingent of guards. "Bring the witch to my office at once," Argblutal ordered.

"Your Grace," Herne said, trying to control his panic, though this couldn't possibly be his fault. "These imbeciles"—he pushed the guards forward—"have failed you. The herb witch was missing when I went to bring her breakfast this morning."

"How could she be missing?" The duke's voice was deadly quiet.

"She must have gotten out by magic, Your Grace," one of the guards quavered. "No one came through this door all night. I swear it."

The duke turned to Tremayne, the head of his forces in the capital. "Search the house thoroughly." Tremayne bowed and moved to carry out the order. "Herne, assemble all guards on duty last night and bring them to me. Have these two taken down into the cellar and prepared."

Argblutal raged as he entered his personal torture chamber. The herb witch's escape could ruin everything. As he'd ordered, the two guards had been stripped and manacled to the wall. He picked up the cat-o-nine, ignoring their pleas for mercy and saying nothing as he began to flay the skin from their backs. Herne and the other guards who'd been on duty during the night arrived to watch him turn their backs into bloody pulp. When Tremayne arrived, Argblutal paused.

"Your Grace, we've searched the house. The herb witch isn't here."

Argblutal turned to the bleeding guards. "Now, it's time you started telling the truth. How have you betrayed me?"

"We didn't, we swear," one of them cried out. "It had to be magic."

Argblutal lashed out again with the whip. The guards' screams did little to salve his anger. "Tell me everything that happened last night."

The guards continued to insist on their innocence and claimed the only person to enter the corridor during the night had been a drunken servant. They claimed not to recognize him, but insisted he was wearing the duke's livery. Under the influence of the lash, they admitted to drinking from the man's bottle. "Your Grace, I swear I had no more than a sip," one of them cried out. They also admitted it was possible they might have dozed off for a minute, but certainly not more.

"Sounds like *keimai*," Tremayne said. "It's a Saloynan drug, Your Grace. It's commonly mixed with alcohol, and the effects are as they have described them."

Argblutal turned back to the two men bleeding on the wall. "You've failed me." He drew his ruby encrusted knife from his belt and approached them.

"Mercy, Your Grace!" they begged.

As the other guards took the men down and pinned them onto the table in front of him, the duke imagined they wore Darhour's face: he had no doubts who had used the Saloynan drug. Ignoring the guards' screams, the duke emasculated them with a few quick strokes of his knife. When he had the princess's guard on the table before him, he'd spend far more time. While mutilating the men brought a certain satisfaction, it wasn't nearly enough. "Throw them in the cell and leave them to contemplate the price of failure until they complete their journey to the seven hells," he told Tremayne.

He turned to the rest of the guards. "These two weren't the only ones who failed me. Who else accepted drinks from strangers?" Two of them paled and backed away, revealing their guilt. He nodded and the other guards quickly disabled the two guilty ones. He barely heard their screams as he castrated them. He turned to his bastard brother. "You were in charge of this. The responsibility was ultimately yours." He nodded to some of his men, and they seized his brother.

"No, Your Grace, this isn't my fault!" Herne cried out as the guards stripped him and manacled him to the wall. "On the life of our father, you can't treat me this way!"

Argblutal ignored the bastard's scream as he whipped his back with his riding whip. He took his knife, still red with blood, and pressed it against the bastard's neck. "Your incompetence has necessitated a change of plans. The princess must die before the old witch can expose me. You will find me a way to get an assassin into her rooms, and you will do it today."

He had Herne unmanacled and turned to Tremayne. "Tremayne, come with me to the palace at once. We must contain this damage before it's too late."

CHAPTER 23

Robrek sat at Myst's table staring out at the night sky. Ronan sat beside him, but the presence of the cat did nothing to soothe his loneliness. Milady had desired him, but he could go nowhere near her. He was still stuck in this Sulis-forsaken Valley, where he had no one to talk to except the horses. As he sat there contemplating what to do, he remembered what other men did when they were feeling low: they went to the inn and got drunk. If so many people did it, it must help. He remembered Myst warning him about the effects of alcohol on a healer. But why should he care? Myst had deserted him. He saddled Wild Thing and headed to the village's inn.

When he reached it, he swung down, taking his staff with him. As always, Wild Thing refused to be tethered. Robrek jingled the few coins in his purse. Most of his money he kept safely at the forest stable.

When he walked in, all talking ceased, and all eyes turned toward him; some of the customers drew the star of Sulis over their breasts. Ignoring them, he walked up to the bar. He took the seat at the end where he could keep his eye on things, propped his staff next to him, and put a coin on the counter. "Ale, please."

The innkeeper looked at him and shrugged; Banagher would have served the entire host of the seven hells if they had the coin. He filled a mug, put it front of Robrek, and took the money. Robrek grimaced as he tasted it. It was foul stuff, but he knew the same was true of most medicines, so he drank more deeply and waited for it to take effect. The inn was only about half full. At a table in the corner, four men were playing cards. They were friends of his brother; two of them were the ones who'd watched Boyden beat him nearly to death.

As Robrek finished half of the ale in his mug, a strange buzzing started in his head. One of the four card players got up and left. The other three whispered and glanced in his direction. Their actions seemed suspicious, but he drank more ale and concentrated on the pleasant floating feeling.

"Hey, you, Boyden's brother," one of the card players called out. Robrek thought his name was Derry or Dermot, something like that.

He didn't like being called Boyden's brother, but it was better than "demon child," so he raised his mug at whatever-his-name-was. "The name is Robrek," he said, and was surprised to find his tongue didn't work quite right.

"Well, Robrek, come and join us. We need a fourth for the game." Some corner of Robrek's brain knew playing cards with the men who'd watched him lick his brother's boots was a dumb idea. But at the moment he wasn't sure why, so he shrugged and got off the stool. He promptly discovered his feet weren't working right, either. He stumbled and had to catch himself on the bar. He concentrated carefully on putting one foot in front of the other. Despite his care, he stumbled again and nearly fell as he reached the table. Derry jumped up to catch him.

"Whoa, there. How much have you had?" Derry asked, as he helped him into the chair.

"This is my first." He waved the mug around. Again his tongue refused to form the words correctly, so he held up one finger to make sure they understood.

One of the other men laughed; Robrek thought his name was Bran. "Can't hold your ale much, can you?"

Robrek wasn't sure why that was funny, but since Bran was laughing, he thought he should, too, so he laughed loudly. He emptied his mug and signaled to the innkeeper for another. He fumbled with his purse and had difficulty getting a coin out.

When Banagher had refreshed all of their drinks, Derry began dealing. "You know how to play, don't you?"

Robrek nodded, but the movement made the room spin, so he decided nodding wasn't a good idea. "I don't have much money, and I've got to get drunk." He emptied his purse on the table, spilling half the coins on the floor.

Bran laughed again. "I think you've already accomplished that."

Robrek found this hilarious and bent over laughing as he tried to pick up his coins. Derry helped him and patted him on the back. "Don't let Bran bother you."

Robrek wasn't sure why Bran should bother him, so he picked up his cards and looked at them. Since he had a hard time focusing, he wasn't sure if he had a good hand or not. He picked up his mug to take another drink, but it was empty. "Hey, what happened to my ale?"

He looked at Bran, who laughed and turned to the other two. "The runt's so damned drunk, he can't even remember what he did two seconds ago." Robrek was sure he hadn't touched the ale, but what did it matter? He signaled for another. When the innkeeper brought it, he showed the man his cards. "Are these any good?" he asked.

Banagher walked away, and Robrek heard him mutter, "Stupid drunk," under his breath.

Bran cleared his throat impatiently. "Are you in or not?"

Robrek thought that three of his cards were fours, and the other two seemed to be fives. He knew that three of the same was pretty good, so he shoved one of his coins out to the middle of the table, but the middle of the table wasn't quite as far away as he thought, and he ended up knocking Bran's ale all over him.

Bran jumped up. "Drunken bastard."

But Derry put his hand on Bran's arm. "Don't worry about it, Bran. He'll buy you another. Won't you, Robrek?"

"Why not?" Robrek signaled again, but he was starting to find it difficult to stay on his chair. He didn't think rooms should be allowed to spin. Again, it was his turn to bet, and he pushed another coin out, more carefully this time. Derry folded, but Bran smiled at him unpleasantly as he upped the bet. The third man, whose name Robrek couldn't remember, also threw down his hand. Robrek was pretty sure he had three of one kind and two of another, so he shoved the rest of his coins out.

Bran's smile broadened. "Any more where that came from? It'd be a pity to stop while we're having so much fun."

Robrek wasn't certain he was having fun. In fact, he was feeling ill, and he had to piss desperately. "It's all I've got."

Bran called the bet, laid down three aces, and reached for the money.

"Wait," Robrek slurred. "I've got three of these." He laid down the fours.

"Aces are higher."

Robrek fumbled with his cards. "But I've also got two of these." He laid down the fives.

As the smile vanished from Bran's face, the third man laughed. "He's got a full house."

Bran looked dangerous as Derry helped Robrek put the money in his purse. Robrek felt too sick to take much note of it. "I don't feel so good. Where do you take a piss around here?"

"Let me show you." Derry helped him to his feet. "I've got to take one myself."

As Derry led him out the back door, Robrek noticed the other two were following. When he got outside, the cool night air cleared his head at bit, and he recognized the danger. He also realized he'd left his staff by the bar. He reached into his pocket for his knife, but found it empty.

"Looking for this?" Bran was trimming his nails with the missing knife.

"Hey, that's mine," he started to say, but something hit him hard in the stomach. The blow caused his already queasy stomach to lose all of its contents all over whoever it was that had hit him.

He heard somebody curse loudly. "He puked all over me! I'll kill him for that!"

Derry let go of him, and Robrek fell face first into his own vomit. He heard the shriek of an enraged horse, and the three men took off running. The last thing he remembered was Wild Thing standing over him.

* * *

Robrek awoke to an overpowering stench. Without opening his eyes, he rolled over. The world spun, and his head was pounding as if it were being repeatedly hit with a hammer, his mouth tasted awful, and his tongue felt thick and coated. He groaned as his stomach flopped, threatening to empty itself again. He felt the presence of Wild Thing and the two magical horses. Somehow he was at the forest stable.

Wild Thing licked his face. *:Not quick enough. Not protect.:* Opening his eyes, Robrek pulled himself into a sitting position. He was shocked to find it was early evening. He'd slept for nearly a full day. *:Man hit. Robrek hurt. Feel pain.:*

"This isn't your fault, my girl." He tore off his filthy shirt. "They didn't do this to me, girl. I drank some really bad stuff. Made me sick."

:We've been trying to tell her that all day,: came the laughing voice of Fancy Man. Robrek glared at the silver stallion. He was in no mood to be mocked. Stripping off his urine soaked trousers, he swore as he realized that both his purse and dagger were missing. He took a bar of soap and his filthy clothes to the river and washed both them and himself. He felt less disgusting when he was clean, but his head still throbbed, and his stomach was far from satisfied. He laid out his clothes to dry, put on some clean clothes he kept at the stable, and made himself a tea of willow bark, rosemary, and pennyroyal. He drank it as he laid his head back against the wall of the stable. Wild Thing remained at his side. The better he began to feel, the angrier he became. *How dare they mock me like this? If they truly knew who I was and what I can do, they'd be too frightened to touch me! But they'll learn soon enough. I'll make sure they pay me back. Every last dram.*

To do that, he needed a new staff to replace the one he'd left at the inn. He could hardly go after them with a sword. He fetched the bronze-hilted knife from Brazen's saddlebags, found an appropriate branch, and carved himself a new staff. With every stroke of the knife, he saw himself crushing Bran's skull or breaking Derry's neck. *And the next person who draws the star when I walk past will find himself with a broken hand.*

By the time he'd finished the staff, it was full dark, and he'd worked himself into a full blown rage. But he'd wait until morning to track down the thieves who'd stolen his things. A full moon had risen, giving enough light to see by. He set the staff aside, grabbed the bronze sword from its peg, and turned to Brazen. "Fight me," he ordered.

:This anger is not good. It is a dangerous thing in a healer.:

"Sulis curse you, fight me!"

No opponent appeared. *:You must cleanse your anger.:*

"Fight me, damn you!"

:Show him,: Fancy Man said. If a horse could sigh, Brazen did so.

Abruptly, Derry, Bran, and the other man appeared, all three with swords drawn. Robrek smiled savagely. *For once, Brazen does something right.* They closed quickly. Diving between them, he rolled to his feet. He stabbed Derry through his kidney before the three realized where he'd gone. Derry dropped, but the others whirled and attacked. With superior speed and skill, he parried the other men's blows. He wore them down with a nick here and small cut there. Wanting to make them suffer as he'd suffered all his life, he took his time. When they were bleeding from at least a dozen wounds each, he ended it. Bran dropped his sword too low, leaving his throat bare. Robrek took advantage of the opening, slicing through his neck and spraying them both with blood. Robrek was momentarily shocked. The illusions had never been so graphic and life-like before. Still, he celebrated Bran's death. With a quick stab to the heart, he finished the third man.

As he was pulling his bloody sword from the body, he heard chuckling behind him and whirled to see Boyden circling with drawn sword. He didn't wait for his brother to attack, but ran at Boyden and hacked at him with such force that, though Boyden blocked, the blow knocked him to the ground. Boyden rolled to his feet and came at him. Robrek parried and drove Boyden back, slashing at him ruthlessly. His blade caught his brother in the right shoulder and the left thigh. Blood blossomed wherever the sword struck. Boyden stumbled, and Robrek crashed his sword into Boyden's head, splitting it in two.

Robrek heard a roar of rage from behind him and turned just in time to block his father's blade. The strength of the older man's anger drove Robrek back. He tripped over his brother's body. His father lunged toward his heart, but Robrek leapt to his feet and countered the attack. His father had size and strength on his side, but Robrek's sword easily slipped past the older man's guard and sliced through his guts, spilling his entrails onto the ground. Angus fell writhing, and Robrek slit his throat to end his screams.

He turned to find Father Gildas. The priest was also armed, but he was less skilled than those Robrek had already bested. Gildas went down quickly, but he was followed by another and another, sometimes singly, sometimes two or three at a time. Every person who had ever laughed at him, shunned him, drew the star of Sulis against him—they all fell beneath Robrek's sword.

At last, he had his revenge.

After a while he ceased to notice who he killed. He merely struck out with the rage he'd carried for years. He was vaguely aware some of them weren't even armed. Through the fog of his battle frenzy, he even heard some of them beg for mercy, but he gave none. He slashed and stabbed. The bodies piled up around him, and the ground became slick with the blood of the fallen. As he pulled his sword free from the body of his latest victim, he heard someone calling his name. He whirled, thrusting his sword toward the sound. Too late to stop his momentum, he saw the auburn hair of the one who had spoken. He watched in horror as his sword plunged through Milady's mouth and emerged from the back of her head. Her eyes looked into his, startled, and she collapsed on top of another woman. As Robrek flung the sword away and dropped beside Milady's twitching body, he realized she'd fallen on top of Cara. Robrek didn't even remember killing her. Beside Cara lay Tegan, the young boy from the horse fair.

He grabbed Milady and held her to his chest. "No!" he sobbed. "I'd never do this to you! I could never hurt you! I love you!" As he sobbed, Milady disappeared, and he noticed the bodies heaped up around him. He collapsed, weeping into the dirt.

When he finally raised his head, the illusions had disappeared. "Why did you make me kill all those people?" he cried at Brazen.

:*We didn't make you. You wanted to. Your gift is too powerful to allow anger to guide it.*:

:*Brazen's right, human child.*: Fancy Man seemed to shudder. :*You're too damned angry. This isn't the dance I meant to teach you.*:

Robrek turned away from them. *Sulis, Father Gildas was right. I am a demon. I shouldn't have been allowed to live.*

CHAPTER 24

The man who Myst finally recognized as the captain of the princess's guard left her in a small underground room in the palace stables—a place far too like her prison cell for comfort. But she wouldn't be here long. She'd tell the princess what she knew, and with luck, she would be back to Robrek before nightfall.

After a short time, the princess, dressed for riding, climbed down the ladder. Darhour followed. With the three of them in the room, there was hardly room to breathe. The princess took the herb witch by the hands. "Mistress, you must forgive me. I never imagined you hadn't returned home. Are you well?"

"I'm well enough, Your Highness," she said, as Darhour presented her with a basket of food. The princess had her sit down at a small table to eat. The princess sat on the cot, and Darhour stood at the base of the ladder.

"Darhour told me the duke has kept you prisoner since Ostara. What did Argblutal want with you?"

"At first, nothing. I was left in the dark without knowing where I was or why. Last night he gave me a book to read—one that should have been destroyed a century ago. I believe the duke wanted me to make the mind-control potion it described."

The princess paled. "Is mind control possible?"

"The potions do have some effect depending on the magical strength of the person making them, but they are erratic. Even with the strongest magic, they can go disastrously wrong."

The princess grasped to her stomach. "Could he have made it already?"

The herb witch shook her head. "The duke couldn't have done it himself. He has no magic."

"What about the high priest?" Darhour asked. "Argblutal has been in frequent contact with Shylah."

Myst shrugged. "I don't know this high priest. How strong is his magic?"

"Very weak, I believe," Her Highness said. "I've never heard of him actually healing anyone."

"If he has any magic at all, he could make the potion. But it would be madness to attempt it. The most likely result would be to drive the victim insane."

The princess began to shake. "That Sulis-cursed bastard! I'll kill him for what he's done to my father!" Her Highness explained what had been happening with the king.

"It's possible the potion could do this, Your Highness, but I can't know for sure without touching His Majesty. But if this potion is the cause of the king's malady, I could make another potion to counter its effects. If my magic is stronger than the high priest's, my potion should be able to undo the damage."

The princess grasped her arm. "But what if the problem isn't the potion?"

"If simple age is responsible for the king's symptoms, it would have no effect and it would do no harm."

"Get started on it at once. I'll send someone to fetch the items you need." The princess turned to Darhour. "Bring Captain Faucon to my rooms immediately. We'll get Mistress Myst in to see the king as soon as possible."

The herb witch touched the princess's arm. "I'll see to the king and do what I can for him, but then I must go home."

The princess got up. "I know you'd like to go home, Mistress, but until Argblutal can be arrested, it simply isn't safe." She hurriedly climbed the ladder, leaving Myst imprisoned. The princess's intentions might be better than the duke's, but she was no more prepared to let her go. Even worse, if the duke went to Valley Fair seeking her, he could find Robrek instead. Myst feared for both Robrek and the entire joined kingdoms if his power ever fell into the duke's hands.

There was only one option. If she couldn't go home alive, she'd have to go home dead. When the princess's man came, she'd have him get ingredients for not one potion, but two.

* * *

Herne chewed paipin leaves to ease both his pain and his panic. If he couldn't provide the duke with a method of assassinating the princess by evening, he'd join the naked and bleeding men in the duke's cellar. And if he ran . . . ? He'd seen the bodies of the men who'd tried.

He paused to allow the calming effects of the paipin to engulf him. He'd never find his way through that maze of documents and diagrams in time without help. He'd have to use the librarian.

When he entered the library, the chief librarian came forward. "May we help you?" the old man said with evident distaste. Herne scanned the library for the man who'd seen him during the night. He was sitting at a far table.

"No," Herne said and walked toward the young librarian.

Druce started to follow, but backed away when Herne glared at him.

"How can I help you, sir?" the young man asked, getting to his feet.

Herne pulled the librarian aside so they wouldn't be overheard. "The princess wants to open her quarters to the servants' corridors, but has been told it's impossible. My lord hopes this is a mistake. He wants to offer her a surprise. If you could help my lord accomplish this, he will reward you well."

* * *

Samantha stared at Darhour. "It simply isn't possible that Captain Faucon died in a drunken fall! I've never seen the Captain even slightly the worse for drink!"

Darhour shook his head. "Few of the guard believe it was an accident."

"Sulis curse it, Darhour! Argblutal must have had him murdered!"

"I'd stake my life on it."

Samantha couldn't swallow passed the lump in her throat. "We can't allow him to get away with this. Bring whoever is taking Faucon's place to me at once."

"I don't think that would be wise, Your Highness. The king has appointed a man named Tremayne. He was head of Duke Argblutal's personal security forces."

Samantha sank down in a chair. "Darhour, we must get Myst to the king at once."

* * *

Herne looked over the young librarian's shoulder as he examined a detailed plan of the palace in Danu's day. Beside it was a contemporary diagram of the palace.

The librarian smiled smugly. "Here are the princess's rooms," he whispered as he pointed to a spot on the diagram. "And here's where the corridors were blocked by the Princess Danu. If we had to go through there, we'd have a demon of a time at it. Danu was a bit excessive in everything she did, and the wall she had made is three feet thick." He moved his finger to a spot behind the princess's bedchamber. "Back here is a room that is rumored to have been used by Danu for sorcery. It was accessible only through her rooms, and it hasn't been used in some time." He pulled the second plan toward him. "Changes have been made in the palace since, and the room is accessible through these servants' corridors." Innis ran his finger along the plans.

"And the princess is unaware of such a room?" Herne raised an eyebrow.

The young librarian nodded. "I'd think so. Princess Morrigan idolized Danu. She had a huge painting of Danu created and placed on the wall of the bedchamber, covering the door to this unused room."

"And you're sure this way in is practical?"

Innis nodded. "As sure as I can be without actually going to examine the rooms myself."

Herne smiled. "Lead the way."

* * *

Innis felt the urge to giggle as he led the duke's man through the palace corridors. Blaine may be working for the princess, but Innis was certain he'd soon be working for Duke Argblutal, and anyone could see he was the true power in the palace these days. He consulted the plans carefully and stopped before a door that was almost hidden in the wall. "Here are the servants' corridors," he told the duke's man, opening the door. Herne followed him inside. Innis led him down the narrow corridor and past several twists and turns. The corridors got narrower and dustier the farther they went . Many of the corridors looked like they hadn't been entered for decades, if not centuries. Eventually, they had to light torches. They had to stop and backtrack a couple of times as they reached dead ends that weren't on any of the diagrams.

"Are you sure you aren't lost?" Herne snapped, after the third such dead end.

"Don't worry. I'll find it." Innis hoped it was true.

Finally, he found the doorway revealed on his diagrams. "This is it." He smiled and pushed against the door. At first it refused to budge. With Herne adding his strength, the door burst open to reveal a dust-covered chamber. Innis choked as the stale air poured out into the corridor. "I doubt the room has been opened for a hundred years," he coughed. Rats scurried into hiding as the two men entered. By the light of the torch, Innis could see rotting tapestries, shelves covered with jars whose contents had long since evaporated, and furniture that had crumbled with the weight of time. A thick layer of dust covered everything.

Innis coughed again. "Of course, this will need a good deal of cleaning before it's a proper path for Her Highness's servants."

Herne smiled. "You said this room leads to the back of Her Highness's rooms?"

Consulting his diagram, Innis nodded. "This way." He led the duke's man through the small room to a doorway at the back. The doorway was boarded over by crumbling and rotten wood.

Herne kicked at the wood, and it broke fairly easily. In a very short time, he'd knocked a path through into the corridor beyond. Again, Innis coughed as bad air rushed in. Using the torch, Herne illuminated the short expanse of corridor. A few feet to the right was a thick brick wall—the one Danu had built.

Innis stepped into the corridor and walked a few feet to the left. "You see the boards here." He pointed to a covering of wood in the brick wall. "This was once the servants' entrance into Her Highness's bedchamber. It shouldn't be much of a chore to knock this out. The only problem is the painting. I've heard the princess is quite fond of it. We'll need to get an artist to look at it from that side if the princess wants to preserve it."

Herne moved behind him. "You've been most helpful. How would you suggest we proceed?"

Innis beamed. "Well, as I said, I think we should get an art—" Before he could finish his sentence, Herne slit his throat.

* * *

Samantha couldn't sleep that night. Faucon's death and Tremayne's promotion made her situation tenuous. Still, all wasn't lost. While Darhour hadn't found a way to get Myst in to see the king, he did have a servant in place who could give the king the first flask of the herb witch's potion in the morning. She prayed to the goddess it would bring back her father's mind. She stared at the painting of Danu, or rather at Danu's horse. The Horsetad reminded her of the day she'd met the peasant boy. Things had seemed so simple then. She longed for the time when her worst problem was getting a decent horse. *Sulis, help me. Holy Mother, give me back my father, and I promise I'll never complain again.*

Samantha heard a commotion in the corridor, and Brice's voice rang out, "Attack!"—the signal word for trouble of any kind. She grabbed her sword from beside her bed and ran to the door of her chambers. She heard the fighting on the other side. The thought of any of her bodyguards in danger was intolerable, but she'd only put them in more danger if she opened the door.

A tremendous crash came from behind her. She whirled to see a man with a sword emerging from her bedchamber. She was so shocked it took her a few moments to remember to yell, "Attack!"

The man laughed "Don't think anyone heard you. It's just you and me, sweetheart. Nobody's coming to your rescue."

Samantha was equally sure her men hadn't heard. She circled warily; she'd never been able to best even the least skilled of her guards. But when the man lunged, she parried his blow with little difficulty.

He smiled nastily. "Oh, the little girl's learned a couple of tricks. It'll make killing you all the sweeter."

He came in again, and this time Samantha not only parried, but also struck a blow on his left arm. "You bitch!" he yelled as the blood began to flow.

Samantha remembered what Darhour had said about an attacker underestimating her skill. This man had, and it had given her the advantage Darhour promised. "Oh, have I spoiled your shirt?" She lunged for his right arm and struck a similar blow. "All better. You match now."

The man bellowed and ran at her, but she stepped to the side and brought her sword hilt down on the back of his head as he passed. She was so surprised the move worked exactly as Darhour had taught her that she didn't press the attack. The man rolled to his feet, calling her every foul name she'd ever heard.

She thrust toward his heart, and the man just barely got his sword up in time. They fought their way around her room, and the princess cut him on the leg. It was a fairly deep wound, and he began bleeding heavily. When he came at her again, she parried and tripped him. When he came to his feet again, the anger in his eyes was overshadowed by fear.

She smiled. Not only was this easy; it was actually fun. "Yes, it is just you and me, sweetheart," she taunted. "Nobody's coming to your rescue."

The man lunged. She'd been so busy mocking him that she parried badly, and his sword sliced her upper arm. "Damn you!" she swore.

She'd end this now. She thrust in for the kill. He managed to parry the blow, then turned and ran toward her bedchamber. The wound on his thigh made him slow. The princess caught him and shoved her sword through his back and into his heart. He dropped to the ground, twitched a few times, and lay still.

She yanked her sword out with a smile of triumph. She *had* become quite good.

She felt something wet on her bare feet; she was standing in a puddle of the dead man's blood. His head turned to the side revealed one of his dead, unseeing eyes. As her gore rose, she clasped her hand over her mouth. This was no game she'd won. She'd just killed a man.

She backed toward the wall and sank to the floor. She began laughing hysterically and fought against tears.

* * *

Darhour heard a shout from the corridors, "Attack!" He leaped to his feet, grabbed his sword, palmed one of his knives, and charged into the hallway and into the middle of a fierce fight. With his sword, he stabbed one of the attackers in the back. Phelan was down, and one of the attackers was about to stab him through the throat. Darhour threw his knife, catching the man in the neck, as Kailen, Conroy, and Bearach also spilled into the corridor.

After that, it wasn't much of a fight. There had been only six men, and either Brice or Phelan had taken out a man before any of the rest could respond. Bearach got one with an arrow, and Conroy stabbed another. Kailen had his sword to the last man's throat. "Don't kill him!" Darhour yelled, but Kailen smiled an icy smile and plunged his sword through the man's neck. "Damn it! I told you not to kill him!"

Kailen glared unapologetically back. "He deserved to die."

"Yes, but it would have been nice if he could have answered a few questions first."

Kailen reddened. "I'm sorry, Captain. I didn't think."

Ignoring the apology, Darhour quickly assessed the damage. He and Bearach were unhurt. Both Kailen and Conroy bore very minor wounds, little more than scratches. But both Brice and Phelan were on the ground with more serious injuries. He saw a small page peek out from behind a statue some way down the hall. "Fetch the physician," Darhour ordered. The boy ran off.

Darhour looked at their six dead attackers. *Only six men? Did they rate our skill so lightly?* He went to the princess's door and knocked. "Your Highness, it's all right. There's been an attack, but we've dispatched it." Darhour stared at the two he'd killed. His knife was still protruding from the one man's neck and his sword dripped with the blood of the other. He'd just ensured his own damnation, but what did it matter? He'd kept his daughter safe.

Hearing no response from within the princess's rooms, he knocked louder. "Your Highness, it's safe now. We've dispatched them."

After a few more seconds, Darhour heard the bolt to the princess's room being slid back. When the door swung open, his daughter stood there with a bloody sword in her hand, her nightdress was covered in blood. His knees grew weak. "Holy Sulis, Your Highness, what happened?"

She gestured with her bloody sword to a man lying dead in the middle of the room. "He just appeared, and I killed him. He tried to kill me, and I killed him. He was just there, Darhour. How could he have been in my rooms?" She collapsed into his arms.

Holding her tightly, Darhour nodded to Bearach and Kailen. "Check for others. Conroy, guard the main corridor." Darhour took his daughter inside her chambers and sat her down, feeling her to find the source of the blood.

"It's just the scratch on my arm," she said. "The rest of the blood is his." She pointed to the dead man.

Darhour tore off a piece of his shirt to bind her wound. Bearach swore loudly from the princess's bedchamber. The princess jumped to her feet and followed the noise. Darhour tried to prevent her, but she whirled out of his grasp. "Danu!" she gasped, as she entered her bedchamber. The painting was torn in half and a gaping hole had been knocked in the wall behind it.

"Bearach, protect the princess. Kailen, with me." Darhour ordered and charged through the hole into the corridor beyond.

Samantha's hand ached. Reaching to rub the ache, she found herself still holding the bloody sword. She dropped it and fell to her knees as her stomach rebelled.

"Physician, at once," Bearach yelled at men arriving in the corridor. "The princess needs assistance." Calum, her father's physician, rushed in. He and Bearach helped her into a chair. Bearach watched the surgeon examine the wound on her arm. Darhour emerged from the hole in the wall. "There's an entire labyrinth of passageways behind here." He turned to Calum. "How is she?"

"She'll be fine," the surgeon reported, as he dressed the wound. "The king may want to think more carefully about who he chooses to protect his heir, however."

Grabbing the man, Darhour slammed him against the wall.

"Stop it, Darhour," Samantha ordered.

Darhour released the man. "I'm sorry. It's my fault. I will ensure nothing like this ever happens again." Darhour's glare scared her, and for the first time she could picture him as the assassin he'd been.

Several members of the Royal Guard poured into her rooms. "Holy Sulis, Mother of us all," Lieutenant Hawk swore.

Darhour rounded on him. "How is it seven armed men can make it to the very door of the princess's room, one into her bedchamber itself, completely unnoticed by the Royal Guard?"

Lieutenant Hawk paled. "I don't know, but I will find out."

Calum finished dressing her wound. "I'll see to the others and then attend to you more thoroughly, Your Highness."

The others? She followed him into her outer chamber. Calum and two assistants were bending over someone in the hallway. She turned to Darhour. "Who was hurt?"

"Both Phelan and Brice have sustained injuries."

Samantha grabbed Darhour's arm. "They will be all right, though?"

"Don't worry about me, Your Highness." Brice's voice was choked with pain. "I'll mend well enough."

Samantha looked to the physician for confirmation. "I'm pretty sure he'll live. The other, I don't know. I've seen men survive wounds like his. I've also seen them die from them."

Samantha inched her way toward her wounded guards. *This cannot be happening. They can't die.*

Darhour pulled her away from Phelan and Brice. "Your Highness, the surgeons are doing all they can. We need to get you some place more secure."

Too numb to protest, she allowed her guards to lead her across the hall into Darhour's rooms. "I thought Argblutal wanted to marry me, not kill me."

"It would seem he has changed his mind."

* * *

Fingering his riding crop, Argblutal sat at his desk and waited for Herne.

There was a knock on his door, but instead of his brother, Captain Tremayne entered. "Is she dead?" Argblutal asked.

"I'm afraid not, Your Grace. Herne underestimated the princess's skill. She took care of his assassin herself."

Argblutal brought his riding crop down hard on his desk. "Where is my pathetic brother?"

"He probably ran."

Argblutal leaned forward in his chair. "Did any survive?"

"The princess and her men were thorough, Your Grace."

"And the herb witch?"

"I don't think she's been found."

"See that she is, and once you've found her, find that bastard brother of mine!"

When Tremayne left, a plan formed in Argblutal's mind, and he sent for Count Morgan.

The count bowed as he entered. "How may I serve you, Your Grace?"

"I need seven Neasarian swords before morning."

Morgan lifted an eyebrow. "They aren't common. How much are you willing to pay?"

"Get them."

"Yes, Your Grace." The count bowed his way out.

* * *

As she paced Darhour's rooms, Samantha hugged herself. Her arm ached, and she felt exhausted. But every time she closed her eyes, she saw the face of the man she'd killed. Although her maids had bathed her, she still felt the wet stickiness of his blood. She'd sent word to her father. The king's council couldn't fail to act. Argblutal wouldn't get away with this.

Before the first light of dawn, Darhour had left her with the other three sound members of her guard and gone to ensure the first dose of the herb witch's potion was given to the king. When he returned, he gave her a grim nod. "It's done."

Please, Holy Mother, let it work! She resumed pacing. Finally, a page arrived with news she was wanted in the council chamber. Trying not to have hopes too high, the princess walked to the council chamber, accompanied by her secretary and her guards. When she entered, the king jumped to his feet. "Samantha, my dear, there have been the wildest rumors! They're saying you were attacked!"

"It's true, Father."

His eyes darted wildly around the room. "This is an outrage!" As the council members took their seats, he turned to the captain of the Royal Guard. "Have you any evidence of who is behind this?"

Tremayne stepped forward. "I'm happy to report we do, Your Majesty. Our first clue was the weapons carried by the assassins." Tremayne placed several swords on the council table.

"These aren't the swords they used," the princess protested, and looked to Darhour for support.

"Indeed, they aren't. Those are of Neasarian make, and those who attacked the princess carried Korthlundian weapons," Darhour said.

Tremayne smiled as if he were consoling a small child for a mistake. "I'm sure in the thick of the battle, you had little time to notice the make of the weapons. These are the swords we took from the dead assassins."

"Proceed," the king commanded.

"But, Father," Samantha protested, "the man in my bedchamber wasn't using a Neasarian sword. These blades are curved; my attacker's was straight."

"What reason would Tremayne have to lie, Your Highness?" Duke Sheen gave an exaggerated sigh, as if the princess were being purposefully difficult.

Samantha turned to answer him, but Tremayne spoke before she could, "As His Majesty knows, such blades aren't common in Murtaghan, so I went at once to question the Neasarian ambassador about where the assassins might have obtained them. Truly, Your Majesty, I had no suspicions he was involved, but the moment I brought up the swords, he became highly agitated. At last, he confessed that he'd ordered the assassination in revenge for the death of his son last summer."

Samantha jumped up. "What had I to do with his son's death?"

The king patted her arm and pulled her back down into her seat. He nodded to Tremayne to proceed.

"Your Highness, I do admit his explanation lacked reason," Tremayne said. "But he seems to believe that his son's death was no simple robbery and that someone from court was responsible. He'd heard reports of his son riding with you and you trusted the offering of condolences entirely to somebody else's hands rather than handling it yourself, as you generally would."

Samantha couldn't believe what she was hearing. "I was in the middle of the Massossinan trade negotiations at the time."

"Calm down, my dear." The king patted her arm again.

"Of course, the notion is absurd, Your Highness," Tremayne agreed. "But the Neasarian ambassador apparently decided you left the burial arrangements in Duke Argblutal's hands because your hands were covered with his son's blood. He's been working on avenging his son ever since."

"But how could a foreigner at court find an entrance to my room that has been hidden for centuries?" As she looked across at the duke, she realized something else for the first time. Argblutal had had Phomello killed, and as she thought back on him coming to offer her condolences, she thought she knew why.

"Good question, Your Highness," Tremayne nodded. "We believe we've found an answer to that as well. A young librarian named Innis Halwnstamm is missing." The princess heard Blaine take a sharp intake of breath. "According to Druce, he claimed to have been given a position by Duke Argblutal."

"I've never met this man," Argblutal declared.

"So we've determined. A man claiming to be in the duke's employ, but who was truly working for the Neasarian ambassador, contacted this librarian. These were found among the librarian's possessions." Tremayne placed a collection of papers and two diagrams of the palace down onto the council room table. Blaine squeaked at the sight. "He'd obviously been researching the palace collections for some time. The first is a very detailed list of all architectural diagrams to be found in the palace library. These other two are diagrams of the palace that reveal the route taken by the assassin to enter Her Highness's rooms. We don't know if this Innis knew why the Neasarian was paying him to do this research. We're searching for him, but believe he may be dead. You'll notice the blood stains on the diagrams."

"We'll have this Neasarian tried at once," the king said. "All will see what becomes of those who plot against our heir."

"I'm afraid that won't be possible, Your Majesty. He tried to run when we went to arrest him. My men were forced to kill him."

Samantha shook her head. *Argblutal has thought of everything!* "Father, the Neasarians can't be responsible for this!"

"Nonsense, my dear." The king smiled indulgently at her. "The ambassador has confessed."

Samantha looked around the table, and all of the council members were nodding grimly. She'd get nowhere protesting further.

* * *

Shaking with rage, Samantha returned to Darhour's rooms. Darhour and all her remaining men accompanied her inside. Darhour looked so fierce she was almost afraid of him.

"Your Highness, we've been out-maneuvered," he said.

"Your Highness, this is all my fault," Blaine said, as white as he'd been after witnessing Kayne's execution. "I made those lists. I gave them to Innis when I left the library. I'd tried to organize Druce's Sulis-cursed catalog. Could I just do what I had been told? No, I spent weeks making sense of that mess. If I hadn't have done that, they never would have found the way in."

With difficulty, Samantha calmed Blaine down and extracted from him the story of how he'd tried to organize the library catalog and been chastised for it and how he'd given the results of his labor to his fellow junior undersecretary. "Your Highness, Innis was a friend of mine. He'd no more betray you than stick his hand in a nest of angry hornets, so to speak. He must have been duped."

"Duped or not, the man's dead if I get my hands on him," Kailen said, and Bearach and Conroy nodded agreement.

Samantha opened her mouth to object, but Darhour beat her to it. "We'll worry about that if he's still alive. For now, we need to know if there are any more such entrances into Her Highness's room. Blaine, see to the repair of the wall and then find out."

Samantha was shocked by Darhour giving orders over her own, but they made sense, and she was too unsettled to object.

* * *

Myst held the potion bottle—the one the princess didn't know she'd made. The Draught of the Living Death, Mother Anu had called it. She'd written a note requesting her body be taken home to Robrek for burial and asked that he be told nothing. Even if the potion hadn't completely worn off by then, a healer as strong as he would surely sense the life within her before he buried her. That is, if there was still life. The potion came with a terrible risk.

Overhead she heard over a dozen booted feet, and Adalardo asked, "What is the meaning of this?"

A man replied, "Official palace business. Stay out of the way." The boots stopped, and the same man spoke again. "Fan out. If you find her, don't let her touch you." The footsteps spread throughout the stables.

Wanting her supposed suicide to be public, Myst knew this was the best chance. She held the potion tightly, climbed the ladder, and opened the trapdoor. "What is going on?" she asked loudly, as she climbed into the office of the Master of the Horse.

Adalardo gaped at her, and footsteps pounded in their direction. Adalardo was pushed aside, and a man Myst didn't know barged into the room with his sword drawn. "She's here," he called, as several other men, also with drawn swords, arrived.

"Come with us quietly, and you won't get hurt," one of them ordered.

"No," she protested. "I won't be taken back to the duke."

"Is there a problem, Captain Tremayne?" The herb witch heard Darhour's voice coming from inside the stable. By the sound of it he had quite a few men with him as well.

"Keep an eye on her. Don't let her escape." A man swept out of the room to confront Darhour. "We've found the king's healer kept prisoner here. What is the meaning of this?"

"The herb witch is no prisoner."

"Lieutenant Hawk and the rest of you," Tremayne demanded, "what are you doing with this man?"

"Captain, he told us the princess's interests were being threatened. We came to lend our assistance."

Myst moved out into the main stable. Keeping their swords on her, the men let her pass, shrinking from her touch. "The princess's interests are being threatened," she called out. "Duke Argblutal kidnapped me. He's poisoning the king with a potion that warps his reason."

"Lies!" Tremayne yelled. "You'll be taken to the duke to answer for your slander!"

"No, I won't. I'll be taken home and buried on my own land." She gulped down the contents of the bottle. A coldness seized her heart and spread outward to every portion of her body. The world went dark, and her strength failed her.

* * *

"Why would she do such a thing?" Samantha cried when Darhour told her of Myst's suicide. "What will Robbie think of me when I send him his mistress's body?"

Darhour's words hissed through his teeth. "He'll think nothing of you, Your Highness. The herb witch's last request states that she wants him told nothing. She wants to be taken home in a simple cart, wrapped in a horse blanket."

Samantha stared out the window toward the stables, feeling too empty for tears. Again she heard the priestess's words. *Oh, my child, it pains me, but dark times are ahead for you. The path ahead of you will not be easy, but it is a path only you can tread.* "No, it isn't a path I can tread," she whispered. "Where are you, O Holy Mother? You must send somebody else to take care of this! I can't!"

* * *

Sick with apprehension, Tremayne walked toward the duke's rooms to report. *It's not my fault. How could I have known she was going to kill herself?* Fortunately, his men had tracked Herne to a paipin den and had secured him at the duke's residence, so he hadn't failed at everything.

"Well?" the duke asked, as Tremayne bowed before him.

"We located the herb witch, but unfortunately, she committed suicide before we could take her." Tremayne explained what had happened, leaving out Darhour's role and the witch's last words. He'd have to be sure the duke never found out that he'd allowed the herb witch to make public accusations.

"Damn the bitch!" Argblutal swore, and Tremayne knew he meant the princess.

"We've located your brother. He's now in your cellar."

The duke's eyes flashed. "Come with me, and you'll witness the price of failure."

* * *

Late that night, Tremayne stumbled into an inn near the docks and ordered the strongest whiskey available. He'd promised the duke he'd never drink again, but he needed it just this once. He couldn't get Herne's screams out of his head. *Holy Sulis! His own brother!*

* * *

Blaine reported that he'd arranged to have the herb witch's body sent home and that the masons had finished the repairs to her bedroom. "I assure you, Your Highness, no one will get in. Lord Devyn is also asking to see you."

"Get rid of him," Darhour ordered before she had a chance to reply.

Samantha glared at him. "Just when did you start giving the orders?"

"You've been attacked, Your Highness. We'll take no risks."

"Devyn isn't a risk." Since any distraction from the aching despair would be a relief, she told Blaine she'd see him.

Devyn bowed as he entered. "Is it true, Your Highness? I've heard the assassins damaged the painting of Danu."

Darhour growled, "Is it the art that concerns you, and not the fate of your future queen?"

Devyn turned bright red. "Forgive me. I didn't mean to trivialize the attack on Your Highness."

"What is your business?" Darhour snapped.

Samantha shot Darhour another glare. "What brings you here, Devyn?" she asked.

"I'm something of an artist, as Your Highness knows, and I know how fond you were of that painting. I came to see if I could repair the damage."

Again Darhour spoke before she could. "You think repairing the painting will get you the throne?"

"N-no, of course not," Devyn stammered. "If my services aren't wanted, I won't impose." He turned to leave.

"Wait!" Samantha commanded. "Please, forgive the captain of my guard. He's overwrought by the attack." She gestured toward her bedchamber. "Please, tell me if you can repair it."

Mollified by the princess's words, Devyn followed her into her bedchamber. Approaching the damaged canvas, he shook his head and made sorrowful noises. "It'll never be quite the same again, but if Your Highness wills it, I can repair much of the damage."

"If you could, I'd be forever in your debt."

"I can begin at once, if Your Highness wishes."

After the young lord had bowed his way out, Samantha rounded on Darhour. "I know this attack has shaken all of us, but it's no excuse for the way you're acting." She wasn't sure how well she knew him anymore. He seemed capable of anything.

CHAPTER 25

Robrek lunged toward the voice. He screamed as his sword pierced Milady's head and blood gushed from her mouth.

Robrek awoke trembling in the darkness of Myst's cottage. It was the third night in a row he'd dreamed of the slaughter at the forest stable. "I'm not like that," he whispered. "I'd never hurt Milady. Never hurt anyone." But even as he thought it, he remembered the pleasure of cleaving Boyden's head in two, and his hands itched to hold the sword. He wanted to make everyone pay for the way they'd treated him. *Holy Sulis, I am a demon.*

Brazen had made him into a weapon. Maybe the magical horses were demon horses, after all. He wouldn't become as evil as his enemies, no matter what Brazen wanted. Making plans to leave in the morning, he drifted back to sleep.

* * *

The sun light blinding him through the window, Robrek woke to the sound of a wagon. Pulling on trousers, he looked out. He didn't recognize either of the men on the wagon seat. He pulled on a shirt and went out to greet them.

"Can I help you?" he asked.

"We're looking for Robrek Angusstamm," one of the men said, getting down from the wagon.

"You've found him," Robrek said.

"Master Robrek, we've been asked to return the body of your mistress to you for burial." He pointed to something covered by a horse blanket in the back of the wagon.

Robrek froze as the man's words sank in. "No! Myst isn't dead!" Pushing past the man, he jumped into the back of the wagon. He pulled the blanket back and gathered the old woman in his arms. She felt stiff and cold.

"She can't be dead," he insisted. "I'll heal her." Barely able to see through his tears, he carried Myst into the cottage and laid her on her cot. The men followed.

He held the old woman's hand and tried to determine what was wrong with her. The icy coldness of her flesh cut through his guts and into his heart, severing him from what was left of his humanity. He rounded on the men. "What have you done to her?"

One of the men put up his hands. "Hold on now, son. We did nothing to the old woman. We were merely told to bring her to you."

Robrek wiped the tears from his face and allowed anger to fill the void left by Myst's loss. "Told by who?" he hissed. "Where has she been?"

"We must be going," one of them said, and they walked out of the cottage.

Robrek grabbed his staff and followed. "You're going nowhere until you tell me what happened to her!"

Ignoring him, they mounted the wagon seat.

Robrek grabbed one of the men, pulled him from the seat, and threw him into the dirt. He put his staff to the man's neck. "Tell me now, or I'll crush your throat."

He heard the second man coming at him from behind. He stabbed his staff back, catching the man in the stomach. Before the man had a chance to recover, Robrek whirled and hit him in the head, knocking him into the wagon bed. Robrek whirled back to the man on the ground. "Tell me or die!"

"I have my orders. I'll tell you nothing." The man closed his eyes and waited for the blow.

Robrek lifted his staff with trembling arms. He wanted to kill him, wanted someone else to hurt as badly as he did. *No, I'm not a demon.* Again, he spoke the lie and fled into the cottage. He knelt down beside Myst's bed and laid his head on her chest. *She can't be dead. I won't let her be.*

As he heard the wagon drive away, he closed his eyes and tried to enter a healing trance, but his grief and anger made it impossible. Giving up on the trance, he attempted to send his energy into her lifeless body. The thinnest trickle of his energy flowed from him. It wasn't enough to cure a head cold, but he foolishly imagined her body growing warmer. Then he heard the faint beat of her heart. "Myst, you're alive."

His relief allowed him to shove his anger aside and better access his energy. Myst's heartbeat grew stronger, and her chest began to rise and fall. He opened his eyes and sat back. The color was returning to her face. The old woman coughed, and her eyes came open.

"Robrek, how?" Her voice was so faint he had to lean in to hear her. "I feel your magic. How is that possible?"

"Shhh, don't try to talk now. I'll make you a tea to help strengthen you." When the tea was ready, he brought it to the herb witch. He helped her lift her head and drink. As she drank, her color improved, her breathing became steadier and her pulse stronger. But the icy chill didn't leave her flesh. She lay back on her pillow and smiled. "Thank you, my child."

She closed her eyes, and her breathing settled into the steady rhythm of sleep. Robrek watched her, terrified her breathing would stop. "Where have you been, Myst?" he whispered. "What happened to you?"

* * *

Myst woke as the first rays of morning light hit her eyes. Though she was wrapped in thick blankets, she felt as if she were encased in ice. Robrek slept in a chair next to her bed. She was shocked by how much older he looked. Somehow, in the two months she'd been gone, he'd become a man.

As the sun rose, Robrek's eyes opened; the vulnerability that had always marked them was gone. Instead, his eyes held strength and a hint of danger, as if he'd seen terrible sights or done terrible deeds. "Myst," he said in a voice deeper than the one she remembered. "How are you? Where have you been?"

"I feel much better. Could you help me into the chair near the fire? And I could use some breakfast."

"Certainly, mistress." He sprang to his feet with the vigor of youth Myst couldn't help but envy. He helped her to the chair, tucked the blankets around her, built up the fire, and began cooking porridge. She noticed his clothing and other signs he'd been living there.

"I see you made good use of my cottage," she said.

He turned from his cooking. "I hope you don't mind."

"Of course not, my child. Have you had problems with your father?" He shrugged.

When the food was ready, he dished up a bowl of porridge. He set the porridge and another mug of strengthening tea in front of her. He dished up breakfast for himself and sat across from her.

"My child, you've changed. What's happened while I was gone?"

"Nothing," he said, but he didn't meet her eyes. "It's just that Father Gildas was right about me." Myst's heart broke for him as he told her what he'd been through and what he'd done—the piles of corpses at the forest stable, the men, women, and little children he'd slaughtered, his sword piercing Milady's head.

By the time he finished, he was sobbing at her knees. "Mistress, I killed them all."

He cried into Myst's lap, and she stroked his hair gently. "My child, no one really died that day."

Robrek pulled away. "Don't you understand? I enjoyed it! They deserved it for what they did to me!"

Myst closed her eyes. "The question isn't what they deserve, but what you deserve. Hatred can warp you if you allow it. Revenge is a horrible thing. By trying to give people what they deserve, you can destroy your own life."

Robrek jumped to his feet and crossed her cottage to stare out the window. "They're the ones who destroyed my life. I want them to suffer."

"They will, my child, and without any help from you. Sin provides its own punishment. Let your anger go, and live your own life."

He whirled on her, and Myst was frightened by the rage in his face. "Don't tell me what to do! You have no idea how I feel!"

Closing her eyes, she breathed slowly. She swore she'd never speak of that day; she hadn't even told Donella about it, but she couldn't let Robrek rob himself of his youth as she had robbed herself of hers. "That's where you're wrong, my child. I know too well how you feel. I nearly let my desire for revenge destroy my life.

Sit down. There's a story you need to hear." With her eyes closed, Myst heard Robrek take his seat. "It began the day I first bled in the way of a woman. I was so proud when I showed Mother Anu my stained sheets. She smiled and, as was the way in my village, tied red and green ribbons to the ends of my braids—green for life, red for the blood that brings it forth. She packed me a basket, and I headed for the woods for a day of meditation. Now that I was a woman, the day was drawing closer when I had to decide whether to take my holy vows. As I walked through the village, I basked in the envious glances of the other girls who saw the ribbons in my hair. I had just reached the trees when I heard the sound of horses. I hid and watched as a band of mercenaries descended upon my village.

"The screaming started almost at once. I could do nothing as my people were slaughtered. At last the screaming stopped, but the quiet was worse. It meant no one was left. The men piled the bodies in the center of the village square. My mother, my friends, my neighbors, Mother Anu, everybody I'd ever known was thrown into a heap. They doused the bodies with lamp oil and set them on fire. I shut my eyes, but I couldn't block out the odor of charred flesh. The soldiers burned the village to the ground and rode away."

Robrek grabbed her hand. "Why did they do such a horrible thing?"

"I never knew. The war was over. My village was a small, unimportant one. But I alone was left. I decided Sulis had spared me to make the soldiers pay. I spent ten long and fruitless years nursing my hatred and attempting to track down those responsible. I starved myself and denied myself any pleasure while I travelled, bribed, stole, whored, anything that might lead to the identity of the band."

"And did you make them pay?" Robrek growled.

Myst shook her head. "I traced the former captain of the mercenaries to a portside tavern. Holding a vial of poison I had prepared, I entered the tavern, intending to learn from him as much as I could of the whereabouts of any others before pouring the poison into his drink and watching him die.

"But when the innkeeper pointed the man out to me, I found I'd come too late for revenge to have any meaning. The officer sat in a corner, his body emaciated and his breath reeking of alcohol and paipan leaves. He could have been no more than forty, but he looked nearly seventy. His hands shook so badly he could barely get his drink to his mouth. His eyes were empty of life or hope. Chasing this wreck of a man I had sacrificed my youth, my virtue, my honor, all the pleasures of the world—only to discover he'd already destroyed himself with no help from me." Myst took Robrek's hand. "My child, learn from my mistake. Let go of your anger. Those who have harmed you will reap the consequences of their sins without any help from you. Hating them will only make you become like them."

Robrek stared out the window, avoiding her gaze. "Mistress, you're tired. You must rest."

Myst tightened her grip. "My child, I felt you use your energy on me. Do you have any idea how powerful you must be to be able to heal both animals and humans? You are too good a man to allow hatred to guide your power."

Robrek pulled free of Myst. "I'm sorry, I'm not the man you think I am."

* * *

Robrek knew Myst meant well, but things didn't always happen so conveniently. His enemies hadn't destroyed themselves. They were all around him, and he needed to determine if the mysterious horses numbered among them.

The two gleaming horses were waiting for him when he arrived at the forest stable. Robrek dismounted and jabbed a finger toward them. "Why are you here? What do you want from me?"

:We were called.: Brazen answered.

"What in the seven hells does that mean? Who called you? Why?"

The silver horse shook his head. *:Human child, let's not waste time in foolish questions when there are so many things to learn.:*

Robrek whirled to face the stallion. "I will have answers. I won't play any more of your games."

:You're right. We have no time for games. You have a lot to learn, and not much time to do it. Manners, court protocol, rules of rank. But I believe we should begin with dancing.:

Robrek stared at the horse. "You can't be serious!"

:The Saloynan waltz would be a good one to begin with.: Robrek heard Brazen object, and Fancy Man snorted. *:Do I tell you which weapons to teach him? But maybe we should begin with something a little tamer—the Basse Dance, perhaps.:*

"Are you mad? I told you I'm not doing anything without answers, and there's no way in the seven hells I'm learning highborn dancing."

:Human child, all the mares swoon over a man who can dance.: Fancy Man chuckled, and an illusion of Milady appeared in the paddock.

Robrek brandished his staff at the stallion. "You'll leave her out of this!"

:That was insensitive of me.: He didn't sound the slightest bit sorry, but he did change the illusion to a faceless, feminine version of the illusions Brazen had him fight.

"I don't care what she looks like; I am not dancing. Now tell me why you're here."

:But you did what Brazen wanted. Do you like her better than me?:

No matter how many times or in how many ways he asked the questions, neither horse would explain their appearance in his life. Instead, Fancy Man continued to whine and plead, and Robrek weakened. As he always had with Brazen, Robrek gave in to Fancy Man's demands. "Fine, teach me the damned dance."

:Ah, thank you, human child. You never know when a good Basse Dance will come in handy.:

Robrek heard music start up in his head. The dance wasn't at all like the wild frenzy he'd danced with Milady at the horse fair. It was much more restrained, as if one didn't want to move too much for fear of ruffling one's hair. Fancy Man opened Robrek's mind to the dance movements. *:Yes, that's it, human child. Now the bransle. Yes, step to the side and sway. Yes, that's it. Very good, human child. Now the demarche. Backwards and shift the weight.:* Robrek had to admit the movement was pleasant, and no-one had ever killed anyone by dancing with them. *:Okay, ending now with the reverence. Yes, bow. Very good, very good, human child. And again.:*

By the end of the afternoon, Fancy Man declared him a fine Basse Dancer. *:Tomorrow we'll work on something a little livelier, the Branle perhaps. I think you'll like that one quite well.:*

Robrek sat on the stump. "Who are you?" he asked.

But Fancy Man ignored his question. *:Now, human child, what do you know about the court?:*

"Nothing, really. We have a king. We live on the king's lands, so we're free from the interference of any lord. I think the king is pretty old."

:Tsk-tsk, this will never do. We can't have you so appallingly ignorant.: Robrek stiffened at the reference to his stupidity. *:The king's name is Solar II. He's kept Korthlundia at peace for fifty years. He cares about his people, as a ruler should. Only problem is, it took far too long for any of his mares to drop a foal. He finally married a young filly, and the Princess Samantha was born. A right pretty thing, she is.:*

"Not as pretty as Milady."

For some reason, the stallion found this hilarious. *:I wouldn't bet on that, human child. But old Solar is losing his mind, and the filly is eighteen.:* Fancy Man went on to explain the workings of the court and the council and how powerful nobles could block the princess's way.

Robrek shook his head as the silver horse finished. "I don't think I would like to be her." Still, he couldn't see what business it was of his.

* * *

Myst showed little improvement over the next few days. She mostly sat in her chair by the fire, wrapped in woolen blankets. Robrek could hardly stand the heat of the cottage. He was beginning to feel trapped, but as long as Myst needed him, he couldn't leave the Valley. He divided his time between Myst's cottage and the forest stable. Fancy Man taught him a great many court dances—the Branle, the Galliarde, the Tordion, the Saltarelli. Robrek found he liked dancing almost as much as he liked weapons work, sometimes more, because when he danced, he didn't imagine himself a murderer of women and small children.

One morning when Robrek arrived at the stable, a huge banquet was spread on a table in the middle of the paddock. The table was piled high with cheese tarts, venison stew, roast salmon, roast pork, mushrooms and leeks, and dishes Robrek couldn't identify. Fancy Man was standing next to the table. "What is this?" Robrek asked.

:Does it please you, human child? I assure you it was no easy accomplishment, and one does like to get things right.:

"What is it for?" Though he'd just had breakfast, the sight of so much food made his stomach rumble.

:It's your next lesson, human child.:

It looked so good Robrek decided not to argue. Instead, he sat at the feast table. As soon as he did so, servants appeared on all sides of him. He ignored them and reached for the loaf of parsley bread in front of him.

:No, no, human child. You haven't washed your hands.:

Robrek noticed one of the servants was holding a basin for him and had an ewer filled with perfumed water ready to pour on his hands. It seemed easier just to do it rather than argue. He held up his hands and washed them in the manner Fancy Man showed him.

When he was finished, another servant filled his bowl with soup. Robrek nodded to the servant, "Thank you." He grabbed the loaf of parsley bread and prepared to take a large bite.

:Stop, human child. First, don't acknowledge the servants. You should take them for granted. Second, the bread must be broken, not bitten. And get your elbows off the table. Did no one teach you how to eat?:

"We're alone in the middle of the woods. What does it matter how I eat?"

The horse sighed. *:Human child, if you're going to eat like an uncultured backwoods peasant, I can make this all disappear.:*

"Fine." Robrek took his elbows off the table and broke off a piece of the parsley bread.

:Not so large a piece.: Robrek glared at him, but said nothing as he broke the bread smaller. He put the bread in his mouth. *:Make sure you chew with your mouth closed.:* He began to chew, but rather than the delicious-tasting bread he'd expected, he tasted nothing at all.

"This has no flavor," he said.

:Now, human child, don't talk with your mouth full. Learning proper table manners doesn't require flavor. When eating the soup, be sure to scoop away from you, and don't let any drops spill on yourself or the table.: Robrek merely stared at the horse. *:Come, human child. It's not so difficult.:*

"You expect me to sit here and pretend to eat food that isn't real and tastes like nothing?" He rose.

:Wait, human child. What would Milady say if she saw you eating like a pig?: An illusion of Milady appeared in the seat next to his.

"You'll leave her out of this!" The illusion of Milady smiled at him as she had when they met at Myst's cottage. "Damn you! Why must you torture me with what I can't have?"

:Sorry, I was being insensitive again, wasn't I?: The illusion of Milady vanished and was replaced by a faceless woman. *:Sit back down so we can get on with it. After this, we'll do some more dancing. How's that?:*

Robrek tried to argue, but as always he ended up giving in to the horse's demands.

CHAPTER 26

Samantha sat in her window seat, watching Lord Devyn repair the painting. Bearach and Conroy stood between her and the young lord in case in a fit of pique Lord Devyn tried to skewer her with his brushes. Using some object of Saloynan magic, Darhour had even checked the paints for poison. Devyn had spent the two previous days spreading canvas behind the original painting and affixing the shreds of the painting to it. Now he was repainting the star on the chest of the Horsetad.

"You do amazing work, Devyn."

"It's my pleasure, Your Highness. I know you appreciate art, as my father does not." Devyn put the brush with the white paint in a solvent and began mixing brown, red, and yellow to try to match the shade of the Horsetad. "Not unless he can see my using it for political ends."

"I assume Sheen hopes my gratitude will cause me to propose marriage."

"Forgive me, Your Highness. It is my father's plan, not mine. I am . . ." Devyn blushed and turned his attention to the Horsetad's neck.

"You're in love with Lady Aislinn. But your father won't let you marry her until I'm married."

"And likely not even then, Your Highness. Her father lacks both importance and wealth."

Darhour entered, "Your Highness, Phelan is asking to see you. I'm afraid he's dying."

Samantha felt an invisible fist crushing her heart. "No, I will not lose one of you to that bastard." Samantha swept out of the room and hurried to the surgery. When she entered, Brice tried to rise. "Your Highness."

The princess laid a hand on his shoulder. "Lie still, Brice. You need to rest."

Samantha went to Phelan, whose eyes were closed. His face was red and clammy. As the princess took his hand, she felt his burning fever. "I'm here, Phelan," she said. "You will not die. I won't allow it."

Phelan opened his eyes and smiled, but his smile was marked with pain. "Y-y-your-r-r-r-r, y-y-y," he stuttered.

"Shh, don't try to speak." She wiped the sweat from his forehead. "You must rest so you can return to my side."

"N-n-n, N-n-n-n-n," he tried again, but stopped as pain flitted across his face.

Calum appeared at her side. "I've done all I can for him, but the wound has festered. He's dying, Your Highness."

"No, he's not," she snapped, but Phelan squeezed her hand.

"M-m, M-m-my." Phelan's voice was barely audible. Samantha leaned closer. "My Queen," he spoke clearly and closed his eyes. His hand in hers went slack. His chest rose and fell three more times, then it, too, stopped moving.

"No, Phelan! I command you to live!"

Darhour touched her shoulder. "Don't let him die, Darhour! I can't lose any of you, not now, not ever!"

"Some things not even a queen can command." Darhour put his arms around her, and she sobbed onto his chest.

Samantha cried until her eyes were red and swollen. All of her guards gathered to pay homage to their fallen companion. Samantha stood by Phelan's bed, looking at the body of the man who'd died protecting her. "Had Phelan any family?" she asked, ashamed she didn't know.

"No, Your Highness, he was an orphan," Darhour answered. "He's from one of the Korthian mountain tribes. His people were nearly wiped out by bandits when he was a child. He requested if he died, his body be burned, as was the custom of his people."

The princess choked. How could she know so little about the men who risked their lives to protect her? She turned to Brice. "Have you family?"

"No, Your Highness. All my family was killed in an epidemic some years back. I always wondered why I was saved. Now, I know." He looked at her with a devotion that hurt. She was unworthy of it. She turned to Kailen. "And you, Lieutenant?"

Kailen looked surprised she'd asked. "Yes, Your Highness, I have a mother and two younger sisters here in the capital. Most of my wages go to my sisters' dowries. I'll see them married well."

"And your father?" she asked.

"He was a member of the Royal Guard and was killed fighting bandits in the Korthian mountains. Five generations of my family have died in the service of the crown." Kailen's icy blue eyes shone with what seemed an eagerness to follow in the family tradition.

She shifted her gaze to Conroy. "What of your family?"

Conroy laughed. "There's a whole brood of us. My father's a fisherman, and all of my brothers have followed him into that profession. He was quite angry when I insisted on joining the guard instead. His brother had done so, and despite my father's objections, my uncle taught me sword fighting when I was a child."

"And is your uncle still with the guard?" she asked.

Conroy shook his head. "No, he died in a training accident some years ago." *So many dead. And for what?*

When she turned to Bearach, he looked away. "My father was a drunken brute. The less said about him the better. I left when I was fourteen. I haven't seen any of my family since, and I never plan to. If I die in your service, burn my body and scatter my ashes to the wind."

She glared at him fiercely. "You won't die in my service! None of you will!"

Darhour cleared his throat. "We can discuss family matters when we have leisure, Your Highness. Should we not see to Phelan's funeral pyre?" Obviously, Darhour was going to tell her no more about himself.

Samantha nodded. "Send for Blaine, and I'll have him arrange everything."

"The guard will arrange it," Darhour said. "Blaine is busy in the library. I'll have no more surprise entrances into your quarters."

* * *

That night Darhour stood in the courtyard next to Phelan's pyre. This was far from the first time he'd consigned one of his men to the fire or the earth, but it cut more deeply this time. Phelan had died trying to save his daughter. Fathering Samantha had been the only good thing Darhour had ever done. If any harm came to her, he was nothing other than a murderer—a killer so notorious he was known throughout half the world. He'd thought to bury The Ghost, consign him to the deepest hell. But as he spoke the warrior's blessing over Phelan's body, he feared that part of himself could never die. He'd killed again, so now his vow was void. *Should I not then kill my daughter's enemy?* He thought of the pleasure the act would bring him, and that thought checked him as nothing else could have. Only a monster enjoyed ending the life of another. But as he lit the funeral pile, he glanced at Samantha and saw her brave attempt to hide her tears. *For her sake, should I not be a monster?*

The thought occupied him as he and Kailen escorted Samantha back to her rooms. Blaine was waiting for them. "I thought you'd been given a task," Darhour snapped.

Blaine straightened and dared to meet his eyes, then glanced at the grief-stricken princess. "A task I've completed, but I'm not sure that now is the time to discuss it."

Why was the milksop suddenly developing a spine? "We'll mourn the dead at our leisure. Is there or is there not another way in?"

"I believe there is." The princess's secretary walked to a heavy table in the corner. "From the diagrams, I believe there is a trap door under here, but I was unable to move the table on my own to verify it." Impatient at Blaine's weakness, Darhour pushed him out of the way. To his chagrin, he needed Kailen's assistance to move the table. Blaine rolled up the carpet, and there, barely visible in the floor, were the outlines of a trap door.

"Open it," Darhour ordered, and Kailen heaved the heavy door up to reveal a long, twisting dark stairwell.

Darhour lit a torch. "Lieutenant, get Conroy or Bearach to help protect Her Highness. Blaine, with me. We'll see where this leads."

The tunnel was a nasty, unpleasant place, and Darhour regretted taking the secretary with him. Blaine seemed continually on the edge of fainting, and Darhour wasn't about to carry him out of the muck. The tunnel wound and twisted as if whoever had dug it kept changing his mind about its destination. At last, they reached a stairway that led back up. The door at the top wouldn't open at first, and he was forced to ask Blaine for assistance. With the combined strength of one-and-a-half men, the door eventually burst open in a shower of dirt. Darhour went through the door and to his shock, he entered the small room under his old office in the stables. He nearly laughed at how perfect this was. With a few well-placed traps that would be tripped by those coming in, but not those going out, this would make a perfect escape route for the princess.

"Well done, Blaine," he said.

Blaine's mouth dropped open at the praise. Darhour wondered if he'd been too hard on the boy.

* * *

That night in her dreams, Samantha saw each member of her guard laid out on funeral pyres. She sobbed, as she set the torch to pyre after pyre and watched the flames consume the bodies of her men. On the last of the pyres, Robbie lay, as dead as the others. She threw the torch aside and collapsed onto his chest. *No! They can't die like this! I won't allow it!* She awoke with her pillow soaked from her tears.

When morning arrived, she fought despair as her maids dressed her. A ray of hope came as a page arrived with a summons from the king.

When the princess entered the king's rooms, he was still staring at the tapestry of the white heron. "You asked for me, father." She prayed he wouldn't ask her opinion on which of the flowers were the most beautiful.

"Yes, my dear." The king tore his eyes away from the tapestry. "A matter of great importance will come up in the council meeting this morning. I want you to handle it. I've sent a proclamation with Gilroy instructing the council I've given you full responsibility to act in my place. That is all." The king turned away from her and back to his tapestry.

Samantha glanced at Darhour, who shook his head as if he were no more able than she to account for the king's pronouncement.

"Father?" She approached the king.

"That is all!" the king snapped.

Wondering what it could mean, she left.

When she reached the council chamber, Duke Argblutal's and Duke Sheen's chairs were empty. After a few moments, the two dukes burst in, arguing furiously.

"This is no matter to trouble the king with," Argblutal insisted. He stopped short when he noticed her sitting at the head of the table. She looked at him with bland unconcern.

"Where is the king?" Sheen demanded with his customary lack of decorum.

Gilroy stood. "His Majesty is feeling indisposed this morning. He has sent me with this document, specifying that he has fully authorized Her Highness, the Crown Princess Samantha, to act in his place today and that any decision she makes should be taken as his own." Gilroy laid the signed proclamation in the middle of the table.

Sheen looked as if he were on the verge of exploding. "Your Highness, I have an issue of the utmost importance—"

"Be seated, both of you!"

"But Your Highness—"

She turned a commanding glare on him. "Your Grace, I said be seated, and then whatever is bothering you may be heard . . . if it's appropriate for this forum."

"It most certainly is appropriate for this forum," the old duke grumbled, but he sat.

"Your Highness—"Argblutal interrupted, still standing.

"I told you *both* to be seated, and Duke Sheen has the floor." As Argblutal took his seat, his glare was murderous. Samantha turned back to Sheen. "You were saying, Your Grace?"

"It's an outrage, Your Highness. My poor daughter is in hysterics, and His Grace"—he glared at Argblutal—"dares suggest I'm overreacting. No girl her age should be subjected to that type of insult. Their nerves are far too sensitive."

The duke's daughter was older than she was. Barely resisting the urge to roll her eyes, Samantha signaled for him to continue. "Your Grace, what happened to cause your daughter so much distress?"

The old duke leaned toward her. "My daughter had difficulty sleeping last night, so she decided to view the galleries. She was accosted by the captain of the Royal Guard with the most indecent proposals. She refused, of course, and tried to return to her rooms, but the man dared lay his hands on her in an unseemly manner. She fought, but he would have taken her virtue if Lieutenant Hawk and a couple of other members of the Royal Guard hadn't heard her cries and come to her assistance. They pulled the drunken sot off her, but not before he'd given her bruises in places no decent girl should be touched before her wedding night. I demand satisfaction, Your Highness, and I will have it."

"Are you saying Captain Tremayne attacked your daughter?"

Argblutal shifted in his seat. He tried to assume a casual pose, but his fingers dug into the palms of his hands. "He was drunk, Your Highness. I swear it won't happen again."

Samantha had a hard time hiding her glee. "No, it won't. Tremayne is hereby relieved of all duties and will stand trial for his offense." She smiled a court smile at Argblutal. "Since Tremayne was appointed on your recommendation, I will leave it to you to see to his arrest."

"Of course, Your Highness," Argblutal said, with an unsuccessful attempt to speak calmly. "I recommend Farrell as his replacement."

Sheen jumped to his feet. "Your Highness, we don't need another of Argblutal's drunken minions. Lieutenant Hawk has served faithfully for years, and the men trust him. If it weren't for him, my daughter would have been worse than murdered last night."

Samantha wanted to object that rape was most certainly not worse than murder, but Sheen's suggestion was exactly the one she'd wanted. "He'd be my choice as well." She opened the table to further discussion. Argblutal tried again to promote Farrell, but seemed to realize he was on shaky ground.

* * *

Shylah cried out as Argblutal burst into his rooms, grabbed him by the throat, and pushed him against the wall. "We are losing control of the king. Rectify this, or pay the price of those who fail me."

Shylah trembled. "There is another potion. It's extremely powerful."

The duke laughed. "If it's so powerful, why not use it to begin with?"

"There are certain . . . distasteful elements involved."

"I care nothing for your distaste. The next excuse I hear from you will be the last thing you say." The duke released him and stormed out of the room.

Shylah collapsed in a chair, gasping for breath. He turned to his statue of Sulis. "I did this all for your glory. Why haven't you blessed my efforts?" The statue stared back impassively.

Shylah went to his cabinet and got out the second book of forbidden magic. He held it and stared at the binding. He had nearly consigned the book to the fire to rid himself of the temptation. The potion it described took three weeks to work fully, but promised progressive control as each dose was administered at weekly intervals.

Again he turned to his statue. "Is it a sin if I'm doing it for your glory? What are three lives measured against the truth?" That's what the potion required, the lives of three innocents, children below the age of fifteen who hadn't known the pleasures of the flesh. And Sulis curse it all, he couldn't even use gutter trash. The children had to be healthy and well-fed. Shylah shuddered as he imagined plunging a knife into a child's heart and filling a vial with blood. He stared at the statue and prayed to Sulis for guidance, but his god remained silent.

Shylah decided to take a walk through the gardens. He opened the door to see a child of seven or eight, dressed as a page, nearly in tears with frustration. The child's face filled with relief with he saw the high priest. "Father, can you help me? I'm lost."

Shylah invited the child in. The child tiptoed inside and gaped at Shylah's altar. "Sit down, child. Tell me your name and how I may help you."

"My name is Eilis, and I'm supposed to be delivering this message"—the boy had a piece of paper in his hand—"from Baron Arawn to Lord Pandaran, but I can't find the way. My lord got me this place when my mother died." The boy's eyes brightened at the honor. "But I'm afraid I'll lose it because I keep getting lost. There are too many rooms and corridors and passageways."

Shylah's heart soared. Sulis was with him after all! "There, there," he comforted the child as he got up to fetch him a glass of water. "New pages are always getting lost." With his back to the boy, Shylah added a few drops of a powerful sleeping potion to the water. He turned and handed the glass to the boy. "Have a glass of water, and I'll set you on the right path."

The boy gulped the water down. "Oh thank you. With your permission, I must be on my way." He tried to rise, but fell back into the chair. "I don't feel so good." Before he could say any more, he dropped into unconsciousness.

The high priest picked up the child's body and carried him to his altar. He bound the boy tightly and waited for night to fall.

* * *

Shylah tried to block out the cries coming from the boy. He was finding it hard to concentrate and wished he could put the boy back to sleep, but the instructions didn't allow an unconscious sacrifice. Fortunately, it was a rather simple potion. *Just a few herbs. A small amount of blood from the king*—he poured in the contents of a vial he'd obtained earlier. *A small amount of my own blood*—he cut his arm and allowed his blood to flow into the cauldron. *Just these few ingredients and the heart's blood of an innocent child.* The potion hissed and bubbled over the fire. It was ready for the final ingredient that would assure the king became compliant to his will. *No, not my will. To the will of the god.*

Holding the bloody knife, he turned to the altar. Eilis struggled against the ropes. "No! Please, don't kill me!"

"Control yourself. Do you not know Sulis reserves a special reward for those who die to fulfill his will? Do you not know the land Beyond the Far Mountain is a place of the greatest peace and the greatest joy? Can you really fear being sent to such a paradise?"

"Please, I don't want to be a sacrifice!"

Shylah's hand trembled. *If Sulis didn't approve, surely he wouldn't have sent such a perfect child.* The clock on his mantelpiece told him he could hesitate no longer. The blood needed to be taken at midnight. Assuring himself of the righteousness of his actions, he raised the knife.

As Shylah began chanting the words of the ritual, the child flailed wildly. "Don't kill me, please! No!"

The high priest strove to ignore the sounds as he traced the god's star on the child's breast with the point of the knife. *Why won't he be quiet? Why can't he see this is for his own good?* The child's cries ceased to be words and dissolved into meaningless terror. *Surely, it's the will of the god.*

The priest lifted the knife and plunged it directly into the center of the star. He felt the warm blood gushing over his hands, as the child convulsed and then lay still. He grabbed the vial and filled it with the last blood to ooze from the child's small heart. *Such a little heart. Such a little, little heart.*

CHAPTER 27

Robrek continued to care for Myst, but despite the power she claimed he had, she remained very weak and icy cold. Most troubling, her healing energy didn't return. She still hadn't said where she'd been or what had caused her illness, always evading Robrek's questions. Early one morning, he decided to search the woods for a certain rare fungus; he hoped a brew of it would help.

Just as he found a good-sized patch, he heard a blood-curdling scream. He dropped his harvesting basket and ran toward it. He found Bran, lying on the ground with blood pouring from his upper thigh. A bloody axe lay on the ground nearby, next to a stack of half-chopped wood. Robrek dropped to the ground beside him, but Bran hissed at him. "Keep your filthy hands off of me, demon boy. My brother's gone for a healer of the goddess."

"You're bleeding to death. You'll die without my help."

"Then I'll die, but I won't be beholden to the denizens of the seven hells." Bran spat at him, hitting him on the left cheek.

As Robrek wiped the spittle from his face, he wanted to do as Bran asked, or better yet pick up the axe and cut his head off, just to be sure he died. *If I'm going to be the villain of a bard's tale, why not start now?* But he couldn't do it, so he grabbed Bran's thigh firmly. "I'm going to stop the bleeding if I can, and your soul can go to the seven hells for all I care." Bran tried to struggle, but the blood loss had weakened him.

Robrek drifted into a healer's trance. But as when he'd tried to heal Cara, he found himself blocked. As he shoved the anger aside and allowed himself to relax, he felt his mind clear. Again, he saw the energy he needed. The rest was simple. He stopped the bleeding, closed the wound, and collapsed to the ground.

* * *

As the sun set, Leigh made his way back to the shrine. The demon summoner had been brought in unconscious late that morning, and almost immediately Father Gildas had given him a huge stack of messages to deliver all over the Valley. It had taken him the entire day. *Another day in which I've learned nothing about my gift.* Sometimes he suspected the priest never intended to teach him anything.

As he reported the completion of his task to Father Gildas, the priest didn't even bother to thank him. Leigh couldn't help comparing the way Father Gildas treated him to the way his father treated his underlings. Leigh shivered at the impiety of the thought. Father Gildas spoke for the goddess, and his father poisoned men's bodies and souls. What did it matter if the priest was a bit abrupt?

Leigh made his way to the room he shared with the two other novices. "Good evening," he greeted them as he opened the door. Parkin and Breasal briefly looked up from their books, but neither bothered to acknowledge him. They looked almost as alike as twins with their thick blonde hair, thick eyebrows that met over their thick noses, thick hands, thick everything. But the two novices weren't even brothers. "Did you pass the day well?" he asked.

Both only acknowledged him with a grunt.

Making one last effort to engage them in conversation, Leigh asked, "Were there any difficulties with the demon summoner?"

Parkin sighed. "A person who doesn't even bother to wake up can't cause much trouble, now can he?"

"I suppose not." Leigh guessed he should be grateful he hadn't had to be the one to tend to the prisoner. He shivered at the thought of confronting someone so evil. Evil had always made him feel a bit nauseous. How would an evil vast enough to summon demons affect him?

* * *

When Robrek opened his eyes, it was so dark he could see nothing. He tried to move, heard a clink of metal, and felt shackles around his wrists and ankles. Scrambling into a sitting position, he tugged against the chains. *Sulis curse it all! Bran must have died! Why didn't I do as the idiot asked and leave him alone?*

Slowly the room started to lighten, and the early morning sunrise peeked through a small window overhead. He was in a cellar of some kind—an extremely large cellar. He couldn't imagine where in the Valley this cellar might be located or why he'd be confined here instead of the village's small jail. The door at the top of the stairs opened, letting in more light. A young man dressed in novice robes descended with a tray in his hands.

The novice smiled nervously. "Did you have a pleasant night?" he asked, handing Robrek a tray containing a small bowl of runny porridge. Robrek didn't bother answering. Sitting on a barrel, the novice looked at him as if trying to decide which species of animal he belonged to. "I would have thought summoning demons would leave a stronger taint of evil on you."

Robrek snorted. "It probably would have if I'd ever summoned one. I used my goddess-given magic, not demons, to try to heal Bran. It's not my fault I failed."

The novice shook his head. "Bran is recovering nicely upstairs."

Robrek gaped at the novice. "If Bran's alive, what am I being accused of?"

"Demon summoning, of course. Father Gildas claims you saved Bran's body at the peril of his immortal soul."

"And the magistrate's agreed to hear such a ludicrous charge?"

The novice looked away. "Well, no, Father Gildas hasn't contacted the magistrate. He's trying you himself."

Robrek laughed. "Unlock these chains! Church courts have no authority to confine anyone! And how can Gildas excommunicate me when he never allowed me into the church in the first place?"

The novice jerked backwards and nearly fell off his barrel. "Surely, you had bestowed upon you the goddess's blessing to which all infants are entitled!"

"You must be new around here. Father Gildas didn't think I was entitled to live. He wanted my father to expose me. He doesn't like foreigners or half-breeds." Robrek nodded toward the novice's nose. "I'm sure he's about as fond of you as he is of me or Myst."

The novice stood and put his hands on his hips. "Don't lump me in with the two of you. You summon demons, and the herb witch is a heretic."

"Do not insult Myst in front of me. She's the most compassionate woman I've ever known, and the only heresy she's ever committed is to be a far stronger healer than your worthless priest."

The novice said nothing and wouldn't meet his eyes. Robrek was about to ask again to be unchained when he heard hammering outside the small window. "What are they building?" he asked.

The novice stared at the ceiling. "The scaffold to burn you on, if you're convicted."

"Holy Sulis, what?" Robrek yanked against his chains. "The church has no power to execute anyone! The only penalty a church court can issue is excommunication!"

The novice backed toward the stairs, still unable to meet his eyes. "Father Gildas doesn't think the king's magistrates will take the charge seriously enough, and if you have summoned demons, you shouldn't be allowed to live." The novice fled the cellar, leaving Robrek alone with the sounds of men building his funeral pyre.

Leigh leaned against the wall at the top of the stairs to catch his breath. *The demon summoner is trying to confuse me. The priests speak for Sulis. Father Gildas couldn't possibly burn a man simply because of mixed blood.* Leigh felt the narrowness of his nose. He might not look as foreign as the man in the cellar, but he wasn't pure-blooded either. Trying to reassure himself of the righteousness of Sulis's servants, Leigh headed down the corridor. At the door to Father Gildas's office, a line of people waited—those the priest had had him take messages to after the demon summoner had been brought in. He heard voices from within.

"The community must see that even his own family has rejected him."

"Father, I know my part." Leigh recognized the voice of Boyden Angusstamm. When he'd delivered the message yesterday, Leigh hadn't liked the demon summoner's brother. In fact, he'd felt evil emanating from *him*, rather than from the one in the cellar. "I've made sure my father hasn't heard about the trial, as you told me."

"You've done well, my son."

Leigh heard satisfaction in the priest's voice.

"The goddess smiles on you and cleanses you of the taint of your mother's blood. I'm afraid only fire can cleanse your brother."

Leigh rushed past and took refuge in his small room. Not only had Father Gildas called Boyden's mother's blood "a taint," but he was attempting to keep the trial a secret from the young man's own father. The bond between parents and children was sacred to the Holy Mother. Leigh thought of his own father. Although their relationship had always been difficult, he knew his father would do anything for him if he were in trouble. No father should be left in ignorance of the peril facing his child.

As he slipped out the side door of the shrine, Leigh heard a wild neigh. He gasped as he saw a Horsetad nearby. *One of Sulis's own!* Leigh had never thought to be blessed enough to see one of the holy creatures, especially not this close. Leigh tried to approach the magnificent beast, but it reared and brought its hoofs crashing down only inches from him. Leigh backed away quickly. *Surely, I'm not worthy to touch such a creature.*

* * *

Myst tried to calm her anxiety as she came awake and saw Robrek's cot empty. *Surely, he has merely gotten up early to take care of some chores.* Shivering with cold, Myst became even more anxious as she realized the fire had gone out. Robrek had never left the cottage without first seeing to her comfort. She looked to his bed. Had it even been slept in?

She wore out the morning in fruitless worrying until she finally heard a horse approaching, but instead of Robrek entering, she heard a loud knock. Struggling to the door, she found Angus on her doorstep.

He pushed his way in. "You've got to come with me. They've taken Robbie."

"Who's taken Robrek?"

"The damned priest." He told her what he had learned from the novice. "They plan on burning him at the stake." He paused, then went on less caustically. "I know I haven't been a very good father to the boy. I never understood him, and he cost me the only woman I could ever love, but that doesn't mean I'm going to stand by and let him be murdered by some pompous fanatic."

"Why do you need me?" The very method she'd used to return to Robbie made her useless to help him.

"Because you're the only one in the Valley besides me that doesn't want him dead. Are you coming with me or not?"

"Yes, of course." Grabbing her warmest shawl, Myst followed Angus out the door.

Too weak to ride alone, Myst rode in front of Angus, his arms around her keeping her on the horse. She'd never had this much physical contact with him before, and it reminded her just how large he was. *Please, Holy Mother, let him be big enough to stop them. Don't let them kill the one who should be my grandson.*

When they reached the shrine, ten men holding pitchforks and scythes stood in front. Angus dismounted and helped her down. He strode up to the armed men, all Valley farmers they both knew well. "Out of my way. You all know this trial is an illegal farce! Gildas doesn't have the authority to sneeze on my son, much less burn him!"

One of them spoke up, "Father Gildas ordered that you and the herb witch not be allowed in."

"If you think I'm going to let that fraud kill my son, you've got another thing coming." Myst watched Angus's hands form fists and knew the inevitable result. He'd be killed or injured too badly to be of any help.

"Angus, no! Fetch one of the king's magistrates. It's Robrek's only hope."

For once Angus decided to be reasonable. He stabbed a finger toward the men. "Tell that bastard priest that if he murders my son, I'll see him hanged." Angus turned to her. "Make sure Robbie stays alive." Jumping back on his horse, he rode hard in the direction of the capital.

* * *

As he was forced up the stairs and into a large chamber, Robrek willed himself to believe it was only a nightmare. The room was overflowing with Valley residents. Boyden smirked at him from the front row of seats, but neither his father nor Myst was present. Father Gildas sat at a table at the front of the room, the novice who'd brought Robrek breakfast behind him. Father Gildas smiled as Robrek was chained to a chair. *Holy Sulis! He's going to burn me alive!* Robrek closed his eyes and breathed slowly. *This can't be happening. The novice has to be wrong.*

348

Father Gildas called the room to order. "Robrek Angusstamm, you have been brought here to answer charges of trafficking in demons. How do you plead?"

Robrek forced his voice to convey a calmness he didn't feel. "You have no legal authority to detain me. I demand to be released immediately."

Father Gildas folded his hands across his belly, making Robrek long to puncture the priest's abdomen with his sword and watch the fat ooze out. "Since the demon summoner refuses to admit his guilt, he will be tried," the priest said. "When found guilty, his flesh will be cleansed by fire, and the Valley can at last be free of contamination."

The room reeled, and Robrek could no longer control the shaking of his voice. "You can't try me. I demand to be taken to the king's magistrate."

Ignoring him, Father Gildas addressed the room, "I call Boyden Angusstamm as the first witness."

Boyden approached a chair near Father Gildas's table. "This time you die, little brother," he mouthed.

"No!" Robrek looked wildly around the room for someone to save him, but all of those present either glared at him or avoided his eyes. He saw Cara and Dillion in the middle of the room. Even they wouldn't look at him. He turned back to Gildas. "If you kill me, it will be murder."

Without even bothering to look at him, the priest ordered, "Silence him." A cloth was stuffed in Robrek's mouth. This was no trial. The priest was merely making a spectacle to entertain the crowd, and the culmination of the spectacle would come when they tied Robrek to a stake and set him on fire. *Holy Sulis, you have to stop him!*

* * *

Robrek heard almost nothing of his trial. He was vaguely aware of dozens of witnesses taking the stand, but he had no idea what any of them said. Instead, his mind kept returning to the time he'd burned his hand as a child. Boyden could whittle amazing figures out of wood, and Robrek had been eager to prove he could be just as good at something. But he'd gotten careless, and the knife had slipped, cutting his finger deeply. He'd yelped and flung the knife away. Too late, he realized the knife would land in the hearth fire. Although the knife's blade was steel, its handle was wooden and would be consumed. His father would beat him, and he'd never have another knife. Panicking, he'd reached into the fire. The pain had been terrible. How much worse would it be when his whole body burned?

Robrek was jerked back into the present by a familiar voice. "And how do you know the accused?"

Amergin Kanestamm shifted in his seat. "I'm ashamed to say it, Father, but when my mare was having trouble dropping a foal, I sent for him."

Father Gildas raised his eyebrows. "And you did so after I warned of his demonic powers?"

Robrek glared at Amergin. *I saved your horse, and now you'll help them to burn me!*

Amergin looked at the ceiling. "I'm afraid so, Father. The mare was in real difficulty. I'm not a rich man, Father. I couldn't afford to lose the horse."

"So you chose to risk your soul instead of your horse." Father Gildas paused, but Amergin said nothing. "And what happened when the accused came to your farm?"

"He went into a kind of trance and started chanting and dancing around the mare. His green eyes flashed, and his black hair shone with unholy light. I was so afraid that demons were answering to his call that I ran." If the circumstances had been different, Robrek would have laughed. The story was absurd—chanting and dancing around the horse. *Who could believe this?* But as he glanced around the room, nearly everyone's head was nodding. "When the demon child was finished, he demanded either a pint of my blood or a piece of my soul in payment." Robrek pulled frantically against his chains, but no one paid him any attention.

The novice was rocking back and forth on his feet, and finally burst out. "But your mare, sir? Did the demons devour her?" he asked.

"Of course not! Both the mare and the foal are doing great. He may be a demon, but he can heal any animal there is."

The novice's mouth dropped open. "But healing is the power of the goddess and not of demons!" Father Gildas shot him a venomous look, and he instantly fell silent, but glanced uncomfortably at Robrek before looking at his feet. *You know they're lying about me, don't you? You're obviously not pure blood yourself.* Robrek looked back at the crowd in the courtroom. Cara had tears in her eyes and seemed to be pleading with Dillion. The sight of her distress frightened him more than Amergin's testimony. She knew he would die. At Cara's urging, Dillion came forward and told of how Robrek had saved Cara's life when she lost her child. But even this Father Gildas was able to twist against Robrek. "Are you saying you allowed another man to touch your wife in such an intimate manner? Is this the work of the goddess, I ask?"

Robrek had to admit Dillion did his best, but he was no match for the priest. The longer Dillion talked the more sordid Father Gildas made his saving of Cara sound. By the time Father Gildas got through with Dillion, the priest had made Robrek look like a rapist as well as a demon. *Oh, Holy Sulis, please help me!* But Robrek was well aware that Sulis had never answered his prayers.

Next, Bran was carried in. Bran started by testifying of Robrek using his powers to cheat at cards and summoning his demonic horse to terrify them. Bran described the star on the horse's forehead and chest.

"But that's a Horsetad!" the novice burst out, staring with wide eyes between Bran and Robrek.

"Leigh Fergalstamm," Father Gildas boomed. "You will not interrupt these sacred proceedings again."

"But sir, if Sulis has showered favor on him by allowing him to ride one of her own, how can we condemn him? There was a Horsetad outside the shrine this morning. Let him claim it and prove—"

Shooting to his feet, Father Gildas slapped the novice across the face. "Go to the chapel immediately. Perhaps a night spent on your knees in prayer will teach you to remember your place."

The novice looked at Robrek, then ran from the room. Robrek knew his last chance left with him.

* * *

Robrek didn't know how much longer the trial went on, but suddenly, it was over, and he was taken back to the cellar to await sentencing. He was seventeen years old, and he wasn't going to live to see another sunrise. Within a short period of time, he would be tied to a pole, kindling and wood would be placed around his feet, and he would be set on fire. He'd die screaming in agony, and he could do nothing to save himself. He didn't want to spend the last few minutes of his life imagining his death.

He'd think about Milady and remember the few glorious hours he'd spent with her. He'd feel her softness in his arms and taste the sweetness of her lips. He felt the ribbon against his chest.

* * *

Desperate for Angus to return with the magistrate, Myst waited in front of the shrine. She'd tried to convince the people hanging around the shrine of the injustice of the trial, but they were all ready to watch a young man who'd done them no harm die in agony.

As the sun started to set, the doors of the shrine opened, and the crowd came milling out. They gathered around the scaffolding that had been built in the village square. She learned the trial was over, and Father Gildas was expected to shortly pronounce Robrek's sentence. *Holy Mother, please help me save him!*

Father Gildas exited the shrine and climbed onto the scaffolding. The crowd cheered. Holding up his hand for silence, the horrid excuse for a priest smiled. It was growing darker, and torches had been placed around the scaffolding. The flickering of the flames gave Gildas's face a sinister look. "Oh my people, I have just received the most grave news." Gildas put his hand on his heart in a theatrical fashion. "The demon summoner's father has gone to fetch the king's magistrate. Our peril is so dire, I thought we could eliminate it before we suffered more grievous harm, but that is not to be. The law of the land takes the demon summoner's fate out of my hands and places it into the hands of those who are blind to the goddess's ways."

Myst laughed with relief, but Gildas wasn't finished. "The king's officer will certainly hear of the danger the demon summoner represents to our bodies and our souls, but in the absence of the goddess's light, he may not see as clearly as we do. He refused to act against the beast when he used his unholy blood to curse an innocent farmer, and he will likely set the beast free again to wreak far greater harm. How many more of you will suffer the destruction of your crops as the wrong-sighted Angus has? How many of you will lose your souls to his hunger? How many of your wives and daughters will have their virtue sacrificed to his lust?"

The crowd roared in fury, and a man yelled out, "Let's burn him now before the magistrate has a chance to stop us!" The crowd cheered in agreement.

"No!" Myst yelled. "There is no harm in the lad!" But her voice wasn't strong enough to be heard over the crowd. She tried to push her way through to the scaffolding, but the crowd closed against her. She was pushed back and fell hard against the ground. She lay stunned, too weak to get up.

Gildas shook his head sadly. "My people, I wish I could do as you ask, but I'm restrained by the king's laws."

Another voice yelled out, "Justice will be done! We won't have this abomination among us any longer!"

The speaker was Boyden. *His own brother! How could he!* Myst struggled to rise, to speak, but she could do nothing as the crowd surged toward the shrine. "No, Sulis, no! Stop this!" she cried in a voice that was little louder than a whisper. *Donella, how can you ever forgive me? I've failed again.*

* * *

The sound of the key in the lock brought Robrek abruptly out of his daydreams. Milady's image faded and was replaced by a vision of a torch lighting the wood at his feet. He jerked helplessly against his chains. The door opened, and the novice ran down the stairs and began unlocking Robrek's many chains. "Father Gildas is in front addressing the crowd. If we hurry, we might be able to get you out the side door before they come for you."

As soon as his hands were free, Robrek tore the gag from his mouth. The novice unlocked the manacles on his feet and pulled him upright. Robrek was stunned by the novice's change of heart, but there was no time to ask questions. The two of them ran up the cellar steps. As soon as they entered the hallway above, a mob poured through the front door of the shrine. "Run that way, quickly." Leigh pointed to a door at the end of the hallway and faded back into the cellar.

Robrek ran for the door, but someone saw him. "The demon's escaping! Get him!"

Robrek felt Wild Thing outside the shrine and gave a frantic command for her to meet him at the side door. Just as he reached it, someone seized him. Grabbing a long candlestick from the wall, he whirled, smashing it into the arm that held him, and flung himself out the door. He flew into the night air and right into Wild Thing.

As Robrek grabbed Wild Thing's mane and pulled himself onto her back, someone screamed, "Don't let him get away!" Boyden grabbed his leg, and Robrek kicked out, sending his older brother reeling into the man behind him. Rearing, Wild Thing took off at a full gallop.

* * *

Robrek rode awoke with the sun on his face. He felt sick and shaky as from a horrible nightmare. But when he felt the stiffness of his clothes and opened his eyes to see them stained with Bran's blood, he realized it hadn't been a dream. He had come within seconds of being burned at the stake. The people he'd grown up among, whose animals he'd healed, had tried to kill him, and they would have succeeded if a complete stranger hadn't decided to save his life. His own father had done nothing. Robrek wanted to take a sword, don one of the suits of armor, and repeat the slaughter he'd committed for real this time. *Why not kill them before they have another chance to kill me?*

He got to his feet. Wild Thing was standing near him protectively, but Brazen and Fancy Man were standing calmly on the other side of the paddock fence. He stabbed a finger toward Brazen. "You made me stay here! I nearly died yesterday!"

:You are alive and essentially unhurt.:

"No thanks to you! You said it was my goddess-cursed destiny! Do you know how close I came to being set on fire?"

:Whoa! Whoa! Human child, Brazen was damned near sick with worry. So was I.:

Robrek rounded on the silver horse. "Then why did you do nothing to help me?"

Fancy Man refused to meet his eyes. *: We couldn't, human child. You'll just have to take our word for that.:*

Robrek picked up a rock and threw it at the nearest tree, shattering a small branch. With all the power the horses had, he couldn't believe there wasn't something they could have done. But they'd never apologize. They'd never explain anything. He wanted to talk to Myst, but her cottage was the first place they'd look. *Oh, Myst, are you okay? Who will take care of you now?*

His stomach reminded him it'd been some time since he'd eaten. He dove into his provisions and found some cheese and bread. He'd neglected his larder at the stable, and there was little else.

:No need stupid cat. Why stupid cat come? Maybe Wild Thing stomp to mash.:

"What are you talking about?" Robrek asked. Before the Horsetad could answer, he heard horses approaching, and through the trees came Myst, riding one of his father's horses and leading another. The second horse was loaded with supplies, and Ronan sat on top. "Myst!" He rushed toward her. Ronan jumped down and rubbed against his leg. As he helped Myst down, she grabbed him into a tight hug.

She sobbed against his shoulder. "Thank the goddess you're alive."

"Don't worry. I'm fine, thanks to another half-breed." She felt weak, so he led her to a tree stump, the closest thing he had to a chair, and told her how the novice had helped him. "But what are you doing with my father's horses?"

Touching him on the shoulder, Myst told him how his father had ridden to fetch a magistrate. Robrek shook his head. He'd thought his father hadn't even cared. "Angus panicked when he rode up and saw the scaffold on fire. They burned it in their frenzy at your escape. He came to me this morning and asked me if I knew how to get supplies to you," Myst said. "He wants me to find out what else you might need."

Glaring at the loaded horse, Robrek cursed his father. He'd reached the point where he could hate his father without reservation. He didn't want to owe Angus anything. Not speaking, he unpacked the horse. There were several warm woolen blankets, clean clothing, an axe, string for making traps, a hook and line for fishing, a good knife, a couple of large cheeses, fresh baked bread, a bag of *bhat* beans, dried meat, dried vegetables, and dried fruit. Still hungry, he took the fresh bread and cut off a large hunk of cheese. He warmed up the brazier to make *bhat* for himself and the herb witch.

:Wild Thing stomp stupid licking thing!:

Robrek looked over. Ronan had found a sunny spot near the Horsetad and was busying licking himself. "Don't be jealous, my girl. You're the one who saved me last night."

Wild Thing snorted. *:Wild Thing help Robbie! Stupid cat just kill tiny, little mice.:* Robrek wasn't sure what Wild Thing had against Ronan, but he smiled in spite of everything.

Myst's hand shook when he handed her the *bhat*. Only then did he notice the exhaustion she'd been attempting to hide. "Myst, you're not well enough to be here. I need to take you home."

"You will do no such thing! You aren't safe anywhere in the Valley! You'll have to get as far away from here as you can."

"But Myst, I can't leave you. You need someone to take care of you."

"What I need doesn't matter. I won't have you risk your life for an old woman. I've already had a full life. Yours has just begun."

"But . . ."

"No more 'but's' my child. Do you have any idea how it tore me apart when I thought I was going to have to watch you murdered? Not for anything will I experience that again. I can make it back to my cottage without assistance. I will try to come here tomorrow or the day after, but you will not come to see me. And if you feel you need to leave sooner, go without giving me another thought."

Robrek knew he could never do that, but arguing would only tire Myst, so he simply helped her mount his father's horse. He watched the herb witch ride away. She was right; it was impossible to stay in the Valley, but he feared she wouldn't survive without him.

* * *

When Myst reached her cottage, she found another young man, looking almost as desolate as the one she'd just left. "Can I help you?" she asked, getting off the horse. She stumbled, and he caught her.

"Mistress, you aren't well. Let me help you inside." Myst was too tired to do anything other than accept his aid. He helped her to her chair near the fireplace and stoked up the fire. The stranger removed his traveling cloak, revealing the robes of a novice.

Anger gave her voice strength. "If you're looking for Robrek, I have no idea where he is and wouldn't tell you if I did."

The young novice collapsed into a chair. "He'd better be halfway to Murtaghan by now. If I've ruined my life freeing him, he should at least have the decency to escape." The novice got to his feet again, seemingly unable to keep still. "Father Gildas knows I did it. I knew he would, but I couldn't stand aside and allow an innocent man to be burned alive. The goddess holds those accountable who watch evil happen and do nothing to prevent it." He paced nervously.

Realizing this must be the novice who'd rescued Robrek, Myst softened. "The road isn't always easy, but the goddess will bless those who follow her will."

The novice nodded, but didn't look happy. "Father Gildas kicked me out of the priesthood and excommunicated me. Mistress, the only thing I've ever wanted is to be a priest."

Myst shook her head. "I'm sorry this has cost you so dearly."

He fell back into the chair. "Robrek said you were a gifted healer and the most compassionate woman he's ever known. Please, mistress, will you take me as your apprentice? If I can't be a priest, please, let me be a healer."

"Come here, my child." The novice stood before her. She grasped his hands in hers, hoping she could grant the young man's request. Closing her eyes, she concentrated. "The power does move within you." She opened her eyes and released his hands. "I'd be happy to take you as my apprentice, on one condition."

He dropped to his knees. "Anything, Mistress."

"You absolutely must tell me your name."

He laughed. "Please, excuse my manners, Mistress. I am Leigh. Leigh Fergalstamm."

CHAPTER 28

"Your Highness, I will be blunt," Duke Torin said, as he sat across from Samantha in her reception room. "Argblutal is your enemy, and half of the council are firmly under his control. The Korthian nobility are growing increasingly uneasy. You're only eighteen, three years away from your majority. You don't have the necessary support to claim regency. If nothing changes, Argblutal will soon be able to force you into marriage." Pausing, Torin took a sip of his wine.

The princess raised an eyebrow. "You are indeed blunt."

Setting his goblet down, he spread his hands wide as if to embrace the world. "Only because I offer you a solution. With me by your side, we could turn the council and get you appointed regent for the king. It's an ideal solution."

Ideal for who? The princess took a sip of her own wine, vying for time.

"Your Highness, without me you have no hope. Refuse me at your peril."

Samantha stiffened. "Are you threatening me?"

The duke's eyes flicked briefly to Darhour. "Of course not, Your Highness. I merely want to emphasize that I must act soon. Argblutal's power grows by the day. It won't be long until he's unstoppable. I, at least, will not be on the losing side." He tossed back the rest of his wine and got up. "I expect a favorable answer within two days."

As the door closed behind Torin, Samantha swore every curse she'd learned in the stables and elsewhere. "Myst's potion better work. If Torin unites with Argblutal, I don't know how I'll fight them."

"Two throats are little harder to slit than one," Darhour said, his eyes darker than she'd ever seen them. As she looked into them, she wondered if she should do it. *Holy Sulis, would it be alright to solve my problems with the edge of his knife? Please, Holy Mother, show me some other way.*

As she was trying to think what that way might be, Blaine entered. "Two of the king's magistrates are asking to see you, Your Highness. They bring most distressing news from Valley Fair."

Samantha didn't know whether to laugh or cry. "I never receive any other kind. By all means, bring them in."

As Blaine showed two men in, Samantha put on the face of a princess. The first was Irvine Keirstamm, the Chief Magistrate of Murtaghan. With him was a younger man the princess didn't know. As the magistrates entered, they went down on one knee before her, a courtesy due only to the reigning monarch. "Your Highness," Irvine said, "this is Flynn Idenstamm, one of our circuit magistrates. He has just returned from Valley Fair. Something sufficiently disturbing has happened that I felt it should be brought to Your Highness's attention."

The fact the chief magistrate had brought the man to her spoke volumes for how the people viewed the situation at court. She turned to the younger magistrate, who stared fixedly at the floor. "What has happened?"

"Your Highness," Flynn Idenstamm said. "Yesterday, the father of a young man being tried by a church court came to Murtaghan seeking our immediate intervention on his son's behalf." Flynn told her of a young man who'd barely avoided being burned at the stake by a local priest.

"That's barbaric! The church has no authority to try anyone. What did the priest have against this young man?"

"From the best I could determine, Your Highness, the priest considers him tainted with demon blood. His appearance is unusual—green eyes, coal black hair, and skin darker than a Korthlundian's, and he is said to be a powerful healer. Father Gildas contends that the power of the seven hells fuels his magic."

Suddenly faint, the princess grabbed the arms of her chair. "Robbie!" she gasped.

The magistrate's head jerked up. "The healer's name is Robrek Angusstamm. Do you know him, Your Highness?"

The princess got up and went to the window to hide her emotion. She fought to stop her voice from shaking. "He healed my horse in the spring. Is he safe?"

"He did escape and is believed to have fled here to Murtaghan. However, it's entirely possible he ran in another direction."

Samantha closed her eyes, remembering the horse fair when Robbie had told her the Valley residents thought him a demon. She'd never dreamed his life might be in danger. "And what of this priest who would so grossly abuse his authority?"

"Your Highness, the young man's father wanted me to arrest him for attempted murder. A case could be made, Your Highness, but the crowd was hostile, and I was alone. Chief Keirstamm said we should seek your will in the matter. Is it Your Highness's desire that I return with sufficient force to make the arrest?"

Yes! Flay the man who would dare do this to the man I love! But things were far too tenuous at court for her to order such a thing on her own. She blinked several times to rid her eyes of tears and turned back to the magistrates, laboring to keep her voice steady. "I'll consult with council. I want you to determine if the young man is indeed safe. I'll be most displeased if any harm comes to him."

"Yes, Your Highness." The two men bowed their way out.

First, I send his mistress home dead, and now this! She turned to Blaine. "Take a message to my father. See if he'll meet with me immediately." *Father, let your mind be your own again, and we will make them all pay.*

* * *

Blaine didn't return for nearly two hours. When he did, he fell to knees, pale and trembling. "Your Highness, His Majesty has turned into a raging bull, so to speak." Shuddering, he wiped the sweat from his brow.

Samantha clutched at her stomach. "What happened?"

"I informed Gilroy I had an important message from Your Highness for His Majesty. He went in to the king and came back and told me that I'd need to wait, so I waited, and I waited, and I waited. I knew Your Highness would be getting anxious, so I told Gilroy it was truly an important matter, and he got all huffy and told me it wasn't my place to rush the king. So I waited some more. Finally, Gilroy told me the king would see me." Blaine paused and shivered. "Both Duke Argblutal and the High Priest Shylah were with him, and there was a mad glint in His Majesty's eye. Not the same mad glint that he's had since Ostara, but a raging bull mad glint, so to speak. I gave him Your Highness's message, and he thundered at me like a spring storm, so to speak. He roared that Your Highness was forgetting your place. He said he'd consult with his advisors and that when he was ready, he would send for you. In the meantime, you aren't to leave your rooms."

Jumping to her feet, Samantha called in Darhour. *Argblutal will not destroy my father!* "We're going to see my father now, and we aren't going to be denied."

* * *

Samantha arrived at the entrance to the king's rooms flanked by the five remaining members of her guard. Brice was still a little pale, but insisted he was fit for duty. A scream sounded from inside the king's quarters.

With the assistance of her guards, the princess pushed past the king's guards, who seemed too shocked by the screams to put up much resistance. Samantha stopped short at what she saw. *No, Holy Mother, please! This can't be happening.* Irvine Keirstamm and Flynn Idenstamm were stripped naked and manacled to the wall. They'd been savagely beaten. Argblutal was standing behind the two men holding a bloody whip. "Father, what in the seven hells are you doing to these men?"

The king's eyes bored into her, and she knew what Blaine meant about a raging bull. "You dare defy our orders!" He gestured at the two magistrates. "You'd make yourself queen before your time."

No, he was getting better! I know he was! "Father, please, you're ill."

"Is that the excuse you've been using to steal the throne? We will put an end to your little games. This wretch informs us that your lover has been trafficking in demons."

"Father, no! Robbie isn't my lover."

"When he's found, and he will be found, he will burn as the priest intended, and you will light the fire yourself."

Samantha ran to her father. "Father, I beg you. Leave Robbie alone. He has nothing to do with this."

"Silence!" The king jumped to his feet and slapped her across the face with such force she staggered. "You will learn obedience if we have to beat it into you."

Her guards stepped between her and the king. Kailen started to draw. She grabbed his arm. It was death to bare a sword in the presence of the king, and the way he was acting now, she knew he wouldn't hesitate to order Kailen's execution.

The king glared at her. "Guards," he yelled, and ten guards entered the room. "Escort Her Highness to her rooms. See that she stays there until I say otherwise."

Samantha's guards moved between her and the king's guards. "But Father, what about these men?" She gestured at the magistrates. "Let them go. Please, Father."

"Their fate isn't your concern. You'll leave now, or you'll be dragged from the room." The king nodded to the guards, who began to close in. Darhour looked at her. Shaking her head, she started toward the door. Whatever had gone wrong with the herb witch's potion, a fight in the king's rooms wouldn't solve it.

* * *

When she had returned to her chambers, Samantha collapsed into a chair and put her head into her hands. "How could things have gone so wrong?" she asked her men.

Kailen's voice crackled with rage. "The herb witch had some magic, but she was no servant of the goddess. A true priestess could cure this madness. Fetch her from the island."

"Of course!" She looked to Conroy. "Go at once to the shrine we visited in the spring."

Conroy's jaw dropped open. "But, Your Highness, I thought we all knew that island doesn't exist. I grew up fishing these waters with my father, and there is no island where we landed."

"Don't be absurd. How do you explain what happened?"

Conroy nodded in the direction of the Far Mountain. "The goddess. There is no other explanation, Your Highness."

If it had been Bearach or one of the others, she might have dismissed his claims, but Conroy wasn't given to wild fantasies. She turned to Blaine. "Go to the library. Bring me all maps of that area of the coast."

"At once, Your Highness." He ran from the room.

Samantha turned to Darhour, who scowled before she could even open her mouth. "The peasant boy will have to fend for himself, Your Highness. I don't even have enough men to protect you. There's nothing we can do."

"That isn't true, and we both know it. I'm not asking you to send one of my men. You're the master spy. Hire someone to find him, and don't tell me you can't. If money's becoming a problem, pawn some of my jewels. I know you didn't like me kissing him, but that's no reason to hand him over to Argblutal."

Darhour's eyes widened. "You're right. We don't want the duke to have someone with the peasant's power under his control. I will see to it, Your Highness."

She didn't like the self-serving line of his reasoning, but if Robbie was found safe, it didn't really matter why. She sent a prayer to Sulis.

When Blaine returned, they confirmed no island existed anywhere near the location of the shrine they had visited. "What do we do?"

"Send Conroy into Korth, Your Highness. The king struck you today. Only a strong healer can save him now."

Samantha turned to Conroy. "How soon can you be ready to leave?"

"At once, Your Highness." Conroy bowed and left.

Samantha went to her window and looked out. "We must plan for the possibility that the priestess can't help. We need Duke Caedmon to return and support my regency."

"If you send Conroy for the priestess," Darhour said, "only four of us remain. We can't spare another."

"I'll send Lord Devyn."

"He's nothing but a boy," Darhour objected. "And he's Duke Sheen's son."

"Darhour, there's more depth to him than his father or anyone else has ever given him credit for."

* * *

Devyn stood before his canvas. There was something that just wasn't right with the sky, but it was hard to concentrate on it with his father yelling at him.

"If you weren't such a worthless oaf, she would have married you already. After what happened to your sister, I'd think you would start to show some responsibility to the family."

Devyn sighed. "The princess seems to have done a fine job without my assistance." He turned back to his painting. *Maybe it needs a bit more green.*

"Damn you! Would you pay attention for once in your life? I should never have allowed you that art teacher. He has ruined you."

Devyn rounded on his father. "He saved me! My art is who I am!"

His father slapped him across the face. "You are my heir! You'll reign as duke after me, and you could reign as king as well. You'll work seriously to win the princess, or I'll see that you never paint again, if I have to break every bone in your hands. Am I understood?"

Devyn clenched his fists wanting to punch his father, but before he could do anything he might regret, there was a knock on the door, and a palace page entered. "Lord Devyn," the page bowed. "Her Highness, the Princess Samantha, requests you wait upon her immediately."

Devyn gaped at the page, and his father smiled broadly. "You know what this means, Devyn? The princess has come to her senses. You won't refuse her." His father wrinkled his nose. "Clean yourself up, and don't forget the paint under your nails."

* * *

Devyn fidgeted as Samantha offered him a seat. "I'm forever in your debt for what you've done for Danu. Now, I must make myself further in your debt."

"Your Highness, I beg you. I thought we agreed I was a terrible choice for king."

"Devyn, I have no intention of marrying you."

"You don't?" The tension drained out of him. "Thank the goddess, Your Highness. I mean no disrespect. I mean, I have nothing against you. I mean . . ."

"Devyn, I know what you mean, and I'm not offended. I have a mission of great importance, and I need someone I can trust to complete it."

"You trust *me*, Your Highness?"

"Am I wrong to have confidence in your loyalty?"

"My loyalty, no. My ability, yes. If you want a picture painted, I can do it, but at everything else, I'm as worthless as my father claims."

"Devyn, it is loyalty more than ability I need. My father is mad. He's being poisoned by Duke Argblutal and the high priest. I need a duke of sufficient power and influence to help me challenge his authority. I need you to go to Korth and bring Duke Caedmon back."

"Your Highness, my father will never allow it."

The princess drummed her fingers on the arm of her chair. "I suggest you not ask his permission. You're old enough to stop allowing your father to dictate your every move."

"But Your Highness—"

"Devyn, I need Caedmon, and I need him now. Without him, my only option is to marry you so that your father will support my regency, something neither of us desires. I have another position in mind for you. I think the court is desperately in need of an official artist. And with such a position, you'd no longer need your father's consent to marry as you please."

Devyn felt his heart become lighter than it'd ever been. "But how do I leave the palace without explaining to my father where I'm going?"

"Tell him I've sent you to make a painting of a waterfall in Korth."

* * *

"She wants you to do what?" Duke Sheen raged as Devyn told him the news. "I won't have you harrying half way across the joined kingdoms to paint some fool picture!"

Devyn put his hand over his heart. "You'll have me refuse the princess's commands?"

"I'd have you do no such thing. But I warn you, Devyn, when you present the finished painting to her, it had better lead to a betrothal."

"Of course, father." Devyn left before his father could question him further.

When he returned to his rooms, he found Aislinn waiting for him. "Oh, Aislinn, there's finally hope for us."

"How so, my dear boy?"

Devyn beamed as he told her what the princess had promised him. "Don't breathe a word of this to anyone. My mission is supposed to be a complete secret."

Squealing, Aislinn jumped into his arms. "Oh, Devyn, I never dared hope! When do you leave?"

"Her Highness wants me to go first thing in the morning, so I need to get my paints packed."

Aislinn raised an eyebrow. "You think you'll have time to paint?"

Devyn told her of the story they'd given his father. Aislinn laughed heartily.

"Oh, Devyn, the princess is truly my kind of woman."

* * *

Shylah watched as the duke's servant took the body of the kitchen boy from the altar. "Dispose of him where no one will find him."

CHAPTER 29

Angus's oldest son stood before him. The one who'd always been his favorite. The one he'd intended to carry on his legacy. The one he'd once believed most like himself. "You'd dare to testify against your own brother!" Angus bellowed. "You'd lead the mob that would tie him to a stake! You'd stain your hands with the blood of kin!"

Boyden glared back. "That demon is no kin of mine."

Angus pointed his finger at Boyden's chest. "He is Donella's son, as are you."

"You're wrong, old man. I'm a true child of the goddess. The demon witch may have ensnared your reason, but the goddess has seen fit to save me from your folly."

"I had children with one woman only. If you aren't her son, you aren't mine! Get out of this house and off my lands before I throw you out."

Boyden crossed his arms. "You can't be serious. Nobody's going to deny me what's rightfully mine."

Angus grabbed Boyden by the shirt, hauled him to the door, and threw him into the dirt of the farmyard. Boyden yelled something obscene and launched himself at Angus, who sidestepped his son's charge and tripped him back into the dirt. Grief and rage mixed within Angus as Boyden rolled to his feet and came at him again. Angus blocked Boyden's blow and smashed his fist into his son's face. He followed with a left hook into his kidney. Boyden staggered, blood dripping into his eye. Angus hit him again before he could recover, flattening his nose. Boyden swung wildly, but Angus avoided his blows. He backed his son against the side of the house and pummeled him in the gut. Boyden growled in anger and attempted to kick Angus. Angus stepped to the side, smashed his knee into Boyden's leg, and threw him into the dirt again. Boyden simply lay, bleeding, at his feet.

Angus looked away. A large group of farmhands had gathered. "Allyn, saddle his horse and bring it here." Some of the female servants stood in the doorway to the house. "Cara, pack his clothes and a few supplies."

Cara obeyed, and Angus addressed the gathered hands. "From this day forward, this man is no longer my son. He's banished from my lands."

"Father, you can't do this." Boyden knelt in the dirt.

"By your own words, I'm not your father." Allyn brought Boyden's horse and helped Boyden into the saddle. Shortly, Cara came out with a bundle of Boyden's clothes and a basket of food. Angus turned his back on Boyden and walked into the house. From the window, he watched Boyden ride away.

What was his wealth worth if he had no son to leave it to?

* * *

Riding to the village, Boyden had difficulty staying on his horse. Although his father had slapped him a few times in the past and he'd had a fair number of fights, he'd never been beaten like this. *Damn the worm to the seven hells! If that slimy mutt ever shows his face again, I'll kill him!*

Boyden rode to the back door of the village shrine. He nearly fell as he dismounted, then staggered to the door. A novice answered his knock. "Good sir! You've been injured!"

"Have I really?" Boyden snapped. "I need to see Father Gildas."

"Of course." The novice stepped aside to let him enter. Boyden stumbled, and the novice supported him as they went into the shrine's surgery, where Boyden lay down on a cot. "I'll fetch the priest, sir."

The novice returned shortly with a basin of water and some salve. "Where is Father Gildas?" Boyden groaned.

"The Father's busy now. I'll see to your injuries."

"I need to see Father Gildas. Did you tell him who was here?"

"Yes, sir. He doesn't have time to see to every drunken brawler."

"I'm not drunk, and I haven't been in a brawl." Boyden stumbled to his feet. "Where in the seven hells is the damned priest?"

"Such language, sir, inside the shrine!" Boyden shoved him aside and headed for the priest's office.

He pounded the door open and found Father Gildas behind his desk. "What do you mean barging in here like a drunken lout?" the priest demanded.

Boyden pointed a finger at the priest. "I did everything you asked! Now my father's disinherited me. You will fix this."

"You've been nothing but an endless series of broken promises and disappointments. Your affairs are no longer my concern."

"How dare you!" Boyden grabbed the priest's robes.

"Control yourself! You forfeit your soul laying violent hands on a servant of Sulis."

The priest's yells brought two novices running. They pulled Boyden off the priest.

The priest adjusted his robes. "Throw this sot out."

"I'm not drunk, I tell you! This shrine is the only home I have left!" But the novices pulled him from Father Gildas's office, dragged him to the temple's back door, and threw him into the street. He landed with a dull thud and heard a small cry. Blair Brianstamm and her sister Lavena were coming out of the general store. They ran to him.

Blair kneeled down beside him. "Oh, Boyden! What happened?"

Boyden tried to raise himself. "Just a minor disagreement with my father and that Sulis-cursed priest!"

Blair gasped, but she helped him to his feet. "We'll take you to the inn and get you cleaned up."

Using Blair as support, Boyden stumbled down the street toward the inn. Lavena took his horse around to the stable, and Blair led him inside. "He needs a room and hot water now," Blair commanded.

Banagher gestured to a room. "Number three isn't in use." Blair nodded and all but carried Boyden down the short hallway. Boyden wondered why he'd never before noticed how strong and confident she was. She laid him on the bed and removed his boots. "Oh, Boyden," she cooed, as she brushed back the hair from his forehead.

The innkeeper's daughter brought in a basin of hot water and a rag while the stable boy carried in Boyden's things. As Blair took the rag and began washing the blood from his face. Boyden again noticed the size of her breasts and realized he'd found the solution to his problem. "Marry me, Blair."

She put her hands on her hips. "Boyden, don't say that if you don't mean it."

He touched her cheek. "But I do mean it. Take my hand, and we'll handfast right now."

Blair giggled. "I don't think you're in any condition to consummate the relationship, Boyden."

"I'll consummate it all right," he leered at her. "Marry me today?"

"You're serious, aren't you?" The damned silly woman tried to throw her arms around him, so addle-brained she'd forgotten he'd been injured. He groaned in protest, but he didn't mind how her breasts pressed against him. "Boyden, I didn't mean to hurt you. I'm just so happy. Of course, I'll marry you. But properly, by a priest."

"Next week, then?" He smiled up at her in the way that had always convinced her to share his bed. "I've been a fool not to have married you already."

Blair's eyes misted over. *Why can't women control their emotions?* "A week isn't anywhere near enough time to plan a wedding. We'll get married in a month, no sooner."

He'd get her to change her mind, but it took too much energy to argue now. Blair didn't pay near enough attention to his injuries. Instead, she rattled off in a scatterbrained fashion about wedding plans. After planning the wedding feast, she had the gall to ask, "And what lands is your father going to give you when we wed?"

"Sulis curse the damned fool! He disinherited me because I did my part to get rid of the worm."

Blair drew back, and her eyes lost their sparkle. "You'll go home tomorrow and work everything out with him!"

"I don't need a woman telling me what to do, and I don't need him either."

Blair stood. "Just what were you thinking we'd live on?"

"Your dowry, of course."

"For your information, my dowry doesn't consist of any land. You have some nerve, Boyden Angusstamm, asking a girl to marry you when you have no means of supporting her. You reconcile yourself with your father before you come asking for my hand again." She threw the rag at him and stomped out of the room.

Damned woman! I never wanted to marry that ugly cow anyway.

* * *

After darkness fell, Angus saw to the latest delivery of supplies to his youngest son. Myst had told him the boy was leaving the Valley before the week was out and had told him of a place near the woods where Angus could leave things. After leaving the cache of supplies, he stepped back into the trees and waited for Robbie to appear. He wanted one last look at his son, to know for sure the boy was indeed alive and safe. But he didn't want to speak to him. This son, too, had defied him.

After a short time, Robbie appeared, looking fit. He carried a staff, and Angus again wondered how the boy had learned to use it. As Robbie gathered the supplies, he stopped and looked in Angus's direction. Angus doubted the boy saw him, but with his damned magic, Robbie seemed to know he was there. He didn't say anything, though. He just took the stuff and left. Angus made his way back to the farm that no longer felt like a home.

* * *

Angry that his father couldn't even be bothered to speak to him, Robrek fought furiously against three armed knights. The bronze-hilted sword flashed in the late afternoon sun. For the moment, he was holding his own. His sword slipped between the ribs of the first man, and he withdrew it quickly to block a blow aimed at his head. From the corner of his eye, he saw the first one go down. Tiring, he fought hard and waited for an opening. He finally found one and aimed for the second knight's throat. The second man fell, but Robrek had left his right side open, and a sword cut him in half.

"Sulis curse it! That hurts!" Although he'd become fairly successful against two opponents, he hadn't yet been able to take on three.

:Few can prevail when outnumbered three to one,: Brazen said.

"And it has to hurt, or I won't try to avoid getting hit. You've told me that at least a hundred times." Robbie walked to cool off and then sat down on the stump. "I'm leaving tomorrow morning early, you know."

:You will be back.:

That was what the horses had said ever since he'd announced his intentions. "No, I won't. I could take you with me, though," he suggested yet again. "If you can hide this place, surely you could hide one near Murtaghan."

When again the horses made no response to his request, he wanted to punch the fence post. Wild Thing came close and nuzzled against him. "At least you'll be with me, my girl. I won't be alone."

:Wild Thing always with Robbie.:

Robrek scratched her neck and then hung up the swords on the stable walls. He looked at the armor and other gear. He'd have to leave it, of course. He packed Wild Thing's saddlebags with everything he planned to take. Then he sat and leaned against the stable wall. Ronan jumped into his lap, and he stroked the cat's head. "I'll take you back to Myst." The cat merely purred, and Robrek wouldn't be at all surprised if Ronan showed up on his doorstep in Murtaghan. If he ever had a doorstep.

* * *

As Leigh healed the child's ankle, he felt more alive than ever. The child had fallen and hurt his leg, and his mother was afraid it was broken. After checking the leg and determining it was merely sprained, Myst gave Leigh his first chance at direct healing. No sensation could be more intense and pleasurable. At last, he completed the task and dropped out of the healing trance. Exhausted, he stumbled and nearly fell. Although Myst had warned of this, he was surprised by how completely drained he felt. The child rewarded him with a small smile before he curled up and fell asleep in his mother's arms.

The mother expressed her gratitude with words and a dozen eggs. They'd have a nice omelet for dinner, a welcome break from the usual bread, cheese, and vegetable stew. It wasn't that they didn't have enough to eat. It was that it was always the same. Leigh had lived the life of privilege as the child of a wealthy merchant and a novice in the church, and he'd had some difficulty getting used to the monotony of the peasant diet. For one thing, they so rarely had meat. Still, he told himself as he collapsed onto the rug, his new life was worth a few privations.

"Why couldn't Father Gildas teach me that?" he asked Myst.

Myst snorted. "Because he can't do it himself. The priests have worked hard to eliminate magic from our land."

Embarrassed by his mentor's heresy, Leigh looked away. Still, he'd felt the spirit of the goddess far more strongly in the herb witch's hut than he'd ever had in Father Gildas's shrine. Perhaps the priest, and not the herb witch, was the heretic.

* * *

Robrek sat Ronan down on the hearth rug next to the chair where Myst was sleeping. The novice who had saved his life sat at the kitchen table. Myst looked so ill, and when he touched her, her flesh was icy cold. She woke and smiled at him.

He knelt at her side. "Mistress, are you alright? You look pale."

Myst patted his arm. "My child, I'm an old woman. All old women look pale."

"Mistress, you're cold," he said, knowing she was making excuses. He took her hand in his and rubbed it. "I'll make you some tea." He got to his feet. "If you need me, I don't have to go to Murtaghan."

"My child, I'll miss you, but I'll be fine. If possible, you must find a way to let me know you're well."

"I will, Mistress. I promise." He talked to her of his plans as he made the tea. When it was ready, he handed her the tea.

Leigh joined them. As well as giving him advice about where to stay and where to look for work, Leigh drew Robrek a crude map of the city. "You won't have any trouble finding a position," Leigh assured him. "One exhibition of your skills, and they'll be lining up to hire you. But Murtaghan can be quite overwhelming to someone who has never seen a big city."

Myst had fallen asleep as they talked. "You'll take care of Myst for me?" he asked.

Waking at his question, Myst gripped Robrek's shoulder. "Don't worry about me." But Leigh nodded. Robrek was glad the novice was there. He wasn't sure he could have left Myst alone, no matter how strongly she urged him.

Robrek reluctantly got to his feet. "You take care, Mistress. I'll never forget what you've done for me." He took her in his arms and felt the icy coldness of her flesh. He kissed her, praying that somehow she'd get well again. He shook Leigh's hand and disappeared into the night.

PART III

CHAPTER 30

The princess sat at her window seat, trying to find the energy to do something other than stare. *Holy Sulis, if my taking the throne is your will, couldn't you have made it easier? Couldn't you have at least left Robbie out of it?* She wondered how she would face him if Darhour did find him. *I should have listened to Myst and left him alone. Surely he'll hate me for deceiving him and putting his life in danger yet again.*

She was jerked out of her torpor when a page arrived with a summons from the king.

* * *

Solar raged as he waited for Samantha to answer the summons Argblutal had forced him to send for her. Two weeks ago, he'd awakened from what seemed one long nightmare, only to find himself in another more sinister one. *I've been king for sixty-five years, and this Sulis-cursed upstart thinks he can reduce me to a puppet!* The man who held his strings stood beside him, giving him his lines for the next act in his play. Solar choked on them. He could think of only one way to save his daughter. *I scoffed at my father's belief in Gloine Torr and the Apples of Airh, but if magic is controlling, perhaps he wasn't such a fool after all. If the old ways truly have power, I'll thwart the bastard.*

"Her Highness, the Princess Samantha," Gilroy announced.

The princess entered with her bodyguards. He stared hard at the one who'd been The Ghost. *They say you were the best. Kill Argblutal!* If the assassin understood, he gave no sign of it. Samantha and her guards went down on one knee. She looked pale, but she held her head high and met his eyes straight on. "You summoned me, Your Majesty."

"Tomorrow is Litha." To Solar's surprise, the strings that held him relaxed as he invoked the name of the holiday. Although the magic hadn't been attempted since Danu refused to take her place atop Gloine Torr, Litha had been the traditional beginning of the ritual. "Since you have refused to name your own consort, our plans for your betrothal will be announced tomorrow in the city square, as part of the celebration." Solar smiled savagely on the inside. He'd been able to speak the words. *Maybe his father hadn't been such a fool.*

"I understand, Your Majesty," she said, speaking the same words in the same tone as she had when he'd refused her a more spirited horse. *You got that horse, didn't you, my dear? I've raised you to be queen. If the old ways can't protect you, be strong enough to protect yourself.* He stared after her as she left the room. *Holy Sulis, I love you, Samantha.*

When the door closed behind her, the king felt the strings snap taut. Argblutal towered over him. "You were to inform your daughter of her betrothal to me."

I'll see you drawn and quartered for this. But he could say nothing other than, "At the festival, we will make our announcement."

"See that you do," Argblutal said, and swept from the room. When the king was alone, his fury faded and despair threatened to close in. *What if this doesn't work?*

* * *

Waiting in the duke's rooms, Shylah cringed when Argblutal entered. "Did he announce your betrothal to the princess?" Shylah asked.

"His Majesty claims the announcement will be made at Litha. But I could see it in his eyes that he's plotting something. We must have tighter control over the king."

Shylah began rubbing his hands together, trying to wash off the blood, but no matter how hard he tried his hands stayed red. He was surprised no one had noticed yet. "Yes . . . yes, tighter control. Much tighter control. We need tighter control."

Argblutal's lips tightened. "You will be pleased to know I've found a child."

"You have?" The high priest rubbed his hands more vigorously. "Yes, that's very good, very good. But are you sure the child is a virgin? The child must be a virgin. Can't have known the pleasures of the flesh."

"I have personally assured her virginity."

"Good, good. No other will do. And is she healthy, well fed? Must be healthy. Must be well fed."

"Why don't you see for yourself?" The duke signaled, and an approximately eight-year-old girl was led into the room. Such a pretty child. Such a pretty, pretty child. She was dressed in peasant weave, but she did seem healthy and well fed. The child bowed before Argblutal. "Your Grace." The child trembled. Oh, yes, be very afraid!

"Deidre," the duke said. "This is High Priest Shylah. You'll be helping him tonight. Go over and let him see you."

"And then can I go home, as you promised?" Deidre's voice shook.

"You'll see your mother again after the high priest is finished with you. Now, let him see you."

Deidre approached the high priest. Such a pretty, pretty child. It's a pity. A pity, pretty child. A red stain formed in the middle of the child's chest and spread outward. "No!" he cried. "Not yet! Not yet!" The child ran backward, and when he looked again, it was gone. No blood yet. But there would be. So much blood Eilis had had. So much blood Cullen had had.

But the god demanded this of him. Eilis, Cullen, and Deidre. Surely, these three lives aren't too high a price to pay to return the truth of the god and magic to the land. "She'll do nicely. Shall I take her with me now?"

Argblutal raised an eyebrow. "I think not. The child will be brought to you in time for the ceremony."

* * *

His left arm wrapped in bloody rags, Conroy limped into the inn. He was dressed in the cheap leather armor of a rather unsuccessful mercenary or bandit and wore an old and extremely battered blade. He was repulsed by his own odor; the man who'd recently worn these clothes hadn't bathed or changed in months.

The innkeeper motioned him to a chair at the bar. "Trouble?" he asked. Wincing, Conroy nodded. "Bandits. Just got away with my life." That was a slight exaggeration; he hadn't had too much difficulty besting them. Still, he'd grown discouraged in the weeks since the princess had sent him north. He'd hoped to find a priestess just across the border in Korth. Now he'd been to Wisteria and beyond. Along the way he'd visited shrine after shrine, village after village, and he'd found no sign of a priestess. The shrines that had been run by priestesses in the past were now either deserted or a priest had taken them over. He'd learned a proclamation had been issued in Korth that named the priestesses an anathema and made anyone conducting religious ceremonies without the sanction of the high priest of Lundia subject to arrest. From his friends at the Winter Palace, Conroy got a list of villages that had been known to have priestesses, but as a member of the Royal Guard and an obvious Lundian from his accent, he'd gotten little cooperation. Then he'd been attacked by a small gang of bandits, taking a minor wound and killing two of his opponents. He hoped an injured traveler in need of healing could uncover the missing priestesses.

The innkeeper grunted and offered him a mug of ale. "Bandits are becoming more of a problem every week. The Royal Guard's more interested in tracking down faithful worshippers of the goddess. Worthless scum." The innkeeper spat, and Conroy was unsure whether he meant the bandits or the Royal Guard.

"Don't I know it! I may have been born in Lundia, but I never trusted those greedy Lundian priests. Have to hand over a hefty donation before they'll even look at you, and not a one of them has a true healing gift." Conroy swallowed a mouthful of ale as if trying to wash away a nasty taste.

"The priestess we had here had a strong gift. The king's guard hauled her away last month."

Conroy swore. "I was hoping you had a healer who could look at my arm."

"My wife can look at it when she gets a moment. She's no true healer, but she knows a thing or two about treating wounds."

Conroy smiled graciously. "That would be most kind, and I'd like a bowl of that wonderful smelling stew in the meantime. I'll also be needing a bed for the night and stabling for my horse."

They agreed on a price, and Conroy produced the coin. He was nearly finished with his stew when the innkeeper's wife arrived. She unwrapped the bloody rags and wrinkled her nose at his stench. "Hardly more than a scratch," she murmured, as she washed the wound, poulticed it, and bound it in clean rags. She wasn't gentle.

* * *

As he sat in Duke Caedmon's reception room, Devyn tapped his fingers on the side of his chair. After leaving him waiting more than long enough to remind him of his inferior status, Caedmon finally entered. Devyn rose and bowed his head. "Your Grace."

The duke nodded and examined him with the same piercing eye that had always made him squirm as a child. Devyn had to fight to prevent himself from squirming now. Taking a seat behind his desk, the duke motioned Devyn into a chair. "What does your father want with me?"

"I come not from my father, but from Her Highness."

The duke leaned back. "I don't recall you being a particular friend of the princess. She's intelligent enough to realize you're unfit for the throne."

Devyn gritted his teeth. "I may well be, but she considered me fit to deliver a message."

Caedmon snorted. "Let's have it." He extended his hand.

"The princess decided it wasn't wise to trust anything in writing in case I was intercepted."

The duke snorted again. "A likely story."

Devyn clenched his fists. "She told me if you doubted me to remind you of the time when she was five years old and took a pearl and emerald broach from your quarters. Later that night, she returned it and begged you not to have her thrown in the dungeon. You assured her if she never stole again, the incident would remain your little secret."

The duke laughed. "The poor little thing was nearly petrified. I'd have given her the damned broach if she'd only asked for it. What does Her Highness want?"

"She asks you to return to court. The king has gone mad, and Argblutal is grabbing power. She needs your support to be named regent."

The duke leaned forward. "King Solar is mad?"

"Yes, Your Grace. As you know, the suggestion to name her as regent must come from one of the four dukes. Duke Argblutal obviously will not do so."

"What about Duke Torin or your father?"

Devyn shook his head. "Duke Torin will only do it if she agrees to marry him, and my father . . ." He felt himself go red as he looked away.

"Your father wants her to marry you."

"Yes, he does, but as you said, I'm not fit for the throne."

"Very well. We'll work up a little surprise to take back to Murtaghan with us before the snow falls."

* * *

Shylah heard Deidre crying as Duke Argblutal tied her to the altar.

As he mixed the few simple herbs the potion required, he shuddered. If they'd just accept their fate quietly, everything would be so much easier. Eilis had cried. Cullen had called curses down on him. Such a foul mouth for one so young.

Deidre was pleading, "But you promised I could go home."

"I'm sure the goddess will welcome you Beyond the Far Mountain and honor what you have sacrificed for her cause," Argblutal told her.

The God Sulis. The God! Such a pretty, pretty child. Why won't she be quiet? They look so different dead. So pale. So cold Eilis had been. So cold Cullen had been. Deidre started screaming. Damn her! How can I concentrate with that going on?

"She's ready. Get on with it," Argblutal demanded.

Shylah stiffened. Where is his respect for the representative of his god? Shylah emptied the vial of the king's blood into the cauldron. He took the knife, cut his own arm, and bled into the cauldron. He has no respect. He referred to Sulis as a goddess. The high priest

381

took the knife, wet with his own blood, and approached Deidre. Tied as Eilis had been. As Cullen had been. Such a pretty, pretty child.

The child cried, "No! Don't hurt me! You promised! My mother needs me!"

"Shut up!" Argblutal hissed. "You'll join your mother soon enough. She made good sport before I killed her."

"No!" the girl screamed. "You're lying!"

The high priest looked between Argblutal and the hysterical girl. "You killed her mother?"

"It isn't your place to question my actions. Your job is to give me control of the king."

"You mean, give us control of the king so that we can restore the truth about Sulis!"

"Yes, of course." But the high priest could tell the duke wasn't telling the truth. *He lied to me, as he lied to this child. He won't support me in bringing the truth back. Eilis died for him, not the god. Cullen died for him, not the god.*

"No!" he cried, raised the knife, and dove for the duke.

Caught by surprise, Argblutal was still able to twist out of the high priest's way. He grasped the high priest, pinned him to the floor, and twisted the knife out of his hand. "You dare defy me? Get up and finish the job!"

"No, no," the high priest whimpered. "No, such a pretty child."

Argblutal kicked him, sending him sprawling and blubbering across the floor. "You started this. You will finish it."

The high priest stared at him with blank eyes. "No, no. Such a pretty child."

Grabbing him, the duke hauled him to his feet and twisted his arm behind his back. Shylah screamed with pain. Argblutal shoved the sacrificial knife into the high priest's other hand. The high priest grasped the knife, but stared at it as if he didn't know what it was. "Finish it now!"

Argblutal twisted the arm more tightly, but Shylah merely cried out and dropped the knife. Time was slipping away, and the high priest had said the sacrifice must take place at the darkest hour of the night. Argblutal picked up the knife and put it back into the high priest's hand, but Shylah's grip was lax. The duke wrapped his own hand around Shylah's and directed it toward the young girl's chest. He slit open her dress, baring her chest. Using Shylah's hand, he began to draw the star of Sulis, as he'd watched Shylah do with the second child.

As the knife began to cut into Deidre's flesh, she shrieked. "Sulis, oh Holy Mother, save me!"

The high priest tried to pull the knife away.

"Damn you!" Argblutal tried to force the knife back to complete the drawing. In the struggle, the knife plunged into the young girl's chest. Deidre convulsed and lay still. Argblutal pushed Shylah out of the way. The drawing of the star hadn't been completed, but could such an insignificant thing matter? Surely, only the blood was important. He quickly filled a vial and took it to the simmering cauldron.

He added the blood to the potion, but nothing happened. When the high priest had added the blood of the second boy, the potion had hissed and turned purple. He cursed. Will it still work?

CHAPTER 31

Before the sun was up, Robrek said his last good-bye to Brazen and Fancy Man.

:Remember what you have learned,: Brazen instructed him.

:Ah, Litha. A wonderful time. Flowers. Food. Music and dancing,: Fancy Man said. *:You could use a little holiday.:*

"This isn't a holiday. I'm not coming back."

:You might be able to find yourself a nice little mare. Release some of that tension you have bottled up.: In his typical lewd manner, the stallion winked at Robrek's groin.

Robrek resisted the urge to punch Fancy Man. *This is serious. How can he treat it like a crude joke?* He swung into Wild Thing's saddle. "Well, goodbye then."

Robrek went through the woods and fields, avoiding the road. As he passed behind the herb witch's hut, he paused. There was no sound from within. "Goodbye, Myst," he whispered. "Sulis, bless her. Nobody deserves it more."

:Why sad?: Wild Thing asked. *:Big Adventure!:*

"That's right, my girl." Robrek urged her into motion again. "Everything will be different for us in Murtaghan." Whatever awaited him had to be better than being burned at the stake.

By the time the sun started to rise, he'd reached the site of the Coan Horse Fair, the farthest he'd ever been from his father's farm. The fair grounds were deserted in the early morning light. He paused beside the area where the dances were held. He touched the ribbon under his shirt and wondered where Milady was now and if she ever thought of him. He shook away such useless thoughts and headed into the unknown.

He had to stick to the road now because he didn't know the way. He stroked his staff for reassurance and checked the knife at his side. "In Murtaghan, we'll be safe, my girl."

:*No worry. Big adventure.*: Robrek laughed, and as he headed into completely unfamiliar territory, Wild Thing's excitement became contagious. He found himself smiling and whistling. Wild Thing looked over her shoulder to object to the horrible music, but she was in too good a mood to let it bother her much.

The road remained empty for some time, and when he finally began to see other people, they were strangers. They stared at him and kept their distance, but they didn't say anything to him. After another hour, he entered what had to be the Setanta forest. He'd heard of it, but he'd never imagined trees could be so big. They seemed to reach for miles over his head, and some were as broad around as Myst's cottage. He shivered nervously, remembering the stories of what else waited in the forest—panthers and bandits.

Wild Thing slowed and looked around warily. :*Trees tall.*: Robrek felt the currents of life. He sensed birds and squirrels, deer and rabbits, but nothing menacing. Wild Thing relaxed after a bit. :*No priests. No brother. No hurt. Big adventure.*:

About midday, the forest ended abruptly. Robrek gasped: a huge pyramid, even taller than the trees, rose out of the plains ahead of him. It was pure black, and its sides looked as smooth as glass. "What in the seven hells is that?" he asked Wild Thing.

:*Big. Black.*:

Nobody had ever mentioned such a thing to Robrek. He heard the sound of a stream and rode toward it. He let Wild Thing drink while he stared at the towering structure. It was too big, too smooth to be natural.

His stomach growled, and he decided this was as good a place as any to eat his lunch. He got down, drank from the stream, and got his lunch out of Wild Thing's saddlebags. He grabbed his staff from the saddle and left Wild Thing's reins looped around the saddle horn; there was plenty of grazing nearby, and she wandered and ate. As he ate his bread and cheese, he continued to stare at the towering pyramid.

When he'd finished his meal, he heard horses approaching. He got to his feet and grabbed his staff.

Two men approached on horseback. They were typical Korthlundians with their blue eyes and blond hair, but they dressed unlike anyone Robrek had ever seen. Their robes were of fine fabric in fantastic colors—brilliant blue and rich scarlet. They stopped when they saw him, and Robrek wondered whether he should bow. He decided on a mere nod of the head. "Hello, stranger," one of them greeted him, speaking slowly as one did to a dimwitted child. "May we share your stream?"

"Be welcome," Robrek said.

Seeming surprised he could actually speak, the men dismounted and watered their horses. "It looks like it will be fair weather for the Festival, does it not?" one man asked.

"Yes, I believe it will stay warm," Robrek answered, feeling out-of-place making such idle small talk.

With his head bowed, the second man faced the huge pyramid. After a few seconds, he straightened and drew Sulis's star over his breast. Robrek shivered. "Is that thing evil?" he asked.

"I should say not. You're obviously a stranger," the man who'd drawn the star answered.

"Yes," Robrek nodded. "What is it?"

"That," the first man declared, "is Gloine Torr, the most sacred shrine to the goddess in all of the joined kingdoms. Taran here fancies himself pious and can't pass it without making his obeisance."

"You could use a little more piety yourself, Braeden," Taran responded. "The goddess placed it here to demonstrate her favor."

Braeden snorted. "Nobody knows where it came from. It's quite a sight, though. There are stairs on the other side, and the view from the top is spectacular."

Robrek nodded, but a shrine to the goddess was the last place he wanted to go.

"Where are you from, my young friend?" Braeden asked. "You speak like a Korthlundian, but you don't have the appearance of one."

Robrek glanced warily at the man. "I'm Lundian, but my mother wasn't. My father married a foreigner."

"That explains it. You had me confused." He turned to his friend. "Taran, have you paid sufficient respects?"

The man shot his friend an annoyed glance. "You'll rot in the seven hells for impiety."

Wild Thing wandered up behind Robrek and placed her head on his shoulder.

Braeden gasped and drew back. "Can that be a Horsetad?"

Being so used to Wild Thing, Robrek often forgot she was anything out of the ordinary. "Yes. Beautiful, isn't she?"

Taran fell to his knees and drew Sulis's star. "The blessing of the goddess must be strong upon you."

Braeden waved off his friend's comment. "How did you tame her?"

Robrek ran his hand through his hair and looked away. "She isn't truly tamed. She won't let anyone but me ride her."

"But why does she allow you?" Braeden asked. "Only in bards' tales does anyone ride a Horsetad."

"I'm an amihealer."

"*Ah.*" He turned to his companion and rolled his eyes. "Come, Taran, up you go now. We must reach the capital quickly if we want a room." He turned back to Robrek. "If you're heading for Murtaghan, will you ride with us?"

Robrek took several seconds to answer the unexpected question. "Certainly," he finally said.

The three men rode along talking mostly about Wild Thing. Both Braeden and Taran asked him endless questions until Robrek started to wonder if riding with them had been wise. The longer they rode the more people joined them. Nearly all of them stared and pointed at him or at Wild Thing. He hadn't thought about the significance of riding a Horsetad into the capital. He held his staff ready. *So much for being able to lose myself in the crowd.*

As they came to the top of a small hill, Robrek slowed. Murtaghan spread out below him. Never in his wildest imagination had he pictured anything so big. The walls were the height of at least five men and stretched outward to the edge of his sight. And on the very edge of the horizon, he could see the beginning of a vast body of water.

:Big people place! Not like home. Small people place bad. Maybe big people place good.: Robrek hoped so.

The closer they got, the more he noticed something else he'd never imagined about the city. The stench of it was almost overpowering: human and animal waste, rotten garbage, thousands of unwashed bodies, spoiled fish, and the tang of salt water. He fought against retching. Braeden glanced at him sympathetically. "It does smell a bit. One gets used to it." Robrek nodded, but he couldn't imagine how.

As Robrek and the two men approached the gate, the pace slowed. What seemed to be the entire population of the joined kingdoms was trying to squeeze through for the festival. When they made it through the gate, the smell became worse, and the sight was horrifying. Little children and old men wearing ragged clothing and sporting open sores begged in the streets. He hadn't enough coins to give even a dram to each of them. Behind the beggars were drinking establishments. Robrek could smell the odor of bad ale and cheap wine. Dangerous looking men lounged in the doorways. Nearly everyone was staring at him and pointing at Wild Thing's stars. He gripped his staff more tightly.

Taking in both his peasant garments and the Horsetad he rode, a girl younger than he ogled him uncertainly. She batted her eyes at him and called, "Hey, magician, want a taste of the big city?" She bared a breast. Robrek had never seen a woman's breast before, and the sight caused stirrings in his groin. But her body was emaciated, and Robrek saw evidence of both old and new bruises.

Braeden leaned over. "No telling what you could pick up from a whore in this part of town. If you're interested in a girl, I could point you to a better place."

Robrek stared openmouthed at the older man. Laughing, Braeden winked at him.

At last, they left the poor section and moved into an area dedicated to shops and stalls. The odor gradually faded, although the air was still rather rank. Hundreds of shops were open and doing a brisk business. Shops selling clothing, shoes, jewelry, wine; an entire shop devoted to ribbons. He saw shops for perfume, candles, candy, and pottery. Another shop sold only books. Shops for musical instruments, pens, ink and paper, knives and swords. Even shops for things Robrek couldn't identify. Everywhere he looked he saw even more things; the variety seemed endless. *Holy Sulis, why would anyone need all these things?*

In the press of the crowd, he'd become separated from Braeden and Taran, and he'd neglected to follow Leigh's directions to where he should stay. Suddenly, he realized he was lost, and he was sure he wasn't in the proper section of town for the son of a country farmer. The inns were large and luxurious, and the people milling about wore rich robes, their necks gilded with gold and jewels. They, too, stared and pointed at him. Trying to decide what he should do and if he dare ask directions, he wandered a bit until he felt a gut-wrenching pain. He gasped, but the pain wasn't his own but that of a horse nearby. He followed the pain into the yard of the most luxurious inn. It bore a sign that read, "The Silk Curtain."

He dismounted and approached the stable. A man who appeared to be the innkeeper glared at him. "We've no need for a new boy," he said. "Beat it."

Robrek held his hand to his abdomen. "There's a horse in your stable that's very ill."

"I said, beat it." The innkeeper approached with a raised fist.

Inside the stables, a horse screamed and kicked at the stall walls. It was all Robrek could do to stop from screaming himself. He rushed past the innkeeper into the stable.

"Hold on there!" the innkeeper hollered, chasing him.

Inside the stable, a beautiful black mare was rearing and kicking, blood dribbling from its mouth. Robrek spoke gently as he neared. "It's okay, girl. Robrek's here. Just let me close so I can help you."

As he put his hand on her, the horse immediately quieted. The stable hands had fallen back from the frantic animal, but now one of them gasped, "How did you do that? I thought she was going to tear the stables down."

Ignoring him, Robrek closed his eyes and reached into the animal's body with his mind. "Holy Sulis. Her stomach is full of ground glass," he said, opening his eyes.

"Just how would glass get into a horse's stomach?" The innkeeper laughed derisively, but the expression on his face said he wasn't entirely certain what to make of Robrek.

Robrek moved his hand along the path glass would have taken to get to the horse's belly. "I'd guess someone fed it to her."

The horse shivered and vomited blood. Robrek pulled out his knife. "Quick, fetch me a spoon and some alcohol." The innkeeper nodded frantically to one of the stable hands, and soon Robrek received the items he'd asked for. He splashed the knife and the horse's belly with the liquor, sedated the horse with his mind, and cut open her belly. He entered a healing trance, where he became aware of nothing other than the animal. He spooned the glass out of the horse's stomach. He healed the lacerations in the horse's belly and up through its throat and then sealed the incision. When he dropped out of the trance, he was dizzy with exhaustion. He briefly registered the faces above him as he collapsed to the stable floor, wondering if what he'd done had been wise. The last time he'd exhausted himself this way, he'd awoken chained in the temple's cellar.

* * *

At a table in the Clothmakers' Guild Hall, Slathek and Abenzio, the barbarian merchant, arranged for the delivery of the linen Slathek had just purchased. Although the price he'd been able to negotiate would make this year's trip even more profitable than last year's, he felt none of the jubilation that a successful business deal had brought him in the past. He was now the last in a long line of merchants. *Just what do I need more money for?*

"And let me say again how sorry I am about your father. He was a good man," Abenzio said.

"Yes, he was." Slathek gathered his papers to hide his emotion. He held out his hand in the fashion of the barbarians. "I'll expect the merchandise delivered to the docks in the morning."

"Yes, yes, of course." Abenzio shook his hand.

As the sun set, Slathek walked through the crowded streets of Murtaghan toward The Traveler's Haven, where his father and he had always stayed. Flowers were being strung from every lamppost and awning in preparation for the celebration of Litha tomorrow. He'd always enjoyed the barbarian holiday, but he had no spirit for it this year. Among the numerous stalls lining the street, Slathek caught sight of an herb seller. The sight and smell of rosemary and comfrey brought back the time he'd spent in Sphry's stillrooms grinding herbs into powder for her and watching her make her medicines and salves. *By the Mother and the Father, I still miss you, Sphry. But at last, our father is at peace.*

Slathek bypassed the inn's common room where he often talked and drank late into the night with merchants and travelers from many lands. He'd be poor company today. In his room, he took off his clothes and retired early, trying to bury his grief in sleep.

He was a child again in Sphry's stillroom. He had a pestle in his hand and was crushing Burdock root into powder for his sister. He looked up to see Sphry adding other ingredients to a kettle. He thought she looked beautiful in the firelight. A wild fox sat calmly next to her on the counter.

"What are you making, Sphry?"

"I'm making an ointment for this poor fox, Slath. See, he's got into something." Sphry pointed to the side of the fox where the fur had been rubbed off, and Slathek could see that the fox's skin was red and inflamed.

He finished with the Burdock root and handed it to her. "Is there anything else I can help you with?"

"Yes, Slath." She leaned against the counter that no longer contained the fox or any of the herbs that had been strewn upon it, and Slathek found himself a man instead of a child. "My son is in trouble, and he needs your help. He'll be in the courtyard of the Silk Curtain tomorrow night. His life and the lives of thousands depend on the strength of your sword. Please, my brother, do not fail him."

* * *

Robrek drifted toward consciousness. When he opened his eyes, he found himself in a luxurious four-poster bed. The sheets felt as though they were made of the same material as the clothing in the magical horses' saddlebags. For a few moments he didn't remember where he was or how he'd gotten there, but slowly, the memory of healing the mare came back to him. He heard whispering and turned his head. Two girls of about his own age were staring at him.

"Look, he's awake," one said to the other. "Do you think he understands Korthlundian, Bree?"

"Who cares what he speaks, Lorna?" Bree winked at him.

Robrek blushed and tried to sit up. Realizing he was naked, he clutched at the blankets. "Where are my clothes?"

Bree's face fell. "He talks like a country peasant."

"Your clothes were so covered with blood and filth that Baron Briac told us to burn them." Lorna wrinkled her nose as if he hadn't bathed in months. "They weren't very nice clothes. He's provided you better." She pointed to a stack of clothing on a nearby chair.

Robrek grabbed at his neck. Milady's ribbon, too, was gone.

"Are you looking for this?" Lorna held up the green ribbon.

"Give me that." He tried to grab for it without exposing himself, but Lorna snatched it out of reach.

"I knew it was important," Lorna told Bree. "Didn't I say it was a token from a sweetheart?" She held it out to him, this time allowing him to enclose it safely in his hand.

"Who is Baron Briac?" he asked, stroking the ribbon's softness.

"He owns the mare you healed. He'd like to speak with you when you're dressed. Shall we help you?" Bree giggled.

"No!" Robrek clutched the blankets more tightly around himself.

"Bree!" Lorna giggled. "You're naughty." They giggled their way out.

Why do girls do that? But as he got to his feet, Robrek realized the girls hadn't found him repulsive. One of them had even winked at him. Maybe Fancy Man was right: maybe he could find a woman in the city who wouldn't mind keeping him company. But as he tied Milady's ribbon back around his neck, he knew it was idle fantasy. How could he ever look at another woman when he loved Milady?

As he examined the clothes the baron had provided, he became irritated. They were blue and red and looked like the livery of a servant. Apparently, this baron wanted to make him one. He'd fetch his spare clothes from Wild Thing's saddlebags as soon as possible.

His knife and purse sat beside the clothing. All of his money seemed to be there. He dressed quickly. The clothing was too large and looked ridiculous. But having no other choice, he opened the door and followed a staircase down to a dining room.

The room bore no resemblance whatsoever to the inn in Valley Fair. The stone floor was polished until it gleamed in the sunlight streaming through windows so large that one of them probably cost as much as his father's entire house. Opposite the windows, tapestries in brilliant colors covered the walls. At small tables of richly polished marble sat men and women in noble dress; gold hung from their necks and their fingers dripped with jewels. As soon as Robrek reached the bottom of the stairs, a man called to him, "Boy, attend me."

Tensing at the greeting, he crossed the room toward the man, who wore brown silk robes lined with fur, a heavy gold chain, a ring on every finger, and a purse at his belt. He was every bit as fat as Father Gildas. Robrek assumed him to be Baron Briac. Sitting next to the baron was a thin man dressed in the robes of a clerk. "Milord, my name is Robrek Angusstamm," he said with the appropriate bow.

The baron waved the information away. "You will get to work at once. Alair here will show you which animals in the stables belong to me." Briac gestured to the thin man, who rose. The baron turned back to his meal as if their conversation were concluded.

Robrek didn't move. "Milord, I have accepted no employment."

The baron turned back to him, his eyes wide with disbelief. "You've donned my livery, boy."

"Since my own clothing had been burned, I had no choice. I have clothes in my horse's saddlebags. I'll fetch them, return these, and be on my way." Robrek started to leave.

"Now wait a minute, boy! Don't be so hasty!" The baron rose from his seat.

Robrek stopped. "As I told you, my name is Robrek Angusstamm."

Turning red, the baron gave him a tight-lipped smile. "Mister Angusstamm, would it please you to dine with me?"

The baron's plate was heaped with eggs, ham, cheese, bread, and fruit, and Robrek was so hungry he felt faint. A good meal was the least he deserved for saving the man's horse. He sat. The baron signaled, and a similar plate of food was placed in front of him. Robrek grabbed a fork, but before he took a bite, he remembered the manners Fancy Man had taught him. Making sure his elbows weren't on the table, he took a much smaller bite than he'd intended.

"You saved a valuable animal of mine. I race horses, and Firebrand is favored to win tomorrow. Apparently, one of my competitors wanted to tip the odds in his favor. How did you know what was wrong with her?"

"I felt her pain from the street and traced it to this inn."

"As powerful as I expected." The baron looked him over with an expression Robrek couldn't interpret. The baron snapped his fingers, and Alair, who'd retaken his seat, handed him a purse. Briac pushed it across to Robrek. "Here, take it."

Robrek glanced at the fat purse, but didn't touch it. "Milord, I'm not seeking employment. I came to see the festival."

"This purse—" the baron waved at it dismissively—"is merely a token of my gratitude for services rendered. How does a wage of five hundred drachma a year suit you?"

Robrek choked on his breakfast. "Five hundred drachma a year?"

The baron smiled. "I take it we are agreed, boy."

Five hundred drachma was twenty-five times the amount his father had paid him, but he didn't like the baron, and he didn't like being called "boy." "I'd like some time to think about it, Milord."

The baron pursed his lips. "Of course, go and view the festival today. I've made arrangements for both you and your horse to be lodged here. In the meantime, take the purse. You've earned it."

After finishing his breakfast, Robrek got up. "Thank you, Milord." He bowed, gathered up the purse, and headed to the stables.

After checking on Firebrand, who was tired but well, he made sure Wild Thing was comfortable. He changed into his own clothing and opened the purse the baron had given him. He nearly dropped it when he discovered it contained fifty drachma. He put five of the drachma into his own purse with the coins he'd brought with him. He'd deny himself nothing today. The rest he left in Wild Thing's saddlebags with the mare as guard. Leigh had warned him about pickpockets and thieves.

With his staff firmly in his hand, he joined the throngs in the main streets. Robrek struggled to keep his mouth from hanging open: his small village's celebration was nothing compared with the sheer spectacle of Litha in the capital. Flowers lined the streets, decorated the vendors' stalls and the ladies' hair; even many of the men wore necklaces made of flowers. Vendors were selling every type of food imaginable, including cakes, cookies, and pies made with seeds and nuts, as was proper for the holiday. He even saw some pies that contained flower petals. He heard it was traditional to use flowers in food for Litha. He bought a couple of pies. One was stuffed with the familiar seeds and nuts. The other seemed to include marigolds. He leaned against a stall wall to eat them. While he ate, he watched a troop of jugglers performing in the street. He laughed as one juggler tripped, causing an egg to smash on his companion's head. When he noticed people putting coins into a hat, he added a few drams of his own. He finished the seed pie and tried the flower pie. It had a deliciously unusual flavor.

He walked the streets enjoying the air of abandonment. Now that Wild Thing wasn't with him, most people paid no attention to him. He also noticed he wasn't the only person lacking the height, blond hair, white skin, and blue eyes of the Korthlundians. He overheard snatches of conversation in other languages.

* * *

Sergeant Farrell entered Duke Argblutal's rooms in high spirits and bowed with a flourish. "Your Grace, the peasant amihealer has been sighted in the capital." He couldn't stop his eyes from flickering to the panther pendant the duke always wore around his neck.

"Have you brought him to my residence?"

"No, Your Grace, we don't have him yet, but we know where he'll return tonight. He's healed Baron Briac's horse. He's staying with the baron at the Silk Curtain. His Horsetad is in the stables, as are his things."

"Bring him to me tonight, and you may name your reward. But remember, I need him alive."

"He'll soon be yours, Your Grace." Sergeant Farrell bowed his way out, contemplating how he would spend his reward.

* * *

At noontime, hearing the king and his daughter would be there to bless the community garden, Robrek moved along with the crowd heading toward the city square. Fancy Man had claimed the crown princess was as beautiful as Milady; now was the time to prove him wrong.

At the edge of the square, Robrek found a box to stand on to see above the heads of the much taller Korthlundians. Soon the crowd parted, and Bearach and another of Milady's men rode into the square. *What can they be doing here?* He didn't have to wonder long because they were soon followed by a very old man and, riding directly beside him, Milady herself. Like most of the women, her hair was braided with flowers. Looking at her, he felt his breath catch in his throat. *How important she must be to be a part of the king's procession.*

As the old man and Milady rode into the square, the crowd broke into a chant. "Long live King Solar! Long live Princess Samantha!" The old man and Milady smiled and waved at the crowd. Robrek looked around for the king and the crown princess, but had difficulty figuring out who they might be amid the crowd of nobles that followed. Looking back at Milady, Robrek saw the old man's crown. And Milady wore a gold circlet.

Holy Sulis! It can't be! But as the people continued to chant, he could no longer doubt the impossible was true. He'd kissed the heir to the throne! The princess herself had touched him and called his green eyes stunning! His future queen had given him the green ribbon he wore around his neck! He clasped his hand to his heart, feeling the ribbon underneath his shirt. *How big a fool am I? I actually thought she cared about me! No wonder she never told me her name!*

Robrek watched as the king, *Milady's father*, addressed the crowd. "Our people, it is by the grace of Sulis that we live to celebrate another Litha with you." Robrek paid little attention to what the king was saying. Instead, he stared at the woman who'd hidden the truth from him, letting him dare love her. She was smiling, but her eyes weren't sparkling as they had when they talked at Myst's cottage. *No, her eyes couldn't have been sparkling for me. For Sulis's sake, she's the crown princess!*

The priest accompanying the royal procession was now chanting and lifting a jug over his head. He handed it to the princess. Robrek felt his spine tingle at the sound of her voice. "Earth, I give you the water of life." She sprinkled water from the jug onto the growing flowers. "Sulis, may you bless this garden and may it be a sign of your blessings upon this land and this people." Walking around the garden plot, she made similar statements and sprinkled water until the jug was empty. She moved with grace and elegance, and he could hardly believe she was the same woman who'd spilled soup on him.

When she'd finished sprinkling the water, she rejoined the old man. *The king, for Sulis's sake!*

The king raised his hands, and all eyes turned to him. "Our people, our beloved daughter and our heir has reached the age when it is time to take a consort to rule beside her." Robrek tensed at the king's words. Of course, he knew Milady wasn't his, but it hurt to watch her given to another. "Having celebrated our ninetieth birthday, we have little time left in this world. For this reason, we've decided to rely upon the old magic to protect the joined kingdoms when we can no longer. At Mabon, we'll place our beloved daughter atop Gloine Torr. There we'll provide her with Apples of Airh. Through three days of competition, those who vie for the princess's hand will attempt to ride their horses up the side of Gloine Torr. Through this competition, Sulis herself will reveal her choice of the man to rule beside our daughter. The contest will be open to all— noble and commoner alike."

The crowd roared its approval.

Milady—no, The Princess—looked giddy, almost as if she wanted to begin dancing around the platform. Suddenly, she froze as if she'd seen something unexpected, and her eyes darted in his direction. She couldn't be looking for him, but he ducked behind the taller people to make sure she wouldn't see him. Between their heads, he saw her grab Scarface's arm and say something to him. Looking annoyed, Scarface shook his head. Her face fell, then she nodded and pasted on a fake smile. *She can't have seen me. They can't be talking about me.* But as the princess's eyes continued to scan the crowd in his area, Robrek wished he mattered enough to her that he could have been the subject of her search. The royal party mounted, and as the princess rode out of sight, she still seemed to be looking for someone.

When she disappeared, he sat on the box and put his head in his hands. *How can Milady be the crown princess?* He remembered Fancy Man laughing when he claimed the crown princess couldn't be as beautiful as Milady. *Damn him to the seven hells! He knew who she was, and he still made an illusion of her for me to dance with! How could he play with me like that? No wonder her men wanted to kill me when I kissed her!*

Feeling claustrophobic amid the crowd, Robrek got abruptly to his feet.

* * *

Robrek wandered the streets for hours, paying little attention to the sights. *How can I be such a fool as to love the heir to the throne?* He walked to the gates of the city and stared at Gloine Torr in the distance. *What is the king playing at? No horse can climb that.* Images of Brazen and Fancy Man flashed into his mind, but he pushed them out. *If she truly cared about me, she would have told me who she was.*

As the sun started to set, he headed back to the Silk Curtain. He'd find out where Baron Briac's estate was, and if it was far enough away, he'd take the job and have enough money to buy anything, except what he really wanted.

As he neared the inn, he heard voices raised in argument. He reached out to Wild Thing to make sure she was alright. *:Different Robbie in trouble.:*

Having no idea what Wild Thing meant, Robrek crept around the inn. He stopped short as he saw the back of a man who had the same curly black hair and dark skin as he did. Standing next to Wild Thing, the man had his sword drawn and was surrounded by six armed men.

"I'm telling you for the last time I'm not this Robrek Angusstamm," the one Wild Thing had called "Different Robbie" insisted. His voice sounded unaccustomed to using vowels.

"Put down your sword, and no one will get hurt," the commander ordered.

Robrek stepped out of the shadows. "What do you want with me?"

They all whirled to face him, and it was immediately evident why they had mistaken the stranger for him. The resemblance between them was uncanny. The stranger's jaw dropped, and the soldiers looked back and forth between them.

One of the soldiers pointed his sword at Robrek. "That has to be the right one. The amihealer's only seventeen."

"Come with us," the commander gestured with his sword.

"They mean to take you to Duke Argblutal, kinsman," Different Robbie said. "He is not a man I'd allow myself to be taken to without a fight."

:Wild Thing stomp bad men to mash. No hurt Robbie: The Horsetad reared, and her hooves crashed down on one of the soldiers. He screamed horribly.

"Kill the beast," the commander shouted, and Robrek rushed to save Wild Thing. He brought his staff down on the head of a soldier who'd been about to stab the horse. As the man collapsed, a horrifying sense of wrongness staggered Robbie. He'd just killed a man. Another of the men whirled to face him.

Robrek almost didn't get his staff up to block in time, but instinct honed by Brazen took over. He blocked and jabbed his staff toward the man's throat, crushing his windpipe. The stranger ran his sword through a fourth. The remaining two fled, and Robrek fell to his knees, retching as nothingness took the place of the life in the fallen men.

The stranger grabbed his arm. "We must get out of here. They'll likely return with others."

Robrek stared at the man. "I've never killed anyone."

"Worry about that later. We must leave." Swaying, the stranger caught himself against Wild Thing. Blood oozed through the fingers that clutched his side.

"You're hurt. Let me look."

The man shook him off. "It's nothing. We must get out of here."

Robrek ran for Wild Thing's saddle and his saddlebags. As he entered the stables, he stumbled over something. He looked down into the unseeing eyes of a man whose throat had been slit. Two other bodies lay nearby. *Holy Sulis!* He grabbed his things and ran back. He saddled Wild Thing and, with her permission, helped the stranger onto her back. Robrek swung up behind him, and they rode out of the inn yard. Different Robbie leaned heavily against him, and Robrek could feel him spasming with pain.

"My name is Slathek. I'm a merchant. Can you get me to my ship? We'll be safe there, at least for a little while."

As the man directed him through little-used alleyways to the harbor, Robrek asked. "What did they want with me?"

"Later," the man said, his voice crackling with pain.

When they reached a ship bigger than any Robrek had ever imagined, the man called out in a strange language. Several men scurried forward, one holding a lantern. They gaped at Robrek, but the man said something to them, and they cleared the way for Robrek to ride Wild Thing up the gangplank. Two of the men helped the stranger dismount and carried him toward a cabin. Robrek followed.

The stranger was no longer conscious when they laid him on the bed, but nobody protested when Robrek took over his care. He quickly took off the man's shirt to examine the wound in his right side.

* * *

A groan woke Robrek, and he sat up from where he'd fallen asleep on the floor. The man settled back into sleep. Robrek had used his magic to stop the bleeding and stabilize him, but he hadn't completely healed the wound. Recent experience had taught him not to exhaust himself completely in situations in which he could be vulnerable. The sailors, none of whom spoke more than a few words of Korthlundian, had brought him food and hot water and medical supplies. They'd also found a stable near the docks where Wild Thing could be hidden.

Robrek sat in the chair and stared at the other man's face in the candlelight. Although the man was approximately fifteen years older than Robrek, he had the same curly black hair, the same nose, the same mouth, the same skin color, and the same shape to his eyes. He also wore no beard, the only man outside the clergy Robrek had seen without one. "Who are you?" Robrek whispered. "What is going on?"

CHAPTER 32

Late into the night of Litha, Shylah sat at his desk, drawing the portraits of those who'd died for Sulis's glory. He drew the poor lost page Eilis, as he lay tied to the altar. He drew himself helping the child to achieve the highest honors the god had to offer. Hand trembling, he reached for his goblet of wine. He downed the entire contents and filled it again. *It was such a little, little heart.*

Shylah pushed his first picture aside. Taking another sheet of paper, he drew the kitchen boy Cullen. He'd caught the child eating treats prepared for the royal feast and shirking his duties. *He had no right to walk in the corridors meant for his betters.* Shylah couldn't forget the curses the child had called down upon him as he drew the star on his chest. *What a foul mouth that child had had! A child shouldn't know such words.* Shylah clasped his hands over his ears. "Be quiet!" he yelled. "It isn't right to scream loud enough to be heard from Beyond the Far Mountain!"

But Cullen refused to stop screaming. Surely, the child's curses could be heard throughout the palace. If Cullen didn't stop, everyone would know what the priest had done. "Make him be quiet! Sulis, make him stop!"

With Cullen's cries continuing to ring in his ears, he reached for another goblet of wine and a third sheet of paper. His hand shook so badly that he had difficulty holding the quill as he drew the third and final picture—the pretty Deirdre whose mother Argblutal had killed. He drew Argblutal's hand directing his hand in drawing the star. He drew the panther pendant the hung around the duke's neck.

"No!" the high priest cried, throwing the quill aside. "They died for him, not Sulis!" He ran to his altar and knelt before his statue of Sulis. "Holy Sulis! Holy Father, how else was I to bring your truth to the joined kingdoms? If you hadn't wanted those children, why did you provide them? There was no other way!"

But the god's eyes sparked with anger. *It was your own ambition you sought,* Sulis's voice thundered. *You want power and wealth. Look at the richness of this altar and deny the truth.*

"No!" Shylah cried. "It isn't true! Killing children for worldly goals is an unforgivable depravity!"

And so it is, the statue seemed to say, and Cullen's curses rang louder in his ears. "How can I atone for what I've done?"

Sulis's stern, impassive features let him know the answer. Taking out the knife he'd used to sacrifice the children, he climbed onto the altar. His hand closed tightly on the knife's hilt, and he bared his chest.

* * *

Early on the morning after Litha, Samantha sat in her window seat staring out at the palace stables. Although she hadn't been able to catch sight of his face, she'd seen Robbie's aura in the city square yesterday. The brilliant bronze, silver, and gold could belong to no other. Worried about him, she'd gotten almost no sleep. *Will Darhour be able to find him? Will Robbie ever forgive me for exposing him to danger? What does he think now that he knows who I am?* She didn't think she could bear to see the love that had sparkled in his eyes turn to hatred. Still less could she bear the thought of what Argblutal would do to him if the duke got his hands on him before Darhour could.

"Damn it all to the seven hells!" she cried and fell to her knees. "Holy Mother, Argblutal's a monster. Is it wrong to kill a beast?" She shuddered as she realized that, right or wrong, she'd have asked Darhour to kill the duke if the king had announced her betrothal. Now, she didn't know what to do. *What will happen when nobody climbs Gloine Torr?*

Darhour knocked and entered. He looked like he'd aged ten years since he'd become the captain of her guard.

She got quickly to her feet. "Have you found Robbie?"

"No, Your Highness, but rumors abound about him. Half the city seems to have seen him arrive on his Horsetad. He is reportedly staying at about twenty different locations, including the palace. That one, at least, I know to be false. I'm working on the others."

"What if Argblutal finds him first?"

"There is only one way to assure that he doesn't."

Samantha knew what he meant, but could she do it? At that moment, Darhour began to glow. The green that had once dominated his aura had faded. What had once been merely shadows of grays and reds dominated the air around him. What had been good in him was slowly leaking away. She had no right to ask him to kill again.

* * *

Entering the council chamber in response to an early morning summons, Samantha saw Argblutal on one side of the king. The duke's face was impassive, but he gripped the arm of his chair as if attempting to crush it. Captain Hawk was also there. Samantha took her seat and accepted *bhat* and pastries from the servants, though she had no appetite.

Count Pandaran was the last to arrive, looking far less groomed than usual. "What is it that requires us to meet at the crack of dawn?" he complained as he took his seat.

Hawk stood. "Your Majesty, Your Highness, my lords." He bowed. "This morning two of my guards patrolling the corridors were disturbed by screams coming from the high priest's rooms. They found the high priest's chambers open. A hysterical maidservant was inside standing over the body of the high priest. He was lying on his altar with a star carved on his breast and a knife stabbed into the center of it. His own hands were on the knife. It has the appearance of a suicide. These were on the desk." Captain Hawk placed three drawings in the center of the table. "The first is of the palace page whose body was found in an alleyway near the palace. The second is of a kitchen boy who's been missing for the last week. The third hasn't yet been identified."

Samantha leaned in to look at the pictures. *Holy Sulis, Mother of us all! Is this how they are controlling my father?*

"The high priest committed child sacrifice within the walls of the palace?" Duke Sheen bellowed. "We must keep this quiet."

Captain Hawk shook his head. "Impossible. The maidservant bolted from the room after seeing the drawings. I'm sure most of the palace staff knows by now."

Baron Teague leaned forward. "There's a second figure in one of these drawings. Isn't that a panther pendant around the man's neck?" The princess's eyes shot from the pendant in the drawing to the one Argblutal wore. The change in her father had happened on the same day the first murdered child had been found. She'd known of the child's death at the time, but had thought the city magistrates fully able to address the issue. Because she'd done nothing, two more children were dead.

"You aren't suggesting I had anything to do with this?" Samantha barely heard the duke's objection. "Your Majesty, you know I'm blameless."

"Of course you are," the king said. "Surely there are dozens of such pendants in Murtaghan." Samantha's breath caught in her throat. A number of the councilors raised their eyebrows. Everyone knew only members of Argblutal's house wore that particular pendant. The king turned to the captain of the Royal Guard. "Captain Hawk, I'd like you to investigate all who wear such pendants."

Captain Hawk bowed. "Of course, Your Majesty." Samantha felt some of the burden melt from her. *He's still in there. My father is still fighting.*

"If there's nothing else . . ." the king said.

"Your Majesty," Gilroy announced. "Baron Briac is seeking permission to address the council."

The king nodded, and Briac entered and went down on one knee. "Your Majesty, I demand redress. A person of my character should be able to safely enjoy the capital and not have my servants attacked by ruffians."

"What happened?" the king asked, signaling the baron to stand.

"Last night, in the inn yard of the Silk Curtain, several of my servants were attacked. My chief groom, along with two hands at the inn, had their throats slit, and a valuable amihealer I recently acquired was kidnapped."

Samantha tensed as the baron went on, "Four dead ruffians were found in the courtyard. I have them here." Briac signaled, and his men brought in four dead bodies.

Samantha cringed, but to her relief, none of them was Robbie. "What makes you say the amihealer was kidnapped?" Argblutal asked.

"Because he's missing, as are his horse and belongings. The servants at the inn heard these four and others attack the amihealer and a man with him. Who the man was, I don't know. The servants only said he sounded like a foreigner. The ruffians made it clear they were after the amihealer on the orders of some duke. The amihealer is mine, and I want him returned."

Glaring across the table at Argblutal, Samantha clasped her hands tightly in her lap. *If you hurt him, I'll have Darhour kill you in the most painful way possible.*

"Baron Briac, I assure you no member of this council absconded with your amihealer," said Argblutal. "A missing peasant isn't a fit subject to bring before this council. You'll refer it to the city magistrates."

The baron started to protest, but the king didn't allow him. "Guards, escort the baron and his corpses out of here." Having no choice, the baron left, still spluttering indignantly.

Grabbing Blaine's arm, Samantha whispered, "Intercept the baron. Bring him to my chambers."

* * *

When Samantha returned to her rooms, she found Blaine and the baron waiting. Briac bowed as she entered. "Your Highness, I hope this means you're taking the theft of the amihealer seriously."

"What was his name?" Samantha asked.

The baron's face went blank. "It was Robert or Ronan or some such thing. What does his name matter? He was odd looking—dark skin, black hair, green eyes."

"Thank you for bringing this to the attention of the court. I'll do what I can to find him."

The baron thanked her and left.

Samantha sank down in a chair, and Darhour put his hand on her shoulder. She looked up at him. "Find him before Argblutal can hurt him. I don't care what you have to do, but find him."

"The duke may not have him, Your Highness. I don't think a Horsetad would allow itself to be taken."

Samantha tried to find comfort in Darhour's words, but couldn't. "Robbie is a peasant. How could he possibly defend himself against trained men?"

"Evidently, the man reportedly with him is a superb fighter."

"Find him, Darhour."

* * *

Argblutal raged as he swept into his quarters. He called for Mahon, the man who'd replaced Tremayne in his employ.

"Four are dead. Where are the others? Where is the boy?" Argblutal thundered when his retainer arrived.

"Your Grace." Mahon trembled. "It seems likely they've failed, and having failed have fled."

Argblutal grasped the knife at his belt. "Find the peasant. Use whatever of my resources you need. Get to him before the princess does."

Mahon bowed his head. "Yes, Your Grace. The peasant will soon be yours."

* * *

Count Morgan approached Argblutal's chambers, knowing his present position had come at the cost of Count Kayne's head. If he was going to keep it, Argblutal had to succeed.

When Morgan entered the duke's rooms, he bowed, and Argblutal offered him a seat and a goblet of the finest Korthlundian wine. "Your Grace, I was wondering if you believe the party who attempted to kill the princess would make another attempt."

Argblutal put down his goblet and fingered his belt. Morgan fought the impulse to look at it.

"The Neasarian is dead," the duke said.

"I understand, Your Grace, but the party might be interested to know that Saloyna trains the finest professionals. I have numerous contacts within the Saloynan community, including an assassin who used to work for one of the Saloynan dukes. Few are better at the craft; it's rumored he was responsible for King Frare's death. Should anyone have any use for such a man, I could fetch him within an hour."

"Bring me this man." The duke paused. "And aren't your estates in Korth falling prey to bandits? The king should send someone to quell this violence. It seems a matter for Captain Hawk to attend to personally, does it not?"

Morgan nodded. "You're correct, Your Grace. I'll bring the matter before the council at once."

* * *

Devyn sat at the council table in Duke Caedmon's study with the other Korthian nobles the duke had gathered to support the princess. Ever since Devyn had arrived with his message, Caedmon had been steadily recruiting men, money, and supplies. He'd now had over three hundred men and a substantial portion of the Korthian nobility behind him. Caedmon was confident more would join them as they marched south. The edict outlawing priestesses had done much to rally support to Caedmon. It didn't hurt that the princess herself was so popular with the people. Devyn had repeatedly heard Her Highness's auburn hair touted as evidence that she was of true Korthian blood.

Devyn wasn't at all sure the princess would be happy with his success. Caedmon refused to consider the political ramifications of bringing an army into Lundia. To do so without the permission of the king was an act of treason, and since they were coming in the princess's name, she could be labeled a traitor as well. When he'd mentioned this, however, he'd been ignored. Duke Caedmon was now discussing the best route for the army to take on its march toward Murtaghan. "The route through Count Pandaran's lands is the most direct. But Pandaran's loyalties are unknown, and he might cause trouble for us."

"May I make a suggestion, Your Grace?" Devyn spoke up. The duke glared at him, and the rest of the table regarded him in an unfriendly fashion.

"Proceed," Caedmon sighed.

"Since this force has been assembled in the princess's name, I think it proper she be consulted before it passes into Lundia." The duke opened his mouth to object, but Devyn hurried on. "She may have some preference as to where and how it arrives. We wouldn't want to interfere with some plan she's developed. I'd be happy to ride to the princess at once."

Caedmon narrowed his eyes at Devyn, but Baron Gwawl spoke up. "I think Lord Devyn has a point. If she's still at the palace when we march south, she may want to ride out and join us. Otherwise, she could find herself caught between two armies."

Instead of ignoring Gwawl as he had Devyn, Caedmon nodded thoughtfully. Despite his bullheadedness, Devyn knew Caedmon truly cared for the princess. He nodded at Devyn. "You'll leave in the morning."

Devyn sighed with relief. He'd ridden north with hopes of gaining the right to his art and Lady Aislinn. Now, his only concern was to stop his country from being torn in half by two power mad dukes.

* * *

Robrek was once again in the inn yard. Both the stranger and Wild Thing had disappeared, and he was alone with the dead bodies. One of the men he'd killed rose to his feet and stared at him with eyes that didn't see. "Murderer!"

"Please, I'm sorry. I didn't mean to."

The corpse laughed. "Some healer. They should have burned you." The dead man advanced on him, and Robrek found himself without his staff.

"No!" Robrek whirled to run, but his second victim stood and blocked his path.

The corpse's breath hissed through his crushed windpipe. "We came to fetch a healer, and we found a killer instead."

Robrek whirled again only to find the other two dead men getting to their feet. "Not a true healer, this one," one of them said. "He and his demon horse should be returned to the seven hells from whence they came."

Milady advanced through the mist. "Murderer! To think I kissed one who would kill." She looked at the animated corpses. "Take him with you to the seven hells."

The dead men grabbed him. "No, I didn't mean to," he cried, as the corpses dragged him away. Milady looked at him without a sign of emotion.

Robrek jerked awake, leaped to his feet, and grabbed his staff. But he found himself alone in the ship cabin with the stranger. Settling back into the chair, he tried to get his heartbeat under control. He stared at the man. *Who are you? What did those men want with me? Was I wrong to kill them?* He thought of the man's sword threatening Wild Thing, but then he thought of the slaughter he'd committed at the forest stable. *Now I am a killer for real. Could I lose control as I did then and kill even the woman I love? Oh Milady, how can you be the crown princess? Why didn't you tell me?*

Groaning, the stranger opened his eyes. "Are you this Robrek Angusstamm they were looking for?" he asked, pronouncing the name as if it had no "o." Robrek nodded. The man squinted at him. "No wonder they thought I was you. The resemblance between us is striking. My name is Slthethkkne. The barbarians call me Slathek." Robrek didn't know who these barbarians might be, but he doubted he could pronounce the first name the man had given. "Robrek isn't a common name, even in Mahngbhayo. How did you come by it?"

"My mother died in childbirth. I was told she named me after her father."

"She's dead then." The man blinked back a few tears. "I always knew she had to be, but the dream gave me hope I was wrong."

"How could you know my mother?"

"When I look at you, I see my sister in your every feature. Robrek is my father as well."

Robrek snorted. "Forgive me if I don't believe such an amazing coincidence. I've learned what my skills are worth."

"Let me tell you my sister's story, and see if I can soothe your skepticism." The story Slathek told agreed with the one Myst had told Robrek about his mother. "If she died giving birth to you, you wouldn't have known her, but perhaps you've seen some painting of her." Robrek shook his head. Still, Slathek took a locket from around his neck, opened it, and handed it to Robrek. "This is my sister."

Robrek stared into the green eyes that could only have belonged to the demon lady from his dreams, then looked at the man who looked so much like himself. He wanted to believe Slathek. His mother had loved him enough that she hadn't even let death keep her from him, and he longed not to be alone in a world that had suddenly gone mad. But the sudden appearance of an unknown relative was as insane as Milady being the crown princess.

"What were you doing at the Silk Curtain?"

"As mad as it sounds, I was looking for you. In a dream, my sister told me you'd be there and need help. I nearly dismissed it as such foolishness, but if I had, Duke Argblutal's men would have taken you."

"What did they want with me?"

"They didn't say, but nothing good can come of being taken by that man. Your mother sought to protect you even from beyond the grave. I often dream of her in this land. I've seen her with two children. I've always thought the dreams a product of my yearning for my sister. Tell me, do you have a brother?"

Robrek grunted. "If you want to call him that." Robrek told Slathek of his trial and Boyden's testimony against him.

Slathek put his hand to his forehead. "By the Father and the Mother, this is too terrible to be believed. No, such a person will have no claim on me. My poor nephew, danger hems you in on every side. You must come home with me."

Jumping from his chair, Robrek backed toward the door. "So you, too, want me for my power?"

"By the Father and the Mother, no! I already have more money than I know what to do with. What I don't have is an heir. You must go with me. Where in this barbaric land do you think you can hide from the king's chancellor?"

Robrek paced the small cabin. Fancy Man had taught him Argblutal was an enemy of the crown princess. He didn't remember much else the silver stallion had to say about the duke because he hadn't thought it mattered. "How could he know anything about me? Baron Briac is the only noble I've ever met"—he wasn't going to tell this stranger about the princess; the kiss and his feelings for her weren't secrets he intended to share with anyone—"and if he wanted me so badly, surely he wouldn't have told someone who could take me from him."

"Baron Briac?" Slathek asked, and Robrek told him about the horse with glass in its belly. Slathek shook his head. "The duke has eyes everywhere, which is why we must leave before he traces you to my ship."

"I'll just have to take my chances. I won't endanger you by staying here, but I'm not leaving my country." He remembered the princess's beauty and majesty as she'd stood in the city square. He couldn't leave without knowing what happened to her.

"Nephew, come to your senses! You have no future here!"

"That's for me to decide." Robrek jabbed a finger toward his so-called uncle. "Not you."

In the end, Robrek agreed to think about it for a day. He needed the time to decide where to go now. But wherever he decided upon, he knew it wouldn't be his mother's country.

CHAPTER 33

Samantha tensed as Count Morgan stood to address the king's council. "Your Majesty, I've received disturbing reports from my estates. Bandit attacks are increasing throughout western Korth at an alarming rate, in addition to the violence against the shrines and temples. I seek the assistance of the Royal Guard in quelling this violence."

Sheen straightened in his seat. "Shrines and temples being attacked? I've heard no such news."

"Your Grace, it seems that word of the high priest's actions has spread into Korth," Morgan claimed. "The edict didn't sit well to begin with, and now the chief Lundian cleric has been found to be guilty of depravity. The people want to force the priests out."

Samantha wrinkled her brow. "What edict?"

"The one that made it illegal to practice the rites of the goddess without the blessing of the high priest." Morgan's tone indicated the answer should have been obvious.

"No such edict passed this council," Sheen insisted.

"The crown doesn't interfere in matters of religion," Samantha agreed.

The king leaned toward her. "If we decide to crush the heretical priestesses, it's no concern of yours." The king turned toward Sheen. "Would you question our judgment as did Kayne?"

Sheen turned red with suppressed rage and spoke through gritted teeth. "I'm sure Your Majesty has the best interests of the joined kingdoms at heart."

Argblutal maintained his usual calm. "Now isn't the time to discuss the edict. The question is how to restore calm. Your Majesty, I suggest you send Captain Hawk north with sufficient forces to quell the violence."

"It will be so," the king said. Captain Hawk stepped forward and bowed.

Samantha exchanged glances with Darhour and then looked back to the king. "Who would be in charge of the palace forces?"

"Kentigern." The king's eyes were dead as he spoke. The king gestured, and a man who'd been standing behind Argblutal stepped forward and bowed to the council.

"Is this another of your raping miscreants?" Sheen asked Argblutal.

Argblutal's court mask remained firmly in place. "Captain Kentigern's honor is above reproach."

Sheen tried to protest further, but the king slammed his hand on the council room table. "We have spoken."

Samantha watched helplessly as Captain Hawk left the room. She had no doubt the men who'd be sent with him would be longtime members of the Royal Guard. Those who remained would be loyal to Argblutal.

* * *

"Have you found the peasant?" Argblutal asked Mahon.

"Not yet, Your Grace," Mahon answered. "But he's too distinct to stay hidden long."

"I'm not a patient man." Argblutal fingered the knife at his belt.

"I understand, Your Grace."

After Mahon left, Morgan entered, accompanied by a man with a thin nose and olive skin, Morgan bowed. "Your Grace, may I present Aposken?"

The Saloynan barely inclined his head. "Your dukeship." He smiled to reveal yellow teeth.

Argblutal stifled his disgust. "You're aware of my desires."

"I've been itching to do another royal."

"How much?"

"I can't say yet. I need to scope out the scene. I'll need a Royal Guard uniform."

"I want it done as soon as possible," Argblutal said.

The assassin laughed. "I do things my way or not at all."

Argblutal grabbed his riding whip and lashed toward the man's face. In a movement too fast to follow, Aposken palmed a knife and severed the whip before it hit him. "The only reason I don't walk out now is because the job interests me. If you're wanting someone you can own, find yourself a scullery maid. Have a uniform sent to my quarters, and I'll let you know how much it will cost." The man left without being dismissed.

He'll pay for his insolence, Argblutal vowed, *but let the bitch pay for hers first.*

* * *

Aposken looked in the mirror as he dressed in the uniform of the Royal Fucking Guard. He hadn't anticipated a job so much in years. Unlike recent boring assignments, this job might just take a little ingenuity, not in killing the bitch—he didn't anticipate much trouble there—but in getting his money from the asswipe of a dukeship without getting killed in the process. Argblutal wasn't the first employer who hadn't planned on leaving him alive after he'd completed a job, but—he blew his reflection a kiss—*I'm not the one rotting in the ground.*

Fully dressed, he headed out to scope out the princess's quarters. The royal bitch was at banquet, so there'd be no one to interfere. He'd already eyeballed the princess's windows from outside the palace, and entering from that direction hadn't looked promising.

Guards stood at both ends of the corridor in which the princess's rooms were located, but none directly in front of her door. He dropped his handkerchief and bent down to pick it up, examining the lock in the process. He froze as a familiar, but entirely unexpected, odor hit his nostrils. The lock was protected by a *kleidaria*—Saloynan magic that would direct a deadly poison at anyone using anything other than the proper key. *How in Hermes's name is there a kleidaria in this piece of trash of a country? Even in Saloyna the things cost a fortune.*

Smiling, he straightened and strode down the corridor. This job was becoming more interesting by the minute.

Aposken went to the banquet hall to get a look at the men guarding the bitch's ass. He'd received a report on them, but he needed to size them up for himself. He entered the banquet hall and joined some of the guards standing at attention. He glanced at the bitch he was going to kill and then at the men behind her. *Holy shit, Hermes, and Athena!* Even from the back of the hall, he had no difficulty recognizing the man on the princess's right. It certainly explained the *kleidaria*.

* * *

Aislinn sat before an easel in her lover's room. She was trying to paint a portrait of Erlina, Devyn's cat, as a surprise for his return, but she wasn't making much progress. The cat wouldn't hold a pose, but insisted on chasing the flies that buzzed in through the open window. It had thoroughly shredded the ribbon she had attempted to tie around its neck. But the cat's antics were only half her problem. Yesterday she'd caught Argblutal staring at her breasts. He'd already raped Count Nola's daughter. Why should he hesitate to do the same to Count Morfran's?

Her father had a small residence in the city. It was understaffed and had no room with light good enough for painting, but to be safe, she'd stay there, at least until Devyn returned.

* * *

Argblutal laughed as the assassin named his price. "You must be joking. For fifty thousand drachma, I could hire twenty assassins."

Aposken shrugged and took a chair without being offered one. "They'd all fail. I don't suppose you've heard of The Ghost."

"You expect me to believe *you* are the legendary Saloynan assassin?" Argblutal sneered.

Aposken smiled, again showing his yellow teeth. "Hardly." Leaning back in the chair, he drew his knife and began trimming his fingernails. "But I met The Ghost once. We'd both been sent after the same duke by different rivals. I entered the man's bedroom, just in time to see The Ghost slit his throat. He grabbed me and pinned me against the wall so quickly I swear I never saw him move. With a knife at my throat, he threatened me with a very short life if I mentioned seeing him. Until today, I kept his secret. It seemed wise." With the point of his knife, the assassin flicked a piece of dirt onto the duke's carpet. "He isn't one I'll ever forget. You see, someone had taken a dislike to his face." Aposken drew horizontal lines in the air with his knife.

"You aren't suggesting Captain Darhour is The Ghost? He's Korthian, not Saloynan."

"I always found that strange myself. I never found out how a foreigner became King Frare's personal assassin. It wasn't considered healthy to ask questions about The Ghost."

"Fifty thousand drachma for both the princess and the captain of her guard."

"Agreed, but I want half in advance." Aposken sheathed his knife.

* * *

Conroy stumbled along the roadway. His horse had dropped from its wounds some miles back, and he'd been forced to kill the poor beast. He feared he'd soon be joining the mount Beyond the Far Mountain. *Sulis curse it! I shouldn't feel this weak! The wound isn't that bad.* He felt the warm blood oozing out of his side.

He'd heard of priestesses hiding out in the mountains between Korth and Lundia. He'd been almost there when bandits had attacked him again; Korth seemed to be infested with them. Even after being wounded, he'd thought he was fit enough to make it to a town or village, but the weakness was overtaking him quickly, and there was nothing in sight. But the princess was counting on him.

He remembered the intensity of the spirit he'd felt in the shrine, when the priestess announced the princess as Sulis's chosen. He was on a holy quest. Surely, the Holy Mother would bless him to complete it. He called out to the goddess for succor, but he heard no answer. The day was darkening, and he knew that the night would mean his certain death. But he wouldn't allow himself to fail the princess.

Maybe after resting for a few minutes, he'd have the strength to go on. He fell down into the weeds on the side of the road, and a gentle warmth crept over him. *I'll just rest a minute. I promise, my princess, I won't fail you.*

* * *

As Lord Devyn rode further and further south, he saw increasing signs of backlash against the clergy. Shrine after shrine lay in ruins, and he saw the bodies of priests hanging from trees and pillars. Although he understood the Korthian anger against the edict, wasn't murder taking things too far? And the mayhem wasn't restricted to massacring clergy, either. With the magistrates busy trying to protect the priests, crime and banditry were growing unchecked.

The grumblings of dissatisfaction could be heard everywhere. As he stopped at an inn for the night, he overheard one group complaining. "I tell you the king has lost his mind. Sulis never intended men to live as long as he has," a man with the auburn red hair and beard of Northern Korth announced.

"I'm sure there's some reasonable explanation for what's happening," a typical blonde Korthlundian replied.

"He's mad," Red Beard insisted. "You heard what that priest of his was up to!"

"The High Priest Shylah wasn't the king's priest, and you know it," Blonde Beard objected. "Besides, you don't believe those stories, do you?"

"I certainly do," Red Beard said. "The king's a raving lunatic! This daft contest he announced at Litha—what is that if not sheer madness?"

Blonde Beard grew glassy eyed. "It is in keeping with the old ways. Besides I wouldn't mind being king. Come Mabon, Hunter and I are going to have a go at it."

Red Beard laughed. "Hunter climb Gloine Torr? You're as mad as the king."

Devyn walked over to the men. "What is this contest you speak of?"

The men looked up at him and bowed as they noticed the quality of his dress. "Milord," Red Beard answered, "at Litha, His Majesty announced that whoever could ride a horse up the side of Gloine Torr would marry the princess. But, if you don't mind my saying so, it's daft. No horse can ride up that surface, and besides, whoever heard of such a mad method of choosing a king except in bards' tales?"

Leaving the two men arguing, Devyn returned to his dinner. The news was disturbing. Silently, he cursed the princess for involving him in this. Life had been so much simpler when all he had to worry about was which shade of blue to paint the sky. If things were deteriorating in the capital, as the men had said, did he have time to reach the princess and make it back to the duke before all seven of the hells broke loose? But what would be the consequences of bringing an army to the capital? He put his head in his hands, knowing too well he wasn't cut out for this type of thing. His head shot up. *The contest! The duke's army can easily hide amid the throng of men that would certainly assemble for the contest! If the princess needs them, they'll be there. If not, they'll arouse no suspicions.* Tomorrow, he'd head back to Duke Caedmon.

* * *

Unable to sleep, Darhour lay awake in his bed. It was only a matter of time before Argblutal tried something else, and he could never be sure he'd anticipated every means of attack. *There's only one sure way to solve the problem. The question is how to do it so no suspicion is thrown on Her Highness.* He entertained and discarded several possibilities, but he felt the delicious rush at the prospect of an assassination. *No, only a monster enjoys killing. There has to be another way.*

Scratching came from the servants' corridors. Darhour froze. Someone was picking the lock on the door that joined his room. Silently, he rolled out of bed, dropped into a crouch, and drew a knife. *Too bad I could only find one kleidaria.* As the door creaked open, he moved away from his bed. Because of the gift of the Saloynan mage, Darhour saw the figure inching closer. The man was good: he didn't make the slightest sound. Darhour's nerves were strung tight for the deadly game he knew so well.

The man held a knife and grabbed for where Darhour's hair should have been. Darhour recognized the technique: grab the hair, pull the head back to provide clear access to the neck, slit the throat before the victim had a chance to cry out. Crude, but effective. At least it would have been if Darhour had been sleeping on the pillow. The assassin froze when his hands found nothing. Darhour briefly registered the fear in the assassin's eyes before he threw his own knife, which buried itself in the man's throat. The would-be assassin gave a gurgling cry and fell noisily to the ground. Darhour lit a lamp and stared down at the body. He knew the man.

* * *

Samantha shook as Darhour told her about the attack. "This can't be tolerated. I will lose no more of you."

Darhour refused to meet her eyes. "That isn't all, Your Highness. Have you perhaps heard of an assassin known as The Ghost?"

"Of course. They say he's single-handedly filled a dozen graveyards." She gasped. "Oh Darhour, Argblutal sent The Ghost after you. I'm glad you killed the murdering bastard." She looked at him with new respect for his skills.

A look of pain crossed Darhour's face. "The dead man isn't The Ghost. I am that 'murdering bastard,' as you so aptly phrased it."

"But Darhour . . . you can't . . . I didn't mean . . ." She broke off, not sure what she didn't mean. She knew he'd been an assassin, but The Ghost . . . ? She clutched at her stomach.

"Not every assassination attributed to The Ghost was truly my doing, but I don't suppose the number makes any difference," Darhour said stiffly. "If knowledge of who I am offends you, I will resign my position as soon as you are safely on the throne."

The thought of Darhour leaving sent panic rushing through her. "No, I don't care if you've killed a thousand men! You will not leave me!"

"Certainly not while you are still in danger." He paused, not meeting her eyes. "Argblutal most likely knows my identity as well. It explains the attempt on my life. I suggest we leave the body outside the duke's rooms as a warning."

Samantha nodded. "Do it. And take steps to better secure your quarters."

* * *

While he waited for Aposken to return, Argblutal sipped a particularly fine wine. The bitch having a dangerous assassin among her loyal apes was an inconvenience that would soon be removed.

He heard a gasp from the hallway, and Mahon entered without knocking. "Your Grace, we have a problem."

"And do we talk of problems with the door open?"

"We do if the problem's right outside."

The duke jumped to his feet. The Saloynan's throat was covered with blood, and his eyes were open but unseeing. "Get him inside quickly." Mahon dragged the body inside and closed the door.

Argblutal threw his glass against the wall, shattering it. "Get Morgan now!"

* * *

Wrinkling his nose against the stench, Count Morgan and two of his retainers rode through the dives of Murtaghan. It was an unpleasant part of town, but nobody understood their business like the Saloynans, and few had better reasons to stay hidden.

He rode down an alleyway and dismounted at a doorway nearly hidden behind a broken cistern. "Stay with the horses," he ordered his men.

He knocked on the door. A peephole opened, and the door immediately followed. Anatloe exclaimed, "Milord, how nice to see you again! Come in! Come in!"

Anatloe led him into a parlor whose opulence was out of keeping with the neighborhood. It was furnished in rich Saloynan carpets, Neasarian tapestries, and furniture made of mahogany inlaid with ivory. Anatloe offered him a seat and a glass of an excellent and extremely rare Mahngbhayon wine.

Morgan removed his gloves and accepted the wine. "His Grace is most displeased."

Anatloe signaled a servant to bring in refreshments. "Aposken's manners may be rough, but he has never failed to take out his target."

"He has now. He was killed by The Ghost."

Looking as if he might faint, Anatloe sank into a chair. "The Ghost? Are you sure? He hasn't been active for years. I thought maybe he was dead."

"According to Aposken, he is now the captain of the princess's personal guard."

"Darhour? The Ghost? You must be joking!" Anatloe laughed.

"His Grace has no sense of humor. He wants to know everything there is to know about the captain." Morgan stood to leave. "You do not want to displease His Grace further."

* * *

After dark, Robrek sneaked off the ship to the small stable near the pier where Wild Thing was kept. Slathek didn't want him to leave the ship, but he needed to see Wild Thing and talk to her about "Different Robbie." He was still only partially convinced the man was his uncle. He would have had fewer doubts if Slathek hadn't been putting so much pressure on him to leave.

When he neared the stable, he heard Wild Thing stomping wildly. He flung open the door to find two of his uncle's men attempting to put a harness around her head.

"What in the seven hells are you doing?" Robrek demanded, calming Wild Thing with his touch.

"Take on ship," one of the men answered in broken Korthlundian.

"She doesn't want to be on any ship."

"Must. We sail before morning."

Damn him! I knew he couldn't be trusted. He rubbed Wild Thing's shoulder. "I'll take care of her myself," he told the men.

The man gibbered to his companion, and they both nodded gratefully. "Must ready first light. High tide early."

After the men left, Robrek hugged the horse around her neck. He had his purse in his pocket and his staff in his hand. There was nothing on the ship he needed. "Where can we go, my girl?"

He didn't like the answer, but he could think of only one place he'd be safe.

* * *

Angus foundered in the blackest pit he'd ever known. Even when Donella had died, he'd been able to console himself that at least he could live for his sons. Now, even with all his money, he was a failure as a man—one whose sons didn't respect him.

Beacan, his foreman, burst into the house followed by several frantic hands. "Master Angus, it's happened again. The demons have destroyed the East fields."

Angus laughed bitterly. "It's exactly what we deserve. Since Robbie isn't around to stop it any more, I'm ruined, and you are all out of a job."

Beacan stared at him as if Angus had gone insane. "Shouldn't we send for the priest?"

"What do you expect that old fraud to do?" Angus pushed past his hands, saddled a horse, and headed for the village inn.

* * *

Slathek awoke early with little more than a slight ache in his side to remind him of the serious wound he'd suffered. His nephew was a powerful healer indeed. He felt the ship moving on the waters and braced himself to face Robrek's anger. He was surprised it had taken him so long to demonstrate it. Slathek dressed with the assistance of a servant and settled into a chair by the table. Breakfast could wait until after he'd talked to his nephew. He hoped he could make Robrek understand, but if he failed, what could the boy do?

When some time passed without the appearance of his enraged nephew, Slathek sent a servant to check on him. The servant returned a short time later. "Master Slthethkkne, Master Robrek isn't in his cabin."

Slathek panicked. "Find him at once!"

The servant departed, and Slathek got painfully to his feet and went up on deck. "Annke," he yelled to the captain of the ship, "have you seen my nephew this morning?"

"No, sir, isn't he in his cabin?"

"The Horsetad? Did you send men to fetch it as I ordered?"

Annke called to the two men who'd been sent for Robrek's horse. As they told him what had happened the night before, Slathek felt an icy pit form in his stomach. Slathek slammed his hand down on the ship's railing. "He ran! Damn him! If the duke gets hold of him, he . . ." Slathek closed his eyes and paused. "Turn this ship around. Head back to Murtaghan."

"Of course, sir, but by the time we get back to the harbor, the tide will be out. We'll have to wait for it to change again."

"I'm aware of that. My nephew will have at least a day's head start."

Annke went to give the orders, and the big ship slowly reversed course.

* * *

Leigh knelt in despair beside his teacher's cot. She refused to take any remedy he prepared. She wouldn't eat, and he could barely get her to drink a cup of water. She'd been willing to cling to life for Robrek, but not for him.

The door burst open, and about a dozen peasants poured into the cottage. Leigh jumped to his feet.

"Where is he?" the leader demanded.

"If you mean Robrek, I have no idea," he answered.

The leader stabbed a finger at him. "The demon child you saved has sent his hordes to attack Master Angus's fields again." Leigh had heard the stories at Robrek's trial about the destruction of Angus's fields, but they'd never been satisfactorily explained. "You tell the demon if he doesn't call them off, tomorrow morning we'll burn this cottage and everyone in it to the ground." The rest of the men murmured their agreement, then stomped out.

Shaking, Leigh knelt back beside Myst. He thought the old woman had slept through it all, but she spoke without opening her eyes. "The Valley has grown unsafe. You must leave."

"Surely Robrek wouldn't attack his own father."

"No, but the last two times, he stopped the attacks. I doubt anyone can stop them now."

"Stop who, Mistress?"

"There's a stable in the woods. If you can find it, you'll know what attacked Angus's fields. But if you can't, you must flee before nightfall." Myst described the location of the forest stable.

"I'll try to find it, then I'll take you to my father's. I don't like what he does, but he'll take us in."

Myst opened her eyes. "I'm going nowhere. Flee the Valley, and let me die in peace." Myst closed her eyes.

* * *

Robrek moved quietly through the trees. Brazen and Fancy Man had been right; he'd come back. He was safe nowhere else. *It isn't fair. I've never hurt anyone.* His memory of the men in the inn yard of The Silk Curtain called him a liar. He remembered the feeling of wrongness when life departed. *But they forced me into it. Why can't people just leave me alone?*

When he neared the forest stable, he heard a person cry out. He dismounted, grabbed his staff, and approached cautiously. Leigh was standing in the clearing, staring at the magical horses and drawing Sulis's star. Robrek wasn't happy to see the novice. He wanted to be free to hate everyone, except Milady and Myst, but Leigh had saved his life, giving up everything he'd ever wanted by doing so.

Robrek stepped out from behind the trees. "They aren't dangerous."

Leigh whirled. "What in the seven hells are you doing here?"

"It's nice to see you, too," he said, beginning to unsaddle Wild Thing. "I'm safe enough here. Brazen hides this place."

Leigh stood with his mouth hanging open. "Who is Brazen? And what are they?"

"Forgive my manners. Leigh, may I present Lady Brazen?" Leigh jumped when the bronze horse bowed her head. "She hides the stable but must have considered you trustworthy. And this is Lord Fancy Man." The silver horse also bowed.

Sitting on the stump, Leigh closed his eyes. "I'm dreaming. When I open my eyes, none of this will be here. Living metal horses don't exist."

Robrek snorted. "These two exist. How's Myst?"

Leigh's eyes popped open. "She's in great danger. Your father's fields have been attacked again. Some men came by. They said if you don't stop it, they'll burn the cottage. Myst refuses to let me move her."

Robrek swore and looked at the two horses. "Don't tell me there's another one of you!"

:*Another comes*,: Brazen announced.

"Another of me?" Leigh asked.

"No, another of them. For some reason, horses like them feel they have to announce their arrival by destroying fields of grain. I'll take care of it tonight. Tell Myst I'll come see her as soon as it's dark."

* * *

When Robrek arrived at Myst's cottage, she was sitting next to a roaring fire. Leigh kept watch outside. The old woman's face was as white as the finest parchment, and despite the stifling heat of the cottage, she was shivering. He gathered her into his arms. "Myst, I should never have left ."

She grabbed him tightly. "My child, why have you come back? It isn't safe for you here."

Robrek dropped to his mentor's feet. "It isn't safe for me anywhere. But if it's a choice between Father Gildas and Duke Argblutal, I think I stand a better chance with the priest."

Myst's eyes widened. "Whatever are you talking about, my child?"

Robrek told her what had happened.

"Holy Sulis, Mother of us all! I thought I had protected you." With some prodding, Myst told him where she'd been during the time she'd been missing from the Valley. "I was trying to protect you, but leaving you in ignorance has only exposed you to greater danger. Can you forgive me?"

"You knew who Milady was, and you didn't tell me! You were the one person I thought I could trust." Robrek abruptly got to his feet. "I have to fetch the third horse."

Slamming the door behind him, Robrek left Myst's and rode toward his father's farm. While waiting for the appearance of the horse, he brooded over all those who'd harmed and betrayed him. His so-called uncle had tried to kidnap him, and even Myst had lied to him. *What's the point of even trying? Everyone's against me. I'll never have any decent kind of life.*

At the darkest hour of the night, a pain-filled cry rang out. He looked across the fields and saw the new horse. It too had an empty suit of armor on its back, but in the darkness, he couldn't tell what color it was. He dismounted and approached slowly, sending out images of comfort and reassurance. The horse walked to him, seeming to trust him immediately.

"I'll take care of you if you follow me," he assured the horse as he removed the bit from its mouth. Robrek swung into Wild Thing's saddle and led the new horse away. Inside the forest stable, he lit a lantern. He gasped as the mare glowed a fiery gold. The equipment on her back was made of gold as well. It was decorated with the five-pointed star of Sulis. "Holy Sulis, where do horses like you come from?"

The horse was in pain, so he didn't question her further. He unsaddled her and began to tend to her injuries. "She's hurt, but she isn't as bad off as the two of you were," he informed Brazen and Fancy Man, who were looking anxiously at the new arrival.

:She's stronger,: Brazen said.

:Stronger, my ass,: Fancy Man objected. *:You know as well as I do that we protected her from the worst of it. Have to look after our baby sister.:*

"Sister?" Robrek stared from Fancy Man to Brazen to the gold mare. Maybe he shouldn't have been surprised. Fancy Man and Brazen often acted like bickering siblings. Still, the idea had never occurred to him. Even the horses had never been truthful with him. He felt the green ribbon against his heart and remembered how Fancy Man had laughed when Robrek had claimed the princess couldn't be as beautiful as Milady. Except for Wild Thing, there was no one he could trust.

CHAPTER 34

Slathek watched the shore come slowly closer, cursing both himself and his nephew. As soon as they landed, he sent one of his men to the Mercenaries' Guild to hire sufficient swords to protect them from the Valley peasants. He knew the gates to the city would be closed before his man could return, and he'd have to wait until morning to go after Robrek. He prayed to the Father and the Mother he could find the boy before anything happened to him.

He called to the captain of his ship. "I'll leave the ship before high tide tomorrow. I want you to sail out of the harbor. If I return safely with my nephew, I'll have Chiamaka fly the signal flag and hire a boat to bring us out to you. If the flag doesn't appear within a week, sail for home."

Annke nodded. "You think the duke may catch you?"

Slathek sighed. "We know he's after my nephew, and we know what kind of man he is. If he does capture me, there's nothing you can do to save me."

* * *

Duke Argblutal watched Count Nola fidget in his chair. "You've been talking with Torin." Argblutal picked up his glass of wine and twirled the blood-colored liquid around the goblet.

"We played a game of draughts. That's all." Argblutal drew his ruby-encrusted knife and began trimming his nails with it. Nola stared at the knife. "He questioned your ability to deliver on your promises, but I swear, Your Grace, I refused to listen to his treason."

"See that you don't, Nola."

After he dismissed the count, Argblutal slammed his fist on his desk. Someday he'd have the power to compel all to do his will, but until he could claim the throne, he would have to reassure his followers.

Mahon entered.

Argblutal scowled. "You better have good news."

"I do, Your Grace. I've just had a report from your man inside the Mercenaries' Guild that a Mahngbhayon merchant has hired two dozen men to take him to the Valley. Some hints were dropped that he needed to rescue his nephew from a fanatical priest. Descriptions of him closely match those of the amihealer. He is almost certainly the foreigner reportedly with the amihealer at the Silk Curtain. He plans to leave at dawn. We could send a force and take him tonight."

Argblutal sipped his wine thoughtfully. "We'll allow the merchant to lead us to the amihealer. Fetch Count Nola to the king's audience chamber, and get men ready to ride at first light. I'll go myself to assure there are no mistakes this time."

* * *

Vaughan crouched behind Roberta in her stall. He'd been grooming Her Highness's horse when the duke's men entered the stables. The duke's men made him nervous. They took any girl they wanted, and he'd heard rumors that some of them preferred boys.

Vaughan heard them ordering the stable grooms to have fifty horses ready to ride at first light tomorrow. Two of the men stopped nearby, apparently checking their gear.

"Why are we going to that goddess-forsaken hole?" one of them asked the other.

"I think it has something to do with that amihealer Mahon has been having us look for," the other answered. "I think he's from the Valley."

"You mean the freak? Goddess bless us, what would green eyes look like staring out of dark skin?"

Vaughan gasped and was relieved that the movement of the horses masked the sound. *Surely, there isn't more than one amihealer. Her Highness has to know.*

When the duke's men left, Vaughan edged carefully out of the stall. When he entered the palace through the kitchen, the chief cook smiled at him. "Get along, Vaughan," she scolded. "We're not handing out leftovers yet."

"Maggie," he whispered. "I have to see the princess. I heard something in the stables she needs to know." Maggie cocked her head, and he was afraid she'd turn him out. He drew the star of Sulis quickly. "Maggie, I swear by the goddess and on my mother's grave that what I have to tell the princess can't wait."

She sighed. "I'll find a boy to take you, but I promise, Vaughan, if you're blaspheming, I'll personally flay every inch of skin off your back."

Maggie went to the entrance of the servants' corridors and found a palace page. "Take this boy to Her Highness's rooms." The page looked at Vaughan as though he smelled bad, and they set off down the corridor.

When they were out of Maggie's earshot, the boy turned to him. "What could the princess want with *you*? I bet her bodyguards tear you apart for trying to talk to her. They're amazingly fierce."

Vaughan laughed a bit uneasily. "They're friends of mine." He had to admit some of them were pretty scary, especially the lieutenant with the icy blue eyes, but he wasn't going to let a snotty page lord it over him.

They wandered up and down corridors and stairwells, and Vaughan was starting to think the page was playing with him. The palace couldn't possibly be this big. Finally, the page stopped and opened a door. As they stepped through into the palace's main corridors, Vaughan gasped. He'd never dared enter them before. The hallway was about five times as wide as the narrow servants' corridors. Gold and crystal chandeliers hung from the ceiling. A huge painting of a knight charging into battle hung in a frame leafed with what he was sure was more gold. The corridors had plush red rugs with gold stars. He hardly dared step on them. When he did, he was ashamed to see his dirty boots left footprints.

Ahead, Brice and Bearach guarded the princess's door. He gave a sigh of relief that one of them wasn't the lieutenant.

"Hello, Vaughan," Bearach called out. "What are you doing up here?"

"I need to see the princess," he whispered. He didn't dare speak louder in a palace corridor. "I overheard something. It's important."

"I'll tell her," Bearach said, and turned to the page. "We'll take care of it from here." Before leaving, the page stared at Vaughan in disbelief. Vaughan gave him a cocky smile. He wanted to say "See, I told you they're friends of mine; they even know my name" and stick out his tongue. But he didn't dare in front of the guards.

Bearach went inside the princess's rooms. While waiting, Vaughan looked at his filthy boots and dirty hands. He was furious he hadn't thought to wash up first. He wondered if his face was dirty as well. Bearach came back and held the door open for him. "Her Highness will see you."

Vaughan entered a room that was even fancier than the corridor. He bowed awkwardly to the princess; she seemed more royal in the palace than she did in the stables. Captain Darhour was with her. "Your . . . Your Highness," he stuttered. He felt himself turning red.

"Bearach said you heard something important," she said.

To Vaughan's further embarrassment, his voice squeaked; it was doing that a lot lately. "Yes, Your Highness. It's about that amihealer you told me about, the one you wanted to marry."

"Robbie!" The princess grabbed his arm.

"The duke's men were talking about him in the stables. They're going after him tomorrow." He told her what he'd overheard.

The princess clutched at her stomach like she was about to vomit. "Darhour, you have to help him."

* * *

When the boy left, Darhour crossed his arms and glared at the princess. "Your Highness, there are only four of us of left! I can spare no one for this peasant! There is nothing I can do!"

She closed the distance between them. "Don't tell me there's nothing you can do! You're the Ghost, for Sulis's sake! I won't let Argblutal have him!"

Darhour merely looked at her. If she allowed herself to stop and think, she'd know he was right. Darhour saw the realization come into her eyes, but instead of the resignation he'd expected, her face crumbled. She turned away from him, and when she spoke, he could hear the tears in her voice. "Darhour, please, there has to be some way to save him."

Darhour groaned internally. Her feelings for this boy were a damned nuisance. "Your Highness, I still have an informant among the duke's men. If Argblutal does manage to catch the boy, I'll have Foy let me know, but that's the best I can do."

Samantha nodded. "Thank you," she whispered, and he longed to take her in his arms and comfort her. But it wasn't his place. *Sulis, should I kill again for her sake? Is killing truly the only thing I can offer her?*

* * *

Nola fought down his panic as he answered Argblutal's second summons of the day. He rigorously repressed the images of his daughter hanging from her bedpost and of Count Kayne's head lying on the council room floor.

Nola went down on one knee as he entered the audience chamber.

"Stand up, Nola," Argblutal commanded, and turned to the king. "Your Majesty, tell the count what you've just signed."

Nola stood. While the king's voice was bland, his eyes were contorted with rage. "We've signed a document giving you control over the king's lands for a year and a day. If you prove a competent steward, the lands will become yours by right."

Argblutal handed the sealed document to the count. "And you doubted me, Nola?"

"Never, Your Grace." He smiled at the document in his hand. *The king's lands! Soon, they'll refer to* me *as "Your Grace."*

"Prepare your men," Argblutal ordered. "We ride to claim your lands in the morning.

* * *

Robrek jerked awake from a nightmare in which Father Gildas had joined forces with Duke Argblutal to burn him at the stake. His so-called uncle had cheered when they lit the wood at his feet. *Damn them, all! Why can't everyone leave me alone?*

His eyes darted around the clearing, looking for danger. He saw nothing, but the gold horse approached him and nudged him with her nose. :*Good thou hast risen. Thou hast far more work than thou dost realize.*:

"What do you mean, 'thou'? You sound like something out of the Holy Writ!"

The gold horse ignored Robrek's complaint. :*Thou must control the vast power that lies within thee.*:

"Finally, something useful." With his full power, he'd be able to protect himself and make them all pay for what they'd done to him. He fetched the supplies he needed to treat the horse's injuries. "Myst has tried to teach me, but something's blocking me. Do you know what it is? Can you help me?"

:I know what it is. Whether or not I can help thee, I know not. In truth, only thou canst help thyself.:

Robrek rolled his eyes. "I've been trying for months, but I haven't gotten anywhere."

:Thou shouldst be grateful thou hast not. Power such as thine, unshielded, wouldst quickly drive thee mad. With the edges of thy power, thou canst feel the pain of a broken leg from a mile distant. Thou canst detect a belly full of glass in the middle of a crowded city. With thy full power, thou wilst feel every sensation of every living creature within miles, and thou wilst feel them all at once. Thou must learn to shield before thy true power thou canst own.:

"Myst never mentioned anything about shielding."

:This land hath not seen one of thy power in centuries, so knowledge of shielding hath been lost. To shield, thou must learn to build a barrier between thyself and the world. When thou hast learned this, we will see if thou canst learn the far more difficult lesson. If thou canst not, all shalt be lost.: Robrek rolled his eyes as the gold horse exaggerated as they all did. *:With shielding, subtlety is difficult. We will begin by creating a total shield, and slowly thou wilst learn to decrease its strength.:*

While he treated her injuries, the horse explained the theory of shields and how they were constructed. It didn't make a whole lot of sense. "Like an invisible bubble surrounding me?" he asked doubtfully.

:The bubble is visible, but not to the physical eye.:

"Like my energy, you mean. I can't really see it, but I can sense it."

The horse nodded. *:Thy mind is quick even if thy heart is stubborn.:*

Robrek resented being called stubborn, but complaining to the horses had never helped before. After he finished treating the horse, he fed it warm mash. The gold horse instructed him to relax. Robrek sat down, but relaxing was much more difficult. He wanted to grab a sword and run somebody through. He was tired of being lied to, tired of his life being in danger for the simple sin of existing.

:Relax,: the gold horse repeated. *:Reach deep inside to the source of thy power. See the edges of it.:*

Robrek tried, but the only thing he could think of was the number of people he'd trusted who'd lied to him and the even larger number who wanted him dead.

: Let go of thy anger. It doth thee ill.:

"That's easy for you to say! How many people want you dead?"

:What I haveth suffered mattereth not. But anger wast not easy for me to let loose.:

The horse glanced at her injuries, and Robrek felt ashamed. She certainly hadn't been having an easy time of it either, and Robrek desperately wanted to learn what the gold horse had to teach. Once he could control his power, he'd be as angry as he wanted to be. Comforting himself with the knowledge of how he could get even, he managed to stuff his anger behind closed doors. He knew he couldn't keep it there long, but for the moment he was separated from it. Then he saw the edges of his energy dancing in front of him.

: Now thou seest thy power. Take hold of it, and mold it into a small bubble.: The horse showed him how to form the thought bubble. *:Good. Now expand the bubble until it floweth out and covereth thy skin.:*

Robrek struggled, but the bubble remained stubbornly small. He tried to force it to expand.

:No!: The warning sounded sharply in his mind. *:Hast thou not learned? Magic canst not be forced. Relax. Breathe. Allow thy breath to expand the bubble.:*

Finally Robrek could feel the bubble expanding. When it was large enough, the horse directed him to cover his body with the energy. That was the simplest part. He merely imagined the energy flowing from within him to outside of him. Soon, he felt his shields snap into place. He gasped in terror. It was as if he'd suddenly gone both blind and deaf, as if every living thing that surrounded him had died instantly. He was cut off from all life, all hope, all that was good in the world. He could see the horses across the clearing and the birds in the trees, but he couldn't sense them anymore.

:Good. Thou hast constructed thy first shield.:

Robrek jumped to his feet. "No! This isn't good! I can't live like this!"

:Calm thyself. Rarely wilst thou need thy shield at this strength, but as I told thee, subtlety is difficult.:

Robrek glanced around frantically, expecting the world to fade and disappear. "How in the seven hells do you expect me to calm myself? Nobody could live in such an empty place!"

The gold horse chuckled. :*Almost everyone doth. Few canst feel the currents of life as thou dost.:*

"I don't care what other people do! I shall die if I feel no more than this! Help me get rid of it now!"

Sit again, and I will show thee how to weaken thy shield.:

"I don't want to weaken it! I want it gone!"

The gold horse sighed. :*Indeed thou art stubborn. Sit. Thou canst not survive the strength of thy gift if thou canst not shield.:*

He needed his full power if he was going to get even, so though every fiber of his being felt drained of life, he sat and listened to what she had to say. Slowly, the horse helped him weaken the shield until he could feel the smallest traces of the world outside. He breathed a sigh of relief as he could again feel the presence of the birds and the horses. Now that he no longer felt completely cut off, he could relax more easily and weaken the shields still more. Still, it was exhausting work.

* * *

Just after noon, Slathek, accompanied by the mercenaries he'd hired, rode into the backcountry farmyard. He couldn't believe this was the home Sphry had been forced to share with a barbarian. It bore signs of neglect, almost as if the owner had recently stopped caring. A huge barbarian came out of the main house. *The Father and the Mother bless this ungainly monster isn't Sphry's husband.*

The barbarian's jaw dropped. "Who . . . who are you?"

Slathek dismounted. "My name is Slthethkkne of Mahngbhayo. I see you recognize my resemblance to my sister Sphrnztegviza and my nephew. Do I have the pleasure of meeting my sister's husband?" Slathek stuck out his hand to shake in the manner of the barbarians. He caught the odor of cheap ale and the stench of unbathed barbarian. *How dare such an uncouth beast touch Sphry?*

The barbarian snorted and ignored Slathek's hand. "Whether you're lying or not, I don't care. They're both gone, and you should follow their example as soon as possible."

Slathek let his hand drop. *I'd have thought such rudeness was beyond even a barbarian.* "I have reason to believe Robrek has returned."

"These murderous imbeciles"—the barbarian gestured wide, taking in the entire countryside—"nearly set him on fire. I can't believe he'd be fool enough to come back. If so, I'm the last person he'd come to. The herb witch Myst is the only one he ever trusted."

"I could see his reluctance to associate with you. Where might I find this Myst?"

"You passed her cottage on the road from Murtaghan. It bears the healer's sign." The barbarian turned his back on Slathek and started for the door. He stopped at his threshold. "If you do find him, get him someplace safe."

* * *

As she lay in her bed wondering if Robrek would forgive her, Myst heard the sound of dozens of approaching horses. Leigh ran to the window. "Holy Sulis! An army is coming, and Robrek's leading them!"

"Robrek's leading an army?" Myst struggled to raise herself, but Leigh shook his head.

"No, now they're closer I can see it's not Robrek, but whoever it is looks an awful lot like him."

The horses stopped in front of the house, and Leigh went out.

"I'm told the herb witch Myst lives here," a man announced. Myst's heart gave a lurch at the sound. This man talked in the same odd way Donella had.

"She does, but she's very ill. I'm her apprentice. Is there anything I can do for you?"

"Please, may I speak with the herb witch? I wouldn't trouble your mistress if it weren't urgent."

"Let him in, Leigh," the herb witch called from her bed. Leigh stepped aside to let the man enter. Myst couldn't help staring. He looked so like Donella, so like Robrek.

The man bowed his head. "May I present myself? I am Slthethkkne, called Slathek by the barbarians."

"Donella said she had a brother, but how is it you know Robrek?"

"I met him in the capital." Slathek related his meeting.

Myst was unsure what to think. If the man's story was true, wouldn't Robrek have mentioned it? "I haven't seen him."

"Please, Mistress, he is in great danger. I must find him."

One of Slathek's men burst into the cottage. "Trouble," he said.

"One moment," Slathek said, and followed the man out.

Leigh went to the window. "Holy Sulis, Mistress, it's Duke Argblutal."

Coldness seized Myst's heart. "Leigh, go out the back window and run to Robrek's stables. If the duke wants magic, he may decide to use you for yours."

"No, Mistress! I won't leave you."

"Leigh, I won't allow another of my apprentices to fall prey to the duke. Run now, before it's too late!" Leigh hesitated. "I'm dying anyway. You must save yourself. Now, run!"

After taking another look out the window, Leigh gathered Myst into his arms. "I'll never forget you, Mistress."

"Nor I you." Myst returned his embrace and then pushed him away. "Go!"

As Leigh went out the rear window, Myst knew it was time. Dying was the last act she could do for Robrek. She directed her energy at her heart, bringing it slowly to a halt.

* * *

Slathek stepped outside to find his mercenaries surrounded by soldiers wearing Duke Argblutal's scarlet and black. To his horror, Slathek recognized Duke Argblutal himself.

The duke addressed the men Slathek had hired. "I am Duke Argblutal, the king's chancellor. This merchant is an enemy of the crown. I doubt you were aware of this, so if you'll surrender your weapons, you may depart in peace. Otherwise, you'll be hanged as traitors."

Slathek swore as the mercenaries surrendered their weapons. For the amount he'd paid them, you'd think they could put up at least a token resistance.

As the mercenaries rode away, Argblutal told the men to take him. Before Slathek could even think about resisting, they had him on the ground with his hands tied behind his back. Slathek tried to tell himself he'd been in dicey situations before, but he couldn't think of one that compared.

One of the soldiers turned Slathek onto his back, and the merchant felt his stomach drop as he met the blue eyes of the duke. "Well, well, well, who do we have here? Bring him inside," Argblutal ordered.

Argblutal's men dragged him back into the herb witch's cottage. The apprentice was gone, and the rear window left opened. The men threw him into a chair and tied him to it.

The duke strode in, and his eyes widened at the sight of the herb witch. "I do not take kindly to being tricked." However, the herb witch's eyes were open and unseeing, and Slathek sensed no life from her. *By the Father and the Mother, she's killed herself to protect Robrek.* When Argblutal realized what she was dead, he swore viciously, drew his sword and stabbed her through the throat.

The duke pressed his sword, wet with the herb witch's blood, to Slathek's throat. "Did you kill the witch yourself or have one of your men do it?"

"I had nothing to do with that." Slathek nodded toward the witch.

"The witch doesn't matter."

Slathek could tell the duke didn't believe him.

"But I will have your nephew. Where is he?"

Slathek laughed uneasily. "I see I've been caught in my own trap. The amihealer is truly no relative. I merely wanted to acquire him. Do you know how rich his magic could make me in Mahngbhayo? I told him some story about a poor kidnapped sister. Unfortunately, he didn't buy it." Argblutal pressed his sword against Slathek's jugular, and Slathek tried not to mind dying. "Please, I don't know where he is. The damned fool ran off, or we'd be far out to sea by now. I tried his father, but the two haven't spoken for years. I thought she'd know where he'd gone." He looked toward the herb witch's body, hoping he'd said enough to stop Argblutal from going after Angus. "But she simply faded and died when I asked."

Argblutal removed his sword. He took his whip from his belt and whipped Slathek's tunic to rags and his chest and shoulders bloody. "To perdition with it all!" Slathek cried. "His magic greatly exceeds that which we of Mahngbhayo possess and could've made me wealthy beyond my wildest dream. But I'd gladly trade him for my life."

Argblutal paused the beating. "*You* have magic?"

Sweat beaded on his forehead. "Very little. Hardly adequate to heal a hangnail."

The duke turned to his men. "Tie him to a horse, and ten of you will ride back with me to Murtaghan. The rest of you stay to make sure Count Nola delivers the amihealer."

* * *

From the shadows of the inn, Boyden watched as a nobleman rode into the village, accompanied by at least fifty soldiers. They stopped in the middle of the village square and waited for a crowd to form. When nearly everyone in the village, including the priest, had gathered, the nobleman addressed them. "I am Count Nola. I seek an amihealer by the name of Robrek Angusstamm."

Father Gildas stepped forward, preening like an overlarge hog. "We had such a demon among us, Milord, but he fled from the judgment of the flames."

"My sources say he has returned to this valley. Anyone who shelters him or gives him aid shall be subject to the crown's justice. Anyone who brings me word of him shall be rewarded. To protect these lands against further infestations, the king has appointed me as your new lord."

"We on the king's lands have no lord," Banagher, the innkeeper, called out.

"By the king's decree, you do now," Nola announced. "I have here the tax rolls." A clerk accompanying him held up a large volume. "Tomorrow morning, all former landholders will report to me, and we will discuss your stewardship. For the time being, I will make the village inn my headquarters."

Breasal, Bran's father, who had no more brains than his son, pushed to the front of the crowd. "Nobody's taking my land."

"You question your lord?" Count Nola looked down his nose.

"I have no lord except the king himself." The farmer spat at the ground in front of the count's horse.

"So be it." Nola nodded to one of his men, who rode over to the peasant and cut off Breasal's head with a quick stroke of his blade. Boyden blinked, unsure what he'd seen was real. Nobody killed so causally. But when he looked again, the head was lying on the ground. *Why should I care? Did he offer to speak up for me when my father threw me out?*

The soldier dismounted, picked up the head by the hair, and brought it to Count Nola. "Put it on a pike in the village square as a reminder." The soldier nodded and obeyed. "Does anyone else object? Two heads would provide a more balanced display."

When no one said anything, Count Nola cleared his throat. "I will expect your reports in the morning. For now, I order you to disperse."

* * *

As he dropped his shields again, he felt exhausted, but smiled savagely. Since he'd accomplished this with minimal difficulty, surely he'd be able to do whatever was necessary to access his full power. As he raised his shields to full strength one last time, he wondered again how anyone could bear to live in such a lifeless void. He dropped his shields and leaned back against the stable wall.

He heard movement coming along the path and got to his feet, grabbing his staff. Leigh burst into the clearing, sobbing. Robrek ran to him. "Leigh, what's happened?"

"Myst," Leigh managed to croak between his sobs before collapsing to the ground.

"No!" Robrek cried. "No, she can't be!" Leigh only curled himself up into a ball and sobbed harder. Once before Robrek had believed her dead, and it hadn't been true. "Stop it! I tell you she isn't dead. I'll heal her." Robrek headed for Wild Thing, but Leigh grabbed him.

"She's dead, I promise you. I watched them bury her. You have to stay here. They're looking for you all over the Valley."

"I'll handle the priest if I have to," Robrek scoffed

"It's not Father Gildas. Duke Argblutal's men are after you. Duke Argblutal killed Myst. Stabbed her right through the throat." Leigh broke off into sobs again. "He followed that man who claimed to be your uncle." Leigh told him what he'd overhead.

Robrek collapsed trembling against the stable wall. *No! Leigh is lying! Myst can't be dead!* Something broke within him. The Valley peasants had tried to burn him. A duke he'd never heard of had tried to kidnap him off the streets. A foreign infidel had tried to lure him into a trap, and now between them, they'd killed Myst. *Myst!* Why shouldn't he become the demon they called him? "I'll kill him! I'll kill them all!"

Leigh gaped at the amihealer. Robrek grabbed a sword from the stable wall and walked into the middle of the paddock. "Fight me," he ordered.

At first, Leigh thought Robrek was talking to him and wondered if the amihealer had gone mad. He gasped as two armed, faceless knights appeared. Robrek attacked ferociously. At that moment, the amihealer certainly resembled the denizens of the seven hells. Maybe Father Gildas had been right about him.

After Robrek cleaved the head off of one of the knights and stabbed the second through the heart, the dead knights disappeared, and two more took their place. Robrek had killed these and at least a dozen more before he dropped beside Leigh. While Leigh couldn't help shrinking away, the amihealer didn't seem to notice. "When it is dark, we will properly bury our mistress. We will mark her grave with a stone that we will carve, and we'll leave her the appropriate offerings of apples and grain. I can protect you if we're found." Leigh said nothing, wondering for a moment whether it was Robrek he needed protection from.

* * *

From across the inn's dining room, Boyden watched the fat count and the clerk who fawned on his every word. This was surely his ticket to something better. Boyden approached the count, but guards blocked his path. "I'd like to speak to Milord. I believe I can be of service."

"Clear off, peasant. The count will receive your report in the morning."

Boyden's hands formed into fists. "It is the reports I want to discuss. He must be aware the Valley peasants will try to cheat him. He could use a man familiar with the lands of every farmer in the Valley."

"Let him approach," the count said, as if he were granting Boyden a crown on a silver platter. The guard stepped aside. "Who are you?"

"My name's Boyden Angusstamm, Milord. My father is the richest farmer in the Valley. There isn't a farm I don't know."

"Angusstamm?" The count lifted his eyebrows and turned to his clerk. "Isn't that the name of the amihealer His Grace seeks?"

"Milord, the demon and I share the same father, but I do not claim him as a relation." Boyden knew it was useless pretending the worm wasn't his brother.

"That is most interesting. Do you know where this *demon* is now?"

"If I knew, he'd be dead."

"Would your brother go to your father for assistance?"

Boyden bristled. "I doubt it. My father threw him off the farm and told him he wouldn't take him back."

"Who might he go to?"

"There are a few servants on my father's farm who might do something for him. I can think of no one else. There's hardly a man in the Valley who doesn't want to see him burn."

Nola eyed him appraisingly. "Give me the names of these servants. Then we'll see if you can be of further use."

* * *

Disturbed by the brief visit from Donella's brother, Angus stared out the dining room window. Shamed at the condition the man had found him in, he'd bathed and changed. *Could the boy really be dense enough to return here?* Just in case, he'd taken some supplies to the place he'd left them in the past, but he could think of nothing else to do. *A father should protect his child. One of the many ways I failed both my sons.*

He'd heard the rumors the king had given control of the king's land to some bastard of a nobleman who'd reduce them all to serfs. Only a few months ago, this would have enraged him. Now, he didn't have the energy to care.

As night began to fall, the nobleman's retainers rode into his farmyard. Angus went out to face them. "What can I do for you?" he asked.

The men initially ignored him. "Surround the buildings. See that none escape," the man in charge said before turning to Angus. "We have orders to bring four of your servants in for questioning. Produce Darien, Allyn, Dillion, and Cara."

"What does His Lordship want with them?" *How could the count know the four who were closest to Robbie?*

"That's His Lordship's business." When Angus failed to answer, the man spoke to the gathering hands. "Point out those named, and no one else will be hurt." It wasn't long before Darien, Allyn, Dillion, and Cara were pushed forward.

"Seize them," the man ordered, and several men dismounted and began to tie up the four terrified servants.

"I'll come with them and see they're treated fairly," Angus protested.

"Suit yourself," the man said.

Angus followed the count's men to the village inn. His servants were dragged inside. Boyden was sitting near the count. "You! How could you betray your own kind?"

"And who is this?" the count asked Boyden.

"Milord, may I present my father, Angus Camlinstamm," Boyden answered.

"I see." The count turned to his men. "Why did you bring him?"

"Milord, when we arrested the servants, he insisted on accompanying us to see they were treated fairly."

"You would question the fairness of your new lord? Do the residents of this Valley need another example?"

The count's eyes bore into Angus, but Angus wasn't afraid. In some ways, he'd be glad if the count put his head next to the one on the pike outside.

"Milord, cut off my head if you like, but I'm certain none of my hands know anything about the whereabouts of my son."

The count smiled smugly. "You'll forgive me if I allow them to speak for themselves."

"We don't know where he is," Dillion cried out. "Please, don't hurt my wife. She's with child. Please, Milord. We haven't seen Robbie since his trial."

Before the count put his head on a pike, Angus had to try to protect his people. "Milord, before Robbie left, he told the herb witch of a spot where I could leave some supplies for him. It's possible he might return there. I'll show you where it is if you let my hands go."

Nola turned to Boyden. "Should I believe him?"

Boyden nodded. "I'd think so, Milord. His hands are more valuable to him than the worm." Angus put a hand to his gut. *Is that true? Have I cared so little for my own blood?*

Nola nodded. "Cut them loose." He turned to the servants. "You may go, but know you'll be watched carefully. If you have anything to do with this amihealer and don't report it immediately, your head will balance the display." Cara and the men hurried from the room. The count turned back to Angus. "My men will provide you with some supplies, and you will show them the spot. Do not try to fool me, peasant."

CHAPTER 35

Slathek had never imagined a situation he couldn't talk, trade, or buy his way out of. But after spending several hours staring at a horse's feet and banging against its side, he believed he'd found one. Ropes cut painfully into his thighs, arms, and wrists and irritated the already painful lash marks. He'd long since stopped being able to feel his hands. When he complained, he was either ignored or beaten. His head hurt abominably.

Finally, Slathek and his escort rode through the city gates and came to a stop at one of the finest residences in the capital. Slathek was dragged in the back door, down a corridor, and into a spacious office, where he was tied to a chair. He was starting to worry his hands might be permanently damaged. *What does that matter? I doubt I'll get out of this alive.*

The duke swept into the room. Slathek bowed his head in acknowledgement. "Forgive me for not rising, Your Grace, but I seem to be indisposed."

"Spirited, I see." The duke smiled unpleasantly as he took his seat.

"Your Grace, I'm a man of business, and I obviously have something you want. Can't we discuss a deal like civilized men over a bottle of wine?"

Argblutal regarded him thoughtfully for a minute. He nodded to the guards, who cut the ropes.

Slathek winced as he looked at his hands. They were swollen and a color between purple and black. Dried blood stained his wrists.

The duke poured two glasses of wine, pushed one across the desk, and picked up his own, taking a sip. "Like civilized men, then. You will make me a potion. The price will be your life."

"Your Grace, I'd be more than happy to oblige, but I've never made a potion in my life. All I've seen require a lot more magic than I possess."

"This one does not." The duke pushed a very old volume across the desk. "The potion has been made successfully twice. You will make a third."

Slathek picked up the book and began to read. Concealing his horror, Slathek forced his face into an expression he used when conducting a dicey negotiation. "It's possible I could do this, but there are several difficulties."

"And they are?"

"Injuries steal energy from a healer. My magic is so weak I could never do this without recovering first."

The duke's eyes flashed. "How long?"

"It'll take at least two or three weeks for my wrists to heal properly, and that is only if I receive proper medical treatment and suffer no further, shall we say, mishaps."

"You do realize if my men find the amihealer, I'll have no use for you."

Slathek nodded. "Which brings me to my second consideration. What assurance do I have you'll let me go after I make the potion?"

"You have my word."

"From what I've heard, that isn't worth very much."

The duke smiled thinly. "Very well. After you complete the potion, I *will* kill you. Do well, and your death will be quick and painless. Defy me, and I'll have you begging me for days to finish the job." He nodded to the guards. "Take him to the cell. Get him medical attention."

Argblutal ground his teeth in fury as the infidel was dragged out of his office. He'd hold onto the arrogant commoner for now, but it was likely he wouldn't need whatever magic the foreigner could conjure. Nearly half of the guard inside the palace had been replaced by his men, and with Duke Torin's pledge of men and support, he believed he had sufficient forces for an attack.

He called for Kentigern. "I need an excuse to bring the rest of my forces into the city. The death of the children caused unrest in Korth."

"Yes, Your Grace, but it didn't have that effect in Murtaghan."

"Another dead child and a few well placed rumors could do so. I want rioting in the streets by tomorrow night."

* * *

Leigh felt weary as he walked down the familiar Murtaghan street. He grimaced as his father's mansion came into view. While most of the houses in the neighborhood had the quiet dignity of old money, his father's had the gaudy opulence of newly acquired wealth. It was blindingly white and trimmed in swirling gold and silver designs interspersed with stained glass in every shade of the rainbow. Gilded statuary and marbled fountains littered the space between bushes and trees, which had been trimmed into geometric shapes, along with flowers in beds so precisely spaced they looked unnatural. Leigh had never seen anything so ugly. He'd thought never to cross the threshold again.

Leigh regretted looking like a beggar when he appealed to his father. He'd stopped at a city fountain to wash the dirt from his hands and his face, but there was little he could do about his robes. They hadn't been very nice to begin with, and nearly two days of walking and a night spent sleeping in the woods hadn't helped. Reluctantly, he lifted the gold-plated knocker and let it fall.

Ennis, a long-time servant of the family, opened the door. "Master Leigh, what a . . . surprise."

"Ennis, can you tell my father I'd like to speak with him?"

"Of course, Master Leigh. This way, please." Ennis ushered him into the parlor reserved for guests of uncertain importance.

His father arrived quickly. Fergal Taranstamm exhibited the same gaudy ostentation as his house. He wore robes of deep crimson lined with sable fur. About thirty gold chains hung around his neck and every finger was bejeweled with a ring inset with some precious stone. Although he wore a stern face, his eyes twinkled underneath it all. "So the prodigal son has returned home with nothing but a filthy robe on his back? Have you finally come to your senses and decided life as a priest isn't a fit occupation for a son of mine?"

"I was thrown out of the priesthood and excommunicated."

"Excommunicated? You?" His father roared with laughter. "This is a story I have to hear. Sit down and tell me, how does the son who doesn't whore, gamble, drink, or steal and who refuses to enter the family business because 'it is a curse on the children of the goddess' get himself excommunicated?"

"I'm glad you find the ruin of my life so amusing," Leigh said, taking a seat. Still, he told his father about Robrek's trial and setting the amihealer free.

Fergal laughed until tears rolled down his cheeks. "Leigh, you're a fool. What was this charlatan to you?"

"Robrek is no charlatan, and I couldn't allow an innocent man burn to death. And there's more." Leigh told him of Duke Argblutal's arrival at Myst's cottage. "If he learns I was the herb witch's apprentice, he could be after me next. He wants someone with magic. I don't know why."

Fergal sobered. "I'm sorry I laughed, Leigh. If Argblutal is involved, this is no game."

"Can I stay, father? Just until I can make sure he isn't looking for me?"

"I never wanted you to leave. Not even when you started all that nonsense about being a priest."

"Thank you, father." Leigh's relief drained the last bit of tension out of him. He felt completely exhausted, and his father was perceptive enough to notice.

Fergal rang a bell, and Ennis appeared. "Show the young master up to his room and have a tray of food sent up to him." He turned back to Leigh. "Your room is just how you left it. Your mother wouldn't hear of anything being touched. Although how she'll react when she learns her most pious son has been excommunicated, I can't say." A twinkle of amusement returned to his father's eyes.

Leigh nodded gratefully and followed Ennis. The fact his father had Ennis show him the way to the bedroom he'd occupied for most of his life demonstrated he wasn't yet accepted back into the family, but he'd have a place to stay for now.

Leigh had allowed no sign of his parents' wealth and bad taste to penetrate his sanctuary. The walls were unpainted wood. The wooden star of Sulis hanging over his bed was their only decoration. Besides the bed, there was only a chest for his clothes, a desk, and a bookshelf.

He'd just removed his filthy robes and put on the plain white nightshirt that was still in the chest when there was a knock at the door. Leigh commanded what he thought was a servant with his dinner to enter, but when the door opened, his mother held the tray.

"Mother," he said, and took the tray out of her hands.

Dympna was a small, slight woman with an even more pointed nose than Leigh's. She wore a blue silk dressing gown embroidered with gold thread. Despite her professed piety, Dympna had never hesitated to reap the benefits of her husband's wealth. "Leigh, my son," she whispered and brushed his cheek with her lips. "Your father is saying the most ridiculous things to upset me. He thinks it's funny to pretend you've been excommunicated."

"I'm afraid it's true, mother."

Dympna let out an ear-splitting wail. "You were my only hope! How will I face my priest now that you, too, are a reprobate? How could you do this to your own mother?" Weeping, she fled from the room.

Leigh sighed and sat in front of his meal. He'd never known how to handle his mother's hysteria. She'd always been distant from her children and spent most of her time recovering from imaginary ailments. In the morning, he was sure to receive a message that, thanks to him, she was on the verge of death. Leigh put his head in his hands and prayed for direction. He couldn't stay in this house long—he'd go mad.

* * *

Darhour sat at his table, waiting for Foy. The darkness of the early morning was relieved by a single candle. A mug of ale waited on the table. The princess was obsessed with that damned amihealer, and the more Darhour learned about the boy, the less he trusted him. He was no peasant farmer, no matter what he pretended. A large part of Darhour was content to let the duke have the boy, but another part of him realized that the two combined might be far more dangerous than the duke alone.

Finally, the knock came at the servant entrance. Darhour opened it, and a man covered by a cloak hurried into the room. Darhour closed the door behind him, and Foy dropped his hood and grabbed for the mug of ale. Darhour noticed the servant's hands trembled. Foy took a large gulp and set the goblet down.

"Well?" Darhour asked.

"He brought a prisoner back from the Valley. I didn't get a look at him, and nobody seems to know his name, but from what others said, he matches the description of the man you're looking for."

Darhour got a purse of coins out and tossed it to Foy. "I've arranged passage for you on the *Farflyer*. It leaves at high tide."

Foy grabbed the coins, but paused before heading for the door. "You'll still see the duke dead? You'll make him pay for what he did to my sister?"

Foy had never told Darhour what the duke had done, but he didn't have trouble imagining. Darhour wondered if he'd truly have to resort to his former profession in order to save his daughter. "I'll take care of him."

Foy nodded and hurried toward the door.

When the door closed behind the servant, Darhour sat and stared into the candle flame. *Damn him to the seven hells! Why in Sulis's name did he have to get himself caught?* He knew well what the princess would want and how difficult it would be. He scratched at the scars on his face.

* * *

One look at Darhour's face confirmed Samantha's worst fear. "Argblutal has Robbie?"

Darhour nodded. "A man matching the amihealer's description was taken into Argblutal's residence."

Samantha clutched at her stomach.

Blaine ran into the room. "Your Highness!" Blaine's face was as white as she felt hers to be. "Another dead child has been found, this time on the steps of the Temple of the Mother's Love. The people think all the priests are ravening panthers, so to speak. They've threatened to tear the temple apart and hang the priests. The king is calling for a special meeting of the council. Argblutal wants his own forces to suppress the mob."

"No! I thought this would stop after the high priest's death."

"The duke has the peasant amihealer," Darhour announced. "He wouldn't need the high priest."

"You aren't suggesting Robbie killed the child?" She glared at Darhour.

"Just how well do you know the boy?" Darhour's eyes now seemed nearly as icy as Kailen's.

She jabbed her finger in his chest. "Well enough to know that he wouldn't kill a child." Samantha told Blaine to bring her regrets to the council meeting and turned back to Darhour. "We aren't going to allow Argblutal the excuse to bring more men into Murtaghan. We're going stop the mob ourselves. Get my guards and as many Royal Guards as you can manage. When the temple is safe, you will rescue Robbie."

Darhour glared down at her. "It's not that simple. Argblutal's residence is swarming with men."

She met his eyes letting him know again he couldn't intimidate her. "They say The Ghost can walk through walls."

Darhour folded his arms and didn't answer.

"Please, Darhour, don't let Argblutal hurt him because of me."

Darhour damned himself for never being able to say no to women. "I'll try."

* * *

Surrounded by her four men and a dozen members of the Royal Guard, Samantha rode to the Temple of the Mother's Love. The area around the shrine was crowded with angry people, and Darhour had several times suggested turning back. If the mob attacked, the number of her men was insufficient to protect her, but Darhour hadn't been able to get more on short notice. As she neared the shrine, she saw a priest standing on the top step, trying to address the crowd. He couldn't be heard over the roar, and his robes were stained with rotten fruit. Far too few city magistrates stood at the base of the stairs.

As she drew near, the people recognized her and parted to allow her and her men through. "Her Highness will see justice is done!" someone shouted.

Dismounting at the bottom of the steps, Samantha climbed to stand next to the priest, Father Hafghan, a man she'd never thought highly of. He was ambitious and self-serving, but that didn't merit being torn apart by an angry mob.

The princess held up her hand for silence, and the crowd quieted. "I understand your anger. Your children are precious, and you fear for their well-being. But Father Hafghan and the priests within these walls are not what threatens them."

"The child was found on the steps of the shrine!" someone called.

"Don't think she gives a damn about some poor man's child!" another man cried out, raising his arm to throw a rotten apple.

Kailen and Brice jumped in front of the princess, drawing their weapons. Bearach nocked an arrow and pointed it into the crowd. "Bearach, no!" she shouted.

Bearach shifted his aim downward, but let the arrow fly. It landed between the feet of the man who'd shouted. Faster than she could see, Bearach nocked another arrow. "I am a poor man's child!" he cried out. "As are all of us whose privilege it is to guard the princess. Her Highness cares about all the people of the joined kingdoms! We will not hear her insulted!"

Warmed by Bearach's defense, Samantha spoke so the entire crowd could hear. "I feel these deaths as deeply as any of you."

"You have no idea what it is to lose a child!" shouted the man who'd been about to throw the apple. "They have my Oran now." He pointed toward the priests. "I'll die before I see him as the next one sacrificed!"

"The priests are murderers!" someone else yelled.

"Give Her Highness a chance! She'll do right by us!"

The princess turned to the priest. "Father Hafghan, will you consent to your shrine being searched?"

"Of course, Your Highness. We have nothing to hide."

"To prove the priests' innocence, the city magistrates will search the shrine for any sign of missing children or human sacrifice. To assure they do so thoroughly, you may send five respectable individuals from among you to accompany them, including Oran's father." The crowd murmured, and after a few minutes, five men mounted the steps.

After they had disappeared inside, the princess paced restlessly. Darhour touched her on the arm. "Be calm, Your Highness. The people must see you project confidence."

The princess started. For once in her life, she'd forgotten she was on display. She stopped pacing, but she couldn't stop her fingers from tapping against her thigh. She tried not to think what might be happening to Robbie at this very moment.

* * *

After an hour, the men emerged. "Any sign of children?" she asked.

"No, Your Highness, we could find nothing," one of the magistrates said.

Oran's father glared at her. "Of course we found nothing! Those priests had plenty of time to clean up. How can I know they haven't hid Oran elsewhere?"

A woman, holding a four-year-old child, stepped to the front of the crowd. "Because he's right here, you dolt. I told you he probably sneaked off to play with the neighbor's kittens."

"Oran!" the man shouted and bounded down the steps. The child wriggled free of his mother's grasp and ran toward his father. As the two met, the tension leaked from the crowd.

"My people, a horrible crime has been committed, but not by these priests. Staining your hands with innocent blood will not bring the dead children back. Do not dishonor their deaths by causing more. Return to your homes. The crown and the magistrates are doing everything within our power to find those responsible, this I promise you."

Slowly the people started drifting away. Some lingered, staring angrily at her and the temple, but without a mob behind them, they lacked courage to act.

Father Hafghan bowed deeply. "Thank you, Your Highness. I was afraid they'd slaughter us all. Can I invite you inside for some refreshments?"

"Perhaps some other time, Father. I must return to the palace at once."

"Of course, Your Highness. If there's ever anything I can do for you, please don't hesitate to ask."

* * *

Having dressed in the duke's livery and disguised his scars with wax and makeup, Darhour surveyed Argblutal's residence from the neighboring roof. In addition to his sword and his many knives, he had a blowpipe and over a dozen darts coated with a powerful sleeping potion.

The property was swarming with men. There were even two stationed on the roof. Taking a dart in hand, Darhour waited for the men on the roof to look away, then jumped soundlessly across the open space separating the duke's residence from its neighbor. He grabbed the first man from behind, clamped a hand over his mouth, and stuck him with the dart. As the man went limp, Darhour lowered him carefully to the roof, making sure he wouldn't fall and alert those below. He crept to the other side of the roof and did the same to the second guard. Tonight the attic window was open to catch the night breeze, and the serving girls were fast asleep. Using his blowpipe, Darhour shot them with darts to make sure they stayed that way. He slipped into their room and out the door on the other side. On the landing below, he saw two guards, both facing away from him. He hit them both in the back with darts; they both fell in less than a second. Darhour pulled them into a nearby closet. The house was relatively quiet, but he passed rooms full of sleeping men. He met two more sets of guards on his way to the cellar and incapacitated them.

Soundlessly, he slipped down to the wine cellar. The door to the torture chamber was cracked open, and he heard the murmur of several voices. Darhour stuck his blowpipe through the door, and before the men realized what was happening, he hit two of them with darts. The others jumped to their feet and began to shout. He got another one with a dart while the fourth fell to the ground with a knife in his throat. Darhour froze, but he heard no sound from above.

Darhour found the keys and opened the cell door. To his surprise and annoyance, the man inside wasn't the amihealer, but an older man who resembled him closely. "Who are you?" Darhour demanded.

The man rose to his feet. "You came looking for my nephew, perhaps? The duke couldn't find him, so he took me instead."

A shout sounded from above, and dozens of footsteps pounded down the stairs. Darhour pulled the man into the adjoining torture chamber. "Quick, hide yourself, and if you're caught, don't breathe a word about me."

Darhour dropped amid the duke's fallen men; feigning unconsciousness, he heard a cabinet door close as men burst into the room. "Holy Sulis, Mother of us all!" one of them swore.

"Find him!" another shouted. "You know what the duke will do to us if he escapes!"

Darhour watched through the slits of his eyes as the men began a frantic search. So far they'd paid no attention to him. He began a slow crawl to the door.

"I found him!" one of the men called, opening the cabinet door. The eyes of all of the men in the room turned toward the foreigner crouched inside.

Darhour took advantage of their distraction to slip to his feet, out of the torture chamber, and into the wine cellar. He heard Robbie's uncle scream, but there was nothing he could do for him. As Darhour reached the steps, two more men descended. "There's a problem with the prisoner!" Darhour told them. "They need your help at once!"

Turning pale, the men rushed past him. Darhour hurried up the stairs. At the top, he found two more guards. "What's going on?" one demanded.

"There has been an escape attempt by the prisoner, but he's been apprehended."

The man looked at Darhour more closely. "Who are you? I don't remember seeing you before."

Darhour didn't have time to bluff, so he palmed two of his knives, grabbed the guard who had questioned him, and quickly slit his throat and threw the second knife at the other man. He drew his sword and ran toward the attic stairs. When he reached the first landing, he heard a cry behind him. The door beside the landing swung open, and Darhour stabbed the man who emerged before running upward. Ahead of him two more men appeared with swords drawn. Without pausing, Darhour drew a knife and threw it at one of them and stabbed the other with his sword. Vaulting over the bodies, he ran up the last flight of stairs. As he neared the top, he felt something sharp hit his shoulder. He ignored it, ran through the servants' room, and toward the open window. As he was about to climb out, he heard the closest of his pursuers approaching. He whirled and threw a knife. A dozen more were coming through the doorway. He jumped out the window and onto the roof. He ran and jumped onto the neighboring roof as the men poured out the window after him.

Men were pursuing him in the street below as well as along the rooftops. Because of his ability to see in the dark, he managed to get some distance ahead of them. But soon he'd come to the end of the block and have to come down. The next house had an open window with a drainpipe beside it. He grabbed the drainpipe and quickly climbed inside the house, where a woman sat up in her bed. Darhour clamped his hand over her mouth and put a knife to her throat. "Make one sound, and I'll slit your throat," he whispered.

The woman froze, and footsteps pounded overhead. When the noise passed, Darhour felt tremendous pain in his shoulder. He looked to see his back covered with blood and a knife sticking out of him. In the heat of a battle, he never felt pain. Now, however, he felt it acutely, and he was beginning to feel dizzy from the blood loss. He loosened his grip on the woman's mouth. "I'm going to let you go, but remember my warning. Do you understand?"

After the woman nodded, Darhour released her and saw her closely for the first time. "Lady Aislinn," he whispered. "Duke Argblutal is looking for me. For the princess's sake, you must hide me." Before he could tell her more, he felt the darkness take him.

* * *

Argblutal burst into the torture chamber to find his prisoner lying on the floor and beaten badly. His arm was clearly broken, lying limply at his side. It would be weeks before he'd heal now. A little more torture could hardly hurt. "Tie him to the rack," he ordered.

The prisoner screamed and passed out as the duke's men obeyed. Argblutal had him revived with a bucket of water. "Who tried to free you?" the duke asked

"I don't know," the infidel hissed through clenched teeth.

The duke grasped a lever, and the prisoner screamed as the rack tore apart his broken arm. The duke released the lever." Now we'll begin again. Who was the man?"

"Please, I don't know. He thought you had the amihealer. Not me."

The duke's hand grasped the lever again.

As the prisoner screamed, Kentigern came into the room, and the duke released the lever.

"Your Grace, the entire block has been searched. There's no sign of him," Kentigern reported.

"How many dead?"

"Six, Your Grace. Another five wounded, one of whom may die."

"Tell me how a single man breaks into my residence, kills six of my men, nearly frees my prisoner, and gets away untouched!"

Kentigern paled. "He was wounded, Your Grace. We found a trail of blood."

"And still he escaped you?" Argblutal turned away. Only one man could have been responsible for this, and the duke knew who'd sent him. *That bitch will interfere no more.*

* * *

Conroy tried to make sense of his surroundings. He was in a cave of some kind. He tried to sit up, but found himself too weak. He collapsed back into the furs, groaning.

"Oh, you're awake." A girl of no more than twelve appeared. She was dressed in the robes of a novice, and her hair was braided into the hundreds of braids favored by the female clergy. The novice had a bowl of broth. "Here, eat this. It will help you recover your strength. I was afraid you were going to die, but now I don't think you will." She looked quite pleased with herself.

"Your mistress?" Conroy asked. "I must speak with her immediately."

Tears formed in the girl's eyes. "She was taken a month ago, and I only just managed to get away and hide in these caves. Now, eat this broth."

Feeling the crushing weight of failure, he closed his eyes and allowed the novice to feed him. "How did I get here?" he asked between spoonfuls.

"My brothers found you with a bunch of dead men and brought you to me. They said you were a gang of bandits. Were you?"

Before he could answer, an older man's voice came from outside the cave, "Oriana."

"Father, I'm back here. He's awake."

The man came barreling into the room. "Oriana, have you lost your mind? I told you to call your brothers to watch him if he woke up. I should have slit the bloody bandit's throat to begin with."

"Sir, if I may—" Conroy struggled to his elbow. "I am no bandit. I serve the princess."

The man laughed. "The princess now employs two-dram mercenaries to attack innocent travelers?"

"Her Highness is a woman of honor," Conroy snapped. "I was the innocent traveler who got attacked, not one of the bandits."

"Yes, of course. You managed to kill all five of them by yourself." The man rolled his eyes.

Conroy nodded, feeling pleased with himself. He doubted the captain could have done much better. "Only the finest are trusted with the princess's life. I swear by the goddess and on my mother's grave I'm one of her guard."

The man looked at his daughter. "He hasn't the slightest taint of evil about him, Father. Surely he's telling the truth."

"What's he doing here then?" the man asked his daughter rather than Conroy.

Conroy answered anyway, "Her Highness sent me in search of a priestess with healing magic. Please, can you help me? The need is most urgent." He told them about the king's madness.

The man made a noise in the back of his throat. "Even if you're telling the truth, I can't help you. There are no priestesses left."

Conroy closed his eyes and sank into the furs. "Then I have failed."

"No, you haven't," Oriana protested. "I'll go with you."

"Are you insane, Oriana?" her father roared. "He might be lying. Even if he isn't, do you think I'd consent to sending you into such danger?"

Oriana put her hands on her hips. "I'll go wherever I believe Sulis calls me."

The man turned to Conroy. "Princess's man, you wouldn't take a young girl into something like this, would you?"

"Under other circumstances, I wouldn't, but the princess's situation is desperate."

"Damn you to the seven hells, why didn't the curse kill you as it's already killed so many?" The man stormed out of the cave.

"What curse?" Conroy asked Oriana.

"Lots of people have started dying, especially the sick, babies, and old people. Nobody knows why. Mother Venetia was trying to figure it out when she was taken."

Conroy dismissed the matter. While it was certainly tragic for those affected, it didn't compare in importance to Her Highness's peril.

* * *

Surrounded by her remaining men and lost in a numb fog of despair, Samantha made her way to the throne room in answer to the king's summons. Darhour hadn't returned last night. *Holy Mother, don't let him be dead. Don't let Robbie be, either. I can't bear to lose either of them.*

She and her men entered the throne room to find the court assembled. Over a dozen of the Royal Guard surrounded her and her men. She approached the throne and bowed before the king.

The king told her to arise. "Our daughter and lords and ladies of the court, we have decided that in order to ensure the goddess's blessing upon the contest, Her Highness, the Crown Princess Samantha, will spend the time remaining before Mabon in prayer and meditation in the shrine atop Gloine Torr. She will leave immediately."

"But Father!" the princess cried.

"Our orders are not to be questioned. We are confident that, with proper prayer and supplication, the goddess will reveal her choice for your consort."

The king's eyes held no warmth or even much life. *Sulis, Mother of us all, is there any hope? Has Argblutal won?*

* * *

Aislinn looked at the sleeping figure on the bed. She'd been shocked when the wax and makeup had been cleaned off his face to find that she'd rescued the captain of Her Highness's guards. She had to admit she'd always been afraid of him. When he had been Master of the Horse, she'd never approached the stables alone. The physician she'd summoned had nearly despaired of the man's life a time or two, but now he'd pronounced Darhour out of danger. She'd tried to get a message to the princess, but had found no way of doing so that wouldn't also alert Argblutal to Darhour's whereabouts.

Sighing, she looked out the window. She was worried about the princess, and she was worried about her Devyn. It had been such a pretty dream to think that it might be possible to marry him, but of course, she should have known better than to believe in dreams. Now she only prayed that both the princess and Devyn survived. *Damn that horned demon who disguises himself as a man!* Aislinn indulged herself in a pleasant fantasy about painting the duke's portrait. She would approach him with her paintbrush in hand on the pretext of taking his measurements. Then when he least expected it, she would jam her brush through his eye socket and into his brain. She'd laugh as he died at her feet. Laying her head down on the windowsill, her fantasy became one with her dreams in which she killed Argblutal in all sorts of interesting and painful ways.

CHAPTER 36

Robrek hadn't cried when he and Leigh had buried Myst, and he wouldn't cry now. He promised himself he wouldn't grieve until he felt Duke Argblutal's hot blood on his hands. After eating a meager breakfast of what little he had left, he turned to the horse that spoke like Holy Writ. "I've learned to shield well enough. You will now help me master my power."

:Thou art too angry. Thou hatest too much.:

"I don't care how angry I am. You said you knew what was blocking me. What is it?"

:Thou dost not understand. It is thy hatred and thy anger that blocketh thee. To own thy full power, thou must forgive all those that hath wronged thee. The duke, the priest, thy father, thy brother, all.:

The horse's words hit him like a physical blow. Clutching at his stomach, he fell to his knees. "No! They've taken everything from me—my childhood, my home, my teacher, my chance to start over again. They've tried to take my life. I will not forgive them! I will have my revenge!"

:Power and anger such as thine should never be combined. I will not help thee own thy power until thou losest thine anger. If thou keepest both, thou wouldst become the demon thou once believed thyself to be.:

"I don't care! Teach me how to kill the duke!" The horse gave no response. "Fine! I don't need you." Robrek jumped to his feet, grabbed the gold sword, and vaulted onto Wild Thing's back.

:Do not go! Thou wilst regret acting rashly!:

Robrek urged Wild Thing into a gallop, trying to flee from the horse's impossible demands. How dare Holy Writ tell him to forgive!

He'd kill them all. Wanting to hurt someone, anyone, he prayed for an attack. As he rode through the open fields behind his father's farm, he heard a shout and turned to see six men on horses chasing him. Ahead he saw another trying to head him off. He looked back at those following and sent terror into the minds of their horses, causing them to rear and bolt. Two riders fell from the saddles, and the others clung on desperately as the horses fled in the opposite direction. He had time to dispatch the one in front before the others could reach him. Letting out a rage-filled battle cry, Robrek lifted his sword to meet the oncoming man's. Their swords clashed with a fury that sent shockwaves up his arm, but he recovered faster than the other man. He brought his sword around before the other man could block, cutting through leather armor and into the man's side. The man fell from his horse, his sword flying from his hand.

Robrek jumped off Wild Thing. He lifted his sword to cleave the man's head in two. Before he could strike, Robrek saw blood seeping from the man's wound. *Holy Sulis, what in the seven hells have I done? He isn't the one responsible.* He looked back at the other men, who were closing in on him. A packet of provisions was hanging from the wounded man's saddle. Since he had hardly any food, he grabbed it as he jumped back onto Wild Thing and sped off.

* * *

Run, Robbie, run! Angus shouted silently as the two men closed on his son. *Why have you come here of all places? When I set the trap, I never expected you to fall into it.* One of the men mounted the wounded man's horse and took off after his son, but the boy's Horsetad left him far behind. *Just what is he? How can he fight like that? Where did he get the sword?*

Angus strode toward the count's men; the uninjured one was leaning over his fallen comrade.

"Get a healer at once," the unwounded man snapped.

"Don't know where I'd get one. Duke Argblutal killed the herb witch, and my son isn't likely to come back to offer his services. There is the priest, but Father Gildas is worse than useless."

"Send for the Sulis-cursed priest," the man ordered. But the man on the ground gasped and went still. His companion rounded on Angus. "Damn your son to the seven hells! You will answer to His Lordship."

* * *

Robrek didn't want to go back to the demon cursed horses, but he had nowhere else to go. *It's Holy Writ's fault! She had no right to demand the impossible of me!* As he neared the forest stable, he raised his shields against the horses.

He wiped Wild Thing down. Then he opened the sack he'd stolen. He found traveler's bread, dried meat, and a flask of ale. Opening the flask, he took a long draught. Whatever it contained was far stronger than the ale at the inn; he drank less than half of it before he collapsed sobbing into the dirt. *I've failed you, Myst. Bards will make me the villain of their tales.* He rolled over and passed out on the ground.

* * *

Samantha knelt at the altar on the top of Gloine Torr. It had been days since she'd sent Darhour to rescue Robbie, and she was torn between praying for their lives and praying for their deaths. If either of them were alive, she knew they'd be suffering, but she couldn't bear to imagine them dead. *Oh, Holy Mother, how can I go on? Without Darhour, will I even survive?*

Hearing a noise behind her, she turned to see Father Hafghan enter the shrine. Bearach moved between her and the priest.

"You look troubled, Your Highness," Father Hafghan said.

Samantha hastily wiped her eyes. "I'm merely overcome by the spirit of the shrine."

Father Hafghan bowed his head. "You have every reason not to trust me. Duke Argblutal offered to support my ordination to the High Priesthood if I'd use my position as a spiritual counselor to spy on you."

Bearach hissed, but the princess silenced him with a look. "Why tell me this?" she asked.

"Your Highness, I'm an ambitious man and a cowardly one, but that day on the steps of The Temple of the Mother's Love you showed me a queen worth serving."

Brice burst in. "Your Highness, it's the captain and Conroy. They're both coming up the steps."

"They're alive?" The princess jumped to her feet and ran to the top of the stairs. Near the ledge that marked two-thirds of the distance up the mountain, Darhour, Conroy, and a young girl toiled upward. Both her men moved stiffly, but they were both very much alive. When they reached the top, Samantha abandoned all royal dignity and threw her arms around first Darhour and then Conroy. She didn't know whether to laugh or cry, so she did both at once. "Where have you two been?"

Darhour swayed on his feet, and Conroy's face was lined with pain and exhaustion. "You're hurt! Come in and sit down." She led them into the refectory and ordered food and drink brought to them. "What happened to you two? How are you together?"

"By chance, Your Highness," Darhour said. "We met at the bottom of the stairs."

"And . . .?" Samantha couldn't bring herself to ask about Robbie.

Darhour understood her anyway. "Your Highness, Argblutal never had the peasant boy." Darhour explained what had happened and who he'd found instead of the amihealer.

"Robbie's uncle? Did he know where Robbie was?"

"We didn't have time to talk." He told of his escape over the roofs and through Lady Aislinn's window. Though the princess felt badly for any man within the duke's custody, she'd gladly trade the life of the stranger for Darhour or Robbie.

Conroy cleared his throat. "Your Highness," he said. "My mission proved more difficult than we anticipated. All the priestesses have either been captured or gone into hiding." He explained the problems he'd encountered. "Korth is in turmoil. Bandits are everywhere. I was attacked and would have died if not for the assistance of this young novice." He indicated the girl who wore a simple peasant dress and straight unbraided hair. "May I present Oriana?"

The girl bowed deeply. "Your Highness, I want to help get rid of the men who persecute my people." Her voice trembled slightly.

The princess smiled to alleviate Oriana's nervousness and hide her own disappointment. "You are most welcome." Although she had doubts about the usefulness of the child, she couldn't help feeling more hopeful now that two of the men she'd feared dead had returned and Robbie was safe. Or at least she forced herself to believe he was.

* * *

When Robrek awoke, Wild Thing was licking his face. He had no idea how long he'd been unconscious, but the fierce ache tearing his insides apart felt every bit as intense. He could feel the horses pressing against his shields. Ignoring them, he felt around for the flask of ale. He found it, but it had been knocked over and was now empty. He swore viciously and dripped the few drops that remained into his mouth. Sitting up increased the pounding in his head. Reeking of ale, vomit, and urine, Robrek was repulsed by his own filth; he went down to the stream to bathe.

Afterward, he ate the provisions he'd taken from the man's horse, but they left him still hungry. *Some legend, Myst. I don't even know how I'm going to keep myself fed.* Darkness was falling, so he decided to check the spot his father had left supplies for him in the past. Perhaps there was something he'd missed.

Listening carefully for danger, Robrek crept through the gathering darkness. When he reached the spot, he found a large and fresh cache of supplies.

At the forest stable, he unpacked them. In addition to flour, dried meat and fruit, *bhat* beans, and grain for the horses, he found an apricot tart.

Robrek ate the tart. Its sticky sweetness increased his anger. Lowering his shields, he glared at Holy Writ. "Am I supposed to forgive him because he gave me a tart? Do you know how many times he ate the last one on the plate, leaving none for me? Do you know how many times he beat my back raw?" Robrek began pacing. "He could never even call me by my name. It was always, 'Boy, do this.' 'Boy, do that.' 'Boy, why are you so damned stupid?' 'Boy, how could I have fathered such a weak, worthless runt?' An apricot tart and a little food are supposed to make that all right?"

:*Abusing a child is never alright. It angereth the goddess.*:

Without warning, Robrek felt himself hit as if by a powerful wind of darkness. He was knocked to his knees, and suddenly he was no longer himself. He was Angus Camlinstamm, and he'd been cursed with the stupidest child ever to be born.

"How could you be such an idiot? Don't you know that the priest wants you dead?" he yelled at his son. Green eyes like Donella's looked up at him from underneath curly, black hair. "I'll teach you a lesson you'll never forget."

He grabbed the boy, tore his shirt off, threw him over the dining room table, and yelled at Boyden to hold him still.

"Please, father, I'm sorry," the boy begged.

Angus hardly heard the boy's cries. Instead, he saw skin the color of creamy bhat as Donella's had been. The boy screamed as he brought the strap down. But he needed to learn. So he hit him again and again, bringing the strap down harder and harder. The boy's hair, so like his mother's, lay across the table. Oh, Donella, why? How could I have traded you for him? He continued to beat the boy until his arm ached. When he stopped, the boy rolled into a ball on the floor, sobbing and trembling.

Robrek threw himself away from whatever Holy Writ had done to him. "I was five years old, damn him! He had no right to beat me like that!"

:He did not. Forgiveness doth not mean the other was right. Forgiveness isn't about the other, but thine own soul.:

Jumping to his feet, Robrek stabbed his finger toward the horse. "He should rot for what he did to me! I will never forgive him! Never!"

:Then thou wilst become like him.:

"I would never do something like that to a child!"

Again the dark wind hit him, knocking him to the ground. *He was in the stable paddock. His sword was wet with blood, and there were piles of corpses surrounding him. A man approached, and he stabbed quickly. Behind him he heard a small noise. He turned, cutting Tegan nearly in half. The child that had reminded him so much of himself dropped at his feet, and he turned to kill another. He crushed the child's hand with his boot.*

"Stop it!" he screamed, wrenching his eyes open. "That wasn't real!"

:It could be.: The body of the slain boy appeared in front of him again. He closed his eyes, but the image still burned in his memory, and again he saw his sword plunging through Milady's mouth. *:How art thou different from thy father?:*

He backed away from the horse. "I don't even remember killing the child; I didn't understand what I was doing."

:And didst thy father understand what he wast doing to thee?:

The dark wind came again. *He heard his beloved Donella screaming from their bedroom. Although she'd been screaming for nearly two days, the baby still wouldn't come. It was all his fault. The herb witch had warned him about having another child. Please, Sulis, please. Let her live. The screaming stopped, and he heard a weak cry. He ran into the bedroom. Donella was lying with her eyes closed, her dark skin nearly as white as a Korthlundian's. The entire bed was* covered in blood. "Do something!" he bellowed at the herb witch, who was wrapping some small hideous thing in a blanket.

He was kneeling by a freshly dug grave as they lowered the body of his beautiful Donella into the cold earth. He'd had to purchase a spot of land just outside the graveyard because the priest wouldn't allow her to be buried on consecrated ground. Would those gods of hers take her? He sobbed as the shovels of earth began to fall onto her sweet body. *She can't be dead. It's all my fault. She can't be dead.*

"No!" Robrek shouted. "It wasn't me that got her pregnant! He had no right to blame me for her death. He deserves my hatred."

:It is not about what he deserveth, but what thou deservest. Sin provideth its own punishment. He chose to indulge his grief and his rage until he hath choked out all that could have been good in his life. He is an empty man when his life could have been full of the joy of his sons. Dost thou desire such emptiness for thyself?:

"I desire nothing but revenge." Robrek's hand itched for a sword so that he could strike off the horse's head..

As always, the horse seemed to know what he was thinking. *:Dost thou believe thou wilst feel any better if thou dost?:*

"Yes, I do!" Robrek ran to the stable and grabbed a sword. As he turned around, he found himself faced with illusions of his father, his brother, Duke Argblutal, and Father Gildas. He rushed his father and, with a single stroke, struck off his head. He turned and did the same to Boyden, Argblutal, and Gildas. As he turned back, he found his father whole and alive. Again and again he killed the four men, and again and again they rose. He slashed and stabbed until he dropped with exhaustion.

"Why won't you leave me alone?" he sobbed. "I never asked you to come! I never wanted any of this!" He gestured wildly at the three horses, and Holy Writ nodded. At that very instant, a profound silence descended into the clearing. He looked around frantically, but he soon realized the silence had nothing to do with the lack of sound. The wind was still rustling through the treetops, and the birds were singing every bit as loudly as they had a moment ago. He could still hear the stream rolling over the rocks. Holy Writ had done as he asked. He could still see the horses, but he couldn't feel them any longer. They'd gone and left this emptiness behind.

Wild Thing edged closer and nudged him with her nose. *:Wild Thing scared. What wrong?:*

"Nothing's wrong, girl. It's just you and me, like it always should have been." Struggling desperately to ignore the emptiness, Robrek rubbed the Horsetad's nose and set about cooking himself something to eat. Every few moments he looked over his shoulder to make sure the horses were still there. Despite how much he fought them, if they left, they'd take half his soul with them. But since what Holy Writ demanded was impossible, he'd have to live with half a soul.

Darkness fell as he finished eating, and with the darkness, the emptiness became unbearable. *I don't need them.* Knowing this was a lie, he wrapped himself up in it and fell asleep.

Dressed in clothes of deepest black, he stood on a dais. Duke Argblutal knelt at his feet; the duke's supporters, servants, and guards knelt behind him. Argblutal begged for mercy. But mercy was dead inside Robrek. Grabbing the duke by the hair, he pulled him to his feet. He used his magic to turn his hands into claws, and with a smile of triumph, he tore deep into the duke's chest and ripped out his still beating heart. The duke screamed and dropped at his feet. Robrek laughed, but the duke's death had done nothing to assuage his grief or his rage. So he grabbed the hair of the first of the duke's men and tore out that man's heart as well. Still, he felt no relief. One by one he ripped out the hearts of every one of the duke's men. But it wasn't enough. He ordered Father Gildas brought before him, and he tied the priest to the stake and set him on fire. Reveled in the priest's shrieks of agony, he danced around the pyre, but when the priest had been reduced to ashes, he felt no better. He had the bonfire built higher and threw in all of those who had testified against him and all of those who had joined the mob that would have killed him. Their cries of pain were music to his ears. But when they had all been quieted by death, he felt no peace. He struck out with his magic at all that came within his reach. He used his power to cause the utmost suffering and pain, as he had once used it to heal. Both the guilty and the innocent suffered and died at his hands. None could stop him because he was the most powerful sorcerer the land had ever known. But the more he killed, the more his emptiness grew. until it became a chasm so vast that not even the deaths of every living soul in the joined kingdoms would fill it.

He awoke, sick to the depths of his soul. *I am a monster.* He tried to tell himself that it had been just a dream, but he knew Holy Writ was right about him. If he lived, he'd be the villain of every bard's tale.

He went to the stable and got the gold sword. Kneeling in the paddock, he placed the point at his breast and closed his eyes.

:Stop!: Three voices shouted in unison, and the presence of the three horses returned. *:This thou canst not do.:*

:No hurt.: Wild Thing wailed.

"I have to," he said. "I won't be like them."

:Then forgive them, but do not destroy thyself.:

Robrek laughed savagely. "Why do you care? Because it's not my 'destiny'? I never wanted a destiny." His hand slipped, and he felt a sharp prick in his chest. Bright blood stained his shirt. He dropped the sword and fell to the ground, clutching the small wound.

:Thou dost not have to feel this pain. Release thy hatred. Forgive.:

"I can't! They deserve to suffer for what they've done!"

:They are suffering. But thou needst no longer punish thyself for what they hath done.:

The dark wind hit him. This time he was his brother. *He was ten years old and a crowd of five boys near his own age surrounded him. "I say he has demon blood, too," one of them said.*

"I do not," he protested.

"His mother was a demon witch," another jeered.

"No, she wasn't."

A third laughed. "Just look at your little brother. Father Gildas won't even let him in the school."

"I don't care. My skin is as white as yours." He shoved his white arm toward them.

"White on the outside, but black underneath," another said.

"Liar!" he shouted at the boy who voiced his deepest fear. Striking out with all his might, he knocked the boy to the ground, but there were five of them. They ganged up on him.

When they stopped beating him, he dragged himself home, and a servant fussed over him. Robbie came into the room and peered up at him. It was the worm's fault this had happened. If it weren't for him, nobody would say things like that . . .

He sat in his room at the inn, counting his coins. What did he care if no one in the village would talk to him? He didn't need them. He had everything he needed right here. He clinked the coins together.

But Robrek felt the emptiness his brother refused to acknowledge—a chasm within Boyden he attempted to fill with greater cruelty, but doing so only widened the chasm. Not wanting to feel Boyden's despair, Robrek struggled to separate himself from his brother, but Holy Writ refused to release her hold on him; instead he plunged once more into the dark wind. He was his father again. *He stood at the back of the room near the pier with the other young men, hooting and making crude gestures at the new whores brought from abroad. "And the next, from the barbarous land of Mahngbhayo," the auctioneer called, as a small, dark-skinned girl was led into the room. He went silent as her green eyes bore into his soul, stirring something in him he'd never felt before—something far stronger than lust. "She doesn't speak a word of the language, but what does that matter with assets like this?" The man grabbed her breast. She slapped his hand away and glared at him with defiance and pride. "A spirited one! She may need some taming, but isn't that half the fun?"*

The girl drew herself up as if she were a queen looking down upon her subjects. Angus wasn't fooled—he saw her lower lip tremble.

"Come on, sweety pie! Show us what you got!" the young man beside Angus called out, and Angus threw the other man against the wall. "Show some respect," he hissed, though Angus had said something similar to the last whore.

He whirled back to the auctioneer and named a price. He glared around the room, daring someone to top it. No one did. He handed the auctioneer every dram he'd intended to use for new stock for his farm. He draped his own coat around the woman to hide her near nakedness from the prying eyes of other men . . .

He saw his sweet elfin girl lying on their bed with his tiny son sucking at her breast. "He's a strong one, like his father." Donella smiled.

His heart bursting with love and joy, he sat beside her. He was a father, and the most perfect woman in all of Sulis's creation was the mother of his child. "He's perfect," he whispered, and gently stroked the soft fuzz on his son's head. He promised himself he wouldn't be like his own father. He'd be gentle and kind and earn his son's respect and love.

"What shall we name him?" Donella asked as she raised the infant to her shoulder and gently patted his back.

"What do you think of Boyden?" he asked.

"Boyden?" She wrinkled up her brow in the way that he'd always found alluring. "Boyden is a fine name for a barbarian without an ounce of color in his skin."

He leaned in closer and kissed her deeply. "Mother of barbarians."

She laughed, and the baby let out a sigh of contentment. He had never imagined such happiness . . .

He heard the small, weak cry coming from the other room. It wouldn't stop. The wet nurse wouldn't be there for an hour. He stomped into the room to pick up the baby himself. It was incredibly small, much smaller than his brother had been. The tears of its hunger fell from emerald green eyes. He ran from the house, leaving the crying infant behind . . .

He sat on the bed at the inn and handed over the coin. The woman dropped her dress and joined him. Closing his eyes, he took her in his arms and tried to pretend she was Donella. But it didn't work. When he'd shared Donella's bed, he'd felt complete. Now, releasing his manhood into the whore's body, he felt emptier than ever.

When he reached home, he found Robbie drawing pictures in the dirt with a stick instead of doing his chores.

"Boy!" he bellowed.

The ten-year-old boy looked at him with terror. "Please, sir, I didn't mean . . ."

He refused to listen to whatever fool excuse the boy had this time. Grabbing the strap next to the door, he threw the boy over the dining room table. He beat the boy viciously, but he got no more relief from the anguish than he'd gotten from the body of the whore.

He stopped and ordered the boy to his room. He couldn't stand the sight of the curly black hair or the rich, dark skin . . .

He watched as his seventeen-year old son mounted his Horsetad and rode away. He'll be back, he told himself. He can't survive without me . . .

He looked at the remnant of the scaffold on which they'd meant to burn his son. Robbie had escaped the flames, but he'd lost both his sons this day: no kin murderer would live under his roof. Where had he gone so wrong? He remembered when he'd watched Boyden suck at Donella's breast. He remembered the promises he'd made to himself. He'd broken them all. His sons had no more respect or love for him than he'd had for his own father. He went to the inn, intent on giving coin to the whore, knowing that doing so would do nothing to fill the aching void inside him.

"No! I can't stand it any more!" Robrek cried. "Why wasn't I the father I promised myself I'd be? Why did I let Donella's death turn me against my own son?"

More visions followed.

Father Gildas's healing continued to fail while the power of those he condemned grew, fueling his fears for his reputation and influence over the people. Duke Argblutal's obsession with kingship, which had twisted his life so that hatred and anger were the only emotions left to him. Unable to tolerate the pain and emptiness, the guilt and despair any longer, Robrek tore himself loose from the visions. He sobbed for the pain those he hated had caused themselves.

:Dost thou see? They have paid the price for their sins. Thou canst hold to thy pain and become like them. Or thou canst release it and be free.:

"Tell me what to do. I just . . . want it to be gone."

:Forgive. Release thy hatred into the hands of the goddess. The Holy Mother can bear all of our griefs.:

"How?" he asked, but then he felt it—the goddess's open arms ready to enfold all of his pain into herself. Suddenly, he understood. Sin, and the pain it brought, was its own punishment. There was no need for him to make his enemies suffer; their own sins would see to that. He could allow those sins against him to turn him into a monster, or he could forgive them and save his own soul. It was a choice between emptiness and joy, between sorrow and love, between destruction and fulfillment.

In other words, it was no choice at all.

"Take it please! I don't want it any more!" Thrusting himself into the goddess's arms, he allowed her to heal his wounds and purge the anger from his soul. As soon as the last vestige of his anger and hatred left, his power poured forth within him. Energy filled his body with exquisite pleasure; every ounce of his flesh was flooded with joy. He laughed with sheer delight and was sure he was glowing with light.

Sensations poured in from all sides. Ronan's simple pleasure while he sunned himself. The hawk's fierce triumph as it took the pigeon, and the pigeon's terror and pain. The rabbit's delight in the new patch of cabbage leaves, and the mother's despair over her wayward child. The bird's bliss as it sang to its mate, and the farmer's joy as his grain pushed its way toward the sun. It was too much, far too much. He collapsed onto the ground and covered his head, but there was no escape. He'd go mad.

Over the whirlwind of sensation, he heard Holy Writ's command. *:Shield!:*

He reached through the chaos for the knowledge of how to shield, grasped it, and snapped his shields into place. The entire world went silent in an instant. Rolling over, he smiled at the sky. He felt spent and abused, but also clean and pure. Although his head ached, he was happier than he'd ever imagined possible. He wanted to dance and sing. He lowered his shields slightly to allow the horses in and felt their pleasure and pride in his accomplishment.

:Thou hast done well. Thou art worthy of thy destiny.:

:I knew you had it in you, human child. Oh, how you will be able to move now.:

:A good beginning.:

Robrek threw back his head and laughed. He hadn't realized Brazen was capable of humor.

CHAPTER 37

Count Nola smiled at Boyden. "You've done well. Without your assistance, these miserable peasants would have tried to cheat me. You've made yourself a lot of enemies."

Boyden nodded. "And I have made many friends as well, Milord." Boyden picked up the stack of coins the count had paid him. "And these friends can't turn on me."

Count Nola patted him on the shoulder. "You'll have as many friends as you wish, provided you continue to serve me well. I must return to the capital for Mabon and the wedding of the heir. I'll leave you in charge here in the Valley in my absence with a dozen of my men for your protection and for the keeping of order. Perform this task with the zeal you've demonstrated so far, and more important tasks will be forthcoming. And if you can deliver your brother to me, you may name your reward."

Boyden bowed. "I'm honored by your faith in me. I won't disappoint you."

* * *

Robrek smiled as he mended a sparrow's wing. He'd felt its panic just after sunrise. Now that his anger no longer interfered, the full power of his healing gift flowered within him, and the bird sat calmly in his hands as he rewove the bone. He was surprised how simple it was. When he finished, he set the bird on a safe perch in the stable to rest and regain its strength.

:Thou hast learned all that I can teach about healing. Now thou must learn to make others see what thou wantest them to see.:

Robrek turned toward Holy Writ. "What do you mean?"

:Thou knowst how thou soothed that sparrow?:

"Yes, I let it know I meant it no harm."

:Thou canst send images in the same manner, but it is terribly costly. The image must be sent into each mind individually, and even thine energy wilst not long sustain such effort.:

"You mean images like the knights I fight and my dancing partners?"

Holy Writ nodded. *:Sit and I will show thee.:*

Robrek obeyed, and like everything to do with his magic now, the lesson was a simple one. Picturing a gray rabbit under the trees, he asked Wild Thing, "Do you see anything by the trees, my girl?"

:Fat rabbit. Not dangerous. Just stupid.:

He pictured a crow on the tree branch above it and again asked the mare. *:Ugly black bird. Not pretty, like Wild Thing.:* Robrek laughed.

Suddenly, he swayed and felt slightly lightheaded.

:It wilt eventually cost thee less, but thy power restest most strongly in the body, not the mind. Thy touch holdest the power of life or death. Guard it carefully.:

"But what will I do with it?"

As usual, the horses gave no answer.

* * *

Leigh approached his mother's parlor reluctantly. He'd been home for a week, and this was the first time she'd sent for him. But as he'd expected, he'd been told she was on the verge of death because of him.

When he was admitted to the parlor, he found Father Mannix, his mother's priest, instead of his mother. The priest was sitting in his mother's chair and drinking a goblet of his mother's finest brandy. He wore robes of silk, tooled with skilled embroidery of gold stars and green vines. Leigh recognized his mother's style. Mannix scowled. "I see you still wear the robes of the office for which you've been disqualified."

Leigh didn't sit. "Father Gildas defrocked and excommunicated me because I stopped him from burning an innocent man. I don't consider his decision valid."

The priest sat down his brandy. "You question the servants of Sulis? Leigh, do you realize your impiety is killing your mother? If you care about her welfare, you will return to this Father Gildas immediately and perform whatever penance he prescribes."

"I care about my mother, but I care more for the goddess. I don't intend to be rude, but I see no purpose in prolonging this conversation. Good day, Father." Leigh left.

As he headed down the hallway, he heard his father laughing uproariously. "Leigh, come here," Fergal called from his office. "I never thought you had it in you, boy."

Reluctantly, Leigh entered. Fergal was putting away the device he used to listen in on his wife's private conversations. It was some piece of Saloynan magic Leigh had never bothered to understand.

"So, you're going to let your mother die for your impiety?" Fergal tried to feign a stern look, but his eyes were twinkling. "You disdain my business, but my impiety hasn't killed your mother yet. Join me in it. Why not add another sin to those you've already committed?"

Leigh clenched his fists. "You know the answer. I'm sorry I had to request refuge. As soon as I can be sure Argblutal isn't looking for me, I'll leave."

"And where will you go?"

"I plan to start a clinic among the poor of Murtaghan, so I can heal them in both body and spirit."

Fergal shook his head. "A fool still, I see. But if you want to starve in the slums, who am I to stop you? Your mother's hysteria over it will be endlessly amusing." Abruptly, Fergal sat up straighter in his chair. "Say, since you're in so tight with the goddess and all, why don't you enter this contest?"

"Contest?"

"You haven't heard? The man who rides up Gloine Torr can claim the princess in marriage. Surely the goddess would choose a pious young man like yourself." Fergal burst into gales of laughter.

But to Leigh, his father's words were a revelation. *I may be the sparrow, but Robrek is the eagle! If any horse could climb Gloine Torr, it's his.* "Father, will you lend me a horse? There is something I need to do."

* * *

Wanting to carve a figure of the princess Robrek sat whittling a stick, but the thing he held didn't look anything like a woman, much less like Milady. Tomorrow was Mabon, and the first day of the contest to win the princess's hand. He tried not to mind that she would soon marry someone else.

He heard a horse approaching and reached for his staff. "Leigh!" he called out as the young man entered the clearing. Smiling, the novice dismounted. Robrek pounded his friend on the shoulder. "What are you doing back?"

"The question is, what are you doing here? The contest starts tomorrow!"

Robrek laughed. "Leigh, this isn't some bard's tale in which peasant boys become kings."

Leigh gestured toward the paddock where Brazen, Fancy Man, and Holy Writ stood. "If this isn't some bard's tale, what in Sulis's name are they? Robrek, the princess needs you! Korthlundia needs you! Who, other than you, could climb Gloine Torr and save her from Duke Argblutal?"

Robrek's hands trembled. "Leigh, you can't know how much I want her, but—"

:I say we get you that pretty mare,: Fancy Man chimed in. :A stallion like you wasn't meant to live celibate.:

Robrek walked to the paddock fence. "Can you three climb Gloine Torr?"

:It would be a most difficult task,: Brazen said.

:Don't listen to the old nag. She's gone without for so long herself she doesn't want to see you get some.:

:Thou dost wrong to promise what thou canst not be sure of,: Holy Writ scolded. :Gloine Torr wast not meant to be climbed.:

"So Leigh is wrong? I shouldn't try."

:Of course you should, human child. These two will preach gloom and doom, but if any horses can climb that mountain, it's us.:

"But what if . . ." Robrek broke off and looked away.

:Ah, human child, can't you see how that mare pants for you? I'm sure when she sees the moves I've taught you, she won't be able to keep her hands off you.:

Leigh came up beside him. "What do they say?" he asked.

Robrek didn't answer. He did have skills that no one else in the joined kingdoms had. And Brazen, Fancy Man, and Holy Writ were something straight out of a bard's tale. He thought of the princess's beauty in the moonlight at Myst's cottage. Most importantly, he loved her, and he couldn't bear the thought of a monster like Argblutal touching her. "I have to try to help her. If she doesn't want me, I can always leave once she's safe."

Leigh smiled broadly. "She couldn't help but want an eagle. I'll help you pack."

With Leigh's help, it wasn't long before Wild Thing and the three magical horses were saddled and loaded with the armor and other items they'd brought with them. Robrek mounted Wild Thing, and he and Leigh rode toward the capital. They'd make it about nightfall.

For the first couple of hours, neither said much. Since no-one on the road reacted to them, Robrek assumed the horses were hiding their true nature. Contemplating the absurdity of what he was about to do, his mind drifted to the day he learned Milady's identity and heard about the contest. It was also the day he'd met the man who'd pretended to be his uncle. Certainly, Slathek had paid dearly for his deception. "Before, you tried to tell me what the foreign merchant said at Myst's cottage, but I wouldn't listen. You said he'd led Argblutal to Myst."

"Argblutal followed him. He didn't do it on purpose. He said he wanted to acquire you because you could make him rich." Leigh told him everything Slathek had said.

"An investment to him? But that doesn't make any sense. He nearly died because of me at the inn when he could have run . . . Holy Sulis!"

"What?"

Robrek doubled over, sick to his stomach. "He lied to the duke in order to protect me! Sulis curse me, I've left him to be tortured when all he wanted was to save my life!"

"Robrek, there's nothing you could have done."

"There is now."

:Thy uncle's fate is not within thy power to change.: Holy Writ said.

He cursed the horses. "How could you let me believe he wasn't my uncle when you knew better! I'm not a child for you to be making my decisions for me."

:Thy uncle is being kept at the duke's private residence guarded by dozens of men. He hath willingly sacrificed himself for thy protection. If thou givest thyself into the hands of the duke, thou makest his sacrifice a thing of naught.:

Reining Wild Thing in, Robrek jumped down to face the horses. "I don't know what you are or why you came here, but I've done everything you wanted me to and asked nothing in return. Now I'm asking. With your help, I can do this."

Shaking her head, Holy Writ refused to meet his eyes. *:I will not help thee destroy thyself.:*

:Your destiny is not to free your uncle.: Brazen stamped her front hoof.

Fancy Man looked from Robrek to the other two. *:He's gotten powerful. There's a chance it might work.:* Robrek wanted to kiss the stallion.

Holy Writ's head jerked up. *:Thou canst not agree to help him in such recklessness. Gloine Torr should be our only focus.:*

"Help me, Fancy Man." Robrek put his hand on the stallion's neck. "I'm going to try with or without you, but I stand a much better chance of living to show the princess my moves if I don't do it alone."

Fancy Man nuzzled Robrek's chest. *:Ah, human child, they will give me grief for a thousand years, but I'll go with you.:*

Robrek threw his arms around the stallion's neck. "Thank you. You won't regret this."

:I already do, human child. I already do.:

* * *

Slathek groaned as the keys jingled in his lock. His arm had never been properly set, and it hurt like all seven of the hells the barbarians spoke of. When the door opened, Duke Argblutal smiled the particular smile Slathek had learned to associate with intense pain. "My sources say you've been lying. Your injuries are no hindrance to your power. Tonight you will perform the sacrifice." The duke's guards pushed a boy of about twelve into the cell. "I found the boy in the stables, cooing over Her Highness's horse. It seems only fitting the princess's fate should be sealed by a friend." The boy let out a small squeak of terror.

"You might as well kill me now," Slathek hissed. "I won't do it."

"We both know that you will. The sacrifice must be performed at the darkest hour of the night. I will fetch the two of you a few hours early. Spend the intervening time deciding how much pain you can endure before you inevitably do as I ask."

As the duke left them in complete darkness, the boy kneeled down beside him. "Master Robbie, are you all right? I thought Captain Darhour rescued you."

Slathek groaned. "I don't believe I've ever been less all right in my life, nor am I my nephew. My name is Slathek. Are you a friend of the princess's?"

"Yes, sir. My name's Vaughan. But what did the duke mean about a sacrifice?"

"I guess you deserve the truth." He told him all about the duke's use of blood magic to control the mind of the king. "He needs one more child sacrificed, and he wants me to do it."

"You're going to kill me?" The boy shrank away.

"Do I look like a barbarian to you?" Slathek objected. When Vaughan didn't answer, Slathek thought the answer might well be yes. *Is the duke right? Will I eventually give in to stop the pain? Oh, Holy Father and Mother, let me die first.* "Vaughan, you should have a full life ahead of you. I wish there was something I could do to save you, but I'm helpless to save even myself. I have very little magic, but I'm going to try to stop my own heart. If you do get out of this alive, don't tell my nephew how I died."

* * *

When Robrek emerged from the Setanta forest, it seemed every man in the joined kingdoms—noble and peasant alike, as well as those from all nearby lands—was assembled at the base of Gloine Torr.

Robrek set up a camp in the middle of a grove of trees, some distance from the pyramid. Brazen assured him she could hide this place as she'd hidden the forest stable. He dismounted and, with Leigh's help, unloaded the horses.

:Thou shouldst abandon thy plan. Save thy energy for the morrow.:

Ignoring her, he unsaddled Brazen and turned to Wild Thing. Wild Thing looked at him mournfully. *:Wild Thing help. No leave behind.:*

Wild Thing had been his best friend for so long he didn't feel right about not taking her. If they needed a quick escape, two horses were better than one.

:Sure, bring her.: Fancy Man winked. *:Having the sweet thing along will help pass the time. But disguise her stars though. The less I have to hide the better.:*

Taking mud from the streambed, Robrek rubbed it over the stars on the Horsetad's forehead and chest.

"Are you sure you should do this?" Leigh asked. "If you fail, what will become of the princess?"

"I won't fail." Robrek swung into the saddle and pulled up the hood of his cloak to cover his dark hair.

As Robrek passed through the gates of Murtaghan and moved along the city streets, Fancy Man didn't hide them so much as send out the suggestion that they were of no particular interest. The city was in the midst of a wild celebration, so it wasn't difficult to get people to ignore them. Fancy Man led him past a row of large and imposing mansions. The duke's was obvious: it was surrounded by what seemed to be a regiment of armed men. "Holy Sulis!" Robrek swore. "How am I going to get in there?"

:*It won't be easy, human child.*: Fancy Man continued a short distance down the street, so they could discuss a plan. :*I can hide you until you get inside, but then you'll be on your own until you come out again. I can't do illusions without being able to see you. Perhaps my sisters are right. Maybe we shouldn't try this.*:

Lowering his shields, Robrek sensed his uncle in terrible pain. "I can't abandon him."

One of the duke's soldiers came out of the mansion. He paused and talked to the men guarding the front gate. Keeping very still, Robrek could hear the conversation.

"Where are you off to, Egan?" one of the guards asked.

"There's a pretty young thing down at The Rusty Bucket waiting for me."

"Give her some for me," the guard said, making an obscene gesture. Egan laughed and continued out the gate and down the street in Robrek's direction. Disguising himself would be a lot less work if he was wearing the uniform of the duke's men. Asking Fancy Man to make sure the soldier didn't see him, he slid off Wild Thing's back. When the man came close, Robrek grabbed him and sent him into a deep sleep. He dragged him into the alley and stripped off his uniform and weapons. The uniform was, of course, too large for him, but he could use Fancy Man's trick of making sure no one looked too closely. He dressed himself and pulled on the guard's helm, tucking his hair out of sight. Robrek stared at the guard's face and memorized its details. Fancy Man did the same.

:*Are you sure you don't want to reconsider?*:

Robrek ignored the horse's question and, in the stolen uniform, approached the gates of Argblutal's mansion.

"That was quick, Egan. Don't have a lot of stamina now, do you?" the guard laughed.

Robrek struggled to keep the nervousness out of his voice and imitate the much lower tones of the other man. "Ask her in the morning how long I can hold out. I forgot my purse."

"Likely story." The guard winked and allowed him to pass.

The guards filling the duke's grounds paid no attention to him as he strode up the walk. As he neared the door, he heard Fancy Man. *:May Sulis guide you, human child.:*

Concentrating on maintaining Egan's appearance, Robrek opened the door. Two more of Argblutal's men stood just inside, one wearing the uniform of an officer. Robrek projected the image of Egan into their minds and saluted.

"I thought you had leave, soldier," the officer addressed him.

"I do, sir," Robrek said. "I don't seem to have my purse. The last time I had it I was near the prisoner."

The officer waved him away impatiently. "Be on about it. The duke has important business with the prisoner tonight."

"I'll be quick, sir." Robrek saluted again. There were two hallways leading off the entrance hall. He concentrated on his uncle, but all that he could tell was that Slathek was somewhere below him. Praying it was the right direction, he chose the hallway on the left.

"Soldier," the officer called, and Robrek turned back. "I thought you said you left your purse with the prisoner. Is it in your quarters?"

"Er, no, sir. Habit, that's all." Robrek turned down the other hallway. The officer continued talking about "preparations."

Two more guards were stationed in front of a stairwell leading down. Continuing to project the image of Egan, he said, "I think I left my purse down there." With no more than a grunt, they let him pass. Robrek went down the stairs into a wine cellar. No one was there, so he momentarily dropped the illusion and leaned against the wall. He felt tired and slightly lightheaded, and he still needed to find his uncle and get the two of them out. Fancy Man was right: this may have been a really bad idea.

After Robrek steadied himself, he moved around a large wine cask and saw a door at the other side of the cellar. He pictured Egan's face and went through. Two guards were playing cards in the room.

"Is His Grace ready for the prisoners?" one of them asked, reaching for a ring of keys on the wall.

"Yes," Robrek answered. "We're to bring them upstairs."

As the guard turned to unlock the cell, Robrek felt a wave of dizziness. He stumbled into the second guard. The man's eyes went wide as he met Robrek's. Before the man could cry out, Robrek sent him into a deep sleep. He lunged for the first guard and sent him to sleep as well.

* * *

Vaughan heard the stranger's continued breathing with relief. *Please Sulis! Don't let me be trapped here with an angry ghost.* Suicide was a grave sin, and any who committed it were prevented from traveling Beyond the Far Mountain. After quite some time, the man uttered what had to be the worst curse ever in a language that had to have come from the seven hells.

"You'll have to do it," the man said. "I've been trying to kill myself, and it isn't working. Please, come over here and strangle me."

"No!" Vaughan squealed and backed as far away as the cell allowed.

"Didn't you understand what I told you? I'm a dead man already."

Vaughan hugged himself tightly and closed his eyes.

"Vaughan." The infidel tried to rise off of the floor, but fell back groaning. "Please, child," he begged. "I don't know if I have the strength to resist. I've never been very good with pain."

Slathek froze as he heard the key in the lock. The duke had come for him, and he was still very much alive. Since the child wouldn't kill him, he'd have to find a way to get the guards to do it. As soon as the door opened, he vaulted off the floor and charged headfirst into the guard. They crashed together onto the floor, and he pressed his good arm against the guard's neck. As he did so, he saw green eyes beneath the guard's helm. "Robrek?" he yelled, loosening his hold. "What in perdition are you doing here?"

"I've come to get you out of here," Robrek hissed. "Now be quiet, or you're going to bring the entire place down on us!"

Robrek's head reeled from smashing into the floor. A young boy looked out of the cell. "Master Robbie? Did Her Highness send you to rescue us?"

Wondering how he knew who he was, Robrek answered, "Not exactly, but I'll get you both out of here. Strip the guards quickly and put on their uniforms. We need to leave as quickly as possible."

The boy seemed to understand much more quickly than Slathek. He undressed one of the guards and put on his uniform. Slathek simply stared at him. "Robrek, you shouldn't have come. Forgot about me and run while there's still a chance." His uncle's arm hung limply at his side, clearly broken.

"I didn't break in here to leave you to die." Robrek stripped the other guard. When he was done, he brought the uniform to his uncle. "I can't spare the energy to heal your arm right now, but I can make it hurt less." He blocked the pain. By that time, the boy had dressed himself. Together they helped Slathek don the uniform. Robrek looked at his uncle and the boy in dismay. The child had had to roll up his shirt sleeves and pant legs, and still the uniform drowned him. Slathek was only a little larger, and he had the added problem of dark skin and hair. It'd be some trick to convince the guards on the way out that there was nothing unusual about the three of them.

As they stepped into the wine cellar and neared the base of the steps, they heard several voices coming from the top. "Duke Argblutal," the boy squealed.

"Robrek, this is madness," Slathek whispered. "Leave us, and save yourself."

"I'll get us out of this," he told them, praying it was true.

Robrek tried to calm his breathing as he came face to face with the man who'd killed Myst.

Argblutal was far harder to fool than his men had been. "I don't believe I've seen you three before."

"My name is Egan, Your Grace," Robrek answered. "These others are recently arrived. They were presented to you." He tried to project reassurance toward the duke.

Argblutal turned to the officer behind him. "Do you know these men?"

Robrek tired to convince the man that he did.

"Egan I know, Your Grace. The other two seem familiar, but I can't be sure."

"Until you can be sure, escort them to quarters and contain them." Argblutal nodded to two of the guards who accompanied him across the wine cellar. Once the duke saw the empty cell all would be lost, so when the duke had rounded the cask, he grabbed one of the guards and put him instantly to sleep. He turned as quickly as he could toward the other, but Slathek's sword was buried in the other man's back.

"Run," Robrek whispered, and the three of them headed up the stairwell.

From behind him, the duke cried out, "Stop! What have you done with my prisoners?"

Drawing his sword, Robrek, followed by the other two, burst into the corridor above, meeting a group of the duke's guards. Not pausing to think, Robrek slashed out with his sword in the manner Brazen had taught him. Before they even had a chance to draw their weapons, all three men lay on the ground. He'd gotten two of them, and unexpectedly, the boy had gotten the third. Robrek froze for a moment. *I've killed again. But what choice did I have?* Steps pounded on the stairs behind them, and more guards were coming from the front of the house.

The boy grabbed his arm. "The rear entrance! This way." He ran in the opposite direction. Robrek sent a mental command to Fancy Man and Wild Thing to meet them in back. He hoped they'd be able to find the way.

As an arrow whizzed by his shoulder, he saw the door up ahead.

"No!" Argblutal shouted. "Don't kill them, damn you! I need them alive!"

The door ahead opened, and two guards appeared. With perfect precision, Robrek struck out with his sword, catching one man across the throat and the other across the thigh; they both dropped. But when Robrek and his charges burst out the door, they found themselves facing a wall of the duke's men. Argblutal and his guards came through the door behind him. They were surrounded, and Robrek was so dizzy he could hardly see straight. *No, it can't end like this!*

Argblutal smiled when he met Robrek's eyes. "I've been searching the joined kingdoms for you. How thoughtful of you to come to me! Now, drop your weapons, and no one gets hurt."

A crash sounded behind them, and Robrek whirled to see an entire herd of horses stampeding through the duke's rear gates. "Look out!" someone called, and the duke's men scrambled out of the horses' way. Robrek, Slathek, and the boy didn't have time to move, but the horses parted and surrounded them.

:Get on, human child, now! I can't keep this up for long.:

The herd was an illusion. Only Wild Thing and Fancy Man stood there. "Quick! Up!" The child was quick-witted and jumped instantly into Fancy Man's saddle. Robrek struggled onto Wild Thing and pulled Slathek up in front of him. His uncle screamed. Robrek had grabbed him by the broken arm. As soon as they were mounted, the two horses fled through the broken fence.

"After them!" Argblutal called, but neither Fancy Man nor Wild Thing were ordinary horses, and they quickly outdistanced pursuit.

:Good rescue,: Wild Thing beamed. *:Need Wild Thing.:* Robrek patted the mare. He could feel Fancy Man's weariness and hoped the horse could prevent them from being noticed until they reached safety. As soon as they were free of the city, they left the road. Fancy Man dropped all magic, trusting the darkness to hide them.

When they reached their camp, Robrek nearly fell off Wild Thing's back. As Leigh ran forward to help Slathek from the saddle, his mouth was hanging open. "You did it!"

The boy had dismounted and was staring at Robrek. "What are you?" he asked.

Robrek shook his head, collapsed to the ground, and lost consciousness.

Vaughan could see little in the darkness, but he watched the princess's man fall. He ran toward him, but the man dressed in novice's robes reached him first. "Is he okay?" Vaughan asked.

"Yes," the novice said. "Robrek has merely exhausted himself. A night's rest is all he needs." He covered the man the princess loved with a blanket. "Please, take care of the horses, will you?" The novice moved toward Slathek. "I'm not the healer your nephew is, but I will do what I can for you."

Vaughan started unsaddling the horses, beginning with the one Robrek had been riding. He finished caring for the first horse and moved on to the second. There were two more horses standing near. He gasped in surprise. In the firelight, he could tell that what he had taken for ordinary horses were nothing of the kind, but beasts of impossible colors—bronze, silver, and gold.

He crept back toward the men. "What are they?" he asked, pointing toward the three horses.

Slathek had just noticed the horses himself and was staring at them with his mouth hanging open. "By the Mother and the Father, they can be none other than the Horses of the West Wind." The man talked the way grownups did in the shrines to the goddess. "In Mahngbhayo, legends speak of them. A powerful sorcerer forged them from bronze, silver, and gold and brought them to life. But a rival sorcerer caused a great storm to come out of the west, which swept the horses into its depths. There they were doomed to be tossed until a worthy human with a vast need could call them forth again. I thought they were no more than a child's story." Slathek turned to the novice. "How did my nephew manage to call them forth?"

The novice shook his head. "When he wakes up, perhaps you should ask him."

CHAPTER 38

"You realize your daughter will marry me when this foolish contest is over?" Duke Argblutal said.

Solar merely smiled. Earlier he'd overheard the duke raging over the escape of some prisoners. Anything that upset the duke pleased the king.

Argblutal put his hands on either side of the king's chair and leaned over him. "How much of what I say do you understand?"

The king glared at Argblutal. *Sulis, if you truly exist, let the ancient ways work. Thwart this bastard and thrust him down to the seven hells.*

Count Morgan entered, looking quite pleased with himself. "The Saloynan has provided me with interesting news, Your Grace. Would you hear it in private?"

"The king is no threat." Solar clenched his fists at being dismissed as nothing more than a piece of furniture.

"According to my contact, the man who calls himself Darhour was once a groom in His Majesty's stables," Morgan said. "His name is Ahearn. He was near Queen Fenella's age and was reportedly her favorite groom. They went out riding alone frequently. There were rumors, and as close as I can determine, he disappeared seven months before the princess's birth."

The king felt his anger rising. *No! I told Connor to take care of him!*

The duke laughed and turned toward the king. "Not your daughter at all, but some peasant's bastard? That would be delicious." He turned back to Morgan. "Find me proof, and you can name your reward."

486

The king wanted to howl. The secret he'd thought safely hidden was in the hands of his bitterest enemy.

* * *

The odor of breakfast cooking woke Robrek when the sun was well above the horizon. His uncle's dark skin was flushed with fever, and Leigh was preparing a broth.

"Let me have it, Leigh," Robrek asked. Leigh handed it to him, and Robrek closed his eyes, infusing the brew with his powerful magic. He handed it to his uncle. "I'm sorry I didn't do more for you last night."

Slathek waved off the apology. "You only saved my life." He looked toward the horses. "How did you call the Horses of the West Wind to you?"

"If that's who they are, they never told me. They just started showing up." Not wanting to think about the horses or the task that faced him, Robrek took refuge in a more comfortable role. He examined Slathek's injuries. Unfortunately, Leigh had done a good job and left him nothing he could do without the use of direct healing magic. If he was going to climb Gloine Torr, he could spare no energy. He nearly laughed at the thought. Who was he to think he could climb a mountain of glass and marry a princess?

"Are you going to climb Gloine Torr on your magical horses?" a voice sounded behind him, and he turned to see the boy frying corn cakes over the fire. When he didn't answer immediately, the boy's head shot up. "You are going to do it, aren't you? Her Highness needs you. She loves you."

"How do you know how she feels?"

The boy thrust out his chest. "She told me herself, that's how. My name's Vaughan, and I take care of Her Highness's horse. She trusts me more than any of the other stable boys."

Can it be true? Robrek felt a surge of exhilaration as he accepted a plate of food from the boy. But the thought of going up the steep side of the colossal mountain tied his stomach in knots. Still, he forced himself to eat.

"You're a knight, I guess?" Vaughan asked.

"No, I'm a peasant farmer. I'm only pretending to be a knight."

The boy shrugged. "If you're a knight, don't you need a squire?"

Robrek set down his food. "Er . . ."

:Don't disappoint the boy, human child. A knight needs someone to carry his colors.: A flag with a green background and a bronze horse head appeared next to Brazen.

:Want to come, too. Boy ride.: Wild Thing insisted.

"But is it safe, my girl? The duke still wants me."

:Stars all dirty. No one know.: Wild Thing's mind voice was pleading, as were the stable lad's eyes.

Robrek sighed, took out some coins, and gave them to the boy. "The contest is scheduled to begin at noon. If you can find clothing appropriate for a squire in that time, you may ride my Horsetad and be my squire."

Vaughan grabbed the money. "I'll be back in half that time!"

* * *

Vaughan was true to his word and returned in less than half an hour with the gaudiest clothing Robrek could have possibly imagined. The tunic was turquoise blue with shockingly pink trimming. The cap was turquoise as well and as tall as Vaughan's head. Three pink feathers stood straight up in its center. "Isn't it fine?" Vaughan beamed. "I'll look like a proper squire in it, don't you think?"

Robrek didn't have the heart to tell him how hideous the outfit was, so he had Vaughan dress himself and then help him don the bronze armor.

He patted Brazen's nose. "Can we do this, Lady Brazen?"

:Only time will tell. Your foolishness may have cost us the chance:

Robrek felt sick, but he couldn't have lived with himself if he'd left his uncle to die. He breathed deeply to calm his nerves. *The boy says she loves me. I'll do it for her.*

"Ride well, kinsman," Slathek said.

Robrek nodded and, followed by Vaughan on Wild Thing, rode out of the camp.

* * *

Samantha paced restlessly atop Gloine Torr. All of her men were nearby, and on the plains below, thousands of men and horses were assembled. Not knowing whether to laugh or cry, she decided a scream of frustration would be most appropriate, but she did nothing other than pace, as she had done for days.

Periodically, she looked at Darhour. As he surveyed the scene below, his gaze rock-hard. She glanced at his sword and then down at her own. She wondered what it would feel like to take her sword and ram it straight through Argblutal's heart. *Do I have the right to blacken Darhour's aura further by asking him to do it for me?*

"All those men want to marry you?" Oriana whispered.

"Not a one of them truly cares for me. They merely want to be king." She saw the small figure of the king on a platform below. Somehow she'd undo what the duke had done to him.

"Do they have to ride all the way up?" Oriana asked.

Samantha shook her head and looked down at the Apples of Airh, which were in a basket near her feet. "Just a third of the way today." As if that weren't impossible enough. "If someone did manage to climb to the one-third marker, do you really think I could throw the apple to him?" she asked Darhour.

Darhour smiled. "You have quite an arm, Your Highness. You might be able to make it."

"And break his skull in the process," Bearach said, as if he wouldn't at all mind if she did.

"The legend does state the Apples of Airh are enchanted," Blaine reminded her. "They're supposed to fly freely from the hands of a true princess into the hands of the goddess's choice for her mate."

Bearach snorted. "You don't believe such nonsense, do you?"

Blaine shrugged. "Someone has to make it one-third of the way before we need worry about whether it's nonsense."

The standard of nearly every unmarried knight and noble in the joined kingdoms, along with dozens upon dozens of foreign ones, paraded in front of the king's platform. Beyond the knights stood a vast crowd of commoners. *Sulis, help me through this madness.*

A cheer loud enough to be heard from the top of the mountain rang out, and a group of about one hundred knights detached themselves from the mob and surrounded Gloine Torr on three sides. No one approached the side with the staircase. A profound silence descended on the plains. Suddenly, a horn sounded, and the men gave a huge shout and rushed the mountain in a confused melee. Some tried backing up a great distance and approaching at a full gallop. Some had contraptions attached to their horses' feet. Some had men or horses pushing them from behind.

No one was making it more than a few feet, let alone anywhere near the ledge that marked one-third of the distance.

"Ouch!" Bearach grimaced, as they watched one rider go down beneath the hooves of the horde.

"Holy Sulis, I hope he's okay," Samantha groaned.

After the first group struggled for about ten minutes with no success, a second horn sounded, and they retired to make way for the next group. Group after group came forward in the futile attempt to climb the unclimbable. She could hardly bear watching the spectacle.

Blaine pointed into the distance. "Holy Sulis, what is that that looks like a piece of the sun come to earth, so to speak?"

Something bright and shining was moving rapidly in the direction of Gloine Torr. It did indeed look like a piece of the sun.

As the bright object came nearer, Darhour swore. "By the goddess! How is it possible for a horse to be that color?"

Samantha gasped. What Blaine had called the sun was a horse that looked as if it had been forged of pure bronze. A knight in bronze armor sat on its back. Trailing the knight was his squire carrying the knight's standard. "Do you recognize the colors?" she asked.

"I've never seen them before, Your Highness," Darhour answered, and the rest of her men shook their heads.

The knight approached the mountain at a full gallop and nearly flew up the first few feet. His horse slowed and seemed to falter, but he didn't go skidding back down. As if it were a spider, the horse stuck to the smooth surface and continued to move upward.

Although the horse's progress slowed to a painful crawl, it didn't fall. Samantha clenched her dress tightly. *Oh Holy Sulis, please . . .* She broke off, not knowing if she wanted the knight to succeed or fail. She picked up one of the gold apples.

The horse faltered about thirty feet from the ledge, and the knight leaned over the horse's neck. Samantha could almost feel magic at work. Immediately, the horse surged up the remaining distance and came to rest on the ledge. The knight bowed to her and held out his hand.

"Who are you?" the princess whispered. "Where did you come from?"

"Throw the apple, Your Highness," Darhour said. "Let's see if Bearach is right, and it does crush his skull."

The princess threw the apple. It seemed to glide through the air and landed precisely in the knight's hand. "They are enchanted," she breathed.

As the bronze knight caught the apple, the crowd erupted in cheers. After he bowed to her again, he and his unnatural horse plummeted down the mountainside. She halfway expected them to crash spectacularly at the bottom, but the horse landed on its feet, and the knight rode off with his squire trailing.

"Your Highness, only powerful magic could have made that possible," Darhour said. "We may be looking at someone even more dangerous than Argblutal."

* * *

As he moved through the crowd, Robrek held the gold apple high. Despite being exhausted from giving his energy to Brazen, elation surged through him. *I've done it. I have the first apple. What will she think when she finds out it's me?* The crowd was cheering and closing in on him, trying to touch him. "Long live the bronze knight!" someone shouted, and the crowd took up the refrain.

The words echoed inside his head as he struggled to break free of the crowd. Brazen was trembling and clearly on the verge of collapse. But finally, they were free, and Brazen used her last burst of energy to put some distance between them and the crowd.

Vaughan and Wild Thing followed closely behind. "You did it, Master Robrek! I knew you would!" the boy cried.

Robrek kissed the gold apple, remembering when he'd kissed the woman who'd recently held it.

As they rode into camp, Slathek let out a shout. "You did it, kinsman! What would Sphry say if she could see you now?"

Robrek stumbled as he dismounted. His head was swimming. Leigh was beside him in an instant. "Are you all right, Robrek?"

He nodded, taking off his helm, revealing hair soaked with sweat. "I'm just tired." He turned to Vaughan. "Can you care for the horses? Brazen will need to be rubbed down thoroughly, and she'll need a large measure of oats." He patted the horse affectionately.

"Of course, sir." He puffed out his chest and got straight to work. Still in his armor, Robrek dropped to the ground beside his uncle.

"You should have seen it, Master Slathek," Vaughan jabbered as he unsaddled the horses. "The whole crowd parted when we rode up.

They knew the bronze knight was no ordinary knight." The boy proceeded to tell Slathek an enthusiastic and only slightly exaggerated version of what had occurred.

"Well done, nephew. This calls for a celebration." Slathek turned to the boy. "When you have cared for the horses and your knight, Squire Vaughan, procure us a feast fit for a king."

"And get yourself another squire's outfit for tomorrow," Robrek muttered drowsily. "The silver knight shouldn't have the same squire as the bronze. You might want something in a more subdued color this time."

* * *

Where Angus stood in one of the many ale tents that lined the plains around Gloine Torr, there was only one subject of conversation among the drinkers—the mysterious bronze knight. He'd come to Murtaghan to sell his harvest, after which he thought he might throw himself into the ocean. But the bizarre events of the day had put a hold on any action. The theories about who and what the knight was grew wilder as the night wore on and more ale was consumed. But Angus had a theory that was even wilder than the one that said the knight was Sulis herself.

Angus had seen strands of coal black hair under the knight's helm and remembered the bronze hair he'd found in the fields that had been destroyed last spring. The horse the knight's squire rode looked like Wild Thing. But of course, it was mad to think the knight could be his son.

* * *

Robrek smiled as he ate the feast Vaughan had procured. To a boy of twelve, a feast fit for a king seemed to consist mostly of desserts. Having always been fond of sweets, Robrek didn't mind, but he narrowly avoided groaning when Vaughan showed him the outfit he'd purchased.

"It's perfect for a silver knight's squire, isn't it?" the boy beamed.

"It certainly is silver," Robrek said. The tunic was of a bright silver satin, but that was hardly the worst of it. It was covered with a crimson fringe so long it swayed in the breeze.

Robrek held the gold apple in his hand, remembering how hard Brazen had had to struggle to make it one-third the distance.

:Don't worry, human child. The old battle-ax has given me a few pointers. I'll get you there.:

Sulis, please, let it be so. When Robrek fell asleep, his dreams were a wild mix of falling from Gloine Torr and taking the princess in his arms. *Ah, Milady, are you within my reach?*

* * *

Samantha listened to her men arguing around the dinner table. Blaine had been jumping with joy since the knight caught the apple. "The goddess has brought her choice to us! He is our light in the darkest night, so to speak!" he insisted for the hundredth time.

Bearach nodded agreement. "I laughed about the apple, but it flew straight into his hand, just like the legend said it would. He is the goddess's choice."

Kailen made a noise in his throat. "He's a dangerous sorcerer and should be eliminated, Your Highness. Have Bearach shoot him out of his saddle as he rides tomorrow."

"Your Highness, his magic is powerful," Darhour agreed. "Climbing the mountain weakens him. If he makes it to the two-thirds mark tomorrow, he will be vulnerable."

"I sensed no evil about him," Oriana claimed.

Conroy seemed to think that settled the matter. "Then he means no harm."

"She's young and half-trained, Your Highness," Darhour objected. "You shouldn't rely on her judgment."

Samantha didn't know what to think. Despite the bards' tales and the stories of magic in other lands, she hadn't really believed magic this powerful existed. Although the apple had felt ordinary, it had flown gently through the air as no natural object should, and the bronze horse had performed an impossible feat. *Danger or salvation? Which is he, Holy Mother?*

"For now we do nothing." Samantha left her men arguing and went to the small cell that was her room on the mountain top. The straw pallet was uncomfortable, and she longed for her feather bed in the palace. *Will I ever be safe and happy again?* She drifted into an uneasy sleep.

She stood alone on the dais in the throne room, the entire court filling the chamber. The crowd parted and cheered as the bronze knight burst through the doors. They chanted, as the peasants had at the bottom of Gloine Torr, "Long live the bronze knight!"

He swaggered to the throne and went down on one knee. He laid all three apples at her feet. "Your Highness, I have won the contest. I claim you as my prize."

The princess stiffened and shrunk away from the knight

"No, you do not!" Argblutal mounted the platform holding a naked sword. "She will marry me or die."

Drawing his own sword, the bronze knight jumped to his feet and stepped between her and Argblutal. "You have plotted against the princess and failed. Now she is mine," he declared in a voice that sounded like the heroes from the worst bards' tales.

Argblutal attacked.

The princess watched the two men fighting and called for her guards to protect her from the victor, but they were nowhere in sight. The bronze knight was more than a match for Argblutal. It was only a few seconds before she saw Argblutal's sword go sailing into the crowd. The bronze knight knocked the duke to the ground and put his sword at the duke's throat.

"I will not shed your blood, but you shall leave the capital, never to return." He sheathed his sword and turned his back on the duke.

Samantha cried out as the duke vaulted off the ground holding a knife, but before the bronze knight could react, the crowd surrounding the platform grabbed the duke and dragged him down. The princess watched, horrified, as the people ripped the duke apart. Despite Darbour's frequent threats, she hadn't believed a human could be torn limb from limb. Nauseated, she turned away.

The bronze knight didn't seem aware of the duke's fate. Instead, he grabbed her arm. "The prize is mine."

The princess tried to pull her arm free, but his grip was painfully tight.

The king appeared besides her. "You have won the contest. She's yours."

"Wait!" she protested. "I'm not a thing to be handed over." Neither the king nor the knight paid any attention to her. Despite her struggles, the bronze knight swept her into his arms, carried her into her bedroom, and laid her on her bed. "We haven't yet married," she protested.

"I've waited long enough," the bronze knight said.

She awoke sobbing into her pillow.

CHAPTER 39

Boyden sat by himself at the inn in Valley Fair. When the innkeeper's daughter brought him his breakfast and slammed it on the table in front of him, he grabbed her and pulled her into his lap. "Davina, is that any way to greet the chief assistant of your new lord? How about a kiss this morning?"

Davina tried to push him away. "Get your jollies somewhere else. You turned your back on your own people."

Boyden tightened his grip. "And which of 'my own people' stood by me when my father threw me off his lands?"

"Let go of me!"

"As soon as you give me a kiss." The room was half full of men doing their best to pretend they didn't see anything. They knew where the power lay now. *And to think I was content to be a peasant farmer.*

The innkeeper came in from the back room. "Get your traitorous hands off my daughter!"

Boyden further tightened his grip on Davina. "Are you saying Count Nola has no right to the Valley?"

"I never suggested any such thing. I merely asked you to get your hands off my daughter."

"It certainly sounded like you were complaining, but I'll be willing to forget the whole thing for a little kiss."

"I'll see you in the seven hells first!" Banagher raged.

Davina stopped struggling. "No, father! I'll kiss you, Boyden—"

"Master Angusstamm," Boyden interrupted.

"I'll kiss you, Master Angusstamm"—Davina's trembling aroused him—"if you'll leave my family alone."

"A kiss is all I asked for." When Davina tried to give him a small peck, he grabbed her behind the head and held her tightly while he kissed her roughly, bruising her lips and forcing his tongue between them. Finally, he let her go. She jumped off his lap and fled into the kitchen. Boyden laughed. *I'll have more from her than a kiss next time.* Banagher glared at him but said nothing more. Everyone else in the inn continued eating and pretending nothing had happened.

The door opened, and Bran and Derry came in, arguing noisily. "You've been chewing paipin leaves. That's impossible," Bran said.

"I saw it with my own eyes. His horse was bronze, and he rode one-third of the way up Gloine Torr. The princess threw him the apple."

When his two former friends caught sight of Boyden, they went silent, but Boyden signaled them to join him. Derry moved toward him reluctantly, but Bran gave him a murderous glare and left abruptly.

"What do you want?" Derry muttered.

"Sit down." He smiled as Derry obeyed. "What's this about a horse riding up Gloine Torr?" Count Nola had told him about the contest, but the nobleman hadn't expected anyone to win.

Derry repeated to Boyden what had happened the day before. "Those who were closer said they saw black hair sticking out of his helm."

Boyden ground his teeth in rage. *No, that's impossible!* But he remembered the metallic bronze hairs from the creature Robbie had summoned. He shivered as he remembered its unearthly wail. *He can't take this from me, too! I won't allow it!*

* * *

Robrek fidgeted as Vaughan, dressed in his outrageous squire's outfit, helped him don the silver armor. "Hold still, sir, or we'll never get this right!" Vaughan complained, and Robrek struggled to comply.

:Don't worry, human child. That pretty little mare will soon be witness to all of your moves.: The stallion gave him a wink, and Robrek blushed.

When Robrek's armor was secure, he mounted the silver horse. Leigh patted the horse's shoulder. "Good luck, my friend."

"Thank you," Robrek tried to say, but he had difficulty getting it past the lump in his throat.

As only another healer could, Leigh sensed his emotions. "Remember, eagles can fly."

Robrek wasn't sure what Leigh meant, but he found comfort in the other man's confidence. Followed by Vaughan on Wild Thing, he rode out of the camp. Robrek noticed the flag Vaughan carried was different today. The banner was silver with the full body of a horse on it; for some reason, the horse was the same shade of green as Robrek's eyes. Fancy Man chuckled. Evidently, the stallion considered the green horse a joke.

As Robrek rode out of the woods and onto the plains, he caught sight of a large group of armed men at the edge of the crowd. Robrek assumed they were waiting for him. Argblutal would certainly try to stop him from winning the contest.

:I'll hide us, human child; don't worry.:

Robrek rode through the armed men without them paying any attention. Once past the soldiers, Fancy Man dropped the concealment, and the crowd broke out in cries of wonder. Again the people parted to allow him through. Robrek noticed a hint of fatigue in Fancy Man. Hiding him from all those men couldn't have been easy.

Gloine Torr loomed before him. Pushing aside his unease, he approached the mountain at a full gallop. Evidently, Brazen's pointers had been good ones because initially Fancy Man took the mountain far more easily than Brazen had. They reached the one-third marker with minimal difficulty. Soon after, however, the silver stallion slowed. Robrek reached deeply into the pools of his energy and poured power into Fancy Man. Even with his help, the stallion struggled. Each step took immense effort, and the horse had to constantly fight to stop from sliding back down. With about twenty feet to go before the second ledge, the stallion stumbled and began to slide. Robrek imagined tumbling to the plains below as they had in his dreams. He drew more deeply on his energy to strengthen the horse. Although they stopped sliding, they didn't regain the distance they'd fallen.

Fancy Man trembled; Robrek patted him. "Steady, Milord, we're almost there."

Fancy Man laughed weakly. *:Don't worry. I'll get you your mare.:*

High above, Robrek could see the princess's auburn hair. Their progress was extremely slow, and the impossible task of climbing a smooth surface taxed Fancy Man's strength nearly unbearably. *We can do this for her. We have to.* He closed his eyes and reached deeper than ever within himself for energy to feed the stallion. For an instant, he thought it was working, but then he blacked out. He was jolted back to consciousness as Fancy Man fell to his knees. *No! We have to make it.* He opened his eyes and laughed; Fancy Man had collapsed on the ledge. Struggling to see through the spots swarming in front of him, Robrek bowed to the princess and held out his hand for the apple. As he caught it, the crowd burst into cheers. They went down the mountainside in what could only be called a barely controlled fall.

At the base of Gloine Torr, Fancy Man stumbled, and Robrek feared he'd remain down. But as the crowd cried, "Long live the silver knight!" the stallion struggled to his feet. The crowd parted to let them through. Swaying on Fancy Man's back, Robrek struggled to remain conscious. Ahead, he saw the armed men waiting. *Holy Sulis, no! It can't end like this!* He saw no hope for escape. Fancy Man had no resources left to hide them, and Robrek lacked the strength to even draw his sword.

:The horses, human child! The horses!:

Robrek thought he had nothing left, but he found one last spark of energy and sent an image of fire into the horses' minds. Instantly, the horses reared and bucked. Some fled in panic. It was the last thing Robrek knew before he succumbed to the darkness.

* * *

Solar sat like a statue in his quarters. Argblutal had brought him there after the silver knight had caught the second apple. There was truth in the old ways after all.

Argblutal interrogated the captain of his guard. "How did this knight get past your men?"

"Your Grace, it has to be magic. None of us saw him until he was nearly to Gloine Torr, and when he left the mountain, our horses went mad. What can I do against magic like that?"

The duke spoke through clenched teeth. "If he gets the third apple, I will be most displeased."

"Of course, Your Grace." The man bowed and left.

Argblutal whirled and faced the king. "Do not think she will marry this knight. I will be king, or I will expose her for the bastard she is."

Solar clenched the arms of his chair as the duke swept out of his room, leaving two of his men behind. He had to warn Samantha.

Solar stumbled to his writing desk. The duke's men followed. The king took up a quill, dipped it in ink, and began to make mindless doodles on the paper. The duke's men glanced at what he was doing for a few minutes, but they soon lost interest and began talking about the women they'd had the night before. With enormous effort, the king managed to scratch out three words:

Duke Knows Ahearn

It would have to be enough. He carefully slipped the paper into the sleeve of his robes. "Summon Gilroy," he commanded.

Although the men rolled their eyes, one of them went to carry out the order. The other looked over the papers on his desk. Seeing nothing other than meaningless scribbles, he went back to looking bored.

Gilroy bowed as he came into the room. "You summoned me, Your Majesty."

"I would like some flowers sent to my daughter. She's always been fond of roses." Shaking with effort, the king slipped the piece of paper into Gilroy's pocket and patted it. The effort nearly caused him to faint.

"Your Majesty, you aren't well. Let me help you to bed," Gilroy said.

"No!" The king's voice shook. "The flowers! Samantha must have flowers!"

Gilroy bowed. "I'll see to it at once, Your Majesty."

* * *

It was dark before Gilroy reached Gloine Torr. "What do you mean, I can't go up? Do you know who I am?" he said to the guards who blocked his way.

"Yes, sir, but upon the king's orders, no one is allowed up until after the competition ends tomorrow."

"The king himself ordered me to deliver these flowers to Her Highness!"

"Do you have a document under Duke Argblutal's seal giving you permission?"

"What does that matter? I have orders from *the king* to deliver these flowers, and deliver these flowers I will!"

"Unless you have an army or a sealed document hidden in those posies, you'll do no such thing."

Gilroy puffed himself up. "I'll see your officer at once."

The guard shrugged and sent for his officer, but the only concession Gilroy could get was an agreement to have the flowers delivered.

* * *

While her men argued over the silver knight, Samantha played with her food. They were divided on whether there were one or two knights. In her heart, she believed there was only one, but she had no insight into his intentions. Brice, who had been watching the steps, interrupted. "Your Highness, a guard from below has arrived. He claims he has flowers from His Majesty."

"My father has never given me flowers."

"Surely it's some ruse of Argblutal, Your Highness," Darhour said.

The princess checked herself from rolling her eyes at Darhour's paranoia. With as many times as people had been trying to kill her lately, a little paranoia might be wise.

"I've disarmed him," Brice said. "What shall I tell him?"

"How about you push him off the side of the mountain?" Bearach suggested.

"No, bring the flowers in," Samantha said. Darhour opened his mouth to protest, but she waved him silent. "Darhour, I'll allow you to search the flowers before I touch them, but if it is another attempt on my life, should we not question the deliverer?" She turned back to Bearach. "Go with Brice, and watch the man until we're sure the flowers are merely flowers."

When Brice returned, Darhour snatched the bouquet from him, threw it on the table, and tore off the wrappings. Near the roots he found a small pouch. He tore it open and removed a simple slip of paper. His face turned white as he read it. "What is it?" she asked.

Looking deathly white and trembling, Darhour said, "It's merely a note from His Majesty wishing you well on the morrow." Instead of handing her the note, he turned to Brice. "Tell the deliverer Her

Highness appreciates His Majesty's wishes." Brice left, and Darhour scowled at Kailen and Blaine.

"Well, I'll just go, shall I? I'm sure I have something important that must be done," Blaine stammered. Kailen merely saluted Darhour and bowed to her.

When they were alone, Darhour handed her the note. She recognized the king's handwriting, but the words made no sense. "'Duke knows Ahearn,'" she read aloud. "What is the meaning of this? Who's Ahearn?"

"I am. I took the name Darhour when I entered the king of Saloyna's service. It means 'Exiled One.'"

"But why does it matter if the duke knows the name you once had? Are you wanted for some crime?"

Darhour laughed without humor. "It was a crime to do what I did, but I don't regret it. My true crime was in coming back."

"Darhour, what is it you've done?"

Groaning, Darhour turned away. "It's a secret I meant to take to my grave, Your Highness."

The way his insides seemed to crumble frightened her. She needed Darhour to be strong.

"The queen . . . your mother . . . I was a groom . . . and . . ." He broke off abruptly and strode across the small room to the window.

"By Sulis, what are you saying?" the princess asked, but Darhour refused to meet her eyes, and she knew the answer. His protectiveness, his paternal manner, his love for her. "Oh, Darhour," she gasped. "You're my father, aren't you?"

Darhour whirled. "Your Highness, I'm so sorry. I never meant for you to know."

Samantha clutched at her stomach. Her father had once been the personal assassin of the Saloynan king—the legendary Ghost.

"Your Highness," Darhour began, still unable to meet her eyes, "I know I'm not the father you wanted, and once you're safe, you need never see my face again."

"No!" the princess cried in blind panic; she couldn't lose Darhour. "You can't leave! I forbid it!" She approached and touched his cheek. "These are because of me. You fled to Saloyna because you were found out, didn't you?"

"You're more than worth anything I might have suffered."

Remembering him making a similar claim as they looked at her mother's portrait, she knew he meant it. "Many men find you frightening. They pale when you do nothing more than glance at them. But from the moment I first saw you, I knew the kindness that lay here." She placed her hand over his heart. "You have been one of my closest friends. I may never be able to acknowledge you publicly, but in my heart, I'd never deny you. Darhour, I love you."

Darhour folded her in his arms. "Samantha, how I've longed to hear you say that." He stroked her hair and kissed the top of her head, as the king once had. It felt so good, so safe. "It is better your guard learn this now, so it will come as no shock if they hear later. If you have no objections, I'll inform them."

Samantha started as she remembered the purpose of the king's warning. "He has to die."

"I see no other choice, Your Highness."

She pulled away. "No, Darhour, I won't have you do it. I've seen what serving me has done to your aura. We'll find some other way."

"It's late, Your Highness, and tomorrow we'll have to deal with the sorcerer." He hugged her tightly, kissed the top of her head again, and left.

* * *

Robrek awoke to the smell of meat roasting over the fire. It was dark, but he could hear the sounds of celebrations across the plain. As he sat up, his uncle smiled. "I was afraid you were going to miss your victory celebration entirely."

Robrek felt dizzy and intensely hungry. "I have two of the apples, but not the third."

"Tomorrow you'll add it to your collection."

Robrek accepted a plate from Vaughan. "The duke's men were waiting for me today. They'll be there again tomorrow. I don't know if I can fight them and still have energy to get up the side of that mountain. Fancy Man gave it all he had today, and we barely made it two-thirds of the way." His hands shook as he brought the meat to his mouth. Had he come so far only to fail?

A brief cloud passed over his uncle's face, but it was shortly replaced by a look of the utmost confidence. "You'll certainly make it."

Robrek turned toward Holy Writ.

:I can promise thee nothing.:
Robrek wanted to refuse the food that felt like lead in his stomach, but Holy Writ would need every scrap of energy he could give her if they were going to have any chance of making it to the top tomorrow.

* * *

Duke Caedmon sighed as the men in the council tent argued endlessly about the mysterious appearance of a second knight or the reappearance of the first. The knight complicated matters in ways he hadn't foreseen.

"One or two, what does it matter?" Baron Teague said. The Korthians from the palace had joined him on the plains.

"It will matter a great deal if the princess has more than one powerful sorcerer to deal with," Sheen objected.

"Only if his or their intentions are hostile," Teague said. "Argblutal's men were set to fall on the silver knight today. If the duke is against him, I say we should help clear the way."

Caedmon thought Teague had a point. *Is not the enemy of my enemy my friend?*

"You think we should let these sorcerers win the princess and control the throne?" Sheen spluttered.

Caedmon spoke from the head of the table."I say we should help them win the gold apple. We'll deal with the consequences as they arise. For now, I can't see the harm in ridding ourselves of a few of the duke's men."

* * *

Samantha again stood on the dais in the throne room. The bronze and the silver knights mounted the platform from different sides. Both of them went down on one knee and laid three gold apples at her feet. She stared in confusion at the six apples. She'd only thrown three.

"I have won the contest. You must marry me," said the bronze knight.

"He seeks to deceive you," the silver knight argued. "It is I who have triumphed."

"Do you suggest I lie?" Drawing his sword, the bronze knight jumped to his feet.

"I do." The silver knight drew and faced him.

Samantha stepped back as the two knights clashed. They fought brutally, but neither seemed capable of gaining an advantage.

"Milady." She looked behind her to see Robbie mounted on his Horsetad. "Come away with me before it's too late."

"She will not." Argblutal and a dozen of his men surrounded the peasant boy. "Seize him!"

"No!" she screamed and looked for Darhour and the rest of her guard, but they were nowhere to be seen. Even the bronze and silver knights had somehow disappeared.

"No more will they come when you call." Argblutal pointed behind her. She turned. Darhour, Kailen, Bearach, Conroy, and Brice hung from a gallows.

"No!" she screamed. "Father, no!"

"This one will join them Beyond the Far Mountain," Argblutal sneered, "That is, if the goddess accepts his kind." She reached for her sword, but her scabbard was empty. Unable to move, she watched Argblutal tie Robbie to an altar, tear open his shirt, and raise a knife. "Before he dies, I will drink his blood and take his magic as my own."

Robbie looked strangely calm. "Your Grace, I'm afraid it is you that will soon travel to the depths of the seven hells. The demons are waiting for you."

The duke laughed, but his laughter turned to screams of agony as the knife in his hand erupted in flames. The cords that bound Robbie and the altar itself caught fire. Samantha jumped back as the fire soared toward the sky, incinerating the duke and all of his men. Somehow Robbie emerged without even singeing his hair. Dressed in peasant weave, he knelt in front of her, laying three gold apples at her feet.

"It is I who have won the contest, Milady. Will you marry me?"

She jerked awake. *Ah, Robbie, why can't it be true?*

CHAPTER 40

Robrek felt like he was preparing for a funeral as Vaughan helped him put on the gold armor. Despite having no appetite, he'd eaten a hearty breakfast, and the food sat heavy in his stomach. When he was attired, he rubbed the gold horse's neck, whispering in her ear. "Holy Writ, we have to prevent her from being forced to marry Argblutal."

:If it canst be done, we shall do it.: This was hardly the reassurance he'd hoped for.

Neither Vaughan nor his uncle seemed to realize anything was troubling him. The boy was bouncing on the balls of his feet, and Slathek was positively giddy. "My nephew, the king!" He roared with laughter. "The son of a poor girl kidnapped by slavers and sold in a foreign brothel rises to take the throne. Oh, what a bards' tale this will make, nephew! Throw in your three horses, and they'll be singing it to the ends of the earth."

Robrek nodded while his insides squirmed so much he was afraid he'd vomit. He looked at the young stable boy. "It isn't safe for you to ride with me today."

Vaughan's face crumpled. "Master Robrek, you have to have your squire. Who will carry your colors?"

:Must go.: Wild Thing insisted. *:No leave! No!:*

Slathek pounded him on the back. "Have faith in yourself, kinsman. No one can stop the gold knight."

Faced with so much opposition, Robrek reluctantly dropped his objection. As he mounted Holy Writ, he tried to shrug off the feeling of doom. *:Tie thyself to the saddle,:* Holy Writ instructed. *:Thou dost not* *want to falter where thou wilst be alone and vulnerable.:* Seeing the horse's wisdom, Robrek lashed himself on tightly.

Vaughan jumped onto Wild Thing's back. His outfit was emerald green and gold. Compared to the others, this one was understated, but Robrek balked at the sight of the flag. On a green background were the five-pointed stars of Sulis in bronze, silver, and gold. "Are you announcing me as the chosen of the goddess?" he asked Holy Writ.

:Dost thou doubt Sulis has brought thee to this point? If thou claimest the third apple today, it wilt be because of her blessing.:

Without giving Robrek time to object, the gold horse moved out of the clearing and onto the flat of the plain. Robrek tensed as he saw the horsemen ahead. "Run back to the grove at the first sign of trouble," he whispered to Vaughan. "Let me handle it," he told Holy Writ. Robrek suspected Fancy Man hiding them the day before had nearly cost them the mountain. He planned on frightening their horses again, but before he could get close enough to do so, dozens of men poured in from the sides and engaged the waiting men in battle. "Who are they? Why would they be fighting the duke's men?"

:This is not thy concern. To the mountain!: Robrek tore himself away and rode wide of the fighting.

The crowd had drawn back from the fight, but they cheered when they saw him riding free of the fray. As usual, they parted to allow him through. Many traced the star of Sulis, and not a few bowed before him. The bows made him uncomfortable. He wasn't sure if they saw him as their future king or as a messenger from the goddess. He cursed Holy Writ's pretentious banner.

* * *

That morning, Samantha watched her guards stare at her, then at Darhour, and look quickly away. The knowledge that Darhour was her father hung heavy in the air, as did the danger it represented.

To break the tension, Samantha asked, "Do you think the silver or the bronze knight will come today?"

"Perhaps they'll both come," Brice blurted. "If they kill each other, that will be one less thing for us to worry about." Samantha started. Brice had never evidenced this type of bloodthirstiness before.

"It will be the gold knight," Bearach said.

Samantha rounded on him. "Why would you say that?"

Bearach pointed into the distance. Samantha looked, and across the plains rode a knight in armor of the purest gold riding a gold horse. While the bronze and silver knights had been spectacular, the gold knight took her breath away.

"Gold armor isn't very practical," Bearach said. "Not only is it expensive, but it's far too soft and so Sulis-cursed heavy I'm surprised it doesn't crush him."

While this was all certainly true, how could he think such a thing while watching the blazing brilliance of the coming knight?

"How dare he?" Kailen hissed.

The princess followed his gaze. This time the knight's squire flew bronze, silver, and gold on a background of emerald green. "Sulis's stars," she whispered.

The gold knight began to climb the mountain at a gallop and made it with seeming ease to the halfway point, but then it slowed dramatically. The knight touched the horse on both sides of its neck, and she could almost see the energy pass between the knight and the beast. The horse immediately gained strength and forged ahead, but the knight swayed on its back.

Darhour noticed this as well. "Your Highness, if he makes it to the top, he will be weak."

"Darhour, you may question him, but no more."

He glared back.

"Father," she whispered. "Please, trust me."

His face softened, and he nodded. "We will do it your way, but if he makes a single wrong move, I won't hesitate."

* * *

Robrek was so tired he couldn't see straight. Feeling as if they were struggling through quicksand, he couldn't tell if they were nearing the top or still had hundreds of feet to go. He tried to feed the horse more energy, but he had little to give. "You can do it, Writ. Only a short way," he whispered, praying it was true.

Suddenly, Holy Writ's feet gave away, and they went slipping down the mountainside. The gold horse scrambled to get her feet back under her, and Robrek struggled to help. Robrek's vision blurred, and he felt so lightheaded he couldn't think. Within moments, he'd stabilized the horse, but they'd lost at least twenty feet. Holy Writ was heavily lathered, and her breath sounded like a wheezy bellows. She seemed to slip one step back for every two steps forward. They'd never reach the top. He looked up, and his vision cleared temporarily. He was close enough to see the face of the woman he loved. The sight of her caused a spark of energy in him. Immediately, he fed it to the horse. Then he blacked out. He jerked himself back into consciousness to find himself hanging half off the saddle. If not for the lashings, he would have tumbled down the side of Gloine Torr. He pulled himself back into the saddle.

Holy Writ crumpled to her knees, but Robrek smiled; they'd made it to the top. To his surprise, the princess with her gold apple drew back, and Robrek found himself surrounded by five of her guards. They had their swords drawn and wore expressions like they'd worn when the princess had kissed him in the spring. Holy Writ struggled to her feet, her legs shaking under her. Robrek met the princess's eyes. *Will she allow them to kill me?*

Scarface glared at him. "Who are you? And what are your intentions toward Her Highness?"

Robrek was unsure if revealing his identity would save him or ensure his death. "Who I am you will learn in time." His voice rasped so hoarsely that it didn't sound like his own. "If Her Highness will give me the apple, I intend to present the three apples before the king on the morrow, in keeping with the rules of the contest. Then if Her Highness will have me, I intend to stand beside her as consort and fight for her against her enemies."

"You expect us to believe one of your power will be content as a mere consort?" Scarface demanded.

"It is the Princess Samantha the goddess has chosen to reign, not I."

"And what if she refuses you?"

Robrek directed his reply toward the princess. "Your Highness, when I bow before you and the king tomorrow, if you do not want me, you need only say so. I will stay to help rid you of your enemies. Then I'll sail far away from Korthlundia, and you'll be troubled by me no more."

Pushing past her men, the princess entered the circle, and Robrek felt his breath catch in his throat. "I trust your words, Sir Knight, but for the sake of my men, can I have your vow?"

"I vow upon the goddess and my mother's grave to abide by your will on the morrow. If you will have me, I vow to serve you faithfully as consort. And if you will not, I vow to exile myself from Korthlundia, never to return."

"I accept your vow. So do my men." She glanced at them, and they nodded somewhat reluctantly. She handed him the last gold apple.

He bowed. "Thank you, Milady." He turned to make the trip back down the mountain.

* * *

"He said all the right things," Bearach insisted as they discussed the gold knight over dinner.

That was partially what was worrying Darhour. He had difficulty believing a man with that much power would accept a subordinate position. When the knight was fully rested, he would be a powerful foe, much harder to be rid of than Argblutal.

Dreamy look in the princess's eyes concerned him further. "He called me 'Milady,'" she said.

"Such an attempt to belittle Your Highness demonstrates the insincerity of his vow," Kailen said.

"Perhaps." The princess nodded, but didn't look as if she believed it.

"Your Highness," Darhour said, "you can't think it's him." But part of him wondered if the strange knight was indeed the amihealer. The boy had always been more than he pretended. Still, he felt guilty as he watched the light go out in his daughter's eyes.

"Of course it can't be Robbie. It's just . . . "

"We all know how you feel about him, Your Highness," Bearach said.

Darhour glared at his subordinate. The princess needed no support for her fantasies.

CHAPTER 41

All night long Samantha had dreamed of making love to Robbie. Now, as she followed the members of her guard down the long flight of steps, she felt more uncertain than ever. *Who is this man who will claim me like a trophy? Do I accept him? Will I have a choice?*

Below, one hundred members of the Royal Guard awaited her. The air nearly crackled with tension; her guards' hands were never far from their weapons. Captain Kentigern bowed to her. "Your Highness, my men and I will escort you to the palace."

Then she saw Lord Devyn's familiar face in the crowd. He was smiling; she prayed he had good news. "May I have a word, Your Highness?" Devyn asked.

"We're in a hurry, Your Highness," Kentigern objected, but she ignored him and beckoned Devyn toward Gloine Torr. She glanced at Darhour, and her men formed a barrier between her and the Royal Guard. Kentigern didn't like it, but he made no move to interfere.

Devyn spoke so only she could hear. "Duke Caedmon has come with an army of five hundred men. Say you have forgotten something, and climb back up the mountain with your personal guards as protection. We will deal with these." He indicated Kentigern and his men.

Samantha wavered. It was a good plan, and every shred of reason insisted she follow it. She didn't have to ask to know what Darhour would advise. But a feeling she couldn't explain insisted she return to the palace. She wished she knew whether she was being led by the goddess or if the way the knight had said "Milady" was interfering with her judgment. "No, not yet," she said.

"But, Your Highness—" Devyn protested. She didn't give him a chance to finish, but strode forward to the waiting horses. Roberta whinnied and nuzzled her.

Her guards mounted, as did Devyn. A group of about a dozen men detached themselves from the crowd and joined Devyn.

"What is this?" Kentigern objected.

"After the events of yesterday, surely you don't object to Her Highness having additional protection," Devyn said.

* * *

"The people have already crowned him king," Morgan complained. "They are chanting 'Long live the gold knight' in the streets. We aren't dealing with an ordinary man, Your Grace."

"And how do you suggest I deal with him?" Argblutal sneered, clearly not expecting an answer.

But Morgan had one. "With a little more help from the Saloynans."

The duke smiled as Morgan explained what he had in mind. "Do it. Except for Darhour. I want him taken alive."

* * *

Robrek awoke with the sun in his eyes and no memory of returning to the grove. He sat up, feeling shaky and lightheaded.

But at the sight of the three gold apples, his entire body filled with light. He accepted a large plate of food from Vaughan and devoured his breakfast.

His uncle had lost the giddiness that had dominated his mood during the contest. "Kinsman, I've been thinking. No matter how many apples you have, Argblutal will never allow you to take the throne. While he has an army, you have only yourself, a one-armed old man, a priest, and a boy. If we enter the palace today, I doubt we'll leave it alive. Give this up, and sail with me."

Robrek saw the princess again as she had appeared atop Gloine Torr. "I won't leave her. I love her. But I won't take anyone else with me. Today I ride alone."

Slathek opened his mouth to object, but shut it and looked at his arm. "I would never allow this, but with my sword arm broken, I'd be more of a liability than an asset."

Leigh made no protest, but Vaughan crossed his arms. "I've known Her Highness all my life, and I care about her at least as much as you do. I know the palace, and you don't. Besides, I have a new outfit and everything."

Robrek wanted to keep the child out of danger, but Vaughan did know the palace and would likely follow him with or without his permission. "Groom the horses until they shine, and clean the dirt from Wild Thing's stars while I take a bath. The princess's consort shouldn't stink."

"Yes, sir!" Vaughan yelled and got straight to work. After bathing, Robrek dressed in the gold silk he'd found in Holy Writ's saddlebags and had Vaughan help him put on the gold armor. Finally, he took the green ribbon out from under his shirt and tied his hair back.

Taking him by the shoulders, Slathek kissed him on both cheeks. "The Mother and the Father ride with you this day, and the spirit of Sphry will surely look out for you."

When Vaughan appeared in his new outfit, Robrek put on his helm to hide his amusement. Today's find was checkered emerald green and gold. The sleeves were extraordinarily puffy and gathered every six inches so that his arms looked like overstuffed sausages. The hat was gold with a wide brim and a cone-shaped protrusion rising out of the center. From the peaked top flew several emerald streamers. "Which one will you ride today, Master Robrek?"

Robrek walked over to his Horsetad. "I'll ride Wild Thing. The two of us have been through a lot together." He patted the mare, and she nuzzled against his chest.

:Let me carry your squire, human child. A boy in a get-up like that deserves to ride in style.:

Robrek laughed. "Fancy Man requests the pleasure of carrying you today, Vaughan."

The boy beamed and bowed to the horse. "I'd be most honored."

After they mounted, Robrek secured the three gold apples on the saddle in front of him. He took the lead with Vaughan behind him on Fancy Man; Brazen and Holy Writ brought up the rear. To prevent Duke Argblutal from mounting another ambush, the horses hid them until they reached the city gates. When the crowd that thronged the streets saw him, they cheered, "Long live the gold knight! Long live the consort!" They parted to let him through, throwing flowers in his path. Robrek had grown used to people trying to kill him, but he had no idea how to respond to people praising his name.

:Nod your head as I taught you, human child. You remember the superior's nod of acknowledgement to those beneath him.:

At the time Fancy Man had taught him that particular gesture, he'd never imagined he'd have occasion to use it. Even now it felt wrong to present himself as superior to these people. Still, Robrek bowed his head and scanned the crowd for danger. He saw none and guessed the duke didn't want so many witnesses.

When the palace gates opened to receive him, the multitudes pressed in. To no avail, the soldiers tried to hold them back. He rode to the base of the palace steps, and grooms rushed to care for the horses. As Robrek dismounted, he heard the horses' voices.

:Go and claim that pretty young mare, human child.:

:It is your destiny.:

:Remember, thou art the chosen of Sulis. Thy power maketh thee a worthy mate for a queen.:

Reassured by their words, Robrek walked through the palace doors and into the corridors, which were lined with members of the Royal Guard. His hands shook, and his heart beat rapidly. In a few moments' time, he'd reveal himself to the princess. He wished he knew how she'd react when she learned he was the gold knight.

* * *

As she stood beside the king, Samantha's palms were sweating. Oriana stood beside them holding the king's hand. She prayed the girl could help her father. Samantha's pulse increased as the fanfare sounded, announcing the knight's entrance into the palace. She tried to slow her breathing and maintain her court mask.

Preceded by more than a dozen of Argblutal's men, the gold knight entered the throne room, carrying all three gold apples. His armor glistened, and he wore his helm with the visor down, adding to his mystery. He paused, and for a moment she thought he looked uncertain, but no man with that much power could harbor doubts. As he strode across the throne room, fear warred with excitement within her.

The knight climbed the steps and went down on one knee before her and the king. He was so near she could touch him. He said,

"Your Majesty, I, on my horses, have climbed Gloine Torr and claimed the Apples of Airh. I present them here today."

"Arise, Sir Knight, and take my daughter's hand. I give her and my throne into your care."

"With respect, Your Majesty, the apples only have I won. To take your daughter's hand and share her throne, I must have her consent." Samantha trembled as the knight turned to her. "Your Highness, at the top of Gloine Torr, I vowed to abide by your will. I have loved you since the day we first met, and I will never love another woman as long as I live. But it would be torture to marry you if you don't share my feelings."

As he laid the three apples at her feet, he began to glow with bronze, silver, and gold. *No, it can't be him! He's a peasant, not a knight.* As he reached to remove his helm, his aura exploded into a halo of blinding white. Samantha again felt the peace she'd felt in the island shrine and heard the priestess's words, "In time, the goddess's choice will appear before you, and when he kneels at your feet, you will know." *Holy Sulis, he is the one!* Unable to breathe, Samantha watched the knight remove his helm. She nearly fainted when Robbie's curly black hair emerged. His emerald eyes shone with both hope and fear. "Will you marry me, Your Highness?"

The princess had difficulty forcing words past the lump in her throat. "Robbie, how can it be you?"

"'How' is a long story, which, if you will have me, I will gladly tell you on our wedding night. If you will not, 'how' doesn't matter."

It can't be. I must be dreaming. This was wrong, so very wrong. The Robbie she knew was no knight, but at the same time, she couldn't doubt what his aura revealed. "The goddess has chosen you, and so do I," she said.

As the king drew his sword, Robbie looked wounded. *No, not Robbie. Robbie is a peasant. I don't know who this knight is.* "What is your name and origin, knight?" the king asked.

"I am called Robrek, Your Majesty. My mother's people come from Mahngbhayo, but I was raised on the king's lands."

The king touched the knight lightly on both shoulders. "Robrek of Mahngbhayo, I dub you Sir Robrek. Arise and take my daughter's hand."

Hesitantly, Sir Robrek did as the king commanded, and she felt the familiar calluses on his hand. He kissed her hand, and his squire approached to help him remove his armor. There, dressed in the most hideous outfit she'd ever seen, was Vaughan. *This can't be real.*

"Through the contest on the holy mountain of Gloine Torr, the goddess has revealed her choice," the king announced. "In keeping with Sulis's will, I announce the betrothal of my beloved daughter and heir, Her Highness the Crown Princess Samantha, and Sir Robrek. Let us feast and celebrate this day, and tomorrow the royal marriage will take place in the palace chapel."

As the court greeted the announcement, Robrek smiled at Milady tentatively, but when he met her eyes, he wanted to disappear through the throne room floor. She looked closer to terrified than happy, and she was the one person he couldn't tolerate being afraid of him. He wanted her alone so he could explain everything, but a mob of courtiers surrounded them as they moved into the banquet hall.

Robrek staggered at the sight of the huge room. A table large enough for fifty, but containing only three place settings, sat on a dais above the others. It was to this table the princess led him. Two tables with seats for about twenty formed a horseshoe with the top table, and the rest of the room was filled with row after row of smaller tables. He was certain the room could seat at least five hundred, maybe even a thousand. He gaped like a backward peasant at the tapestries on the walls. The colors were far brighter and richer than any he'd even imagined existed, let alone seen, and the artistry was so superb it looked like the hounds and hunters might leap off the walls and trample through the hall. The chairs at the top table were flaked with gold and gems and cushioned in velvet. *Who am I fooling? I don't belong here.*

"Sit beside me, Sir Robrek." The princess's use of the title reminded Robrek just who he was supposed to be and how he was supposed to act. Suppressing the peasant, he took refuge in Fancy Man's training.

"I hope the food will be to your taste," Samantha said, using the idle small talk with which you address a stranger. No sparkle lit her eyes. If she'd just smile at him like she used to, he thought he could handle the rest.

As he sat, something sharp jabbed his leg. He winced slightly, reached under his leg, and pulled out a needle. His healing senses became aroused, and he felt a poison begin to spread. *So this is the duke's plan. It's not a very good one.* It was a slow acting, yet powerful poison, but he neutralized it easily. Argblutal was glaring at him from the head of one of the longer tables. Robrek bowed his head in greeting. It was the bow of equals, and Robrek could tell it infuriated the duke. He turned to the princess, wondering if he should say something, but she was still smiling that fake smile, making it difficult to talk to her.

A servant stood at his side with a basin and a pitcher of water. He held out his hands for the servant to pour the water over and repressed his impulse to thank the man.

"Sir Robrek," one of the nobles sitting at Argblutal's table said. "Since you have claimed the right to be king, forgive my curiosity in wanting to know something about you. Your lineage, perhaps?"

"We haven't yet been introduced," he said, startling himself with the perfect correctness of his words and tone. The silver stallion had been an excellent teacher.

"Sir Robrek, may I present Torin, Duke of Oirthir?" the princess said, in that horribly formal voice.

Robrek bowed his head in the precise manner to indicate a relationship of equals. "A pleasure."

"Likewise, I'm sure." Duke Torin responded with an equivalent bow. "As to your lineage?"

For a brief moment, Robrek was tempted to claim he was a Mahngbhayon prince. But he remembered the reason Holy Writ claimed he belonged by the princess's side. "My father is a farmer from Valley Fair, and my mother was the daughter of a merchant from Mahngbhayo," he said as if he were announcing himself the son of Sulis herself.

"A son of farmers and merchants?" Disdain dripped from Duke Torin's voice. "You would joke about so important a matter as lineage?"

"Whatever reason would I have to joke? Having mixed blood is what has given me magic powerful enough to ride up Gloine Torr. It is this magic, not a noble lineage, I offer in service to the princess and the joined kingdoms."

* * *

As the food was served, Samantha stared at the stranger she'd thought she loved. Although he was the goddess's choice, she was certain of nothing else about him. Surely no peasant could know just the right words and tone to parry the nobles' challenges, and no peasant ate with the unselfconsciousness of one who'd spent a lifetime banqueting at court. Robbie certainly hadn't when he'd eaten the soup in Myst's cottage. *Just who are you, Sir Robrek of Mahngbhayo? And why did you lead me to believe you were the peasant boy named Robbie Angusstamm?*

When the dessert was served, she noticed Vaughan sitting among the other squires. Unlike Sir Robrek, he had no notion of court manners and ate like the stable boy he was. "Tell me, Sir Robrek, how is it my stable boy is now your squire."

Sir Robrek didn't respond immediately, and when she looked at him, he cleared his throat, looked down at his plate, and lowered his voice. "Duke Argblutal took my uncle prisoner. When I came to rescue him, I found the boy in the same cell. The duke intended my uncle to sacrifice Vaughan to perform some type of blood magic. I got them both out. Vaughan insisted a knight needed a squire and begged to be mine. I didn't want to bring him with me today, but he insisted he cared about you every bit as much as I do."

Care about me? You don't lie to those you care for. But Holy Sulis, you're powerful. How could you do what Darhour could not?

At that moment, the king announced the beginning of the ball. Taking Sir Robrek's hand, she led him into the ballroom. When they entered the room, the knight stopped abruptly and gaped like an ignorant peasant. But as she watched, the sheen of a courtier fell over him, and he bowed to her. "May I have this dance, Your Highness?"

Wondering if she'd imagined what she'd seen, Samantha let him lead her to the middle of the room. When the music started, Sir Robrek moved with an effortless grace that infuriated her. *Just what kind of game was he playing with me when he pretended to be so clumsy at the horse fair?*

* * *

As the sorcerer began to dance with the princess, Argblutal had difficulty maintaining his court mask. This sorcerer didn't act like a peasant, and the poison showed no signs of affecting him. *Is this sorcerer mortal? Or is he a demon, as those of the Valley believe?*

Argblutal signaled Kentigern. "Get my best archer on the balcony above the ball room. Shoot him as he dances with the princess. We have no more time for subtlety."

* * *

Kailen's icy blue eyes swept the ballroom for danger. The duke would hardly stand by and allow this marriage to occur. There was also something very wrong about this upstart the king had betrothed to the princess. Kailen dearly wished Bearach had succeeded in killing the boy in the spring.

Kailen felt a sharp prick in his neck and slapped at an annoying insect.

* * *

Brice's gaze darted around as he stood near Duke Argblutal. The captain had told him to stay near the duke and watch for any suspicious movement. *What movement of the duke's isn't suspicious?* The duke didn't dance, but merely watched the princess and the peasant boy or whatever the mysterious knight was. He felt a sharp prick in the back of his arm. He looked around, but no one was near.

* * *

Conroy glanced briefly at Oriana, who still maintained a position beside the king. He prayed she could help. The tension in the ballroom seemed near the boiling point, and Conroy recognized few of the Royal Guard present. The captain believed them to be mostly the duke's men. He noticed several wearing Lord Devyn's colors, but even so, the odds certainly weren't in their favor. Conroy swept the room, looking for any sign of danger to the princess or her betrothed.

He slapped at his neck as he felt the sharp prick of an insect bite.

* * *

Bearach slapped at his neck and returned to scanning the ballroom for danger. *Robbie is the goddess's choice? Whoever would have thought it?* Bearach had taken a liking to the boy when he met him at the herb witch's cottage. Although there was clearly more to the amihealer than he'd let on, Bearach couldn't be anything but happy for the princess. He smiled at them fondly.

Out of the corner of his eye, he caught sight of movement from the balcony. "Watch out!" he yelled, as with the quickness of long practice, he grabbed his bow, nocked an arrow, and released it at the same moment that the archer in the balcony released his.

* * *

Samantha's anger and confusion bubbled under the surface as the royal musicians began to play the Saloynan waltz. She'd ordered that the song never be played at court, but apparently the music master thought her betrothal was an exceptional circumstance.

As he heard the sensual music, Sir Robrek smiled and reddened slightly. He put his arm around her waist as demanded by the dance. She felt her breasts brush against his chest as they swayed to the music. *Just how can he know all the court dances unless he's noble himself? But why has he created such an elaborate game?*

"Watch out!" Bearach's voice reverberated through the room. Before she could figure out what to watch for, Darhour charged into Sir Robrek, knocking him aside. The knight stumbled into her, and they fell together to the floor. She heard the twang of an arrow, and Darhour dropped, the arrow piercing his chest. "No!" she screamed.

Kailen grabbed her by the arm. "This way, Your Highness. We must get you to a more secure location."

"No!" Samantha tore her arm out of her guard's grasp. "Oh, Darhour, don't die!" She dropped down on her knees beside her father.

Dropping next to the fallen captain, Robrek placed his hands on either side of the arrow. He had to work quickly. He hurriedly broke off the arrow's shaft and turned the man to pull the arrowhead free. He closed his eyes and became one with the wound. Darhour's life aura was flickering. Although Robrek's healing powers had increased markedly, healing a hole through the most powerful muscle in the body was no simple task, especially since he had to heal it with a single burst of power so that the princess's man didn't bleed to death. As the hole through the heart closed, he felt himself sweating and trembling. But the heart lay limply within the guard's chest; he was still dying. Reaching deeper into his energy, Robrek poured his power in to rebuilding the damaged tissue and setting the heart into motion again. As he felt himself losing consciousness, he hoped he'd acted in time.

Samantha watched in numb disbelief as Robbie collapsed on the ground beside her father. "No, Robbie!" she wailed.

"That one is a most powerful healer."

The princess looked behind her to see Oriana. "What do you mean?" she asked.

"He sealed a hole through the captain's heart. I never imagined such was possible."

"Sealed the hole? Darhour isn't dead?"

"I'm sure he's not, Your Highness," a boy's voice said. Vaughan in his ridiculous clothing came up beside her. "There isn't anything Sir Robrek can't do. He just passes out like that afterward."

Willing something to make sense, Samantha closed her eyes. It wasn't possible to survive an arrow through the heart. When she opened her eyes, men were carrying Sir Robrek and Darhour out of the room. "Where are they taking them?" she cried.

"To the surgery, my dear," the king said.

Samantha forced her mind to clear. "Bearach, Conroy, go after them. Move them someplace safe." Rather than obeying, Bearach looked toward Kailen. "I command here," the princess snapped. "Move them to safety!"

Devyn joined them.

"Take some men and join them," she commanded, and they left the room, followed by Vaughan.

The king held out a hand to her, and she allowed him to help her to her feet, his other hand clinging desperately to Oriana's.

Argblutal strode up, followed by members of the Royal Guard carrying a dead man with an arrow sticking out of one eye.

"Murderer," she hissed.

Argblutal ignored her. "Your Majesty, it appears the princess's guard was able to take down the assassin. This note was found on his body." The duke handed the king a slip of parchment. "It indicates he was offended by the notion of a peasant on the throne and was determined to stop it. He surely acted alone."

"Liar!" she said. "Father, he is behind this."

"The princess is hysterical," Argblutal said. "She should be sent to her room before she creates even more of a scene."

"Go to your rooms now, my dear," the king commanded. "Let the guard be sure there are no others."

"Please, Your Highness," Kailen said. "There is nothing more you can do here."

Samantha didn't want to leave and was certain she protested, but without realizing how it happened, she found herself entering her own chambers followed by Kailen and Brice. Collapsing into a chair, she put her face in her hands.

Kailen knelt at her side. "Your Highness, we should flee into the tunnel immediately and get you to safety."

"No, I won't go until I know they're safe."

"Your Highness, if the captain could speak, he would order us to abandon him," Kailen argued.

She ignored this. "What about the men Devyn brought?"

"They are just outside the door."

"Bring them here, and we'll hide them in the tunnel. You and Brice guard the door as you normally would until one of the others returns with news."

Kailen growled with frustration, but he offered no further argument. Soon Lord Devyn's men were down in the tunnel. Kailen made sure the heavy table blocked their reentry. Brice shoved Blaine into the room. "His Grace doesn't need any more hostages," Kailen said. He left, slamming the door behind him.

* * *

Scratching at a nasty insect bite on the back of his neck, Bearach hurried with Conroy, Lord Devyn, Vaughan, and one of Devyn's men toward the surgery.

"One of the buggers got you, too?" Conroy asked, scratching the back of his arm.

Bearach nodded. "This is my fault. Something stung me while Her Highness and Sir Robrek were dancing. If I hadn't been swatting at it, I might have had the murderous scum before he got the captain."

They burst into the surgery. Vaughan tripped over his own feet as he came through the doorway, and his ridiculous hat fell under one of the tables. The boy scrambled after it. The surgery assistants were taking the captain and the amihealer off the litters. "Leave them," Bearach shouted. "We're taking them elsewhere. Her Highness's orders."

"Where?" the king's surgeon demanded.

"None of your business." Bearach pushed the physician aside and directed the others to the litters. Bearach chose the one that held the amihealer for himself. Sir Robrek was a hell of a lot lighter than the captain.

He hadn't had a chance to lift it yet when Duke Argblutal and over a dozen members of the Royal Guard appeared in the doorway. Bearach drew his sword and placed himself between the princess's betrothed and the duke's men. Conroy, Lord Devyn, and his man did the same. "Get out of the way," Bearach ordered, sizing up their chances against the greater numbers. "Your men may get me eventually, but I'll be sure to take you with me."

Drawing a small blowpipe from his belt, the duke merely smiled. "I very much doubt that. You won't even have the strength to hold that sword much longer."

Bearach tried to laugh, but his sword did feel unreasonably heavy. Sweat was running into his eyes, and he swore the room was starting to spin. Conroy looked every bit as bad.

Argblutal tapped the blowpipe against his hand. "The Saloynans are truly an ingenious people. You have to admire those who have made murder an art."

Conroy suddenly collapsed to the surgery floor, and Bearach clasped a hand over what he'd thought was an insect bite. "Poison," he whispered.

"Yes." The duke's smile widened. "My man tells me you were the last stung, so you probably have a few more moments before you, too, fall."

With the last of his strength, Bearach lunged toward the duke, but he collapsed before he'd crossed even half the distance.

Devyn felt his knees go weak as the two members of the princess's guard fell to the surgery floor.

"I had sent men to fetch you," Argblutal sneered. "But you've walked right into my hands."

"You can walk right into the seven hells," Devyn said, trying to project bravery, but the trembling of his voice made it so he didn't fool anyone.

"Maybe later. Right now, I require your assistance. Drop your weapons before I have my men kill you and end this farce."

Devyn didn't see an alternative, so he lowered his sword to the floor and nodded to his man to do likewise. One of the duke's men kicked the swords aside. Devyn stood straight. "Kill me if you must. I'll do nothing to aid you."

"Again, you're wrong." He nodded, and one of the duke's man skewered his companion.

Devyn gasped as the man fell, but he turned his eyes to the duke. "I still won't help you."

The door to the surgery opened, and several more men entered holding a woman in her nightdress. "Let me go, you spawn of toads!" the woman shrieked.

"Aislinn!" he cried and moved toward her, but the points of ten swords stopped him. "Let her go! She has nothing to do with this!"

The duke approached Aislinn and rubbed his hand across her cheek. "Wrong a third time. She's essential."

Aislinn's eyes shot daggers at the duke, and when his hand neared her mouth, she clamped down hard with her teeth.

"Gutter-born bitch!" Jerking his hand away, the duke slapped her across the face. Devyn's knees buckled as the duke hit her again. "Now, Devyn, unless you want me to continue, tell me what you and your men are doing here."

"Don't tell this mud-dwelling, tadpole-humping slime anything," Aislinn swore with the passion that had won his heart long ago. Duke Argblutal slapped her again, cutting her lip, then shoved his handkerchief deep inside her mouth, muffling her cries.

"I just wanted to check on the princess's betrothed. That's all." Devyn heard his voice squeak and knew it was obvious he was lying.

"Isn't that loyal of you?" The duke grabbed Aislinn and bent her back over a surgery bed. He pinned her hands tightly with one of his own, and with the other filthy hand, he caressed her breast. "Would you like to watch while I take her now? When I'm done, I'm sure my men wouldn't mind enjoying whatever's left."

"Keep your hands off her!" Devyn cried.

The duke slapped Aislinn again. "Tell me what you are doing here."

Devyn tried to silence the voice that called him a traitor, but he couldn't watch them hurt Aislinn. "Her Highness sent us to fetch the peasant healer and her chief bodyguard and hide them."

The duke released Aislinn. "And where were you to hide them?"

"I don't know." Devyn pointed to one of the fallen guards. "Conroy was to direct the way." He watched the duke unhook a riding crop from his belt and raise it over his beloved. "I swear I don't know where we were to take them, but once they were there safely, I was to go to the princess and let her know."

The duke lowered his whip. "You'll relieve her mind soon enough, but for now, we'll discuss your travels on the princess's behalf."

Aislinn's eyes told him to say nothing more, but did she honestly expect him to watch Argblutal rape her?

* * *

Under the bed, Vaughan lay frozen. How could he help? If the duke caught him, he'd tie him to the altar and sacrifice him as he had the other children.

He watched the duke's men carrying Sir Robrek and the rest of the princess's men. A squire didn't desert his knight, but Argblutal had told his men to take them to the dungeon!

As he lay there struggling to calm the pounding of his heart, he knew what he had to do. He had to hide until the duke left, and then he needed to run and tell the princess what had happened. The princess would know how to rescue Sir Robrek.

CHAPTER 42

Oriana drowsed in the bed beside the king. She was exhausted from trying to leach the poison from His Majesty's body. When she'd first touched him, she'd been overwhelmed by the horror of the king's condition. But she remembered what Mother Venetia had told her. "Never underestimate the power of small magic. A little at a time can conquer even the greatest of diseases." Although she didn't have anything like Sir Robrek's power, she was helping. The king had even told her so before he fell asleep. She was drifting into sleep herself when the door burst open.

The king sat up. "How dare you barge in here?" the king said to the evil duke who'd poisoned him.

Oriana cowered behind the king, not sure the duke had noticed her. He emanated so much evil it made her nauseous.

"We've played this game long enough," the duke said. "I've secured the princess's betrothed and guards in the dungeon. She is without protection. Tomorrow, you'll hand her over to me in front of the entire court."

Oriana wanted to shout with joy when His Majesty rose to his feet. Despite being so terribly old, he looked everything a king should.

"I most certainly will not," the king said, not sounding at all feeble.

"You will marry her to me, or I'll expose her in front of the entire court as the bastard child of a Saloynan assassin."

"You will have my daughter over my dead body," the king hissed. Oriana gasped as the king grabbed a sword from beside the bed.

The evil duke just laughed and drew his own sword. "I'd have preferred it otherwise, but if you insist."

"No!" Oriana shouted, as His Majesty lunged for the duke. The duke parried and aimed a blow at the king's heart. The king was too old to move fast enough, and the duke buried his sword in the king's chest. Oriana vaulted off the bed and ran toward the far door.

"Guards," the duke yelled, as she struggled to open the door. "Seize the child." She flung the door open, but someone grabbed her. She sent out a shock, and the man yelled, letting her go. She slammed the door behind her, grabbed a chair, propped it under the door handle, and ran down the corridor.

Men smashed against the king's bedroom door as she tried the other doors in the corridor. She wanted to cry when she found so many of them locked. Finally, one opened, and she threw herself inside. Behind her, she heard the king's door crash open. She locked the door behind her and found herself in an empty bedchamber. Diving under the bed, she prayed to the goddess for protection as the other locked doors were broken down. Her door crashed open, and two men entered. All she could see were their feet. Focusing on them, she sent one thought into the mind of the closest one. *You already looked under the bed. You already looked under the bed.* She trembled with the effort.

"Any sign of her?" the evil duke asked.

"No, Your Grace, she isn't in here," one of the men answered.

"Did you search thoroughly?" he asked, and Oriana was afraid the sound of her heart would betray her.

"Yes, Your Grace, I looked everywhere."

The evil duke cursed in frustration, and the three sets of footsteps moved on. As the searching men moved farther and farther away, tears trickled down Oriana's cheeks. She wished she were as strong as Sir Robrek so she could have saved the king.

* * *

As he came awake, Robrek stretched. He froze when he felt shackles attached to his wrists and ankles. Jerking his eyes open, he could see nothing but blackness. He heard pounding from without. *Holy Sulis, they're building my scaffold. It was nothing but a dream! I'm still in the temple cellar! Idiot! How could I ever even dream I had a chance to marry a woman like her? But you'd think in a dream she would have been happier to see me.*

He smelled the metallic tang of blood and felt the stiffness of Bran's blood dried on his clothing. He pulled against the chains binding him, and the cloth of his garment rubbed against his arms. It was smooth and soft—silk, not peasant weave. The pounding he thought he'd heard earlier was nothing other than his own heart. *Where am I? What's going on?*

Lowering his shields, he felt for life surrounding him. Five men shared his confinement—one healthy but asleep and four near death from poison. He recognized their minds: the princess's men were dying.

Robrek scuttled around, feeling for the closest body. The chains restricted his reach, but his hand closed around the arm of another man, Bearach—the one who'd seemed the least hostile to him. Robrek was tired, but fortunately, poison was an easy problem to handle. He drew the contaminant from the man's body into his own and neutralized it.

Almost immediately, Bearach gasped and sat up. "Where am I?"

"I have no idea," Robrek answered, rolling to the other side and reaching for the next closest man. He strained against his chains. Finally, he felt the tip of the man's fingers against his; he didn't know this one's name. Again, he drew the poison from the man's body into his own and neutralized it. The tenuousness of his hold made it much harder and more time-consuming, but at last he'd leached all the poison out of the man's system. The man jerked awake. "Where's the princess?" he shouted.

"The others are poisoned, too; there's no time for questions," Robrek answered. Robrek scrambled to reach another man, but the others were beyond his reach. "Can either of you touch one of the others? Perhaps I can reach them through you."

He could hear the other men searching around in the darkness. "I got someone," the second man shouted.

Robrek quickly grasped the man's fingers, but released them abruptly. "The captain hasn't been poisoned. What about the others?"

Darhour felt someone grab and release his arm. He kept his eyes closed, delaying his first view of the seven hells, where he would spend eternity. He was here, but Argblutal still lived. To save the life of the sorcerer, he had stripped his daughter of protection when she needed him most. He could think of no words strong enough to condemn his betrayal. If it was his destiny to rot in darkness, why had he not at least brought his daughter's enemies here with him? He froze as someone spoke.

"I've got one." It was Bearach's voice. Darhour tried to sit up, but he found himself too weak to move. He was in a cell of some kind with the sorcerer and his men. *No, I can't be alive. I took an arrow through the heart.*

The sorcerer spoke, "It's no use. He's dead, and I can't bring the dead back."

"No! The lieutenant can't be dead! Try again!" Bearach's voice rang with the desperation of the damned. *The lieutenant dead? He couldn't possibly mean Kailen!* But Kailen lay still on the other side of the cell.

The others scrambled in the darkness that must be too thick to allow them to see, and the sorcerer spoke again, "There's nothing more I can do. The other two are dead."

"Try again!" Bearach demanded. "Don't tell me you can do nothing!"

"Bearach," Conroy said, "he's a healer, not a god."

The significance of those confined with him sunk in. He jerked himself up into a sitting position. By some miracle of the goddess, he still breathed. "Who is with the princess?" he demanded.

"Kailen and Brice are dead, captain," Bearach said. "I guess no one's with the princess."

Darhour tugged furiously against his chains. "How could you let yourselves be taken?"

"We're sorry, Captain," Conroy replied. "We were poisoned."

Shuddering at the thought of the duke touching his daughter, he turned to the sorcerer. "You claim to have strong magic. Get us out of here," he ordered.

"How?" Robrek tugged against the chains. "My power only affects living things."

"Just who are you?" Darhour snapped.

"You know who I am."

Darhour's words bit into him. "You're the man who pretended to be a peasant, deceived the princess, and tricked her into falling in love with you. I have no idea who you really are. I'll have no more of your lies!"

Robrek sagged wearily against the wall. *That's probably what she thinks, too. That's why she was so cold.* "I've never lied to you or Her Highness. I don't expect you to believe me, but can you keep your suspicions at bay until Her Highness is safe?"

"Captain, he saved your life. Ours, too," Conroy said. "If he meant her ill, why would he have done so?"

A heavy silence filled the cell, and Robrek feared the captain was contemplating the best way to get rid of him. Finally, the older man said, "Let me make this clear. I don't like you, and I don't trust you. But for whatever reason, you seem to be on Her Highness's side. I'm willing to agree to a truce until Duke Argblutal is dead, but after that, all bets are off."

"Agreed. I only ask that before you slit my throat, you discuss it with Her Highness."

To Robrek's surprise, Darhour chuckled. "Fair enough. But I *will* slit your throat if the occasion calls for it."

* * *

The sun was beginning to rise as Oriana crept through the palace corridors, jumping into alcoves and shadows whenever she heard footsteps approaching. She blinked to rid her eyes of tears. *Holy Sulis, Mother of us all, why did you let it happen? I could have made him well. I have to find the princess. But the palace is just too big! Please, Sulis, help me.* She saw a couple of guards ahead and hurriedly slipped through a nearby door. She ran straight into the boy with the ridiculous hat and sausages for arms. "You're Sir Robrek's squire, aren't you?"

"Shhh!" he whispered. "Don't betray me, I beg you."

"Of course I won't," she whispered back. "Do you know where the princess's rooms are? I have to warn her."

"I know, for all the good it will do us." He wiped at his eyes fiercely as if trying to deny he'd shed any tears. "Her door is surrounded by guards. I can't think of any way to get by them. Duke

Argblutal took Sir Robrek and Her Highness's guards to the dungeon."

"There has to be a way." Oriana wrinkled up her forehead. "Flowers," she said. "Do you know where I can find flowers?"

The boy stared at her stupidly. "What good are flowers?"

Oriana rolled her eyes at the boy, who obviously knew nothing about weddings. "It's supposed to be Her Highness's wedding day, isn't it? If I had some flowers, I could tell the guards I was bringing them to dress Her Highness's hair, couldn't I? Now, do you know where I can find some flowers?"

The boy screwed up his face in concentration. His face brightened, and he nodded. "This way." He headed down the corridor.

* * *

"What could be keeping them?" Samantha asked for the thousandth time as she paced the floor. Far too restless to sleep, she'd been pacing all night. She kept expecting Bearach or Conroy or Devyn—someone—to return and tell her what was happening. Even Kailen and Brice failed to answer when she'd pounded on the outer door. Although she'd promised she wouldn't open the door unless one of them assured her it was safe, she'd reached for the heavy bar, but Blaine, in an unprecedented show of defiance, had blocked the door and insisted she could skewer him like a roasted pig, so to speak, but he wouldn't allow her to expose herself to danger. *Sulis curse it! He's right. If it were safe, someone would have told me.*

As the sun peeked over the horizon, Blaine's face took on the same expression he'd had when he blocked the door. "Your Highness, we have to get out of here. If they were coming back, they'd be here by now."

Samantha sank into a chair, knowing, but not wanting to admit, that Blaine was right. She'd never forgive herself for not doing as Caedmon wanted and escaping to the plains when she had the chance.

A knock sounded at the door. "Your Highness. It's me." Samantha felt giddy with relief when she heard Lord Devyn's voice. "Please unbar the door. I have excellent news."

She nodded at Blaine, and he took down the bar, letting Devyn and two of his men inside.

Devyn bowed low. "I apologize for the delay, Your Highness. You must have been frantic. But the palace has been in turmoil and has only just quieted. The healer you brought to the king has restored his mind. More of the Royal Guard were loyal to His Majesty than we thought. He's managed to have Argblutal and his men arrested. Sir Robrek is well. Your guards are outside, and the king has instructed I tell you to prepare for your wedding ceremony. It's to be held in an hour."

"This is too wonderful to be true." She wanted to leap, to dance, to sing. But her spirits crumbled immediately as she realized Devyn wasn't meeting her eyes and none of her guards had accompanied him into the room. They never would have allowed Devyn and two strangers to come in unescorted.

Devyn had betrayed her.

She'd roast Devyn's entrails, but first she needed to get to Caedmon. She hid her pain and fury behind a court smile. "I'll see you well paid for your part in this. If you'll excuse me now, I must dress for my wedding."

"Of course, Your Highness." Devyn bowed and left.

Ardra approached her smiling. "Can you believe it, Your Highness?"

Fighting against a wail of grief, Samantha clutched at her stomach. "Devyn's betrayed me. They're all dead. They must be."

Blaine and her maids stared at her as if she'd suddenly lost her mind. She would have explained, but she heard voices on the other side of the door and drew closer to listen. "Her Highness is preparing for her wedding. No one's allowed in," a male voice said.

"But how can she do that without any flowers for her hair?" Oriana protested. *At least the child's still alive.* "No woman, especially not a princess, gets married without flowers. It simply isn't done."

She couldn't hear the man's response, but someone knocked on the door. "It's Oriana, Your Highness. I've brought your flowers."

"Let her in, Blaine."

As soon as the door opened, the novice hurried into the room. She dropped the flowers she'd been holding, ran to the princess, and clutched her hands. "Your Highness, Vaughan's been trying to get to you, too, but I had the flower idea. The duke has thrown Conroy and Sir Robrek and the others in the dungeon. He's going to make you marry him."

Samantha grabbed Oriana's shoulder. "They're not dead? There's still hope?"

"They'll be dead if we don't save them."

"What about my father?" she forced herself to ask, but she already knew the answer.

Oriana burst into tears. "I'm sorry, Your Highness. The evil duke stabbed him right through the heart. I'm not powerful like Sir Robrek. There was nothing I could do."

"No!" she cried. "No, Father, no!"

"Your Highness, what will we do?" Blaine asked. "If Devyn's men are traitors, too, we're trapped."

He's right. There truly is no hope! But she heard again the words of the priestess on the island. *"Take comfort, my child. The goddess will walk the path beside you, and your friends will stay true to you when many turn against you."* Those friends were now in danger, as was Sir Robrek. She couldn't afford to feel emotion, so she carved a hole in her heart and stuffed all her grief inside and shut the door She rose like the queen she now was. "Get the trap door open, Blaine. We'll have to risk trusting Devyn's men. Help him, Malvina. Ardra, get my armor. We're going to rescue them. I'm leaving none of you behind."

Blaine looked as if he might vomit, but he and Malvina started moving the heavy table. Ardra, however, stood still. She was ghost white. "You don't have enough time to free them before the duke discovers you gone, Your Highness."

"Get my armor." She wouldn't allow herself to think that.

"I'll wear your dress and your veil and walk down the aisle with the duke. That should buy you enough time."

"No, Ardra! Do you have any idea what Argblutal will do to you?"

Ardra nodded. "But I'll do my part to stop that monster from taking the throne."

"Ardra's right, Your Highness," Malvina said. "You have to get free. I'll stay and help her. The dress has about a thousand buttons up the back; she'd never be able to get it on without help."

"No! I said I'm leaving none of you behind!"

"You have no choice, Your Highness. If we don't buy you time enough to escape, the duke will kill us all," Ardra said.

"No," she said. "I would never ask this of you."

"That's why I'll do it, Your Highness," Ardra said.

"I'm so sorry, Ardra. If there were any other choice." Stuffing her fear for her maids into the hole with the rest of her emotions, Samantha turned to Oriana. "Go to Father Hafghan. Vaughan can show you the way. Tell the priest it's my will he perform the longest wedding ceremony in the history of the joined kingdoms. Then, you and Vaughan find a place to hide and stay there. Vaughan will know of one."

"Yes, Your Highness." The girl bowed and left.

Ardra quickly dressed the princess in her armor while Blaine and Malvina struggled to get the trap door open. When they finally succeeded, the officer in charge stood and bowed to her. "Captain Irving, Your Highness. Can we be of assistance?"

"Duke Argblutal has murdered my father and imprisoned Sir Robrek and my personal guard. I'll need your help in rescuing them."

Irving gasped, "Your pardon, Your Highness, but we must get you to safety first."

"No, we'll rescue my men and my betrothed. I am your liege, and these are my orders."

Captain Irving bowed. "Of course, Your Highness."

She grabbed Ardra in one last tight hug and followed Devyn's men down the staircase. Blaine brought up the rear. She told herself she wouldn't think of Ardra—bloody and dead. She refused to imagine the king with Argblutal's sword piercing his heart. She wouldn't envisage Darhour hanging from a gallows or Sir Robrek tied to the rack. But her maids closed the trapdoor, shutting out all light from above, and the tunnel was a place to bring dark thoughts even to those who weren't already living a nightmare. The soldiers' torches did little to cut through the absolute blackness, and the constant drip of water seemed to be the blood dripping from the bodies of those she loved. The floor was slick with it, making footing treacherous and progress slow when every moment's delay might make her too late to save her men. Mold and fungus grew everywhere, adding to the dangerous footing and producing the sharp stench of death and decay. When they finally reached the bottom of the staircase, rats scurried away from the light, and her feet crushed the bones of small animals. *How can a successful rescue begin in such a horrible place?* As they neared the end of the tunnel, she shoved this thought into her heart.

When she climbed the ladder into Adalardo's office in the stables, Captain Irving had a knife at the Master of the Horse's throat. "No,

Captain," she ordered. "Adalardo and the stable hands are loyal to me."

"Can you be sure?" Irving hissed.

"I've known Adalardo since I was a small child. I'm far more sure of him than I am of you."

Looking stunned, Irving withdrew the knife. "Your Highness, you have my complete loyalty."

"I'm betting my life and the lives of those I love on that."

Oriana and Vaughan came pounding in, gasping for breath.

"I thought I told you to hide."

Oriana rolled her eyes. "That's what we were going to do, Your Highness. After I delivered your message to Father Hafghan, Vaughan said he knew a place in the stables."

"Use it," she commanded. "Adalardo, I need thirty horses saddled and ready when we return."

"Wait, Your Highness," Vaughan protested. "It would be faster if we take the horses with us. Me and Oriana and a couple of grooms can hold the horses. We don't have to worry about them being seen. Sir Robrek's horses can hide them and us. The silver one helped Sir Robrek break me out of the duke's cellar."

The bronze, silver, and gold horses nickered as if confirming the stable boy's words. *What are they? Just who is this man I thought I loved?*

* * *

As Malvina fastened the buttons on the back of the glorious dress, Ardra admired herself in the mirror. "Her Highness would have looked so lovely."

Malvina smiled through her tears. "She would have. But she would have complained the entire time about how uncomfortable the dress was." Ardra gave a half laugh, and Malvina finished buttoning and came around to survey her friend. "I haven't time to dress your hair proper. I'll just have to hide it under the veil."

Ardra shrugged. "Doesn't matter. Nobody will be looking at my hair."

"Ardra, I wish it could be me instead."

Ardra shook her head. "It has to be me. I'm small like Her Highness."

Malvina sobbed as she attached the veil to Ardra's hair, making sure not a trace of blonde showed. She took a small sheath out of her pocket. "Here, take it. You might want it."

Ardra held the small knife. "You be thinking I can take on the great duke with this little bitty thing?"

"No, but you might be wanting it anyway."

"Ah," Ardra said, and tucked the knife into her bosom. She drew her friend into a hug. "As soon as they come for me, hide. One of us has to be around to dress Her Highness for her real wedding. We can't be trusting anyone else to get it right."

Malvina squeezed hard. "Don't be worrying about me. Oh, no, I've mussed your dress." Malvina straightened it.

When the knock sounded on the door, Malvina drew the veil down over Ardra's face. She dried her eyes and unbarred the door.

The court ladies entered to escort the princess to the chapel. Accompanying them were about a dozen members of the Royal Guard. The officer in charge bowed to her, as if she were the princess. "We're your protection until we get to the chapel, Your Highness. Your personal guard will meet you there."

How daft do they think the princess be? Like the captain would ever trust anyone else with Her Highness's safety! But Ardra merely nodded her assent.

Two of the court women gathered up her train. The others preceded or followed her, strewing flower petals and singing the wedding hymn. As she left the room, she glanced briefly at Malvina; her friend gave her a smile holding no hope they'd meet again. She fought against her own tears and walked with the slow dignity of a princess. Ardra prayed that no one would notice her trembling. Did the nobles of the court know what was going on? If she really was the princess and she cried out for their help, would they leap to her assistance? Or were they all as much traitors as Lord Devyn?

* * *

Vaughan must have been right about the magical horses because they crossed the palace grounds without anyone noticing. Few of Argblutal's men were around; Samantha guessed most of them were guarding the palace chapel. Two guards stood in front of the small side door nearest the dungeon, but Irving's men dispatched them.

535

The men pulled the bodies behind a bush, and Samantha left Vaughan, Oriana, Blaine, and a couple of stable grooms with the horses. The rest of them slipped through the door into a deserted corridor. As they turned a corner, they met a patrol of five men. Her men quickly killed four of them, but the fifth turned and started to run, so she palmed her knife as Darhour had taught her and threw it. To her complete shock, she caught him square in the back. She'd never thrown that accurately before.

This part of the palace was deserted, and they didn't meet any more guards until they reached the dungeon entrance. Her men dispatched the two guards there, but not before one of them yelled, "Attack!" The shout brought more than a dozen men running up the steps from the dungeon below. Irving's men tried to protect her. She hadn't fully appreciated the expertise of her own men until she fought with Irving's. Several men got past their guard and in reach of her own sword, but because of Darhour's rigorous training, not a one of them marked her. Her sword became stained with blood as they fought their way down the dungeon stairs. Men fell and died, and in the confusion of the battle, Samantha wasn't sure how many of them were hers.

Despite the carnage, the fight was brief, and when she reached the bottom, only two of the dungeon guards remained. They both dropped their weapons and raised their hands.

"Do you support regicide and usurpation of the throne?"

The men looked at the bloody sword in her hand. "No, Your Highness."

"My betrothed and my guard have been imprisoned. You will bring me to them and free them." When the first guard seemed to waver, she pressed her sword against his throat. "I don't need you both. You have three seconds to decide if you want to live."

"The keys are right over here," he stammered. "I'll show you the way."

Samantha eased her sword away from his throat, and the man fetched the keys from the guard's desk. "How many guards stand in our way?" she asked.

"I think you killed them all, Your Majesty, except the two in front of the sorcerer's cell."

Samantha had her men tie and gag the second guard, and they followed the one with the keys down the corridor on the right.

* * *

Feeling weak and hungry, Robrek could tell Darhour still didn't trust him. They'd come up with an escape plan, but he wasn't at all sure it would work. Its biggest flaw was that it relied on someone unlocking the door and coming into the cell. Unfortunately, none of them could think of anything better.

Suddenly, he felt over a dozen men approaching. "About a dozen men are coming." They all assumed their positions, but Robrek had less hope then ever. They hadn't counted on so many.

To Robrek's surprise, the first part of the plan worked perfectly. A key turned in the lock, the door swung open, and someone came far enough into the cell for him to grab his ankle. Robrek sent him crashing to the floor and into a deep sleep. A nearby thud told him one of the others had gotten another one. Robrek reached for another, and the light from the corridor poured into the room. There, like a goddess surrounded by a halo of light, stood the princess.

The captain saw her at the same instant. "Your Highness, what are you doing here?" he asked, removing his hands from the throat of the man he'd been attempting to strangle.

"Rescuing you. What does it look like?"

A soldier entered the cell, took the keys from the guard Robrek had sent to sleep, and kicked him out of the way. "He isn't one of us," he said as he unlocked Robrek's shackles.

Robrek smiled as he got to his feet. "In the bards' tales isn't it the knight who rescues the princess, Your Highness?"

She laughed, and for a moment her eyes sparkled, and she'd never looked so beautiful as she did at that moment.

"There's no need to worry about those two," Darhour said, pointing at the bodies of the guards he'd been unable to save.

"No!" the princess cried. "They can't be dead. Robbie, do something!"

"I'm sorry, Your Highness. I tried, but I was too late."

"Your Highness," Darhour said, "we'll mourn the dead later. We must get you to safety. You shouldn't have risked coming for us."

"How could you think I'd leave you to Argblutal?" Her Highness said to Darhour, and Robrek felt sick. The princess loved her guards, not him. But Robrek loved her, and he would see her safe.

As they left the cell, Robrek picked up the sword of one of the dead men. They ran down the corridor and to the dungeon steps, the area around which was strewn with dead and dying men. The healer within him recoiled at the sight, but he pushed his way to the front. "Let me take the lead," Robrek insisted. "I may be able to hide us."

Two men flanked Robrek as he led the way up the staircase. The sword felt hot in his hand. At the top of the staircase, he ran into another pile of bodies. *Holy Sulis, how many have died to set us free?* He tried to tell himself it'd been necessary, that if Argblutal was allowed to claim the throne far worse would happen, but seeing the loss of so much life sickened him.

Feeling a single guard coming around the corner, he tried to project an image of himself and his companions as fellow guards. Although it seemed to work for a few seconds, Robrek was too weak to maintain the illusion. The guard's eyes widened, and Robrek thrust before the man had a chance to cry out. He froze as the man dropped at his feet. The others ran past him, and he forced himself to follow. They met no more guards, and those in the lead were running out a door. When he burst through after them, Vaughan grinned at him from Fancy Man's back. Wild Thing, Brazen, and Holy Writ were all there. The princess and most of the other men were already mounted.

He vaulted onto Wild Thing's back. *:No more dungeons. Wild Thing scared.:*

He patted her neck to comfort her. "I was scared, too, but I'm here now."

They took off at a gallop toward a small side gate. Bearach fit an arrow to a bow he must have acquired from one of the dead guards. Other archers among them did likewise. The battlement guards had no idea what hit them as the arrows began to fly.

* * *

Argblutal swore under his breath, as Father Hafghan repeated for at least the dozenth time, "The sons and daughters of Sulis should be united in love and harmony."

The priest's marriage sermon had already been about four times longer than was typical, and still he showed no sign of drawing it to a close. When the ceremony was over, Argblutal vowed he'd do the joined kingdoms a favor and have Father Hafghan hung, drawn, and quartered so he didn't bore anyone else to death. The princess stood like a statue beside him. Her hands trembled slightly, but she portrayed as little emotion as she had when he'd informed her outside the wedding chapel of the change of groom. He merely had to threaten to kill the king and all of her men, and she'd nodded her acquiescence. If she just lay there and let him do what he wanted in the marriage bed, she'd be little entertainment.

The door of the palace chapel burst open. "Your Grace, there's an attack on the palace walls," one of his men reported.

"Finish it now," Argblutal snapped at the priest. "Just the vows."

The priest paled. "Do you Argblutal, Duke of Handgriff, take Her Highness, the Crown Princess Samantha and Heir to the throne of the joined kingdoms, as your wife under the eyes of the goddess from this day forward, as long as you both shall live?"

"Yes, of course!"

The priest turned to the princess. "Do you Samantha, Crown Princess and Heir to the throne of the joined kingdoms, take Argblutal, Duke of Handgriff, as your husband under the eyes of the goddess from this day forward, as long as you both shall live?"

"Her Highness sure wouldn't, and I don't, neither!" an uncultured voice said from under the veil.

Argblutal tore off the veil to see he'd nearly been tricked into marrying the princess's maid. "Where is she?" he hissed.

"Attacking the palace walls, I be guessing."

Argblutal slapped the impudent wench, knocking her into the altar. He drew his sword and pointed it to the priest's throat. "You will pay for your part in this!"

"I swear I had no idea it wasn't Her Highness," Hafghan said.

He turned to his men. "Put him in a dungeon cell, and take her to my quarters. With me!" he yelled to the others and led the way out of the palace.

He reached the courtyard in time to watch what had to be the princess and her men disappearing through the far palace gate. His men were offering no resistance; it was almost as if they couldn't see the fleeing men. "Shoot, you idiots! Kill them!"

Still, they did nothing. With growing rage, he realized they must have betrayed him to support the princess. Promising himself he'd kill them all as slowly as possible, he yelled for horses. When they arrived, he vaulted into the saddle, but quickly found himself on the ground. Someone hadn't cinched the saddle tightly. "Damn the bitch!" he yelled. One of his men scrambled to saddle his horse properly, and others checked the rest of the saddles. They were all loose. The stable grooms would die as well, but for now, he and his men roared out of the palace gate in pursuit of the princess.

Although the princess had a head start, he was able to gain on them by trampling anyone foolish enough to get in his way. By the time they neared the city gates, he'd almost caught up. The sorcerer looked back at them, and Argblutal's horse and those of his men reared and bucked in panic.

The duke fought to control his frantic beast. Some of his men were thrown, and their horses fled back to the palace. Finally, he and about twenty of his men regained control of their mounts and raced through the gates after the princess. They'd lost substantial ground, but he still thought they'd be able to catch them. But he reined in hard as he saw about one hundred fighters riding to meet the princess. He swore a horrible oath, whirled, and galloped back to the city walls. He heard the cries of his men as arrows took some of them from behind.

* * *

Ardra struggled as two of the duke's men threw her onto a bed to join Zinerva's lady, Lady Aislinn, who was tied to the bed. "Another toy for His Grace," one of the guards who brought her said to the two already in the room, and then left.

The guards in the room looked up from the game they were playing. "Are you going to be a good girl and lie still, or do we have to tie you up like that one?"

Ardra felt Malvina's knife against her bosom. "No, please, please, don't hurt me," she simpered. "I'll be good. I won't stir without your say-so."

"See that you don't," the guard said, looking her up and down and leering at her breasts before turning his attention back to the game.

Ardra made a quick survey of the room. Lord Devyn was gagged and hanging by his wrists from the ceiling. Hoping he was in even more pain than he appeared to be, Ardra considered using her little bitty knife to cut the traitor's heart out, but she decided whatever the duke had in mind would be worse than anything she could think of. There were only the two guards, and they were engrossed in their game. She took Malvina's knife out of her bosom and leaned close to Lady Aislinn. As she cut the rope binding the lady, she whispered in her ear, "If I distract them and get one of them with my wee knife, do you think you could knock the other over the head with something?"

Lady Aislinn nodded, her eyes flashing with rage. Zinerva had said her lady was fiery. Adjusting the dress to reveal more of her breasts, Ardra scooted to the edge of the bed and hung her legs over, taking care to show a good deal of them.

"Who said you could move?" the guard snapped at her, his eyes wandering freely from her breasts to her legs.

"I don't be meaning no harm. I just be scared and kind of lonely."

"Lonely, is it?" the other laughed. "Come over here, and I'll keep you plenty good company."

"I don't mind if I do." With the knife concealed in her right hand, she strolled across the room and sat on the man's lap. He grabbed her rear and buried his nose in her cleavage.

"Careful, Clust, you know how the duke feels about used goods," the other guard said.

"I've been used goods for some time now." Ardra smiled suggestively at the disapproving guard. Lady Aislinn was moving slowly to get behind him. "But I don't mind being used a bit more. I wouldn't mind at all giving you a turn when I'm through with this one." She turned and licked the side of Clust's neck.

"Clust, I'm warning you—"

"Stay out of this, Sloane. I've never refused a willing cunt yet, and I'm not about to start now."

Ardra lowered her mouth to Clust's. His tongue felt repulsive, but she teased it with her own, moving her arm behind him to the spot Captain Darhour had said was the best for killing a man from behind. She thrust her knife in hard. Clust cried out in surprise. At the same moment, she heard a loud crash behind her. She turned. Sloane had slumped down in his chair, and Lady Aislinn was holding a broken water jug and smiling savagely.

"Do you think he's dead?" she panted.

"I don't know, Milady, but now don't be the time to be worrying about such things." Ardra disentangled herself from Clust, who was surely dead. She grabbed Lady Aislinn's hand and pulled her toward the entrance to the servants' corridors. "Quick. Before anyone else comes."

"Lord Devyn?"

"I'll not be wasting time rescuing traitors," Ardra protested.

Lady Aislinn grabbed Ardra's other hand, the one that still held her small knife. "I know he shouldn't have, but he's never been strong, and the duke threatened to do horrible things to me if Devyn didn't do exactly as he wanted."

Ardra reluctantly let her have the knife, and she cut Devyn free. He stumbled and grabbed Aislinn for support. With the other hand, he pulled a wadded handkerchief out of his mouth. "You should have left me, Aislinn. I deserve to die."

"We be worrying about what you deserve when we get away from here," Ardra scolded, and headed into the servants' corridors.

CHAPTER 43

When Samantha rode into Duke Caedmon's camp, the old duke hurried forward to help her dismount. "I can't tell you how happy I am to see you alive, Your Highness. What madness caused you to walk into Argblutal's trap?" Duke Sheen, Baron Teague, and a host of lesser Korthian nobles gathered around her.

Samantha ignored the question. "Duke Argblutal has murdered my father and taken control of the palace."

"Solar? Dead?" Caedmon put his hand to his heart. "That is a most grievous blow." He shook himself. "We will mourn the dead later. Now, we must put the rightful queen on the throne."

Samantha took Sir Robrek's hand and drew him up beside her. "May I present my betrothed and future consort, Sir Robrek of Mahngbhayo."

Robrek bowed appropriately for the occasion, and the nobles returned the gesture with little enthusiasm and even a glint of hostility. "The wounded, Your Highness. I should see to them," Robrek said.

"Yes, of course." She released his hand, ashamed she'd forgotten some of Captain Irving's men had been wounded. "Duke Caedmon, I need to see you privately for a moment."

"Of course, Your Majesty."

"I haven't yet been crowned. Let's leave it at Your Highness for now."

"One moment, Your Highness," Sheen interrupted. "Is my son with you?"

"I'm sorry, Your Grace. He didn't make it out, but he was alive when I last saw him." She didn't think now was the time for Sheen to learn of his son's treason. Since there was little likelihood Devyn would survive, Sheen might never need to know.

Caedmon led the way toward a tent. The meeting wasn't exactly private because Darhour refused to leave her side. Conroy and Bearach remained outside to make sure no one overhead.

"I know what this is about, Your Highness," Caedmon assured her, patting her on the shoulder. "We'll take care of that foreign sorcerer."

"You most certainly will not!" Samantha, said, the duke jerked his hand away. "Sir Robrek is my betrothed! He is the chosen of the goddess!"

Caedmon smiled at her as if she were a five-year-old asking for a treat that would spoil her dinner. "I'm sure he's handsome enough, Your Highness, but we'll discuss his appropriateness later."

"No, we won't. If I am queen, Sir Robrek will be my consort."

"What do you mean, if you are queen? Surely you don't doubt we will prevail against the traitors?"

She shook her head. "That may not be my greatest difficulty. You were close to the king. Did he ever tell you the truth about my father?"

Opening his mouth, Caedmon looked toward Darhour. "This is not something to discuss before witnesses. Indeed, it is not something you should ever mention again. You are Solar's chosen heir."

"Darhour already knows, and he isn't the only one. Somehow Argblutal has found out. He isn't likely to keep it a secret. I believe we can control the damage better if the news comes from me rather than the duke. What would you advise?"

Caedmon nodded. "I think it would be best if you allowed me to broach the subject. We will meet in the council tent as soon as you've had a chance to freshen up."

* * *

Fortunately, none of the wounded had life-threatening injuries. After caring for them, Robrek left them with a young novice and followed Vaughan to a tent that had been prepared for him. He washed up and changed out of his blood-stained clothes into the silver silks and belted the silver-hilted sword around his waist. As he passed through the camp, every eye followed him, sizing him up and finding him wanting. If Her Highness didn't seem to share their opinion, it wouldn't have bothered him so much.

Ahead he saw the princess emerging from a tent; she'd also washed and changed into fresh clothing. As she joined the men around the council tent, he stopped to watch her. She was little taller than he was, but she was far too regal to be overshadowed by the men surrounding her. Three of her guards were with her, including the one Robrek knew she loved. *Would she have even cared if I had been one of those lying dead on the dungeon floor?*

The princess smiled as she caught sight of him, but her eyes didn't sparkle. She beckoned him to her and took his hand. "You look far better than when I found you this morning."

"I clean up well." He smiled.

"So you do," she said, barely looking at him. "Duke Caedmon is assembling the council of nobles to discuss a plan of action. You will sit beside me so there is no question you are my betrothed."

How can she still plan to marry me when she feels so little for me? But he couldn't leave until she was safe.

As Samantha led Sir Robrek into the council tent, she felt hollow. This sorcerer, this knight, bore little resemblance to the handsome peasant boy who'd filled her dreams for over a year. She tried to console herself. *I never expected to marry for love.*

Taking her place at the head of the council table, she gestured the knight to the seat at her right. Caedmon took the one on her left. After the rest of the nobles were seated, Caedmon stood. "Defenders of the joined kingdoms, I'm sure you have all heard that Duke Argblutal has murdered our rightful king, Solar II."

"I will see him drawn and quartered," Sheen fumed. There was a chorus of agreement.

"But Argblutal's foul deeds do not stop there," Caedmon continued. "He attempted to force Solar's heir, the Princess Samantha, to marry him. When that failed, he began spreading rumors that Her Highness is not Solar's true daughter."

"How dare he!" Baron Gwawl protested.

"Clearly, there is no foul act the duke wouldn't attempt," Caedmon said. "The question is, shall we let him get away with it? Shall we believe the slander of a regicidal usurper? Will we allow such lies to stand unchallenged?"

As the nobles answered with a resounding "No!" Samantha stared at Caedmon. *How dare he say he'd handle it without telling me what he intended to do! He's trapped me. I can't contradict him now without handing Argblutal the crown on a silver platter. He's treating me like a child!*

As the tent erupted with cries of "Long live Queen Samantha," she rose to her feet. She'd show Caedmon that he couldn't dismiss her so easily. "I thank you for your loyalty, and be assured it will be well rewarded. Allow me to introduce the goddess's, and my own, choice for consort, the bronze, silver, and gold knight who through his magic and Sulis's blessing has done the impossible—Sir Robrek of Mahngbhayo." Staring into Caedmon's eyes, she took the sorcerer's hand and raised him to his feet.

"Long live Sir Robrek!" Baron Gwawl called out, and the rest of the tent took up the cry, but less enthusiastically than when they had praised her. Her gesture seemed lost on Caedmon, who remained resolutely silent. She wanted to cry, scream, or punch something; she didn't need this difficulty from her most important ally. She shoved her frustration into the hole in her heart with her grief and carefully maintained a court mask. "Now we must plan the best manner to eliminate the regicidal usurper. If it can be done without many casualties, I would prefer it so. But at this point, I am open to any suggestions."

The nobles were disappointed when Sir Robrek assured them he couldn't call fire from Beyond the Far Mountain and simply incinerate the duke's men—a plan that, even if it were possible, didn't meet her criteria of minimal casualties. Nor did any of the other ideas presented. It seemed as if the Korthian nobles wouldn't be satisfied unless they had shed barrels of Lundian blood. Argblutal had to be gotten rid of, but if she alienated all of Lundia in the process, she could find herself with even worse problems.

After being silent for hours, Sir Robrek finally spoke, "The duke is a brutal man." The men's eyes registered surprise as they turned to her betrothed. It seemed they'd all forgotten he was there.

Caedmon laughed contemptuously. "Yes, thanks for reminding us that the murderer of our king is, as you say, 'a brutal man.'"

As the men waited to see how Sir Robrek would respond to the blatant mockery, the tent went deathly silent. Samantha wanted to ram her fist through Caedmon's mouth and out the back of his head.

Sir Robrek's skin darkened. "Brutal men do not inspire loyalty in their followers. Those who support them do so either out of fear or greed. Isn't it likely that many would simply surrender if Her Highness could convince them to be more afraid of her than the duke, or demonstrate that Argblutal couldn't deliver on his promises?"

"How would Her Highness do that?" Sheen demanded.

"On the morrow, we could ride until we are just out of arrow range of the palace walls. My magic affects all things living, so I believe I could amplify Her Highness's voice so it could be heard throughout the palace. Her Highness could convince the duke's men of the weakness of their position and the injustice of the duke's cause. If the words are chosen well, I think it likely many would choose surrender over battle. They couldn't have been expecting an army of this size so soon."

Samantha's embarrassment for her betrothed turned into a smile of admiration; she was ashamed at how quickly she'd discounted him.

Baron Gwawl laughed. "The idea is simple, yet brilliant. If it works, it would not only save hundreds of lives, but would be far less likely to turn Lundia against Her Highness. I like it."

Caedmon cleared his throat. "It would be nice to believe it could be resolved so easily. But what if the duke's men choose not to surrender?"

Sir Robrek met the duke's challenge with remarkable poise. "When you fought beside King Solar, did you ever know him to have just one plan?" Samantha wanted to laugh. Without seeming to insult the duke, he'd reminded them all Caedmon had never seen battle. He'd been a child of ten when her father had ended the civil war and started an era of fifty years of unbroken peace. Indeed, none of those in the tent had experienced anything more formidable than skirmishes with bandits. Robrek might not be the boy she'd thought she loved, but maybe she wouldn't regret the goddess's choice of him.

Baron Teague wiped his mouth to hide a smile. "There can certainly be no harm in giving it a try. If it doesn't work, we can always make the palace walls run with blood, as His Grace desires."

Caedmon's court mask was insufficient to hide his fury that a mere boy had outmaneuvered him. He could look like a fool by continuing to mock Sir Robrek or he could graciously accept the plan. Despite his flaws, Caedmon had never been a fool.

* * *

Argblutal stormed into the palace. "Draw all my men into the palace grounds," he snapped at Kentigern. "Mohan!" Argblutal shouted as he pounded down the corridors toward his quarters. "The damage?"

Mohan answered, "Twenty-five men were killed as the princess made her escape through the side gate. At least another thirty bodies have been found throughout the palace. Another ten didn't return from your pursuit of her."

"Are you trying to tell me I lost sixty-five men, and not a single one of the bitch's was killed?"

"We've found half a dozen bodies that appear to be her men."

Argblutal burst into his chambers to find his bed empty of women, and the two men he'd left to guard them slumped over in their chairs. One was clearly dead, but the other seemed to have been knocked unconscious. "Get me that priest," he hissed at Mohan.

* * *

Father Hafghan walked with as much dignity as he could muster in his chains. When he entered the corridor to the duke's quarters, he could hear screaming and begging. His guards knocked on the door, and after a moment, the door opened to reveal two large soldiers dragging a half-naked man out of the room. The man wore no trousers, and the blood covering his lower body didn't hide his mutilation. Hafghan nearly vomited. Hafghan was forced inside where the duke stood, holding a bloody knife. "A simple discipline problem. I'm sure you understand."

When Hafghan's guards forced him down on the table, the other man's blood soaked into his robes. The duke placed the tip of his knife near Hafghan's groin. "How is it that you dared to marry me to a common whore?"

Hafghan struggled not to turn into a blubbering idiot. "I swear I had no idea it wasn't Her Highness."

Argblutal ripped a hole in Hafghan's robes with the knife. "You expect me to believe you preached the longest and most boring wedding sermon in the entire history of the joined kingdoms on a whim?"

Hafghan closed his eyes so he wouldn't have to see the knife. *It will merely ensure that from now on I keep my vow of celibacy.* "Her Highness requested I draw the ceremony out as long as possible, but I swear on my honor as a servant of the goddess I had no idea why."

"You swear on your honor? I guess I'll have to believe you then," the duke said, and Hafghan wasn't sure whether to be relieved or more afraid. "As I am a man of mercy, I'll give you a chance to atone for your part in the deception.

* * *

Ardra stood in the vast cellar next to Lady Aislinn. "Is this really necessary?" Lady Aislinn asked, looking over at Lord Devyn, who was tied to a barrel of sausages. Ardra's handkerchief was shoved into his mouth, and two palace footmen stood with their arms crossed on either side of him.

"He's lucky I didn't have them kill him for what he did to Her Highness."

"You won't hurt him, though, will you?" she pleaded.

"I'll let Her Highness decide what to do to him. If I were her, I'd have him drawn and quartered."

Lady Aislinn paled. "Her Highness will be merciful."

In ones and twos, the palace servants answered to the pages Ardra had sent. Adalardo, the Master of Horse, and all of the stable boys and grooms came as well. Soon, Malvina arrived. When she saw Ardra, she gave a squeal of delight, rushed toward her and nearly crushed her in a hug. "Oh, sweets, I never thought to see you again. How did you get away?"

"Oh, it wasn't hard," she smiled mischievously. "The wee bitty knife of yours did come in handy after all."

"The duke? You didn't!" Malvina gasped.

"Nah, not the duke, but I did be making good use of it on one of his men. Her ladyship here broke the other's skull." Malvina nodded proudly and patted Lady Aislinn's hand.

Maggie, the chief cook, bustled in. At this point, it seemed that nearly all the palace servants Ardra felt she could trust had arrived.

She cleared her throat to get their attention. "As I'm sure you've all heard by now, Argblutal has done the king in. Her Highness got away, though, and has gone off to get some help."

"Thanks to you," Malvina beamed at her.

"Well, I did help a wee bit, and I heard the stable hands did their part as well." The stable hands grinned, and the remainder of the servants chuckled.

Adalardo nodded modestly. "I barely got all the grooms and lads down the princess's tunnel before the duke gave the order to hang us all. But we'd better keep this down. If we're heard, we'll be slaughtered."

The servants' faces sobered immediately. Ardra continued in a quieter voice, "Lord Devyn told Her Highness that Duke Caedmon has an army waiting for her out on the plains. This might be a lie because he turned traitor." She gestured toward the young lord, who was shaking his head vigorously and trying to speak.

"He appears to have something to say," Adalardo suggested. Adalardo pulled a knife from his belt and approached the lord. He put the knife to his throat. "Heir to a duke or not, cry out, and I will slit your throat." Lord Devyn nodded, and Adalardo pulled the gag from his mouth.

"I ask for no mercy," Devyn said. "But I swear Duke Caedmon's army awaits Her Highness. We rode south with five hundred men, and more have been joining us on the plains surrounding Gloine Torr. Soon they're sure to try and retake the palace."

"The duke is having himself crowned as we speak," a palace footman said.

"I don't care what that bloody usurper is doing," Maggie said. "Queen Samantha is the only monarch I'll go down on one knee before." There was a mutter of agreement.

"Which is why we have to help her take the palace back." Ardra finally got to the reason she'd asked the others to meet her here.

"How? What can we do against armed men?" Adalardo asked.

"We haven't any weapons," a stable groom added.

Ardra rolled her eyes. "You men, you think a big old fight is the only way to handle anything. Of course we can't grab our brooms and kitchen knives and take back the palace. But if we think more deviously, perhaps there are things we can be doing to make it easier for Her Highness."

* * *

The door to the throne room opened to the sound of the orchestra playing the song that hadn't been heard in over sixty-five years, the song reserved for the coronation of a new monarch. The courtiers bowed low as the duke made his way to the throne where Father Hafghan stood waiting to place the crown on his head.

Mounting the dais, Argblutal turned to face the court. He held up his hand for silence, and the orchestra brought the piece to a graceful conclusion. "My lords and ladies of the court, we are gathered here today on what should have been an occasion of celebration, but the joy has been marred by tragedy. Our great King Solar has finally succumbed to age, but even more troubling are the words he spoke to me on his death bed: he confessed the one we have known as the Crown Princess Samantha was a result of Queen Fenella's dalliance with her stable groom." The crowd gasped, and the duke paused to allow the information to sink in. "Out of his great love for the princess, he couldn't publicly denounce her, so he begged me to marry her and take the throne for myself. When I agreed to do so, he called the princess to him and gave her the same command. We both thought she agreed.

"This morning, however, she practiced the most brazen of deceptions by sending her maid in her place. She has fled the palace and joined the forces of Duke Caedmon, who seeks to subjugate Lundia to the will of Korth. Will you allow yourself to become a subject people in your own land? Do you bow before the bastard of a stable groom or a man who can trace his lineage to the beginnings of the joined kingdoms? What say you, my people?"

"Long live King Argblutal!" Count Morgan cried out and went down on one knee. Count Weylin and Baron Arawn followed. Soon the entire court took up the chant.

When quiet reigned again, Argblutal turned to High Priest Hafghan and went down on one knee, the last time he'd ever bow to anyone.

CHAPTER 44

The meeting in the council tent was winding down when a messenger entered. "Your Highness, Count Tierney is without and seeks admittance."

She recognized the name as belonging to the one who'd been so rude to her and Vaughan at the palace stables. "Send him in."

The messenger returned, followed by Tierney and six other minor Lundian nobles. They all went down on one knee. Tierney spoke for the group. "Your Highness, on the day I mistook you for a stable groom, you could have ruined me, but you demonstrated what true nobility meant. We would like to dedicate ourselves and our men to putting the rightful queen back on the throne. Our forces aren't large, but we can offer you one hundred and fifty men. If you'll have us, we're at your service."

At this evidence that at least some in Lundia supported her some of the tension left her shoulders. "Your offer is both kind and welcome. Make room for the Lundians at the table," she commanded.

* * *

Angus approached the camp where, rumor had it, the princess was encamped. The idea was absurd, but Angus was certain the man betrothed to her was his son. The name Sir Robrek of Mahngbhayo had moved like a whirlwind through the camps surrounding Gloine Torr. Could there be another by that name in the joined kingdoms? Three times his fields had been attacked, and the mysterious knight had ridden three different horses up the side of Gloine Torr. Yesterday he'd watched the gold knight's procession to the palace. The horse he rode undoubtedly had been Wild Thing. Angus's mouth felt dry. Had he beaten his future king nearly senseless, not once but dozens of times? When he'd done it, he'd told himself the boy needed to be taught a lesson, but Angus now realized he beat the boy for reminding him what he'd lost when Donella died.

A sentry stepped forward to challenge him. "Recruits to Her Highness's cause are gathering to the right." The man pointed, and some distance away Angus saw peasants, like himself, joining the princess's army.

"I'd like to speak with Sir Robrek, if I may. He's my son."

The sentry laughed. "Get a load of this guy, Errigal," he called to one of his companions. "He claims to be Sir Robrek's father. Don't he look like a mighty sorcerer from Mahngbhayo?"

Errigal frowned. "I'd be careful if I were you, Liam. Rumors say Sir Robrek's father is a backcountry farmer."

Feeling more out of place than he'd ever felt in his life, Angus shifted his feet. His son might be Sir Robrek, his future king, but Angus knew he was no father for a king. Liam signaled to another soldier. "Search him for weapons. Then take him to Sir Robrek. He says he's His Lordship's father." Stunned by hearing his son referred to as "His Lordship," Angus barely heard the soldier's instructions to raise his arms.

The soldier searched him thoroughly, taking his knife. He led Angus toward the center of the camp. Far ahead, the flap of a large tent opened, and a host of nobles poured out. Among them, standing next to the princess, was a short man dressed in silver silk. He had dark hair, dark skin, and green eyes, but that is where this man's resemblance to his son stopped. Sir Robrek mingled as if at ease with the nobles. The princess took His Lordship's hand. Sir Robrek may have once been his son, but he was no longer. "I see he's busy. It can wait," Angus said to the soldier who'd been guiding him. He fled in the direction of the peasant recruits before Robbie could catch sight of him. The soldier didn't try to stop him.

* * *

Samantha drew Sir Robrek away from the others. She'd need to call Caedmon to task over what he'd done, but first she needed to find out who the stranger she'd agreed to marry was. She sank on the grass at the edge of a small stream. Sir Robrek sat near her, but not close enough that their bodies touched. Not knowing how to begin, she stared at the sunset.

"Milady," he whispered. "Can you at least look at me?" When she looked at him, Sir Robrek was gone. Somehow, Robbie had taken his place. The eyes that met hers had none of the power of a mysterious knight, but held the vulnerability of a peasant boy whose heart was breaking. "You haven't looked at me since you rescued your men from the dungeon. I know you don't want to marry me." He ran his fingers through his hair, loosening the green ribbon, and allowing his curly hair to fall free. "I'll help you get your throne back. Then I'll leave. You don't have to marry me."

Samantha laughed, but cut it off when she heard her own hysteria. "Yes, I do. The goddess has chosen you as my consort. But I don't know if I want to. You've made a fool of me. You pretended to be a country bumpkin when you're a knight of incredible power. You even went as far as to dance like a clumsy oaf when you can move more gracefully than any man I've known. Why did you lie to me? Why have you been playing games with me?"

The knight looked as if she'd slapped him. "I am a 'country bumpkin,' and the day we met I could dance no better than an 'oaf.' I would never play games with you, and I have never lied to you."

He got up, moved a few feet away, and leaned against a tree. "I don't blame you for doubting me. Your men wouldn't believe me, either. The captain is probably out there waiting to slit my throat as soon as my guard's down. Milady . . . I mean, Your Highness, sometimes *I* have trouble believing what's happened to me. It's them; they've changed me." He gestured behind her, and Samantha turned to see the bronze, silver, and gold horses emerging from the gathering dark. "They helped me claim my full magical power. They taught me to fight like a knight, how to act around nobles. That one"—he pointed to the silver one—"taught me how to eat and dance so I wouldn't disgrace you."

"What are they?" she asked, not knowing whether to believe his words.

He shook his head and sat with his back against the tree. "They'd never say. My uncle calls them the Horses of the West Wind, but I know little else about them. Whatever they are, they have a habit of destroying grain. It all started the day after we met." He told her the most wondrously strange bard's tale she'd ever heard. She scooted closer to him as he talked. By the time he finished, she was sitting near enough to touch.

He met her eyes. "I know how impossible it all sounds, but I swear by the goddess and on my mother's grave that every word of it is true. Milady, I love you. Since the day we met, you're the only thing I've wanted. When I sleep at night, it's always you in my dreams, and I wake longing for you."

When she touched his face, his cheeks were wet with tears, and she knew that, whatever else he'd become, at heart he was still the boy she loved. "Robbie, I fell in love with you that day at the horse fair. It hurt when I thought you'd been deceiving me, but believe me now when I say I will be the happiest woman in the joined kingdoms on the day we marry."

"Do you mean that, Milady?" he asked.

She threw her arms around him and answered him with her lips. As she felt the warmth of his body, all the emotions she'd repressed since learning of the king's death came pouring out of the hole in her heart. She collapsed against his chest. "Robbie, these last few months have been so hard, and I've lost so many dear to me." She sobbed into his chest, soaking his shirt with her tears.

He enclosed her in the safety of his arms.

* * *

Samantha cried until her face felt raw and her throat dry. She allowed the fullness of her pain to rip her heart apart because she knew she had someone to help her put the pieces back together. When she had no more tears left, she lay against Robbie's chest. He stroked her hair and made soft soothing noises. "There's something I have to tell you," she said. "The rumors Duke Argblutal is spreading about me are true. Robbie, I'm a bastard. King Solar isn't my father. Darhour is."

"The captain?" Robbie gasped. "No wonder he always looks at me like he wants to castrate me."

"I only found out the truth about him a few days ago. He was my mother's stable groom. The king knew about the affair, but said nothing because he needed an heir and knew he couldn't father a child. He raised me as his daughter and until recently I believed I was.

Does it make a difference to you that I'm not truly the daughter of a king?" she asked, her heart pounding in her throat.

"How could you think it would? The captain makes a rather imposing father-in-law." She could hear his heart beat matching her own. "But I love you, for you, Samantha, not because of who your father is."

Tears glistened in her eyes. "I never thought anyone would ever say that to me and mean it. I've been courted by hundreds of men. But none of them were interested in me. They only wanted to wear a crown. Robbie, I don't want to wait another minute to make you mine. Don't peasants have a custom for a kind of marriage if a priest isn't available?"

Robbie's voice was husky as he answered. "Yes, it's called handfasting, and it's good for a year and a day or until a priest can be found to add Sulis's blessing to the union."

"And how does it work?" she asked, sitting up.

"The two who desire to be handfasted clasp each other by the right hand."

She took his hand in hers. "Like this?"

"Yes, just like that." His hand was trembling.

"And then what happens?"

"Well, the woman usually goes first, and she says, 'I,' and her name, 'do take you,' and the name of the man, 'by the right hand. I pledge myself to you for a year and a day, and such is my solemn vow before Sulis.'"

"I, Samantha, do take you, Robrek, by the right hand. I pledge myself to you for a year and a day, and such is my solemn vow before Sulis."

Samantha had difficulty breathing as Robbie spoke. "And I, Robrek, do take you, Samantha, by the right hand. I pledge myself to you for a year and a day, and such is my solemn vow before Sulis."

"And then?" She leaned closer.

"And then they kiss." He turned his lips toward hers, and she met them eagerly. They were soft, smooth, and delicious, but she needed more of him. Breaking the kiss, she pulled him to his feet. She led him to her tent and drew him down beside her on the bed.

"Samantha," he breathed. "Are you sure this is what you want?"

She ran her fingers through the silky smoothness of his hair. "Make love to me, Robbie. I want to be yours, and I want you to be mine."

"As long as you want me, nothing will ever divide us."

As they removed each other's clothing, Samantha reveled in the beauty of his body and thrilled at his gentle touch. As he cupped her breasts in his hands, she felt the hole in her heart beginning to fill. No matter how many she had lost, she knew she could go on as long as she had him. One by one he took her nipples in his mouth, and in doing so gave her back the love that Argblutal had tried to strip from her.

She felt his maleness pressing against her leg and knew she must have him inside her. She shifted her body until he rested between her legs. She cried out in pain and pleasure as he entered her. As she raised her hips to meet him, the entire world dropped away, and she felt as if she were a ship lapped by warm ocean currents. Robbie moved deeper and deeper inside her, and she writhed until something burst in wave after wave of indescribable wild completion and joy. Robbie gave a small cry and collapsed on top of her.

"Holy Sulis! I love you, Sam!" he whispered, and her heart swelled with joy at the sound of her name on his lips. He rolled off her, but she followed, wrapping her arms and legs around him.

He gasped as she took his nipple in her mouth. "Does it feel as good when I do this to you as when you do it to me?" she asked.

"Oh, yes," he sighed. She moved her hand lower, and he stiffened again at her touch. "Samantha, you had better stop now if you don't want to do it again."

She didn't answer, nor did she have the slightest intention of stopping.

* * *

When Darhour had watched his daughter sob in the peasant boy's arms, he'd felt as if his own heart were being ripped out of his chest. He'd failed her. What right had he to ignore the priestess's warning and take that vow? How could he have allowed his own flesh and blood to pay for his oath? Killing was the only gift he had to give his child, and he'd denied it to her when she needed it. What was his soul worth when his only child was in pain?

He'd left his daughter by the stream, in the arms of the sorcerer who loved her and would keep her safe. Now The Ghost crept into the dark city through the drainage ditches. Like the disembodied spirit for which he was named, he slipped through the city streets, into the palace, and entered his own rooms. He looked into his small mirror and drew a knife. One by one he hacked off the braids he'd worn in the Saloynan style to symbolize his vow. He got out wax and make-up to disguise his face.

* * *

When the princess awoke, the smell of Robbie lingered on her pillow and on her skin. She'd have liked to see him in the first light of dawn, but she'd reluctantly allowed him to go back to his own tent while it was still dark. What had happened between them was no one's business but their own.

She got up and, having no maid, washed herself. She pulled on a simple tunic and called out to her guards to summon Caedmon. When the duke arrived, Conroy entered with him. Samantha was surprised Darhour hadn't come in himself. She didn't offer Caedmon a seat and had Conroy help her on with her armor as she spoke to the duke. "Do you accept me as your liege?"

"I'm of a mind to forgive it, but I find your asking such a question offensive."

"Not as offensive as I found your stunt yesterday."

Caedmon waved the matter away. "Your Highness, confirming Argblutal's accusations when they can so easily be denied would have been a disastrous mistake. Solar would have handled it exactly as I did."

"And what would Solar have done with an advisor who made a public announcement of this importance without consulting him?"

Caedmon sighed. "Do you wish me to enumerate all the reasons confirming Argblutal's slander would have been a mistake?"

Fully armored now, Samantha buckled on her sword. "No, I would have liked it if you had enumerated them yesterday. Caedmon, I asked for your advice, and instead, you took the decision out of my hands. I will not tolerate your going behind my back like that ever again."

Caedmon looked at her as if she were an infant who suddenly stood up and called him an offensive name. "Your Highness, you're making far too much of this. I assure—"

"The only assurance I want from you is that it will never happen again."

"Of course, Your Highness." If Caedmon had patted her on the head, his attitude couldn't have been any more condescending.

Samantha wanted to scream, but she knew anything more she said or did now would weaken her position with the duke. Her father had taught her that any monarch who has to argue her underlings into obeying her commands doesn't rule. "Samantha, my dear"—she blinked back the tears as she heard her father's voice in her head— "always project the belief that you will be obeyed, and you will find that you nearly always will be. Then have good spies for the times you are not." It hurt to think so, but she was certain she'd have to ask Darhour to watch Caedmon.

She dismissed the duke to see to the readying of the army and, with Conroy, emerged from her tent, hoping she might have time for breakfast with Robbie. The blood rose in her cheeks thinking of the gentleness of his touch. Outside her tent only Bearach waited for her. "Where's Darhour?" she asked. It simply wasn't like him to trust that none of the hundreds of armed men in the camp would be struck by some mad desire to skewer her.

Bearach and Conroy exchanged glances, and Bearach coughed uncomfortably. "We don't know, Your Highness. He left last night when you were speaking with Sir Robrek by the stream."

She felt as if a cold fist tightened around her heart. "He's gone to kill the duke, hasn't he?"

"He didn't say, Your Highness," Bearach answered, not meeting her eyes.

No, please, don't let him have done it. But she could think of no other reason for him leaving. She tried to take comfort in the knowledge that this was hardly the first time Darhour had sneaked into a guarded palace and killed someone, but it didn't help. She couldn't bear the death of another dear one. *Sulis, I beg you, keep him safe.*

* * *

Dressed in the bronze armor, Robrek went looking for Samantha and found her outside the tent where he'd made her his wife the night before. *Holy Sulis, she's beautiful!* He wanted to wrap her in his arms and twirl her around the camp. He wanted to take her back inside the tent so badly he was certain the entire camp would read it in his face. He tried to assume a more somber expression, but he was simply too happy.

When Samantha saw him, she smiled back and blushed. But the smile faded quickly. "What is it?" he asked.

She looked nearly ready to burst into tears. "It's Darhour. He's gone after the duke."

How could her own father hurt her like this? "Why would he do that? How could he hope to succeed?"

"Easily," Bearach said, and the princess's other guard nodded. Both showed insane confidence in the captain's success.

Robrek touched Samantha's arm. She grabbed his hand and squeezed tightly. "Darhour was an assassin, Robbie, and a very good one. The odds are in his favor, but I can't think about that now. I can't afford to feel." As Robrek watched, a mask seemed to flow over Samantha's face, and the grief and fear leaked away. It was almost inhuman.

A sentry approached. "Your Highness, Sir Robrek, a man claiming to be Sir Robrek's uncle is at the edge of the camp. He's asking to speak to Sir Robrek."

Samantha turned to him, and he nodded.

"Allow Sir Robrek's uncle through," she commanded.

A few minutes later, Slathek strode into view, his broken arm in a sling. He was grinning broadly and accompanied by Leigh. When they reached him and the princess, the two men went down on one knee. "Your Highness, Sir Robrek." Slathek's voice rioted with giddy joy.

Robrek turned to the princess. "Your Highness, may I present my uncle, Slathek of Mahngbhayo? With him is Leigh Fergalstamm, the novice who saved me from being burned."

The princess held out her hand and lifted Slathek to his feet. She spoke formally and little resembled the woman he'd made love to last night. "Any relative of my betrothed is most welcome." She lifted Leigh to his feet. "For saving my betrothed, you have my gratitude. When I've regained my throne, you may name your reward."

Leigh blushed. "Your Highness, I have need of little. I seek only to serve the goddess."

"I appreciate your piety and will not forget it. Since you are a healer, I would ask you to take charge of the medical tent and prepare for casualties."

"Of course, Your Highness." Leigh bowed and went in the direction she'd indicated.

Samantha squeezed Robrek's hand and gave him a quick smile. "We ride shortly. I must check my troops." She moved toward the gathering of nobles and officers. Robrek watched her leave, marveling at the gracefulness of her bearing and the beauty of her curves.

Slathek pounded him on the shoulder. "Kinsman, I'll help see you king, and you shall bed that handsome wench yet."

"Uncle!" Robrek tore his eyes away from the princess, blushing furiously.

Slathek laughed. "My dear nephew, you haven't bedded her already, have you?" he whispered.

"Uncle!" Robrek blushed even more deeply.

"Oh, good show, kinsman, good show! A good bedding always helps prepare a man for battle. Not that I'd know myself, but all the stories say it is so."

Vaughan approached holding Brazen's reins. "Her Highness told me to tell you they're ready to ride."

Relieved at the interruption, Robrek swung into Brazen's saddle, said "good-bye" to his uncle, and joined the princess. As soon as he joined her, she gave the signal to move off. Robrek felt a chill of fear as the vast army moved toward the gates of the city. The army had swollen from the five hundred Caedmon had brought to well over a thousand.

Men with a battering ram led the way, but when they reached the city gates, they found them wide open, and the city magistrates waiting to greet the princess. They went down on one knee.

"Your Highness," the one who seemed to be their leader said. "We would join you if you'll have us. We support the rightful heir to the throne, not the usurper."

She nodded with the dignity of a queen. "You are most welcome."

As they rode through the city streets, men and women armed with battered swords, staves, axes, clubs, or kitchen knives came out of their houses and joined the princess's march on the palace. From the upper windows came cries of "Long live the queen!"

As they neared the palace, a horrible odor filled the air. "What in the seven hells is that?" Samantha asked.

Robrek lowered his shields and felt an intense cramping in his bowels that nearly doubled him over. "Someone has fed Duke Argblutal's men aloe juice mixed with burdock root. It's caused them to . . . Well, it's given them . . . They can't . . . " He couldn't think of a delicate way to discuss the massive outbreak of diarrhea, but the odor made it so he didn't have to.

"Who would have done that?" Samantha asked.

Vaughan spoke from behind them. "I'll bet Maggie put it in their food. She's threatened me with it a time or two." They turned and looked at him. "You didn't think the servants would let the duke take the palace without a fight, did you?"

The princess laughed. The help of the servants hadn't occurred to her.

* * *

Disguised as a palace footman, The Ghost slit another guard's throat as he neared the duke's chambers. He hadn't counted how many men he'd killed to get this far. He no longer cared. They were all responsible for Samantha's tears. They would all pay for her sorrow. He could hear voices coming from the open doorway ahead. "What is the condition of my men? Can they fight?" Argblutal snarled.

"At least half are in less than prime condition, Your Majesty," a second man responded. "They can't make it to the privies, and a good quarter of them have broken out in a terrible rash. But they'll fight as ordered. They know what it means to displease Your Majesty."

How dare he take the title that belongs to my daughter?

"And the bastard's army?" the duke asked.

"It's larger than we believed, at least two thousand strong. Some of them are untrained peasants, but we are still outnumbered nearly five to one. The people throng into the street to join her."

"How can they want a bastard on the throne?" The duke's voice dripped with venom.

The Ghost took two more strides, threw a knife, and the duke's underling fell face down into the room. He stepped over the body. "Because she's far more fit to rule than you," The Ghost answered.

"Guards!" the duke yelled.

The Ghost laughed. "There are no guards to hear you. I've been most thorough."

Argblutal grabbed his sword. "Do you honestly think you're my match?" he sneered.

"Easily." The Ghost drew his sword. He could have killed the duke with a throwing knife. But that would have been too quick. The monster had to be made to feel all the pain he'd caused Samantha. That wasn't possible, though. It took a heart to suffer as she had. The Ghost lunged in for a quick attack. Argblutal parried, but The Ghost's sword made a shallow slice across the duke's upper arm.

"You think the people will bow the knee before a bastard?" Argblutal tried to taunt him, but The Ghost didn't answer. Words were wasted breath. Relentlessly, he battered Argblutal toward the wall. Blood sprang from wounds on the duke's legs and arms. The Ghost was vaguely aware the duke had scored a few hits of his own. But The Ghost was no longer mortal. He didn't feel pain.

Argblutal was weakening, and he again yelled for assistance. As his parries became wilder and clumsier, The Ghost saw his opening. He swung his sword toward the duke's stomach, slicing open his midsection and spilling his entrails. The duke clutched at his guts and dropped to his knees. The Ghost bent down beside him.

"Who are you?" Argblutal hissed.

The Ghost pulled the wax off his face.

"Darhour, is it?" Argblutal sputtered. "Do you really think you can put your bastard on the throne? Do you think they will bend the knee to the daughter of a stable groom?"

"You'll never know if they do or not." The Ghost looked at the duke's stomach wound. "You could take three days to die of such wounds. It's a pity I can't spare the time to watch." He drew a knife. "I've heard you remove the manhood of those who disappoint you."

* * *

Duke Torin stood on the excrement-covered battlement atop the palace walls, watching the princess and her army draw up before the palace gates. Counts Weylin, Nola, and Morgan stood beside him as well as Kentigern, the captain of Argblutal's guard. *If only the damned bitch would have married me when she had the chance!* Still, he cringed at the thought of linking his name with that of a bastard. Next to the princess he saw the peasant sorcerer. A peasant and a bastard without a drop of royal blood between them couldn't be allowed to reign. Torin ground his teeth. "Where is Argblutal?"

Looking far from well, Kentigern clutched at his guts. "His Majesty will be here shortly. Today will be the day of his final triumph." Despite his words, Torin could tell the captain was nervous at the size of the princess's forces.

Torin started as the princess's voice rang out. Using what had to be magic, the princess's voice carried to every corner of the palace. "My people, why do you stand against me?"

"Do you think this people will bow the knee to a bastard simply because she commands the skills of a sorcerer?" Torin shot back.

To his surprise, the princess laughed. "You would believe the lies of the man who slew your king? My father gave this nation over fifty years of peace and prosperity, and this is how you repay him? By accepting the self-serving slander of a traitor guilty of regicide? My people, Argblutal treats you as children who can be fooled by bards' tales. Reject the man who would mock the good name of the greatest king this land has ever known. Accept Solar's rightful heir, and you will be forgiven. Argblutal will die for what he has done, but no one else needs to die this day. Throw down your weapons, my people. Come out and swear your loyalty to Solar's memory and his daughter, and no blood need be spilled."

From beside Torin, Morgan cried out, "His Majesty King Argblutal speaks nothing but the truth. A stable groom shared Fenella's bed and fathered her child. The throne of the joined kingdoms will not be polluted by such common blood." Jeers and hisses from the princess's forces greeted Morgan's words.

"Are you certain of this information?" Torin whispered to Morgan.

The count nodded grimly. "The captain of the princess's guard fathered her."

"Darhour? What proof do you have of this?"

"Enough," Morgan answered, but Torin realized it wouldn't matter who was telling the truth; the winner of the battle would write its history.

"So says the murderer of your king!" The princess's voice carried far more clearly than Morgan's rebuttal. "My people, you are outnumbered, and you are ill. If you choose to fight, you will be defeated! Wouldn't it be better to lay down your weapons? Surrender, and my betrothed can heal you."

Grim resolution spread across Kentigern's face, and he gave the command, "Prepare catapults. We'll see how well her lies stand up to stone."

Cries of fear and dismay sounded behind Torin. He whirled and saw the catapults had burst into flames. *Holy Sulis, no! He can't be that powerful!*

"The fires!" Morgan said. "They're unnatural!"

"Of course they're unnatural!" Torin snapped. "The sorcerer has brought them up from the depths of the seven hells!"

"No, the sorcerer has cast an illusion," Morgan breathed. "They do not burn."

Torin saw what Morgan meant. The fires burned without consuming the catapults. Torin smiled and turned to Kentigern, who was looking between the fires and Morgan in confusion. "Send men to the catapults. It's a trick."

Kentigern looked doubtful, but gave the command. The soldiers within the walls were starting to panic. "We have to surrender, or we'll all die!" someone cried out. "How can we fight demons? "

"Where's the king?" Torin hissed, knowing only Argblutal would give them time to prove the fires were a harmless trick. He caught movement from the palace balcony. To his relief, Argblutal's head appeared over the railing. At first, the soldiers greeted the sight with cheers, but the cheers quickly turned to cries of dismay; the head wasn't attached to his body, but was impaled on a pike. *Damn you, Argblutal! You started it! How dare you get yourself killed before finishing it!* However, another thought occurred to Torin. If Argblutal was dead, certainly he had a better claim to the throne than the bastard. Torin put up his hands, calling for quiet, but he didn't get it. He tried to shout over the noise. "It's the work of the bastard and her sorcerer! Shall we not repel such demons?"

Torin doubted that many heard him over the cacophony of cries coming from the forces within the palace. Although they appeared equally divided in seeing the situation as the work of demons or the goddess, they were united in their unwillingness to fight. "We must surrender before she kills us all!" one voice sounded above the others.

Kentigern turned to Torin. "We won't fight for a dead man. Open the gates and surrender."

"No!" Nola cried out. "Do you not realize we'll all be executed as traitors? Men, keep up your courage! Do not quail at the sight of evil!" The panic in his voice served only to build the fear of those on the battlements.

Kentigern yelled down at the princess. "Do you vow that we may have our lives if we open the gates and surrender?"

"Upon the goddess and on my mother's grave, if you open the gates, throw down your weapons, and pledge your loyalty, no one will die."

Torin grabbed Kentigern by the shoulder and pulled him away from the edge of the battlements. "If you will not fight for Argblutal, fight for me! We must not surrender!"

"We both must and will." Kentigern nodded to the men on the wall, and Torin and his fellow nobles faced the points of dozens of swords. "Drop your weapons, or die," Kentigern commanded.

Nola and Weylin dropped their weapons immediately. Torin wanted to draw his sword and run Kentigern through but saw the futility of it. He glanced at Morgan, and as one they dropped their weapons. Kentigern had them seized and their hands tied behind their back. He forced them to the edge of the battlement. "I am Captain Kentigern. We've taken these four for you. I, for one, am ready to surrender and accept your vow." The captain dropped his sword. "Men, I order all of you to do the same, and open the gates."

Weapons rained down in front of the palace walls. The gates opened, and the princess's forces began to stream inside.

Samantha laughed as the weapons began to fall and the gates creaked open. "I thought you said you couldn't call down fire," she said to Robbie.

He shook his head in bewilderment. "I didn't. I can't." But the silver stallion winked at her, and she knew who'd been responsible. She laughed again.

"Harm none who surrender," she shouted to her men. A hundred of her men streamed through the gates before her to make sure it was no trick.

She and her betrothed followed. As soon as she entered the courtyard, she saw soldiers approaching with Torin, Nola, Weylin, and Morgan between them. They forced them to their knees before her. Baron Arawn and Count Ultan approached her unescorted and dropped to one knee.

"Forgive me, Your Highness," Weylin blubbered. "I didn't know what he was like. I swear I didn't."

"Your Highness," Arawn stated with much more dignity. "We're at your mercy."

"Like the bastard has any," Torin hissed. "I will not bow down to a bastard and her sorcerer. We both know Argblutal wasn't lying."

Samantha wondered if it wouldn't have been better to admit the truth, but it was too late for that now. She kept her face impassive. "Do you choose to believe the murderer of your king, or are you prepared to swear your loyalty to Solar's heir?"

"I will bow before no bastard." Morgan struggled to get to his feet, but the solider forced him to remain on the ground. The count spat at the princess's feet.

"Nor will I," Torin said, but didn't bother with useless struggle.

"I will, Your Highness," Weylin blubbered. "I always knew Argblutal was lying. The aura of royalty surrounds you. I vow my loyalty by the goddess and on my mother's grave."

Samantha started at the use of the word "aura." *Does he know?* Looking at him, Samantha decided his choice of word had merely been coincidental. "Cut him loose," she ordered.

"I'll give my vow as well," Arawn promised, as did Ultan.

Nola stared at her with hatred. "You maintain my rights to the lands the king has given me, and I'll give you my vow."

"The king's lands will remain as such. They belong to my betrothed."

Caedmon stood next to her. "I say we cut off their heads at once, Your Highness," he said.

"That won't be necessary," Nola stuttered. "I'll give my vow."

"Very well," the princess nodded and turned to Morgan and Torin, who stared back defiantly.

"Put them in the dungeon for now," the princess commanded. "We'll deal with them later." Torin and Morgan were dragged off.

When they were gone, Captain Kentigern turned to her; he was clutching his gut. "Your Highness, you promised your betrothed could do something about our bowels. We beg you to fulfill this promise."

"Yes, of course." She nodded to Robbie.

"Light a large fire in the courtyard," he commanded. "Bring me the largest cauldron you have and fill it with water." The princess smiled as she watched him give orders as to which herbs should be brought to him. She ordered a dozen men to ensure his safety.

Samantha heard a squeal of delight and turned to see Ardra and Malvina hurrying toward her. "Ardra!" she cried, tears springing to her eyes. She threw her arms around her maid, not caring who might censure familiarity with her servant. "You're alive! How did you escape?"

"With the help of a wee bitty knife," Ardra smiled mischievously, pulling away. "Did you like our little surprise?" She held her nose against the stench. "It was Maggie's idea."

"I told you it was," Vaughan said, puffing out his chest.

Behind her maids, Adalardo and several of his stable grooms, dressed as palace footmen, came escorting Lord Devyn tied between them. Lady Aislinn walked with dignity beside him.

"What is the meaning of this?" Duke Sheen spluttered. "Release my son at once. He was the first to pledge his loyalty to the princess."

"And the first to betray her," Adalardo said, forcing Devyn to his knees in front of her. "My men and I were tempted to hang him from the battlements, but the Lady Aislinn has persuaded us to bring the matter before Your Highness."

"Your Highness, what is this nonsense these servants mutter?" Sheen demanded.

"I am afraid it isn't nonsense, father," Devyn said, staring fixedly at the ground. "I have disgraced myself and you, and I ask for no mercy. I'm a weakling and a coward. I deserve to die for what I have done."

Sheen stared at his son in shock, but Aislinn fell to her knees before the princess. "Your Highness, Devyn made a terrible mistake, but I beg you not to kill him. Duke Argblutal threatened to rape me before his eyes, then throw me to his men. It's no excuse, and I told him to let them do it. He made the wrong choice, Your Highness, but do you not understand what men will do for love?"

The princess looked up at Argblutal's head. She knew who had placed it there. There was nothing Darhour would not do to protect her. How could she condemn Devyn for doing the same for the woman he loved?

"Strip him of his rank, imprison him, banish him if you must," Aislinn pleaded. "But Your Highness, I beg you not to take his life."

The princess turned to Sheen. "Your Grace, your son has played a key role in Duke Argblutal's plot against me. I cannot allow him to remain your heir."

"I quite agree, Your Highness. I won't plead on his behalf. With Your Highness's permission, I will make my second son, Cedric, my heir. He was always more fit for command than this one, anyway."

"So be it," the princess said, and turned back to Devyn. "Because of your actions, I can't trust you with any position of importance. I find you fit only to be court artist and nothing more."

"Court artist?" Devyn gaped at her as if he didn't believe his ears. "But Your Highness, I betrayed you. I don't deserve to live."

"Do you question the desires of your queen?" the princess asked.

"No, Your Highness." Devyn blushed.

"Thank you, Your Highness," Aislinn bowed and kissed her feet. The princess felt uncomfortable with such homage and dismissed the lovers. Again she looked around for Darhour, but could still see no sign of him.

The commoners were flooding in through the palace gates, breaking into cheers and dancing. Caedmon leaned close to her. "Your Highness, you should address them from the palace balcony."

"Yes, of course," she said. Certainly, Darhour would be waiting for her there with the head of the man he'd killed. She glanced at Robbie who was busy with the cauldron; then with Bearach and Conroy by her side, she headed into the palace. All the nobles who had supported her followed in her wake.

As she walked through the corridors and up the stairs toward the balcony, she kept expecting Darhour to appear. She hoped he hadn't been seriously wounded or . . . *My father is not dead. I know he isn't. I would feel it.*

When they neared the doors leading to the palace balcony, Samantha saw something on the floor. Her guards placed themselves before her, but she recognized the thing on the ground as a body, and she had no doubt whose it was. It had been disemboweled, castrated, and beheaded. She gagged, nauseated by the sight. He deserved this, but it disturbed her to think of her father committing the butchery. She looked up from the body and saw Bearach detach a piece of paper from the door. It had been stuck there by Argblutal's ruby-encrusted knife. Bearach handed the paper to her. "Your Majesty," she read. "Please accept this final gift from one unworthy to serve you."

The paper went limp in her hand. She turned to Bearach. "What does it mean? Where is he?" Bearach and Conroy exchanged glances, looking stricken. "No, he can't be gone! He wouldn't leave me!"

Caedmon came up beside her. "Your Highness, is there a problem?" He looked down at the butchered corpse of the would-be king. Samantha handed him the note. He read it and smiled with satisfaction. "And a fine gift indeed. I see he was smart enough to see the undesirability of his continued presence."

"No! He isn't gone!" She rounded on Bearach and Conroy. "Find him now!"

"Your Highness," Conroy objected, "the captain wouldn't want us to leave your side. If he doesn't want to be found, he won't be."

She fought against tears. "I don't care what the captain wants! He does not rule! Find him, damn you! He can't leave me!"

"Your Highness, this emotional display over a guard is unseemly," Caedmon whispered. "You are queen now! Comport yourself as such!"

No, he can't be gone! He couldn't have left me!

But she knew he had. He'd slaughtered her enemies and left her alone to pick up the pieces. She was queen now and had to act like it no matter how much it hurt. She straightened and stepped over Argblutal's body onto the palace balcony.

Cheers greeted her appearance beside Argblutal's head. She strode up to the balcony railing, and the nobles who had rallied to her cause closed in around her.

Robrek heard the crowd break into cries of "Long live Queen Samantha!" He looked up and saw her on the palace balcony. *Holy Sulis, she's beautiful! Can she truly be mine?* The man in front of him groaned, reminding Robrek of what he was supposed to be doing. He filled the stricken soldier's cup with the potion he'd made.

"Thank you, Milord," the soldier said, startling Robrek with the use of the title. He wondered if he'd ever get used to it.

Robrek filled another cup, then looked back at Samantha, again forgetting his job. A servant came forward and bowed. "May I, Milord?" The servant reached for the ladle. Robrek relinquished it, but felt awkward about doing so. He wasn't used to standing around while others worked.

Up on the balcony, Samantha held up a hand, and the crowd fell silent. "My people! Duke Argblutal murdered your king and tried to steal my throne. He has suffered the fate Sulis intended for such betrayal. Let us celebrate this victory, achieved with so little loss of life."

The crowd roared its approval, and Robrek beamed up at her. She was a woman meant to rule. No one could have sounded more regal than she had when she'd talked the soldiers into surrendering. He knew becoming her consort would take some adjustment, but with her by his side, he felt ready to take on the entire world. Joy far greater than any his magic had ever brought him filled his body, and for the first time in his life, he gave thanks to Sulis.

As the crowd broke into sounds of celebration, Samantha tried to feel a sense of victory, but she couldn't. She'd lost both her fathers within little more than a day. Solar had died trying to defend her, but Darhour had made the choice to desert her.

Caedmon took Argblutal's head off the pike. He raised his hand for quiet. "Let us remember the fate of those who raise their hands against the goddess's chosen!" Caedmon dropped the head into the midst of the crowd. The crowd roared and tossed and kicked the duke's head about.

Samantha was glad the duke was dead, but his death did nothing to fill the hole caused by those she'd lost. Then she saw Robbie smiling up at her from across the courtyard. He'd given her what she thought she could never have, loving her for herself and not just her position. Joy sparked within her as she remembered the night she'd spent in his arms. Somehow, it would be all right. She had nothing to fear from the future.

If you enjoyed the novel, please leave a review on Amazon or Goodreads.

To follow the continuing adventures of Samantha and Robrek, read the next book in the series, *The Soul Stone*. I have an excerpt below. If you enjoy it, the novel can be purchased on Amazon

Also, subscribe to my mailing list to
get monthly updates on my writing, specials,
and advanced news on upcoming releases.
You will also received a free ecopy of my short story collection,
Blood Cursed and Other Tales of the Fantastic.
http://jamie-marchant.com/newsletter/

THE SOUL STONE (EXCERPT)

The Kronicles of Korthlundia
Book 2

By Jamie Marchant

PROLOGUE

As she braided Awena's hair, Mother Venetia shivered. Their undyed wool robes were not warm enough for the freezing dungeon.

"I'm so cold, Mother!" Awena cried.

"I know, child." Venetia rubbed the young novice's arms to warm her. She and Awena were two of hundreds locked up due to Father Shylah's edict. How the Lundian high priest had got the king to ban and imprison female members of the clergy, Venetia couldn't imagine. Perhaps the rumors were right, and the king had lost his mind.

It was so cold she could see her breath, but Venetia shivered for another reason. Tonight was the night of the new moon, the night all priestesses throughout Korth would perform the ritual to keep the ancient evil contained behind the shield of Armunn's soul. Since her village of Balley Beg was closest to the source of that evil, Mother Venetia's role in the ritual had always been pivotal. This would be the third month in a row she'd been unable to play her part, and because of the mass imprisonment of Korthian priestesses, she was hardly the only one absent. Prophesies spoke of a day when Armunn's shield would fail. She feared the weakened ritual might well bring such a day.

She abruptly stopped braiding as she felt warm tingling through the soles of her shoes.

Awena grabbed Mother Venetia's arm. "What is it, Mother?"

"It's Mother Bensaggyrt. She's sending a call through the earth for all of us to gather."

"Why would she do that? That will only make it easier for the Royal Guard to arrest more of us!"

Mother Venetia shook her head. "I don't know, child." But she could think of only one reason. Had the ancient prophesies come true and evil been loosed to ravage Korthlundia again?

CHAPTER 1

In the palace courtyard, Robrek Angusstamm stirred the cauldron, brewing the potion that would cure Duke Argblutal's former forces of the mass diarrhea caused by the princess's supporters in the palace. Argblutal had attempted to usurp Samantha's throne, and Robrek had just helped her retake it. The potion was ready except for the final ingredient—his magic. Robrek spread his hand over the cauldron and closed his eyes. Pure joy and pleasure flooded his body as his magic flowed out of him. Nothing felt this good. He smiled as he opened his eyes. The potion would provide a nearly instantaneous cure.

Robrek took the ladle from the waiting servant and began ladling out the potion to those waiting. They were bent over from discomfort, and the smell was atrocious. Robrek tried to breathe only through his mouth.

The crowd broke into cries of "Long live Queen Samantha!" He looked up and saw Samantha on the palace balcony. *Holy Sulis, she's beautiful! How can she truly be mine?* It still seemed like a dream that they'd been handfasted the night before and that she had spent the night in his arms.

The man in front of him groaned, reminding Robrek of the task at hand. He filled the stricken soldier's cup. "Thank you, Milord," the soldier said, startling Robrek with the use of his new title.

Robrek filled another cup, then looked back at Samantha. A servant came forward and bowed. "May I, Milord?" The servant reached for the ladle. Robrek relinquished it, but felt awkward doing so. He wasn't used to standing around while others worked. He supposed it was just one of many things he'd have to get used to as consort. *Can I truly be king?* He shook his head at the absurdity of the idea. Only in bards' tales did peasants become kings, but what had his life been if not a bards' tale?

Up on the balcony, Samantha raised a hand, and the crowd fell silent. "My people! Duke Argblutal murdered your king and tried to steal my throne. He has suffered the fate Sulis intended for such betrayal. Let us celebrate this victory, achieved with so little loss of life."

The crowd roared its approval, and Robrek beamed at her. Duke Caedmon stepped onto the balcony beside Samantha, and Robrek frowned slightly. Caedmon disapproved of him, didn't think him worthy of the princess.

Caedmon removed Argblutal's head from the pike. Robrek suspected Darhour, the captain of the princess's personal guard and a former assassin, had put it there. *Where is Darhour?* Robrek would have expected him to be by Samantha's side, but the only two guards with her were Bearach and Conroy.

Caedmon raised his hand for quiet. "Let us remember the fate of those who raise their hands against the goddess's chosen!" Caedmon dropped the head into the midst of the crowd. As the crowd roared and tossed and kicked the duke's head about, Robrek felt a surge of nausea. For what Argblutal had done he'd deserved to die, but did they have to desecrate his remains?

Samantha's eyes sought him out in the crowd, and she smiled down at him. Lost in that smile, he forgot everything else.

The thousands of peasants who had joined Samantha's army as she'd marched on the palace and who now filled the courtyard erupted into dancing and celebration, and Robrek was swept up in the dance. People pounded him on the back and beamed at him, accepting him as he'd never been accepted in the village of his birth.

At the edge of the crowd stood Wild Thing, his Horsetad mare, with Brazen, Fancy Man, and Holy Writ—the magical bronze, silver, and gold horses who had changed his life and helped him win the contest that allowed him to claim Samantha as his bride. Now, the despised youngest son of a peasant farmer would be king. Now, surely, he'd be able to do what he was meant to do and heal in peace. Beyond that he couldn't imagine what his new life would be like.

But having Samantha in it would be enough.

:She liked your moves, didn't she?: came the laughing voice of Fancy Man, who taught him how to dance, among other things. *:Now I've taught you all I know.:*

Holy Writ nodded her head and snorted. *:Thou hast done well.:*

:It is your destiny.:

Robrek laughed as Brazen again said her oft repeated line. Robrek felt happy and at peace. With the horses and Samantha beside him, he had nothing to fear.

Robrek danced over to the horses and gave each one a hug around the neck, ending with Wild Thing. *:Wild Thing and Robbie big heroes.:*

He scratched her neck. "Yes, my girl, I guess we are."

He looked over at the line of soldiers waiting for the remedy and noticed one limping badly. He approached the man as his cup was filled by the servant. "Your foot pains you?" he asked.

The man started and turned to Robrek, eyes widening when he saw who had addressed him. "Er . . . er . . . yes, Milord. I stepped on a nail about a week back, and I'm afraid it's began to fester. I fear I might lose it, Milord."

"Not while I'm here you won't. Drink it down." He pointed to the cup. "Then come with me." After the man drank the remedy, Robrek led him to the nearby mounting blocks and had the man sit and remove his boot. The foot was swollen and red. The nail wound on the bottom was oozing pus and turning green. Red lines of infection travelled up the man's foot. If it weren't for Robrek's skills, it would definitely have to be amputated. Robrek reached out to touch the foot, and the man flinched. "I have to touch you if I'm going to make it better," Robrek said. "It won't hurt."

The man nodded, but he was trembling slightly. Robrek put his hand on the foot, closed his eyes, and went into a healing trance. He gathered the infection and pushed it toward the hole in the foot, so that it streamed out with pus and blood, but after a few moments, the pus stopped flowing, and the foot slowly reduced to normal size. The greenish tinge and the redness disappeared, and finally Robrek closed the small puncture wound.

When Robrek opened his eyes, the man's eyes were wide with awe. The man fell to his knees. "My life for yours! How may I serve you, Milord?"

"You can't," a voice spoke beside Robrek. Robrek turned to Hawk, captain of the Royal Guard, who was looking down at the man with loathing. "His Lordship has no need for traitorous scum. You will depart with the rest after you've sworn your loyalty to Her Highness." He gestured toward the front door of the palace. There stood Samantha, with Bearach and Conroy on either side of her and one of Argblutal's men kneeling before her. A line of men, all who'd fought for Argblutal, waited behind him.

The man whose foot Robrek had healed looked between Captain Hawk and Robrek. "But, Milord, I only served Argblutal for the money. I will give my life for yours."

"Once a traitor, always a traitor," Hawk said, and signaled two Royal Guardsmen over to him. "Escort the traitor to Her Highness."

The Royal Guardsmen took him by the arms. The man was so upset at being taken Robrek thought he should say something, but nothing came to mind. He had no idea how he could make use of the man and no assurance he could be trusted. Hawk called two more Royal Guardsmen over. "You and you are now guarding His Lordship."

"I have no need of guards," Robrek protested.

"Her Highness's orders," Hawk said. "Too many traitors still in the courtyard, not to mention all the peasants." Hawk gestured toward the dancing commoners, all of whom were armed, mostly with makeshift weapons. "Her Highness requests your presence."

Robrek smiled at the thought Samantha wanted him and followed Captain Hawk. The two men Hawk appointed as his guards followed as well and took up station on either side behind him. They were large, imposing men, at least a head taller than Robrek. He felt intimidated rather than protected.

Samantha acknowledged him with a slight smile, but otherwise, her attention was taken up with the men kneeling before her. She held a piece of paper in one hand, and Robrek sensed something was wrong, but he wasn't sure why she wanted him there. She didn't seem to have anything for him to do.

A lot of men had followed Argblutal, and Robrek soon found the oath taking tedious. He scanned the crowd for signs of injury, but couldn't find anything major. Still, wouldn't healing scrapes and bruises be better than doing nothing? He shifted from one foot to the other, wondering if he should go back to ladling out the potion.

Samantha touched his arm. He relaxed at her touch and smiled at her. She smiled in return, but the smile seemed forced somehow and not her true smile. Robrek wondered if he'd done something wrong, but he couldn't imagine what.

When the last of Argblutal's supporters had finally pledged their oaths and been escorted from the palace grounds, Samantha turned to Captain Hawk. "Make sure the palace and grounds are thoroughly searched for any stragglers."

Hawk bowed. "It's being done as we speak."

She turned to Caedmon. "Now, I'll see to my father."

Of course. That's what's wrong. Robrek cursed himself for being so thoughtless. Argblutal had killed her father. Unlike Robrek's relationship with his father, Samantha's with the king had been close.

Still clutching the paper, Samantha took Robrek's hand in her free hand and led him into the palace. Caedmon and their bodyguards followed. The entry hall was overflowing with the nobles who'd sided with her against Argblutal. Although Robrek had been in the entry hall before, he couldn't help staring around like the country peasant he was. Chandeliers full of candles dangled from the ceiling. Robrek wondered how the candles had been lit. Wall sconces provided more light. Between the sconces were brilliant statues of long dead heroes, crossed swords, and suits of armor.

Surrounding him and the princess, the nobles danced and celebrated the nearly bloodless victory. "Long live the queen!" resounded all around them, and the nobles pressed close, congratulating her and reminding her of the part they'd played. She smiled that false smile he found so disconcerting. "Let the wine cellar be breached," she announced. "And all celebrate the joy of our victory!"

Cries of "Hear, hear!" broke out. However, joy seemed to be the last emotion Samantha felt as she moved among the courtiers.

Slowly, they worked their way to the edge of the crowd and down a deserted side corridor. Samantha led him past rich paintings of distinguished looking men and women in gilt frames, bright tapestries of knights and battle, more statuary and suits of armor. The floor was polished flagstone, and large windows provided light. The corridors were wide and the ceilings high. His father's entire farmhouse could have fit in that corridor. *Can I truly be a part of such a world?*

Samantha slowed. She seemed to be in no hurry to reach their destination. She clung tightly to his hand, and he squeezed back to comfort her. But he had no idea what to say. *How can I comfort a queen?*

* * *

Clutching the note Darhour had left pinned to the door above Argblutal's corpse in one hand and Robbie's hand in the other, Samantha approached the room where the king lay dead. *No, Father! You can't truly be gone!* Their steps echoed off the stone floor in the vast emptiness, reminding her of the emptiness of her own life. The air seemed to thicken about them, and she slowed. If she never reached the king's bedroom, maybe she could make his death a lie.

After a few moments and an eternity, she stood before the king's chambers. She hesitated, squared her shoulders, and pushed open the door.

The king lay on his bed, his eyes closed as if merely asleep. His body had been washed and dressed for burial. Seeing him lying there reminded her of when she'd had nightmares as a little girl; she'd come to him and crawl in bed for comfort. He had held her, stroked her hair, and told her stories. She'd snuggled against his long white beard until she fell asleep.

Will I ever feel that safe again?

She was certain she wouldn't. Not when Darhour, too, had deserted her. Darhour had been the captain of her guards, her friend, and as she'd discovered only a few days ago, her true father. Now, according to the note left near Argblutal's body, he'd left her. "My final gift to you," he'd written. "From one unworthy to serve you." *How dare he think of himself that way?*

She forced thoughts of his betrayal out of her mind and looked around the room—everywhere but at the king's body. Above the mantle across from the bed was a portrait of her sitting in her window seat and looking out at the palace grounds. Every two years the king had had a new portrait of her painted to hang in his bedroom. He'd told her he wanted her to be the last thing he saw before he fell asleep.

Maybe it's all a mistake. Praying for life to flow back into him, she knelt beside the bed and took the king's hand. It was freezing and felt more like marble than flesh. Robbie laid his hand on her shoulder. "Can you do something?" she asked him.

To ask anyone else the question would have been absurd, but Robbie was the most powerful sorcerer Korthlundia had seen in centuries. He'd saved Darhour's life when he'd taken an arrow through the heart. Could he not heal her father's heart now, through which Argblutal had thrust his sword?

He shook his head. "I'm sorry, Sam. Maybe if I'd been here at the time. But I can't bring back the dead."

"Holy Sulis, how can I go on without him?" She let go of Solar's lifeless hand and rested her cheek against the coverlet. She wanted to sob, to wail out her grief, but the man who'd always soothed her tears was dead. Robbie knelt beside her and put his arm around her. He didn't tell her the lie that everything would be all right or say any of the trite things people say to comfort those in grief. He just held her.

"Damn Argblutal!" she choked.

Before disappearing, Darhour had done a thorough job of killing the duke—eviscerating, castrating, and decapitating him. Still, she wished Argblutal was alive, so she could kill him with her own sword, rip his heart out of his chest with her bare hands. But nothing she could do to Argblutal could heal the gaping hole in her own chest as she knelt beside the greatest king Korthlundia had ever known and the best father a child could have.

She dropped the note to the floor. Robbie picked it up. His mouth dropped open. "Is this from Darhour?" he asked. "Has he gone?" She nodded and turned away, unwilling to cry over a betrayer. Robbie engulfed her in a hug. "Oh, Sam, I'm so sorry."

She clutched him tightly, grateful for the one thing she hadn't lost.

* * *

His inadequacy in comforting her was like a knife in his heart, Robrek held Samantha and smoothed her auburn hair with his hand. *Why doesn't she weep?* He knew how much she'd loved the king and Darhour, too. The pain in her face was nearly unbearable.

He heard a noise behind him, and Samantha stiffened in his arms. Duke Caedmon was entering the room. "What do I do now, Uncle?" she asked him. "How do I go on?"

Caedmon didn't meet her gaze. "It would seem a celebratory feast is in order. The preparations shouldn't take long, seeing Argblutal had been preparing for a marriage feast that never happened. The people need to celebrate the victory of the rightful queen. Tomorrow you can declare a week of mourning for the king."

She tore away from Robrek and stood. "Are you mad? My father lies dead!" She snatched a gold and gem horse figurine from the mantel. "I gave him this when I was a mere child! He kept it here with my portrait. He loved me! How dare you suggest I celebrate?"

Caedmon held up his hands in a gesture of surrender. "You asked my advice. I have given it."

Samantha glared at Caedmon for a moment more; then the grief flowed off the princess's face and an expressionless mask took its place. The mask made her seem less human somehow. "Very well. Tell Blaine and Maggie to arrange. . . a celebratory feast."

Samantha grabbed Robrek's hand and, without another glance at her father, led him out of the room. She sped through the corridors, her jaw set.

"Where are we going now?" Robrek asked.

"Anywhere but here," she snapped.

They arrived at the edge of the swarming crowd; nearly all the people held glasses or bottles of wine. Glasses were shoved into his and the princess's hands, and the princess halted to propose a toast. "To victory! To another fifty years of unbroken peace!" She drained her goblet, and someone immediately filled it.

The hallways rang with cheers, and when no one seemed to be paying attention, Robrek emptied his glass into a potted plant and set the glass aside. Healers couldn't tolerate alcohol. But before he knew it, someone had shoved another glass into his hand.

Dozens of men Robrek had never seen before pounded him on the back, congratulating him and the princess. They made passage through the corridor slow and difficult. Again, cries of "Long live the queen!" broke out on all sides. The princess smiled at everyone, but the smile didn't reach her eyes. Every time she emptied her glass, it was soon filled again. Robrek merely held his, brimming with wine.

By the time they made it to the banquet hall, where their betrothal had been celebrated two days previously, Samantha's gait was unsteady, and she leaned against him for support.

* * *

"What happens now?" Count Nola asked. "We just sit back and let a bastard reign over us?"

He and the other Lundian members of the Royal Council were sitting at the dining table in his townhouse. Nola, Counts Ultan and Weylin, and Baron Arawn had all sided with Argblutal in his failed attempt to usurp the throne.

Arawn sighed. "Argblutal's accusation about her bastardry was certainly self-serving. Perhaps it isn't even true. Just who is supposed to be her father, anyway?"

Weylin took a large gulp of his wine and waved the matter aside. "Who cares if it's true or not? She has the throne. If Argblutal failed to take it from her, which of us could?"

Ultan's lips tightened. "It is wrong to even speak of it. She gave us our lives when few monarchs would have, and we gave her our sacred oaths of loyalty."

Nola stood. "Words! That's all an oath is. Mere words, spoken under the threat of the axe." The three other men stared at him, mouths hanging open as if the mere thought of breaking their oaths would damn them to the seven hells. "All I want to know is, will she honor Solar's bequests?"

Weylin laughed. "You're concerned about the king's lands?"

Nola turned red. "Shouldn't I be? I have the deed right here." He held up a piece of paper. "Signed by Solar himself. If she's truly the late king's daughter, she won't break her father's word."

Arawn chewed a grape and seemed to consider his words carefully. He spat out the seeds onto a plate before him. "If I were you, I'd figure on kissing those lands goodbye."

"Not while there's still breath in my body. And what about the promises Argblutal made to the rest of you? Are you willing to let them go so causally?" He leaned over the table. "We have to unite on this, or she'll rob us blind."

* * *

Father Faolan knelt before the altar on a plush crimson and gold rug. He fingered the fine silk cloth that had once covered the high priest Shylah's personal altar. The cloth was embroidered with a gold star surrounded by baskets of fruit and roses of the deepest scarlet. He lit the candles on either side of the statue of Sulis. The candlesticks were of gold, inlaid with silver roses and rubies. The statue itself stood two feet tall. Made of pure white alabaster, it depicted Sulis dressed in long, flowing robes. In contrast to most depictions of the Holy Mother, it lacked the curves that differentiated a woman's body from a man's. The goddess's hair, traditionally depicted in long braids interwoven with flowers, was here hidden under a priest's cowl. The statue's face had a strong chin, a pointed nose, and a stern expression. Indeed, it looked far more masculine than feminine. Its sculptor seemed to understand, as very few did, the truth about Sulis, the truth Father Shylah had taught Faolan.

Faolan had taken these things of Shylah's to honor the high priest after his supposed suicide. Faolan, however, wasn't fooled. Shylah had been far too great a man to take his own life. He had been murdered both physically and in reputation. The accusations of child sacrifice were slander of the basest variety, and Faolan knew who was responsible: the bastard who would reign on the great Solar's throne and the abomination she'd taken to her bed.

There was a knock on the door, and Father Eadoin entered. His blonde hair was shaved to a fine buzz, and he had small, beady eyes that avoided looking directly at Faolan. "Am I interrupting?"

Faolan shook his head and got to his feet. "No, I was just praying, asking Sulis for a way to restore the high priest's reputation. What's on your mind?"

Eadoin rubbed his fingers over the silky smoothness of the altar cloth, still not looking at him. "It's the high priesthood, Father. Until the new high priest is chosen, I'm afraid of your flaunting your closeness to Father Shylah. Few believe he was not guilty of the crimes with which he was charged. Your chances of being chosen the next high priest would be greater if you were to repudiate—"

Faolan put his hand on the younger priest's shoulder. "I will not repudiate Korthlundia's greatest high priest merely for worldly ambition. I will find a way to clear his name and trust in Sulis to guide our fellows in the selection of the one most fit to lead the church in these troubled times." Times in which a bastard and an infidel were set to take the throne. Such a travesty must be prevented, and who better than the church to stop it?

* * *

With Samantha laughing somewhat hysterically beside him, Robrek entered the banquet hall. Robrek wondered what was funny. All he'd seen and heard in the entrance hall was nobles boasting of their own feats, when really they had done nothing except ride with him and the princess to the palace. Samantha led him up to the high table, and Robrek felt small as a sea of nobles followed them and sat. As Samantha took her place, she called for music, and soon the hall rang with songs of long-ago battles and bright victories:

> And he marched up to Boirche,
> And rode it round about:
> 'O where's the lord of this castle?
> Or where's the lady of it?'
> But up spoke proud Lord Armunn then,
> And O but he spoke high!
> I am the lord of this castle,
> My wife's the lady gay.
> 'If thou art the lord of this castle,
> So well it pleases me,
> For, ere I cross the Borderlands,
> The enemy's force was nigh.'
> Armunn took a long spear in his hand,
> Shod with the metal free,
> And for to meet the Demons there
> He rode right furiously.

Robrek didn't know who Armunn was or why they'd be singing about him now, but it was obviously a popular song at court; the nobles pounded the tables and sang along with the bard. Samantha merely sipped more wine and leaned her head on his shoulder.

Bard after bard sang until the servants began serving the first course—a leek and chicken soup. Robrek took a spoonful of the soup, remembering to eat in the manner Fancy Man had taught him. But Samantha picked up her goblet instead. Worried about her, Robrek put his hand on hers. "Eat something."

She shook her head, took another sip of wine, and commanded the bard to sing a romantic ballad. Robrek grinned and blushed as the song reminded him of last night in the princess's tent. Hungry from healing, he ate heartily, but he had a hard time getting Samantha to even try the food. All that alcohol on an empty stomach wasn't a good idea.

Midway through the feast, people tapped their forks against their glasses and called for a speech. Samantha rose unsteadily to her feet, her hand on Robrek's shoulder to keep her balance. "Lards and. . . ! I mean Lords and Ladies! Nobles of the land! All of you who helped the rightful queen regain the throne, I thank you! My consort thanks you! If my father were still here, he would thank you! But he was foully murdered." She swayed, but Robrek steadied her. "Argblutal has paid the price for his treachery, and this we celebrate here today!"

Cries of "Long live the queen" broke out again.

"So on with the music!" she said, nearly falling into her chair.

* * *

Duke Sheen watched the princess down goblet after goblet of wine; the wench could hold her own with a sailor. He'd thrown everything he had behind keeping her on the throne; he hoped he hadn't backed a sot. In all the years he'd known Solar, he'd never seen him the worse for drink. Could Argblutal's accusation be true? Was she a bastard? Did it matter if she was?

He frowned at the peasant boy sitting beside the princess, then looked away. "That will never do."

"What won't?" Baron Teague, his fellow Korthian Royal Councilor, asked.

Sheen looked askance at the Baron. He hadn't really intended to speak aloud, but now that he had, he might as well let his opinion be known. "Are you willing to see a peasant, and a mere child at that, in the place you once sought for your own?"

Teague frowned. "Tonight we celebrate our victory against the Lundian scum. Tomorrow's soon enough to worry about who the princess marries."

Next to them, Count Pandaran took a sip of his wine. "His fashion sense is appalling. And look how he positively dotes on her. It's almost putting me off my food."

Sheen grunted. Pandaran's complaints were trivial, as was everything about him, but who cared, if they got him on Sheen's side? The important unknown was Duke Caedmon. Would he support a Lundian peasant on the throne? If Korth united against her, they could force her to realize the absurdity of her peasant lover. Solar had adeptly performed the tricky balancing act between the Korthians and the Lundians on his council, but after the Lundians' betrayal, the princess wouldn't have that recourse. With the Lundian interference out of the way, Korth, not the princess, would direct the course of the joined kingdoms.

Sheen smiled and lifted his goblet. Yes, it was a new day in the joined kingdoms.

* * *

Robrek led the princess through the corridors toward her quarters, the princess leaning against him, giggling, and singing a verse from one of the ballads:

> "But who will bake my bridal bread,
> Or brew my bridal ale?
> And who will welcome my brisk bride,
> That I bring over the dale?"

Her bodyguards had to show him the way; she was in no condition to do so. The two men Captain Hawk had appointed were still following him. Both they, Bearach, and Conroy stopped at the door to Samantha's quarters. Robrek followed Samantha in.

When they were alone in her bedroom, she wrapped her arms around him and kissed him. Gently, he pushed her away. "You're drunk, Sam."

She clung to his shirt. "Please, Robbie, make love to me. Touch me like you did last night in my tent."

Despite himself, his body responded, and he wanted nothing so badly as to give in. But it wouldn't be right. "Sam, I can't take advantage of you when you're like this."

Abruptly, she collapsed sobbing against his shirt. "Robbie, I feel so alone. They're gone! Both of my fathers are gone!"

He led her to the bed. He lay down beside her and let her soak his shirt with her tears. *Holy Sulis, she's lost so much.* At least she was crying now. It seemed inhuman to withstand so much loss with dry eyes. He wouldn't have been able to.

After a long while the sobs subsided and were replaced by a soft snore. She'd fallen asleep on his chest. He gently extricated himself and stood. For the first time, he looked around her room. One entire wall was covered by a painting of a princess, resembling Samantha, riding a Horsetad. Horsetads ran free on the Reidhlean plains, and people said they could never be tamed. Robrek had never known anyone other than himself who had ridden one. He thought of Wild Thing, his Horsetad mare, down in the palace stables, and he reached out to her with his magic. She was sleeping contentedly in the paddock and didn't want to be disturbed.

Besides the painting, the room held two huge wardrobes, carved with horses and stars in intricate detail. He opened them and found them full to bursting with dresses in silk and satin, lace and velvet, so many she could wear a different one every day for an entire year. Robrek shook his head. Although his father had been considered wealthy by those in the Valley, Robrek had never had more than a couple changes of clothes. Figurines of horses in gold, silver, jade, crystal, and precious stones arrayed themselves on the mantle. Ten years' proceeds from his father's crops couldn't have afforded one of them.

Last night the princess had had him leave her tent before dawn— they'd been camped at the base of Gloine Torr waiting for today's battle—so it wouldn't be known they'd slept together. Tonight he didn't know where to go. Robrek left the princess and walked into her reception room. A life-sized horse made of smoked crystal dominated one corner. It had a gold mane, tail, and hooves and wore a gold saddle studded with emeralds. On the wall was a huge tapestry of a white mare at the edge of the forest, helping her newborn foal stand. The mare reminded him of Roberta, the horse he'd helped Samantha choose at the horse fair where they first met. The mantle was covered with more horse figurines. There was enough wealth in this room to support the entire Valley for a hundred years.

What in Sulis's name am I doing here?

Not wanting to wrinkle his bronze silks by sleeping in them, he removed them and placed them over a chair. Then he wrapped himself in a blanket and fell asleep on the rug in front of the fire.

ABOUT THE AUTHOR

Jamie began writing stories about the man from Mars when she was six, and she never remembers wanting to be anything other than a writer. Everyone told her she needed a back up plan, so she pursued a Ph.D. in American literature, which she received in 1998. She started teaching writing and literature at Auburn University. One day in the midst of writing a piece of literary criticism, she realized she'd put her true passion on the backburner and neglected her muse. The literary article went into the trash, and she began the book that was to become *The Goddess's Choice*, which was first published in April 2012. Her other novels include *The Soul Stone*, *The Ghost in Exile*, and *The Bull Riding Witch*. In addition, she has published a novella, *Demons in the Big Easy*, and a collection of short stories, *Blood Cursed and Other Tales of the Fantastic*. Her short fiction has also appeared in the anthologies--*Urban Fantasy* and *Of Dragons & Magic: Tales of the Lost Worlds*—and in *Bards & Sages*, *The World of Myth*, *A Writer's Haven*, and *Short-story.me*. She claims she writes about the fantastic . . . and the tortured soul. Her poor characters have hard lives. She lives in Auburn, Alabama, with her husband and four cats, which (or so she's been told) officially makes her a cat lady. She still teaches writing and literature at Auburn University. She is the mother of a grown son, who is a fantastic young man.

OTHER BOOKS BY JAMIE MARCHANT

The Kronicles of Korthlundia

> *The Goddess's Choice*, original edition (2012)
> *The Soul Stone* (2015)
> *The Ghost in Exile* (2016)

The Bull Riding Witch (2017)
Blood Cursed and Other Tales of the Fantastic (2016)--short story collection
Demons in the Big Easy: A Novella (2013)

Story Collections including her work
> *Waiting for a Kiss: A Princess Fairy Tale Anthology* (2017)
> *Of Dragons & Magic: Tales of Lost Worlds* (2014)
> *Urban Fantasy* (2013)
> *Best Genre Short Stories Anthology #2: Short-Story.Me!*
> *(Volume 2)* (2010)